RED MOUNTAIN

 A NOVEL OF THE BOOM DAYS IN COLORADO

D1478608

WESTERN REFLECTIONS
PUBLISHING COMPANY

This is Mildred's Book

With the exception of actual historical personages,
the characters are entirely the product of the author's
imagination and have no relation to any person in real life.

Library of Congress Catalog Card Number: 63-7704

ISBN: 1-890437-35-2

Cover Design SJS Design (Susan Smilanic)

Western Reflections Publishing Co.
PO Box 710
Ouray, CO 81427 USA

Foreword to *Red Mountain*

by Duane A. Smith

"What made them go was a sort of urge, a frame of mind, ... Yes, that's right. That's what built Red Mountain - the frame of mind of the people." That frame of mind of the people - that could explain why men and women went into the high and inhospitable Colorado San Juans, or the hot desert of Tombstone, Arizona, or almost anywhere else they thought they could get rich "without working" by finding a rich gold or silver mine. The mining west moved and stopped, and moved again, with just such an attitude for well over fifty years. Those caught with "the fever" tracked from California to Nevada, east to Colorado, north to Montana, and up to the Arctic Circle in Alaska.

Nevertheless, the mining West was more than chasing a golden rainbow. Near the end of *Red Mountain*, author David Lavender has one of his main characters, freighter Walt Kennerly, try to explain to newcomers why people went to Red Mountain. They could not understand why, or what motivated them to work and live at nearly 11,000 feet. Walt struggled in his mind how to do it. "What frame? Oh Christ," Walt cried silently in his agony. "They believed," he said. They did believe in real life too.

They believed that over the mountain, looming on the horizon, or in some nearby nameless canyon, they would find their bonanza. They believed that the next round of blasting deep into the earth would uncover a vein of gold or silver unimagined until then. They believed that in the aborning mining camp, they would find their latchkey to fortune. They believed then that all the privations, the hard work, the loneliness, the lost years of their youth, the busted dreams would be vindicated. They believed.

They believed in themselves. They believed in their destiny. They believed in Red Mountain. They believed in the future.

Many people today, when they are visiting the Colorado San Juans, the highest mining district in the United States, cannot understand what motivated these people, either. That is where *Red Mountain* provides the key to unlock a sense of time and place that are as foreign to us today as the revolutionary war era was to the pioneers who rode and walked into the valleys and mountains of the San Juans in the last quarter of the nineteenth century. Some walked out almost as fast. As one old miner said as he tramped down the mountain, "He would be damned if he would work where there were three months of mightily late fall and nine months of winter."

David Lavender grew up in these mountains. Born in Telluride, he called the region home when old-timers still told tales of the pioneering days first hand. Dave worked on a cattle ranch and as a miner in one of the district's famous mines, the Camp Bird. He also is a master story teller. In a 1979 interview, he jokingly recalled that his mother said he was "always making up stories from the earliest on." Dave, however "doesn't remember doing it."

Native born, with a love for the region and the experience of living there, he has the background to spin a well-told tale. Having all that, there is still more. Dave believed, as he wrote in his fascinating autobiographical look backward at his youth, *One Man's West*, in this philosophy.

Came a day when I wanted to get married and needed a stake. To my youthful optimism, geared as it was to the 'thirty-a-month-and found' wages paid cowboys, the vast affluence of five dollars a day in the gold mines seemed to offer the quickest solution.

Then, as he commented, "I myself knew no miners and nothing about mining." That mattered little. He believed. No one is better qualified to take the reader back to the boisterous nineteenth century days of the opening of the San Juans to permanent settlement.

Spanish prospectors and miners had first ventured into the rugged La Plata and San Juan Mountains long before, in the eighteenth century. They came and found some minerals but did not stay. The region was too isolated, the Utes opposed them, and Spain's outward thrust withered away, far from this isolated outpost of empire. They left behind place names, lost mines, stories of buried treasure, and the legend that here in the San Juans would be found the mother lode of mining. Here, in the veins shooting through these mountains, nestled the bonanza spot in which the gold and silver originated.

In the decade that followed, the stories continued to drift about. Like the wind blowing down the canyons, you did not know where they came from, but they persistently would not go away. The 1849 California rush, followed a decade later by the Pike's Peak rush, turned dreams into reality.

By the 1860s prospectors had reached the heart of the San Juans. A mini-rush followed the next year, but little success in finding gold, the ever present Ute, isolation, and distance drove the adventuresome and all others out. Within a decade, they were back, this time eventually to stay. By the mid-1870s, little camps appeared in the valleys, high and low in the mountains.

In the generation that followed, there was not one San Juan rush, but nearly a score. The district names became famous - and so did their towns. Silverton, Telluride, Ouray, Rico, Creede, and a host of smaller communities all had their day of fame and fortune. The mining west was an urban west. The Red Mountain district boomed and busted as part of this larger whole. Its apex of production and prominence came in the 1880s.

The story of the San Juans is the saga of western mining in the second half of the nineteenth century. It offers the story of the women and men who came to a new land to work out their personal destinies. Few made a fortune, most just a living, and some failed miserably. Not all persevered and many drifted onto another dream. A zest for life and adventure is mingled with sadness and disappointment.

Out of all of this, David Lavender has spun his story of Red Mountain. It is well grounded on research into history and his extensive knowledge of local geography. From this point, he then takes the reader beyond where the historian can go. He tells the story through fictional characters who reflect the ideas, attitudes, hopes, and dreams of the generation that came to open a mineral treasure box. These people are, as he said, "figments, more or less, designed for the story, not from any historic prototype."

The story is firmly placed geographically. The St. John Mountains, as the reader will quickly understand, are the San Juans. Fictional Argent is today's Ouray, Baker is Silverton, Montezuma is Durango, San Cristobal is Lake

City and Summit City, the now ghost site of Congress. There was a real Red Mountain City in the district, although in the book the location is moved.

The road that John Ogden works so hard to build is the forerunner of today's highway 550, the Million Dollar Highway from Silverton over Red Mountain Pass (originally Sheridan Pass) and northward to Ouray. As Dave wrote in his original edition, "Other geographic disguises and shifts will be apparent to those who wish to run them down."

Of the characters in *Red Mountain*, two have actual prototypes. Otto Winkler is based on Otto Mears, Colorado's famous toll road king and narrow gauge railroad builder. Al Ewer and his newspaper, The True Fissure, are molded around Ouray's colorful, outspoken newsman, David Day. His Solid Muldoon was one of Coloradans' favorites, when Red Mountain glowed at its peak. Day was damned and praised in turn. However, he kept people reading, and laughing, as well as swearing.

There are actually three Red Mountains lined on the east side of the district. They not only guard the district, they also provide an insight into the story and the author. In a January letter, Dave wrote:

I did have some vague symbolism in mind. The three red peaks are obviously suggestive of the trinity of faith, and I suppose if you strain at it you can make Johnny out to be a sacrificial victim of faith that suddenly appears empty.

And of course the readers find symbols wherever they look, which is okay. Whenever a specific shape or event stirs response, it is also on the edge of becoming representative of the moods and so on that the story, poem, or whatever is being read is presenting. An author never has more than 10% control over his readers anyhow; if they want symbols, let 'em have symbols, say I.

Come back then to the exciting, heart breaking days when mining, newly crowned as king of the San Juans, beckoned to one and all with the promise of the fulfillment of dreams.

I

"1"

Old Man Hedstrom bore a harrowing tale. He began it as soon as he had tossed his reins to the hostlers and had slid stiffly from his freight wagon seat onto the soiled loading platform of the Argent City Livery and Transport Company. He continued beside the flagpole in the middle of the town's single street intersection. He ran through it once again on the long verandah of the Dixon House, where the new pine boards behind his head looked cherub-pink under their scumbling of white lead paint. After each shift he left behind him a loose group of men standing just as the old photographs of the new mining camps always showed them standing—both hands thrust into the front pockets of their baggy-kneed trousers, their shirts minus collars or their collars minus ties, and in back of them, as unreal as a flat of vaudeville scenery, the great lift of the Colorado peaks.

Unreality. That was the first reaction. Then someone would say, "Why, the yellow sonsabitches!" and the bald condemnation would send a ripple of questioning through the group. Perhaps there was more to what had happened than they were hearing. . . . Well, by God, I've heard a-plenty. The ones who said that were generally the ones who broke away from the argument and followed Hedstrom to his next stop, to listen once more to what he had to say.

Betrayal—that was his theme. A few nights before—on the last day of September 1880, to be exact—he and his freighters had halted their three wagonloads of mill machinery and fence wire at a handy camping site on the road that wound through the Ute reservation into Argent City. Two drunk Indians had made pests of themselves around the wagons. As a reminder for them to keep their distance, Young Hedstrom, Old Man Hedstrom's nephew, had fired through the darkness. By sheer bad luck he had hit one of them. The other had fled. That meant that soon half the tribe would come squalling back, wanting the freighters' blood in vengeance.

Was the killing really an accident? Hedstrom mimicked the question savagely. Accident? His lips stretched behind his gray whiskers; his voice climbed. The boy wasn't fool enough to do it on purpose, was he, only four of them with valuable freight alone there in the middle of the whole Ute nation? Of course it had been an accident.

Only four of them. And they'd had to protect Young Hedstrom. They had hitched up and had driven back over the hilly road to Mort Tally's trading post in Curecanti Valley, thinking they could fort up among friends. But Tally, practically a Ute himself, had feared that a battle might destroy his post. Others traveling the road had feared that a fight might trigger a general uprising that would engulf their wagons and camps. So the cowards among them had persuaded Walt Kennerly to ride to the Ute agency at Los Alamos and bring back the new agent, Andrew Cushman, to pacify the red devils. Yeah, big, yellow-haired Walt Kennerly, the one who had lived with the squaw so many years. Because Kennerly was a squaw man, it was supposed that the Indians would let him through. That's right—Indian-lovers, all of them: Tally and Kennerly; Hal Banner for another, wetting himself lest a war close the road and keep him from delivering the deeds to his mining claims before the options lapsed. And John Ogden.

By now the telling had moved inside the Pastime Saloon. The listeners stood close around, their shot glasses damp in their thick fingers. At Johnny Ogden's name the old-timers among them looked into the amber lights of their whisky and gave their heads little wiggles of uncertainty and—yes, embarrassment. Betrayal? Johnny Ogden? It was as if something unexpectedly naked had stepped into the room.

Old Hedstrom settled back on his heels and glared out of dust-reddened eyes at the ring of faces. "Yes, Johnny." He let the challenge hang a moment and then shrugged. "I hain't God or anybody to go reading into another man's mind. It hain't for me to say what made any of them do what they done. But I do know those mules that Ogden was packing in here from Gunnison were his own property, the first things except his hat he ever owned. I know that his contract for taking those store goods to Gabe Porcella on Red Mountain was his first fling, you might say, his first time to cut away from day wages and start working on his own. If he didn't deliver because of an Indian war or anything else, he was ruined. Like I say, I hain't God. But you figure it."

Go on, go on.

Well, Kennerly came back from the agency with Cushman, "Cushman and twelve dragoons." Old Hedstrom stayed flat-footed, lips back, letting the number sink in. That's right, twelve—commanded by a baby-faced lieutenant fresh from West Point. Hadn't never before seen a mad Indian. And by that time there had been at least a hundred mad Utes boiling around Tally's, yammering that all four of Hedstrom's party be handed over to them in return for one drunken pest shot by accident.

Sure, Cushman was new on the job. But not so new-green that he thought he could hold off the Utes with twelve soldiers. It had been a deal from the beginning—pretend to protect the road while giving the Utes the blood they wanted. Measure it for yourself. Cushman was the one man there whom the Indians would listen to. They knew he was on their side. The pious-mouthed, missionary son of a bitch—hadn't he said publicly a dozen times to tan-bellies and white men both that his church board and the government had sent him to Los Alamos to protect the interests of the Indians, even against his own race?

Go on, go on.

So right away Cushman had set up a huddle with old Shavano, the father of the pup that was killed. He promised Shavano that the guilty man, the one who had fired the shot, would be taken to the nearest court, at Gunnison, for trial according to the laws of the land. That had seemed fair. No white man's court would hold against the boy, and naturally—Old Hedstrom wagged his head—naturally the freighters had supposed that Young Hedstrom would be protected on his ride outside. But instead Cushman had made a lot of talk about how the settlers' wagons along the road would be a temptation to the aroused Indians. With that as an excuse he had ordered every vehicle between Tally's and the agency, including Old Man Hedstrom's three, into a train and had put his twelve soldiers to watching them. Meantime, four civilians, each one of them a friend of the Utes, had volunteered to escort Young Hedstrom to Gunnison. Looking back, it was plain to see how each one of them stood to gain. Tally saved his post; Hal Hoyt, Tally's helper, saved his job; Hal Banner delivered his deeds; Johnny Ogden kept his mules.

Why hadn't Old Hedstrom protested? Why, everything had looked aboveboard—then. Mighty cute: enough soldiers to appear brave but not enough to do their job: and then a preacher arranging the deal so it would smell sweet, but being careful not to go with the escort himself. And then having John Ogden ride along as one of the guards.

Hedstrom leaned over and spat. "They knew they had to keep me off the escort, 'cause I'd of fought when the Indians come to take the boy. So they rang in Johnny. I didn't suspicion a thing with him along. Would you? Why, I trusted John Ogden like I trust my own right arm. Besides, I had to deliver that mill machinery on schedule. So I started on with the train."

And then the Indians had come to a spot agreed on by the four civilians. Young Hedstrom had been given to them without resistance. Post, job, deeds, mules—everything saved. Except Young Hedstrom.

The old man's face crumpled under its whiskers. Poor orphan boy he'd practically reared, hardly old enough to be shaving yet——

"Just about as old as Johnny Ogden," someone said.

Hedstrom drank and wiped his nose on the back of his hand. "I hain't God. I hain't a mind-reader. I'm just saying how it was. One of their own kind, delivered up like——"

Sonsabitches. Insistence, repeated throughout the night, bred its own belief. This was murder. It was murder as surely as if the planner, Andrew Cushman, and the escort themselves had pulled the trigger—or had lighted the pyre, for by now a large part of the town was convinced that Young Hedstrom had been burned at the stake. A mighty righteousness coalesced. With Old Hedstrom grim in their midst a knot of men clumped out of the saloon to visit the justice of the peace. On the strength of Hedstrom's affirmations warrants were issued for the arrest of Agent Andrew Cushman, Mort Tally, Harold Banner, Harry Hoyt, and John Ogden. Charges: Murder, conspiracy to murder, accessories before the fact. A net as tight as that ought to catch and hold the guilty ones. Betrayal . . .

"2"

The warrants were handed to Sheriff Charles Gaw for execution. A tall, brown, earnest young man, Gaw was fortified in his calling by a practical turn of mind; and it occurred to him to wonder what he would do if he reached the agency at Los Alamos, where Cushman had full charge of the United States troops assigned to maintaining order on the reservation, and found that the culprits declined to submit to his authority. Could he, the sheriff of one small county, rightfully defy the federal government?

As Gaw hesitated, the mail carrier arrived in his buckboard and announced that he had passed John Ogden and Walt Kennerly plodding in complete serenity toward Argent with their mule train. Amazed at his good fortune, Gaw decided to stay in town, where he was sure of himself, and make his first arrest there.

The news of Johnny's approach created intense excitement. At least an hour before he could be expected, men began to gather around the flagpole at the intersection to see what would happen. At this point two of John's friends, Pat Edgell and Gabe Porcella, decided something had to be done. They thought of trying to warn him, but it was too late for them to slip out of town undetected. They thought of trying to form a protective cordon of his well-wishers, but Old Hedstrom's reiterations had built up so ugly a feeling among Argent's large complement of Ute-haters that the issue was perhaps better left unforced. Physical methods being thus unpromising, the pair reluctantly sought out the elder of the town's two lawyers, but the fellow had political aspirations and declined so controversial a case. In desperation, therefore, the friends hurried to the town's other barrister, a young newcomer named Harmon Gregg. Their request to Gregg was utterly direct—to protect John, not necessarily to prove him innocent. It was not their office as friends, and perhaps not Harmon's as a lawyer, to judge. But Gregg's circumstances were such that the question of guilt kept intruding.

"3"

Protection. Harmon Gregg drummed his fingers softly on the raw pine table that served him as his desk and regarded, with what he hoped was judicial aloofness, the two agitated young men beseeching his aid. Give us this day our daily writ, he thought sardonically. For thine are the books, the power, the salvation, amen. Majesty of the law? To this pair the law was a genie to be whisked out of a container of fine black print and then put away again when the emergency was ended, all to the tune of the proper incantations. Habeas, supersedeas, thy will be done.

Well, why not? With wry self-honesty Harmon glanced from his visitors to the cabinet of tomes he had arranged against the muslin curtain that separated his office from his living quarters. He was tall. His thin face was topped by brown hair as fine as cobweb; his voice was soft. He was a little flabby through the middle, though he was not yet thirty years old. There was a gentleness in his mouth—or a weakness. To hide it he had grown a silky brown goatee, hoping to look as

vigorous, as lascivious even, as the animal from which such whiskers had
drawn their name. Instead he looked sad.

The books in his cabinet were also pretense—forty-three assorted
volumes, dull tan or scuffed black, bought at a sale in Denver for
eighty-four dollars he could ill afford. Blackstone and Kent's *Commen-
taries* as usual, Greenleaf on *Evidence*, Parson on *Contracts*, Jenkins'
Legal Forms, Morrison's *Mining Law*, a mixture of supreme court reports from several states. He had arranged them in a rickety, homemade,
glass-fronted case, interspersed with gaudy mineral specimens from
nearby silver mines, and had placed the cabinet so that the books'
learned spines would be the first things to impress visitors coming
through his door. But how many of the volumes did he himself consult with familiarity, beyond the annotated copy of the revised statutes
of the state of Colorado, Bouvier's *Law Dictionary* now and then,
and most particularly Jenkins' *Legal Forms*. Jenkins' offered set formulas
for nearly every routine. But not for murder, or at least not for the
strange concatenation of events that the Argent City justice of the
peace, under pressure of the town's growing outrage, had chosen to
warrant as murder. And if the bulk of the citizenry really demanded
murder, they might well get it, even though not a single one of Young
Hedstrom's charred bones was turned up in evidence. Yet Harmon was
supposed with a wave of his hand to dispel society's threat against
John Ogden. Incantations. From ghoulies and ghasties and burnings
that go bump in the night, deliver us, O Genie.

"Then you will defend him?" Pat Edgell pressed. He had a most
curious snub-tipped, shallow-bridged nose. His eyes were shallow also,
set wide apart in an almost flat countenance. With no brows beetling
over them and with short lashes ringing them they looked strangely
round. A smudge of freckles lay underneath them and across the slight
swell of his nose. Generally he was merry and laughing; but he had a dis-
concerting ability to stare a man into uneasiness and people said that
when the boogers were riding him he could be mean. He had been in
Argent since before the town's incorporation. Like all senior citizens,
he assumed oracular gifts. The pioneers were, in their own minds, a fraternity apart. To hear them talk, one would suppose they had subsisted
during the days of their strength largely on snowballs and rabbit tracks.
They had survived lower temperatures, larger grizzly bears, and more
thunderous avalanches than had been vouchsafed to later mortals. Out
of the brotherhood born of their experiences they had created for themselves a superior caste. John Ogden was part of it, although neither he
nor Pat Edgell had emerged from their teens when first they had looked
into Argent's cliff-girt basin and had absorbed its silver promise.

How tight a part would those invisible bonds play in the case now shaping up, Harmon wondered. It was not the pioneers who were hollering murder. Old-timers like Pat Edgell and Gabe Porcella evidently saw nothing wrong with trading a white boy's life for the preservation of the vision they had glimpsed. The anger blared from recent comers, the ones who had arrived to cash in on the promises advertised by the pioneers and then had found the would-be town and their would-be trade choked by the Ute reservation—a foreign principality, in effect, lying across the ingress road they needed, and shutting them away from the farmlands they wanted. They therefore despised the Indians. They despised anyone who would deal with Indians. In their minds the government's troops should be used to drive the tan bastards out of the state, not to set up a betrayal.

Harmon drummed his fingers. He was a new man in a new town, and a case like this could make or break him. The majesty of the law? Or the expediency of his first big opportunity? What did he really know about John Ogden? For that matter, what did he really know about this whole Indian-infested, silver-obsessed country?

Misreading his hesitation, Gabe Porcella said, "You'll get your pay. Johnny, he's been one to save his money. He's got those mules and all."

"He owns a couple of residence lots up on Vinegar Hill," Pat put in.

Gabe nodded vehemently. "Don't be fooled just 'cause Johnny looks like a pecker-necked kid."

This condescension about age from the height of Gabe's—what?—twenty-eight years at the most. He was the homeliest man Harmon Gregg had ever seen. Mountain sun and wind had made his huge red face look raw. He had a frog-wide, wistful mouth and no mustache, but he did wear scraggly puffs of orange sideburns low down on his meaty jowls. There were smaller tufts of orange hair between the knuckles of his beefy hands. Obviously he possessed enormous strength, but to judge from his expression he had little idea what to do with the power beyond lifting barrels and shoveling muck. On learning that his full Christian name was Gabriel and that he owned a flute which he sometimes piped to himself on lonesome evenings, jokesters often called him Angel for the sheer incongruity of it. Angel Gabe did not care. He had a simple-minded craving for friendship that absorbed even insult without recognizing it. Anyway, simple-mindedness was not necessarily a demerit up on the bright flanks of Red Mountain, where Gabe, tired of prospecting, had tried to attract company by stacking up a handful of groceries and dry goods in his tent and painting the word STORE in huge uneven letters from one end of the sloping canvas roof to the other. When the supplies had run out, John Ogden had agreed to go to Gunnison with fifteen pack mules for replenishments.

Fifteen mules—security for a lawyer's fee. Or, as Old Hedstrom would have it, the price of a white boy's life.

How did one find the truth? Or, the truth obscured, where would the best defense lie?

"Ogden may want something to say about who represents him," Harmon temporized.

Pat Edgell waved his hand impatiently. "You wrote to the legislature to get a toll-road charter for Johnny, didn't you?"

"Yes."

Your petitioner therefore prays. One charter, cost five dollars, granting exclusive right to build within the next two years a toll wagon road from the town of Argent, seat of the county of the same name, up whichever side of Ute Canyon proved necessary, to a terminal site at or near the principal mines of Red Mountain. Lawyer's fee, five dollars also. The annotated statutes, plus a sheet of foolscap backed with blue to impress clients, had been guide enough for that. But when white men turned one of their own kind over to the Utes—

"That sounds to me like Johnny was satisfied with your work," Pat insisted.

Harmon Gregg's mouth twisted ever so slightly. If the client was satisfied with his lawyer, then automatically the lawyer was satisfied with client. But was he?

Make—or break. His grimace grew. What was he so afraid of? Faint heart, fair case. This was what he had hoped to find in Argent, was it not—an opportunity to start again? If there was a whisper of a chance against the roar of the town, some solid explanation in John himself that a lawyer could polish to brightness and hold up before judge and jury. . . . Give us this day. He looked backward, searching.

"4"

He had seen John Ogden just once, a week ago. It had been afternoon. Waldo Trumbull, the local waterman, had been going with his ox-drawn, dripping water barrel along the two blocks of Main Street on his last round of the day. The wooden runners of the sled carrying the barrel gritted over the pebbles. Waldo's voice was equally gritty.

"Bring out your buckets! No more till tomorry less'n you pack it yourself! Bring out your buckets!"

Harmon had reached behind the muslin curtain for his galvanized pail and had gone outside. This was his third day in Argent and still the basin overwhelmed him, as if the ringing peaks of the St. John Mountains were going to drop personally, maliciously, onto his head. In the bottom of so gigantic a cup the town was no more impressive than a scattering of coffee grounds—flecks of cabins around the edges and a thicker cluster of stores along the north-south main street and the single cross street, named Silver Avenue.

Harmon's log-and-plank office and dwelling sat in the middle of the Main Street block to the south of the intersection. Between him and the corner was the principal saloon, the Pastime, and across from the Pastime was Lincoln Hotchkiss's general store—MINERS' SUPPLIES, GRO-CERIES, GENTS' READY TO WEAR, printed on a whitewashed board pro-truding at right angles from the store front across the plank sidewalk. The courthouse, its jail wing forming a stubby wooden L at the rear, occupied the corner farthest from Harmon. Across from that was the only two-story structure in town, the hotel, the Dixon House, fronted by a long porch where men were always rocking and spitting and wait-ing for a dogfight or the arrival of the triweekly stage.

In the center of the intersection was a flagpole, a large fir tree which, so Harmon had been told, had been trimmed, painted white, and erected for the Fourth of July celebration two years before, in 1878. A braced crossarm reached perpendicularly out from this pole. Hanging from the end of the arm on a short iron cable was a rusty circular saw blade at least five feet in diameter. The blade had been erected as an alarm gong after the Meeker massacre in the northern part of the state in 1879. During that debacle, a dozen white men had been slain, three women kidnaped, and a column of troops brought to the verge of another Custer's fall. When word of the battling reached the south-ern Utes, they had grown tremendously excited. Straightway wild rumors whirled through Argent. The local Indians were going to emulate their northern tribesmen. They were smuggling in arms and ammunition; they were going to cut the single access road which ran for a hundred miles through their reservation; they might even attack Argent City itself. To forestall the last threat, volunteer militia industriously heaped up in the narrows below the town a rude fort of sandstone boulders. To sound warning the saw blade had been suspended from its cable and a singlejack for ringing it had been hung beside it from sixty-penny nails driven into the flagpole.

For three weeks nothing had happened. Then one frosty night a drunk had given the gong a few experimental licks. He was caught doing it by the terrified men and women who had poured half-clad from their cabins and tents, and things might have gone hard with the man if a few gayer souls, including John Ogden, had not taken charge. Instead of tarring and feathering the prankster as originally proposed, the mob contented itself with tossing him half as high as the flagpole in a blanket. After that there had been no more false alarms. But the Indians were still about despite the government's offering them a new treaty if they would leave; and the blade still hung on its cable, symbolic, Harmon thought, of the teeth that most of the citizens of Argent would gladly direct toward their red neighbors if opportunity ever afforded.

The town had reason for feeling trapped. It was almost completely circled by bands of maroon-colored sandstone, layered like a cake and speckled by brush and trees wherever growth could find a hold, the frosted aspens and cottonwoods showing yellow swatches among the evergreens, now in late September. Above the horizontal bands humped vertical ribs of igneous rock. Remnants of the year's first snowfall glinted on their upper, gray-brown reaches. On above them, to the west, rose the square top of Whitehouse Peak. A rock rolling off that towering summit, Harmon thought with a shiver born of the flatness of his Kansas boyhood, might not stop until it splashed into the river which lay between the scraggly ends of the town and the lowest band of sandstone cliffs.

Eastward there was more space. In that direction the rim of peaks curved back to form a vast gray amphitheater. A bright green mound named Vinegar Hill sat well forward in the center of this amphitheater, at the borders of the town. The crystal brook from which Waldo Trumbull filled his water barrel foamed past one side of Vinegar Hill. Here and there around the other skirts of the hillock lush thickets of box elders marked the sites of numerous hot springs. A few enterprising householders had piped the almost boiling water into their cabins, and it was generally agreed that as soon as the Utes were out of the way and Argent began to grow, real estate values on Vinegar Hill would soar. (Later Harmon would remember Pat Edgell's saying that John Ogden owned two lots on Vinegar Hill, valuable lots if the Utes could be kept from going on the warpath and depressing prices.)

At the basin's lower, or northern, end the sandstone bands were sundered by a gap seventy or so yards wide. Through this gap the Ute River poured into the reservation-gripped valley below. This was the Narrows, only possible route whereby wagons could arrive from outside. At the upper end of the Narrows stood the town's fort. At the lower end was a surveyor's pyramid of loose stones marking the reservation boundary. Would-be squatters on the rich bottom lands along the river regularly pulled down the pyramid as a sign of their impatience. Just as regularly it was rebuilt by indifferent troops sent out from the Los Alamos agency by Andrew Cushman.

Southward, the main peaks of the St. John Mountains reared up even higher than did the summits to east and west. In this direction the rising land was split by the gorges of the streams that funneled together to form the Ute River. Up at the head of those gorges lay the mines—or the hope of mines. Prospectors were burrowing everywhere along the fringes of timberline, Harmon understood, trying before winter locked the approaches to find the leads they were sure were there.

It was one such visitor from the high country whom Harmon saw approaching Waldo's sled just ahead of him. The fellow was lithe. He carried a blanket roll in a horseshoe over one shoulder. Though flushed from exertion, he seemed unwearied. He was perhaps twenty-two or -three. He was smooth-shaven, though most young men in the area tended to sprout beards to prove their maturity. His head was strong and bony; his dark skin someday might be florid. Something (a mule's hoof, Harmon learned in time) had broken his nose. The slight sideways cast left by faulty healing gave his expression a faintly quizzical look. Other than that, he appeared as average as a score of other adventurous young prospectors wandering the neighboring mountains: height medium, shoulders heavy, feet light in their thick boots, hands strong with cracked, soiled nails.

What wasn't ordinary, Harmon saw as he drew nearer, were his eyes. Later, as the lawyer tried to evaluate John Ogden, those were the features that kept returning to him—their utter, their incredible serenity. Blue as a baby's and with as absolute a naïveté. Could such—innocence was the only word Harmon could make fit—could such innocence, if total enough, be the father of a ruthless betrayal?

Johnny slipped the blanket roll from his shoulder and asked Waldo for a drink. The waterman filled the tin dipper hanging by its crooked handle to the barrel's rim and passed it over, a community fountain at ten cents the ladleful.

"Johnny Ogden!" Waldo's sunken cheeks moved in and out over his toothless gums like a chipmunk's. "I thought you were workin' on that new road of Otto Winkler's over on the other side of the mountain, past Baker."

"We got paid off day before yesterday."

"Where's Pat 'n the rest?"

"Still in Baker. There's a new sporting house over there with a lady twenty-one dealer. Pat liked the way she smiled when he said, 'Hit me!' She was still a-hittin' when I left."

He handed back the dipper for a refill and reached into his pocket as if for silver. But his fingers came out empty and he looked suddenly embarrassed. Waldo eyed him mistrustfully. Holding tight to the refilled dipper, he said,

"That'll be twenty cents—a dime each."

Johnny winced. "Twenty! Why, I was just going to hit you for a dollar."

"Me? A dollar?" Waldo's cheeks caved in. "Just 'cause I sell a bucket for only four bits"—he took Harmon Gregg's bucket, splashed in the dipperful Johnny had reached for, then immersed the pail into the barrel—"there's some as think a dipper ought to be free. But how many dippers do you think a townful of moochers can drink in a day? Jesus, a man's got a living to make."

He handed the dripping pail to Harmon. Ostentatiously he pocketed the lawyer's fifty-cent piece. Johnny watched it all, wide-eyed, and it was Waldo who grew more and more fidgety. "You acquainted with Gregg here?" he asked. "A new lawyer. Johnny Ogden, Harmon Gregg."

Johnny nodded but declined to be diverted. He kept looking at the dipper, sorrowfully, as if disappointed in far more than the lost drink. Waldo squirmed.

"If you're that short," he said ungraciously, filled the dipper again, and thrust it forward so rudely that water sloshed onto Johnny's feet.

John accepted the container gravely and drank slowly, all the while watching Waldo over the rim. At last Harmon grew suspicious. This was a deliberate leg-pull, though to what end he could not fathom.

Waldo turned aside to another customer. Sighing satisfaction, Johnny poured the last few drops from the dipper onto the ground. As Harmon had learned, this was a characteristic gesture among mountain dwellers, almost like a libation, although John Ogden no doubt would have been baffled if Harmon were to ask him what he meant by the instinctive ritual.

Then Johnny challenged, softly, scarcely opening his lips, "I got the drink. I'll bet you a dollar I get the dollar, too."

Harmon nodded; Johnny turned to Waldo.

"About that dollar—"

Waldo shied like a frightened rabbit. Just then two Ute squaws padded out of Hotchkiss's store, twin braids of jet hair hanging over their floppy breasts. Waldo ducked for their shelter.

"Look at them goddam Utes," he said.

Walking backwards away from each other, the pair paid out between them a hank of crimson Germantown yarn, to make sure it was full measure. Satisfied, they rewound the skein, passing without notice the toothed saw blade, and waddled back into the store to haggle about price while the clerk leaned his black sleeve-protectors on the counter and with a pencil stub rapped out his boredom against his teeth.

Waldo spat in profound disgust. Even a waterman was superior to that kind of dealing. "I don't know why we let 'em in town. They'll spend a whole morning dickerin' over two bits' worth of string."

Johnny grew reflective. "If you could get them to work the same amount of time for two bits, it would be cheap labor. Do you reckon they would work for yarn?"

What kind of feint now, Harmon wondered. He was fascinated. Complete guile, and at the same time that untouchable innocence. Children absorbed in play had just such an intentness as Johnny's. And there was no other end than the game for the game's own sake. The dollars were an emblem only, the sparkle of victory.

Waldo had no idea what was happening. He lumbered along his original path.

"The Utes wouldn't be comin' to town to bother us, either, if that preacher-agent at Los Alamos, that Cushman, would pin 'em down to signin' the treaty so we could get 'em out of the state."

Johnny shrugged. "Just what you said—they like to dicker. Maybe they'll string the negotiations out long enough for me to hire a passel of 'em."

This time Waldo stopped. He looked at Johnny and then at the door through which the squaws had disappeared. His cheeks worked and it was obvious that he was asking himself at last whether or not he was being victimized.

"I guess I didn't hear you right," he said.

"I need somebody to work on my trail."

"Trail where?"

"To Red Mountain."

"They already is one."

"That thing! Down logs, slide rock, spruce bogs, cliffs—let a burro lean too far out over the edge and good-bye burro. I mean an honest-to-god graded, corduroyed, all-weather mule trail four feet wide clear up Ute gorge to the top."

"The gorge! Why, in a hundred years you couldn't—"

"We surely can. We'll raise the money by subscription. The boys decided on it in a meeting last night in Gabe Porcella's store."

"Gabe's what?"

"He put a plank across a couple of barrels in his tent. He can call it a store if he wants. You call this the Argent water department."

"Ain't ary other one in town," Waldo said pridefully.

"No other store at Red Mountain, either. They need one, too, and a way to bring goods in and take ore out. The boys agreed to subscribe half the cost of a decent trail if you merchants here in Argent subscribe the other half. That's where your dollar comes in."

"Me!" Waldo hung the dipper back on the barrel rim. "I ain't goin' to Red Mountain."

"Why, you nickel-nursing old skinflint. Look here. A good trail means more supplies for Red Mountain. More supplies mean more ore being mined for treatment down here in Argent. More ore means more people drinking water. Hell, you'll have to buy another barrel."

"Can't afford it."

Johnny laughed in delight. "You're all right, Waldo," he said. He glanced at Harmon. His blue eyes said serenely, You think you've won; but not yet. Soberly he said to Waldo, "The whole town working together can afford it."

Waldo's cheeks moved in and out. How serious was this? "I don't know. It's pretty rough up there."

They looked south, up the gorge. Everything triangles. At the end of the V-shaped trough, perhaps three miles from town, rose the colossal pyramid of Ute Peak. At either side of the peak were smaller, inverted triangles carved by the forkings of the river. The main branch foamed through the chasm to the left, through Hudson Gulch. Down from the right-hand triangle plunged Red Mountain Creek, as rusty-looking in its iron-stained bed, so Harmon had been told, as an oxidized nail—proof of mineral somewhere up there, everyone agreed. But so gaunt a land! Even the firs clinging to the rocky sides of the gorge were triangles, stiff black isosceles. Everything stiff, everything unyielding. But not to John Ogden, Harmon realized. He really meant to make the gorge surrender. This byplay about a silver dollar was just part of the yeast that was working in him, the froth of the exuberance that was bubbling to come out. The old piss and vinegar, the town would say. Up and go, on the wings of the morning.

"We can do it," he declared solemnly. "It'll be work, but like you said yourself, Indian labor is cheap labor."

"Me! I never said no such thing!"

"Reliable, too. Indians wouldn't get the prospecting bug and run off the job every time they heard of a new strike on the other side of the hill."

Waldo snorted. "They're too lazy to run. Or to work, either. You're crazier'n hell, Ogden."

The squaws emerged from the store and waddled toward the hitching rack where their ponies were tied. Johnny watched them thoughtfully.

"Maybe you're right, Waldo."

The waterman swelled with the flattery. "'Course I'm right."

"Instead of bucks, I'll hire squaws."

"Squaws!"

"They're used to hard labor, like cutting tepee poles, packing wood, butchering. I imagine they'd learn shoveling pretty quick."

"Squaws on a white man's job! You'll get run out of town!"

"I'll get a medal, you mean—keeping the Utes out of trouble and building a trail besides." Johnny gestured toward a sign projecting from the log building adjacent to Harmon's office. THE TRUE FISSURE—JOB PRINTING. "I'm going in there now and have Al Ewer write it up for next week's newspaper. Biggest story he's had this fall. Front page, I'll guarantee. I'll have him put your name in, too. Waldo Trumbull, first subscriber. That ought to be worth a dollar of anybody's money."

A vagrant breeze swayed the saw blade. The rub of one of its teeth on the cable set up a faint humming.

"You're crazy," Waldo grumbled again. He jabbed the sleepy ox with his goad. "Gid up, Brigham!" He raised his singsong. "Waterman! Bring out your buckets!"

"Waldo!"

"Now what?"

"You forgot your twenty cents."

Waldo scowled at the dimes. "I thought you said you were short." He pocketed the coins and then began a late and sour smile. "Didn't get your dollar though, did you?"

"I will."

"Huh!"

"I mean what I say about building a road to Red Mountain."

"Yah! So the trail has growed to a road now! Plumb easy—on hot air."

The tongue lapse, if it had been a lapse, did not bother John Ogden. "Trail first, then a road. You'll see."

"Yah! You get me a contract for haulin' water up to your Ute shovelers. Then I'll subscribe."

With a triumphant cackle Waldo moved away, crying his gritty cry. They smiled after him. Johnny handed over a dollar to Harmon, and the lawyer said, greatly pleased with this joyous young man, "If you hadn't dragged in that nonsense about the Indians, you could have persuaded him."

Johnny shrugged. Shoot for the moon: that was the fun of games. Now this one was over and already he had forgotten it. His blue eyes turned up the gorge; he put his hands in his hip pockets and rocked back and forth, ever so slightly, from his heels to his toes. Suddenly he said, interrupting Harmon in the midst of small talk,

"You're a lawyer."

"Yes."

"Do you know anything about toll roads? I mean, what you have to do to get a permit for building one—"

"A franchise, it's called, or charter."

"Do you know how much the permit—the franchise—costs, and if it's exclusive, and things like that?"

"I can soon find out."

There must have been doubt in the lawyer's voice, because John turned that utterly candid glance on him, not amused now, and said,

"I'm not joking. I was studying about routes and grades while I was walking down from Red Mountain this afternoon. Oh, patching up a trail will do for a start. But when the boom hits, there has to be a road. In fact, they feed each other. The boom brings the road, and the road builds the boom. I've watched it happen, over on the other side, where we built the road from San Cristobal past Engineer Point down into Baker. And it isn't a road, really, just a scratch that can be used only in summer. Even so—you ought to see."

The yeast was in him, swelling, working. He had to let it out, had to talk. Harmon smiled indulgently.

"Come on over to the office," he invited.

And now in the office a week later with Gabe Porcella and Pat Edgell, he remembered the enthusiasm and the confidence of that talk and from it tried to understand, in part, why Young Hedstrom had had to die. If, indeed, any such death can be excused. The law says . . .

"5"

The law said this also: For as long as the streams shall run and the grass shall grow—in the usual language of Indian treaties the Utes had been allotted all of Colorado west of the 107th parallel of longitude. Almost immediately thereafter silver had been discovered in the St. John Mountains, whose western fingers reached across the parallel into the reservation. To satisfy miners who wanted to cross into the inviolate land, the government after long negotiation had purchased from the Utes a rectangle of ground embracing the coveted fingers. Straightway haphazard log settlements had sprung up in scattered basins formed by the junctions of the frothing streams. The earliest of these settlements were, of course, in the eastern part of the mountains, where they could be reached by abrupt trails over the Continental Divide. From there prospectors slowly worked outward, clinging to the high granite ridges, safely beyond reach of the Utes.

Thus they had first gained the site of Argent, at the farthest edge of the St. John purchase. But the would-be town, despite its sheltered beauty and the true fissure veins that surrounded it, had grown slowly. Wagons could not follow the high ridges. They had to circle the northern flank of the St. John Mountains, bumping through the reservation to Los Alamos and then turning up the Ute River through the Narrows. The Indians allowed the traffic grudgingly. There were continual scares and frequent small clashes. Even so some men were willing, for the promise of silver, to risk the savages' unpredictable displeasure, hoping that still another new treaty (for as long as the grass shall grow) soon would push the Indians completely out of the way and leave the roads open. But the Indians refused to sign, high hopes drooped, and Argent languished.

It was different among the towns in the eastern part of the purchase. Stridently, in an effort to attract population for developing its prospects, each hamlet proclaimed itself the gateway to the future. None was more vociferous than Baker City.

It wasn't what Johnny Ogden said about the early days in Baker so much as the way he said it that let Harmon grasp what the young road builder had experienced—or thought he had experienced. Silver!— pale splendor lapping the peaks, filling the canyons. Come one, come all—heaven by the silver stairs. No questions, no doubts: the world for the taking. Confidence, which was a form of innocence, and impatience strode hand in hand across the passes, up the glacial gorges.

Burros sufficed for transportation at first. An entire smelter was dismantled and brought into Baker on their tiny backs. But as more mines opened burros ceased to be good enough; and finally in '79, bushy-bearded little Otto Winkler had decided to risk hacking out a freight road.

Johnny had worked for Otto before, first in Winkler's store and freight corrals at Saguache, east of the divide. Later he had helped transport the agency to its new site at Los Alamos, west of the 107th parallel. The movers had had to build their own road as they traveled across the reservation, and that had been Johnny's start in construction projects. As he had grown in heft he had also developed a knack for handling blasting powder and, more gradually, for keeping Otto's Mexican laborers from indulging in too many siestas during their twelve-hour working day. So when Otto had decided times were ripe for constructing a toll road over the mountains into Baker, he had decided that Johnny too was ripe—the boy was twenty-one the spring of '79— and he had invited him to come over as one of his foremen. Pat Edgell was to be another.

Past San Cristobal they drove their drill holes and scrapers, up the flanks of Monument Peak, around Engineer Point, down into the gray glacial trough of Los Padres River, on toward Baker. Two summers it took them. Grunt, heave, dig, blast—no road on earth had yet climbed so ambitiously, nearly thirteen thousand feet to the top of Baker Pass.

A highway? Johnny grinned his crooked grin. God, no—chuckholes, loose log spans where ice water bubbled up through the interstices, sidling curves that stood a wagon driver's hair on end. But it was a way to get wagons through so long as snow held off, and each little cloudtop town had gone wild with welcome as the builders had brought the first wheels turning through what at last could be properly termed a street.

For enjoying one reception too much, Pat and Johnny and some others had been haled before a magistrate at Engineer Point and fined. Johnny's grin broadened as he told Harmon about it.

"I'll appeal!" Pat had blustered on principle. "I'll take it to a higher court."

"You cain't," the judge retorted, blandly pocketing the fine. "This yere is the highest court in these U-nited States."

The next day a scraper team had run away, over the cliffs. One long shriek of agony. Honor the dead. But how? Engineer Point possessed no sawn lumber for a coffin. That afternoon Johnny and Pat directed the man's friends in lining the grave with hand-split logs. They put a layer of grass in the bottom, and at sunset lowered the tarpaulin-wrapped corpse into the hole with reins taken from a harness—freshly oiled reins that left black streaks on the canvas.

A cold wind moaned among the crags that night. In the morning half a dozen Mexicans walked off the job. Johnny had to ride clear to Saguache to find replacements. Two days' hard travel both ways— hurry, hurry, hurry, heaven by the silver stairs. A mountain of high-grade ore was waiting in Baker for the wagons that already were lining up behind the road builders, the drivers eager to hand their coins to Otto Winkler's representatives waiting at the tollgates. An army of promoters paced the streets in Baker, the hotel lobbies, the assay shops, the supply houses. Silver, mister. You can't miss: massive chlorides from the grass stems straight down to the roots of the world. Grunt, heave, dig, blast—spruce bogs they beat with their road, slide rock, flood channels. And so down into the Los Padres Valley, with smooth sailing the rest of the way to town. To Johnny the names of the mines they passed were like the drum of the wind in the firs—San Juan Chief, Mastodon, Vermilion, Old Lout, Sultan, Red Cloud. Silver, mister! Come one, come all!

More than greenhorns fell for the blandishments. One day Pat Edgell rode into Baker for supplies, returned at dawn sour-breathed and puffy-cheeked.

"Look here!" he said, shaking Johnny out of bed and smoothing, under the pale candlelight in their tent, several crumpled certificates for mining stock. "Look what I bought!"

Arching across the face of each parchment was the company's name, taken from the stream—Los Padres Silver Mining and Milling Company, Ltd. Beneath this was engraved a picture of paddlewheel steamboats plying Los Padres River. One steamer was represented as lying moored at a dock fronting a chimneyed mill. Beyond the mill was a mine entrance. A throng of workers carried bags from the tunnel mouth to the mill, from the mill to the steamer. Presumably each bag was full of silver ore.

"You loony!" John said. "Steamboats! There's not a place on the Los Padres that would float more'n a rowboat—and it would wreck in the rapids."

"Sure it's a fake," Pat said, admiring the crinkly feel of the parchment. "Brighter'n a button, too. I snuck in early. Now I can catch me a greenhorn and unload at a profit when the promoters edge up the price for a come-on."

"How much of your wages did you sink in that?"

"Don't worry about me." Pat's tongue wagged happily. Loony? These steamboats were mild. Remember the Ennis brothers back at San Cristobal, paying a lady spiritualist for advice on how to drive their drifts in the Highland Mary? The tunnels snaked like a bad dream; superstitious miners would not venture into them except in pairs. But the Highland Mary stock was still going up. Silver, mister. Hurry, hurry, hurry!

"Johnny?"

"What now?"

"Do you figure to keep on working for Winkler the rest of your life?"

"Today is worry enough."

"And tomorrow. What do you aim to do after we finish this road? Prospect?"

"Hell, no."

"Drive team?"

"I don't know."

"Buy some more mules with Kennerly?"

"At least I'll have something to show for my money."

"Mule piss, that's what. Johnny—"

"Did you sleep with somebody's talking crow down there?"

"I'm just asking. What are you so sore about?"

"I'm not sore." Johnny jerked on his pants and cinched up the belt buckle. "Steamboats! And next winter you'll be wanting a loan."

"What we need is a proposition of our own. Something cute like these—"

"I'm going out and get some breakfast."

Late in September the road reached Baker City. Its boss and owner, tiny, bearded Otto Winkler, put a load of dignitaries into the first stagecoach ever to cross the pass and rolled them over the hump to receive the keys of the ecstatic town. Councilmen pontificated; the Silver Cornet Band of the Baker City Volunteer Engine Company Number One (no engine yet) puffed their faces as red as their uniform coats. Meanwhile Johnny and Pat and two or three others sat it out in the Big Swede's saloon. They had driven a buckboard loaded with tools down ahead of the stagecoach to clear away rocks that had rolled off the hillsides and to make sure that the last-minute bridge timbers had been spiked down so that some prancing horse would not put a foot through a crack. They galloped into Baker about half an hour ahead of the ceremony, feeling very pleased, but no one gave them a key to anything. After listening through the open window to a third speech from the temporary platform in the street, Pat borrowed a bung starter from Emil and climbed unsteadily onto the bar.

"On this momentous occasion—" Outside, the cornets hit an unscheduled high. Pat paused to hiccup.

Someone else carried it on. "It is altogether fitting and proper—"

"That we take this goddamn town apart!" Johnny interrupted with a howl like a Ute.

Still carrying the bung starter, they marched arm in arm over to Blair Street. Ought to be a welcome somewhere.

At dawn they amused themselves getting even with a waitress. She had declined to join their party on the grounds that her steady escort—her solid fellow, in the mountain way of saying—might object. Solid fellow? A'right. They stole a wooden cigar-store Indian and while she was opening the café lugged it with stifled whispers and giggles into her roominghouse and put it into her bed. They could only imagine her reaction when she found it, but they were sure it would be the funniest thing that had ever happened. They could hardly get back through the door for leaning on each other and laughing.

John fell asleep after that. When he awakened in midafternoon, the taste of the party had turned gummy in his mouth. Leaving the others, he rented a livery-stable horse and rode through the long chill shadows of the September evening north up Mineral Creek toward the pass that led beside Red Mountain to Ute Gorge and on to Argent. Just as twilight was vanishing, a swollen moon floated up over the peaks. It helped him find a way out of the black spruce onto the grassy hillsides that lined Mineral Creek's deepening canyon. He could hear aspen leaves rattle as he skirted occasional groves, and running water was a lonesome sound in the canyon. The slope rose as steeply as a cow's tail. The Baker horse's progress dwindled to a series of lunges—

hunch, jump, stop and blow. Leg-weary, back-weary. Each time it paused, its eyes rolled apprehensively toward the inky gulch to its right. Finally John dismounted, tied the reins to the saddle horn, and shooed it downhill. Like all self-returning horses of the mining camps, it would go straight home.

He set fire to a dead log. Lying down on a flat spot between the blaze and a ledge of rock that caught the heat, he slept until sunrise. Hungry and stiff, he climbed on through dew-drenched grass to the pass. His eyes turned surveyor, as they always did when he saw a workable gap in the ranges. This one was a natural, only eleven thousand feet high and tree-sheltered against winter storms. From either direction, from Argent to the north and Baker to the south, racketing chasms climbed almost as straight as arrows out of the town basins to meet here at this saddle. Lots of blasting, but no sharp curves to reduce the pulling power of the big freight teams. Only twenty-five or thirty miles separated town from town. Traffic flowing both ways. . . . Oh, sure. On ore not yet found, money not yet raised. Hitching his blanket roll around to the other shoulder, Johnny pushed ahead through the gap to where the ground began tipping the other way, toward Argent.

Overhead, the early morning sky had been scoured so clean by the wind that it was a glow rather than a mere blueness. To his left, a long line of peaks lifted snow-streaked skulls out of the gorge leading to Argent. Erosion-battered pinnacles crowned their round tops. Their standard hue, above the green collars of alpine grass, was the familiar gray-brown of volcanic tuff. To his right, however, the mountains blazed —three cones of red rock, two of them standing at either end of a curving cirque and the third separated from the twins by a gaudy water channel. The name Red Mountain blanketed all three peaks. Yet not red, he thought. Rust and maroon and orange and tan, yellow in spots, crimson streaks—a paint pot slushed up and spilled over. Thus when he studied it. Yet when he glanced away, the after-image blurred into red. Not quite blood color. Not sunset scarlet. Just . . . red, until he surveyed it again and the blend tantalized him for a specific he could not find.

As he dropped lower, streamlets coursing the sides of the peaks gathered to form a creek rusty-bottomed with iron salts. On either side of the creek's slit of a channel rolled a welter of odd, hummocky hillocks. Geologists, as he knew, speculated that these overgrown gopher humps were actually the debris of ancient landslides that had run down from the peaks and long since had been covered by vegetation. Blanketing as they did the true skeleton of the ground underneath, the hummocks made prospecting difficult. And travel, too. Complicating their maze were clusters of spruce windfall through which he had to clamber, slide rock that threatened to turn his ankles, briar patches that dragged at his trouser legs but yielded enough tiny ripe raspberries to cut the stickiness in his mouth.

A curious atavism walked with him, an impression that he had been here ages ago. The feeling would flash up when he stepped around a corner and glimpsed the thrust of a cliff ahead of him, or saw the lean of some lightning-struck spruce above a spine of rock. These were familiar mountain sights, of course. But the sense of having been here before, of belonging, was something else. He caught himself listening. A rock clanked on a talus slope. Wind gusts thrummed. Footsteps. A voice around the bend. . . . Nuts, Ogden. Boogers. Hangover nerves.

Someone was there, though. He came across a trail and followed it around a point of red earth to a prospector's shelter built partly of brush, partly of logs, partly of canvas. Nearby, where a vein seamed the rocky slope, the mouth of a shallow tunnel gaped. He looked in, smelled stale powdersmoke. In blue-fogged light from a candle held by a pointed iron stick thrust into a timber he saw the stooped figure of a miner. Johnny called. By and by the fellow emerged, bent over by the low tunnel roof and by a leather sack on his back. He had no mine car, no wheelbarrow. He brought out the muck from each shot this hard way. He was a tall, gaunt Finn with deep grooves in his face and lank, dirty hair curling to the back of his collar. He coughed and blinked and smelled sourly of smoke and sweat. One shoe sole was splitting away from its upper. He was glad to see company and grinned, and there were snuff stains on his uneven teeth. His name, Johnny learned later, was Aino Berg. He had been running this tunnel all summer.

He shrugged the sack off his shoulders and began sorting the rock, tossing waste off to one side and putting the ore in a pile at his feet. The ore was garish—peacock shine of copper, gleams of lead—but color didn't necessarily make it rich enough to merit packing out of these mountains.

"How'll it run in silver?" Johnny asked.

"We see," Aino said. He ground up a chunk in a mortar, placed the powder in a test tube he took from its case in a hole bored into a block of wood. He added nitric acid. The mixture fumed violently.

"Pyrites," Johnny said.

"Ja." In went water. After the liquid had settled a while, Aino poured the contents onto a small flat piece of copper plate, then washed the plate with cold water. Probably he had run this crude assay every time he pushed the tunnel a few feet farther into the vein, and probably he grew just as excited every time.

A black smudge of silver salts formed on the plate. Too thin. Johnny was as disappointed as if it had been his own mine.

"Only so-so," he said.

"Ja."

They hunkered side by side, not talking much, looking across the creek at the tumbled landslide hillocks and above the hills at the ruddy slopes of the peaks, bright in the morning sun. Only so-so. But the next round . . .

"Prospecting?" Aino asked.

"Too much like work for me," John said, and explained what he had been thinking about a road. It was no sillier than dreaming of mines.

"A road!" Aino approved in his singsong, the inflection rising at the ends of the sentences. "Now maybe Gabe can bring in something to eat for his store."

"Angel Gabe? Has he a store up here?"

"He calls it that."

Aino pointed north to where the creek flattened out onto a long meadow dotted with two tiny lakes and bordered by aspens frosted as golden as the stroke of a bell. For the first time Johnny noticed a wisp of smoke rising from the trees at the upper end of the meadow. Two—no, three wisps. A regular settlement. He grew excited. But Aino was scornful. Those were placer workings down there, and placer mines were soon stripped and forgotten. Deep veins would last. He poured his shiny pebbles from one palm to the other.

"Veins. Dot mountain, she is rotten with mineral stain. Ore is here somewhere. We don' see it quick because dose little hills cover the outcrops, I t'ank. But I'll find dem."

"And then?"

Aino's glance turned inward. But he was not ready yet to tell all he saw—only as much as he knew was expected.

"A girl first. One dot smells good behind her ears. You take your hand—" He swallowed.

"There's a lot of that coming into Baker already," John said. "A sure sign of prosperity. Maybe we'll even persuade some of 'em to come up here and you won't have to go all the way down to smell 'em. A store already—" He shook his head. "What do you know!—old Gabe. But I wouldn't bet he can get what he needs down in Baker. Everybody's bidding for winter supplies as fast as a wagon comes in over the new road. Prices are higher than this mountain. Can't Gabe buy what he needs in Argent?"

"He say supplies are short dere, too. Not many freighters travel dot way. They afraid the Utes."

"The Utes won't last. The northern ones are already on the way out because of the Meeker massacre. As soon as the southern tribes sign this new treaty the government is offering them, they'll go too. Then this whole end of the mountains will open up."

"For a year I hear dot," Aino said. "But not'ing happens." He flung one of his pebbles at a marmot that had appeared on the slide rock. "If powder I have and one more sack of flour I can work six weeks yet, perhaps two months in luck, before the snow grows bad. I t'ank I go to town myself for t'ings I need. But it takes two days, whichever way I go, and in two days drilling up here maybe I find— who knows?"

"An independent packer could go clear outside to Gunnison and bring in Gabe's orders for him—if there's enough stuff in the order to make the trip worthwhile." Johnny stood up. A job of hauling! A mine. More hauling jobs—then there would have to be a road! "I've plenty of time now," he said. "And mules that Walt Kennerly has been using for packing to the agency. Walt has wagons, too, if he's finished with them. I reckon maybe I'll talk to Gabe."

And Aino said, "Dis place might amount to somet'ing." He looked inside himself again and what he saw there slipped out. "A man might be somet'ing, too." He stood up beside Johnny. "Let's go to Gabe's."

"6"

That was the way Harmon remembered John Ogden—down out of the mountains, ring-tailed with his own kind of genie, conjured up with his own kind of medicine. A dozen miners, some coughing from the smoke of their tunnels, some with the skin of their legs as blue-numb as death from the cold wetness of their placers had gathered in Gabe Porcella's canvas store, had peered at the empty shelves and had seen—what? Not a tunnel breast or a sluice box, any more than John Ogden saw only the trail he was commissioned to build for taking out the ore that was piling up beside the prospects. Already the vision was beyond that, growing, swelling. Next year and the next. . . .

Do you know about toll roads? he had asked. I've seen, I tell you! What did Baker have compared to Argent? Notice how the St. John Mountains lay (he drew a map on Harmon's pine table with his index finger) protruding like a square peg into the Indian lands. Argent lay at the tip. To get there you skirted the mountains and came up the river. Elevations were low; grass and timber were available every mile of the way—a year-round route. To reach Baker, on the other hand, you had to cross the range on the summertime road Johnny had just helped build. There was no comparison between the two approaches or the two towns. Once the Indians signed the new treaty and left the land open, Argent would boom. For one thing, the region could supply itself. Look at the farmlands below the Narrows and the yellow pine lumber on the foothill ranges. Nothing like that could be found in Baker's high sterile basin. Baker was limited to mines that would have to import from outside everything they used. Oh, Argent was the town with the future.

Harmon grinned. "You sound like a promoter." And then he regretted the words when he saw Johnny's frown. Steamboats on Los Padres—a proposition, as Pat Edgell would say. John had not meant that.

"You've never been at Red Mountain," he protested. "Three peaks on fire, I tell you. Mineral in every fissure. You get rust on your teeth just drinking from those springs." His eyes grew reflective. "There was a geologic survey came through here a while back. Walt Kennerly and I packed for them. One of the fellows said a single volcano blowing its head off might lay down a few hundred acres of ashes and lava maybe two or three feet deep. Why, Jesus, there's miles and miles of it up there, in places two thousand feet through, according to what he showed us on the cliff faces. It must have been a whale of a blowing, if what the fellow said was true." He looked up the deep V of the gorge, the crook of his face very quizzical. "Do you believe it?"

Gregg shrugged. "'And God said, Let the waters under the heaven be gathered together unto one place and let the dry land appear.' Take your choice. I gave up straining my believer a long time ago."

"You think I'm crazy too, like Waldo does, don't you? But one day before long there'll be a call for that road. Fissure veins running every which way up there. Reaching deep! This is hardrock country. It'll last!"

Exuberance unalloyed by doubt. "Hardrock Johnny," Harmon murmured, feeling envy, and after that he always thought of him as Hardrock—solid, unshakable innocence. Yet Old Man Hedstrom said he was a killer.

"7"

Harmon looked across the pine table in his office at his visitors, at Pat Edgell and Gabe Porcella, and drummed his fingers.

"Do you think he's guilty?" he asked bluntly.

Gabe rubbed his sideburns, startled. Lawyers did not ask such questions; lawyers waved their wands.

"Cushman, Tally—maybe they tricked him."

The refuge of the simple-minded: someone had taken advantage of them. Pat Edgell gestured in annoyance.

"What the hell? Young Hedstrom wasn't such a much. He's been locked up plenty right here in town for his troublemaking. All right, he kills a Ute and the Utes kill him. It's no loss."

Old Hedstrom is making a loss of it, Harmon thought, and just then a newsboy came shouting out of the print shop across the street, waving aloft the newest release of Argent's weekly paper, *The True Fissure.* Harmon secured a copy of the four-page sheet and spread it on his desk.

The crudely engraved masthead showed a picture of a prospector and his burro gazing raptly upward at a granite peak creased by veins emitting rays of light labeled "Prosperity" and "Truth." Typographically, the paper was as tight as a stack of dried lumber. No headline was more than a single column wide. To compensate for this lateral constriction, editor Al Ewer piled up black rows of banners like cribwork, achieving some visual change of pace by varying type styles and line lengths. The multiple decks of the Hedstrom story reached halfway down the front page.

INHUMAN GHOULS

A Crime That Has
No Parallel
In Ancient or Modern
History

A. D. Hedstrom
Who Kills An Indian
In Self-Defense
Deliberately Turned Over
To The Red Devils
FOR TORTURE

Indian Agent Cushman
Capt. Mort Tally
Hal Banner, Hal Hoyt
and
JOHN OGDEN
are
THE GHOULS

The Citizens of Argent
Are Sworn To Avenge
This Dastardly Outrage!

On Sept. 30 four freighters—J. H. Hedstrom of Del Norte, his nephew A. D. Hedstrom, and two companions were camped for the night between Captain Tally's trading post and the Ute Agency at Los Alamos. About seven o'clock two drunk Indians, Johnson, son of war chief Shavano, and Henry, a known bad actor from the Blue Divide country, rode into their camp demanding food. An altercation developed . . .

Harmon's eyes jumped down the story. It was a distillation of what Old Hedstrom had been saying now for twenty hours. The shot that had killed Shavano's son; the freighters' seeking refuge in Tally's post; Walt Kennerly's riding for help to the Agency; Cushman's promise to the Indians that the killer would be taken outside for trial; the escort of which John Ogden had been a member; and finally by prearrangement with the savages—so *The True Fissure* repeated—the surrendering of the boy to the Utes in order that they could torture him and burn him at the stake.

. . . the worst dastards of history could not have acted in a more cold-blooded manner. To plan the death of a boy whose only crime was the defense of his friends is beyond the conception of men who wear a heart. The mere thought that a so-called civilized white man could turn over one of his own countrymen to be killed with all the fiendish cruelty the fertile minds of the savages can devise is sufficient to goad honest men to desperate doings. Agent Cushman and John Ogden on one end of a rope and Capt. Tally and his henchmen on the other end, with the middle of the rope resting on a substantial bough of a tree would be a sight that should offend no lover of justice.

"Oh, for Christ sake," Pat Edgell said and started a slow, flat, violent cursing of the paper and its editor. Gabe Porcella, who was only halfway through the story, looked up in alarm.
"What's the matter?"

"You can read, can't you?" Pat growled and then in angry triumph glared at Harmon Gregg, as though the lawyer's acceptance of the case was now a foregone conclusion.

Our daily writ, Harmon said again to himself. Majesty of the law. One young man on the threshold of his life's fulfilment, as guaranteed by the statutes of a free society, conspired in the death of another young man on the threshold of ditto. And what were the reactions? The Angel Gabriel forgave because he thought John had been duped. Pat Edgell shrugged the whole thing away as fair exchange. The voice of the town cried protest not so much about the death of the boy but about delivering him to the Indians whom they hated. But who protested the arrogance of a handful of private citizens taking it unto themselves to decide it was time to end another citizen's life? Indeed, the town's answer, spoken through *The True Fissure*, was similar arrogance—a lynching, as ungraced by fair trial as Hedstrom's death had been. Meanwhile, up at the head of the creek, three mountains of blood-colored stone rose serenely above tumbled hillocks where, if certain mules arrived in time, enough silver might be discovered to justify the whole episode.

What was Red Mountain, essentially? And what was this town? And what had Young Hedstrom been as his flesh had begun to burn? And John Ogden—what was he as he had helped betray Young Hedstrom toward that burning?

And why was Harmon Gregg, runaway lawyer, asking himself these questions? His gentle mouth twisted above its goatee. You know damn well why, he told himself. It's not the incorruptible majesty of the law. You just want to be sure the daily writ will work, that's all.

Gabe finished reading the story. "A hanging!" His meaty face looked like boiled ham between the orange sideburns. "Godamighty, Mr. Gregg! Hadn't we better do what we started to do, and ride out and meet Johnny and head him off?"

Harmon avoided their eyes, letting his own glance slide from the dull spines of the lawbooks to the saw blade at the intersection, and then back to the masthead on the paper. Truth. Prosperity. John Ogden, ghoul, trading a human life for fifteen mules and two residence lots. Or Johnny Ogden, the shine of innocence on his face, trying to guarantee a dream, a road up the silver staircase to everyman's hope.

Which was correct?

Which, ten years from now, would this town accept as correct?

He said, "Has Johnny friends in town you can count on?"

"For what?" Pat asked.

"For getting him through the street into the courthouse?"

"Jail, you mean?"

"He has to be arraigned before he can be tried."

"We can round up some fellows," Pat said.

Gabe hesitated. "Johnny, he's popular all right. But a lot of people came in here this summer, while he was over on the other side of the hill, that don't know him. And they do know the Utes."

"Will the sheriff help protect him or will he stand aside?"

"Gaw? He'll do his job," Pat said.

Gabe was still not convinced. "If Johnny lies low until this blows over—"

"It won't blow that fast. Besides, he'll look guilty." Harmon let his voice grow barrister-precise. "It's my advice, so long as you think you can control the situation, to let him ride in here as if he had every right on his side. Let Gaw serve the warrants that issued from the Argent justice court. As soon as that is done, John will have the start of a case— lack of jurisdiction on the part of the county. The offense, if there was actionable offense, was committed on federal land and involved wards of the federal government—the Indians. John can then apply to the district court in Denver for a writ of transfer. That technicality alone may free him. In any event, the trial will be shifted into a court where this total prejudice against all things Indian won't cloud the issue and where a plea of self-defense—or whatever emerges from Johnny's side of the story—will have some chance of being judged fairly."

This was what Pat had been waiting for—the genie. "We'll get him in," he said, and cracked his knuckles in anticipation.

Gabe asked anxiously, "You'll handle the case—get it set up like you say?"

"I'll hear Ogden's story anyhow," Harmon temporized.

"Will you come to the Narrows and meet him with us?"

And commit myself too soon? Harmon wondered. "I'd better stay here," he said, waving vaguely toward the bookcase, "and do some research."

Alone at last, he leaned back in his wooden chair and regarded the faded gold letters on the back of Jenkins' *Legal Forms*. The ritual of civilization brought in a worn trunk by a snail-slow wagon through the lands of a vanishing race. Were the old forms the right forms here in this new and eager world? Or would outworn standards have to be betrayed along with men?

"8"

When Gabe and Pat and the little cavalcade that was escorting John Ogden's mule train came clattering into town, the evening air was sharp with fall. At the foot of the lower cliffs shadows were darkening, and back under the trees, away from the flat-faced main business block, a few cabin windows and canvas tents glimmered with early lantern light. Eastward, high above, where the ring of peaks pulled back to form the basin's enormous amphitheater, alpenglow shone on the rocks with a passion of brightness. Suffused reflection from it touched the tips of the evergreens and lay ruddily on a pile of new pine boards beside the courthouse. Harmon wandered out into the intersection. A straggle of men, including Old Hedstrom, were already waiting there. More were clustered around the Dixon House verandah. Random, dim-red shimmers of light appeared and disappeared on the rusty sides of the saw blade that hung to the flagpole.

Sheriff Gaw stood among the waiters. Where Silver Avenue opened onto the intersection four riders sat on hang-headed horses. They were Johnny's friends. Harmon nodded approval. Mounted men, especially if they knew what they intended to do, had the strong moral advantage of elevation over disorganized pedestrians—and so far as he could see, none of Old Hedstrom's following had thought to get horses.

As the string of mules drew nearer, it had to ripple sideways around the stump of a huge fir that no one had yet bothered to remove from the road. Fifteen mules. Candles, boots, gloves, blasting powder, pick and shovel heads. Flour, pinto beans, slabs of salt pork, five-gallon kegs of hooped wood full of whisky for softening chills left by the damp tunnels and icy streams. And back on the reservation the remnants of Young Hedstrom. A fresh spasm of doubt pulled Harmon's mouth back against his teeth. Craning, he tried to see Johnny's eyes.

Men shouldered past him and the handful of riders with the mule train came to an enforced stop beside the flagpole. Johnny was up front. The stiff canvas jacket he had put on against the cold made him look almost square. The fading light striking under his hat brim touched his face a deep pink, so that his crooked grin would have made him resemble a ribald satyr. But there was no grin in him. His glance moved around the other pink faces staring up at him. He did not seem frightened or angry, so far as Harmon could determine, but only bewildered. It was a lonely bewilderment. The other men who had been involved in the surrender evidently had chosen not to come into town.

There were mutters and catcalls. Big, round Al Ewer, editor of *The True Fissure*, undertook the job of spokesman. "Well, John," he said. Over to one side, Old Hedstrom, bleary and slack from twenty-four hours of drink and staled emotion, snarled "White Ute!" The epithet swung Johnny's friend, Walt Kennerly, aside. He was very tall, Harmon noticed, morose-looking, with long yellow hair and a long straw-colored mustache. He leaned over the saddle horn, speaking softly to Old Hedstrom.

"Listen, you son of a bitch. You were quick enough, when the Utes were wanting blood at Tally's, to point your finger at the one of your party who killed Johnson. Your own nephew! That's just about enough finger-pointing out of you, you understand."

Hedstrom glared up at him and then around at the watching men. "Anybody smell anything bad?" he sneered. "Hell, Kennerly wasn't anywhere near Tally's when things were tight. But he's fartin' big now."

"How big would you be if that alarm was ringing now?" Kennerly said, nodding toward the saw blade.

Hedstrom's slack face twisted with venom. "So that's the drift! Ogden saved the town from Utes. Well, we're particular who saves us. That right, boys?"

Gaw came pushing through. "Open up, open up! He's under arrest!" And Ewer: "If you've any statements to make, John—" And Harmon Gregg: "Not here! Don't talk here!" And Gaw, recalling things he had read about his job: "That's right. I got to tell you that anything you say can be used against you."

Ewer swung to the lawyer. "Are you representing Ogden? What about Cushman and Tally and the others? Have they retained you too?" Harmon was about to answer when a voice shrilled over his shoulder, "Yella bastards, hiding behind a lawyer's dirty skirts!" and he let what he had been about to say remain unspoken.

Gaw waved a signal. Porcella took the lead rope of the mules from John and shifted enough so that the long string of pack animals formed a blockade of sorts against men striding up from the lower part of town. Then John's four mounted friends edged their horses into the press. The mob growled and jostled, but nobody stood his ground so firmly that a horse had to topple him to advance. We're all right, Harmon thought, and glanced at John's puzzled, stricken face. Gaw thrust his palms, not too hard, against the chests in front of him and repeated insistently, "I'm taking him in. Now get out of the road. I'm taking him in."

They wedged John close to the sidewalk and off his horse and up the three steps to the courthouse's little stoop, an uneven platform of boards under a triangle of roof held by two crudely lathed wooden pillars. Down on the walk Hedstrom tried to gather his wits together. In falsetto imitation of a woman's terror he shrilled,

"Oh Johnny, Johnny! Save me from the Injuns!"

He defeated himself. There was the tiniest of pauses and then some of those who might have been persuaded to crowd up the steps chose instead to halt and save face with jeering laughs and shrills of "Save me! Save me!" Anger came to Johnny then. He turned back, bayed. His mouth opened; he breathed as if he had choked on soot. Before any words could work out, however, Gaw gripped him just above one elbow.

"Come on, come on!"

They pulled him inside and slammed the door, leaving Pat on the stoop, his flat eyes hard in his flat round face, grinning and spitting and grinning again while the mob began to unravel.

"9"

What Gaw called the formalities did not take long. Afterwards, the sheriff said that Harmon Gregg could confer with the accused and with Walt Kennerly in the sheriff's office. Harmon waved Johnny ahead and then felt Walt's touch, restraining him.

"Listen," Walt said, and then produced nothing to hear. His long, narrow eyes were miserable, the skin at their outer corners crumpled like pale brown paper which someone had wadded into a ball and then had tried ineffectively to smooth again.

"I'm listening," Harmon prompted.

"I wasn't at Tally's when it happened."

"That's what Old Hedstrom said," Harmon reminded him. He was puzzled. Walt did not look like the sort that would make so careful a point of building an alibi for the time of the trouble. What was behind the insistence?

"I know what happened just the same," Walt went on. "Johnny won't think to tell you. If all you ask him about is Tally's, that's all he'll say. That's not enough. You've got to see this town the way it was when John first saw it, and the way it is with the Indians sitting across the only road we can use to get in here, and the way the town can be, if luck breaks. And you've got to see Johnny the way he is. He's just a kid still, I don't care how old a timer he's supposed to be. Look at him. Listen to him just five minutes and you'll know what I mean."

Harmon nodded. "I've noticed those eyes. Complete—oh, simplicity. Like a sixteen-year-old virgin's."

Walt frowned, suspecting Harmon of facetiousness. "He's not stupid."

"Or a virgin either?" Harmon smiled faintly. "I said simplicity. It's not the same." The smile faded. "But even kids can be guilty of murder."

"You won't listen!" Walt cried in protest. "Murder! You keep trying to make it like—like shooting somebody you find in bed with your wife. It wasn't that way."

Harmon pounced. "So they did arrange with the Indians to have Young Hedstrom killed."

"You're sitting in the middle of big trouble. You see the only thing that can be done—"

"And on your own responsibility you condemn another man to death." Harmon ran his tongue around the dry insides of his mouth. A new lawyer in a new town. Make—or break. "You're not making his defense any easier," he said.

Walt's anger grew, bringing a stain of color high on his cheeks. "You're like everybody else, smarter than hell about what the decisions should have been after the thing is done. The least Johnny's lawyer ought to give him is an open-minded hearing."

"With you putting in your licks, too, to make sure it's open-minded in your way?" Harmon asked sarcastically, and thought with belated prescience, Maybe Walt had ducked out of Tally's when John needed him most. Maybe remorse over something like that was his reason for trying so hard now.

"I've known him since his family brought him to Saguache," Walt said. "And that's part of it, too. You can't just stop at Tally's."

"Sounds like a long night," Harmon said. The majesty of the law, aloof from human passion. What had Johnny's family to do with this? Guilt or innocence should be as direct as that. Legal forms. Give us this day . . . His gaze dropped from the thrust of Walt's eyes and he found he could not repeat his original mockery even to himself. Our daily bread, he finished. Hunger, eternally and achingly in a man's breast. Make or break. For thine is the power, the glory . . . the writ. Oh, damn: the questions, the doubt, the self-contempt all over again. He motioned toward the door.

"I'll listen," he said.

John looked up as they came in. He had taken off his hat and coat. Light from the sheriff's coal-oil lamp, placed strategically on the top of a ponderous, gilt-decorated safe labeled ARGENT COUNTY, fell strongly down across his tangled hair and bony face. He had been reading *The*

True Fissure story and the bewilderment of his glance came at Harmon like the cry of a child pinched by the world's unexpected cruelty.

"That's not the way of it!" he blurted.

"That's the way Old Hedstrom says it was," Harmon retorted with deliberate malice and watched the flush that darkened Johnny's already dark skin. Ghouls with virgin eyes. Was such a mingling possible? He looked at Walt.

"Suppose you two get together and decide where to start."

"You're definitely going to be his lawyer?"

"I want to know first what I'm up against."

"I'd think a lawyer would want to know what Johnny is up against."

"It comes to the same thing," Harmon said. Well, he owed them this much at least: "If you make me believe in the case, I'll find a way to make the jury believe in it."

They began to talk, pulling back and forth at each other. Walt had his way and in spite of Johnny's impatience, took the account clear back to Saguache in '74, but the story as a whole came out confused and blurred. Afterwards Harmon had to spend a long time sieving it, rehearing parts of it, asking questions where reticence had left holes, and then ordering it into a pattern. In the beginning he supposed he was trying to discover the past. But as the aspirations and the dreads and even some of the half-spoken secrets emerged, he realized that he was really trying to outguess the future, his own and John Ogden's and Walt Kennerly's and how all of them might fit—or not fit—into this embryo town which itself had not yet achieved its pattern.

II

" 1 "

The thing John remembered first, after Walt's insistence had hauled him backward to the Saguache he wanted to forget, was the white, stark set of his mother's face. He knew now that the look had been born of hatred.

He had noticed it first when his father had met them at the railhead in the mountains, after their long, jolting, cindery ride from Altoona. The family had not seen Henry Ogden often during the past fourteen years—and that too, Johnny realized now, was the way Henry Ogden and his wife Deborah had really wanted things. At the very outset of the Civil War, Henry had resigned his job as bookkeeper in the Altoona ironworks to join a troop of horsemen being formed by a backslid Quaker named William Palmer. In the mud and the drills and the chill night gallops, in the swift coppery excitement of bullet whines, even in the slowness of boredom and the maddening ignorance about the reasons for so many of the things he was compelled to do— throughout the long welter, where his destiny was not really his, he had found satisfactions that had eluded him in the placid order of his home.

When Palmer had written shortly after the war, asking if Henry would rejoin his former commander and some of his old comrades for railroad work in the West, Ogden had packed up overnight. He tramped the Plains with grading crews of the Kansas Pacific, bossed tie camps in Colorado. When Palmer extended his surveys to the Pacific, Henry was made foreman of one of the crews. They crossed the front range of the Rockies and turned down the San Luis Valley into canyoned deserts. Thirst parched them, Apaches stalked. The red sand reached and reached. Fifteen hundred miles out to the blue Pacific, fifteen hundred miles back to a vision Palmer had caught in the San Luis Valley—and so far as Johnny could tell from his father's accounts, joy had shone on every mile.

Returned to Colorado, Henry had settled down to helping spiral Palmer's tight little narrow-gauge railroad, the Denver & Rio Grande, over the foothills toward the future quarries and mines and farms he had glimpsed in the valley. When snow blocked the work, he occasionally reappeared in Altoona, staying long enough to father two more children, spindle-legged daughters, and to stroll on sunny afternoons with his wife along the sidewalk, her fingers resting possessively on his arm while she nodded in apparent pride to her neighbors. She had made a legend of herself in Altoona, the faithful Penelope waiting for her wanderer, and in public she let the legend sparkle. Even as a child, however, Johnny had noticed that when his parents were alone together they had little to say. Most of Henry's talk was for his son, stories of Indians and hunts and horsebreaking that made the boy ache with longing.

Too soon for his vague yearnings the stories would trail off into absent-mindedness. The intensities, mostly mixed with anger, that Johnny overheard from the bedroom would cease. Presently Henry Ogden would leave. The monthly letters would start once more, as dutiful as clockwork. Deborah Ogden would make a ceremony of receiving these at the post office and afterwards would sprinkle purported quotations around the town. But Johnny knew, from spying for stories, that the communications generally contained little else than funds. Neither tears nor wistfulness on the part of his mother ever made him suppose that she wished for anything more.

The silver panic of '73 stopped the checks. Work on Palmer's railroad dragged to a halt. Lacking a job, Henry decided to fill the time by jumping ahead of the rails and taking up a homestead in the San Luis Valley, near the new adobe-brick town of Saguache. The region enthralled him and for the first time he tried to pass on some of his anticipation to his family, perhaps because there was nothing else he could send. Only a sneezing Indian, so he wrote, could pronounce the town's name properly, but white men made out by calling it Sí-wash. Deborah was not amused. And then he said that Deborah and the family could join him or not as she chose, but she could expect no money from him for an indefinite time. And finally he suggested, almost as a postscript, that here in this land of beginnings, perhaps they could begin their lives again also.

Deborah wept the night the letter arrived. The next morning, dry-eyed, she announced throughout Altoona that she was going West.

Johnny, having secured the letter as usual, thought hopefully that his father's closing words had wrought the decision. Later, watching his mother as the train chuffed away from the security of the patterns she had manufactured for herself, he wondered if the dread of being exposed poverty-stricken before the town might not have been the more powerful motive.

Henry Ogden must have had his own moment of hope as the train pulled into the depot. He caught Deborah by the elbows as she stepped onto the platform. For a moment he held her so, searching her eyes. Then a grayness overlaid him. Turning, he scooped up his daughters, tickling laughs out of them; and perhaps their wigglings and Johnny's rapture over being shown a new repeater rifle and twin Colt pistols hid from the depot loungers the fact that the reunited husband and wife had not spoken a word to each other.

Henry had brought a wagon to the railhead to pick up their goods and also the stove and bedsteads and churn he had ordered for setting up housekeeping on the homestead. Evidently the vehicle had seemed commodious enough until he faced her grips and telescoping bags and wicker baskets and parrot cage and her yellow-brown, foot-pedaled harmonium.

"Debbie—"

"If this must be my home, I am going to make it be like home."

Giving in, he rented a two-wheeled cart which Johnny drove with the overflow behind the wagon. The last day on the trail they nooned beside a cabin of gray cottonwood logs chinked with plastered sticks and roofed with earth and straw. Whoever owned the place had no great concern for it. The door was open, but even the raw March wind could not push Deborah inside the building's dank, rat-musty interior. They huddled against its sunny wall, where Henry built a fire to warm coffee, and ate in silence, regarding the while the scrofulous patches of old snow lingering under the sagebrush and the miscellany of rusted junk scattered between the house and the corral of sway-backed poles. Two Indians loped by, black eyes staring out of round moon faces. The branches of the leafless cottonwoods along the little creek were restless whips across the gray sky. In the distance they could see the few tawny cubes that comprised most of the little town of Saguache. Henry Ogden watched his wife's pinched, taut face. Abruptly, after hours of silence he began to talk.

He tried to tell her what coming into the valley the first time had been like. Everything he groped for and said she could see right there in front of her—on one side of the valley tall peaks white with a promise of unfailing water for irrigation; on the other side the rolling hills of timber; and in between, as far as the eye could reach, the grasslands and potential grainfields. Here was where Palmer had taken fire, the heartland for which his rails would be arteries. Mines, stock ranches, new cities untrammeled by the cramping hand of the past . . .

She stirred restively, Henry changed his theme. Though when you came right down to it, the valley had its traditions as well as Altoona had. Why, parts of Pennsylvania had been untouched wilderness when the first settlers had come into the San Luis Valley from Sante Fe, itself an older town than Philadelphia, older even than Boston. Johnny was puzzled. Henry Ogden, preaching age, as if he thought that to a woman oldness somehow brought confidence: birthing and dying, life's continuity assured. But age alone wasn't enough. An inward pull of her shoulders dismissed the history. "Mexicans," she said scornfully.

The tightness Johnny had learned to dread grew around his father's mouth. "They're good people when you get to know them."

"I will not live on a homestead like one."

"We've got to meet residence requirements to get the deed. Virgin land, Debbie, to make of it whatever—"

"New! New! It's people who stay and are satisfied who make a place fit for living. Anyway, you did not come here first because you wanted something new. I know you."

"Debbie—"

"You came to get away from me and your children. You came because you hate me. Virgin land won't change that."

"Debbie—"

"I will not live on a homestead. I will live in town, like a white woman."

And she did. She planted herself in Saguache's sole, deplorable hotel until her husband was at last able to rent one of the town's few frame residences. She prevailed on him to build a picket fence around the yard against stray cows and burros; she put net curtains at the windows; she erected a fresh barrier of pretenses against the newness of her unwanted world—the genteel wife bravely accepting the strokes of economic disaster until her engineer husband could return to his proper work of railroad building. To help finance the town house, she allowed Johnny, after a scene with her husband, to go to work for Otto Winkler, local storekeeper and freight contractor. She also took in Walt Kennerly as boarder and roomer. Henry had encountered Walt earlier in the Arizona country when Walt had been packing for Palmer's surveyors. Now he was packing for Winkler, which meant that he was absent from the house for days at a time and hence no great bother. And when he was home he too became part of Deborah Ogden's defense and pretense.

Oh, indeed she was genteel. Henry grew perverse about showing Saguache how Altoona lived. No matter. She trained Walt Kennerly to file his broken fingernails, to pass cups, to rise when she entered the room. Heaven knew how she managed him. Certainly Saguache did not know. Indeed, the town never had understood the man. A hell of a Walt, his fellow freighters would say and let the matter go at that. The whole underneath of him ran contrary to his golden surface. Fixed for town with his long yellow hair curling over the collar of his black frock coat, he looked like a tinhorn gambler, but Henry Ogden had never seen him touch a card except to play solitaire. Breaking horses or bringing a sledload of logs down an icy hill, he seemed crazy-reckless. Yet when the reckless ones tried to talk him into joining their exploits— guiding them on hunts for lost mines in the southwestern deserts or riding to California to trade for mules—Walt always refused.

"I reckon not. Too chancy for me."

He fascinated Johnny, who pestered his father for information, but Henry could reveal only this: during an Indian fight in Arizona Walt somehow had become separated from the rest of the survey party. On foot and alone he made his way with desperate hardship back to Santa Fe. Later, hearing that Palmer was in Saguache (misinformation, as events developed) he tried to rejoin his old boss but lost his way in a blizzard and was almost dead when his horse brought him, by instinct, into Otto Winkler's freight corrals. The two experiences evidently had dried up any recklessness he'd had. From then on he had stuck like glue to Winkler.

This suited Otto, who needed a dependable foreman. Besides, Walt had savvy. "You vant to learn," Otto would say to Johnny. "You vatch Kennerly." It was unnecessary advice. John tagged Walt everywhere, working over wagons and mules with him, pitching horseshoes, or just sitting silent in the sun against an adobe wall while Walt's thoughts turned inward onto memories of which he never spoke.

He was nine years older than Johnny and in love with Johnny's mother, which the boy sensed well enough. It made him angry with her rather than with Walt—every betrayal so far had been hers. He sensed, too, that Walt had never before seen such a woman, so genteel and all. The freighter would sit like a stunned man when her fingers lingered against his while passing a plate. A puppy-love crush, except that Walt had been too long in the mountains to stay content with puppy love. She would smile up at him in the lamplight and then deliberately turn away, knowing well enough how his eyes followed the motion of her back across the room. Suddenly, with a look of black despair, he would plunge outside. He did not care then what he found, Mexican or Ute or some worn prostitute eking out another year or two so far out on the fringes that men could not be particular. Deborah knew of those evenings, but there was no change in her expression when at length he returned, content again just to touch, to look. This was a mastery she could have without danger—oh, no scandal about her and Walt. Furthermore, her defenses needed him more than ever. Henry was spending longer and longer periods at the homestead, and the town was beginning to wonder why she did not join him. Ah, but she was needed in town to help raise money by caring for her boarder; to watch over Johnny, whose job kept him in Saguache and who was growing toward the age of wildness; to raise her girls, who had to remain near their school. The faithful mother of the little flock. She would go to her husband as soon as these other duties released her.

And so the months slipped by, from March of 1874 to the late summer of 1875. Johnny put on muscle. He swept Winkler's store, weighed nails, carried ashes, dickered with the Utes who came to trade. He loaded and unloaded wagons, curried horses, patched harness, shoveled manure, pumped the bellows for the blacksmith. Best of all, he listened to the endless talk that swirled about him.

Saguache in '75. Ute Indians whooped over Cochetopa Pass to swap muskrat furs and buckskin for the whisky that was illegal on their own lands. Discharged soldiers from Fort Garland, farther south, wandered in hunting homesteads. Red-shirted prospectors collared every traveler to ask about the St. John Mountains, which the government, for a niggardly price in shoddy annuity goods, had recently carved out of the reservation beyond the divide. Anticipation throbbed everywhere. Worried about his father, Johnny tried in his inarticulate way to make his mother acknowledge the vigor of the land, even if she could not share it. She would not.

Genteel—oh, indeed. One day in a cattle camp a few miles outside of town, an itinerant peddler killed a popular cowhand in a quarrel over a pair of overshoes. Nearly every male in Saguache rode out to see justice done. Winkler stopped Johnny, however, and delegated the boy to take care of the store, probably for his mother's sake. Further humiliation occurred when Deborah herself visited the store later that morning, ostensibly to buy groceries but actually, so Johnny suspected, to make sure her son had not slipped away to partake of the violence she abhorred.

While she was consulting her list and he was up on a ladder reaching for brown sugar, ten or twelve of the town's married white women appeared in the doorway. Most of them carried sledge hammers or axes. Seeing Deborah Ogden, they peered uncertainly. High-class. Could they be sure of her?

The big-boned, graying woman in the lead spoke up defiantly.

"Most of that posse, they call themselves, was drunk by seven o'clock this morning on liquor they bought here." She glared around for Winkler. Just to the right of her nose was a wart with long hair growing out of it.

"I know," Deborah said.

"The peddler that did the shooting was probably drunk too."

"I imagine."

"There's too much of that around, and this is where it comes from."

"Yes."

"There's nobody here now to stop us."

The flat statement could have been taken either as a threat or a question. Deborah smiled.

"Nobody," she agreed.

They went to work. First they attacked the whisky keg lying on its side on the counter, a tin dipper hanging beneath. Then they marched to the storeroom at the rear of the building. Belatedly Johnny bobbed after them, making futile noises of protest. Otto was not going to like this. Compact, easy to freight, and in so ready a demand as to need no salesmanship, whisky yielded more profit per pound than any other item of merchandise. In addition, it lured buyers into the store—one could get a drink from the dipper for five cents—and so loosened their purses for other things. No, indeed, Otto was not going to like this. Johnny waggled his arms and bleated. The women ignored him. He appealed to his mother for help. She looked right through him, watching the destruction with an expression he had never seen before—almost of exaltation.

Smash! Bang! Perhaps the women were remembering the town fandango of the previous week when liquored Americans had run the Mexicans off the floor and the liquored Mexicans had retaliated with a bombardment of stones and cowdung hurled through the doors and windows. Perhaps they were remembering that a favorite sport of drunk Indians was to grimace through lighted windows, to watch the women and children jump. Smash! Bang! They panted. They grew disheveled. And it came to Johnny that the spasm of protest went beyond just whisky and was a dumb, passionate, irrational attack on every indignity and privation and denial which they had suffered in being brought to this raw newness where most of them had never wanted to come.

Looping, awkward blows. But they destroyed. Spattered whisky soaked their cotton stockings and the hems of their dresses. The room reeked. A squaw coming through the door giggled in astonishment, squatted, and began to scoop at a puddle with an unwashed hand. In grim triumph the women marched past her toward the outside. For the first time they saw, as Johnny belatedly did, that Winkler had entered the store during the vandalism and was standing behind the counter, methodically writing on a sales pad. The women paused, terrified as always by any threat to their little resources. Then the gray-haired woman with the wart pulled them back to their victory. "We'll do it again if we have to," she spat at Winkler and they stalked on, chins high.

At the end of the month a bill for whisky came to the husband of each one involved, including Henry Ogden. Henry and Otto were friends, but this was too much.

"I'll be damned if I'll pay!"

"You'd better."

"You didn't help those harridans. Johnny says you just—"

"In my heart I rejoiced."

"Debbie—"

"Pay!" she said. Too genteel to swing an ax but not too genteel to rejoice. Her whole cheap triumph over the valley and its dream was compressed in that one word. "Pay!"

Henry sank back in his chair, his fists clenching the cloth of his trouser legs. "Papa," Johnny said. "Papa—" Slowly Henry's fingers uncurled and Johnny knew unmistakably the truth which for weeks he had tried to avoid: whatever Saguache and this valley once had meant to Henry Ogden, it was over now. And because Deborah had wrought better than she realized; because her son had believed the lie she had created for her vanity back in Altoona, the dream was done, here in Saguache, for Johnny too. Helplessly he watched as his father straightened. Henry looked at his son, and tried to speak. Johnny could not help him. The words slipped back into Henry's throat. With an indecipherable gesture he picked up his hat and vanished into the night.

"2"

Saguache—breath of a hundred winds. In Otto Winkler's adobe store, its dusky interior smelling of every compass point, John Ogden stood first on one foot and then the other, trying to hear the man-gossip around the replaced whisky barrel while the dumpy squaws he was serving haggled over rectangular looking glasses and copper pots. In Otto Winkler's freight yard, smudged with axle grease and sweating from the weight of the bales he was loading, he heard the name of places just-beyond. The glitter of the horizon: the prospector's eternal fever: one more round of holes and we'll find it. All on wheels, the symbol of America. A promise with every spoke. Life is going to be right; if it isn't, why, drop the pieces of the dead dream and move on to where a new one can live again. Every day Johnny watched a fresh wagon trail its plume of dust out of the East into the town, hunting the promise. Every day he watched a new mule train curve westward up Cochetopa Pass, over the roadless backbone of the land. Soon wagons would be moving westward, too. Wagons in need of bridges, grades, openings. The heart-hunger, the longing. And there was nothing here any more.

"Please let me go, Mr. Winkler!" Otto held a contract for building the Indians' new agency at Los Alamos on the Ute River and for constructing the road that would be necessary for hauling in the annuity goods which various treaties had granted the savages. Johnny felt he could help with any of that. In the past year and a half he had learned to work logs almost as smooth with an adze as if they had been planed. He could drive jerkline, shoe balky mules. He had picked up considerable Spanish and some Ute. Whatever else he might need to know did not worry him; learning came easy. "Please Mr. Winkler!"

"Your mother might not like—"

"You can take the money for the whisky out of my wages."

"That whisky iss not your problem."

"I can do a man's work."

Seventeen—young and cocky. But not here. Over the horizon. Winkler smiled sadly behind his whiskers. "Iss not picnic, Schonny."

But for Johnny it had been a picnic. His first job had been to help drive the Indians' beef herd to a new location near the agency. After turning the steers over to their herdsmen he had gone to work under Walt Kennerly on the road. It was inevitable that whites would soon begin to use the route. Oddly, however, the first travelers had come not from the outside, but from the western mountains, from Argent itself. Johnny first heard the name of the town when Walt and he and some others chanced on a group of five men with fuzzy pack donkeys surrounded by angry Indians. They entered the altercation, quieted the Indians, and learned that the quintet were bound outside to buy supplies for themselves and for companions still at work back in the mountains. But these louse-bitten Indians were trying to forbid them passage, trying to make them go back where they'd come from. The five glared at the Utes, who glared right back.

Walt said uncomfortably. "The treaty doesn't allow trespass. You'll be safer if you go out for your supplies the same way you came in."

"Across those mountains!" The five looked south, although from this particular point the peaks could not be seen. One of them, grizzled

and powerful, swore violently. "Man, you must not know those mountains! The way we came from Baker—past three peaks red as fire and
then down a gorge that if you fell it'd take you three days to hit the
bottom of it. My God! This time of year? A snow catch us up there,
we'd never get through. Besides, we need supplies to carry us the whole
winter. That means wagons, not these runt-gutted burros, goddamn an
animal all ears and orn'iness and nothing else, and the only way to
bring in wagons is around the mountains, not over them. What in
Christ name you building this road for anyway—Injuns?"

"Yes," Walt said while Johnny wriggled with embarrassment. Cold-
handing their own people this way! "You can't use the road without
permission from the tribe—or, to be more practical about it, without
permission from the agent at Los Alamos."

"Permission be damned! When did the Injuns take to running this
country?"

Walt glanced at the muttering knot of bucks. They looked ludicrous enough on their scrawny ponies, dressed in an incongruous medley of Indian blankets and moccasins and white men's suit coats and
black sombreros with tall, uncreased crowns. But they knew how to
shoot the rifles in their saddle scabbards, once the proper momentum
was generated among them.

"There's enough of them to run you," he told the blusterers. And
when they saw that Walt and the road builders were not going to
back them, the prospectors simmered down and let him work out a
compromise.

He started quietly, with introductions all around. That was how
Johnny Ogden first met Pat Edgell. Pat was the youngest of the five,
no more than a year or two older than John, a merry look in his shallow
eyes and recklessness stamped plainly on his round, flat face. The two
of them sat side by side as the elders began their palaver with each
other and with the Indians, whose language Walt knew how to talk.

The violent, grizzled man, who titled himself Judge Short, said to
Walt, "Do you know the Ute River?"

Walt nodded.

"Just back of where it breaks out of the mountains, there's a basin."

Again Walt nodded. He and Johnny had ridden, mere look-see,
into that tremendous pocket shortly after bringing the cattle herd into
Ute Valley. Only two men had been camped in the basin then, in a
ragged tent. Now, according to Short, sixteen men had claims there.
He shook some pebbles out of a sack he pulled from a pannier on one
of the donkeys.

"Gray copper and galena, high in silver, we think. We're taking
samples from each claim outside for accurate assaying. In addition,

Brunton here and young Edgell and I have platted a townsite in the basin. We want to file a claim to it in the nearest land office. Argent City we call it," he added, proud of the way the name evinced his learning.

Walt asked, "Didn't you come by the agency on your way out?"

"We never even heard about any agency until just now. We were working our way around the toe of the hills, hunting a route a wagon could use. About the time we stumbled on this road, these Indians stopped us. But by God, if they think—"

Walt said quietly, "We've been over that, remember. And I still tell you that if you want to be sure of getting yourselves out or a wagon back in time to do your friends in Argent—City, you say?—any good, you'd better swing around by the agency and make it legal. Don't forget, you'll want to bring other wagons in and out too, or else your . . . city isn't going to amount to much. But if you want to bite off your nose to spite these Indians, why, then, just go ahead the way you are."

Short growled and swore on principle, but the others overruled him and went with Walt and the road crew to the agency. The agent, caught on the horns of the dilemma that Walt had shifted to him, reluctantly granted the prospectors the right to cross the reservation to Saguache and return along the agency road with no more than two wagons. To salve his conscience, the agent—not Cushman but a predecessor—exacted in return a promise that the quintet would not bring whisky, even sealed and wrapped, onto reservation land with them. And that was how the first wagons reached Argent City. Others would follow on the strength of their precedent. Having let the first vehicles through, inertia would persuade the Utes to let others pass, until Otto Winkler would put up tollgates at two strategic bridges and have his men collect fees from travelers just as if the whole thing were legal and not a complete contravention of the government's written treaty with the southern Ute nation.

The agent who granted the original permission soon lost his job during a change in administrations and the original town promoters forgot his part. Walt Kennerly—and John Ogden, too—were accorded full credit for breaking the blockade. Shortly after the initial wagons reached the basin in December Pat Edgell rode to the agency to express appreciation by inviting the pair to join the town in its celebration of Christmas Day.

Johnny bubbled with enthusiasm as Walt and he cut each other's hair for the occasion. Not half a year since their first visit to the basin and already a town was taking shape!

Walt shrugged. "A paper town."

An unformed town, Johnny countered—as unformed as Saguache

had been when Henry Ogden first had seen the San Luis Valley.
The glow again. The dream. This time. . . .

"If they hit ore—"

"If. And if they find capital to work the ore. And if they don't go
broke hauling it outside. And if the Indians stay quiet."

Johnny grunted in annoyance as they went outside to saddle up.
"Why are you always backcapping?"

Walt smiled sourly. "Don't stick your neck out and you won't get it
chopped off. That's another thing you've got to learn out here where
the fast-talk boys are selling off the world as if it was a great big cherry
pie." He turned somber, looking south at the wall of peaks glittering
under their December snow. The soft exhalation of his breath made
a little white veil in front of his blue eyes. "If anyone asks what your
Uncle Walt ever gave you, tell 'em it was a piece of advice about
cherry pie." He roused himself with a little shake and picked up his
bridle reins. "Well, let's go see what the boys have stewed up for
dinner."

Eighteen men, each one carrying his own tin plate, tin cup, and
cutlery, crowded into the largest of Argent City's four hurriedly constructed cabins. They sat on the earthen floor, on log rounds and packing boxes, on canvas ticks rustling with cottonwood leaves. Johnny
ate until his eyes bulged. Venison, grouse, sourdough biscuits, canned
tomatoes, coffee made from beans pounded fine in a sack on the
hearthstone. Dessert, too. Pat Edgell rolled out a crust of dough, spread
on a coating of applesauce made from dried fruit, rolled it up, tied the
ends, put it in a sugar sack and boiled it like a pudding. With sweetened
sauce dripped over it, it went down Johnny's throat as smooth as honey.

Afterwards he threw a handful of wood ashes into the cooking pots
to cut the grease, and helped wash the dishes. Pat dug out a fiddle he
had carried over the hill from Baker and sawed away, one foot flapping,
until Logan Whitlock belched loudly. Pat decided he was being in-
sulted.

"So?" he said belligerently. "What kind of music do you favor?"

"Well," Whitlock drawled, "I reckon a bass drum well beaten exceeds
anything else I ever heard."

Pat got red in the face. "Frig you." Then he laughed. "How's this?"
He swung into a slow mournful air. Two or three sang softly:

> Long ago, sweet long ago,
> On the golden shores of sweet long ago,
> There are buds and blossoms rare
> Bound with threads of auburn hair;
> There are crowns, there are scepters fallen low,

There are kisses fond and sweet,
Pressed by lips no more to meet,
On the golden shores of sweet long ago.

It was the wrong tune. They fell silent, each man hugging his knee and staring at the fireplace, thinking Lord knew what. Christmas. And outside the chill of the mountain night was flowing down the canyons, down the cliffs, pressing, pressing. Snow wrinkles on the cliff faces, snow tufts on the evergreen boughs, and straight overhead a snow-cold moon hung in a frosted sky a million miles deep. Like living in the bottom of a well, someone said. Judge Short gave his shoulders a shake.

"How about the map, Brunton? Walt and Johnny haven't seen it."

Lank, taciturn Bill Brunton lifted a long roll from the rafters, removed its oilcloth cover, and spread the paper over the adze-flattened saplings that had been lashed onto four legs by way of a table. The corners of the map kept curling, as if trying to grow congruent to the shape of the basin. Brunton placed chunks of ore on the paper to hold the town flat.

"That's it," he said. "Streets named, business and residence lots marked off. Everything."

"Except people," Walt said dryly.

"They'll come!" Judge Short said. His hands spread over the map—a regular peddler showing his wares; after all, he and Brunton and Pat Edgell had dreamed this thing up. "Mountains of mineral on every side for making us a real living, and in this sheltered basin a real place to live. A second Eden!" His fingers moved along the hatching of lines. "This is Main Street. Intersecting it here is Silver Avenue. On this corner of the intersection the town company is donating a lot for a courthouse. Up here is another free lot for a school. There'll be a park and a bandstand on the meadow at the north end of town."

"And the whorehouses down by the river," Pat said. "Johnny and Walt can bring us some Utes." The freckled skin beneath his shallow eyes tightened with desire. "I saw the squaw that met your wagon at the agency, Walt, and then carried your bedroll into her tepee. Red meat for Christmas. What the hell are you doing up here?"

Johnny rubbed his hands up and down his pants legs while he stared at the paper. Suddenly he blurted, "How about selling me a lot?"

It took them by surprise, as if until this moment they themselves had not quite believed in their paper town. But promoter Pat recovered quickly.

"Now you're talking! Which one do you want?"

"They're all open," Brunton said, "except the ones the boys here got for helping put up the filing fees and all. Discoverers' privilege, you might say."

"Most of the ones they picked run along the creek here," Judge Short chimed in. His finger hovered expectantly. "I recommend you move in beside them, convenient to drinking water and near where the stores will be."

Johnny's finger moved the other way. At the edge of the townsite, as he knew, a low brushy slope rose to a small flat. Except for surveyor Brunton's orderly instinct to bound the city with straight lines, that isolated bench probably would not have been included in the plat. Packing up water and supplies would be laborious. Nonetheless the hill was where Johnny pointed.

"I'll take those two lots."

"You're sure?" Brunton demurred. "You can have anything you want."

Then Pat plowed in with his merry grin. "That's what I call confidence. Ogden figures the town is bound to grow and he don't want to be crowded."

Short, the perpetual optimist, nodded benignly. "Rightly choice, when you think on it. Johnny'll have a view out over everything." He wrote Johnny's initials, J.O., across the purchase and then snapped his suspenders. "Our first outside customer. On Christmas, too. We ought to have a drink to celebrate. But the law wouldn't let us bring anything back through that miserable, missionary-bound reservation. Every time I think on it I get so mad I—"

A bottle of vinegar stood on the crude shelf beside the fireplace. Johnny interrupted.

"Got any baking soda?"

"Why?"

"I'll show you."

He mixed water and vinegar in a tin cup. A pinch of soda made it foam. "A kind of sody pop. We used to drink it back home in Altoona in the summer when we were kids."

He handed the rollicking liquid to Pat, who sniffed, sipped, grimaced, and started to derogate. Then he read Johnny's face and changed his mind.

"Anyhow, it's different," he said. "Altoona, huh? Kind of a Dutchman place, ain't it?" He sniffed again. "Let's not deprive these other thirsty souls of this pure old Pennsylvania brew."

Cups were filled. Each man added his own pinch of soda. The fizz made a whispering throughout the room. Pat raised his cup to Johnny.

"Here's to your new home! Here's to Vinegar Hill!"

Home! Johnny looked around at the circle of cups and the tasting lips and did not hear a single one of the wry jokes. But he could not tell afterward what did pass through his mind. Not Altoona, surely. Nor Saguache, which might have been Henry Ogden's home. Vinegar Hill—he raised his own cup and drank it off without pause for breath.

Then Pat said to Walt, "How about you, Kennerly. You'd better have a lot, too."

"Me?" Walt sounded startled and for a moment Johnny feared that he was going to say something about cherry pie. But Walt also read the boy's face.

"I've no use for residence lots." He spoke kindly and felt kindly, and so never grasped the disappointment that his denial brought to the new eagerness stirring in Johnny, an eagerness which for its un-crippled birth needed a sharer.

"3"

Three weeks later they returned to Saguache on one of their endless errands. On walking into Johnny's former home, Walt's boarding-house, they found Henry Ogden and Deborah at the splintering point of a furious quarrel. A wedding *baile* was to be held at the ranch of wealthy Juan Sandoval just outside of town. A few select Americans were being invited to join the elite of the Mexican colony and Juan had wondered shyly to Henry Ogden whether they might borrow his wife's golden-oak harmonium for the occasion.

"My harmonium! At a Mexican dance!"

"It won't come to harm. I'll wrap it carefully. I freighted it from the railway without scratching it."

"You may not take it."

"Deborah, I promised Juan—"

"*You* promised *my* harmonium!"

"Think how it will please them. Many of these people never heard a harmonium, especially the Spanish—"

"Papists!"

"I am not going to argue, Debbie. I'd rather you would agree. But this time, even if you don't—"

"I'll leave you."

"That's not a bad idea, either."

"Ma!" Johnny said in anguish. "Papa!" and Walt said, twisting his hat in his hands, "I reckon I'd better get on up to my room."

Henry Ogden growled a word that reddened his wife's face, then stamped around the house to the barn, saddled, and rode to the incompleted cabin on the homestead that his wife had seen once on a picnic and had steadfastly refused to visit again. Evidently he tried to work his anger out with an ax. He could not have been heedful, however. The big aspen he felled toppled in such a way that it struck another tree. The butt kicked sharply back and struck Henry Ogden in the head. It was not the manner in which death might have been expected to come to so experienced a hand.

Juan Sandoval postponed the *baile* out of respect; the town's women flocked to Deborah's help; and Henry Ogden, with fifty-cent pieces on his eyes, lay in state in a nice pine coffin set on trestles in the parlor. Otto Winkler paid the widow more for her equity in the homestead and for Henry's three horses and cow and sharp, well-kept tools than John privately thought they were worth.

Three days after the burial, Deborah began preparations to return to Altoona and the claims a sorrowing widow, martyred relict of a pioneer, might legitimately make on her relatives. While she picked things up and put them down and sighed and aimlessly began again, her two daughters, Johnny's sisters, took over the washing and ironing and folding. *Please don't ask me to go with you,* Johnny thought wildly as he brought in the grips from the shed.

She never did. Perhaps she sensed that he had ridden too far away during the past few months to be recalled even by her wiles. She turned to Walt, her eyes bright with tears.

"Take care of him for me, Walter. He's strong for his age, but he's still only a boy."

Kennerly made some kind of sound and reached for her hand. She slipped away.

"I've always tried to bring him up to be a . . . good man." This time she herself took Walt's hand, squeezed it gently. "Take care of yourself, too, Walter."

"Sure," he said, his face gray and stricken. "Oh sure."

"4"

Shortly after Johnny returned to the agency with another load of Indian goods, Logan Whitlock went outside for his wife. Eager that she be the first white woman to reach the town in the basin, he brought her back through a bitter March storm. Johnny helped them buck a way through the last snow-heaped miles, and was almost as excited as Logan when he stowed away inside the new two-room cabin her boxes and rope-bound trunk and the geranium slips carefully packed inside slit raw potatoes which she somehow had kept from freezing. He was almost as distressed as Logan when she immediately came down with pneumonia. After the crisis had passed and word spread through town that she might be able to hold down a little fresh trout, the entire male populace rushed to the river to fish through the ice. No luck. Dreadfully agitated, Johnny threw down his pole and climbed to his flat on Vinegar Hill, where he had seen several ruffed grouse feeding a few days before. Fool grouse, they were locally called. A plump one whirred up onto a spruce limb and then sat there craning its neck this way and that while Johnny threw four useless stones, and then, taking a deep, careful breath, finally felled it. He dressed it out with as much solemn eagerness as if he had been the town's high priest preparing a propitiation.

Although Stella Whitlock perked up, Argent continued to languish. The prospects in the basin were not ample enough to support a whole town. The bright mineral stains of the high country seemed to offer more promise—"Ten times out of nine, Silver comes at timberline," local doggerel put it—but an army of searchers would be needed to scour each gulch and cirque and saw-toothed ridge. That meant, in turn, supplies and trails and money. But none of these things would move in freely—nor ore out—so long as the reservation circled the town's jugular like a garrot. Oh, damn the Utes.

A stagnant town. One evening in a poker game Pat Edgell carelessly bet away his third interest in the original townsite. Judge Short was killed by lightning while bringing in a load of poles, and his heirs back in Georgia sold off his share for a song. At about the same time, Brunton vanished after the custom of prospectors. By chance, the new county of Argent was just then formed by politicians in Denver who were gerrymandering more Republicans into the state legislature. The new county treasurer promptly seized Brunton's third of the townsite, forced a division, and sold off the lots to help fill the abhorred vacuum in his ledger. Thus, one way or another, each of the property owners who had celebrated the town's first Christmas together let his holdings slip away until only Johnny Ogden's two parcels on Vinegar Hill remained unalienated.

The formation of the county and the selection of Argent City, the only incorporated settlement in the district, should have been followed by a rush of new population. But within months the northern Utes had wiped out the Meeker agency on the White River; catching the blood-fever, the southern Utes began beating drums and setting the forest afire near the mining camps; and as a result of the uneasiness the number of new wagons rolling around the toe of the mountains could be counted in dozens rather than the hundreds the founding fathers had hoped for.

A dead town—but to the amusement of people like Pat Edgell and the exasperation of newcomers like Al Ewer, owner and publisher of the county weekly, John Ogden did not seem to understand how moribund it really was. He would come back from hauling freight or patching road for Otto Winkler and give a whistle of pleasure as he counted the stores that had been started along Main Street during his absence or the new homes that were being built along Silver Avenue, leading back toward Vinegar Hill. He admired extravagantly the courthouse for whose construction the bankrupt county had had to borrow money from the state. A dozen times he went up to his lots and paced off the outlines of the grand house that he was going to build there—some day.

A mere hope was enough to uncork a demijohn of plans. The fire department, for instance. Early one Sunday evening the roof of Josh Gibney's new cabin caught ablaze from its poorly plastered chimney. A swarm of citizens, summoned by Josh's shouts and beatings on a dishpan, joyfully put out the flames by throwing snowballs at them and then repaired to the new Pastime Saloon to keep up their spirits. There with much laughter and hooting they formed a volunteer fire department, nominating Logan Whitlock as captain and John Ogden as lieutenant, despite John's perfunctory protests that he was likely to be gone much of the time. No other lieutenant was apt to be permanent, either. John was elected, and that was enough to set him off. For days he wandered through the town, pacing off routes for ditches by which water could be diverted anywhere within the city limits from Portland Creek; and at strategic intervals he staked spots for digging basins deep enough for dipping it up. He sent away for catalogues of engines and pumps and ladders and bright uniforms. He even talked about a reservoir and pipelines. Nothing materialized, of course. Too poor to hire ditch diggers or buy fire horses, the town settled for a few leather buckets that could be used in hand brigades. The shrinkage did not bother Johnny. Buckets were a start, weren't they?

A brighter start emanated from Washington, where Colorado senators drew up a treaty offering the southern Utes certain inducements if they would leave the state with their massacre-guilty northern tribesmen. Argent sparkled with hope. Miners hurried along the agency road, and with them came farmers, eyeing covetously the rich bottomlands on the reservation just below the Narrows. But the Utes—oh, damn the Utes—declined to sign the document; and their new agent, Andrew Cushman, insisted that until they did sign, their rights on the reservation would remain inviolable. Damn Cushman, too—using his office and his troops against his own people. Tempers sharpened. The editorials in Al Ewer's *True Fissure* grew more and more intemperate. The names "Ute" and "Cushman" came to be spoken like obscenities. By late September 1880, when Johnny walked down from Red Mountain with his bedroll over his shoulder, the virulent hatred of the red men had reached concentrations more intense than Johnny, long absent on Winkler's road into Baker, was prepared to sense. Yet even if he had been in Argent that summer, so Harmon Gregg was to speculate later, would he have acted differently? Harmon doubted it: how often was innocence ever prepared for its ambushes, no matter what the warnings?

"5"

By chance Walt Kennerly rode into Argent that same afternoon from the agency. He and Johnny welcomed each other as boisterously as Walt ever let himself be, and repaired to the Pastime. There Johnny told about the supplies he planned to fetch back for Gabe Porcella, about the proposed trail to the mountain, and about the application he was making, with the new lawyer's assistance, for a toll-road charter. He wanted Walt to join him in everything. Walt shrugged off the construction projects as more pipe dreams, but did agree to go with John to Gunnison for Gabe's food and tools. Wagons being in short supply, they decided to use the mules which Walt had been keeping for Johnny down at Los Alamos.

Their start was delayed by a heavy night rain that raised the streams. Noon was warm overhead before they rode past the fort at the upper end of the Narrows, through the canyon, and out into the widening valley of the reservation. There, less than two miles below Argent, they encountered the first of the episodes that would lead directly to the death of Young Hedstrom.

Where Shavano Creek coiled down to the river from the peaks to the right, a handful of dragoons in blue coats surrounded a canvas-covered wagon. Around the dragoons Indians eddied. Interspersed here and there, watching stolidly, were white travelers bound to or from Argent.

"Squatters," Walt explained to Johnny as they rode toward the throng. "Three kids—two girls and a boy. The oldest one is some looker. I'd have thought every stud in Argent would have heard of her by now. Name's Nora—Nora Brice."

Johnny grinned. "You forgot to mention her last night. Private claim?"

Walt ignored that. "I told them when I came by here yesterday afternoon that they couldn't stay. But the old man is a fool."

"The old lady?"

"Dead. Just Nora to keep the rest hanging together. It's pretty bad. And her just a kid." He smiled faintly. "In some ways, that is."

Johnny eyed him sideways, remembering suddenly that in all their talk last night Walt had not mentioned the squaw, gone to fat now, who had borne him two half-breed children and whom, for reasons unaccountable to Johnny, he called Alice. A hell of a Walt, men said. A queer one. Not because of his squawing; a certain amount of that was standard on the reservation. But to Walt the cohabitation had been a relief more than merely physical. It was as if some insecurity deep in him needed the assurance of arms that would receive what he was willing to give and would demand no more; as if he needed the steadfastness of a place where, when snow blocked the land against his normal anesthesia of work, he could lie on piled sheepskins, his hands locked behind his yellow head, and forget the past of which he never spoke, the future for which he never planned. But to turn to Alice! She was no cleaner or more fragrant than most Utes. To Johnny's thinking she was not pretty, either, and she chattered like a magpie. Yet for four winters Walt had gone back to her as a matter of course. This September, however, he had not uttered her name, although Johnny, in the course of their long talk, unconsciously had given him several opportunities. Why? Was the white world from which he had so long stayed aloof catching up with him at last, in the shape of a looker there in that wagon? For an envious moment Johnny felt left out. Dragoons, squatters, a girl named Nora—crossruffs of tension were building here that he had totally missed over on the other side of the mountain. He plunged into questions, and Walt, in his dour manner, recounted what he had learned on his ride up from the agency the day before.

His first intimation of the settlers had been the abrupt lift of his horse's head. Following the direction of its ears, he saw a girl sitting on a drift log. Willow brush almost screened her from the trail. But it probably would not screen her from the hunting party of Utes he had seen riding out of the piñons half an hour back, if they chanced to turn in this direction. He reined toward her, noting that she was on her way back from packing water from the river. A half-filled pail sat on the ground beside her. A wet spot on her skirt suggested that she had sloshed herself with the other half, probably through slipping while climbing the bank.

She watched him without rising, without showing fear or even interest. He touched his hat. If she had stood, he thought, she probably would have been taller than most of the women he was used to. Though her gray dress was loose and threadbare, it did not conceal the fullness of her thighs and breasts. Yet she appeared to Walt to be only eighteen or nineteen years old. She wore no sunbonnet. Her hair, pulled back across her ears into a large, rather unkempt bun, dropped two or three strands across one cheek. The hair looked reddish in the afternoon light, but away from the sun it would probably be ordinary brown. Her eyes were brown, too, long-lashed and enormous. Her chin was rather small. Somehow, just from the way her skin lay across her cheekbones, he sensed she did not often smile.

"You're camped near here?" he asked.

Her lips mocked: Did he suppose she was picnicking? He grew impatient. Dismounting, he picked up the pail.

"Which way?"

Indifferently she indicated an opening through the brush. He stood back, waiting for her to go ahead. She gave him a long look, almost scornful, then obeyed.

They emerged onto a meadow scalloped around the edges with yellowing cottonwood trees. Fallen leaves lay like gold coins on the drying grass and on a gray patched tent and on the nearby covered wagon. The brightness did not hide that the entire outfit was hangdog, not quite slip-slop, yet certainly not shipshape. Two children, the boy perhaps ten and the girl twelve or so, played in the dirt nearby. Out of sight in the cottonwood grove an ax rang. In the meadow three draft horses grazed beside a big black mule and a runty saddle pony.

Walt set down the pail by the fire-blackened cooking pots and nodded to the boy. "Hello, sonny. I see you've got a horny toad."

The boy stared back without answering, his grubby hands cupping a spiny-backed varmint. The younger girl smiled. She was fuller of face than her sister, with lighter hair done up in short, ribboned pigtails. Her sunburned cheeks shone like cherries. She was friendly and she was bored. She wanted to talk, but since her sister stayed silent, so did she.

"Did you just pull in?" Walt asked, fumbling for conversation.

"This morning," the younger girl said. Her name was Mabel.

"Bound for Argent?"

"Pa says he likes it here."

Pa had better not like it too much, Walt thought. But it wasn't his business to go around frightening children.

"That your father out there?" His head gestured toward the sound of the ax.

"He's cutting enough firewood so he can spend tomorrow staking a claim."

"We're goddamn land boomers," the boy said.

"Tommy!"

"That's what the man in Gunnison called us when Pa up and quit his haying job to come over here." Tommy put the horny toad on his shirt front. It clung motionless to the sun-faded fabric, and he ran an experimental finger under its throat. "Is that right, mister? Will they squirt blood out of their eyes?"

The older girl, Nora, looked defiantly at Walt. "Do you know what a land boomer is?"

"Your father's business is his concern," Walt said uneasily and sought refuge in the horny toad. "Sometimes they'll ooze blood out of their eyes if they're tormented."

"He'll learn cruelty without teaching," Nora flared. A fury had been smoldering in her for a long time, he sensed—perhaps since their father had dragged them away from Gunnison—and now he was fresh fuel onto which she could blaze. "We sneak first onto new land, file a homestead claim that someone else might want, sell it, and move on. That's what a land boomer is. Now go ahead and tell me this land isn't open for filing."

Walt shrugged, angry in his own turn. "Why should I waste breath telling you what you already know?" As he let his eyes thrust back into hers, he felt a stir in him to feel her flesh under his hand.

"Then tell me what I don't know. Tell me what we're supposed to do if we're evicted and have nowhere else to go."

"Look, miss, I'm just riding through."

"Then why did you stop?"

Her breast rose and fell. He watched it a moment and contemplated telling her about the Utes he had seen a little earlier. But that would be a cheap victory, if it impressed her at all, and anyway she had probably endured fear and humiliation enough already. Why else was she so snappish? Yet he could not let these children just sit there.

He tried bantering, an approach that did not suit him well. "I learned a long time ago not to talk to a man, or to a woman, with a mad on—especially a woman. If your mother is around, or if your father wants to ask some questions about the country for answers and not for fighting, why, then I'll be glad to oblige as much as I can."

The boy Tommy said, "Ma's dead." Whenever it had happened, it had been long enough ago so that grief had left him. He put the horny toad on the back of his hand and scratched a fingernail along the spine on its back, trying to make it run up his sleeve. "Nora's mad at Pa, not you. She gets that way ever so often and then nobody can't suit her. Like the mad mule—ever hear that one?"

"Sho' now, I'm sorry," Walt murmured. So that was the bottom of her trouble—stuck to a life she despised because there was no one else to look after the children. "Maybe if I talk to your dad—"

Tommy was determined to tell his joke. "Like the mad mule that kicks somebody else on Friday for what you done to him on Monday." He grinned at her, obviously liking her in spite of the tumultuous quarrels they undoubtedly indulged in. "She'll larrup me for this, too, after you've gone."

Mabel, the younger girl, interrupted. "Here comes Pa now."

He had heard voices and was walking from the grove to see who had arrived, his double-bitted ax held loosely just below the head. His name was Ira Brice. He looked like an animated turnip, the top of his head being smaller than his fleshy chin and heavy jowls. A bush of graying beard increased the disproportion. A worn, short-brimmed hat was jammed down tight on his grizzled hair. He looked strong. But the axhead lacked shine and tiny nicks flecked the cutting edges. Like the rest of his possessions, it was get-by, no more. He gabbled rather than talked, miscellaneously friendly, and his jowls jiggled like the wattles on a turkey. He made about as much sense as one, too.

"They's a treaty," he kept replying to everything Walt tried to say about the land not being open yet to settlement.

He was not the first would-be farmer to have jumped at conclusions on hearing that a treaty for removing the Utes had been prepared back in Washington—as though the mere putting of words on paper turned a possibility into a fact, without the agreement of the Indians. Throughout the summer ragtag wagonloads of squatters had evaded Cushman's harassed guards at the agency, swearing solemn oaths that they were bound for Argent and then plumping themselves down wherever the curve of the stream or the smell of the soil suited their fancy. Some honestly meant to raise crops and livestock for the new town; more were land boomers, speculators hoping to pick up choice sites they could sell at a high profit as soon as the Utes left the

reservation and a stampede of miners into Argent raised prices throughout the vicinity. But the Utes declined to sign the treaty. Angry at the
premature trespassing, they had frightened away some of the trespassers.
Troops under Agent Cushman had moved more.

Walt told Ira Brice all this and then grew exasperated. "You don't
see anybody else around here, do you? What makes you think you're
so special you can get away with it?"

Brice was impervious. He hunkered on his thick hams, crumbled
dirt in his thick fingers, and repeated, "They's a treaty."

"Not until both sides ratify it. How many times——"

"Indian signatures! Hell, don't ask the red bastards, by God tell 'em.
This spot right here is practically gov'ment land right now, and that
agent down at Los Alamos is a gov'ment man, servant of the people
you might say, not of the Injuns, and the likes of him have no call
to say that the likes of me can't come out here and better ourselves. I'm
staying."

"The Utes might have different ideas."

"This ain't wilderness any more. They's a town on one side of
'em an' sojers on the other. They saw how fast the troops come in up
north after the Meeker trouble. They may bluster, but the way I
figure, they'll by God think twice about gettin' rough, if a man just
has nerve enough to call their bluff."

"Your children——"

"They ain't worried none." Brice grinned and spat. "That Nora,
she can shoot a rifle like a man. Got a temper like one, too. It's the
Indians you ought to be frettin' about, not her."

There was no use talking to a man like that, and Walt couldn't
talk to the younger children. Nora had gone into the tent and showed
no disposition to return. He gave up and started on toward Argent.
He'd done what he could in a matter that really was not his concern.
Yet his conscience nagged him; and when he met the mail carrier
hurrying to reach Los Alamos before dark, he soothed his vague feelings
of responsibility by giving the man a note to Agent Cushman and
five dollars to press his horses still faster. Now let the government
worry. A damn fool was too much for private enterprise.

"6"

Cushman and a detachment of troops reached the flat the next noon, just behind a band of Utes. After endless talk and jostling, Brice was persuaded to break camp, a maneuver which Nora and the younger children had already commenced while the old man gabbled. Seeing Walt and Johnny ride up, Brice once again stopped working and in full detail expatiated on what had happened.

"It gave us a turn, I'll admit that. Just as I was getting ready to mosey out and set up corner stakes where I'd stepped off the sweetest piece of hay land you ever saw—I'll bet it'll go, oh, I don't know how much an acre . . . all right, Nora, in a minute. Well, anyway, I'd just got the stakes sharpened when this bunch came bustin' up. 'Ute land. Vamoose pronto.' I told them by God they's a treaty. No, no. Ute land. Then this one"—Brice indicated a fat sub-chief whom the whites at the agency called Modesty because he wasn't—"he points at our horses grazin' out there on the flat. 'White man heap like Ute grass— um, um.' They made us—all four of us, would you believe it—they made us get down on our knees and by God I truly do believe they would have made us eat grass, too, if the sojers hadn't showed up right then. Then this feller"—he indicated Cushman, striding toward them in open annoyance—"he sides the Utes. We've by God gotta leave. But I 'spose he's bound to do his job as he sees it."

He grinned at Cushman without animosity. How Walt refrained from saying I told you so, Johnny did not know.

The agent said sharply, "If you're going to get out of here while there is still light enough to travel—"

"Hold your water," Brice said amiably and sauntered off. He heaved a last box into the wagon. The boy Tommy swung onto the runty buckskin saddle pony. The two girls were helped by a willing soldier onto the wagon seat. Brice fiddled with the harness. Indians and travelers sat their horses in a loose ring, staring. Andrew Cushman sighed and said to Walt, with whom he had become acquainted at the agency,

"I never before encountered so complete a zany. Yet the children seem quite capable, perhaps because they've had to be."

John Ogden eyed the man curiously. Cushman had reached Los Alamos only a few months before, while John had been working on the road to Baker, and they had not met. Like many of his unhappy profession, Andrew Cushman had been appointed to his job by the

Indian Bureau in Washington from a list of candidates recommended by the missionary boards of various churches. Rumor said that he had meant to be a preacher but had failed and this was a way of easing him out of the pulpit. Duty was his ruling word. He was bony and loose-jointed. His forehead was high and pale. His thick black hair and the beard that muffled him almost to his eyes were so glossy that John wondered fleetingly if he oiled them. When he talked he had a trick of throwing back his head and looking down his nose, as if he held at least a sergeant major's rating from God Almighty—which in a sense he did, being the ultimate arbiter of every Ute in southwestern Colorado.

The whites in the neighborhood detested him. He had arrived at Los Alamos with a flat announcement that he had been sent by church and government to look after the interests of the Indians and he purposed to do exactly that, no matter what worldly opposition he encountered. After reports of the declaration had traveled to the miners' huts, the mildest epithet used in referring to him was "that Ute-lovin' son of a bitch," and each time his soldiers ejected a white squatter from the reservation the Argent newspaper, *The True Fissure*, printed a frothing editorial. There would be another editorial this week, Johnny thought, after the Brices reached Argent. There would be the usual rumors, too, that Cushman was fleshing out his meager salary by abstracting sides of bacon, sacks of flour, and bolts of calico from allotments intended for the Indians, and selling them to shady speculators whom no one ever clearly identified.

Ira climbed up the wagon wheel to his seat and clucked his team, three horses and the big black mule, into the river ford. Johnny was surprised. Although Argent was less than two miles away, Brice was heading back into Indian lands.

"Are you making him go clear back to Gunnison?" he asked Cushman angrily.

"Only to Los Alamos," Cushman said. He grew unctuous. "As the young lady pointed out rather insistently, you can't just turn people loose, with nowhere to go, at the beginning of winter. Fortunately I need a man to help in the blacksmith shop and to keep things tidied up around the yards. The work will tide him over until he can settle legally."

Pleased with himself, he mounted a horse a trooper brought him and fell in behind the wagon. Johnny and Walt followed, threading a way among the sullen Utes. Pretty cute, Johnny was thinking. Nora not only had landed a job for the old man but had landed it in a strategic spot where Brice would be among the first to hear when the reservation lands were at last declared open for settlement. He could then dash in ahead of the rush and pre-empt the choicest plot available. No other settler had managed Cushman so well.

"She really must have rubbed Mr. Missionary up with those brown eyes of hers," he drawled to Walt.

"Let her alone," Walt snapped back. "She's got troubles enough."

Johnny raised his eyebrows, stung by the tone and mildly surprised. "Well, all-l right. If that's the way it is . . . Look at the fool now!"

Unable to find the regular ford across the river because of the high, muddy current, Brice had let the team veer away from the beaten path. The right front wheel dropped into a hole. The top-heavy wagon listed sharply. Startled, the girls raised their feet and grabbed at their skirts to keep clear of the water bubbling over the footboards. The team meanwhile found solid footing on a gravel bar. Ahead of them the murky channel deepened. A drift log bobbed by close to their noses, and when Brice tried to urge the animals on, they balked.

Young Tommy Brice, motivated by some vague notion of helping, tried to push his buckskin pony out to the vehicle. Frightened by the stalling, the creature tossed its head and made meretricious little hops without getting its feet wet. Tommy was sure everyone was laughing at his helplessness.

"This Jesus-forgotten plug," he piped to Walt, trying to sound like a man. Tears came in spite of him. "Now what'll we do?"

"Don't worry," Walt reassured him. "There's plenty of lariats around. We'll tie on and snake the wagon out in no time."

A grinning dragoon rode up beside the wagon seat, held out an arm hooked into an arc, and offered to carry Nora ashore, slung over his shoulder like a sack. She refused. Then Walt splashed up.

"It's got to be done," he said, "to take the weight off the wheel— and maybe to keep you from getting pitched out headfirst."

His gesture suggested a more graceful carry. Finally she slid one arm around his neck and let him pick her up. Johnny took the littler one, Mabel. When they lowered the girls to the ground, their skirts ruffled up above their knees. The Utes and the soldiers who had already reached the bank lolled in their saddles and grinned broadly. The skin across Nora's cheekbones looked so tight that Johnny thought it must surely ache.

Someone brought Brice's ax from the wagon. Walt and Johnny found two dead, dry logs, cut them into sections, trimmed them, and towed them to the wagon. Brice jumped down to assist. Drenching themselves, they lashed a timber onto either side of the box to help float the vehicle. They tied two ropes to the end of the wagon tongue and handed the loose ends to mounted soldiers. Brice, who was an efficient worker once he was lined out, then climbed back onto the seat, holding one foot and then the other into the air to let water drain out of his boots as he talked.

"We'd of made it the first time," he said in self-defense for having caused the fiasco, "except for Mule. He's tuckered, Mule is—had a hard trip from Gunnison. But you give him one little boost with those ropes and watch him dig in. Yes, sir, just one little boost."

Mule looked to Johnny to be in better flesh than the horses. Mule wasn't tired, Mule was wise. He stood directly in front of the dropped right wheel and when the pull came he would have the hardest part. But Mule didn't look like the straining kind. As Walt and Johnny splashed ashore, Johnny said, "What do you bet they don't get out the first try?"

One of the troopers with the lariats called to Brice, "Now!" They set spurs to their mounts. Brice swung his reins. The three horses of the team set their shoulders into the collars. Mule just pretended, and the wagon stayed tilted in the hole. On the bank the sergeant of the dragoons said with an oath, "I'll untucker that mule!"

He cut a long willow switch and rode into the river. The whip rose and fell. Mule shuddered. Beside him on the bank Johnny heard Nora's sudden, fierce whisper, "Don't give in, Mule! Don't!" Johnny glanced at her in puzzlement. A pet? A long-eared nuisance that had hung around the back door of a slovenly farm waiting for whatever tidbits the barefooted children would bring it, unnamed and so growing by default into this fool name Mule?

"Don't!"

But eventually Mule did. In a fury at the animal's resistance, the sergeant stood in his saddle seat, gave a flying leap, and landed astride Mule's back. Mule was astounded. Mule was more than astounded when spurs raked him and the sergeant's stiff hat battered his long ears with buffets that popped like promises of eternity. All four animals lunged. The wagon gave an almighty lurch and a moment later stood dripping on the grassy flat beside the entrance to the ford.

Mule sagged in the traces, flanks heaving. Nora had sagged also. Even her lips were pale. Would she have had the wagon stuck there forever rather than have that malingering mule jerked alive? Johnny said reasonably,

"There was nothing else to do."

"I know." She had had her own humiliation out in the river, too. Her glance traveled from the wagon to the stream to the mountains to the troops to the Indians and back to Johnny. "Oh, I know. You always have to give in. Or die, the way my mother died. And it's brutal and it's cruel and the only thing you offer in exchange is, 'There's nothing else.' Oh, I know. And that's why I hate you all."

"7"

The passion was still on her the next day at the agency. It was a water-bright morning, blue crystal for far seeing. Johnny went outside of the barracks where Walt and he had slept, scratched leisurely, and looked at the distant peaks shining in the new sunlight. Hearing ululating shouts, he wandered around the building to the pasture fence, where Andrew Cushman was watching the agency's Mexican herders drive in a dozen or so steers for the routine beef ration. By and by Brice joined them.

A group of younger Indians on barebacked ponies raced out to meet the steers. On reaching the animals they leaned low over their horses' necks, split into two howling columns, and circled back in a melee of excitement. The steers scattered, the herders screeched protest, the flat became a confusion of horsemen and panicked beef.

"They sure must like their meat preheated," Brice drawled.

"No," Johnny said, "they just like chasing it—pretending it's buffalo or something. They'll pretty soon shove the steers into that killing corral over there, and then each man that's drawn a critter will ride up beside it and shoot it and feel like a brave. But when the meat butchers out smoking, the squaws won't much like it and they'll likely throw half of it away in the arroyo with that pile of guts stinking yonder. I don't think I'd relish your job, Cushman."

"You can't change a people's way overnight," the agent said stiffly. "But because the Indians will not adapt to civilized standards on the instant, critics like you and that newspaper in Argent call them savages and demand that they be ejected from their lands."

Johnny said, "If that isn't savage, what would you call it?"

The slavering steers had been bunched again and were being crowded toward the killing corral. Jabbering Indians streamed out from the tepees clustered behind the agency's squat adobe buildings. Some wore blankets around their shoulders, some had on store-bought coats and vests or bright sateen shirts, some were bare-chested in the cold fall morning. Beadwork ornamented the mingled cloth trousers and buckskin leggings. A few of the men and women had braided their hair; more let it stream in greasy hanks.

Finally the steers were pushed into a small pen opening off the main enclosure. Children yelled, dogs yelped. Gesticulating bucks climbed onto the earth roof of the stable bordering the far side of the main slaughtering corral. Squaws leaned over the top rail of the fence, waving shiny butcher knives and hatchets. A sequence of killers, each armed with a loaded rifle, pushed their tossing ponies close to the swinging gate that controlled passageway from the small pen into the corral. As soon as the order of shooting had been determined by Cushman, the killing would begin.

On the way to join the throng, Brice and Cushman and Johnny Ogden passed a raised platform of willow poles laid horizontally across crotched branches. Underneath the poles wood had been prepared for fires.

"Here's where the squaws will dry whatever meat they decide to keep," Johnny told Brice. "They'll cut it in thin strips and spread it on those willows. They'll glaze it with smoke so the flies won't blow it and then let it hang in the sun until it's dry enough to pack in sacks. Then they'll take it with them to their camps in the hills. When they need more grub, they'll come back for another ration allotment."

Imps of mischief danced in him. Besides, he owed Cushman a score.

"It's part of the adapting process Mr. Cushman was talking about," he said very dryly. "Like he says, an agent's main job is bringing civilized standards to these poor abused savages. Biscuits, for instance. The Utes like biscuits—if somebody else bakes them. They'll prance into every camp they pass on the trail and beg for biscuits. But if you bring 'em raw flour, the way the government does, they'll mix it in water and drink it. Bacon, though, they want raw. When they cook it at all, it's so they can save the grease for pouring into their coffee."

Brice sensed the banter. He glanced solemnly at Cushman. "Is that a fact, now?"

The agent glowered. "Tastes differ. Some white men eat oysters."

"And calico—there's civilization for you. Do you know how the Utes tan buckskin, Ira?—chew it and rub it with brains until it comes out most as white as paper. Soft! Fringed, beaded, hung with elk teeth— some of the young ones are prettier than you might think." John made a stroking gesture, remembering. "So the government sends calico. But sewing skirts is a trouble. Instead, the squaws scissor the cloth out square, cut a hole in the middle, pull it over their heads, and cinch it around their waists with a piece of rope. Civilized, see."

"I see, all right," Brice said, grinning at the calicoed rears hanging over the fence.

"And pants," Johnny went on. "I remember freighting in the first consignment, back in '75. Two hundred pair. The bucks didn't know what to make of them. They were used to leggings, which don't go no higher than the crotch. They adapted, though. Each one cut the seat out of the pair of pants issued to him, to make it feel more natural. More convenient, too. A sight, though, to watch them waddling around the compound. The agent's wife—pshaw now! Not Mrs. Cushman. An earlier one."

Angrily Cushman said, "What would you have? The things the tribes once depended on are gone. Their lands are shrunken, and will soon shrink still more. They can no longer provide for themselves. They must be taught new methods." His head went back; he glared down his nose. "Those who are too high and mighty to assist in the process are generally the first to resort to trivial humor about it."

He stamped away, stiff-backed. On his arrival at the swinging gate, the din soared into frenzy. The squaws shrieked, rifle shots reverberated, steers bellowed in agony. The half-wild, always hungry Ute dogs, maddened by the odor of death, snarled and fought. The uproar frightened the babies which the mothers had left in leather carriers leaning against the fence posts; their round black eyes wrinkled like dried plums and great howls echoed unnoticed from the containers.

Johnny shouldered out standing room for himself and Brice. Ira's nostrils flared—smells of blood and manure and the acrid bite of black powder smoke; the sweetish stink of overheated animals, the sour reek of sweating Indians. Inside the enclosure three or four steers soon lay dead. Another, wounded, stood spraddle-legged in a corner, blood and mucus roping from its nose. Several youths goaded it with sharpened sticks from its refuge. As a mounted Indian bore down on it with cocked rifle, it leaped frantically across the dead animals in its path. The Indian fired into its head, and still the terrified beast did not drop.

The Indian reloaded and took after it again. Brice looked as if he wished he could hide behind one of the posts.

"He'll kill somebody."

"They never seem to," Johnny said. "They shoot at such close range that the bullets always lodge somewhere in the meat."

At each ineffective shot the watchers screamed their scorn. Whereas one or two bullets had sufficed to kill the first steers, the excitement quickly tightened to such knot that aims wobbled and eight or ten discharges were required to drop each of the remaining beasts. As the last one sagged, the squaws swarmed shrilly over the fence, brandishing their hatchets. Furious disputes arose over ownership. Cushman, assisted by a *tawats*, or headman, and looking green under his whiskers, settled distribution. Some of the victorious women, eager for brains to use in tanning, split the skulls. Others skinned and butchered. Bloody arms plunged in elbow deep, hunting the pancreas for immediate consumption. Dripping sweetbreads were passed about; gourmets among the males flavored their raw bits with roots of camas and thistle.

"Look how the squaws pull those butcher knives toward themselves and never slip or get cut," Johnny marveled. He glanced at Brice's jowls. "Seen enough?"

"God yes!" They turned away. "And it's for that we can't go settle on our own land."

Johnny nodded. "Cushman thinks they should be cared for here on the reservation until they learn new methods. Trouble is, they only half learn. Like I told you, they want to hunt buffalo. But the buffalo are gone. So the government gives them beef and corrals and guns and knives. But the old way was to ride up beside a buffalo and kill it with a bow and arrow at a dead run. That proved a man was a man— a meat getter. So they try to use their new things in the old way. What comes out is what you just saw—a mess."

He gave his head a shake, half sorrowful, half impatient. He had lived weeks at a time with the Utes, had hunted with them, raced horses against them. He had spent many a night trying to master their gambling game-of-hand, which looked easy and actually was as sly as the shell-and-pea manipulation of a bunco artist. There had been a dusky girl or two in the meadow grass. Loafing around the wickiups, listening to the chatter and the bragging and the tribal lore, he had liked some of the Utes fine—as individuals. Utes in the abstract, how-ever, were something else.

"I can see Cushman's side. But Jesus, the Indians had these mountains for a thousand years and never made a thing out of them. Now the time has come for them to move over for someone who will." He recalled a line from an editorial in *The True Fissure:* 'The Utes adapted themselves to their environment and remained stationary; the whites have adapted their environment to themselves and have pro-gressed.' Remake the world—a road to Red Mountain. He hitched at his trousers, afire again. "Wait until the Indians aren't sitting across our only way in and out. Then you'll see a boom that really is a boom."

That was when they noticed Nora, standing a little distance ahead and looking as taut and angry as she had been the day before at the river crossing. Walt was bringing young Tommy to her from the corral. They reached her simultaneously.

"At least you might have spared him that," she flashed at her father.

Ira sighed and his jowls quivered. "I didn't notice—"

"You never do. He'll grow up as wild as one of those Indians for all you care."

She caught Tommy's hand and hurried him toward the sod-roofed cabin into which the family was moving from the wagon. Then they saw that Mule had slipped his picket and was making toward a herd of Indian ponies grazing where oak brush feathered onto the bottomlands. Walt's horse was already saddled. He ran to it and took off to retrieve Mule. Tommy pulled loose and scampered after him. Ira had already dropped behind to escape his daughter's tongue, so that Johnny was now left walking alone, uncomfortably, at the girl's side.

Back by the corral dogs snarled over the offal; the squaws gabbled. He gathered his breath.

"You can't keep the boy from things like that if you stay here."

"What other choice do we have?"

"You should have gone into Argent."

"A sod house deeper in the mountains—why is that any better?"

"Argent's not like any other town." He groped for a way to make her see. "Hot springs all around. Some folks have even piped the water into their cabins for laundry."

"Mineral water? It must smell."

"It beats chopping wood. And that's not all——"

But she was not listening. And out of nowhere he glimpsed again his mother in '74 riding the jouncing wagon seat down the long gray trough of the San Luis Valley, so infinitely remote from her native Pennsylvania. The slow creep of the wagon and cart, the gray cabin. *I will not live on a homestead.* Old unhappiness rippled through him. He tried to escape it by hurrying ahead with his words.

"It's a good town, Argent is," he insisted. His tone brightened artificially: Henry Ogden's son, trying to present reassurance through a pattern a woman could recognize as familiar. "There's a church already. A literary society, a school where Tommy and Mabel can go—stuff like that. Trees. Flower gardens—prettiest place in Colorado. You ought to go look."

"And have Pa catch the prospecting fever and run off and leave us in a tent for winter? I know him too well."

"I own two lots—hot springs on one side and a good cold creek on the other, just a little hill to pack the water up. You could camp there. Fine neighbors. They'll help."

"Sympathy. A name in their mouths. I know that, too. This will do, until . . ."

She did not finish, but he guessed. "Until you can coax your father into going back wherever you came from. That's why you turned him this way—to have a start on your road home, away from things that might distract him again."

"It's the first time I can recollect that he wasn't going somewhere that was supposed to be better but never was . . . an Argent. I've had enough."

"8"

Later, after Mule had been retrieved and Walt and he were riding on toward Gunnison, Johnny said out of a long silence,

"That girl Nora puts me in mind of my mother."

"Your mother!" Walt was startled. "She was a lady." Then he turned thoughtful, his head bent. He needed a haircut, Johnny noted absently. His yellow hair rippled behind his ears and down the nape of his neck as thick and as glossy as a cat's fur. "What makes you think she's like your mother?"

Johnny glanced toward the cornering ranks of peaks, where the gorge of the Ute River broke through the huge basin holding Argent. For the second time in his life he sensed that to two women at least a wall of mountains might seem like the end of the earth, not a beginning.

"Because," he said sadly, "neither one of them will . . . believe."

"9"

In the transfer corral at Gunnison, Johnny pulled the knot of the last hitch tight and grinned at the fine sight the fifteen mules made. "Let's go!" he said. Snow would be coming soon, covering the outcrops. Hurry, hurry, hurry—the silver stairs. It was not their intent to stop in the middle of the second afternoon at Cap Tally's trading post in the Curecanti Valley, but rather to push on until darkness stopped them, camp, and so reach Argent the next evening. On arriving at Tally's place, however, they were engulfed in such an uproar that they had to halt.

The valley was broad and well-watered, a natural gathering place for the nomadic Utes. Tally had begun his business with the Indians in a cramped, two-room cabin built of square-hewn logs and roofed with pine shakes. Johnny could remember when the man had cooked and slept like a hog in the rear room and had used the odorous front room to swap clothing, pots, awls, beads, mirrors and whatnot for furs and deerskins. Then the silver strikes at Argent had started pulling a few freighters and travelers along the road by his door, the road Otto Winkler had built originally for supplying the agency. Because Tally's post was roughly halfway across the reservation, in a valley that offered grass and water and firewood, it became a stopping place. The trader added barns and sheds to accommodate the wayfarers, acquired a slatternly wife to serve them meals, and last summer had built what he called a hotel. His original building then became a storehouse.

He was inordinately proud of the hotel and boasted, incorrectly, that it was the only two-story building west of the divide. But surely it was the most visible one. It rose out of the hoof-pounded flat like a monstrous square box, its raw pine boards as brightly yellow as a pair of new high shoes. Downstairs was a long pine bar over which no liquor could be legally sold until the Indians were moved, a cracked mirror, a long dining table covered with stained oilcloth, a kitchen, and invisible somewhere in the rear, the dark boar's nest where Tally holed up with his wife. Upstairs, running across the entire front of the building, was a large bedroom for special guests. Behind this were eighteen uncarpeted cubicles barely large enough to hold cots. The halls that bisected this warren were reached by an outside staircase, and nervous sleepers wondered what would happen if the place ever caught on fire. Such a structure on the reservation was quite illegal, but since even zealots like Cushman recognized the necessary function it performed, no action had yet been taken against it. As a faint disguise Tally still referred to the place in formal documents as a trading post, and continued to operate a sizable mercantile business with the Utes from his side door.

Tally himself had been around the country for a long time. This and not authentic rank had given him the title "captain." He was a little man. The back of his brown neck was crosshatched with deep wrinkles full of dirt. His eyes were muddy-looking and bloodshot from constant rubbing. Indeed, the whole of him had been muddied and curdled by constant buffets of sleet and rain and wind and dust. He greeted everyone with a loud "Hi-ho" devoid of cheerfulness. Criticism of any sort put him into a fury. He resented Al Ewer in particular for a yarn in *The True Fissure* about a man who awoke one morning at his mining claim, saw a woodchuck, and remarked to a companion that it was the biggest bedbug he'd faced since spending the night at Tally's new hotel. After reading the story Tally had started gunning for every woodchuck in the valley; perhaps he thought to quiet the jibe but of course his antics merely delighted his clientele into perpetuating it.

When John Ogden and Walt Kennerly drew near the establishment they saw three big freight wagons parked beside the hotel. They recognized the vehicles at once, from familiarity and from information gleaned in Gunnison: Old Hedstrom's outfit, bound for Argent with machinery for a new lixiviation works to be built beside the river near the fort at the Narrows, and rolls of fence wire for a hardware-store owner speculating against the time when the farmland below town would be declared open for settlement. Other wagons stood about, including two that contained a total of three women and seven children. In addition, four or five saddle horses were hitched to the rack in front of the hotel's narrow stoop. All told, as Johnny counted later, twenty-seven people had gathered there, including Hedstrom's party of four— a driver for each of his wagons and himself as general roustabout. The quartet stood bunched warily at the rear of one of their vehicles. Most of the rest of the people ringed them in a loose semicircle, regarding them with open animosity. Except for the Hedstrom party, the wayfarers were strangers to Johnny—immigrants, apparently.

The immigrants were strangers to Mort Tally also. When he at last saw two familiar faces drawing near, he greeted them with a flood of talk. The night before, it seemed, Old Hedstrom and his crew had been camped eight miles farther along the road toward Argent. A fracas developed with some Indians. One was killed. No, Tally did not know details. He obviously did not care; his immediate troubles were absorbing enough. For rather than go on to the agency and risk encountering vengeful savages en route, the freighters had turned back to hole up at Tally's. Other travelers, meeting them, also turned back. Still other groups had stopped, just as Johnny and Walt had, to learn what the excitement was about. One driver was so panicked by the news that when he broke a rear wheel in his hurry, he took off the other wheel, set the wagon box on skid poles, and dragged the vehicle into Tally's that way, pretty well scrambling his possessions during the bumpy flight.

John exchanged glances with Walt, asking silently, Do we stay or go on? Walt shrugged, Let's find out more.

Tally thrust out a chapped underlip and blew air across the end of his nose, a mannerism he had when angry or nervous.

"If a big enough bunch of Utes come after those fellers, they'll burn down my hotel to snake 'em out. Brand-new—that sign over the door—TALLY'S, MEALS AND BEDS AT ALL HOURS—I put it up July eleven, not three months ago."

Johnny started to say, A fire would clean out those big bedbugs, then thought better of it. Tally was in a state.

"I'm Christ glad to see you boys. Most of these greenhorns wouldn't be worth a pinch of dung in a fight. You got any ammunition on those mules? I'm short—illegal to trade it."

"No ammunition," Johnny said. It occurred to him then that the whisky they carried could be more destructive than gunpowder if the

Indians got hold of it. Perhaps they had better stay here forted up with the others, after all.

Tally went on chattering. "If we can get rid of that Hedstrom crew— hell's hubs, they had no business coming here, putting us all in trouble. They ain't about to leave, though. Hardcases, if ever I seen any. They got those tenderfeet walkin' sideways. Well, you know Hedstrom's nephew, Young Hedstrom. He don't fool." Tally blew across his nose. "What'll I do?"

Walt said mildly, "The first thing is to make up your mind who you're going to fight."

"What do you mean?"

"If it's going to be Indians, you'd better clear those wagons and everything else that's cover for an attack away from around the house."

"But——"

"If it's going to be Hedstrom, you'd better start before the Indians get here."

"Will you help?"

"If it comes to a fight with Indians, we will. But maybe you can stave that off by sending to Cushman for troops. I'm surprised you haven't done that already."

"Who'd go? Nobody here knows the country. Or the Utes."

"You do."

"I got the place to look after." Tally swallowed unhappily. "You know Hedstrom. Maybe if you'll talk turkey to him—"

"No," Walt said. "We're not going to tell anybody they've got to leave shelter and go wait for the Utes." He paused thoughtfully, his booted toes thrust forward against the flat bottoms of his stirrups. No one around, not even Tally, knew the Utes as well as he did. He sighed faintly. "I'll go to Los Alamos, if you want."

Tally brightened. "You will! You'll have to hurry. I mean, night riding and all—but if the soldiers get here in time—that's great, Walt. I won't forget this."

"I'd like to talk to Hedstrom first, so I can tell Cushman exactly what happened."

"We'll have to unload, too," Johnny said, "and get this whisky inside, out of everybody's way."

"10"

The confusion of clearing out a field of fire around the hotel and of arguing about strategic positions for posting riflemen frightened the immigrants still more. When John put his Red Mountain whisky inside the hotel, the travelers clamored to move in their goods also, an impossibility. They vociferated to Tally, who shook his fists and grew red with rage. Walt meanwhile was trying to find out from the freighters exactly what had happened. The quartet responded in sullen monosyllables. As Walt gradually read things, only the hatred surrounding them at Tally's kept them from splintering into bitter recriminations among themselves. Young Hedstrom, sharp-faced and fidgety, snapped at Walt to keep his nose in his own business, and the two hired hands said viciously, Why ask them?—it was Old Hedstrom who set himself up as the know-it-all.

Old Hedstrom had the outlines of a tale ready—the same story which, without names, he would repeat later in Argent. Two drunk Indians demanding handouts had caused the trouble, he said righteously. The shooting was accidental, an unfortunate outcome of a perfectly justifiable effort to frighten off the obstreperous pair.

Who had fired the shot? What was that to Kennerly? The four of them were in this together. No bunch of soreheads at the post were going to pin any blame onto one of them for what had been the mutual defense of all. Cushman did not need names to send in troops for keeping order. As soon as the four knew that their rights would be respected, they would spell out the details to the proper authorities— not to Walt Kennerly or Mort Tally or to the Indians or to anyone else. See?

The two hired hands obviously were not pleased by being so included in this bond of eternal brotherhood. The looks they gave Young Hedstrom made it clear enough who had pulled the trigger, and they were puffed up like toads with the poison of having to share the guilt. Yet they dared not protest. The two Hedstroms, hard-driving and vicious of temper, were an immediate dread far greater than an unknown number of Indians off in the uncertain distance.

And indeed Young Hedstrom was something to fear. He was thin but as resilient as a wagon spring; slouchy in posture but as lithe as a panther when he chose. He had a pale, wedge-shaped face, topped by long albino hair. A cruel bright humor danced in his white-lashed eyes.

Some women found him handsome. Gossip in Argent said that one of the town's handful of prostitutes regularly turned her earnings over to him. He was a notorious bully, but no coward. He enjoyed fighting. Not long before, he had figured prominently in a donnybrook in which a miner had been knifed almost fatally. Town whispers put the blame on Young Hedstrom, though legal proof was lacking. In most of the villages where freight runs brought him he had been jailed for drunkenness and disturbing the peace, yet he still had several months to go before he would be as old even as Johnny Ogden. Fear rather than family affection quite possibly was motivating Old Hedstrom's loyalty to him as much as it was that of the two hands. Well, Walt was under no obligation to turn prosecutor. If Cushman felt that he, as guardian of the Indians, must pinpoint guilt before moving into this affair, that was the agent's business. Walt had done what he could.

He borrowed a fresh horse for the ride to Los Alamos. As he made sure of its cinches, he watched Johnny laughing and joshing and reassuring the women as he carried their wicker suitcases and canvas bags upstairs to the front bedroom. It was far more fooforaw than the females could possibly use before the troops came. But in their fright they wanted it with them, and that was enough for Johnny. Walt felt a stir of resentment. Johnny was a born sucker. Trouble was on its way here. Why should Tally or the immigrant women or Hedstrom or anyone else expect those who had no stake in the turmoil to become involved? Well, they need not expect it of Walt. At Los Alamos he would unload his share of the unwanted burden onto Cushman, who was paid to handle it, and be done. Hence his offer to go. And Tally had gibbered, "That's great, Walt. I won't forget." But it was relief, not gratitude, and Tally would forget, a raw truth that Johnny had not yet learned. And so Johnny lugged suitcases and pickabacked children, and the memory of his wholesale altruism would be a booger on Walt's back for—how long? *Take care of him, Walter,* Deborah Ogden had said. Sure. Oh sure. But Johnny would not leave Tally's now. Johnny was totally committed by his fecklessness, just as he was committed to Gabe's empty store, and to a Red Mountain trail that he had promised to build without reckoning finance; to toll road charters and to whatever else excited him about this country he called "his." Here at Tally's he had made himself within minutes as much a part of the immigrant gathering as if he had crossed the divide with them, one more innocent for Cushman and his troops to fish out of hot water and put back on the road of their desiring. If the troops got here in time . . . and to that extent Walt also was involved. Go on, sucker, ride.

"So long, Johnny."

"So long, Walt."

"11"

While daylight lasted he kept back in the trees, out of sight of trails where he might be swooped upon by Utes hot for vengeance. At dark he dropped back to the easier riding of the road, counting on the horse's sharper hearing to warn him of the approach of any considerable body of horsemen. Not a sound troubled him. Knowing the erratic nature of the Indians, he was not surprised. They would probably react in a hash of ways to the word of the killing. Some would want to summon reinforcements; a few might urge that they first consult with their agent. Someone would bring out a war drum. Women relatives of the dead man would begin their public wailings. The daubing on of black and yellow war paint, medicine fires, dances and orations would precede the gathering of the horses. Indians relished emotionalism too much to let it chill off in planning. No calculated maneuver was likely to have been launched yet. Still, one never went wrong by being careful. Even though most of the southern Utes knew who Walt Kennerly was, he nevertheless had a white skin and in a hot enough frenzy that might be the only thing the younger bucks would consider.

In time even apprehension can grow monotonous. As Walt rode without disturbance through the starlight, his mind slipped out of its shackles of concentration and wandered back across the frozen, empty years to other Indians, to other towns. The village in Ohio, for one. Whether or not he had been born there he couldn't say. A foundling, he had been entrusted by the state to a family that made a trade of raising orphans. He had been well enough cared for: he ate what the family's own children ate; went to school with them until he was thirteen; wore, as all the younger children did, the castoff clothing of the older boys. But from the beginning he knew that he never quite belonged. Although he was generally chosen among the first in games because of his sturdiness, in quarrels he either became the community target or else was ignored, as not being passionately enough bound to anyone to be permitted to take sides. In sickness the touch on his forehead never lingered quite as long as it did on the others. When there was a buttoning up of winter coats, he did not receive the last quick kiss on the end of his nose. He was the outsider, the loner.

For a period after his schooling ended, he had been apprenticed to a harness maker, a morose Swede whose silence at last grew so oppressive that Walt ran away to a high-toned livery in Cleveland. There some of the customers' fine talk and fine manners had rubbed off onto him, but nothing had filled the emptiness inside. Even his foster parents would have been preferable to such meretricious warmth as he tried to buy out of his meager salary, but he dreaded rebuff and so let his pride drift him on from town to town. Unobtrusive, adept with animals and willing to work, he seldom had difficulty finding a job. In Missouri he hooked on with a caravan of freight wagons bound for Santa Fe. He had liked the dusty adobe town, the hunting in its mountains, the crispness of its summer mornings, the soft slur and undemanding openness of its olive-colored girls. In Santa Fe, too, he had met one of the few men for whom he might have been willing to risk himself. This was William Jackson Palmer, who paused in Santa Fe for several weeks gathering men and materials for a railroad survey to the Pacific. Walt was hired as one of his mule packers. Henry Ogden had been on the same trip, but they were in different messes and seldom did more than nod on passing.

In the country draining out of the San Francisco Mountains into the Rio Verde the group had run afoul of Apaches. They tried to escape by stealth. Bad guidance landed them in the bottom of a rocky canyon whose far side was too rough for their animals. Tautly aware of the danger of ambush, they stumbled down the gorge between towering cliffs, the burdened mules at the rear of the line lunging and falling over the white boulders. The attack started with an avalanche of rocks rolled from above. Arrows followed, shrieks, and a weird medley of echoes booming and rolling until one had no idea how many or where the enemy were.

Improvising a counterattack, Palmer sent scattered parties up both sides of the canyon, protecting each other with a crisscrossed covering fire. The mule herders tried to follow. But evening was near, a fog of dust thickened the twilight, and the shattering din further frightened the animals into rebelling. Swearing and yanking at them, three of the packers became trapped behind a palisade of rock they could not surmount. Their predicament went unnoticed by the rest of the whites, who chased the Apaches out of bullet range and then marched hastily westward along the canyon lips, hunting a place where they could regroup.

Indians closing in behind the main body spotted the three whites and started rolling more rocks. Abandoning the mules at last, the trio found a crevice in which they were relatively safe. Walt's and one other man's horse were amazingly unharmed. A hind leg of the third was cut and swelling rapidly. The thing to do, they decided, was to wait for full darkness and then go afoot down the canyon leading the two sound animals until riding was safe. Then, doubling up alternately on the horses, they could strike after the rest of the party.

They were weary and fearful and bruised. But the worst of their torments was thirst. They had not stopped for water since their nooning, and the violence of their recent exertions had dehydrated them. Yet in spite of the discomforts Walt was happy. He was fully a part of their small unit, every resource in him devoted to a common end. When one of his fellows groaned that he did not see how he could continue without a drink, Walt volunteered in the exaltation of his well-being to worm his way two or three hundred yards up the canyon to a side gulch where lush greenery gave promise of water close to the surface.

The canyon was absolutely silent. Carrying a small folding shovel which one of the men had strapped to his saddle, he soon reached the gulch, dug down to moisture and carefully filled a canteen. On his return, footsteps and a soft voice froze him to the ground. The sounds soon faded but he dared not move lest he draw attention not only to himself but to his companions as well. Then, as he lay there, a new fear pierced him. Perhaps the prowlers had seen him or his footprints and were after reinforcements. In that case he should give warning.

He fled down the canyon, running bent from shadow to shadow, clutching the canteen. When he reached the crevice, it was empty. For a while he refused to believe. Indians—but no, he'd have heard the ruckus or seen some sign. This evacuation had been deliberate. The pair had gotten rid of him, then had taken his horse and had departed.

Big-hearted Walt. The water-gatherer.

Never again.

What happened to the pair he never learned. Throughout the next day he had to lie hidden in the crevice, sucking on his unshared canteen while Apaches prowled the rim above. At dark he retraced his party's route upstream and after a week whose agonies were blurred in his memory by fatigue and hunger, he reached a base camp. From there he made his way to Santa Fe. Eventually he received his pay check and, somewhat assuaging his bitterness, a solicitous note from Palmer. Army packing then took him to Fort Garland in the San Luis Valley of Colorado. There he first met the Utes. There too he heard that Palmer, now president of the Denver & Rio Grande Railroad, was planning to lay track through the valley and that a construction base would be established farther north, at the town of Saguache. One lonesome winter day he decided impulsively to rejoin his old boss. En route a blizzard engulfed the trail and he barely reached Saguache alive. While he was still thawing, racked with pain, he learned from Henry Ogden that his information about the railroad had been wrong. There was no construction camp. Because of the panic of '73, Palmer had halted his grading crews; when work continued, if ever, the line would run not near Saguache but near Fort Garland, which Walt had just left.

No more. Life had betrayed him enough. From now on he'd sit tight.

"12"

Firelight glimmered on the conical tops of the Indian tepees beyond the agency. Drums thumped. Because of the alarm they engendered, lamplight still glowed in the windows of the barracks and in the cantonment offices. Walt rode on past the army area into the agency compound and reined toward the bit of fence surrounding Cushman's square residence. From daylight visits he knew the yard was as bare as the parade ground, save for a leggy bush in one corner of the fence and a few dry fall flowers at either side of the narrow, pillared stoop, but at least the enclosure kept the Utes from taking their horses right into the front door.

Walt hitched his own horse beside the gate and felt his way along the uneven plank walk. Lamps burned behind Cushman's windows, too, but he had to knock loudly before he heard Mrs. Cushman call in agitation for her husband to see who was there. When the agent at length appeared he was yawning and haggard, his clothes rumpled as if he had been sleeping in them.

Walt gestured toward the racket in the Indian camp. "I guess you've heard at least part of the story."

"The killing?" Cushman hit himself across the jaw with the heel of his own hand, trying to awake. "Runners came into the village from one of the other camps just before dark. There was a lot of fuss and some of the young bucks got their horses and galloped off. Then the drums began. We've had men down there all evening, trying to learn exactly what did happen. I must have dropped asleep while waiting for a report. It's been a terrible day." He grew petulant. "I don't know why the Indians didn't come straight to me with the whole story. They know I'm here to protect their interests." He shook his head again, hard. "What is it you want, Mr. Kennerly?"

Walt told him.

Cushman closed his eyes wearily. Praying, Walt supposed, recollecting that the man was a missionary.

"I have no soldiers to send," the agent said. "There has been trouble on the Dolores—I had to send two companies over there yesterday. Today I finally stationed a detachment up at Shavano Creek. I'm tired of riding back and forth from here. Every day some squatter tries to sneak in on those meadows, just the way that outfit did." He waved toward the shed that had been turned over to the Brice family. Firelight shone ruddily out front, showing the canvas-topped wagon still standing where it could serve as supplementary sleeping quarters and storeroom. Walt had been watching the place throughout his brief talk with the agent.

"And I am not going to strip this place to go to Tally's rescue," Cushman finished angrily. They could hear Mrs. Cushman moving about inside, trying to keep herself occupied until her husband let her know what was happening. It was not difficult to surmise her thoughts. Almost exactly a year earlier the White River Utes had destroyed their agency in the northern part of the state, killing a dozen men and forcing Agent Meeker's wife and daughter and one other woman into what the newspapers politely called marriage. "There's no telling what would happen if the Indians thought we were undermanned here."

Walt did not answer. The silence wore. Cushman chewed his lower lip. "I suppose," he burst out at last, "that I can spare twelve men."

"Twelve!"

"That's inadequate?"

"It's enough to make the Indians mad, maybe. Or to tempt them. Not enough to stop them if they get started."

"I'll accompany the soldiers. The Utes trust me. On second thought, I'll invite a contingent of them to go with us to Tally's."

Walt inhaled as if to protest, then shrugged. "You know your own trade, I guess."

"There are times, Mr. Kennerly, when we must trust that God's will will be done." Cushman paused, waiting. Receiving no answer, he thrust bluntly. "Do you plan to return?"

"To Tally's?" Walt stood listening to the drums, to Cushman's breathing, to the far-off whispers of the night. Over by Brice's shed a woman's figure passed in front of the fire. "No," he said.

Cushman sighed. "I'd better go alert Lieutenant Kelley." He turned back into the house to speak to his wife, then checked himself. "Thank you for bringing the message," he said, very politely.

Walt took his horse to the stable, rubbed it down and fed it, and walked to the Brices'. The old man was sitting on a box, punching holes through a leather strap. Nora sat on a piece of cottonwood log that had been dragged up for burning, her long dress pulled tightly down and around her knees. The boy Tommy leaned against her side, playing sleepily on a mouth organ. The other girl, Mabel, was not about—inside the shed, probably asleep. Walt hunkered down at the edge of the fire aura; the wood had now crumbled into embers, pulsing alive occasionally under fitful runs of little blue and yellow flames.

He told them what had happened. Nora seemed to understand some of the potentials. Her father did not. He dismissed the whole problem by repeating, as he had the first time they had talked to him, "They's by God a treaty," then drifted off into speculations about taking up a timber claim instead of the farm he had first contemplated.

Tommy fell asleep. Nora interrupted her father's monologue. "Why don't you take him to bed?"

Brice protested, "Me? You're—" Then he slapped his knee. "Yup, yup, by God, yup. Come on, Tommy. We're in the road out here."

Walt felt hollow with embarrassment, but Nora seemed indifferent. She sat with her chin between her fists, never looking up from the fire, and after the old man at length had gone inside the shed and had shut the door, her silence grew annoying. Walt said awkwardly, to break it,

"You're getting along all right?"

She kept on watching the embers. "We eat. We have a place to sleep."

Walt watched the glints in her hair, the faint ruddiness along the line of her cheek. Impulsively he told her, "John Ogden says you remind him of his mother."

Nora did not respond.

"She hated this country too. 'Wouldn't believe,' is the way Johnny put it."

"Where was she from?"

"Pennsylvania."

"We came from Illinois last summer. Forty-two days in a covered wagon to Cañon City."

"Colorado?"

"Yes—east of the mountains. Papa bought a farm he thought he could resell at a quick profit and went to work for the man who sold it, to meet the first payment. We never had any cash, except a little Mama and I earned late in the fall. We'd put in a vegetable garden when we arrived, that's all the planting there was time for, and the frost held off long enough for some of the things to make. Then Mother and I bought a second-hand wheelbarrow. We filled it in the mornings with pumpkins and squash and cabbages and turnips and pushed it into town and around from door to door, peddling. One day it rained. She was never well after that. When she died, the people we'd sold vegetables to got together and bought the coffin for her. A while later Tommy was helping a man bring in fence posts. He killed a porcupine with a stick. We ate it for Christmas dinner. Better by God than pig, Papa said. But it wasn't."

She smoothed her dress across her lap. She had small, strong hands. "What did John Ogden's mother have for Christmas dinner?"

"The one Christmas she was out here? I don't know. John and I celebrated that Christmas up in Argent. Only three–four cabins there then. Now it's a town." He caught himself. "Am I sounding like Johnny?"

"No." For the first time her eyes met his. "You're more like me."

"What makes you say that?"

"I can feel it. Johnny would have gone with Cushman back to that trading post. He'd want to be in the middle of whatever happens, telling everybody things will be all right. You're . . . different."

"A loner," Walt said and moved over and sat beside her on the log. The embers were fainter now than the star glitter overhead. "I don't know how you figured Johnny out so soon."

"He talked all the way down here from the creek where we met you."

"And he still couldn't make you 'believe'?"

Her hands went back to smoothing her dress. "In Cañon City Papa heard about the stampede to Gunnison and believed it and gave up his farm and the payment he'd made and drove over. In Gunnison he heard about the lands over here being opened up. He believed that too. Today he's been talking to a man who says timber claims are the coming thing. Tomorrow . . ."

"Why don't you leave him?"

"What of the children?"

"I didn't think."

They were silent. The drums had stopped. He listened to horses' feet moving from the agency barns along the road toward Tally's. More hoofbeats, pounding urgently, sounded from the direction of the tepees. Uneasiness touched him. Twelve soldiers. Just enough to make the Indians mad. Then Nora said,

"Why should his mother believe? What is there to believe?"

The familiar ache of loneliness filled him and the small routines with which each day he tried to keep it away receded into impotence. He took her hand.

"This," he said. "I can't say it, exactly. But—"

"I know."

A little later she said, "It'll be better in the wagon."

There, shut away by the arching top from even the loneliness of the starshine, he heard the rustle of her clothing, felt the searching of her hands.

"Be good to me, Walt."

"Oh my darling."

"13"

About the same time, out in the same star-hung loneliness, where the hills were a darker looming against the sky, a scout raised from where he had been crouching over the road. To Cushman he said, "There's been another bunch of Utes swing in ahead of us from the Cerro villages. Traveling fast."

Cushman said, "All right." And to Lieutenant Kelley he added, "If the horses can stand it, we had better speed up."

"14"

The first group of Indians traced the freighters to Tally's a little before dawn. They made no attempt to come quietly. Tally's was a familiar place. They knew they could talk to the owner; and also they expected more of the tribe to follow them shortly. If talk failed, then there'd be enough of them to fight. So they swooped up with an arrogant clatter, firing their ancient guns into the darkness by way of announcement, and ordered the guards whom the whites had posted about the yard to send Tally out to palaver with them. Alone.

Inside the post, nerves twisted tight. The men who had been sleeping in the rear cubicles had piled at the first shots down the outside staircases with a clatter of boots. The women stayed upstairs with the children in the front bedroom. "That ain't good," the men agreed belatedly about the outside approach and by lot selected two reluctant sentries to stand guard at the foot of the stairs.

Having thus provided for the women, they gathered in the parlor. They wanted whisky, though throughout the night Tally had been insisting that he possessed none—liquor was against the reservation laws. Now they turned on Johnny, trying to cajole him into tapping one of the kegs which everyone knew he had stored in the rear of the building. He refused. It gave their ill will a focus. They were bitching and bickering with him and with each other, growing uglier by the minute, when Tally reappeared through the dark doorway enormously agitated, blowing great gusts of air across the end of his nose.

He glowered at the freighters. "It's just what I said it would be. Either we hand over all four of you, or they'll come in here and get you."

Young Hedstrom ran the pale tip of his tongue around his pale lips. The freighters were still declining to say openly who had done the killing, though by now everyone was sure. Young Hedstrom's vanity fed on their knowing, yet he too kept up the pretenses.

"That's interesting," he said. As long as the four of them stuck together, they could make a formidable opposition. The prospect even seemed to please him.

Old Hedstrom snarled, "Don't be so goddam cocky. What did you tell them?" he asked Tally.

"They promised to wait until Cushman gets here."

"That Indian-lover!" Young Hedstrom grinned at Tally. "Anything to stop a fight and keep your hotel from getting shot up, is that it?"

Johnny asked Tally, "Did you tell the Utes that Cushman would be bringing soldiers?"

Tally evaded that. "They promised not to do anything until they talked to Cushman," he repeated. He was quivering with outrage and nervousness. "Do you know who you shot?" he demanded of the freighters. "The squint-eyed buck they call Johnson. Shavano's youngest son. That's who!"

"Shavano!" Johnny said. *Nagoto tawats*, one of the war leaders. Memory leaped five years back, to the time Johnny first had seen the man.

Los Alamos that summer five years before had been a piled confusion of thousands of adobe bricks, sun-drying in their molds. Haphazard around the spot stood clusters of painted elkskin tepees. In front of the wickiups blanketed braves sat sullenly among swarms of puppies and fat-bellied children. The beef herd wound slowly toward them through the sagebrush. White man's doings. Very well, let them do it alone, without help. Except Shavano. He rode out to guide the herd to its new grazing grounds between the agency and the mountains. The ceremonial clothes of fringed and beaded buckskin and the V-shaped breastplate of small parallel bones that he had worn during the signing of the St. John purchase agreement had been replaced by a pair of dirty red flannel leggings. On his round head was a black hat, its tall crown uncreased. Twin braids of glossy hair flopped on his breast. A fat man. But, Johnny noticed, he did not ride fat. His knees pressed the pony here, there—through the piñon trees, across rims of tawny stone, in and out of the rocky side gulches, following his beaked nose straight toward the silver mountains that his people no longer owned. Only a mile or so short of the uplift, where a tributary creek coiled through meadowlands toward the river (and where Ira Brice later had thought to squat), Shavano drew rein. "*Aquí.*" They turned the cattle loose in grass waist tall. Shavano Creek they named the side stream, partly as a matter of good politics; and it pleased the old warrior.

In the hazy twilight, as supper steamed in sooty pots, Johnny sat on the chuck-wagon tongue and watched the peaks turn black against a water-green sky. Spang across the whole world they seemed spread, crannied, carved, the river gorge leaping back and back into impenetrable shadow.

Shavano padded by and smiled at him. "*Bueno,*" he had said— *wāno,* as he pronounced the Spanish word. Good. Probably he was looking at the cattle grazing contentedly beside the creek that had been named for him. But he might also have been looking at the mountains and saying in his own way, It's all right, we can live together. *Bueno.*

That had been five years ago. Neither of them had known then that a handful of prospectors had just crossed the pass beside Red Mountain and were already scratching away in the basin where Argent later would be founded.

"Shavano!" Johnny exclaimed. "Is he out there now?"

"No," Tally answered. "But they're expecting him." He glared at Young Hedstrom. "You couldn't have killed an ordinary buck, could you?"

Hedstrom grinned and lolled. "What makes you so sure I did it?" he drawled, all but hugging himself.

One of the hired freighters exploded at last, "It's as plain as the silly grin on your silly face. To hell with you. Why should the four of us hang together to save your hide?"

And Old Hedstrom said unexpectedly out of his growing fright, "That's right. You didn't have to fire that shot. The Utes were leaving."

Young Hedstrom uttered an obscenity, soft with venom. Then he looked at Tally and at John. "How was I to know who Squint-eye was? He was just a drunk hog stumbling around the fire and upsetting the mulligan I was cooking and boasting big about what the Utes were going to do to every 'Mericatz this side of the mountain." He made himself grin again. "A chief's whelp! Well, while I was at it I'm glad I got me a good one."

"You talk too much," the angry freighter said.

"You'd admire shutting me up?" Hedstrom retorted. His white eyes danced.

John was disgusted. "Go ahead, fight it out with each other. Save the Utes the trouble."

The words pulled the spectators inside the room back from the diversion of the immediate quarrel and they shifted uneasily, remembering the Utes outside. Hedstrom tried mocking them through the quick silence. No one snapped back. They were too intent on the windows, searching for the first thin pallor of dawn.

Tally was called outside again. After what seemed an endless wait he reappeared, huffing air. Behind him came six Indians. Each had a black bar of war paint daubed horizontally across his face under his eyes. Each carried a naked weapon, either a knife or a hatchet or a pistol.

"The whole bunch wanted to come in and watch you to make sure you didn't slip off," Tally said uneasily. "I talked 'em down to these six."

Young Hedstrom laughed. "That was right obliging of you." He kept himself smiling as the Indians ranged themselves around the freighters. The savages did not speak a word, just looked. Hedstrom's smile tightened into a grimace.

"Go on, stare, you tan bastards." He was leaning forward in his chair now, legs spread, the palms of both hands gripping the front edge of the wooden seat. His albino glance jumped about the room. "Are you all Indian-lovers? Are you gonna let 'em tramp you this way—you, white men? You, Banner? You, over there in the canvas coat? Ogden, you? Whose side you on?"

No one answered.

Upstairs a woman screamed. And again. And again, an ascending spiral of terror. It lifted Johnny by the nape of the neck, outside into the thin dawn and up the staircase on the heels of the two startled guards. The sound quieted and by and by he came back down to the bottom of the stairway, laughing but with the humor shallow in his eyes.

One of the women had been stretched out on the bed, he explained to the men grouped there. She dozed off. She woke with a jerk, you know how you do, and saw daylight making and thought she'd look out the window to see what she could see. It was still dark inside the room. She staggered a little and reached out to steady herself and put a hand on a head of hair. She thought it belonged to a crouching Indian and began yelling. But it was one of those hanks of false hair—what do you call them?—that women use to puff up their own hair. She'd taken the hank off herself and put it on the table beside the bed, before lying down. Like old Arkansas Hank, you might say, biting himself when he sat on his own false teeth.

A ripple of snickers and oaths greeted the tale, though no one really thought it funny—yet. More Indians had just arrived, in the quarter light it was impossible to gauge how many, and were milling about the compound, some on foot, more on horseback. Scattered shots punctuated the hum of hoots and calls. Johnny went on inside the parlor. Everyone was still staring at the Hedstrom crew. When John repeated the story about the hair it fell completely flat.

More Indians galloped up. Finally, as the barn and the stack of meadow hay and the lighter-hued horses were beginning to absorb color from the sky, Cushman arrived with his soldiers. Still more Indians rode in front of and behind his small squadron. Johnny's heart sank. Tally, standing beside him at the window, began to swear.

"Nine, ten—twelve of 'em! Great Christ A'mighty! There must be anyhow a hundred and fifty Utes out there!"

Cushman reined toward a fat Indian on a motionless horse. Shavano! He sat stolid and impassive while the agent squirmed and gestured. Lieutenant Kelley, his apple cheeks shiny and soft, dismounted his soldiers and stationed them around the building. From the way they got their backs against the wall and let their eyes shuttle left and right, it was plain they were frightened. Johnny too began to feel fear at last. The appearance of the dragoons had acted like morning frost on water shimmering in a wagon rut. The aimless rippling of the Indians ceased and they congealed into an icy ring around the spot where Cushman and Shavano conferred. The agent spoke volubly, the Indian only occasionally, now and then underlining his words with one of the broad, fluid gestures of sign talk.

Presently Cushman nodded and turned away. Dismounting, he gave the reins of his horse to one of Tally's workers and with Lieutenant Kelley entered the parlor. His black hair, when he took off his hat, was matted into crow's nests. He looked leaden with weariness. First he sorted out the people inside, and then his words.

"The Indians," he said at last in so low a voice the listeners had to lean forward to hear him, "want all four of the party who fired the shot that killed Johnson delivered to them for justice."

"The hell—" the angry freighter burst out and Young Hedstrom laughed his nervous, defiant answer. "We've heard that before. Tell 'em they can—"

Cushman's mouth grew pinched with distaste and he interrupted, "I promised them, on my word as their representative whom they can trust, that the guilty man will be taken to Gunnison and given to the authorities to be tried according to the laws of the United States. I said that the government would accept no other solution."

There was not a sound in the room.

Cushman's hand stirred in a weary gesture. "Obviously I must know who the guilty man is."

Old Hedstrom said, "Will the Indians accept that solution?"

"I think they will."

Young Hedstrom spat, "*You* think!"

"They want to know first who the guilty man is and what story he tells."

Again there was silence. Then Old Hedstrom pointed a thumb at his nephew. "Ask him," he said.

The boy uttered the same soft obscenity.

Cushman closed his eyes. Even here, Johnny thought, the agent could not forget that he was a preacher. "That sort of talk helps nothing." His tired eyes grew almost beseeching. "Will you tell me how it happened? Or will I have to ask your uncle."

Young Hedstrom hung fire, measuring his uncle's throat as if he would like to slit it. Then he wrinkled his lips and laughed.

"Sure, sure, sure. I'll tell. These double-crossers wouldn't give it straight anyhow."

The night before, he said, they had camped near the Cerro bridge. His uncle had gone out to look for a deer while the others picketed the teams. It was Young Hedstrom's turn to cook. He put the coffee pot on the fire, made bread in the Dutch oven, opened the tomatoes, cut up the meat and potatoes for stewing. Then he sat down on a grain sack to braid a whip he was working on. It was twilight by then.

Cushman tried to hurry him along. Young Hedstrom said impatiently, "I'm telling you, ain't I? Then these two Indians come up, see. Drunker'n hoot owls. It's supposed to be agin the law to have alcohol on the reservation. But they'd sure got hold of some somewhere."

He looked at Tally, who bristled. "If you're hintin'—"

"Let him talk," Cushman said.

"They wanted handouts. They kept saying, 'Biscuit, biscuit.' You know how they do."

"Yes, yes."

"I told them the food wasn't ready. They didn't believe me. They got off their horses. Both of 'em had rifles in their saddle scabbards. Both of 'em were wearin' pistols. That's more gun than is legal, too, ain't it?"

"Not out on the range hunting. Go on."

"Well, that squint-eyed one tried to take the lid off the Dutch oven. He burned his fingers. I laughed and that made him mad. He kicked

over my stew pot, right in the fire. I jumped at him with my whip—
it was braided enough. He ran to his horse and jerked his rifle out
of its scabbard, and he levered in a shell. Then my uncle hollered. He
was coming back from hunting and seen what was happening, and he
slipped behind the crotch of a tree and pulled a bead on 'em. There
was still light enough for the bastards to see they were covered."

"Is all this correct?" Cushman asked Old Hedstrom.

"About."

"What do you mean, 'about'?"

"Yeah, it's right."

"Like hell," the angry freighter said. "I didn't see the Indian lever
in any shell. I didn't see that he even got the rifle out of the scabbard.
He was just runnin' toward his horse and you guessed he meant——"

"You were out of sight by the front of the wagon," Young Hedstrom
interrupted softly. "Sitting damn tight too, both of you."

"We—"

"Just tell the story," Cushman said.

"My uncle ordered them to throw down their guns. They sure as
hell didn't want to. But he had them pinned. They obeyed, finally.
Then they rode off a-ways. At full dark we heard 'em coming back.
They stopped far enough out so we couldn't see and began hootin'
threats."

"You could make out one of them against the light trunk of a cottonwood tree," the angry freighter said.

"I'm telling it," Young Hedstrom said, very softly again. "We jumped
away from the fire. They might have had other guns we didn't know
about. They kept jeerin' at us—not preacher talk, either. Enough was
enough. I snapped a shot, to warn them."

"With one of their own rifles?"

"Why not? I had it in my hands, curious-like, lookin' it over. I
wanted to see how it would shoot."

"Were you satisfied?"

"I just snapped the shot, I said. The horses galloped off. I went
about patching up supper. My uncle wandered out. Then he hollered.
He'd found that squint-eyed one lying there."

"Dead?"

"Dying. We did what we could—"

"I'll bet," someone said from a corner.

"—but toward morning he cashed 'em in. We talked it over and decided that the one that run off might rouse a whole passel and we'd
better come back here." He could not let it rest with that, but had to
add, "If I'd of knowed then who it was, I'd of took his scalp."

Cushman looked at the uncle. "In your opinion the killing was as described—pure chance?"

"I wouldn't be liable to say anything else, would I?"

"You might wish to see justice done, if justice is called for." Cushman's glance passed on to the angry freighter. "What do you say?"

The man stole one quick look at Young Hedstrom, then shrugged. "He admits he did the shooting. That's all the Indians care about, isn't it?"

"I am not asking only for the Indians," Cushman said stiffly. "This is a matter of concern for everyone. For example, the entire treaty negotiations are likely to be upset by this incident."

"So what are you aiming to do about it?" Young Hedstrom challenged."

"Get you to court first. I promised Shavano that unless I was satisfied that the killing had occurred during a fair fight, the shooter would answer according to law."

Hedstrom looked at the Indians still watching him. He listened to the hoofbeats outside, to the ululations and shouts. Right now court seemed the lesser worry. He lolled back in his chair.

"Why, that appears reasonable," he drawled, "providing the Indians agree to let us through."

"I told Shavano I'd talk to him again after I'd heard your side of the story."

He went outside with Tally. Johnny thought, *Does he really think he can talk those Indians over?* He walked as far as the doorway and from there watched still another conference between Cushman and Tally and Shavano, the three of them afoot now in a little cleared space on the packed earth in front of the hotel. Cushman appeared unutterably tired, as if all he could think of was getting this thing settled so that he could go home and sleep forever.

By now the Utes were growing unmanageable. The soldiers in particular were drawing their ire. Now and then a young buck would race his pony full tilt toward one of the dragoons and a split second before collision would jerk it to a rearing stop. Whenever a soldier flinched the Indians jeered triumphantly. Then others would walk by and spit at the flincher's feet. One blue-coated youngster, he looked about eighteen, was growing edgy. Kelley went over and stood beside him. The Indians shifted their attention then to the dragoons' horses, tied under a single guard at the hitching rack. They raced up behind the animals with loud din, making them plunge and kick, and then laughed uproariously at the efforts of the guard to keep the frightened animals from breaking loose. The noise rather than the malice upset

Cushman. Frowning, he spoke to Shavano and the *tawats* waved that particular devilment to an end, at least for the moment.

White faces crowded the door beside Johnny and peered through every window, trying to read their own next moves from whatever was being decided out there by the talkers. Hal Banner, an Argent miner bound outside to sell some claims he owned, said angrily to John,

"That holy-mole of a Cushman has let things get out of hand. He should have brought the soldiers inside and forted up, instead of scattering them all over the yard. The way it is the Indians can split into gangs and ride the troopers down one by one. Hell, they're all but doing it now. That's what comes of letting a goddam preacher have the say of things. Who else would have come into this hornets' nest with only twelve soldiers?"

"He figures God is on his side," someone drawled.

"God had better be—on ours too."

"The Utes would surely like to take on those soldiers."

They surely would, Johnny thought. And that was exactly what would happen if part of the troopers, or even all twelve, tried to march Young Hedstrom back through the reservation to Gunnison. Courts, hell. The Indians wanted direct vengeance. Furthermore, the lack of resistance they were meeting here was inflaming them more and more. What made Cushman think that his promises, or Shavano's either for that matter, could hold them in check?

Yet as certainly as sunrise, if the Utes tried to take Hedstrom away from the soldiers, the soldiers would fight. It would end in a massacre most likely. And then, great Jesus—the whole Ute nation running wild for blood . . .

"Why in Christ's name don't they get that jaw music over with out there?" Hal Banner said out of the rawness of the waiting.

Tally's post would be indefensible. An hour after the first fire arrows lodged on the roof it would be a black heap. The immigrants here and along the road, helpless. The Indians roaring drunk on Johnny's Red Mountain whisky—and the Red Mountain miners giving up because of short supplies and retreating across the pass to Baker—not to Argent; that town would be too hot. The saw blade clanging. Even if the town was not attacked directly, its supplies would be cut off, and winter lay dead ahead.

Banner said, "There's even armed Utes inside the house. Old Shavano is ridin' on top and he knows it. Look how the fat pig chops the air with that hand of his every time Cushman tries to tell him something. And for what? A Swede puke like Hedstrom. I say, let the Indians have him."

An uprising would set Argent back for years, Johnny thought. Oh, relief troops would come bugling over the passes soon enough and in time, no doubt, they would bring the Indians to bay in the rocky gulches. But in the meantime the treaty would blow up. Everything would be uncertain. Traffic would cease, Baker would capture the Red Mountain trade. There would be no need of the trail he had been authorized to build, or the toll road he projected. His lots on Vinegar Hill, the entire town . . .

"Here they come!" Banner cried.

Shavano turned aside. Cushman and Tally started toward the doorway. A buck named, approximately, Tah-koo-ni-ca-vats spurred insolently in front of them, blocking their path. A troublemaker, Tah-koo-ni-ca-vats was. The whites around the agency called him, in sour irony, Happy Jack. He leaned over and began talking to Cushman.

"Just what I said!" Banner exclaimed furiously. "Hotheads like Jack there can run this show to suit themselves. The whole business has been preacher-handled into the ground from the beginning."

His temper and his fear took over. Giving his pants a hitch, he strode out to join the vehement council between Cushman and Jack. Johnny was about to follow, but Lieutenant Kelley caught his eye and asked him by a shake of his apple-cheeked head to stay where he was in the doorway, presumably so that Johnny could see any untoward developments inside and at once relay a warning.

Finally Cushman and Tally and Banner came on again, into the room. The travelers who had been holed up in the post through the nerve-twisting hours crowded in behind them, even one of the women. Cushman halted in front of the four freighters. He tried to look at them but his gaze slid away to the floor.

"It's decided," he said. He worked his lips behind his beard. He was red-eyed and exhausted and seemed to be having trouble picking his words. "We'll put the freight wagons and the immigrant wagons together and send them on to Argent in a group. Shavano promises that the wagons won't be bothered. But you saw how uncontrollable the Utes are getting out there—more of them than have been assembled in one place since—oh, for a long time. It strikes me—and Mr. Tally as well—as unwise, under the circumstances, to rely too completely on Shavano's ability to control the excitement. Considering the Indians' present state of mind, the wagons may look—oh, tempting. Therefore Lieutenant Kelley's troops will escort you."

A long and nervous way of saying it, Johnny thought. All around him he heard the immigrants' exhalations of relief. The woman said loudly, "Thank you, Lord. Amen!" Cushman glanced at her and for a moment her beaming approval soothed some of the haggardness from his face. "Amen," he repeated.

"And me?" Young Hedstrom said like a knife. "Any amens for me?"

Cushman still did not look directly at him. "Shavano agrees that you be taken to Gunnison," he said in so low a voice Johnny could scarcely hear it.

"Who's taking me?" Hedstrom demanded. "If the soldiers are going with the wagons—"

"An escort of civilians."

No soldiers, Johnny thought in relief. Cushman was smarter than he had thought: there would be no fight to start a general war.

"Who's in the escort?" Hedstrom asked.

"Tally—"

"My pal!"

"Banner, here. And Hal Hoyt."

"Who's Hoyt?"

"He works for Tally. The Indians know they can trust him."

"Can I?"

"That's not your choice." Cushman said with his first flash of anger. "After all, you are the cause of this trouble. If you don't like the escort that is being assigned to you, perhaps you'll try riding to Gunnison alone. It's the Indians we are satisfying, not you." His eyes slid again to the floor. "They want to make sure you do come to trial."

Hedstrom sneered, "Indian-lovers!" but the epithet drew no answering ring from the stony silence in the room. He ran his tongue around his lips. "Are any of the Utes going along?"

Cushman nodded. "We had to accept two of their representatives."

"Who?"

"Piah Bill and Tah-koo-ni-ca-vats."

Hedstrom's teeth showed. "Another real pal!"

"There are only two Indians and four whites." Cushman said impatiently. "Those proportions ought to suit you as fair."

"Are you the fourth white . . . man?" Hedstrom said scornfully.

"No. I have to return to Los Alamos. But Shavano agreed that we could pick a fourth who would be agreeable both to you and to the Indians."

That was when the hunch that had been nagging at Johnny matured to a certainty. *They've made a deal to surrender him and avoid a fight.*

"Who is it you think I'll agree to?" Hedstrom said.

For the first time since he had entered the room Cushman met another man's eyes directly. He looked at Johnny. "Will you go, Mr. Ogden?"

"Agh!" Johnny said in total surprise. He glanced at Hal Banner, who nodded encouragement.

"It must be on your own free choice," Cushman insisted.

"Johnny Ogden!" Hedstrom said. "Well, that's something, I guess."
He glanced at his uncle, who said, "Yes, I'll feel better about things
if Ogden goes along."

"But not good enough to come with me to Gunnison yourself,"
his nephew jeered.

"I've got delivery contracts on this freight. As soon as I hit town,
I'll hunt you up a lawyer."

"Thanks, pal."

"Don't worry so. No white court is gonna blame you——"

Lieutenant Kelley put in restively. "If we hope to get these wagons
to the agency by dark, we had better line out." He was pale and young
and eager to be away from this tactically hopeless position. He began
to draw on his gauntlet gloves. "As soon as Mr. Ogden has decided . . ."

Johnny's surprise remained so absolute that he even forgot that Walt
was not there. He looked around to ask his advice. Then he remembered. He drew a breath.

"Why," he said, "why, yes, I'll go."

"15"

They saw the wagons lumber away toward Argent before they themselves took the road back toward Gunnison. Hedstrom's eyes, like those
of everyone else, were bright with sleeplessness. But escaping from the
oppression of the room and the sullen red guards who had stood over
him for so long with drawn weapons had swung his erratic temperament
back to high spirits. "It right certainly was touchy in there for a while."
Now he was moving, all but free. As his uncle had said, no white
man's court was going to stick a white man for standing up to a couple
of drunk Utes. His well-being was such that he did not protest even
when Banner insisted on taking his revolver and handed it to Johnny,
who wore no gun, to buckle about his waist. The only thing that
unsettled him momentarily was catching sight of a flashing mirror in
the hands of one of the few Indians still hanging around the post.

"What's that feller doing?"

"Playing," Tally said. "They're worse'n kids. They'll sit around a
whole afternoon blinkin' those things."

They jogged on. It was a soft day, big clouds lazing overhead and
near the ground scarcely enough breeze to twinkle the golden aspen
leaves on their spatulate stems. Tally and Hal Hoyt rode ahead, then
Hedstrom with Banner on one side and John on the other, and in the

rear the two Indians. The three in the middle gossiped about mining claims; Johnny told them about the Red Mountain prospects, the trail, and his application for a toll-road charter. Hedstrom was interested for a while. Then the morning warmth made him sleepy and he began to catnap to the sway of his horse.

About six miles, an hour and a half, from Tally's, fifty or more Utes poured down a slope screened by russet oak brush. Except for a few yips from youngsters in the rear, they were surprisingly quiet. Shavano was not with them—or at least not visible.

Hedstrom jerked wide awake. He kneed his horse toward John. He had his own kind of courage. "Toss me my gun," he whispered urgently.

Johnny sat like a stone. Hedstrom's eyes shuttled from one to the other. He knew now that he had been betrayed. But he could not quite make the top part of his mind believe it. "Johnny!" he cried for denial and Johnny's mouth fell open and he started to cry "I didn't know!" but he had known, without words, just as Hedstrom knew. Then Tah-koo-ni-ca-vats jerked the bridle reins from Hedstrom's hands. Another Indian struck Hedstrom's horse across the rump with a quirt. As the animal bounded after Tah-koo-ni-ca-vats' lead, Hedstrom almost fell. He caught the horn.

Twisting back, he shouted, "Johnny! My gun!" and then a quirt struck him across the mouth and they were out of sight among the trees.

"Well," Tally said. He blew across the end of his nose. "Well."

Johnny felt a strange sensation of wanting shade. He looked around. The big Mexican rowels on Banner's spurs, the spot on the shoulder of Hoyt's horse where the hair had grown in white over an old wound, the color of the leaves. Everything the same. He gave his head a shake. The queerest sensation. No sleep and on top of that no breakfast.

"I'm hungrier'n hell," he said and stared around at their faces. Speech gushed, washing away at the experience as if only the parts that were talked about were the real parts. "That was sure enough slick the way those Indians hid. The first thing I knew, there they were right on top of us. A whole friggin' mob—and not a sign in advance."

It pulled the plug on all their tongues. Chattering, they rode toward the post, their horses' shod feet stepping crisply onto the tracks they had made coming out. How many Utes would you say? A hundred? Not that many actually in sight, but probably there'd been more hidden in reserve, just in case. Oh, the Utes knew how to use cover, you had to hand 'em that. The soldiers wouldn't have had a chance. Like a fellow Banner knew, telling how they had jumped Thornburg's column up on the White River. . . .

III

" 1 "

The recitation in the sheriff's office frayed away into repetitions and irrelevancies. Hedstrom's two hired hands might have added more, but they had left him in anger on reaching the agency, and the freighter had driven on to Argent with strangers who had not been at Tally's. For the time being it was Johnny's story—and Walt's—against Old Hedstrom's. Still, Harmon thought, additional details probably would not affect the general picture. Even after allowing for the shadings of self-interest, the account had sounded factual enough. If he accepted the case, his problem as defense attorney would be to search out and shore up the weak spots revealed by those facts.

He drilled again at John, following lines he was sure the prosecution would take. "Cushman and Tally and perhaps Banner are the ones who evidently made the arrangements with the Indians. You yourself did not hear what was said."

"No. You see, I—"

"Just answer what I ask. Now, when the man came back into the post after the talks with Shavano and Tah-koo-ni—whatever his name is and picked you to go with the escort, was any word dropped to let you know a deal had been made?"

"Not in so many words. But it was obvious the Indians—"

"Just answer."

"No."

"On the way to Gunnison was anything said, in so many words, to lead you to expect the Indians to appear?"

"I . . . No."

But it is perfectly plain you knew anyway, Harmon thought, just as you know when a girl is ready even though she does not murmur a sound. Somebody had been clever—Cushman, probably. Tired, harassed, and desperately aware of every nuance of the situation, the agent had gotten the soldiers out of the way (how he must have regretted bringing them in the first place!) and also had contrived his own exit, all without incriminating words. There was a childishness about it, like a boy holding his fingers crossed behind his back to negate what he said. At least John Ogden was honest. In that monumental, that impervious innocence of his he was willing—actually eager—to tell what he had done. And he would be ripped to pieces for it. Right now was none too soon for him to start looking at what he must confront.

Bluntly the lawyer said, "Old Hedstrom is claiming around town that you're the one who pulled the wool over his eyes. He says that except for you he wouldn't have let his nephew go where the Indians could seize him."

Johnny turned red. "That's a damned lie. He didn't care what happened to the kid. He was quicker than a fox to let the escort run their risks with his nephew while he saved his own hide by skinning out with the soldiers."

"Why were you willing to run the risks? For Young Hedstrom's sake?"

How could you answer that without sounding pompous? Johnny couldn't. His hand made a looping, frustrated gesture. The people on the road. The town. Everybody.

"Red Mountain?" Harmon insisted. "Your mules?"

"Why not? The supplies might mean a lot to them up there."

And to you, Harmon thought. He exhaled unhappily. The hole in the case gaped like a cave. Five minutes after the boy was in the witness chair, any clever prosecutor could wring from him the existence of an understanding, never mind whether it was spoken or not, and then could drive the last nails into the scaffold by showing what certainly would look like motives of black selfishness. Walt had been right: to understand, you had to go clear back to Saguache. But would any trial in this town be permitted to go that far back, or would any Argent jury heed him if he tried?

Yet just as surely, John Ogden did not consider himself guilty. To him the killing had been like beating that Brice mule in the river crossing: you did what you had to do. To be reviled then by his own town for accepting a duty imposed by that town's need for safety was an ultimate irony. Nonetheless a case based on contentions of need would not stand. Even the most ignorant country prosecutor would have no trouble showing a jury that in cases of life and death it was man's law, not the passions of any one man, which determined what should be done. Yet so far as Harmon could tell, neither Johnny nor Walt Kennerly had faced that truth. Pure in their own eyes, they expected their lawyer with a wave of his hand, with the summoning of a genie, to dismiss contending claims and make the purity evident to all.

Could he?

Should he?

If this was to be his town also, where did his own duties lie?

It was late and he was tired and muddled, and Johnny's eyes watching him expectantly did not clarify matters.

"Let's sleep on it," he said and stood up.

"2"

Informed that the conference was over, Sheriff Gaw scratched himself in embarrassment and said he reckoned that it had become necessary for him to take Johnny to his free new boardinghouse.

"I'll appreciate it if you'll all come along," he added awkwardly. Now they too were embarrassed, but there seemed no way to refuse the odd request. In a tongue-tied group they clumped along the corridor into the jail wing. There, recoiling, they grasped the reason for Gaw's discomfiture.

In spite of a loan from the state, the commissioners of the new county of Argent had lacked money for proper buildings. Until more mines were brought into production and the tax situation improved—as soon as the Utes were gone, Al Ewer's *True Fissure* editorialized—many of the functions of government had to be improvised under temporary shelter. Most expedient of the structures was the jail. After the ramshackle L that was designed to house it had been erected, no funds remained for proper cells. Instead, a local blacksmith had welded together a cage out of flat strips of iron two inches wide and a quarter of an inch thick. Roof, floor, and divisions between the individual cells were of the same sort of latticework as the sides, each cubicle scarcely wide enough to hold a slop basin and an iron cot. This square, squat contrivance sat like a tumor in the middle of the cavernous, ill-heated, ill-smelling room. Gaw was unhappy as he rattled his keys.

"I keep telling the commissioners this place ain't fit even for criminals," he apologized. "But so far I got nothing else to offer. I wanted you all to understand."

Walt caught Harmon Gregg's arm. "He can't stay in there. We'll scare up bail."

"This late at night?" Gaw shook his head dubiously. And Harmon said, "I am not sure the offense is bailable. There'd have to be a hearing."

Johnny managed a grin. "I'm tired enough to sleep anywhere," he assured Walt. He drew a breath, ironed the instinctive grimace out of his face, stepped inside, then turned and nodded a pleasant goodnight to them.

"3"

On the street Walt said to Harmon, "Drink?" He had already slipped away from Johnny's story-telling for three or four snorts with Gaw, but to keep him from further imbibing was not Harmon's reason for refusing. He saw light in the office of *The True Fissure* and he wanted to talk to Al Ewer. He said goodnight in his own turn and started away.

Walt haled him back. "Are you taking the case or aren't you?"

"I want to think about it some more," Harmon said and then realized from Walt's gesture how the statement could be interpreted as a demand for a high fee. If both Harmon and the town's other lawyer refused the case (and Harmon supposed that Yount had refused) then Johnny's friends would have to go clear outside, to Baker or Gunnison or farther, to hire an attorney, one who would be a total stranger both to Argent and to John. The situation gave Harmon considerable power.

Go on, use it, he told himself. Why had he come here in the first place? As he hesitated, little flicks of memory touched him. The sponge of debt soaking up his energies in Topeka. The termagant landlady. Her absorptive daughter who had got Harmon into bed and then had set up more claims than even his complaisance could endure. After pilfering the petty-cash drawer in the office where he was reading law, he had fled to the new mining camp of Leadville, in Colorado. There a certain shyster who needed errands run for him at the state capitol in Denver had helped him gain admittance to the Colorado bar, for which he really wasn't prepared yet, largely through string-pulling and the gift of a barrel of whisky to the examiners. But the price of the aid had been the man's contempt as he had handed Harmon his crumbs. Harmon had started hunting surcease, in Denver, at Mattie

Silk's crystal sportinghouse on Larimer Street. There one night he had overheard a snatch of big talk by a little man trying to impress one of the whores: "That's what I said, Argent. You mark my words: that town is going to boom, as soon as the Indian treaty is signed. I don't know another spot in Colorado where a girl like you that wants her own house could do any better." Harmon had had to go to the post office to learn where Argent was. As for the girl, there was no indication that she had been so gullible: ostrich plumes and lavalieres come from developed booms, not potential ones.

So here he was, at the end of the road in a log-shanty town in the middle of the overwhelming peaks of the St. John Mountains. Where next, if he bet wrong now?

"It's not just the fee," he said.

"No?" Walt's tone had the polite rub of contempt that never failed to make Harmon shrink.

"I'm trying to get established in Argent."

"You mean you want to pick the winning side."

Anger coiled around Harmon's chest. Walt wasn't invulnerable enough to risk that kind of remark: why had he stayed with Nora Brice the night of the surrender, leaving Johnny at Tally's? But direct attack was not integral to Harmon's gentleness—or weakness. He made himself shrug, biding his turn.

"After all, John Ogden is guilty—not of murder perhaps, since he didn't pull a trigger. But Young Hedstrom deserved fair trial under due process of the law. He didn't get it. Furthermore, he had no chance. He was promised one thing but given another. He was betrayed."

"How much trial did Hedstrom give the Indian he shot?" Walt retorted.

"Two wrongs don't make a right—in case you haven't heard the saying."

"How much due process is this town giving Johnny? Have you a saying for that?"

"It's a pretty study in irony," Harmon admitted. He held up a hand. "Now, hear me out. Basically John wanted to keep the road open in order to benefit Argent and the immigrants bound for Argent. He thought this could best be accomplished by pacifying the Indians. Right?"

Walt's mustache lifted impatiently. "What else did we spend half the night talking about?"

"But most of the people in Argent think that pacifying the Indians just leads to more trouble. They think Cushman's twelve soldiers should have defied the whole tribe. If a war had started, all the better. The merchants would make money contracting for the army. Meanwhile the cavalry would drive the Indians out of the state, and the road to Argent would be open—a better road than the current one, probably, after the army repaired it. Then Argent would be ready to boom. Kowtowing to the Utes has spoiled that, in the town's opinion. As a symbol of their loss they are making a martyr of Young Hedstrom—"

"That punk!"

"—not because he was sacrificed illegally, but because he was sacrificed to Indians. Now let's suppose I am able, through some technicality or perhaps through a stirring plea to an unprejudiced jury if we can switch the case into another court—suppose I am able to have John Ogden acquitted before the law. Will this town acquit him?"

"What are you driving at?"

"He'll want to come back to Argent, won't he?"

"Naturally. Everything he has is here."

"It may seem to the good citizens of Argent that he was freed because he did pander to the Utes, the people they despise most. Are they likely to appreciate that? You saw how they ganged up on him around the saw blade when you first rode into town. How long can Johnny or anyone else keep swallowing that kind of treatment?"

Walt's gaze turned toward the intersection. Just enough light was seeping from the Dixon House and from the Pastime to touch into visibility the outlines of the whitewashed pole and its burden.

"I heard too, there at the flagpole, what they said about a lawyer's dirty skirts," he mocked.

"That's right. They may not acquit me either for defending an Indian-lover. I may never get another case."

"Particularly if you lose." Walt's gaze shifted to the lamplight in the office of *The True Fissure*. "That's why you want to talk to Ewer—to sound him out and see how far you can risk your luck without getting hurt."

"Partly," Harmon admitted.

Walt gave his head a shake. "You worry too much. As soon as the Indians are gone, the town will forget. People are always moving in and out. If there's a rush in here, a few big strikes—"

"At Red Mountain?"

"As likely a place as any."

"Then Johnny and his fifteen mules—and I, his defender—then we're heroes." Harmon grimaced to himself: give us this day our daily . . . hope. But was hope alone enough for this decision? "Singing our praise would be irony, too. Because John Ogden is still guilty. Perhaps the town will forget. But when Johnny wakes up at night, say, ten

years from now and hears Young Hedstrom crying through the darkness
for a gun—will John forget?"

Walt exhaled explosively. "He was tricked!"

"No. He chose. He did not have to go with that posse."

"He did what he believed in."

"Oh, certainly. Look at those baby-blue eyes. He thinks he's innocent. But if all a man has to do is believe, then everyone becomes his
own law. Any defiance of society, murder or whatever, can be excused
on the ground of good intent."

It was more language than Walt could cope with. "You goddam
word-splitters," he said bitterly. "You make yourself sound high and
mighty with your talk about guilt and society, but you're still thinking
about Number One. All right, how much do you want?"

And now Harmon did strike. "Why should I lose my shirt believing
in what John Ogden believes in? How much believing did you do
when you left him at Tally's?"

"Someone had to go to the agency."

"You could have come back, especially when you saw how few
soldiers Cushman was taking."

Walt fell silent as a stone.

"If you had gone back to the post, would you have accompanied
the escort in Johnny's place?"

Silence still.

"Would you have let John go, knowing of the deal with the Indians?"

"I didn't know!" Walt choked out with a depth of anguish that
startled Harmon. "Don't try if-ing me to clean your own hands. I
never knew about any deal. How could I have guessed Cushman would
do that?"

He wheeled away, across the intersection. Harmon hesitated, ashamed
of himself. Could one really better his own self-respect by reducing
someone else's? Not liking the thought, he started toward Al Ewer's
office.

As he reached for the doorknob a hideous clangor froze him. The
saw blade! Walt had strode into the middle of the street, had taken the
sledge hammer from its nails on the flagpole. Spraddle-legged, he
was swinging on the alarm with wide, circling blows, again and again,
until the basin shuddered with the sound.

"4"

Harmon ran to the corner. Where shadows lay between the pale drift-
ings of light from the hotel and the saloon he stopped, instinctively
trying to shelter himself. "Kennerly! Kennerly!" But Walt stood fixed,
listening to the town. Then he hauled off and struck the blade again.

The immediate reaction was a chorus of more dogs than Harmon
had supposed Argent contained. Then lights flared in the second-story
front bedrooms of the Dixon House. Dark figures crowded out of the
Pastime. "Kennerly!" And still Walt stood there, one hand loosely behind the head of the sledge, the other at the end of its short handle.
What was in his mind? "Kennerly!" This time Harmon called aloud,
in full exasperation. Perhaps the fool thought he was showing the town
what an Indian scare was like. But fear always engendered anger,
and anger always sought a focus. "Kennerly! Come on away from——"

Doors banged, voices called, a child screamed. Lanterns bobbed out
of the Pastime and up Silver Avenue from the livery stable. Two or
three pine torches blazed ruddily. Each moving pool of illumination
attracted a cluster of men, their arms akimbo as they tried simultaneously to run and clutch rifles and shrug into coats. There was no cohesion. Some of the blobs of light careened toward the fort. Some
grouped and paused, a shimmer of wild gestures. Voices howled questions. The compulsion to congregate drew more and more of the erratic dots toward the flagpole.

Harmon joined the first group that ran from the Pastime into the
intersection. "If you're trying to prove something to me—" he began.

Walt gave him the barest of glances. "You?" Anything else that
might have been said was drowned under the cries of the gathering
mob. Where were the Utes? How many? Who had brought the message?
When was the attack likely? Walt said not a word. He looked very
tall beside the saw blade, his light blond hair and mustache pale in
the shifting light. His lips were parted, probably for breath, but the
expression looked like a smile. Against his apparent amusement the
questions drained away, a silence spreading from the closest circle
back through the outer ripples, until the more distant shouts served
to intensify the bewilderment around Walt.

No Indians. The mob could have understood a drunk trying to be
funny. Or a group of Halloween-minded boys hitting the blade a lick
and scampering like rabbits. But Walt seemed utterly controlled—and

deliberate. He had his back to the circular blade, so that its teeth surrounded him like a gigantic devil's halo. The sledge in his hands could have mowed out another circle several feet wide around him. The mob halted circumspectly.

Old Hedstrom wormed up, still whisky-bleary and still looking as if he had not taken off his clothes for days. Walt grinned at him.

"You're not on the reservation now," he mocked. "What are you so afraid of?"

Hedstrom's face puckered with rage. "If this is your idea of a joke—"

Gaw jostled past him. The sheriff was still buttoning his jacket and was as nonplused as everyone else. Pat Edgell's flat face appeared over someone's shoulder, and beside Pat loomed Gabe Porcella's orange sideburns. The word "joke" bubbled back through the crowd. The mob, needing some kind of justification for its continued existence, tried a tentative growl.

In lieu of any other idea, Gaw said, "You'd better go home, Walt."

Walt glanced toward the jail wing of the courthouse. The windows were dark. No one was in there to look out and explain things to John Ogden, immobilized in his cage. Yet John surely had heard the clangor. Unquestionably he was already beside himself with apprehension. What was happening out there by the saw blade which his sacrifice of Hedstrom should have kept quiet?

Someone shouted, "Ride him out of town!" and Hedstrom cried, "Get a blanket!" and Walt drew back his lips again and ran his hand up and down the helve of the sledge. Whatever he was trying to achieve by this idiotic challenge of the town, he was quite willing to fight for.

Sheriff Gaw warned, "Now listen, Kennerly, if you don't go quiet . . ."

Harmon thought, Go where, other than to a cot in the livery stable or to one of the town's two roominghouses? He saw Walt look at the jail again; and in a flash of divination the lawyer knew at last what Walt was up to. He was denying his desertion of Johnny, that critical night when he had stayed with Nora Brice. He thought that by pounding a loud enough clamor from the blade he could tell Johnny—could tell the whole town—that he was still on John's side.

Harmon pressed a way through to the sheriff. "He's under arrest, isn't he?"

Gaw looked blank.

"For disturbing the peace," Harmon prompted.

"Well, I don't really like—why, sure."

Getting Walt into the courthouse was largely a repetition of what had been done earlier with Johnny. The town lacked solidity. Half its energy was down at the fort. More was being wasted in shouts along the street. Some of the men at the periphery of the crowd still expected to hear something about Indians. Those who were beginning to grasp that this was some kind of trick realized that it lacked humor and were therefore too uncertain of its nature to decide what to do. Against that vacillation, a set purpose was enough to open a path. When Harmon had time later to analyze events, he was struck by how little force an uncoalesced rage actually has. He also remembered that some jokester, recalling the evening's earlier face-saver, squalled shrilly, "Save me from the Injuns!" Others took up the cry, so that Johnny probably heard it, too. Years later, in the lonesomeness where every man must evaluate himself, might he hear it again—*save, save*—echoing down the corridors of whatever he had done? Could he answer then: Could he tell what he had saved—and at what cost?

"5"

For light Gaw allowed the prisoners a single candle set in a cup of sand placed on a box in Johnny's cell. A draft troubled the flame. As the men lay on their cots and looked up through the iron lattice-work, they saw monstrous shadows of the bars moving vaguely across the dim, far-off ceiling of the room, lacing and relacing until Walt felt tangled in an impenetrable net. His breathing deepened spasmodically, as happened on occasion when he crawled into bed on the ground at high altitudes. He lay rigid until, by counting, he edged himself back to normal.

He answered Johnny's questions in grunted monosyllables. Presently the younger man gave a short laugh.

"So they really jumped, did they?"

Walt did not reply.

Johnny continued, "Now that they know what an honest-to-God attack would have made them feel like, perhaps they'll quit listening to Hedstrom."

That isn't the reason I hit the gong, Walt thought. He felt disappointed and grew angry at himself. Exactly what had he expected anyhow?

"Go to sleep," he said.

But in a minute Johnny was talking again. "Is Gregg going to take the case? I thought he seemed pretty knowledgeable." Even support purchased for a fee was justification and hence comfort of sorts.

"He's thinking about it."

"What's holding him back?"

"He's new—feeling his way."

"It's that sonofabitchin' Hedstrom," Johnny burst out. "He soured the whole town, hurrying up here ahead of me to clean his own drawers by putting out the story his way. And that sonofabitchin' newspaper, printing only what Hedstrom said, without waiting to hear our side . . . How long do you reckon it'll be before I get out of here?"

"How should I know? A couple of months maybe."

"Months!" Johnny flopped upright. The draft from his violence reached the candle flame, and the shadows of the bars raced across the ceiling. "I've got to get up to Red Mountain!"

"Gabe can take the stuff."

"The trail—"

"You couldn't do much work on it before snow flies."

"I can start. Can't that lawyer get bail?"

"He said something about murder not being bailable," Walt said and then bit his tongue. The word fanned Johnny's bitterness.

"Murder! That's Hedstrom's talk, too." He lay back. The shadows slowed to an uneven drift. In anguish he cried out, "What would this town rather have had—a war?"

"You don't need to argue with me," Walt said, though he knew that what Johnny was actually doing was arguing with himself. The hatred that had met him at the saw blade, the darkness of this cage—for the first time doubt was beginning its whispers, just as Gregg had predicted. At the same time the innocence he felt inside him, stirring out of its first shock, was protesting, Why? What answer was there to give? In lieu of anything better, Walt held out the same thin comfort he had offered the lawyer earlier in the evening.

"By spring this town will be so full of other business it'll forget."

Johnny shook it aside. He did not want Argent to forget, if what he had done had been right. He went on trying to find something other than his own act to explain away the animosity of the town—his town.

"They're as scared as old women of the Indians, that's the trouble. But the Indians have their laws, too. That white-tallow bastard, pulling down on Johnson the way he did—what did the town expect? That Shavano would give him a medal or something?"

"You'd better get some sleep, Johnny."

"That paper saying Hedstrom was tortured and burned at the stake! Where did Ewer get such crap? Nobody has seen one of the Utes that took him."

"It sells papers. Don't worry about it."

"It makes me sore—using guesses to condemn a man."

It's not such bad guesswork, Walt thought. But he did not say so. He did not have to. The same dread was boring at Johnny. By and by it came out.

"You don't reckon they really did burn him?"

Kind of late to wonder, Walt reflected. Yet at Tally's, wondering probably would have seemed irrelevant. It had been necessary for a hundred Indians raging outside the post to vanish and the vanishing had been arranged, without questioning. Innocence again, Harmon would say. The word no longer seemed so strange to Walt. But how do you reassure the girl who has just lost her virginity?

"You can't ever tell what Indians will do to a prisoner," he temporized.

"Old Shavano might know."

"Why dig up something you can't change?"

"If I could show this goddamn town the truth!"

"Forget them," Walt said. He turned pointedly on his side, so that his back was to Johnny. "It's been a long day."

"A longer night," Johnny said. He lay on his back, watching the shadows. After a time he said softly, "Walt?"

No answer.

"You awake?"

The humped form did not stir.

"It was kind of lonesome here until that gong began to ring."

Still no answer. Johnny leaned over and blew out the candle.

"I just wanted to say thanks for coming."

The cot creaked a little as Walt shifted himself into a more comfortable position. He'd heard, all right. Gradually his breathing grew less deliberate, and he really was asleep, not so troubled any longer.

"6"

On leaving the courthouse after Walt's incarceration Harmon Gregg fell in with Al Ewer and returned with him to the office of *The True Fissure.* In the tiny front room a kerosene lamp burned smokily on a littered desk isolated from visitors by a pine counter. On the public's side of this counter was a splintery wooden settee on which no one ever sat and, invariable to each business house in Argent, a glass-fronted cabinet displaying mineral samples. On the counter itself stood a cut-glass vase holding a wilted bouquet of yellow-centered, lavender-petaled fall asters. Harmon smiled. Poor old Al. The flowers meant

that one of the town's few housewives had come in lately with a notice
she wanted printed about some meeting or another, and had used the
occasion to speak to him once again about modifying the barnyard
tone of his stories.

Ewer led the way ponderously through the front office to the shop
at rear. He was overweight and leaden-looking. His big round face was
always tired and mournful. So far as Harmon could determine he almost never went to bed. Perhaps he was too destitute to dare. In his
own words, his makeshift shop looked like a widow-woman outfit for
fair. Greased brown paper that would pass some daylight while ex-
cluding some drafts covered the holes in the dusty windowpanes. Beside the compositor's rack coffee simmered on a stove contrived of
rocks and flattened lard cans. Mingled with its odors were the sweetish
smells of ink, melting lead, wood smoke, and cleaning fluid.

Until the saw blade had interrupted, Ewer had been taking the forms
of the last edition off the press, washing away the ink, and unlocking
the chases prior to distributing the hand-set type in its racks. On returning with Gregg he absently resumed operations, picking up a
damp sponge and wiping it across the type. Suddenly he bent, peered,
and motioned.

"Ever see type lice, Gregg?"

Harmon grunted. To see type lice you bent close to a crack. Ewer's
thick fingers snapped the metal blocks together and a tiny squirt of
water hit you in the eye: jobbed again—each trade had its routines.

"Old age is making you forgetful, Al. You pulled that one on me
last week."

Ewer grinned back. "Like the steer said, it never hurts to keep trying."

They got along. By the nature of their professions they were rather
more literate than the bulk of Argent's population. Though each hoped
to live indirectly on prospecting and mining, neither was inclined to
indulge in such operations for himself. Thus set apart, lonely yet not
given to saloon haunting, they had fallen into meeting beside the coffee
pot in the print shop and talking until late at night. On one of those
nights Ewer had talked more about himself than perhaps he meant.

He was from Arrowrock, Missouri, where he had been clerk in a
general store. His voice, telling about it, grew sad with nostalgia.
"That's where I met my wife, fitting her for a new pair of shoes. She
said I tickled, but she kept putting her foot back for more—the romance
of commerce. Fired with love and ambition, I cut out corn liquor and
random fornication until I owned a fifty per cent interest in that store—
and a hundred per cent of the managing, my partner having decided
to retire on the strength of my enthusiasm. Then I borrowed money
from him for a—well, venture. It didn't work and after that I didn't

own any per cent. I was dead broke. My partner said I could keep on clerking. I began fitting patent leather pumps again, planning to climb back up the ladder, when in the middle of one afternoon I asked myself whether there wasn't some better way. I bought two second-hand mowing machines and headed West, thinking maybe I could cut hay while the prospectors were hunting gold and then make a killing by running up the price of their mule feed when winter came. Over in San Cristobal I chanced across some printing equipment. About the same time, I heard that the legislature was setting up Argent County. There'd have to be a newspaper for legal notices, if nothing else. So I traded my mowers for the press and high-tailed it over here to get the county business before anybody else could."

"You started this paper without prior experience?"

"Not exactly." Ewer hesitated; no man likes to confess his foolishness. "That was my venture. Local politicians back in Arrowrock decided to subsidize a newspaper to support a candidate. I undertook to run the paper, thinking I'd cash in when their man was elected. I borrowed all I could raise to get started—oh, the others were going to help, sure. But their man lost and they forgot their promises. That left me holding the bag." Ewer glowered at Harmon. "All right, I was a sucker. And so here I am again. Well, I'll tell you why. That taste of ink made me wonder what it would be like to break out of the old molds and run a paper to suit just yourself. If you can't do it in a town that's just being born, brand fresh, where can you do it?"

This evening, as Harmon poured a cup of coffee and settled down in one of Ewer's homemade chairs, on a canvas cushion stuffed with shavings, he remembered that statement. And he thought, *There's no mold more traditional than poverty.* Al had had the devil's own time getting started. Throughout the winter he had chopped firewood before and after office hours, selling it out of his back lot in order to meet his rent. Such drifting employees as he managed to hire he generally had to pay with due bills against stores that owed him for advertising. As a result he seldom had help. For at least half his issues he inked his own Washington flat-bed press, wrote his own stories, solicited advertising, read proof, placated offended townswomen, gossiped with the town windbags about politics and distant prize fights, and at midnight swept out the shop—if it was swept at all. For subscriptions he accepted garden truck, venison, hides, and shares in moribund mining claims. Meanwhile his wife and a stack of children were back in Arrowrock, waiting to join him as soon as he wrote them that he was established.

He had to sell papers, mostly by dint of what he called fearless personal journalism. Each day he made a regular tour of the spots where men congregated, the livery stable and hotel lobby, the saloon and the

street corners, a slow, fat beetle, antennae aquiver. By press time each
Friday he had evaluated in full the week's usual fantastic crop of
Indian and mining rumors, the items of public concern emanating
from the courthouse and recorder's office, and a potpourri of personal
doings; he knew almost exactly what opinion was held or likely to
be held by the majority of his readers about each of these items. He
then reflected these opinions back to his readers with dashes of obscenity, prejudice, and intemperance, in proportions designed to appeal
to an audience largely masculine. The account of the Hedstrom killing
was an example of his reporting a major happening. At the other
extreme was his long-drawn-out tale, in the previous week's issue,
about Tom Watrous's broken leg. Tom it seemed, had gone looking for his burro in the dark and had fallen into a prospect hole. Delighted with the overtones, Ewer had spun out the story in infinite
detail, closing it with what he called his snapper, three lines of
characteristic doggerel:

> At last the man has been found
> Who can't tell his ass
> From a hole in the ground.

Well, entertainment was sparse in Argent. So was news. Ewer
managed to fill his paper each week by mixing the two, and readers
were beginning to slap each other on the back and ask whether they'd
seen the *Fissure's* latest. But this night, blowing on his coffee, Harmon
wondered whether Al still thought that he was running the paper to
suit himself, without coddling to anybody. Probably he did. A man
seldom questions the foundations of his own illusions.

Ewer squeezed out his sponge and poured himself a mugful from
the pot. "What," he said, to start the conversation, "do you suppose
got into as sensible-appearing a man as Walt Kennerly to make him
chivvy the whole town thataway? He didn't look drunk."

"Why, as I see it," Harmon reflected, "he sat tight the other night
at Los Alamos when he figured he should have been at Tally's with
John Ogden. Now he's trying to catch up."

"Is that lawyer talk or are you trying to say something?"

"It means that Kennerly announced to Johnny and the town whose
side he's taking."

"And you?"

Harmon said, "Half an hour ago I started across the street to talk
over that very question with you—to ask your advice about the best
course for an ambitious lawyer eager to build a clientele. You know the
currents of opinion as well as anyone in Argent."

"It's my business to know." Like everyone else, Ewer enjoyed being consulted as a sage. He sat ponderously on a box, his thick legs spread. His round face grew solemn with decision. "I don't think I'd buck the town on this one. There's a lot of heat."

"Kennerly thinks it's quick heat and won't last."

"In other words, you are going to defend Ogden."

"Probably."

Ewer grew injured. "Then why ask my advice?"

"I said it was half an hour ago that I was going to ask. Now I'm telling you."

"For publication?"

"If you want."

"Your tone suggests that I won't want."

Harmon waved his coffee cup. "The basic split is simple enough. John contends that he joined the conspiracy to turn Hedstrom over to the Utes in order to benefit Argent. The majority of the citizens of Argent contend, on the other hand (and this is the line you followed in *The True Fissure*) that he helped kill that apparently undesirable young man in order to benefit himself. Fundamentally, a decision as to which contention is true is a question of fact to be determined by a jury of his peers."

Ewer grunted. "Do you really think you can get any jury to believe that that crew—Mort Tally, for instance—was thinking of preserving *The True Fissure*, say, instead of saving his new hotel from being burned down?"

"I am talking about John Ogden."

"Johnny, then. Are you saying he wasn't thinking about his mules or his freight contract with Gabe Porcella? That he was bleeding just for us?"

"Oh, no doubt the mules were mixed up in it. But the mules are also part of the ideal he sees shining up there on Red Mountain. The bright new heaven arching over the promised land of Argent."

"Complete with the Angel Gabriel? Some heaven!"

Harmon chuckled. "I hadn't thought of that particular heavenly body. Yes, complete with Angel Gabe—and with you and me. Do you remember telling me why you happened to come to Colorado?"

"Has the question anything to do with John Ogden?"

"You came for a new start. That's also why I came." Harmon paused, his mouth pursing above his silky goatee. He knew he would later regret exposing too much of himself, but the intensity that had caught him beside the saw blade was still carrying him along. "I wasn't very happy with myself in Denver, hiding from debts, doing shyster jobs for a Leadville double-talker, and trying to look big to myself in Mattie Silk's mirror. Argent sounded like a place where I could shake loose and remake the picture closer to my vision of myself—a new beginning."

"Some of us came just to get ahead in the world," Ewer said.

"Ahead to what?"

"To . . ." The editor paused, staring into the dregs of his coffee. "Have it your way . . . to what we would like to be. But I'm not sure everyone here is so ambitious. A lot of yonkers blew in just for the hell of it—adventure, seeing the elephant, having a fling before settling down, recovering from a sad love affair, just drifting—as many reasons as there are people, I imagine. And even as regards your 'new starters,' I'm not sure that many of them intend to *stay* in Argent once they've made their pile. The town is a means, not an end, and what does that do to your second-heaven theory?"

"Nothing. I'm talking about Johnny Ogden, who probably hasn't thought one way or another about leaving. And I'm not sure you'll leave, either, if this town catches hold and your paper grows with it. And that is what Johnny is seeing—the town catching hold. It's part dream, of course—a fever, a disease if you like, that he contracted at an age when dreams can be more real than fact. It's a little hard to analyze right off, unless you've had dreams yourself, and even then you end up sounding mushy when you try to explain. But—"

"But you'd like to practice before carrying an argument in front of a jury."

"If I can make *you* understand, a jury ought to be easy," Harmon grumbled. "Anyway, the first thing to realize is that Johnny as a young-ster never knew his father very well, but out of one thing and another, a lot of it fed to him by his mother during the process of fattening her own vanity, he created a tremendous hero picture of the man. This hero—and in a sense it was Johnny himself, his root and his strength—was out West, doing a hero's proper job in helping build a new world for everyone who needed a new world—the American ideal, if you like."

"So the copybooks say."

"When Johnny actually came West it should have been like walking right up the golden stairs. Instead, he saw his hero chopped down and the new world shrink to . . ." Harmon hesitated and his eyes roamed instinctively around the dingy, littered, impoverished print shop. ". . . to grubbiness."

Ewer's round face reddened. "Thanks, my friend."

"But Johnny refused to accept the shrinkage. He was still too young to be cynical. He still envisioned things as they might be, not as they were. Which is the way you're really seeing this print shop, isn't it?"

Ewer let his own gaze tour the room. "No comment," he said.

"If Saguache had been Altoona, the shrinkage might have been permanent in spite of his—innocence is the word I keep coming back to. But a new area was opening up across the divide. John had shared the beginning of it himself when he celebrated Christmas here in this basin and bought two lots as a guarantee that the dream would stay real. If Argent succeeded, he succeeded."

"Mules and all."

"I don't mean just materially. Everyone draws his substance out of what he believes in." Harmon stared into the bottom of his cup. "The trouble is, you have to keep guaranteeing the dreams. Most of us run out of steam after while. So far Johnny hasn't. It's reassuring, for the private dream each of us had about this town, to think that he'll keep on shining it up for us, in spite of the Hedstrom mess."

"Maybe Hedstrom had a dream too, until it got toasted out of him." Ewer gave his heavy head a shake. "It won't wash, Gregg. Even if Johnny wasn't thinking entirely of his own ambitions, what you're twisting the mess into is, 'Greater love hath no man than this: that he lay down somebody else's life for his friends.' No, no. You can't make that sound like idealism to me. Why didn't Johnny fight the Utes and risk himself?"

"And everyone else in this part of Colorado?" Harmon sighed. "One life instead of many lives—that's the way the idea presented itself there at Tally's. Furthermore, the sacrifice wasn't Johnny's idea. That's part of his innocence, too."

"Eating the apple the snake held out wasn't little Eva's idea, either. But she got wised up fast."

"Wised up by the Lord—not by the other inhabitants of Eden."

"I'll settle for the town in this case."

"The town isn't so dangerous. You heard Kennerly defy them all with that gong, didn't you?"

"So that's what made up your mind!" Ewer mocked.

"Partly. At least it showed me for the second time today that a few men can walk through a whole mob just by knowing where they are going."

"To jail, in both cases! A great destination!"

"Jail's just a stop on the way."

"On the way to this heaven you've been talking about?"

"Yes. And that's the rest of what finally decided me to bet on Johnny Ogden. He's working to preserve something he thinks is worth preserving, even though he probably couldn't put what he's after into words. The town is negative—just mad at his methods—"

"With reason. He and the others used Hedstrom like a poker chip."

"But the only substitute the town comes up with is that there should have been a fight." Harmon gave his hand an angry wave. "When you get down to it, the town's as bad as it thinks Johnny is. We're all out here in a hurry-up sweat to get what we want and to the devil with whatever stands in our way, Hedstrom or Utes or whatever."

Ewer gave a sardonic grunt. "Hell bent for heaven, is that it?"

Harmon checked himself. No use being irritated by smart-alecky remarks at this point. "There must be something to the idea," he said dryly. "The world has been working on it long enough."

He shoved chips into the stove and sat back while the constraint between them feathered away, and wished the doubts beneath his surface assurance could be dispelled as easily. After he finally got outside he paused, looking toward the dark windows of the jail.

Wised up, he repeated to himself and hoped Ewer was wrong. No dream could stand too much wisdom, and if this one failed, then where did he go? *I'll still bet on Johnny Ogden,* he thought, and how much of his decision was wistfulness and how much was conviction he never really knew.

I

"1"

On the sharp blue afternoon of the same day that John Ogden had left Red Mountain to go outside on his fatal trip for supplies, a tall, thin young man walked toward Gabe Porcella's store, driving a lightly packed donkey. Accompanying him and helping urge on the burro was a shaggy, solemn dog, mainly black but smudged here and there with traces of gray and brown. Its muzzle and one foot were white. Its fangs were enormous.

The dog's owner regarded the legend STORE on Gabe's tent with amusement, tethered the burro outside, and ducked through the flap. Gabe was mending socks. The heat from his little sheet-metal stove and the smells it released were stifling. The air glimmered yellowly from sunlight filtering through the canvas. Gabe's orange sideburns and meaty red face looked bilious as he glanced at his visitor. A short exchange revealed that the fellow's name was Parley Quine and that he had just followed fresh tracks across the pass from Baker. "They'd be Johnny Ogden's," Gabe said. The visitor then asked for a loaf of bread.

Gabe put a finger through the heel of a sock and sighed. He was not sure that he approved of Parley Quine's bland, presumptive eyes. "Do I look like I was running a bakery?" he said crossly.

Quine was not offended. "Any crackers?"

"No."

"Any flour?"

"I aim to get some shortly."

"Any beans?"

"No."

"Any venison?"

"No."

"Any ham?"

"A quarter of a slab of salt pork."

"I can live that well out of my own pack. Any tinned tomatoes?"

"No."

"What do you have?"

"Some sardines," Gabe said. "Some chewing tobacco. A couple of pounds of dried apples. And there's a few of the boys who like to smell the old whisky barrel."

"A kind of poor camp," Parley Quine observed.

Gabe bristled. "There's enough colors showing so most of the boys plan to stay at least until snow flies. I'm having supplies brought up for them."

"That's good enough for me," Quine allowed. "Is there any place where a man can camp?"

Gabe waved a meaty hand. "Help yourself."

"I mean shelter." Lest he seem too lazy, Quine added, "I haven't time enough before winter to waste building a cabin of my own. My syndicate wants a report as soon as I'm sure of what's here."

"Syndicate?" It was an impressive word. Gabe pushed more fir splinters into the stove. "You mean you want to *buy* a mine?"

"I'd like to pick up some options at least, to hold while we run scientific developments on whatever seems promising."

"You talked to anybody yet?"

"I wanted to establish headquarters first."

Gabe deliberated. He still did not like Quine's expression, but that should not be relevant in a matter involving the entire district. "Well," he said at last, "there's Jake Euston's cabin up at the edge of the trees. Jake wanted me to sell the place for him if I could, but if you're going to help the camp by bringing in some capital, I don't guess he'd mind you using it for a few days."

"I'll be beholden," Quine said. He gossiped a while, asking about the most promising claims and their owners. When he felt he had won Gabe over, he went back outside. Gabe followed him, trying to stave off loneliness. The big dog rose to its feet the instant its master appeared. Gabe clucked admiringly.

"Looks like a fighter."

"He'll oblige."

"What's his name?"

"Joseph."

"Coat of many colors?"

Quine chuckled. "Never thought of that. I named him for my uncle, because he's a son of a bitch too."

Gabe, who liked animals, scratched the dog behind the ears. Joseph accepted the introduction gravely, with neither friendliness nor animosity.

"Dogs are good company out here in the hills," he said, and then added quickly, covering the moment's nakedness, "These people you represent, do they live in Baker?"

"They operate wherever they can find good mines," Quine said grandly. He untied the burro. Gabe pointed out Jake's cabin and said,

"Like I told you, the boys think this camp has a good future. Look at that mountain! Ever see mineral stains to beat them? You ought to have a picture painted to show your syndicate, except no paint could get it right."

"I'll tell them about it," Quine said.

He turned the driving of the burro over to the dog Joseph and with long swinging strides walked perhaps a quarter of a mile beside the rust-bottomed creek to a squat cabin standing where the tawny meadow ended and the dark spruce began climbing toward the pass. It was a low-doored, ill-mortised, greenhorn place in a greenhorn location: a moist hollow that would cup whatever cold settled down from the peaks. Quine grimaced, then shrugged, unpacked his burro, and carried his bedroll inside.

A bedstead of poles covered with a packed matting of dry spruce boughs was built into one corner. A fireplace of mud and sticks occupied the wall opposite the door. Inside the fireplace's maw was an iron bar to which pots could be hooked, and on the crude mantelpiece above were a few tin dishes and cups turned upside down against mouse dirt. A canvas had been stretched overhead to fend off leaks from the mud-covered roof. Water stains made irregular patterns on the fabric, and it sagged in the middle where pack rats had built a nest. Quine heard their dry scurrying as he entered. For a time he amused himself by following the ripples of their running and stabbing at them with a fork. Then he shrugged again and went outside to cut firewood.

The next several days he spent prowling the neighboring prospects. A few of these, like Aino Berg's claim, which Johnny had visited on his way over from Baker, were located near the stream course. Most of the miners, however, had climbed high up the red flanks of the peak to get above the frustrating landslide hillocks that covered whatever outcrops might have surfaced on the lower slopes. The majority of the cramped tunnel mouths were clustered above the meadow holding Gabe's store, but a few adventurous souls had struck farther afield, walking along the side of the peak above the hillocks and here and there staking claims along a contour that more or less paralleled the scraggly trees of timberline.

Various shelters housed the workers. Some men shared fairly substantial cabins on the meadow near Gabe's store and each morning walked to their work up steep, zigzagging trails. Others sought to save time by living in hovels near their tunnel mouths or shaft openings. There was also a handful of placer miners working their sluice boxes beside the stream that meandered through the meadow. Including these placer miners, the population of the district numbered almost forty men. Another twenty or thirty had staked claims but because of the dearth of supplies and the approach of cold weather had drifted away.

Parley Quine visited every holding with his burro. To the owners who were still about he talked knowingly of the differences between milling ores and smelting ores. He discussed sampling procedures which would yield fair assays, but he was content to accept the specimens which the claim owners themselves handed him as representative of their veins. He sacked these fragments and loaded them onto his donkey for transport back to the pile of similar sacks growing beside the cabin he had appropriated. These samples he said he assayed during the evenings. Actually he seldom did more than spit on them, shine them, and look at them through a magnifying glass. He would then return to the owners, talk vaguely of his syndicate, and make what seemed to be astronomical offers for the properties, all predicated on options for which he offered very little besides conversation. A few placer miners whose work was being frozen out by nighttime ice listened to his blandishments. So did two or three deep-rock miners who had grown discouraged and thought that they might as well get at least a promise in exchange for their summer's work. Most of the owners, however, said wisely to each other that they would talk business when they saw the color of Quine's money. To Quine they said that they thought they would wait until John Ogden arrived with his supplies. Then they would drift their tunnels deeper into the mountain and see what their holdings turned into. Good showings would change their asking prices.

Save for such credulous souls as Gabe Porcella, they all understood clearly that Quine was a promoter. There was no syndicate. Quine used the term as a maneuver to secure options. These options obtained, he would go to Baker and wave them around, hoping to create an actual syndicate which would buy several adjoining properties and work them as a single economical operation. If such a purchase took place, Quine would claim a commission from each claim owner and from the syndi-

cate as well, plus a small percentage of the property, as his pay for promoting the transaction. Not a great deal of money would be involved
in amalgamating these untested claims, but it might be enough to let
him survive the winter without resorting to manual labor, and if the
holdings should chance to turn into a real mine, his percentage would
guarantee him a good return. Such a mode of existence seemed to him
no more uncertain than prospecting, and it served a useful purpose.
As one miner put matters to Gabe, "We've got no time to go outside
and find capital. Or connections, either. We've got to depend on promoters like Quine. It's when fellows like him start coming into a camp
that you begin to stand a show of getting a little of your money back.
It just don't pay to be in too big a hurry with 'em, is all."

When Johnny Ogden did not appear on time with his supplies,
Gabe Porcella went down the hill to learn what was the matter. By
that time Parley Quine was hungry. The pot of beans he kept simmering in the fireplace was almost empty: the potatoes he had packed up
on his donkey were gone and he was regretting that he had not saved
the peelings. When a scuff of snow fell one night and he saw fresh
deer tracks the next morning, he forgot about options. Loading his
rifle he followed the trace into tangled gulches among the landslide
hummocks. The tracks led into one particularly deep, steeply inclined
trench between two of the mounds. In its bottom was a shallow, ocher-
colored water channel. As he started to step across this, he saw a
magnificent buck bounding among the scattered firs on the slope ahead.
Balanced precariously, he jerked up his rifle. The shot went wide; the
deer vanished. In a temper Quine banged down the gun and chipped
a fragment off the top of a round boulder.

The gray sheen of the exposed surface caught his eye. He picked
up the chip. It was heavy for its size. Galena, almost certainly. And in
this country that probably meant silver. A claim of his own to sell,
down here in the hillocks where the smart prospectors had not thought
it worth their while to look! He spit on the fragment, rubbed it on his
shirt sleeve. In his time he had made superficial evaluations of a great
deal of lead-silver ore and he was familiar with its showier characteristics.

Excited suddenly by what he saw, he picked up the boulder from
which the fragment had come. Grunting with exertion, he hurled it
against a larger stone, checked it with his foot from rolling down the
hill, and then heaved it again. And again. He grew winded and red in
the face and mashed his toes painfully, and twice he looked around to
see if the racket had attracted attention. Finally the rock shattered.
Fingers trembling, he reached for piece after piece, scrutinizing each
rapidly and shoving it into his pocket with the rest. Then he got hold

of himself. Walking out onto the hillside where the snow had melted under the climbing sun, he made himself sit on a log until his heart quit thumping.

Calmer at last, he returned to the shattered rock. Carefully he studied the manner in which its outer surface had weathered. Then slowly he worked his way up the gulch, hunting for more pieces of float, or, if his luck held, for the outcrop from which the original boulder had rolled.

Presently the gulch forked. In the right-hand branch, concealed from chance observation by a patch of gooseberry bushes, he found what even his inexperienced eyes recognized as the exposed surfacing of a vein. Tracing out what he hoped was the direction of its course, he stepped off a claim fifteen hundred feet long by three hundred feet wide, the maximum size allowed under Colorado mining law. At three of the corners he made flat places on the precipitous slope and heaped up small cairns of stones. At the fourth he sliced the bark off a spruce tree. On the yellow-white wood beneath he penciled the necessary legend of possession. He knew that gum oozing from the cut next spring would probably obliterate his writing. This did not concern him. By spring he did not intend to own the claim. Developing and operating a mine took too much time and ran into too much work.

His eagerness betrayed him. As he was hurrying down the hillside, his heel caught. He fell and tumbled headlong into the rocky ravine. For a moment he hovered on the edge of unconsciousness. When he aroused, his entire right side ached, but the sharpest pain centered in his buttocks. Exploring gingerly he found that he had split his only pair of trousers completely apart and that a raw scrape underneath was oozing blood. Groaning, he hobbled on down the hill.

He knew that in spite of his discomfort he must go immediately to Argent and enter the claim with the county recorder. This involved reclothing himself. To obtain material he pulled down Jake Euston's canvas ceiling, choking and swearing in the odorous cloud of dust released by the pack rat's nest. For a pattern he finished splitting his old pants apart. He then laid them out flat on the canvas and cut around the edges with a butcher knife. He whittled an oak awl from a hammer handle and sewed the fabric together with twine borrowed from Gabe's untended store. It tickled his fancy to leave ravels of twine along the seams in mockery of buckskin. The two safety pins he happened to have with him he used for fortifying the more strategic junctures.

In his hurry to finish and start for town, he failed to leave ample room in the seat and so was badly chafed during his walk down the rough trail. En route he passed Gabe, bound uphill with fifteen loaded mules. Surprised to see the promoter in such wise, the Angel asked questions, but Quine was not ready yet to tip his hand. He passed Gabe off with remarks about girls and limped on, grumbling alternately at his sore toes, his sore crotch, and his sore behind.

"2"

Leaving the county recorder's office, Quine walked painfully along the board sidewalk, past amused stares, to the assay shop. Business was slack and he had no trouble cajoling the assayer into rushing through a quick preliminary determination on some of the galena samples from the mountain. Twelve hundred ounces of silver per ton! This shook even Parley Quine. *Sonny boy,* he told himself, *think fast.* Tenderly he rubbed his lacerated rear.

Quine's specimens were the richest the Argent assayer had ever handled. By no possibility could such news be kept secret. Let it leak, Quine decided. Let some fellows rush up there and file next to me. Follow them and wait until the winter got cold enough and talk turkey to them and get the whole hillside under option. And this time maybe he'd join the purchasing syndicate himself—not a syndicate for operating the property, except as might be necessary, but for floating a stock issue.

His spirits soared. "R.A.M.," he told himself exuberantly. "That's what I'll call the mine—Ragged Ass Mine." Ram for short. The story would spread fast among mining men. Descriptions of his canvas pants and limp would help it spread. Potential buyers of stock would laugh over the episode, and their chuckles would help the name stick when the syndicate turned its issue loose among investors. Yes, Ram would be much better than Rainbow, which was the name he'd first given the recorder and which would have to be changed.

He followed the assayer outside and watched while the excited man showed a copy of the report to the first acquaintance who walked by. Within five minutes a crowd had started to gather. The canvas pants were part of the show. The dog Joseph drew still more people by fighting savagely with a town cur and winning. Attracted by the uproar, a round-headed man with a walrus mustache came ponderously out of the newspaper office up the street, pencil and pad of paper in hand. Quine graciously granted him an interview, with at least a quarter of the town's population craning on tiptoe to listen in.

"Ram!" Ewer laughed explosively. Right down the doughhead's alley,
Quine thought in happy self-congratulation. Innocently he said,

"Why don't you ride up the hill with me—as soon as I get a new
pair of pants—and then come back and write up a first-hand account
of the strike?"

Ewer hesitated and Quine surmised that he was probably contemplating the horrors of hoisting his fat bones onto a horse. Then Ewer
asked,

"Do the people in Baker know about this strike yet?"

"No," Quine said. But they soon would. The faster the news spread
the better.

"Then I think I'll stay here and put out an extra—first one since the
paper started."

Quine shrugged. Having the Ram the cause of an extra could not
hurt him any.

"The strike is in Argent County," Ewer said. He was talking to the
entire crowd now, not just to Parley Quine. "It is important that
the news appear in the Argent first, so that people will realize that the
mines will be tributary to us and not to Baker. Gentlemen, this is a
big day!"

He hurried back to his shop to begin preparations. On the compositor's rack was a story he had begun about Johnny Ogden's arrest,
together with some mention of John's side of the Hedstrom story, as
it had filtered to Ewer through lawyer Gregg. The editor hesitated
over the account for a moment, then pushed it aside. Feed the people
what they wanted. Red Mountain and Parley Quine and R.A.M. and
even the dog Joseph were the news today, not Utes or John Ogden.
He picked up his compositor's stick. As his heavy fingers moved lightly
over the type—he composed and set the story simultaneously—he realized that he had time and information enough for no more than a
half-sized sheet printed on one side only. And this time he would
forget his single-column heads and run big type completely across the
page. A queer looking product it would be, like a handbill. Then he
thought that here might be a chance to attract publicity to *The True
Fissure*. Extra revenue, too. He would hold an auction on the sidewalk
in front of the building. He would sell to the highest bidder the first
copy of the historic extra to come from the press.

He did not flatter himself that the bidding would be for the paper's
news value. Everyone in Argent would know of the strike long before
the extra reached the street. What the town would be paying for would
be the color which Quine's Ram gave to its own hopes. For the confirmation, in print, that each man's judgment in coming to this remote

and chancy spot had been sound after all. Red Mountain was going to make something of them yet. That assurance ought to be worth a few dollars at anyone's auction.

"3"

Pat Edgell learned the news at the livery stable. He had gone there to help Angel Gabe pack the mules and afterwards had sat around gossiping with the hostlers. Three men with bedrolls, a few tools, and a dab of grub arrived in a breathless hurry to rent horses. They were secretive at first, but when they were riding out the double doors, their excitement slipped leash. Very confidentially they told Pat that they planned to find Quine's Ram—that was a hot one, R.A.M., get it?—and file claims of their own adjacent to it. Twelve-hundred-ounce ore! Man!

Within twenty minutes eight more miners had clattered into the stable on their hobnailed boots. The rental price on horses rose from a dollar to three dollars a day and one of the hostlers quit to join the rush. He wanted Pat to accompany him, but when Pat thought about the high meadow where Gabe's tent stood, white above the white hoarfrost, he shook his head.

"That mountain won't go anywhere before warm weather," he said. Besides, there were easier ways of making money out of a rush than by digging. He had learned that in Baker.

He stood in the doorway, thumbs hooked in his waistband and heels hooked over the manured cleat boards transversing the stable ramp. His shallow eyes watched the curve of the trail rounding the hill just above town. Three groups went by, one of them afoot. It was fair, therefore, to assume that more men than had come into the stable were already hurrying toward Red Mountain.

And I thought Gabe was crazy, taking fifteen packs there, with winter already knocking.

The shadows in the doorway whetted the edge of the wind blowing down the gorge. Pat moved into sunlight. From his new stand he could see a large knot of men clustered around the flagpole. Two riders jogged by them toward the trail. There was a waving and catcalling. No use being sneaky now; everyone knew.

If this keeps up, he thought, supplies are going to get tighter than a wet knot. Old Gabe! That lucky son! Pat kicked at a rock. There must be some other proposition that a man could figure out. Corner all the shovels in Argent, maybe? The crosscut saws? It was said that during the early days of the Baker stampede, a man in town with a carpenter's kit made far more money than did a man out in the hills with a shovel. And a man who owned good building lots had it over all of them. Pat kicked again. His building lots, a third of all Argent once, had vanished in a poker game. Well, next time he'd know better.

That Gabe! Fell in and came out smelling like a rose! Everyone in town knew he had taken those supplies up and now they were counting on it. By dark he'd be selling stuff as fast as he could push it across the counter. Fifteen mule loads wouldn't last a week. Suddenly Pat snapped his fingers. A man with a string of pack stock could make a fortune just renting the animals. Johnny Ogden owned those fifteen mules Gabe was using. Walt Kennerly owned still more. But both of them were in the calaboose where they couldn't do a thing. They might appreciate a little help.

Purposeful now, Pat strode up the tilted street. He paused to crane his neck at the man in the canvas pants and then went into the courthouse, intending to ask if he might visit his friends. He was diverted, however. Several of the town's leading citizens had gathered in the sheriff's office and were heatedly discussing the portents of what had just happened. Linc Hotchkiss, who owned the general store, was there. Mayor Rubin; Luke Dixon of the Dixon House; George Yount, the town's elder lawyer and most active politician; the sheriff—people like that. They glanced at Pat, nodded vacantly, and went on talking. Much of the conversation traveled in circles or onto side tracks like a half-trained hound, but pretty quick it would be whistled back again. Oh, this strike might be the very thing they had all known was coming. The need now was to corral it and herd it so that Argent and everyone in Argent might benefit as fully as possible.

"There's not half as much stock in my store as there should be," Linc Hotchkiss was moaning. "Not half."

"Bring in some more."

"I don't know how much farther my credit will stretch. And the cost, man. Freighters are scarce."

Luke Dixon growled, "Those damned Indians along the road smelling blood. Cushman! And Ogden! They ought to be hanging from that flagpole right now!"

Gaw said mildly, "The Utes might of been more than just smelling for blood if the sojers had come."

"Soldiers would have opened the road," Dixon said, chipping out his words like a fierce dog barking. "As far as that goes, I thought you were going to take a posse onto the reservation after Cushman and Tally and the rest."

"The district attorney ain't sure I got the authority. And I ain't sure I can deputize a big enough posse, now that everyone who's free to leave his job is already on the way to Red Mountain."

"This Quine, now," Mayor Rubin said. "He's a slick article, I'd say— pure promoter. He may be starting rumors just to sell his claims."

"You can't kiss off twelve-hundred-ounce ore as rumor."

"It takes more than one assay to make a mine."

"Especially if you don't really know where he got those specimens."

George Yount said, "We can send a man—Gaw here, perhaps—to the telegraph office at Gunnison and wire the commander at Fort Garland that a state of emergency exists and we need troops to keep traffic open."

"Fort Garland, hell!" Dixon barked. "Go to the top! Wire Granny Schurz at the Indian Bureau in Washington. Tell him to stir up his ambassadors or what the hell ever they are. Put Otto Winkler on the job. Get the Indians' signatures on the treaty and then get the tan-bellied baboons out of here!"

Mayor Rubin said, "I think I'd better ride up the mountain tomorrow and look at what Quine really has. I'll take that fat newspaperman with me. We'll print an honest, official report and mail it to every town in the state before the Baker people wake up. That will pull freight through here rather than Baker."

"Are you willing to go through the reservation to the telegraph office?" Yount asked Gaw.

"Red Mountain is in Argent County," Hotchkiss said to Rubin. "It's just natural for business to come this way instead of through Baker."

"I'm not so sure," someone else retorted. "That trail through the gorge would be hell to move any large amount of ore over."

"I'll go," Gaw told Yount unhappily, "if the county commissioners order me to."

"Trails can be fixed."

"You can arrest Tally on the way and take him to Gunnison with you."

"You can't do much trail fixing before winter."

"We can do more than Baker will do. For one thing, look at the advantage we have in distance. From here to Red Mountain is at least nine miles shorter than from Baker."

"Trails! Christamighty! This is big! We need a road!"

Road. The word teased at Pat, but in this swirl of talk it slipped away before he could grip it.

"Road! Just where do you think the money's coming from?"

"That's how to get left behind—sit on your tail saying a thing can't be done right while the other fellow is out doing it."

"We don't know for sure what's up there."

"That's why I want to go see," Rubin repeated. "A true report."

"I think I'll go with you," Dixon decided.

Hotchkiss laughed harshly. "You stove huggers! You'll freeze your knockers up there."

"Might as well be frozen as rusted, the way they are."

Pat remembered. Without thinking, he blurted, "How about John Ogden building the road? He has a franchise."

"4"

"Ogden?" The whole room stared at Edgell. Dixon's lip curled. "I'll see John Ogden roast in hell with Young Hedstrom first."

"Franchise?" Yount asked. "What franchise?"

"To build a road."

"Up the gorge?"

"Yes."

"When did he get it?"

Pat did not have to answer that question. Gaw interrupted with an incredulous wag of his head, "Like I say, just where does Johnny Ogden think the money is comin' from to build any such road."

Mayor Rubin agreed with a solemn nod. "It's not a job for individuals."

"Not for a white Ute, anyway."

"It's a county job."

"The county had better do it, too, before Baker builds up from their side and steals our own camp right out from under our own nose."

"Baker? They'd have to lift freight over the divide both ways."

"Look at the divide they're already lifting stuff over."

"I wouldn't hurry any road on just one pocketful of rock."

"A promoter's canvas pocket, at that."

"If it was spring, with enough time really to prospect that high country—"

"You'll feel damn smart, won't you, if the merchants over in Baker get together and decide to push ahead of us—"

Pat slipped outside. No one seemed to notice. In the hallway he paused. Concentration scoured vertical furrows above his bridgeless nose. One thing seemed certain: whoever got in first on that road was the one who'd cash in. Poor old John, trapped in the clink . . .

Rousing abruptly, Pat went to Harmon Gregg's office. The lawyer had taken from his bookcase a ponderous volume on pleading and another whose title Pat neither saw nor tried to see. He acknowledged them, however, by asking,

"Are both those books for Johnny?"

Harmon nodded and leaned back in his chair and rubbed his eyes. To judge from his looks, he had not slept much since his late interviews the night before.

"Do you reckon you can get him off?"

"We can make a good stab at it."

"How soon?"

Harmon exhaled uncomfortably. "I'm afraid it may take a while. For one thing, I want to shift the case into another court."

"Will it take weeks?"

"Months, perhaps."

"The hell! That'll be hard on Johnny."

"There's not much help for it."

"I was just heading for the jail to tell him about the strike at Red Mountain."

"The what?"

"Twelve-hundred-ounce ore. Fellow named Quine. He calls it the R.A.M.—Ragged Ass Mine, get it, 'cause he scratched his butt while he was prospecting. Where have you been all morning?"

"So that's what has had people running up and down the street!" Harmon gestured at the books in explanation of his ignorance and then brightened somewhat. "This will please John. It should take some of the heat off him, too."

"Maybe," Pat said dubiously. "They're still cussin' him, though, when they happen to think of it." He paused and then asked the question that had been on the top of his mind all this while. "What about the road franchise you applied for?"

Harmon pursed his lips. "By George. It had slipped my mind. To Red Mountain!"

"Have you heard anything definite about it?"

"Not yet."

"Is it likely to come through?"

"Those things are generally routine."

"Once he's got it in his pocket, is he the only one who can build up the gorge?"

"Probably, unless another applicant proves a need for a second road paralleling the same route." Harmon looked bluntly into Pat's shallow eyes. "Why?"

Pat grinned at him. "Not because I aim to buck him, if that's what you mean. What about the county? Can they take his franchise?"

"Under eminent domain I suppose they could."

"They would have to pay?"

"Yes."

"How much?"

"It's impossible to say. First there would have to be an appraisal. If John did not like the figure, he could go to court. Why?"

"He's in the clink," Pat said, "and you say he's likely to stay there a while. But things are happening fast. He may need help getting his road started—a company set up and maybe enough stock sold to begin work so that nobody can step in and take the road away from him on the grounds that he's not able to swing it."

Harmon kept his eyes steadily on the flat, merry face. "Pure, disinterested friendship?" he asked.

Pat smiled again, unabashed. "As disinterested as you being his lawyer. Anyway, what's wrong with helping ourselves while we're helping him?"

Harmon dropped his eyes. "I deserved that," he apologized. He rubbed his goatee in embarrassment and sought refuge by turning to his books. "Talk to Johnny and then let me know what he says."

Pat walked back toward the courthouse. A crowd was still clustered around Quine at the flagpole, some individuals now and then spinning off and others taking their places. Edgell's wide mouth smiled exultantly at them. Go on, dig. He thought of Gabe again. All right, if you can't be lucky, be smart. As for mules—peanuts! This road was what would help Johnny and Patrick O'Shaughnessy Edgell to boot. Whistling cheerily, he took the courthouse steps in a jump and asked Sheriff Gaw if he might see the prisoners.

"5"

On their tacit promise not to escape, Walt and Johnny had been freed from the cage and allowed the whole of the jail wing. Another tacit understanding had delayed until afternoon Walt's hearing on the charge of disturbing the peace, so that he could keep Johnny company through most of the first hard day. The companionship was tacit, too. Walt was playing solitaire with a deck of cards borrowed from Gaw, and John was staring morosely out of the window, when Pat burst in on them with a headlong account of the day's events.

Mountain moonshine on an empty stomach at twelve thousand feet could not have hit Johnny harder or faster. "Ha!" His eyes shone. "At

Red Mountain!" He tried to see over the store tops to the gorge. "I knew it!" He flung out his right hand as if he were the one who had made the strike. "That'll show some of these soreheads whether they needed the supplies up there."

The strike had occurred before the supplies had arrived. Pat sneaked at Walt a faintly sardonic glance, but Walt kept smiling at John as if everything really was the image of what John wanted. Oh, why argue? Pat told himself. That was Johnny: he always read things the way he wished. If anyone challenged him on the timing of the strike, he would say that the miners would not have hung around the mountain if they had not been expecting goods; and without mines Quine would not have appeared to find the outcrop. So let it go. The main thing was to cheer him about the road.

Pat worked into his proposal much as he had worked into it with the lawyer, but slower, giving Johnny time to blow off steam over one shock before going on to the next. He told about the delay which Harmon Gregg predicted, waited while John paced back and forth— "Months! My God, I can't—" and then reminded John of the toll-road franchise and said he figured it was important to form the road company right away. "Months!" Johnny's hand sawed the air. "How—" Awkwardly Pat offered himself as a solution.

"It's not just a matter of the work, either," he said and stared at his hands in embarrassment and exhaled. "This is a mean thing to bring up, John, but, well, a lot of people have been listening to Hedstrom and reading *The True Fissure* and, well, there's some that feel pretty hot about it. Right now wouldn't be the time for you to go out, or even send somebody out in your name to try and hire men or raise money."

"If I could talk to them!" Johnny cried. "If Ewer would print both sides!"

"I know, I know. But, well, we've got to work with things as they are. Now look. This is what I've doped out and you see whether you like it or not. I'll front for you. We'll set up a company partnership, fifty-fifty or whatever suits you, and give it a name something like, oh, the Ute River Transportation Company—how does that sound to you?"

Johnny responded as Pat had hoped. He got outside himself, he began to plan, his eyes sparkled again. He didn't like the name Pat had suggested, however. "The district will be called Red Mountain, and the name ought to show what area the road is serving. Don't you agree, Walt?"

"I guess," Kennerly said.

"Red Mountain, then," Pat said. "Red Mountain Toll Road and Transportation Company. That sounds good, and the soreheads won't even need to know your connection with it, till things quiet down. Meanwhile I can move around selling stock——"

"Stock?"

"It's going to cost, building a road up that gorge. Subscriptions and work donations won't do, Johnny. This is big—as big as anything we ever worked on for Otto Winkler. We've got to handle it big, too, or the people over in Baker will form a company and build in there ahead of us."

"I never thought of that," Johnny said. He nodded vigorously. Pat was right; this road had to be good enough to guarantee the ore for Argent.

They talked about that, and about ways and means. They tried to predict the weather and how many men Pat ought to begin with, and then John said impulsively to Walt, who had spoken scarcely a word,

"Why not come in with us on a three-way partnership?"

Walt ran the cards with his thumb and shook his head. "I don't hardly see how I can. I've all I can do, packing for the agency."

"That agency isn't going to be there forever."

"There'll be other hauling."

Johnny looked at the cage. His frown was bewildered. The poor kid, Pat thought. Walt had got himself arrested to share the lonesome part of the night with John, but he would not share the road. Too risky. Like some of those gasbags in the courthouse, he'd hold back until he was sure what the mountain would produce. Well, there was no gain without risk. And that was what Pat was willing to share, the risk as well as the gain.

"I'll go see the lawyer," he said, "and he can rough up some papers and you can study them out and make whatever changes you want, and then I can start the work."

"That's great, Pat. I appreciate it. I—hell, you know what I mean. And look, Pat. There's one more thing."

"Whatever you want."

"We've got to keep the trail open, too."

Pat hesitated. "I'll be busy down here." He smiled brightly. "Gabe can work the trail enough to keep supplies moving."

Johnny wasn't satisfied. "It's my responsibility. I promised the boys. They'll expect—well, you know Gabe."

Seeing that he was going to be insistent, Pat gave in. "We'll keep her clear as long as the weather gives us a fair shake."

"Thanks, Pat. I won't forget."

"Oh, I'm figuring on my fifty per cent," Pat said candidly. He felt warm and virtuous as he went outside. That deadhead Kennerly! It was just as well not to have him in the company. This job was going to take git-up-and-go. Johnny running the work as soon as he was clear. Pat handling the business end. A team! They'd make Argent notice, they surely would! And they didn't need anyone else, just themselves.

II

"1"

Winter passed into April. Snow was gone from the foothills when the little narrow-gauge night train from Denver roared and shook and crept south along the front range and then bent into the mountains through the vast granite canyon of the Arkansas River. At the rear of the train was a parlor car with individual plush seats that leaned back and also rotated on their bases like barber chairs. Ahead of this was a single Pullman with diminutive berths. The other five passenger cars were coaches, packed full.

In the smoking section of one of these coaches, Johnny and Harmon sat jammed into a single seat. Harmon felt congealed with misery. Outside, the wheel flanges shrilled against the curving rails. Echoes of the engine's labor swelled and faded with the shape of the granite walls. Inside, the air was rank with stale tobacco and the stench of kerosene from the faulty wick of one of the overhead lamps. The grimy red plush of the coach seats smelled of coal smoke and old food and outraged flesh. The heat from the stove at the end of the car was stifling. Shadows leaned and straightened and leaned with the sway of the car. Lolling faces looked slack and ocher-colored. Harmon tried to flex his tendons against creeping paralysis. Leg room must have been designed for an undernourished midget. The flat part of the seat was too narrow, the back too straight. Human joints could not bend to such angles.

None of it bothered Johnny. Harmon glared at him. Wedged upright between the lawyer and the streaked window, he slept with his head slumped forward onto his chest. Bubbly noises pushed through his slack lips. Now and then he gave a jerk. His head lifted, his eyeballs rolled whitely, and then he fell asleep again.

Harmon looked at his watch. Four-eighteen A.M. Nine hours of purgatory behind. Forty-two minutes more to go before they could disembark at South Arkansas for the stage ride across the Continental Divide. Dear Lord and Father of mankind, he murmured and rose and went to the brass water container at the end of the car for another tepid drink. There, partly in self-defense, he lit another cigar, taking his time, and amused himself, as he had earlier, by looking through the smoking section's open doorway at the handsome young woman in the front seat of the general section.

She was asleep finally. She had taken off her big brown hat and brown cashmere jacket. The puffed sleeves of her high-necked blouse were crumpled. Her head, its heavy jet black hair piled high above her forehead in a pompadour, leaned sideways against a small square of pillow that she had purchased from the news butcher. Her black lashes intensified the pallor of her thin cheeks. The unawareness of sleep made her look very isolated to Harmon, very tired. She had evidently come a long way. Earlier when she had taken off her gloves while nibbling dispiritedly at a sandwich, he had seen a gold wedding band. Probably, he surmised, she was traveling to join her husband in one of the remote mining towns, and he could not help wondering how she would like it when she saw what it was.

His mouth felt rubbery from too much smoke. He dropped the half-consumed cigar into the overflowing spittoon and crowded back into his seat. Johnny wakened. He yawned, grunted, and cupped his hands around his eyes to peer through the car window into the darkness. "Where are we?" he said thickly.

"About half an hour from South Arkansas," Harmon answered.

"Almost there!" Johnny humped his shoulders to stretch his back. As he grew more alert, he regarded with fresh interest the medley of faces, the festoons of coats swaying on their brass hooks, the duffel bags, suitcases, and paper sacks piled on the filigreed rack overhead. "Full house!" He had said exactly the same thing before, in the same exultant tones. "I wonder how many of them will be going over the mountain to the St. Johns." He scratched his ribs. "How'd you sleep?"

"Not the way you did," Harmon said enviously. Some of the speculations that had filled his wakefulness while he had watched and listened to Johnny's sleep returned to him. He still did not find the young man quite credible. Nothing that had happened throughout the winter had quite suppressed his serene faith that each morning's sun would rise again.

"2"

It had been a winter for crushing spirit, too. Harmon's maneuver in challenging county jurisdiction had succeeded almost too well in that it had alerted the federal prosecutors. Federal indictments had followed. The charges had been a repetition of those made in Argent: first-degree murder, conspiracy to murder, accessories before the fact. Cushman had been included as had Hedstrom's escort—Ogden, Tally, Banner, Hoyt, and the Indians Tah-koo-ni-ca-vats and Piah Bill. Other warrants, concerned with the actual slaying, were sworn out against Shavano and various John Doe Utes.

The Indians disappeared. Sending marshals to find them and the remnants of Young Hedstrom if any, had roused the tribe to fury. To keep treaty negotiations from breaking down entirely, the Indian Bureau had stepped in and had ordered the search postponed until a more propitious time. Meanwhile, on the strength of the change of venue from Argent, Cushman, Tally, and the others of the escort had surrendered to a federal marshal. John Ogden, released by federal court order from the Argent County jail, where he had by then spent more than a month, had been rearrested immediately and taken to Denver for trial.

Delay piled on delay. The Indian Bureau appointed a high-powered Washington counsel to defend Agent Cushman, and there was a long wait while the attorney came West to familiarize himself with the case. For Johnny, the days had been harrowing. Not just the claustrophobia and the smells and the bad food. Argent had offered those. But in Argent he had been able to look out the window at the peaktops. Visitors could come in and sit with him; his occasional cellmates had been limited, for the most part, to good-natured drunks. The Denver prison had been different. There, killers and rapists and thieves had tried to accept Johnny as one of themselves. Infuriated by his aloofness, they then had learned that he was charged with betraying one of his own kind to the Utes for torture and death. After that they had scorned him as beneath themselves, and had subjected him to indignities which Johnny had never detailed but which Harmon had guessed something of just by the look of the boy's face.

Red Mountain had sustained him. While Johnny had still been in Argent, Parley Quine had ridden, in a new pair of pants, back up the hill; and in Gabe's store had made an astounding agreement with a pair of Cousin Jacks, as Cornish miners were called. If the two Jacks would do the necessary development work on the Ram—sink a shaft and run a drift out from its bottom—they could keep, in return, whatever ore they extracted. Everyone laughed at the Cornishmen. Average run-of-the-mine values were not likely to match Quine's twelve-hundred-ounce specimens, and transportation costs on mule back, as everyone at Red Mountain knew, would prohibit the shipping of merely average ore. Quine, in short, would probably end up not only with the Jacks' free labor but with their abandoned rock as well.

To the county's amazement, the assays stayed high. Just before Johnny was rearrested, a syndicate of Argent businessmen offered Quine thirty thousand dollars for a prospect explored very little more than thirty feet. He turned them away with a wave of his cigar.

The eager Cousin Jacks quickly progressed beyond hand effort and clamored for better equipment. With herculean effort, Walt Kennerly packed up rail, a little dump car, hoisting apparatus. To keep the machines busy, the Cousin Jacks employed helpers and then sent outside for catalogues of fine clothing and elegant furniture, though neither was married. In spite of vile weather, Red Mountain's population grew. Gabe Porcella hired snow shovelers to keep the trail passable and rented Johnny's mules to bring in more supplies.

Although Johnny's resentment over Ewer's stories on the Hedstrom affair stayed white-hot, he subscribed to *The True Fissure* so that even in Denver he would miss no Red Mountain news of significance. Harmon brought more details when he came outside to confer with the lawyer retained by the Indian Bureau. Even the Denver dailies began to show interest in the new strikes. Great bonfires of spruce wood, Johnny read, were being used to thaw the frozen ground along the flanks of the peak; and because Quine's lucky find had showed where ore might be expected, other strikes followed. Weather prevented accurate appraisal. Even so, a hurry-up settlement began to take shape. Walt built a barn to shelter his pack stock. He helped Gabe cut logs and sled them down the hill for a new store. There was even a hotel of sorts, and a saloon, and a dozen log cabins. Johnny chuckled over the description of the town, imagining the way the young city would list next summer when the snow melted under the foundations. But, anyway, it was a town, and until snowslides in March piled more debris across the trail than hand-shoveling could clear away, it maintained fairly regular communications with Argent.

Furthermore, and this he learned from the bragging of *The True Fissure*, people headed for Red Mountain were crossing the reservation to Argent; they were not risking the trails into snowbound Baker. Argent, Ewer crowed in one editorial, was the logical approach to the new mines. He added that the advantages of the Argent route would soar the following spring when a graded road was constructed up Ute Gorge—a road that could be maintained throughout the year. He did not say who was building the road. He did not admit why the reservation was safe for travel. Eventually, though, he would have to.

John Ogden, president of the Red Mountain Toll Road and Transportation Company.

A ghoul, was he?

Guilty?

Harmon wagged his head, awed and even a little dismayed at the store Johnny was setting by the road. That confidence, too, was part of Ogden's young innocence. It would seem that every evening after the cell door shut behind him and he could snatch a few minutes' privacy, he would unfold his copy of the incorporation papers which the lawyer had filed with the Colorado secretary of state, would admire the colored ribbon and the great seal and the flourishing official signatures, and then would read and reread the printed matter until he knew it by heart.

Know all men by these presents that we, John Ogden and Patrick Edgell of Argent County, do hereby associate oursleves together for the purpose and object of becoming a body corporate under Chapter XIX of the Revised Statutes of the State of Colorado, and for that purpose and object do hereby make, execute, acknowledge and deliver these our Articles of Incorporation.

Article 1
The corporate name of the Company shall be the Red Mountain Toll Road and Transportation Company.

Article 2
The objects for which this said Company are formed are to build a wagon road between Argent City and the principal mines of Red Mountain, to maintain the thoroughfare all months of the year, to build stations for collecting such tolls as are authorized under the laws of the state, and to conduct such other business as may be proper.

Article 3
The capitalization of the Company shall be $50,000.00 represented by ten thousand shares of non-assessable common stock, par value five dollars per share. . . .

At this point in the reading Johnny would pause and some of the exaltation would leave his face. The stock had not been the sesame envisioned.

By agreement made in the Argent jail with Pat, he and John were each to hold, in payment for their enterprise and labor, twenty-five and one-half per cent of the stock, or 2550 shares apiece. One hundred shares had been given Harmon for his work as company lawyer and company treasurer. The remaining 4800 shares were deposited in the treasury, to be sold as construction needs demanded. Potentially the sale of these shares could produce twenty-four thousand dollars for building the road. Neither partner had ever before contemplated such a sum as an actual rather than purely hypothetical figure. Just the munificence of its sound rolling off their tongues seemed a guarantee of success. In the heady contemplation of the power it would make available to them, they mentally foreshortened the span of the gorge and let its barriers shrink to mere inconveniences.

Pat had launched himself into the selling with an enthusiasm bred by these rosy pictures. Results surprised and mortified him. People did not buy. Some of the men he approached scoffed openly at the possibility of building the road with three times that money. Winter doldrums and Argent's normal lack of cash discouraged others. But the biggest obstacle, Pat said baldly to Harmon after a few weeks of discouragement, was John Ogden's unfavorable reputation in the town. Many of its inhabitants, still outraged by the Hedstrom affair, did not wish to associate themselves with him in any venture, no matter how attractive it was. As a result Pat had been able to sell only a few odd lots of stock, scarcely enough to provide tools for starting the preliminary grading.

Johnny's confidence swallowed even that insult. He insisted that as soon as he was cleared and as soon as summer came, sales would pick up. Meanwhile, he wrote Pat, they should start work with such resources as they had, to show the countryside that they were serious and not just speculating. Instead of following this advice, however, Pat traveled clear to Saguache over stormy roads to see Otto Winkler. He had hoped to sell Otto at least a thousand shares. Winkler bought a hundred at a discount, and acted as if even this was an indulgence to former employees rather than an investment. The only reason he gave for his niggardliness was to say, "Iss not ripe."

Johnny cracked his knuckles in exasperation when Harmon came to the visitors' room in the Denver jail and reported the words. "What does he mean by that?"

"I didn't talk to him," Harmon said.

"Maybe he's afraid we can't produce. Has Pat done anything to get the work started?"

"He's surveying."

"Is that all?"

"He can't do much more in winter."

"Maybe not in the gorge. But he could begin the first grades out of town."

"He's been concentrating on selling stock."

"I don't like it, Harmon."

"You've about got to. The way things are . . . well—"

"With me locked up and him out, you mean?"

"That's about it. You've got to let him use his own judgment about what needs his attention most."

"I suppose," John said gloomily and then began pressing as eagerly as ever for information. "Where is he running his survey lines? Is he going to leave town at the end of Main Street or down behind Fat Terwilliger's barns, the way we first talked?"

Harmon regarded the floor. "Neither."

"But we agreed—"

"He changed his mind. He's had his survey crew living in a cabin at the old Mineral Patch and studying the best way up the west side of the gorge. They've had a rough time of it in some of the storms."

"West!" At the mention of the word Johnny jumped to his feet and began pacing the narrow visitors' room in agitation. "Pat and I argued that a hundred times in Argent. The east side is best."

"Pat says the rock work will be too expensive on the east side. On the west there's already the start of a road as far as the Mineral Patch. You can take that over fairly cheaply, which I must admit is a sound consideration. Money evidently is going to be harder to raise than we thought."

"But—" and Johnny plunged into talk about curvatures and snow-slides and tributary roads until he realized that he was wasting his breath. Railing four hundred miles away from the job to a lawyer unfamiliar with road work was not going to realign any grades. He hooked his fingers through the wire netting, his face miserable with frustration.

Harmon felt like a child-beater. "We're doing all that's possible. These things can't be rushed."

After interminable conferences, Gregg and the lawyer representing Cushman decided to ask for bail. This involved a review of the three counts on the indictment, first-degree murder, accessories before the fact, and conspiracy to murder. The first charge was attacked on the ground that no body had been found and that if any crime had in fact been committed the white defendants obviously had not partici-pated directly. The Washington lawyer next pointed out that existing federal statutes contained no provision for punishing any such offense as accessory before the fact. Harmon dug up precedent for admitting to bail men charged with conspiracy to murder. After hearing the arguments, the judge allowed the plea. Tally, Banner, and Hoyt could not raise the amount set, however, and stayed in jail. The Indian Bureau became surety for Cushman, who returned righteously to his duties at Los Alamos. Otto Winkler and Walt Kennerly signed Johnny's bond. By this time he had been more than three months in different jails and was fever-bent to hurry to Argent and line out the road the way he thought it should be done. Once work was progressing satisfactorily, he insisted, the money would come in, for the advantages of the road were plain.

Sell us this day our daily stock, Harmon thought with a twist of familiar irony. Have faith and the Lord will provide. That unshatterable innocence! One could not help warming to it, and yet Johnny had to be prepared for reality.

"You're not clear yet," he said bluntly. "That was just a bail hearing. If you go to Argent now, you'll just be inviting . . . well, whatever Ewer or anyone else wants to say."

Johnny's dark face turned darker. "That son of a bitch. I'm not afraid of him."

"Pat is."

"I don't see—"

"He's having a hard enough time selling road stock as it is."

"What we need is some good solid work for a change," John said sulkily. "Something to show the investors what they're buying."

"You can't do much work without money for wages and equipment. Don't make things any tougher for Pat than they already are. Besides, you won't have time to do much work. Within a few weeks you'll have to turn around and come back for your trial."

"I can at least get the road started up the right side of the canyon," Johnny insisted stubbornly.

Harmon felt his patience slipping. "You just won't look a fact in the face, will you?"

"What do you mean?"

"Things are happening fast over there. Otto Winkler and Fred Fossett have gone into the reservation to help the Ute Commission negotiate the treaty, and it looks now as if the tribe may sign."

"Whatever that's got to do with me going to Argent—"

"Use your head, will you? As soon as the Indians are out of the way, a whole new rush of people will pour into the town. Like Walt Kennerly has said all along, the entire atmosphere of Argent will change."

"Are you saying Walt thinks I should wait?" Johnny asked miserably.

"He thinks, and I agree, that the new excitement will give folks other things to think about than—oh, Al Ewer's worn-out bleats, for example."

"That son of a bitch," Johnny said again. "He never has printed my side of the story."

"Listen to me, will you?"

"I'm sorry. It's just that I get so darn . . . Go ahead, I'll shut up."

"When the Utes and the snow are both out of the way, the development of the new strikes will be the only thing on people's minds. One of the biggest demands will be for a road to Red Mountain. That's the time for you to go back. By then you'll have had your trial and be clear, if we're lucky. Ewer won't be able to hurt you so much. But if you go back now, he can keep on printing anything he pleases. He can do the road real hurt. Don't give him the chance. Let Pat raise as much money as he possibly can for you to start work with in the spring."

Johnny took an unhappy turn around the room. At last he let his hands drop, palms out, "I suppose you're right," he conceded reluctantly.

While he waited, he found a job in the railroad shops in Denver, for he was nearly broke by now. Meanwhile, the Washington lawyer had insisted that Cushman's trial, essentially simpler than that of the other defendants, should be separated from theirs. Since the agent had not been with the escort, the only charge against him that held much strength was the one about conspiracy. This promised to be difficult to prove, and Cushman's attorney did not want the prosecution to dodge it by concentrating on the charges against the other defendants.

Harmon at once agreed to the change, for of course the failure of the charge against Cushman would inevitably weaken the government's case against Johnny. He further agreed with the Washington attorney that Cushman's trial be held first.

The strategy proved effective. The court granted the attorney's plea for separation of the cases, and Cushman's hearing was scheduled for the latter part of April. In preparation, the government prosecutor started looking for Indian witnesses. None were forthcoming. The tribe, still agitated by the earlier search for the actual slayers of Young Hedstrom, misunderstood the new quest and believed that surrendering a witness to the marshal would be the same as delivering the man for hanging. The chiefs breathed defiance; war drums boomed. A reporter sent to the agency by a Denver newspaper wrote back that a thousand troops would be required to produce a single witness. Winkler and Fossett, deep in the reservation and on the point of success in their negotiations, fired out protests. One of Colorado's senators began to rumble. The Indian Bureau, rumor said, added words of its own. When the federal marshal returned and certified that his subpoenas were unserviceable, the prosecutor let go the matter, *nolle prosequi*. Cushman thus freed, the case against the other defendants was also dropped.

Johnny walked out of the railroad shop grinning from ear to ear. "I can go home tonight!"

Harmon was less exuberant. He had achieved his victory in about the manner he had hoped. Yet the incompleteness of it bothered him, and it was his nature to postpone forcing issues in the hope that new developments might remove the need.

"I'm not sure it's wise to go straight back," he said.

Johnny scowled. "Wait for spring, wait for more people. Now what do I wait for?"

"It's early yet. Why don't you go up to Red Mountain the back way, through Baker? You can stay with Gabe or somebody, do some work on that end of the road, and wait for Argent to get used to this—it might as well be said—this tricky, easy escape of yours. Then when the rush builds up—"

Time? Tell a drowning man how good the swimming will be tomorrow? Johnny's scowl deepened. "You didn't stand by that saw blade last fall and hear people you thought were your friends hollering to lynch you. You didn't have jail scum spit on you. I've waited long enough. I'm clear, ain't I?"

Harmon worked his lips in and out above his goatee. Beyond wanting to return to his work, the boy ached for vindication. That was natural enough. But vindication for what, exactly? From the charge that he had shared in a murder? Or for his public shaming? Unhappily the lawyer said,

"Technically, you're not clear. There's been no verdict."

Johnny sucked in his breath. "Do you mean they can arrest me again if I go to Argent?"

"They can, but it's not likely. We've pretty well established that a county warrant would not be valid. I don't think that the federal authorities will reopen the case. Furthermore, of course," he admitted, "until you are actually found guilty, the law presumes you innocent."

Relief flooded back. "Then I don't see what the worry is."

Was the dream so bright that no shadow whatsoever could touch it? Harmon took a deep breath.

"Not everybody over there will presume what the law presumes. Some people still say that Hedstrom was burned at the stake."

That stung. Blood rushed to Johnny's cheeks. "The marshal's posse never found a trace."

"Without a verdict to the contrary, they are likely to keep on saying it."

"Ewer, you mean?"

"Probably."

"I'm damned if I'll wait again for Al Ewer. You said yourself that the big cry is going to be for a road to Red Mountain. All right, then!" Once more exaltation touched Johnny's young face. "The sooner we get that road built, the sooner we can bring the ore down to the mills in Argent and then ship the bullion out where everyone can see what our mines have. That ought to mean something even to a backcapper like Al Ewer."

"As easy as that," Harmon murmured. What was it the poet had said? —follow it, follow the gleam. Enthusiasm too bedazzled to remember a dead man's charred bones. Jenkins' *Legal Forms* contained nothing about a case built on that kind of faith. And perhaps Johnny was wiser than Jenkins. The lawyer grew envious. "No, no problems at all."

Johnny misunderstood. "Oh, it'll be a job," he said, "getting past those Wolf Creek cliffs. But like I told Pat . . ."

By the time they boarded the train for the first leg of the journey home, he was completely serene again, right under Harmon's marveling eyes. He could even sleep while sitting bolt upright in a narrow-gauge railroad coach.

"3"

The train began slowing. The conductor lurched down the aisle, bawling, "South Arkansas!" The young lady in the blouse awoke with a start, looked dazedly about, and reached for her jacket. The conductor smiled benignly upon her and made a ceremony of lifting down her grip from the rack overhead and hauling out a larger suitcase that had been standing on its end in the corner by the door into the smoker. To the rest of the passengers he granted the merest tag of his attention. "Change for the West Slope stages! South Arkansas!"

About a third of the passengers scrambled stiffly down to the narrow brick runway lying between the tracks and the yellow depot. After the brassy heat of the coach, the predawn mountain air went into their lungs like steel splinters. The travelers paused, pulled their collars around their necks, and then slowly began to ravel away on their individual paths. Everything shifted, flickered. Light from the engine's firebox glinted ruddily on steam leaking out of the cylinders. Lanterns bobbed, baggage carts rattled, people milled and called. Then Harmon saw beyond the puddle of confusion, beyond the depot roof, the solid black lift of the Continental Divide. Johnny saw it, too. He stopped abruptly, shaggy in a long, black bearskin overcoat, and stared upward. The young woman, straining behind him with her two heavy grips, had to step around him. He did not notice. Harmon doffed his hat and gestured at the bags. She shook her head and disappeared with her burden into the depot. Johnny roused himself. "Let's get some breakfast," he said and they carried their own light grips into the station restaurant.

This time he did notice her and spent most of the meal watching her sip at bitter coffee she did not appear to enjoy. Fifteen minutes later as they prepared to board the stage, she was ahead of them at the scales, being bullied by the baggage master.

"Thirty pounds is the allowance, ma'am. Excess is a dollar a pound to Gunnison."

"Just to Gunnison!" she gasped.

"That's what I said."

"I have to go clear on to Argent and Baker. Will there be additional charges?"

"I'm not responsible for Argent and Baker."

"It's an outrageous rate. I—"

"The stages are overloaded and the roads are bad. Why not leave the big suitcase?"

"Those are my samples—material for dresses."

"A dressmaker?" The baggage master's eyebrows slid up into a leer. Prostitutes in the mining camps by almost universal convention called themselves seamstresses. But evidently she did not know this and the innuendo dropped unheeded.

"No, I am not a dressmaker. I take orders for—oh, what difference does it make? Can I send the big suitcase by freight?"

"You'll have to ask at the freight office, one block up. Opens at seven. Next, please!"

"I'll miss the stage! Does freight go through promptly?"

"Madam, I am not the freight agent. And these gentlemen are waiting to be weighed. Next, please!"

She wandered away, hesitant and distraught. When Johnny caught up with her she was standing behind the three West Slope stages backed up to the street side of the depot, waiting for passengers. The drivers were struggling to stow baggage and awkward canvas sacks of mail into the rear boots of the vehicles. The young woman was preparing to accost one of them, probably with intent of bribing him to take her suitcases. Her cheeks looked stiff and hard and embarrassed.

"Let me do it," Johnny said. He picked out the man he wanted. What the determining factor was, Harmon could not tell. To him the fellow looked as ordinary as the others. He wore the same sort of black cap with earflaps, gauntleted gloves, and a canvas coat on whose sleeve he kept wiping his nose. Maybe John figured that he was an old-timer in the mountains and that they would speak the same language. Anyway, he picked up a mail sack and helped mash it into place.

The driver nodded obligation and turned around to see what else needed attention. Johnny said, "I'd like to make you acquainted with Miss . . ."

"Mrs. Montgomery," she said, underlining the Mrs.

The driver touched the brim of his cap. "Pleased," he said and waited.

"Don't you think she's pretty enough to be twins," Johnny asked.

The driver remained noncommittal.

"Thirty pounds of baggage for each twin, too."

"I see." The driver glanced with distaste toward the baggage master. "Are you traveling on this same stage?" he asked John.

"I am."

"The road's pretty boggy in spots. We might get stuck."

"Then you might need help shoveling." Now that they understood each other, favor for favor, the driver picked up Mrs. Montgomery's suitcases and crowded them into the boot. " 'Board!" he sang out.

Johnny took Mrs. Montgomery's elbow and propelled her toward the door. She said, "I can't thank you enough." And then she asked, "How much did you give him?"

"Give, ma'am?" Johnny repeated blankly.

"So that I can repay you."

He shook his head. "He wouldn't have taken anything."

"Please." She halted and faced him. "I pay my own way. It is very important to me."

She was taut, as though perhaps she thought she could ward off the world's teeth if she defied it fiercely enough. Johnny made a little gesture of resignation.

"Two dollars," he said.

It satisfied her and she snapped open her shiny black reticule. "Thank you." Now the boards were clear between them and she could smile. "I do appreciate it," and her fingers rested briefly on his wrist.

"4"

The thawing roads were too difficult for regular Concord stages. These three vehicles were mudwagons, enclosed on both sides by canvas roll flaps and roofed by another canvas that afforded no room for passengers. The only outside seat was the one by the driver. Since the temperature was below freezing that morning, most of the passengers scrambled for the interior. There might have been arguments over space if Johnny had not paid off part of his obligation to the driver by reluctantly letting go of Mrs. Montgomery's elbow and climbing topside. "Ge'oup!" the driver cried and the four matched horses sprang out through the sleeping town at least five minutes ahead of the other two sections.

Dawn strengthened into daylight as they pulled steadily upward around sprawling hairpin curves. They smelled wood smoke and passed the tents of a railway construction camp. "Grading crews," the driver explained to Johnny. "The steam cars'll have us out of business by the end of summer. The next summer they'll be at the Utah line, with spurs tapping the St. Johns."

"The Indians haven't pulled out of the way yet, have they?" Johnny asked.

"They will. You know Otto Winkler?"

"I've worked for him off and on."

"A smart old Jew, they tell me. Well, him and Fred Fossett—you know Fred?"

"Loved him like a brother. He's Winkler's old paymaster. Everyone knows Fred. I hear Otto is setting him up in a bank at Argent."

"That's the fellow. Well, the story is that Winkler got tired of all the stalling over the treaty and him and Fossett went out into the reservation with a barrel of silver dollars to get the bucks to put down their marks. In two weeks they came back with fourteen hundred Xs."

"Out of one barrel?"

"That's the story. Anyhow, the treaty's signed. It'll take a while for the Utes to round up their horses and do a last hunt and make their medicine and finally get moving. But already people are pouring over the divide, to be on deck as soon as the bugles blow opening the lands for filing. Look at us, running three–four mudwagons every day already. What'll it be when the roads dry and warm weather comes?"

"A sight," Johnny agreed. And this line under construction was just one of the new railroads reaching west. Farther south, according to the papers, the tracks his father once had worked on had finally leaped La Veta Pass into the San Luis Valley and were making for Montezuma at the southern end of the St. John Mountains. Speculation said the rails might even push up the lower part of Los Padres Canyon into Baker. Railroads coming in toward Red Mountain from both sides! Oh, the boom was on! He hugged himself inside his bearskin coat and breathed the cleanness of the spruce after half a year of choking behind bars, no taint here in a morning so clear it felt alive, and he lifted his face to the sunrise soaking the sky and he kicked his cold feet and watched the ears of the rear team rock back and forth and he thought, At last, and forgot the pressure of eyes on him and the curl of lips and the ring of questions, even his own questions and his own doubts, and he felt good again and tingling and eager, even though the stage itself was traveling slower and slower.

The ruts were thawing. First the ground was a paste, then a mush. The laboring horses had to stop every hundred yards or so to blow. Johnny shed his coat. Water squeezing out of the dirty snow banks on the upper side of the road carved transverse gullies across the way, so that the mudwagon lurched on its thorough braces. Now and then they passed loads of heavy machinery whose drivers had given up and had pulled off to the side until the evening freeze would let them move on again. Just short of the summit, the soft snow closed in across the way. The wheels sank into it so deeply that the axles dragged the surface. The horses stopped, flanks heaving.

"Up till the last day or so this stayed froze enough to hold us," the driver said, "but now they're gonna have to get shovelers up— late like always." He leaned over and shouted at the windows. "Everybody out and walk!"

Johnny jumped down. The male passengers slid grumbling through the door. When Mrs. Montgomery saw them ankle-deep in slush, she hesitated. Johnny said to the driver, "She doesn't weigh much."

The driver said, "Twins is twicet as heavy." But he nodded and let her stay—she was the only female passenger—and with the wagon now nearly half a ton lighter he urged the horses on.

The men, each of them experienced enough to be booted, slogged and slipped along behind. At eleven thousand feet most of them soon ran out of breath. The tails of their greatcoats dragged, their muscles failed, they straggled in an unhappy line. Johnny and Harmon soon found themselves far enough in front to be able to gossip freely.

Harmon was impressed with Mrs. Montgomery. Real class, he said.

A mighty courageous little woman, too. She was a widow, he gathered, and had a little boy, Lennie, three years old, living with his grandmother back in Chicago.

"Three?" Johnny said. "She doesn't look that old."

To support herself, Harmon continued, she represented a fancy Chicago modiste—

"A what?"

"Dressmaker shop. Sounds better in French. As I understand it, the firm she works for imports fine materials and Paris styles. Then they send saleswomen out to the small towns to persuade the local social set that they can be right in the swim by just looking at the pictures in the book, picking out the material from the samples, getting measured, and handing their orders to the traveling representative."

Johnny gave a soft whistle. "What do you know!" he said, "Paris gowns in Argent!"

Harmon stumbled in the slush. "At times it does seem incongruous," he admitted.

Ahead of them the stage bogged in a soft spot. Johnny helped dig it out. After he had wiped the mud from his hands on a snowbank and had rejoined Harmon, the lawyer continued,

"Even you'll have to admit that this is pretty rough traveling for a woman. Boiled cabbage and bedbugs in hotels built for he-boars who are in too big a rush even to notice the color of the wallpaper. Crowded in stagecoaches with men smoking cigars and smelling of the whole winter, and worse. That drummer, now—the one with the black mustache grunting along at the end of the line. Just because she's a saleslady, he thinks she's cut from the same cloth he is. He had a seat next to hers. He pretended to be asleep. First his hand would slide over onto her knee and then his head would roll onto her shoulder. She frosted him plenty, and polite as a queen the whole time. Real class. She deserves to sell a lot of clothes."

"This seems like a long way to come from Chicago, for a fact."

"She says the lady who worked Leadville last year made a killing. That turned the company's attention to the mining camps, but since Mrs. Montgomery is new with the firm, she had to take the leftover areas."

"Leftover!"

Harmon smiled. "In spite of the stories which the Chicago papers occasionally run on their inside pages about the Red Mountain strikes, this country still doesn't mean much back East. But Mrs. Montgomery

decided to take the chance. Now of course she's wondering what she's
gotten herself into."

"I'll talk to her," Johnny said.

"That's what I told her," Harmon said dryly.

"5"

The stage labored across the summit and paused between swollen
snowbanks to wait for the walkers. As they waded up, Mrs. Montgomery retreated to a corner and pulled her skirts back to make room.
Johnny looked at their soaked trouser legs and at the drummer holding
his bowler hat in his hand and leering. Leaning through the door, he
said,

"It's warmer now. Maybe you'd like to ride on top and see the
scenery."

"Oh, I would!"

He helped her up. Ignoring the exchange of glances among the men
still standing in the snow, he clambered up beside her. She sat stiff
and restrained between him and the driver, trying to grow used to them
and to this mountaintop world, and replied to their attempts at conversation in polite, diffident monosyllables. The stage rolled slowly on
between timberline evergreens grotesquely grained and twisted by the
wind. Don't rush things, Johnny thought. Then they rounded an open
point and suddenly he rose in his seat, pointing to the southwest.

"There! There they are!"

The peaks of the St. Johns. A hundred crow-flight miles away, they
were scarcely distinguishable from the clouds that lay among them on
the misty horizon. After he had made sure she had seen them, he settled
back into the tight seat beside her.

"Even the air is better on this side," he said and grinned at her.
"Gregg—he's the lawyer with the chin whiskers, Harmon Gregg—he
said I wasn't to tell you anything except the gospel truth."

She smiled back. Her black brows made her eyes seem intensely
blue. Or perhaps it was the effect of the sunlight.

"Truth about what?" she asked.

He swung an all-inclusive gesture around the mountains. "Whatever you want to know."

They dropped out of the snow into mud, out of the mud onto firmly
packed earth. At a relay station they changed teams. With good footing
underneath and a downgrade ahead, the driver flicked the fresh horses

into a run. The willow shoots at these lower elevations were turning red with spring; the tips of the spruce boughs were blue with new growth. Where snow drifts had lain not long ago, pasqueflowers bloomed in pale masses, furry-stemmed—"Their winter overcoats still on," Johnny said. Iris flaunted in the meadows; bluebirds whistled softly. Juncos skirred away with white flickerings of their tails. The driver drawled, "What springtime they do have up here sure is nice." And the woman said "Oh, yes!" with unexpected verve, turning her dark head left and right to see everything that they pointed out.

The road leveled. As they careened at a fast trot beside a flooding creek, they opened their lunches. The driver said solemnly, "Be careful of crumbs."

"Why?" Mrs. Montgomery asked obediently.

"That's the way wolves pick up the scent of the stages. They're hungry this time of year, before game has started moving back up into the high country."

Johnny said, "I hope you remembered your fire extinguisher."

"Wouldn't be caught without it."

"Why?" Mrs. Montgomery asked again.

"When you race the wolves," Johnny said, "the wheels turn so fast they smoke and sometimes they set the coach afire."

"Gospel truth," she said and laughed, quite unrestrained for the first time that day, perhaps for several days, Johnny thought. He winked at the driver: I knew we'd get her unlimbered: and the driver winked back and soon they were giggling like children. Again they changed horses and pounded on past new shoots of wild hay, the coach rocking so that the men inside took hold of the arm braces and wondered what kind of medicine those on top were indulging in now.

Her name was Lucille. Until this spring she had never been twenty miles away from Chicago. She was intensely curious about each of the towns of her district, San Cristobal and Argent and Baker. What kind of place, for instance, was Baker?

John clucked his tongue. "They have to pry the snowslides out of the way so the sun can rise."

"And Argent?"

"Warmer. Best way to avoid prickly heat is to sit in the shade of the banana trees."

"No doubt it's because the air is better on that side," she said, and Johnny grinned in delight. Perhaps living over here was rough for a woman, but this one knew how to pick up a man's banter. She'd make out.

"What about Red Mountain?" she asked.

"It's not a town," he said. "It's a mining district." Exactly what that

was he tried to explain as well as he could. He put in about the Red
Mountain Toll Road and Transportation Company, too.

She frowned. "Do you mean the road isn't built yet?"

"It will be by fall."

"And there's no regular passenger service between Argent and Baker?"

"Not by stage."

He watched the day's brief carelessness leave her eyes. Towns without
roads! Could one sell dresses in such a land?

"Both places are in my territory," she said. "How can I get from one
to the other?"

The driver said, "You can go around the mountain by coach. It's
a long pull, though, and the connections aren't good."

Johnny suggested, "It would be quicker to ride horseback across Red
Mountain Pass."

"Horseback!"

He tried to reassure her. "It's not just any old ride. You'll like it.
There's not another twenty-five mile stretch in Colorado that can
touch it for sights, not even this one across the divide. The creek
down at the bottom of the gorge is like a ribbon somebody dropped.
Those three red peaks—" He broke off, eyeing her face. "But I don't
guess you came for scenery, did you?"

She shook her head mutely. The tired horses dropped into a walk
and the driver did not pick them up. The setting sun lowered into
their faces; shadows lengthened. Aspen trees gave way to long sagebrush swales that rose in the distance to buttes crenellated with ragged
rimrock. The silence grew oppressive.

Johnny broke it insistently. "You'll do all right. It's a good town."

"I'm sure it is. Except . . ."

"Except what?"

"It doesn't sound the way I'd pictured it after hearing about Leadville."

Johnny dismissed the comparison. "Oh, that." He spread out the
bearskin coat as a lap robe against the gathering cold. In the crowded
seat he could feel the rounding of her hip. "Leadville just got a couple
of years start on us, is all. But our turn's coming, now that the Indians are on the way out. You'll see. When ore starts moving into
Argent from Red Mountain and when the railroad comes up from
below and people realize the opportunities—"

It didn't work. He paused, feeling how absolutely motionless she was.
He drew a deep breath. "Ma'am," he said. "I guess this is the time for
some of the real gospel. You've just come from Chicago and Denver and naturally our towns look kind of little to you. Kind of raw
and crude, too, I expect, and that's the extent of what some back-

cappers—they're people who run down their own country—that's all some backcappers see in them. I know. I've heard 'em. My own mother was one. They laugh at our talk about how big and fine we're going to be. They won't . . . believe. But, ma'am, Argent *is* going to be as good as I'm telling you. So don't set your opinions entirely by what you see or hear along the road, or the way it looks when we first get there. Tomorrow is closer than a whole lot of people realize."

She thought it over. Then she said in a voice so low he could scarcely hear, "Some of us can't wait for tomorrow."

"What do you mean?"

"Your friend seemed to think times weren't right yet for me to sell many dresses in Argent."

"Did Harmon say that?"

"I inferred it."

"Well, I'm saying you will."

"How can you be sure? No roads or . . ."

He gestured impatiently, as though anyone ought to understand just from the taste of the air, just from the day's journey from snow to grass. Release. Ice melting, water frothing. Expectancy . . .

"Winter's over. A man curries the rough hair out of his horse and sees that his tools are sharp. He stakes a claim or cuts logs for a new house or does whatever else his mind was thinking on all the time he was snowed in. A woman—well, what would her way be of showing that she too was staking out a new prospect on the springtime for herself? She just naturally would go out and buy a dress if an up-and-coming mo-mo—what do you call them?"

"Modiste, do you mean?"

"That's it. If a right spruce modiste was there to sell it, wouldn't she?"

The sun dipped out of sight; the stage rocked gently; a great moist star shone over their left shoulders. Lucille touched Johnny's wrist.

"And that's the real gospel?"

"Ma'am, I never talk anything but gospel to mo—modistes," he said, proud to have mastered the word, and to have made her smile again. "Not to good-looking ones, anyhow."

"6"

They spent the night in Gunnison and would go on again in a different coach at five the next morning. After a greasy supper in one of the hotels, Lucille found a lumpy bed in a small room whose window

was so near the sidewalk that she could have reached out and interrupted the passers-by. She locked it and pulled the blind and then
lay listening to the creaks inside the building, the continual tramp
of feet outside, the distant tinniness of a band trying to lure customers
inside a variety hall, and to one sharp crack that might have been a pistol shot. Winter's over, she said to herself. She was dreadfully tired, yet
she could not fall asleep. Tomorrow, she whispered experimentally. It
sounded very strange, fading through the empty darkness. When, for the
last four years, had she said, Tomorrow? When, since she was just past
eighteen and had been forced at last to admit to herself that she was
pregnant and that the boy across the street had run away rather than
marry? Tomorrow: dear God: not ever tomorrow.

Her grandparents, kinder than her father, had helped her through
the desolate, endless years, had let her assume her great-grandmother's
maiden name, Mrs. Montgomery. But it had been too close to home;
people whom she knew showed up just often enough so that every
time she said "Mrs." she felt the muscles tighten across the back of her
shoulders, and she had to force herself to stare straight ahead lest the
weakness come and she let her glance slide about to discover whether
anyone was near to overhear and smirk. Jobs came and went. Then her
grandmother began to fail. Quite by chance, during that period, she
went into a dressmaker's shop, hunting work. The brassy, hard-mouthed
female manager had looked her over critically and had said, very knowingly,

"You've got style, dearie. You'll knock 'em dead in the mining
camps. It's the quickest money I know of."

"But isn't it . . ."

"Just hold your head up," the woman said. "Use that style you've
got."

Hold your head up. Yes. She had worn her humility long enough.
Somewhere she could live again.

"Act like a duchess and you'll be treated like one. Only . . ."

"Only what?"

"You'll have to expect to be lonesome most of the time."

"I'm used to that."

"Unless you get yourself a man."

"No," Lucille said. Not ever again.

"One to fetch and carry, I mean, and to have a sign on you to
keep off the ones you don't want. The men are lonesome, too. There
aren't many women to go around. They'll be glad to do whatever
you'll let them do, and no worry about pay, if you know what I
mean."

"I won't trade on being a woman."

"With your style? Don't be foolish, dearie. Just walk down the street—walk like a woman. The men will come around and perhaps that will make the women catty. But the women will buy. And that's what you want, isn't it?"

"I . . . yes, certainly."

So here she was. Mrs. Montgomery. Once she had practiced the name again and again in private lest she neglect to answer when someone addressed her unexpectedly. But the syllables had never fit easily. Mrs. Montgomery—a stranger to her name and now a stranger to everything else in these surging mountains. For a while after boarding the night train in Denver she had been terrified—that wall of granite and fir closing in around her. But the little mudwagons had gone up and over, and strangeness was becoming normal. An amazing day, racing down into newness, rocking, singing, joking.

That exuberant young man! Feet tramped outside, a hoarse laugh sounded farther down the hall, the shop manager's advice rushed back. Someone to fetch and carry and no worry about pay if you know what I mean. The real gospel, Mrs. Montgomery—gomery—omery. On his lips the syllables weren't strange. He accepted the identity she handed him and she need not fear his fetching and carrying no pay if you know. Tomorrow . . . believe. Turning, she burrowed her head into the pillow and drifted asleep.

"7"

A little before five o'clock the next morning, sleepy passengers bound for the St. John Mountains began crowding around the stove in Gunnison's cramped stage office. One miner in a canvas coat and hobnailed boots slept noisily on the end of the bench. As people kept stepping over the man's sprawled legs, Johnny began to grin. He motioned with his head at a neighbor, who instantly understood. Not that John needed help, but sharing made a practical joke more fun. Moving with elaborate care, the two of them piled the sleeper's duffel bag and bedroll beside the stove, then elevated his feet onto the mound so that the hobnails would absorb the heat. The drummer meanwhile was trying to entertain the room with an account of his lodgings the night before.

"Every place I went to was so full the proprietors were sleeping with their own wives. I couldn't even find standing room until I came to this spot they call New Hotel." He turned his cigar in his moist lips, making sure the audience was listening to him and not watching the jokesters. "Anyway the boards were new. You could smell the resin in 'em two blocks away. The whole place was built out of twelve-inch planks, rough-planed and stood on end with cracks between them wide enough to throw a cat through. To hide the cracks the rooms are papered, you might say, with a thin, sleazy kind of muslin. The light comes right through, of course. Sound does, too. The shape of the place magnifies noise like a banjo box."

The sleeper stirred and twisted his feet. The crowd eyed each other and smiled. The drummer scowled at the distraction and raised his voice. "Well, this yonker came down from the hills on his honeymoon and he didn't notice how thin the muslin was. He started talking baby talk while he peeled off the girl's stockings, commenting on the well-filled bundles. Everybody held their breath to listen, except one feller who let out a snort and said loud enough for the whole hotel to hear, 'By God, if I ever get married I'll honeymoon on a camping trip.' The yonker froze. Spoiled his fun and the fun of thirty more besides. Some people never do learn when to keep their mouths shut."

Johnny laughed with the others and then saw Lucille Montgomery standing in the doorway, pretending not to have heard. He started toward her. The sleeper woke with a mutter, jerked his legs away from the stove and stood up. The hot nails pressed against the soles of his feet. He danced and howled; the room guffawed. "I can lick the man who done that!" he roared. Everyone looked expectantly at Johnny: a man had to back his own jokes. Mildly Johnny said, "Would you rather try it here or somewhere farther down the road where you won't be hopping around too fast to take a swing?" The room guffawed again and with ill grace the victim decided to accept the jobbing. Johnny went on over to help Lucille get settled.

This time she had to pay for her excess baggage, but only fifteen cents a pound. The coach that wheeled up to the stepping blocks was no mudwagon, but a full-sized Concord, bright red, and it racketed over the cobblestones behind its six gray horses like a fire engine.

"That was mean," Lucille said, referring to the joke. The traces of a smile teased the corners of her mouth, however, and she pleased Johnny enormously by riding outside the stage. She took the seat of honor beside the driver and bundled herself against the cold in a red stage company blanket that left only her blue eyes and the tip of her small nose showing. The other outside fares, Johnny and Harmon and two or three more climbed to the dickey seats above and behind her. The stage sprang ahead with a lurch. Lucille clutched the handrail, braced her feet on the mail sacks heaped against the footboard and set her back against Johnny's knees.

Already the town was coming to life. Smoke curled from the chimneys; early risers drifted like sleepwalkers along the sidewalks, shoulders humped and hands thrust into the front pockets of their trousers. Wagons were swinging from the freight yards and turning toward the St. Johns. Trace chains jangled, mules brayed. The stage clattered across the river bridge and hit a soft spot that dropped and then lifted the hind boot with a frame-cracking jolt. Sunrise flamed. Lucille tipped her face back to Johnny.

"This is exciting!"

Strings of traffic coiled along the road—horsemen, pack trains, a high-sided freighter and trailer creeping behind a dozen yoke of oxen, immigrant families with crates of resentful chickens lashed to the rears of their covered wagons and milk buckets dangling underneath. But what really bugged Johnny's eyes was the junction at Lake Fork, which they reached a little after ten o'clock.

Here the road split. One branch continued on through the agency to Argent; the other, on which Johnny and Pat had worked for Winkler during the previous two summers, curved up through San Cristobal, over the high pass at Engineer Point, and dropped down into Baker. The stage changed horses at the junction; freighters rested their stock; immigrants camped while they made up their minds which way they wanted to go. Hobbled horses and mules and donkeys grazed wherever new grass showed through the gray-silver clumps of last year's growth. A blacksmith and three or four vendors had set up booths near the stage company's corrals. Two boys astride a single donkey saw the big red Concord swinging onto the flat. With heels flying and the rear lad swinging a flat board, they belabored the little beast into a twinkling trot toward the station, crying out "Here she comes!" A straggle of bored men and a few women drifted out of the gray tents to watch the arrival.

"I golly!" Johnny said as he helped hand Lucille down, "the whole world's moving to the mountains."

The driver warned, "Those of you who're going through to Argent, we leave in fifteen minutes. Those who are transferring to San Cristobal, that buckboard over there at the gate leaves at the same time."

A tall, turkey-necked, cadaverous man among the watchers said loudly, "If they are looking for real opportunity, they'll go to San Cristobal and then over to Baker—not to Argent."

Johnny gauged him instantly. "A runner," he told Harmon.

"What's a runner?"

"The hotels and freight yards and eating places in Baker sent him over here to turn traffic their way." Johnny smiled good-naturedly at the runner. "Things must be in a bad way over there if they have to lure trade by paying someone to soft-soap the suckers."

The runner instantly accepted the challenge.

"Do you call it soft soap if I enlighten the ignorant and encourage the faint of heart?" He sounded downright grieved at being so misconstrued.

Johnny grinned back, relishing the duel. "Have you enlightened them about that outfit?" He waved grandly toward sixteen big brown mules hitched two abreast to a high-wheeled wagon that had been stripped to its running gears. Lashed to this framework was a ponderous steam boiler.

"Aimed toward Argent," Johnny said. "That boiler means a big mill. A hurry-up job, too, or they wouldn't be tackling the road this early, while it's still soft from winter. But who's hurrying to Baker?"

The runner declined to be impressed. "There's already two big mills in Baker." He appealed to the stage passengers. "Look, friends, at these two clippings, fresh from the Baker *Herald*, and then decide for yourselves which way wisdom lies."

He passed around a piece of newsprint backed by cardboard and shielded by isinglass. Johnny craned his neck to read it over the drummer's shoulder.

"Great Jesus!" he exclaimed to Harmon. "Parley Quine just sold a three-quarter interest in the Ram for a hundred and twenty-seven thousand dollars!"

"To a Baker syndicate," the runner crowed. "Not to anyone from that left-behind town of Argent. Those of you who are interested in Red Mountain—and who isn't?—had better plan to make your headquarters in a wide-awake city. I mean Baker obviously."

Johnny was totally agog. A hundred and twenty-seven thousand dollars! When this news spread across the divide, the St. Johns really would go wild. He almost loved that runner. A hundred and twenty-seven—!

"Have you told them," he said, rallying himself, "how soon the snow will melt on the pass so they can get into those tail-end headquarters of yours? Maybe next Fourth of July if they're lucky."

"Shovelers are at work right now," the runner said. "It'll be only a few days. And since you brought up the subject of roads, as I'm glad you did, listen to this."

Unctuously he unfolded another, longer clipping. It was an editorial, also from the Baker *Herald*, and was entitled "Hard Facts for the Consideration of the Public." The runner read in a loud, high, inflectionless voice:

"For months the so-called newspaper across the hill in our rival town of Argent has been trying to mislead the public as to the Red Mountain Mining District, contending that because the accident of arbitrary political lines has included Red Mountain in Argent County, the mines are of necessity tributary to the dying county seat. However,——"

"Dying!" Johnny interrupted. "Why, Argent has grown more in the last few—"

"Shut up!" several voices growled and the runner continued,

"However, the fact that Baker capitalists were able to pay $127,000 for a seventy-five per cent interest in the oldest and most famous mine on Red Mountain while Argent promoters could only make promises is sufficient to prove the case. Red Mountain is tributary to Baker City. We earnestly hope therefore that from this point on no member of the traveling public will be gulled into trying to reach the mines by journeying through Argent."

Here the runner interrupted himself and looked over the edge of the clipping at Johnny. "If you think the road by San Cristobal is bad, get a load of this." Again he read,

"No one using the Argent route will be able to reach Red Mountain before June. Anyone who tries will be taking a desperate chance of being swept by snowslides a thousand feet into Ute Gorge. The so-called trail from Argent to Red Mountain has been closed since February. Although it is true that a company has been formed to build a toll road up the gorge, it is in the control of irresponsible parties—"

"Irresponsible!" Johnny bleated.

"—one of whom is currently being tried in Denver for conspiring with Indians to murder an innocent freighter."

Blood rushed to Johnny's face. So far this had been a good-natured bicker, but now the rival paper was hitting below the belt. "Like hell the freighter was innocent," he blurted.

"Take it easy!" Harmon warned.

The runner from Baker raised his voice joyfully. "My friends, the truth unsettles this lost and benighted soul from Argent. And we've only begun. Listen!"

"There is no possibility that the present Red Mountain Road and Transportation Company, or even an honest company, can construct a road over the fearful terrain between Argent and Red Mountain before 1890. Meanwhile, enterprising citizens of our own community, including Parley Quine, discoverer of the Ram, are engaged in forming a syndicate which will build a modern, graded highway up the easy slopes of Mineral Creek from Baker. They are taking subscriptions for stock now, and guarantee to complete the construction before snow flies next fall."

Johnny looked at Harmon in agitation. "Had you heard that?" he demanded.

The runner caught the whisper. "There seems a great deal you haven't heard, my friend," he mocked and read on:

"No doubt the exposure of these facts will not redeem the citizens of Argent from the error of their ways. Led by the misrepresentations of their newspaper, they have been engaged so long in trying to deceive the outside world into believing that Argent is a mining camp that they have partly deceived themselves. We sympathize with them and with the last agonies that lead to the lies they tell, but we must warn the public nevertheless. Baker is the town with the future."

Lucille laughed. "How extraordinary! Towns squabbling like children over the best way up a mountain!"

"Not any mountain, ma'am," the runner chided her. "A mountain of pure silver, all set to flow into Baker."

The traveling salesman, who fancied himself as a narrator, saw an opportunity to capture the limelight. Loudly he said, "That business about the freighters conspiring with the Utes. The paper should have said more. It's quite a story. Are you people familiar with it?"

Johnny's face muscles stiffened. Harmon said in attempted diversion, "If just half these rumors are true, there's enough ore up there for both towns," but it was too late. The drummer was launched. Last fall, he said, looking with satisfaction at his auditors, a group of hardcase freighters had been camped a little way ahead on the Argent road, inside the reservation. They had molested some Indian women—he leered at Lucille—and a war party had surrounded them. Finally they had bought their way clear by handing two of their own party over to be burned at the stake.

Johnny said, "Are you dead sure of those facts, Mister?"

"That's what they tell me."

"Who's they?"

"Why, everybody around Gunnison."

"Nobody around Gunnison or any place else in this country is telling lies like that."

"I know what I heard."

"You heard wrong. No squaws were molested. Only one man was involved. He wasn't burned. A federal posse combed these hills, looking. They didn't find a trace." Johnny appealed to the stage driver. "That's right, isn't it?"

"I'm new on this run," the driver said carefully. The Baker runner cried triumphantly, "Anyhow, it didn't happen on the road to Baker. You don't need to worry about that road, friends!"

"Oh for Christ sake," Johnny said. He refused to heed Harmon's efforts to interrupt. "I'm sick of this crap—people and newspapers twisting the story into lies to make business for Baker and kill our roads."

"Are *you* so sure of your facts?" the salesman sneered.

"Damned right I'm sure," Johnny said. His head lifted and he glared at Harmon. "I'm not about to be ashamed of it, either—here or in Argent."

And he told them, in stark outline, exactly what had happened.

"The court in Denver couldn't prove any conspiracy and dropped the case," he finished, talking directly to the Baker runner, for the salesman did not count save as an accidental catalyst. "When you get back to Baker, tell that loose-mouthed writer—they're all the same, even in Argent, all talking out of half the facts—tell him to print the whole truth in his next editorial."

The runner sniffed. "Soldiers could have kept the road open."

"Oh, sure, sure. That's what everyone says who was a hundred miles away, not looking at those Indians when they came. But if the troops had marched in—"

He checked himself. While he had been talking, the freighter in charge of the big boiler on the stripped-down wagon had walked from the corral with his red-bearded swamper. Johnny knew the man—Eb Sinsabaugh. They had worked together in the days when John had been helping move goods into the agency at Los Alamos. He pointed.

"See there!"

The passengers' necks swiveled. Eb was walking along the line of animals making minor adjustments to the harness. "E-he," he kept droning. He could hoodoo a mule with the touch of his hand, the slur of his voice. "E-he," and the big beasts understood.

Limber-legged, he swung into the saddle on the near-wheel animal. His hand closed over the jerkline.

"Let's get ready!" he sang out.

The lead team felt the twitch of the line and braced themselves. The motion made the bells on their collars jingle. The sound was a signal for the others to prepare.

"All right, you long-eared sons!"

The signal of Eb's hand ran along the jerkline to the jockey pole. His long whip curled with a crack like frozen wood breaking. Thirty-two hind legs straightened in unison. On foot, Eb's red-bearded swamper ran down the line, shouting and banging on the ground with a broad-thonged leather popper.

The team curved into the road. The long tug chain attached to the wagon tongue veered at an angle, reducing the forward pull. "Ho now, ho!" Eb yelled. The swing team hopped across the chain so that they could achieve a straightaway thrust. The swamper danced and whooped. The wagon gathered momentum. As the direction of the pull straightened, the swing team hopped back into position on either side of the chain. Panting, the swamper returned for his riding horse. Eb relaxed in the saddle and looked around, surprised at being the center of so much attention.

His hand went up in recognition. "Hey, Johnny!" he called. "I heerd they let you loose!" Down the road he went, the tinkle of bells and the creak of running gears an audible boast of his skill. No soldiers. Just himself and his swamper, unprotected, through the heart of the reservation.

"See!" Johnny said proudly. "That's what I mean."

"8"

To Lucille the episode was totally unreal. No one seemed to know how to respond. The people around the stagecoach stood like photographers' subjects waiting for a time exposure to tick past. The cadaverous runner clutched his newspaper clippings in his bony fingers and thrust his nose toward the vanishing freight wagon like a contemptuous vulture. Spots of color shone high on Mr. Ogden's cheeks, under the corners of his eyes, and he looked as if he would enjoy a contradiction that would justify him in using his clenched fists.

No one spoke a word until finally the driver clucked, "Well, well," and pulled on his thick gloves and said into the silence, "We're two minutes late."

The uncertainty broke into a scurrying. Three men picked up their grips and changed to the San Cristobal stage. Their places were taken by a couple who had grown tired of waiting for the pass into Baker to open, a seedy-looking little man and his enormous wife, her upper arms as big around as most men's thighs. The driver asked her politely, as a courtesy extended to each female passenger, whether or not she would like to ride on top of the coach. She vented a great gust of laughter. "Laws' sake, man, I'd never get up there!" she cried joyfully, caught the rails on either side of the door and boosted herself inside, her husband hopping anxiously along behind. The thorough braces swayed. The drummer looked furious as the other passengers, scrambling back to their original seats, left him a tiny opening beside her.

Mr. Ogden leaned over the edge and called at the runner, "How about that? You picked up a net gain of one for Baker. But there's eight, no, nine of us still in here for Argent. That's hardly worth paying your board for."

The runner made a sulky and, Lucille surmised, an insulting gesture. "You'll sing different when Quine gets that road from Baker up Red Mountain," he retorted. "'Cause you ain't gonna put a road up your side just by a murderin' dicker with the Utes."

"Yah!" The hardness edged Mr. Ogden's voice again. "We got the people by gettin' the Utes out of the way. We"—the stage lurched and he was almost unbalanced—"we'll get the road, too!"

He settled back, but Lucille could tell from the shifting of his knees against her back how restless he was. "I hope Baker isn't going to steal a march on us with that road," he fretted to the sad-looking lawyer with the chin whiskers. The next minute he gave a laugh of pure exuberance. "Some rags in that ragged Ram! One hundred and twenty-seven thousand of 'em!"

"And Quine still owns a quarter interest of the property," the lawyer said. "For a winter of other people's work, he's done all right."

"It surely did start a rush," Mr. Ogden said, completely enthusiastic again. "There are probably people all over the mountain right now, digging in snow up to their belly buttons. And I don't suppose the Ram tunnel has been developed more than a hundred feet, either. Couldn't have been, even if Walt did take up cars and track before snowslides closed the trail—in March, not February, the way that lying paper said. When the mine starts real stoping and the other prospects begin shipments—no wonder Quine's thinking about a road. I wonder why Pat didn't see him about buying stock."

"Quine's from Baker."

"But to get ore to Baker you've got to lift it over the pass. The gorge is better than that. Damn! I hope Pat's off the dime. We haven't a day to lose. I knew I should have come back the first chance I had, instead of sitting there in Denver."

He fumed and wriggled. But the top of a stagecoach was no place for sustaining impatience. The vehicle rocked; the horses' feet made a steady thrum. Gradually Mr. Ogden simmered down. Then, after a time, she heard him say matter-of-factly to the lawyer,

"That's where they grabbed him. You wouldn't believe fifty Indians could hide up there behind those scrub oaks, would you? A hillside sure looks different when it's bare. But in the fall with the leaves turning red from the frost it made a good hideout."

Lucille glanced at the gnarled, naked branches of an oak patch running down the hill toward the road, and beyond them at a prickle of stark white aspen trunks holding aloft cold black limbs. Indians! She had known she must cross a reservation, just as she had known she must cross the Continental Divide, and her grandmother had fussed evening after evening about both prospects. "This isn't the landing of the *Mayflower*," Lucille had said. She still could not picture a flux of savages pouring out of the colored leaves, the tails of their ponies streaming. Yet it wasn't out of a book. It had happened. Here, this spot. And this man, his knees in her back, had turned another man over to them in order to keep this road open for people like herself and the fat woman and the salesman.

And this was the country to which she had committed herself. Paris gowns!

She saw the freight wagon with the boiler plodding ahead of them. "That's what I mean," Mr. Ogden had said. Twisting awkwardly around, almost off balance, she said to him,

"It must have been a frightening experience."

"What makes you say that?"

The sudden, leaping defensiveness nonplused her for a moment. Then she recalled that he had been taken to Denver for trial, and although she did not understand just what that had involved, she could imagine how the lawyers had hammered at him with their questions and their insinuations, much as her own father had thrust and thrust at her: why, why; didn't you know, a daughter of mine; what did you suppose, couldn't you see, why, why, why . . .

Apologetically she explained, "You said there were fifty of them—"

"In round figures. I'd have counted if I had known so many people were going to put so much store in the exact number."

"And only six of you——"

"Four. Two of the escort were Indians."

"Weren't you frightened?"

"Why do you want to know?"

She grew annoyed. "Forgive me if I'm being nosy. I simply thought it was a brave, fine risk for you to have taken and I didn't suppose you would be so touchy over telling more about it."

She faced around. The stage swung wide to pass the freight wagon.

The man riding the off-wheel mule waved and called, "Save some beans for me!" and Mr. Ogden answered with a great ringing whoop, "Hey, Eb! You're lookin' good!" and then, as the stage careened back into the center of the road, he leaned again over her shoulder.

"That's the first time anyone has asked me about being afraid."

Was he ashamed of it? "I didn't mean to offend you."

He laughed joyously. "I was scared stiff."

He grew sober again, but not prickly. He looked along the road, remembering, and then began to talk to her about the reservation, about Argent and treaties, squatters and cavalry, about Vinegar Hill and Ute Gorge, a Finn named Aino Berg and a storekeeper called Angel Gabe and three round peaks flaming with the promise of mineral. Promise— out of all his talk that was the one thing she truly understood. It was a voice whose whispers she had heard first when the brassy dress manu- facturer had told her of the silver towns of the mountains, of quick money and lost identity. Until then every pressure she had experienced during the past four years—her father's tight lips, her grandmother's sorrowing eyes, her own isolation—everything had informed her that expectancy was finished, that henceforth she was to accept the shackles of her days with resignation and humility.

They were wrong, she told herself exultantly. She knew it now because yesterday afternoon she had been able to sit on a swaying seat and sing and laugh and joke about fire extinguishers while the stagecoach crossed the divide from the past. Because today she had watched rapt faces listen to the blandishments of rival towns hungry for people to come their way, to drive impossible roads up unimagi- nable gorges to what Mr. Ogden said was a land red with the fire of hope.

Her father would never understand. Probably her grandmother would not. But perhaps some day Lennie, her son, would. And for just an instant the ache of regret twisted again.

She was even younger than John Ogden, just as impetuous and in her own way as warm-hearted and as proud. Perhaps she was just as naïve. In spite of everything, tomorrow could be better. That was what she heard John Ogden say while he talked, that was what she wanted to hear. Throughout the rest of the journey no other voice quite man- aged to intrude.

"9"

While he was yet talking the stage dipped over a hill and stopped at an extraordinary yellow box of a building that reared alone, like a wart, in the valley bottom. The sign across its front cried, TALLY'S— MEALS AND BEDS AT ALL HOURS.

Mr. Ogden jumped to the ground and reached up to help her descend. At the same moment, a strange-looking man with blood-shot eyes swooped out of the building and engulfed them with a rasping, "Hi-ho, folks, hi-ho!" He must be Mort Tally, she surmised, a codefendant of Mr. Ogden's in Denver, and this must be where the Indians had first appeared. She looked around, half expecting to see several of them, tall in feathered headdresses, aloof with folded arms. There were none. For a frightening instant everything seemed very small and barren.

Evidently Tally had preceded Mr. Ogden home by only a few days. He still wore city clothes, as rumpled as if he had slept in them. He was elated, perhaps because his yellow hotel, having escaped destruction, now served as official meal stop for the Argent stages.

"Ho-ho, everybody! Step right inside! Dinner's waiting and hot— Tally's for the best. The wash benches are out back, ladies to the right, gents to the left. Johnny Ogden! Hi there!" He slapped him on the side of the arm. He saw the lawyer and slapped him, too, and cried to the passengers, "Here's the best damn jawsmith in the mountains, if ever any of you want loose from the law, like John Ogden and me! Hi now! Right through this door, folks!"

The lawyer's long face grew longer with distaste. Mr. Ogden looked embarrassed. But neither could escape. Tally trapped them in his twines of conversation and led them away. Smirking, the drummer moved up beside Lucille. To avoid him, she made league with the fat woman and passed through the odorous hall to the wash benches in the rear.

She could not bring herself to wash in the grimy basin or use the grimy towel she was supposed to share with her new friend. Over on the other side of the doorway, the male passengers had no such scruples, save for the drummer, who did pat his cheeks dry on his own silk handkerchief. Like the rest of the men, he then smoothed down his hair with his moist palms and went to the bar in front of a cracked mirror, where whisky was being sold even though, the lawyer remarked, the reservation laws had not yet been rescinded. Lucille followed the

fat woman to one of the two rough wooden benches lining the long
dining table. Her companion lowered herself with a sigh of content.
Lucille was more gingerly. The table was covered with cracked, stained
oilcloth and decorated with bottles of sauce crusted around the tops.
At each place a napkin that had been used before was folded into a
peaked triangle. Mrs. Tally, so Lucille supposed her to be, emerged from
the kitchen. Thick white platters teetered precariously on her arms and
her cheeks shone from the heat of the stove.

"It's on," she said crossly and banged the dishes down with a peremptory clatter. The men tossed off their whisky at a gulp and repaired
to the table. Johnny found a place across from Lucille, the drummer
one at her side.

The fare was stringy, lukewarm venison, boiled potatoes, red beans
cooked to a glutinous thickness, and a viscous pie of dried fruit. Lucille
toyed with her fork. Everyone else ate in profound concentration. The
clack of utensils, the squeak of the benches, and the noise of chewing
were the only sounds. As each diner finished, he wiped off his thick
crockery plate with a piece of gray bread, swallowed it, pushed
back his dish, reached for a toothpick from the cut-glass holder in the
center of the table, and bolted outside. Soon only Johnny and the drummer and the fat woman remained with Lucille. Seeing that each of the
men was determined to outwait the other, Lucille rose and turned outside. The fat woman said, "What's the rush?" and reached for another
piece of pie. At the very most the dining had occupied ten minutes.

The wagon with the boiler came plodding up to the corral. Johnny
said, "Old Eb! Greatest freighter in the mountains! I want to talk to
him." He bounded over. The other stage passengers stood on the
stoop of the hotel, waiting for a fresh relay of horses to be hitched to
their vehicle. The sun felt warm on their backs; their dinners rested
heavily in their stomachs. The salesman took a cigar from his vest
pocket, bit off the end, and belched loudly.

"Our friend Happy Jack out there would have been smarter to have
let the Utes burn the place down," he said. He rolled the cigar between his lips to moisten it, watching Lucille and waiting for her
to join the answering titter that reduced Tally's establishment to
complete shabbiness and Johnny's actions to pettiness.

"Perhaps we should consider ourselves lucky to have anything at all
to eat," she retorted and turned her back.

The driver called them to their place. The drummer grimaced at the
sight of the fat woman climbing aboard and switched to the first
of the dickey seats on top. Undeterred, Mr. Ogden came running
back and joined him and the lawyer, so that now three of them were
wedged in the single seat. The stage toiled up a long, brushy hill;

the sun began its long slide down the western sky. The driver gave
Lucille a pair of green goggles to cut its glare. The salesman told about
better stages he had ridden, and Mr. Ogden repeated new statistics about
Argent's growth that he had picked up from Eb Sinsabaugh. Now and
then he interrupted himself to show her tiny blossoms in the new foliage
or little cottontail rabbits dodging away among the pungent sage bushes.

They crossed a low divide and rolled west into a broad, dusty valley.
"Ute Valley!" Mr. Ogden said. "Now we're getting there!" The ridge
to their left fell away, opening a view to the south. He had been
craning his neck for this, but purple thunderclouds swaddled the high
peaks he wanted his fellow passengers to see. It was not in him to stay
disappointed, however. "These spring thunderstorms generally don't
last long," he said. He told them about the first time he had seen the
area with a herd of cattle and then discussed the possibilities of stock
raising and hay farming, now that the Indians were leaving, and in truth
he grew rather monotonous. Lucille dozed behind her green spectacles.

At the Los Alamos agency the horses were changed for the last time.
During the brief pause the drummer looked at the dark, dirty, ragged
Indians standing apathetically around the adobe buildings, and said
with loud contempt, "They certainly don't look dangerous to me."
Mr. Ogden ignored him. He was standing on the teetery seat to count
the cluster of immigrant wagons on the meadow by the river, their
canvas tops bleached by the weather as white as bones. "Seventeen!"
he exclaimed. "Just on this one campground, and spring hardly begun!"
As the stage started up, he wormed back into his seat. "A customer
for a French gown in every wagon," he joked to Lucille. The drummer
snorted: "Paris gowns are just what they need—like that one." He
pointed at a bony woman carrying an armload of firewood sticks who
turned up a gaunt, sallow face as they rocked past. She's so tired,
Lucille thought. But not far away was Red Mountain, where Parley
Quine had stumbled onto a mine that he had held for scarcely
half a year and then had sold for a hundred and twenty-seven thousand
dollars. How many Paris dresses would that buy?

So strange a land!

"I wish we could see Red Mountain," she said.

The view of the range was blocked out now by foothills reaching
long fingers toward them. The road climbed steadily; the six horses
labored. The valley grew narrower and shaggy with piñon pines and
junipers. Great dun boulders, rolled ages since from the hill's high collar
of rimrock, crowded the road close to the river's edge. Lucille saw yellow
flood water curling around the brush roots, heard the *shush-shush* of it
against the bank. Clouds of insects pirouetted above the swampy marge.

Nervously she said, "It looks deep."

"It always is, this time of day in the spring," Mr. Ogden told her.

The salesman asked skeptically, "What has the time of day to do with it?"

"Each morning the spring thaws start a gush of snow water out of the mountains. The rise starts getting down here to the crossing late in the afternoon and lasts until midnight. Evening floods, we call it."

Patches of snow appeared, a sequence of dirty, ice-crusted old drifts alternating with bogs of hoof-churned mud. The big Concord wallowed past wagons that had pulled aside onto higher, gravelly spots. Weary immigrants were unloading them in order to lighten the vehicles for the stretch ahead; obviously they would have to return for the piles of furniture and the bulging boxes over which the women were hovering anxiously.

Across the river Lucille saw a broad bottomland where a tributary stream coiled down from the left. Several tents were pitched here and there, and near a patch of willows stood a squat, small cabin.

"Are we going to have to cross?" she asked.

The driver reassured her. "You'll stay dry up on top. But if you're nervous, there's a fellow runs a rowboat back and forth. The passengers inside generally go with him. Fellow name of Brice," he added to Mr. Ogden.

"The hell!" Mr. Ogden exclaimed. "So he got back here in time to grab the land he wanted." Chuckling, he told how he and a friend named Walt Kennerly had fished the Brice family out of high water last fall. Now the Brices were helping fish out other folks. "That girl Nora didn't like living out here," he said. "A pretty girl, too."

As if prettiness had anything to do with it, Lucille thought, eyeing the rushing torrent.

"Nora, she's gone up to Argent to open a restaurant," the driver put in.

"The hell!" Mr. Ogden said again. He wasn't even aware of the word, Lucille decided. "So she finally quit the old man!"

"Took the little girl with her, too. What's her name? Martha, Mabel—?"

"Mabel."

"She'll help Nora sling hash and wash dishes when she isn't in school."

"The old man is going to poison himself, trying to batch without them."

"Oh, he's got him a woman."

"The hell! Who?"

The driver glanced at Lucille and patently reworded what he had been about to say. "Some . . . seamstress that came through the agency last winter on her way to Telluride."

"Well, I declare!"

Ahead of them two wagons had camped under the bare cotton-woods, waiting, Mr. Ogden said, to cross at low water in the morning. A woman in a gray sunbonnet was milking a Holstein cow into a metal-bound wooden bucket. Her menfolk were at the river bank, belaboring a reluctant donkey into the water. A man on horseback was pulling on a lead rope; the others were behind pushing. There was a great deal of shouting and laughing.

Lucille leaned forward to see better. "What's the matter with the poor thing's ears?"

"A burro will drown in deep water unless its ears are tied up," Mr. Ogden told her.

"I don't believe you," Lucille said. She appealed to the driver. "He's teasing me?"

"That's the story I've always heard, ma'am."

Launched at last, the donkey disappeared completely under the flood. "He's drowning anyhow," Lucille gasped. Mr. Ogden said with an absolutely straight face, "He breathes through his ears; that's why they're tied thataway." Just then the donkey's head emerged. The little animal swam strongly behind the horse. Arrived at the shore, the rider dismounted to undo the donkey's bindings. "His voice'll come untied with his ears," Mr. Ogden said, and sure enough the donkey's sides heaved in and out as it raised its bray in a wild trumpet call of rejoicing. Lucille giggled. "I'll never learn this country," she said.

A large rowboat put out from the opposite shore, following a guide line made of pieces of rope knotted together and stretched across the current. A man and a boy sat side by side on the center seat, rowing occasionally but in general letting the current do the work. The stage driver called to the passengers inside the coach that they would keep drier if they crossed in the boat. Fifty cents extra. They descended, grumbling that the stage company ought to pay. The driver leaned over and spat and said contemptuously that lots of cheapskates who would rather save their money than their clothes crossed inside the stage. That was their privilege, but the company hadn't guaranteed to run boats too, and no there wasn't any more room on top, either.

The man with the rowboat jumped onto the bank and pulled the prow a foot or two onto dry land. He had a good-natured, fleshy, turnip-shaped face that needed a shave. As he approached his unhappy clients, he saw Mr. Ogden on top of the stage.

"Hey John!" he yelped. "We heerd you was out. But some of 'em in town were bettin' you wouldn't come back."

Mr. Ogden turned dark red. "I hope you took some of that money."

Brice laughed uproariously. "Hell, no. I'll by God lose four dollars if'n you go on."

Mr. Ogden thrust back by changing the subject. "While you were building that ferry, why didn't you make it big enough to carry wagons? Hi there, Tommy," he added to the boy. "How's tricks?"

"Good," Tommy said. "Walt brought me a new Indian pony, a calico."

His father said simultaneously, "Too much work for a short season. No customers, anyhow. The big wagons go acrost on their own and the little ones wait for low water in the morning. All I get are hurry-up fellers who want to stay dry. There's a passel of 'em comin' in, though. More by God every day. Like I keep sayin' around town, you boys did a job quietin' the Utes last fall. If they was still on the prod, this country would still be dead. Now the railroad is even surveyin' for a line. They thought they were bein' mighty sly, but I know where the right-of-way is gonna run next to the mesa yonder. I by God aim to move over there and—"

"Here we go!" the driver said and slapped the reins and the big horses edged into the water. "You heard him!" Mr. Ogden cried triumphantly to Harmon Gregg. "A railroad! And Brice admits we're the ones who kept the Utes quiet!"

The coach lurched. Lucille clutched the handrail. Looking down, she saw the yellow ripples cleaving, curving, folding. The coach slipped sideways. She felt herself spinning. Mr. Ogden's hand gripped her shoulder.

"Don't look at the water!" he ordered.

She wrenched her eyes upward and the dizziness passed. On the meadow they stopped to wait for the passengers in the rowboat. "Oh dear," she said weakly and knew that she was paper pale.

Mr. Ogden exclaimed, "Why, that's one of my mules over there— two, three of them. And there's Walt!" His voice rose in what Harmon Gregg later told her was a Ute war yell. "Hey, Kennerly! Oh, you've got to meet him," he said excitedly to Lucille. "Walt Kennerly—greatest fellow in the mountains!"

Off to one side of the small cabin by the willows a tall man in a heavy woolen jacket and a broad-brimmed black hat was nailing wire to a fence post. He heard Johnny's shout. Carefully he hung the hammer by its claws between wire and wood, waved back, and walked toward the stage. Johnny swung to the ground and strode to meet him.

Lucille took advantage of the moment to ask the driver in an embarrassed whisper whether there was a comfort station near. As gingerly as if he would rather not admit to owning his hand, he pointed

toward a woman working industriously in a kind of lean-to behind
the cabin.

"You'll have to ask her."

As Lucille skirted the cabin, she glanced through the open doorway
at a crude fireplace plastered over with adobe. The carpet on the floor
was made of coffee and flour sacks stitched loosely together. A crude
ladder led to the loft, its ceiling so low that even the boy Tommy could
hardly have stood upright under it. According to Mr. Ogden, this
was the first settler's cabin to be built on the reservation. To him it was
impressive.

The shelter behind the cabin consisted of crooked piñon posts holding some poles across which a wagon canvas had been stretched. A clumsily lettered sign nailed to a post facing the road announced, CLOTHES
WASHED $3 A DOZ. Two galvanized tubs resting on rods of steel, miners'
drill steel she learned to recognize later, simmered over a deep pile of
embers glowing in a rock-lined trench. Nearby were more tubs, scrub-
boards, a wringer. Shirts and overalls and long underwear dangled wetly
from multiple wires out back. The place smelled of steam and yellow
soap and starch. A very bony woman with untidy graying hair turned to
welcome Lucille. She wiped her hands on the front of her dirty dress,
and her perspiring temples on her bare, moist upper arm. They exchanged pleasantries and the woman, presumably Mrs. Brice, pointed
toward a dim path leading through newly leafed willows. Historic, Lucille thought again.

Emerging from the abominable privy, she lost her way in the
willows and came around the far side of the cabin. Voices stopped
her just short of the corner, John Ogden's and another that probably
belonged to the man Kennerly. It was the latter's that became distinct first.

" . . . drizzle-mouth will tell you anything. Why, he said right out
that he was having trouble keeping his hands off his own daughter
when this woman came through the agency."

Johnny's voice clucked. "A common whore, the driver said."

Lucille gasped. The driver had said seamstress.

"She was down on her luck," Kennerly went on, "half starved and
half sick, heading for some camp far enough out that the men wouldn't
be particular and maybe she could hang on and rattle for another
few months. Brice picked up with her and married."

"She seems to be making him a good wife."

"She works like a hungry dog for him. Grateful, I suppose."

"Well," Mr. Ogden said, "at her age I don't imagine many of them
get a chance to start over again. I gather Nora didn't cotton to her,
though."

"Oh, I don't know as Nora objected to the woman so much as she wanted to cut loose on her own. The woman furnished an excuse."

"She's opening a restaurant in Argent, the stage driver said."

"The Bon-Ton."

"Where's she getting the money?"

There was a pause. Then Mr. Kennerly said, "I'm staking her."

"Is she any happier than she was last fall?"

"How should I know?" Mr. Kennerly said, rather snippily, Lucille thought.

Mr. Ogden perhaps thought so too, for he changed the subject. "And you're renting this pasture down here, to boot—besides building the fence Brice ought to be building."

"Hay's a short bite in Argent," Walt said. "I haven't time to wait on him."

"Suppose he moves out from under you? He talked like he might relocate on the railroad right-of-way, hoping to hold them up for a big price."

"I know," Kennerly said. "The damn fool! He's got the best meadow in the valley here, and up in town a quick market for all the hay and dairy stuff he can raise. Well, I'm hoping Nora and Tommy and his woman and I can change his idiot mind. . . ."

Lucille retreated back around the cabin. Mrs. Brice ran a pair of overalls through the wringer, tossed them into a wicker basket, and looked up at her and smiled, perfectly content. Lucille felt she should respond somehow, but nothing would come. A common . . . she would not say the word even in her own mind because the only tone it would have would be the one she had heard from her father's turned-down lips. Common . . . Making a helpless gesture, she fled back to the stage. Dear God, she thought and looked up the valley opening to where the storm clouds were beginning to break into long, tumultuous streamers.

"10"

She was alone at the vehicle. The passengers had wandered off, some to watch the clumsy rowboat bring across its second load of fares, some to gossip with campers who had pitched their tents by the tributary stream. The driver was digging a rock out of the front hoof of one of the lead team. As Lucille stood collecting herself, the lawyer Mr. Gregg appeared. He helped her to her accustomed place and then settled himself into the dickey seat behind. From their elevation they could see that John Ogden had gone with Walt Kennerly behind the cabin and was talking to Mrs. Brice, swinging out his arms in hearty gestures.

"Is he always so enthusiastic?" she remarked to the lawyer. "Whatever he's concerned with is perfect—his town, his road, his friends, everything—even that wo . . . even this ranch."

"That's Hardrock Johnny," the lawyer agreed and explained the name: deep veins in solid granite; this country will last. Then he added, "You have been good for him, Mrs. Montgomery."

"I!"

"You've let him talk about the things he values."

She laughed. "I could hardly have done anything else."

"A shared belief is a strengthened belief. John needs that."

The seriousness of the tone mystified her. "Why?"

"In spite of what John likes to call the rush, Argent is not yet a large town. You'll almost certainly see him fairly often during the next weeks."

"I hope I'll see both of you." Men to fetch and carry. "You'll be the only people I know."

"You should understand that to many in Argent, John Ogden was guilty of a criminal act in surrendering that freighter to the Utes."

"What else could he have done?" she protested.

Mr. Gregg sorted his words. "Do you remember how he responded this morning to your question about whether he had been afraid when the Indians appeared?"

"He said no one had ever asked him that before."

"His accusers never asked because they do not believe he was afraid."

"I don't understand."

"They believe that the Indian attack was framed in advance. They believe the escort sold Hedstrom to the Utes in exchange for their own lives and property, and therefore they knew they would not be molested."

"How terrible!" Lucille whispered. And yet this interpretation of the story had been evident ever since the runner at the road junction had read from the Baker *Herald*. But Mr. Ogden's version had been preferable and she had looked only at it. "The court freed him," she said defensively.

"The court dropped the case. It is not quite the same as a verdict of innocent."

"Are you implying he was guilty?"

"By law, Mrs. Montgomery, all men are innocent until proved otherwise."

"That's not what I asked," she insisted. "You defended him. Doesn't that mean you believe—"

"That no mistake was made? Not necessarily. But if surrendering Hedstrom was a mistake and if John Ogden is guilty, still he acted in . . . oh, innocence." The lawyer gave a deprecatory smile. "I keep saying that, and I guess it is not very clear, is it?"

Lucille watched Mr. Ogden carry Mrs. Brice's wicker basket out to the clothesline. "I don't know enough about it to judge," she replied. A familiar clutch of regret was tightening inside her. Something lost. "Why are you telling me this?" she cried.

"You should know the whole situation, in case the town calls on you to take sides."

"I'm a total stranger. There's no reason—"

"You've listened to him, Mrs. Montgomery. In a short while you'll be meeting for yourself the things he's told you about. He will watch your reactions to see if you bear out his estimate of his town and—and, in a way, his evaluation of himself."

"A woman to fetch and carry," she murmured ironically.

"Pardon?" Mr. Gregg said.

"Nothing. Just a saying."

He frowned uncertainly, then shrugged and finished, "I am not suggesting that you fetch or make any active declarations that will hinder your own business. I am not even sure that the town cares any longer about John Ogden and what he did. I am simply telling you that you may hear sneers and whispers, and even read malice in the local newspaper. For you not to be turned away by such things while he is getting established again could possibly mean a great deal to him. He's going to be hard on himself, I'm afraid, even if the town isn't."

Not to be turned away. She watched John Ogden say good-bye to Ira Brice's new wife and stride toward the stage with his friend. She shrank inside herself. Must another person's despair be piled on her back too? And she saw again her father's loveless eyes.

"I—" But there were no words for the contradictions she experienced as he came beside the stage and beamed up at her and introduced her to his friend, with open pride in both of them.

"Like I said," he told Walt, "she's bringing Paris styles right here to Argent. How about that? The old town's coming along for sure, isn't it?"

Handsome and blond and reserved, Mr. Kennerly nodded gravely.

"I hope you'll like Argent, Mrs. Montgomery."

"If it likes my dresses, I'm sure I shall."

"I keep telling her," Johnny said, "that she's going to do a land-office business."

They talked small talk while the driver hurried the rest of the passengers to their seats. The horses set themselves against their collars. Johnny leaned out over the edge of the vehicle. "So long!" he bawled inclusively. "See you in Sunday school!" They waved back, Tommy and the campers and Walt and Ira Brice and, out under the clothesline, the woman. Lucille hesitated. Then, diffidently, she waved too.

"11"

The stage rolled through the Narrows. "Now!" Mr. Ogden said, watching her face exactly as the lawyer had said he would.

The sandstone bands ahead of them spread apart in abrupt concaves. Color—that was her first impression. Color everywhere, filling and overflowing this round, tremendous basin. Fuzzes of white mist floated out of bright green shrubs that Mr. Ogden said were nurtured by hot springs. Aspen trunks glistened. Water cascaded down the side gulches. Oak brush ran lines of contrast between the tiers of red sandstone. Above the cliffs rose brown buttresses of rock. The black bristles of spruce trees between these ribs were slit by old avalanche scars, softened now by patches of lighter, fresher growth. Overhead, the storm had broken into pieces. Cotton clouds of baby pink floated in a baby-blue sky. Stray shafts of sunlight slanting through the rifts touched with unexpected brilliance the snowy knobs and slopes of the amphitheater that formed the left-hand, or eastern, side of the basin.

Straight ahead of them, rising out of the deep canyon that cleaved the southern wall of the basin, was a pyramidal block of mountain, its top lost in swollen, purple-gray clouds. "That's Ute Peak," Mr. Ogden said. "The main river comes down from the left. Red Mountain Creek is there to the right, in the bottom of that deep, narrow slit. The streams come together right smack at the foot of Ute Peak and flow on down the gorge to town. You can see where our road will probably go. See that ledge along the left side of the gorge? I figure the best way is to follow it, cross the main river, go around the front of the peak and on up through the slit where Red Mountain Creek breaks down from the high country. You can't see Red Mountain itself from here. It begins three–four miles farther back, out of sight behind Ute."

Lucille did not even try to follow the pointing of his finger. There was too much closer at hand, first a loose sprawl of industrial buildings and then, at the upper end of the basin, the town, squatting stolidly where pines and aspens had been cleared away. It looked very new and, from this distance, very clean.

"Oh it's beautiful!" she murmured.

"Sure is," Mr. Ogden agreed, as if he had arranged even the water-falls. "And look how it's grown!"

On the first wide spot above the Narrows a sawmill whined. Even this late in the evening two wagons were backed up to the platform, their owners snatching up the green planks as fast as they came from the blade. "I wouldn't want to live in the shack they build out of those boards," the stage driver remarked. "They'll shrink until when you say 'Scat!' the cat won't even have to look for a door." Meanwhile Mr. Ogden was pointing first to the untidy heaps around the new brick-yard and then at plumes of smoke trailing from tall iron stacks—a smelter *and* a lixiviation works, he said. "I golly!" He had been used to a log town. Bricks and iron stacks were permanent, like the cap-ital city, like Denver.

"Most of this grew up in one winter and a piece of spring," he said. "Wait till summer! Man, I hope Pat's got that road going!"

On the meadows immediately below the town immigrant wagons were parked in the cottonwood groves. A score or more tents leaked streamers of fragrant blue wood smoke from crazily canting chim-neys. An antlike line of men tramped from the camp to the town to see the sights and then come back with armloads of groceries. They waved as the stage rattled past—men in boots, men in frock coats, men in fur caps; farmers, charcoal burners, miners. But there were not very many women, Lucille thought unhappily. "They're inside, cook-ing supper," Johnny said when she murmured something about it. And dreaming of Paris gowns, she said to herself. Here, in this setting.

A congregation of donkeys was nosing about the refuse at the end of an alley. As if on a signal they united in a strident braying. "A cross between an earthquake and a woman who's stepped on a mouse," the stage driver said of the din as Lucille laughed. Then she saw that a pair of them were mating and she looked away in horrified embarrass-ment, up the street which the stage was just entering. Wagons and buck-boards and saddle horses lined the hitching racks that paralleled the wooden sidewalks. Beside some of the vehicles small fires burned. Lu-cille looked down on them in amazement. "Why, they're cooking!" she exclaimed of the booted men squatted beside the steaming tin cans and rusty skillets.

Everywhere men were tramping, tramping. Like tigers, Lucille thought, caged and restless and bored. When a dog fight racketed be-tween two cabins, nearly every lounger on the street surged over to watch, then turned back to hoot at a small spring wagon going down

the street in the opposite direction to the stage. In its open bed a
man wearing a red coat and black plug hat pounded furiously on
a drum. A banner on the wagon's side proclaimed, "You Can't Beat
Emmett's!" Ben Emmett, so the stage driver explained to Mr. Ogden,
owned the town's newest variety house, whatever that was. Near the
corner a vender was hawking patent medicines and a cure-all electric
battery. Behind him, on the narrow verandah of a hotel, the Dixon
House, men sat in rocking chairs or leaned against the pillars. Talk
stopped and each eye turned to follow the stage, estimating what new
interests it might be bringing.

In the center of the intersection rose a tall white flagpole. Hanging
from a crossarm attached to the pole was a huge circular saw blade.

"What on earth is that?" Lucille asked.

For once Mr. Ogden did not respond.

"An alarm," the lawyer said after a moment's silence.

"Fire?"

"Indians."

Oh dear, she thought, and Mr. Ogden said angrily, "They haven't
needed it for months. Why don't they take it down?"

The driver warned, "Hang on!" and gathered his reins for the showy
dash to the depot, located around the next corner where there was
room to park. As the horses began to run, Mr. Ogden cried, "Look
at that safe!" A massive iron strongbox stood on the sidewalk in
front of a two-story brick building still too new to be occupied. Gilt
letters on the building's window announced BANK OF ARGENT. Mr.
Ogden soared back to enthusiasm. "Hey, Fred! Fred!" he yelled at
someone on the sidewalk. "Fred Fossett," he explained to Lucille.
"He used to be our paymaster when I worked for Otto Winkler.
Now he's starting up the bank here." The words were hardly finished when his wonder shifted again. "Look at the line in front of the
Bon-Ton! Half of them carrying their own tin cups and plates, too!
Nora Brice will make a mint. Oh, I said you'd like this town!"

The stage swooped to the corner. The driver leaned forward, his
wrists bending against the reins. The leaders raced past the middle of
the intersection, then wheeled at a full gallop into their turn. The
swing team came around at a lope, the wheelers on a trot in the narrowing arc. A soft aspiration escaped the driver's lips. His foot touched the
brake. The mud-spattered Concord rumbled to a stop, swaying gently
on its thorough braces. A crowd of idlers rolled up, whiskery faces
lifted, eyes shining whitely in dark faces. Every jaw seemed to chomp
in unison. A woman. Lucille fancied the word ran through the crowd
like a sigh.

The interior passengers climbed stiffly through the door. Runners from the rival hotels assaulted them.

"Bags, mister? The Belvedere Hotel, newest in town—"

"Not if you want comfort, folks. Those rooms are so small you have to hold your breath to turn around. Now at the Dixon—"

A round-headed man with a walrus mustache pushed between the runners to confront the fat woman. He waved a pencil and notebook. "I'm from *The True Fissure*, ma'am, Argent's only newspaper. If you'll favor us with your name as one of the day's two fair arrivals, and a statement of your impressions about our city—"

"That's Al Ewer, editor of the paper," Harmon Gregg told Lucille when Mr. Ogden refrained from his usual rush of explanation. "If it seems like a good idea to you, let's get some publicity for your dresses by having him give you a private interview tomorrow, rather than waste the opportunity with one of these name-and-impression routines he hands every newcomer here on the platform. What do you think, John? Al will go for something different—a story, say, on the new styles for his women readers. He doesn't get much to please them."

Mr. Ogden did not answer. He had sat motionless since their arrival, his hands gripping his knees. His eyes, though, kept sliding back and forth, across the watchers, to Ewer, and on to the restless men tramping along the main street, and back to the staring faces. Lucille glanced at the lawyer. He returned a faint nod: go ahead, give him a boost. A woman to fetch and carry.

Aloud she asked, "Can you help me down?"

Just then a voice caterwauled from somewhere in the crowd, "Hey there, John Ogden! How's the Injuns!"

It was almost as if this were the trigger he had been waiting for. His lips stretched into a smile; his gaze steadied on her. "Why, surely," he said. He stepped lightly onto the ladder fixed to the side of the stage, from there to the top of the wheel to the protruding hub to the splintery boards of the platform. "If you'll get out of the way," he said coolly to Ewer. His glance pushed out enough room for him to maneuver in and he nodded up to her. She slid to the edge of the seat, trying to keep her ankles from showing. He gave the crowd a look as if he were about to make a presentation. "This is Mrs. Montgomery," he said. Reaching up, he caught her under the arms and swung her down onto the platform.

III

"1"

Harness for eight draft horses held a lot of black straps. Johnny wanted every one cleaned and oiled, and every knob on every hame polished, and every browband fixed with a center rosette for holding a plume. Even with Walt and a stableboy helping, the afternoon was dwindling before he completed the job to his satisfaction. Hurriedly then he hitched Walt's clean-limbed, blood-red trotting horse to the buggy he was hiring by the week from the livery and went up town to fetch Lucille.

She had rented a shop in one side of the new bank building. To guarantee privacy for her clientele she had backed the single small front window with dark cloth. Inside the alcove thus formed she had framed between a pair of egrets a large hand-tinted fashion plate which she changed from time to time. This day it was a drawing of a low-necked satin evening gown with a flaring bustle. Two miners in muddy trousers were staring at it in profound silence as Johnny rattled the knob of the entry door. He heard a scurrying inside and then Lucille appeared. Her forehead looked very high and cool under the upsweep of her pompadour.

"Oh, it's you! Come in!" To another woman silhouetted against the pale square of the rear windows she added, "It's Johnny, Nora." And to him again as he came from the street glare into the dusky, fragrant interior, "We've been finishing our princess costumes for the parade."

She gestured toward two streamers of some kind of gauzy material draped across the back of an upholstered chair she had borrowed from Mother Marsh, at whose roominghouse she was living. Johnny smiled benignly. The flair of finger and eye by which she could twist and fluff

and curve ordinary cloth into something striking was a continual wonder to his angular ways of thinking. Having set up her display table for
her, he knew it was nothing but raw pine boards on sawbucks, covered
by a bed sheet. Then presto—a few folds, some evergreens and pussy-
willows, a calculated placing of her fashions books and pink order pad—
well, it wasn't anything he could even have guessed.

Still more starkness had been taken from the raw little room by
colorful hooked rugs hanging on the board walls. Because of the dim-
ming of the windows, she extravagantly burned, even at midday, a
coal-oil lamp whose yellow glare was softened by a Brussels shade. At
the edge of the glow she had placed a small table. On this was a tea
set of hand-painted china, rented from one of the stores. The smells
of her routine afternoon brew and of her powder and perfume created
an illusory world into which the townswomen loved to drop, to talk
of styles and look at her books. Johnny enjoyed dropping by, too, if
there weren't too many women around. He believed that other men
did also, when dragged there by their wives, although afterwards they
reared back their heads and snorted and said it was nothing but a damn
trap, like fence wings funneling into a wild-horse corral. Your woman
got the gate sprung closed and those pictures on your lap and that
Chicago woman making limber motions off the ends of her wrists and
how did you get out again?

"We've fixed the harness and wagon too," Johnny said proudly.
"You'll be knockouts. Let's go see the silver. There's a picture taker
down there, I hear, if he isn't finished by now. I've a buggy outside."

"As soon as I tidy up," Lucille agreed. She dropped snips of cloth
into a wastebasket, moved scissors around, took a tortoise-shell hairpin
out of her pompadour and held it in her mouth as she patted at the
glossy black waves on her head. Nora, who still had not said a word,
picked up some bundles. She chanced to move so that lamplight flowed
up across her small round chin and full cheeks. Again it struck Johnny
how pretty she might be if she would just give herself a chance. But
she had cut her hair short, to help prevent its being smelled up by
everything she cooked, she said; she parted it severely in the middle
and for decoration wore some frizzy bangs across her brow. The only
dress she owned for street wear was gray and graceless, with black cuffs
and a black choke collar and a row of closely spaced black cloth buttons
marching up the front. "No style whatsoever," Lucille had said once
in despair. Yet the lack did not keep men from watching whenever
Nora walked along the street with that unconscious, swift vitality of
hers. "She has such a lovely figure," Lucille had said. "If she just
wouldn't hoard every penny she makes. She's still afraid, I think. Notice her mouth when she supposes she's alone. And she's only twenty."

"You'd be afraid too," Walt had defended her, "if you had lived the way she has."

Two women could not possibly be more different; yet since the night of the stage's arrival, when Johnny had taken Lucille to supper at the Bon-Ton, they had gotten along famously. They were in and out of each other's places whenever slack moments came, helping each other with dishes and laundry, consulting about mysterious problems, sharing in their own way the special fact that, save for aging Mother Marsh, they were the only two unattached females older than sixteen who were completely and respectably on their own in Argent City.

"Aren't you coming with us?" Johnny asked Nora as she turned toward the back door.

She faced him with the angry look that he swore she reserved especially for him. "Just who will get dinner if I go?"

"Half an hour," he urged, as much to be contrary as anything else. They never did agree. "Those old boars you feed won't notice if you're a few minutes late one evening. Mabel—"

"Mabel has all she can do, cleaning trout."

"A pack horse loaded with nothing but trout," Lucille marveled. "Imagine!"

"Uncleaned," Nora said. "The lazy creature I bought them from said he hadn't had time. But I got them at half-price. Now I can undercut the Dixon House." She would not stay pleased in front of him, however. "And now," she said, her lips pinched again, "I've got to do something with the guts."

John sighed aloud. "Relax and come on and enjoy yourself for once. We'll throw the guts off at the dump on the way to the smelter."

"That will make a pleasant ride, I'm sure," Nora said. She did not want to be placated. He had known it and should not have roused her with that sigh. She scorched at him. "Why not route your fancy parade through the alley tomorrow and show Winkler and Mayor Rubin and Ewer and that banker and the rest of the big visitors and civic boosters what this town is really like? You don't want to see, that's why. Silver! Did you ever try cooking in a kitchen crawling with flies?"

"The council—"

"—will pass another resolution, I suppose, and Ewer will write another editorial. But the manure heaps are still in the street and garbage is still rotting wherever anyone drops it in the alley, and those dead burros are still down at the town dump where they were dragged last winter. Maybe the council thought they could pass a resolution against thaws. But summer came anyhow. Even you ought to be able to notice when you ride by."

I won't get mad, Johnny told himself. But he did. "All I asked was whether you wanted to ride down to the smelter to see the ceremony. Tomorrow will be the biggest day Argent has seen yet—nothing special or anything. Just the first parade and—oh, what's the use?"

"Stop it, both of you," Lucille broke in. "You're worse than children." She took the ruffles out of their tempers, as she always managed to do, but she could not persuade Nora to go with them to see the silver.

"I don't mean to quarrel with her all the time," Johnny said after she had gone out the back way to her restaurant. "But she's so darn scratchy. I'm tired of her always picking on me for everything she thinks is wrong with the whole state of Colorado."

"She's not mad at you."

"Strange how I get a different impression."

"She's mad with the way life has treated her. And you are always so optimistic—"

"Should I sit around and moan with her? I offered to take those fish guts to the dump. But no, she enjoys complaining."

"Give her time to loosen up, Johnny. She can't believe yet that things won't go wrong once more." Lucille giggled suddenly, partly to change the subject. "Walt is buying her a dress."

"That old coyote!"

"He wants it to be a surprise. I managed to take her measurements while we were working on the costumes. I'll have the shop hold the final touches until I am back in Chicago myself and can make sure everything is exactly right. Oh, I do hope he's satisfied."

"She's the one who'll wear it."

"He selected the pattern, even the colors."

"Kennerly, buying she-duds!"

"John Ogden! If you tell him— Please! I promised!"

"Will you mail the dress straight to her or to him?"

Lucille grew suspicious. "Why do you ask?"

"Just wondering."

"I don't think I trust you," she said and switched the subject again. "Why doesn't he marry her, John?"

He deliberately did not look at her while he wondered whether she knew that after the Mexican dishwasher and the regular customers had straggled away from the Bon-Ton at night and after Mabel had fallen asleep on her cot in the storage pantry off the kitchen, Walt as often as not went to bed with Nora, without marriage. What would she think? He could not estimate, and suddenly that bothered him, for he thought he had grown to know her very well indeed during the past month.

"Oh, I don't know." He could feel himself being almost too casual as he shrugged. "Maybe Walt isn't the marrying kind."

"When a man says that, it just means he's completely selfish."

"He's buying her a dress."

"You know what I mean."

"No, I don't."

"He seems so kind and gentle. But underneath he's aloof . . . untouchable."

"He gets things done."

"If that's your criterion, so does a mule. If he hurts her—"

"You women! Always looking for the worst—"

"I'm sorry." She touched his wrists with her fingers, apologizing. "Don't let's quarrel. We've only two days left."

He winced, his irritation forgotten. "Let's not talk about that either. It's too soon for you to leave."

She turned away from him. "If we're going to reach the smelter before everything is over, we'd better go."

"2"

Johnny had left the buggy top down, knowing how she liked to watch the evening light retreat up the sides of the basin to the turreted rim, where snow still glinted. For a moment after he had handed her in, she sat quietly, her head back against the seat, but as he came around to his side of the vehicle, she straightened, her glance shifting this way and that, taking in the entire growing, busy town. Very brightly, so that he knew she was trying to restore the lightheartedness that was more normal between them than was this last restraint, she said,

"Argent's first parade! I'm really excited. So is Nora, even if she does pretend to be crusty."

The parade was part of a celebration generated by the excitement attending the removal of the Utes. After weeks of dickering and preparation the Indians finally were going to leave their ancient home, escorted across the desert to a new reservation in Utah by a heavily armed troop of cavalry and fed by a long train of government commissary wagons. Winkler had landed the contract for freighting to the agency the materials necessary for the long march. After making sure the goods reached Los Alamos in acceptable condition, he planned to continue on up the river to Argent and discuss certain business procedures with Fred Fossett, his companion in negotiating the Ute treaty and the man whom he was now setting up in the Bank of Argent.

On learning of Winkler's plans, Al Ewer had proposed through the columns of *The True Fissure* that Argent hold a testimonial banquet for the two men at the Dixon House. Mayor Rubin and the council agreed. Promptly the Argent City Silver Cornet and Drum Marchers had attached themselves to the ceremony. The band played voluntarily for Fourth of July programs, Election Day rallies, horse races, baseball games, the acquisition of the town's fire engine—anything. Moreover, they recently had assessed themselves to buy new peaked hats with patent-leather visors and scarlet jackets with braided black frogs, and as yet they had had no opportunity to display the magnificence. Accordingly their leader had written an open letter to the paper suggesting that the honored guests be transported in fitting style in a decorated buggy along Main Street to the Dixon House, preceded by cornet and drum music. Ewer caught up the notion and elaborated. Let the mayor issue a proclamation, naming the event Good Riddance Day, in celebration of the Utes' departure. Let a slogan be devised for the town so soon to burst from the bonds imposed by the Indians. Ewer himself would donate a five-year subscription for the best phrase. (Ben Emmett of Emmett's Variety House had won with "The Town Without A Bellyache.") Let this slogan be the keynote of a parade of floats, prepared by patriotic merchants and civic groups, to accompany the buggy on its triumphal tour. Again *The True Fissure* would award five-year subscriptions, plus certificates of merit, to all participants connected with the winning float, the newspaper staff to act as judges. (Staff, Ewer wrote proudly. He had recently been able to afford both a full-time printer and a part-time office boy.)

As a climax to the gala day, the Argent Guards, a militia group formed during the first Indian alarm, decided that this would be an appropriate time to disband formally. The ceremony would be the occasion for a public ball to be held in the Dixon House after the testimonial dinner.

Johnny had not intended to participate. Although he had been one of the founders of the Guards, they had let him know quite clearly, several months ago, that they no longer considered him a member. Nor had anyone invited him to the testimonal dinner. To hell with them. Winkler had agreed, in a one-line answer to a voluminous letter of Johnny's, that while he was in Argent he would look at the beginnings of the Red Mountain road. That was celebration enough for Johnny. He had overcome Pat's preference for the cheaper westside route up the gorge, and the initial part of the grade was now curving grandly upward toward Wolf Creek Falls and the tremendous boiler-plate cliffs on the east. Surely Otto would be impressed by what he saw. Surely then he would unbend and give his ex-employees the help they were beginning seriously to need. Let the Guards go ahead

and dance themselves out of existence. For Johnny the weekend was a
beginning.

At this point a complication developed which brought him back into
the picture quite beyond his will. Lucille was invited by the banquet
committee to be Otto Winkler's dinner companion, in lieu of Mrs.
Winkler, who declined to endure the long ride over from Saguache for
an evening of speechmaking.

While Lucille hesitated over accepting, three members of the Argent
Guard had entered her shop with an additional invitation. They were
very much in awe of her and correspondingly awkward—a modiste,
intellectual enough to be writing a weekly column of incomprehensi-
bly high fashion notes for Ewer's paper, yet beautiful as well. They
stood paralyzed inside the door of what she referred to as her salon. By
chance Johnny had been lolling at his ease beside the teacups. The
visitors glared at him without ingenuity enough to maneuver him out
of hearing, and since Lucille did not come to their rescue, they had
to blurt out their errand in his hearing. Winkler, they said, did not
dance and so would put in only a token appearance at the ball. Therefore they were offering themselves as her joint escorts for the rest of
the evening.

Lucille's hand had sunk in dismay. A complete actress: every woman
was under such circumstances. "How sweet of you!" Each of the trio
was personally convinced that she would not have offended him
for worlds. "But I just promised Mr. Ogden to go with him. I am sure,
though, that if you'll ask he'll save places for you on my card."

The Guards started sentences they could not finish, glowered afresh
at Johnny, and stumbled into each other as they backed outside.
"You're not angry?" she had asked afterwards. "No," he had said,
though at first he had been. But there was no polite way of rejecting
the interference. She was trying, rather obviously, to use the celebration
as a means of towing him back into the stream of the town's hopes
and ambitions where she said he belonged; and he half suspected
Harmon Gregg of putting her up to it. "I'm honored," he had said. He
went outside stiff-backed. Across the street the three Guards were talking together and still scowling. To hell with them. It was a public
dance. They could not keep him away. What was more, she preferred
going with him and in effect had so told the entire town. Of a sudden
it had been all he could do to keep from throwing his arms toward
the sky and letting out a yell.

That same night he had conceived the idea of the float, for the
parade was also public and he could not be kept from that either. Walt
had just finished bringing down to the Blair Reduction Works below
town the last of five mule-train loads of the hand-sorted, high-grade

silver and lead ore which the two Cornishmen had taken out of the
Ram mine in the course of its development. The silver and lead would
be smelted from the ore at the reduction plant and molded into eighty-
pound pigs for shipment to a refinery in Denver. Red Mountain's
first mineral! Why not put the pigs on a decorated wagon and haul
them in the parade. Have the two Cornishmen stand proudly behind
the pyramid of bars, and in front of it, representing Argent, the Silver
City of the St. Johns, the town without a bellyache, place a pair of
lovely princesses, Nora Brice and Lucille Montgomery. Sponsor of the
float would be the Red Mountain Toll Road and Transportation
Company, the conduit by which future silver would flow into the
eager town. Pat had agreed instantly—man, that'll help sell stock—but
the Cornishmen had been fearful until Johnny had promised that
Sheriff Gaw would post armed deputies along the route. Then he remarked in an offhand way that he hoped they would not mind riding
through the town in cutaway coats and plug hats. The heat of that
vision evaporated the last of their resistance. It also led Roscoe Blair
of the reduction works to ask his first big customers to pose for pictures on his loading platform, beside his handicraft. Quickly the town's
love of novelty turned even this into a ceremony. Parley Quine promised to amble down to make a speech; Ewer would be there for interviews and to collect material for an eye-witness account; Blair's recently
married daughter would wield a bottle of Catawba wine over the metal
pigs—no champagne had yet reached the town. The christening of an
era, Johnny had said, and was envious that he himself had not thought
of the stunt in time for Lucille to perform the symbolic wine act. It
made more sense, after all, than dinners or dances.

He flicked the bay into a ringing trot down the long street. As they
approached the main intersection, Lucille exclaimed involuntarily, "The
saw blade is gone!"

Johnny had noticed the gap on the way up from the stable. "The
Argent Guards took it down," he said sullenly. "I hear they aim to use
it in some kind of float."

She watched the set of his face. "We don't have to go to the dance,"
she said.

"Don't be silly." Then he realized that that kind of compliance
could be more rude than rejection. He made himself smile. "It'll be fun.
The ball is where they'll announce the prize for the winning float. You!"

Her fingers touched his wrist in the gesture he had learned well: thank
you Johnny. With unexpected shyness she said, "Perhaps I shouldn't
have forced you into this. I know the past month hasn't been easy."

His pride would not unbend. "There hasn't been any trouble," he
said. They had just passed the courthouse and he heard workmen

hammering inside the jail wing, replacing the cage with standard cells. Rumor said that the entire structure soon would be replaced by a fine building of red brick, with granite steps leading to a white door, a fanlight above, and on top a white cupola. No more savagery. He had braced himself for brutality, but Walt had been right; the town was busy and nothing more than gossip had met him. Still, isolation could be as cruel sometimes as open scorn. He would round a corner to the sunny side of a barn and the booted men yarning there would end their talk abruptly and he would know that his had been the last name in their mouths. Or he would go into a saloon, road dust and powder smoke thick in his throat, and would catch the flickering exchange of glances in the mirror. Sometimes when he saw men lounging on the verandah of the Dixon House he would veer off, in spite of himself, through the alley, rather than walk past the silence and feel it break into ripples against his back. It would have been a relief, at such times, if someone had yelled openly once again, "Hey Johnny, save us from the Injuns."

But there had not been any trouble.

"The town is changing," he said. "They're forgetting."

"They shouldn't also forget what you've done for them," she said.

"It's past. All I care about now is getting that road built."

She persisted. "I want to say one thing before I leave."

"Nothing needs saying."

"It's been good to see that a mistake doesn't have to be the end of everything."

Instantly he flared. "It wasn't a mistake."

Flustered, she tried to explain. "I didn't mean it was. I'm only saying some people thought it was. What you've had to go through because of it would have turned many men sour. But you're still yourself. You still . . . believe, as you put it once to me. Seeing that, when I was coming out here alone and afraid, meant a great deal to me. More than I can really tell you." Her glance dropped to her gloved fingertips. Her voice was a whisper. "I just wanted you to know."

He sat staring at the horse's ears. Despair caught her. "Oh, what use are words?" she cried. "We try to say something out of our hearts and nobody understands."

"It wasn't a mistake," he repeated stubbornly.

By now they had emerged from the lower end of the town. As they circled the new fairgrounds, Johnny let the bay slow to a walk. Several men were in the long grass in the center of the racetrack, practicing baseball for the merchants' team. Ben Emmett was hitting fungo flies. John listened to the crack of the bat, watched the white ball loft clearly against the bank of evergreens across the river, and he remembered

abruptly, through his hurt, the Sunday afternoon when he had brought
Lucille here to see the town's favorite mare run against a black cavalry
horse which a swaggering lieutenant had brought up from the cantonment at the agency. She had let him bet five dollars for her. He remembered again the roar of the crowd, the mare out front on the back-
stretch, Lucille's eyes dancing; and then her knuckles hard against her
mouth as the black came up fast out of the last turn, tears in her eyes,
the profound silence of the home rooters and the yells of the soldiers. It
wasn't money. When your town's horse got licked, you felt licked too.
The prim and proper townswomen, who thought it somehow wasn't
quite ladylike to go to the races, would never understand that. Lucille
did.

He turned to her. "Don't go to Baker yet," he said.

"I've already put it off once."

"More people keep coming in. There'll be more strikes in the high
country now that the snow is melting and prospectors can get their
shafts down. More business—"

"I've sold only two dresses in the last week, one of them Nora's.
And Mr. Fossett has written the bank in Baker to rent me a showroom,
beginning Monday."

"Another week here won't hurt sales over there."

"You wouldn't stop work on your road for a week."

"You won't be stopping, just—"

"I've been away from Lennie too long as it is."

"I suppose," he grumbled. She always brought up the boy just when
he wished she wouldn't.

Her fingers touched his wrist. "It's been a wonderful month, Johnny."

"Less two days."

"We still have the parade and the ball, and on Sunday the ride over
the pass to Baker. I can't wait to see your red mountains."

"I suppose," he grumbled again. But he could not make himself
return her smile. It hadn't been a mistake, and he wished she would
stay here long enough to realize that it hadn't been.

"3"

When they reached the reduction works, the wine-splashing and the
photography were over. Parley Quine, as cool as a dog's nose, was on
the loading platform winding up his speech. He wore a broadcloth coat
over a fawn-gray flannel shirt, and striped trousers tucked into shiny

black boots. Polished spurs glittered on his heels. Beside him was a
section of pine trunk standing on end and covered by a bright Navajo
blanket. Above the blanket rose an imposing cribwork of twenty-six
silver-colored bars, each one looking something like an elongated loaf
of bread. Beyond the silver tower sat the two Cornishmen, caricatures
of their own aspirations in long-tailed coats, their plug hats placed
carefully on the dusty platform beside their wooden chairs. Out front
in a ragged arc was an audience of fifty or sixty people, mostly men,
some afoot, some lounging sideways in their saddles, a few in wagons.

Quine was telling them, at first, what they expected to hear. Fore-
sight and courage. Transportation the key. Roads from Red Mountain
over the pass to Baker, down the gorge to Argent. Railroads from the
outside guaranteed for the next summer, bringing in capital for un-
restricted development. He was a Baker man himself, of course, and
the new coal deposits recently discovered near Montezuma at the
lower end of Los Padres Canyon meant that most smelting ore would
go out by way of Baker. But let this be no cause for jealousy. Red
Mountain held riches enough to content both towns. Prosperity,
fraternity . . .

Until Quine had grown condescending about Argent, Johnny had
kept nodding in vigorous agreement, not noticing the half-smile with
which Lucille watched him. But when Quine twisted his speech into a
flagrant promotion of Baker, John became vastly annoyed. Baker,
nothing. With the pass blocked by snow, the first silver had had to
come to Argent and Quine himself had come down to see it—and now
was mocking at the town that held it. To show his disdain, Johnny
cocked one foot indifferently over the dashboard of the buggy, yawned,
and flauntingly regarded the audience rather than the speaker.

Presently his interest focused. "There's your solid man for tomorrow
night's dinner."

"Mr. Winkler? Where?"

"Standing yonder beside Fred Fossett."

He wondered if she was disappointed.

The trader's appearance would hardly have signaled him out as
cause for celebration. The spade beard that had been glossy black during
Johnny's days as a clerk in Otto's Saguache store was now streaked with
early gray. His narrow face and beaked nose rode forward on a scrawny
neck. He wore a dust-colored hat with an absolutely round brim, and
although the evening chill had not yet settled with the shadows into the
basin, he had thrown what appeared to be a discarded army greatcoat
over his shoulders like a cape. Hunched under it, his hands clasped behind his back, he looked misshapen.

"Oh you'll like him!" Johnny said. He had told her something of

Winkler's career—how, after being discharged from the army in Santa Fe following the Civil War, he had drifted north into the Ute reservation with a packload of trinkets for the Indian trade. Peddling had grown into the store at Saguache and contracts to supply the agency at Los Alamos. His first roads he had built for moving his own goods. Soon he was building toll roads everywhere that traffic flowed. His investments spread with them—an interest in a warehouse in one town, a wheat farm near another, in mines and freight lines and in the Argent bank, whose president was nominally Fred Fossett. It was said that he and Fred had persuaded the Utes to sign the treaty of removal by riding from camp to camp leading a pack horse loaded with specie and offering each male two silver dollars in exchange for a laboriously scrawled "X." Fourteen hundred signatures, rumor said, had been rounded up that way while Agent Cushman and the commissioners from Washington waved their hands in pious horror. Certain Congressmen from the eastern states had also trumpeted derogation and had demanded investigations of mysterious financial interests behind the Indian Bureau. Such righteousness had outraged the towns of western Colorado. Otto Winkler knew the way to action: two shiny dollars in sight meant more to the Indians than did Congress's vague promises about future annuities. Tomorrow's testimonial was not only a tribute to Winkler's and Fossett's expediency; it was also a raucous gesture of defiance to their critics. Good Riddance Day. Let the carpers carp. This way lay success.

Quine finished his talk. The Argent audience granted him a perfunctory handclapping, and then Roscoe Blair shot forward, his bony hands upraised.

"Just a minute, folks!" He was a long, thin man, sallow, young of face but prematurely bald. "Seeing as you're already here, we might as well make this visitor's days at the Blair Reduction Works and show you around. Any as want to see silver bars in the making, step right up."

What he meant was that he wanted to lure Otto Winkler inside. He shot off the platform, buttonholed his prey, and presently started inside at the head of a small procession. Quine attached himself to Winkler's other side. The Cousin Jacks, feeling left out, shook hands with each other and went over to where two whores with pink parasols were waiting in a carriage.

Johnny had long since visited the smelter, but Lucille had not; women did not venture into man's domain except on special occasions.

"Do you want to see the place?" he asked her.

"I'd love to."

He hitched the bay and swung her down. On the platform they stopped under Gaw's benign watchfulness to examine the metal bars, damp still from the wine Blair's daughter had broken over them.

"Must be a ton of it here," Johnny said, as proudly as if he had mined the ore himself.

"This little bit—a ton!" Lucille was properly amazed. "How many silver dollars will it make?"

"By weight it's mostly lead," Johnny admitted. "The silver will be recovered at a refinery."

"Oh." She was disappointed. "I thought it was pure."

"Ore in these mountains always carries base metals."

"Base?" She ran a finger along the top bar. "The day's philosophy—there is some dross in everything."

"Oh, lead is worth close to five cents a pound."

She laughed. "Johnny, there is no one else like you."

He was puzzled but pleased. "I don't see—"

"Never mind. Tell me about the silver."

"It's down a little, about a dollar-eleven an ounce, I think. I don't know how many ounces these bars will assay. There may be fractional values in gold, too. Anyway, even after deducting expenses, the boys have made themselves a lot better than day wages."

A worker pushed an iron-wheeled dolly clattering along the boards of the platform. Johnny helped him pile on a load of six bars, which he took to a wagon that would transport them to the bank, where they would be stored in the vault until the parade. Sheriff Gaw drifted off to watch the transfer, and as the wheels went rumbling away Lucille said half wistfully,

"After tomorrow I'll probably never again see anything like this."

The opening had been bound to arise sooner or later, and during the last yards of the buggy ride Johnny had determined to seize it. All at once dry-throated, he blurted out,

"You will if you marry me and stay here."

She stood absolutely still.

The silence panicked him. "You must have guessed . . ."

Still she did not speak. For all he could tell she was admiring one of the buttons on his shirt.

"Are you sore?"

"Oh Johnny!" Her eyes lifted.

"Then—"

"No. I can't."

Now it was he who ran a hand back and forth across one of the bars. "You mean you won't."

"I can't."

"Why?"

She dropped her eyes, not answering.

"If you think you can't ever love me," he stammered miserably.
"Johnny, don't."
"I love you." There, it was out, and not as difficult as he had feared
it would be. He regarded her in amazement. "I don't know why I
couldn't get up nerve enough to say that before. Or even to kiss you."
· Her eyes stayed fixed on his button. He plunged on, "This is a
poor place, I guess. It slipped, kind of—proposing I mean." His neigh
of embarrassment sounded ludicrous in his own ears. "Oh damn. I mean,
if you'll let me ask you later, in a better place."
"It wouldn't be fair, John. I can't."
Despair touched him. "You seemed to like it here. I know it's a crude
town in some ways, like Nora says. But—"
She shook her head, gesturing in place of words, and he saw the
shine of tears in her eyes.
"Lucy—"
"No, John."
"Why?"
"You're just starting. I know the struggle you're having for money."
"Is it because of . . . Hedstrom?"
"You know it's not."
"Then—"
"You shouldn't be burdened now with another man's son."
In the silence he heard Sheriff Gaw say something that made the
silver carter laugh. He drew a deep breath. "Maybe I'm the one to
judge about that."
"No." She shook her head. Her cheeks were stark. "No." In a whisper
he could scarcely hear she said, "I have to be fair to Lennie, too."
"I get along with kids. We'll learn to know each other."
"John, no!"
"But—"
"Don't harass me so!"
Harass? Then he heard the returning rumble of the dolly's wheels.
He had to vanish somewhere, hide. The buggy? That long, empty
distance back up the road into town? He couldn't, yet. As he stood
drained and helpless, he felt her fingers slip inside his arm. "We'd better
go after the others," she said and in silence they fled from the carter
into the dusky, noisy, cavernous upper floor of the plant.

"4"

Forlornly they passed through the storage rooms where ore from different mines was stored in separate bins, passed the sampling heaps, and walked into a din so intense that they blessedly did not need even to try to talk. Iron-jawed crushers were pulverizing gray ore from the high country with thunderous vibrations. The red-shirted workers feeding the machines looked curiously at the belated sightseers. They fled on. A dusty, sooty stairway took them below the crushers, amid a fretwork of beams and pipes, into a room full of boilers and brick-and-iron furnaces. Here they overtook the others. Roscoe Blair was so excited about showing off his plant that he stripped off his good coat and shirt, revealing sweaty gray long underwear, and himself threw open a furnace door. "There!" he cried.

An incandescent mass pulsed redly. Lucille peeked obediently in her turn, her white cheeks lighting like cherries in the glow. Trying to make her smile, John said, "It's like a great big stomach ache." She glanced at him wanly and responded, "Argent is supposed to be the town without a . . . stomach ache." Neither of them laughed.

Roscoe prodded the mass with an iron lance. Yellow, green, and blue flames blossomed angrily. Roscoe grinned like a magician and slammed the door with a ringing clang. "Watch!" He opened the slag spout. Red metal gushed with a fury of sparks into a conical iron vessel held on four legs. When the container was full, a man rushed up with an iron cart, grappled the slag pot, and wheeled it glowing and fuming out to the dump.

"Where is the silver?" Lucille asked, though she did not seem really to care.

Johnny pointed at what he called a well, located some distance beneath the slag spout. "The silver and lead ooze down into it out of the slag. It's ladled out into those iron molds yonder. I guess there isn't enough stored in the well yet for Roscoe to give us a demonstration of the ladling."

The visitors trooped back to the stairway. Roscoe put his coat on over his underwear, wiped the perspiration off his bald head with his shirt, and draped the garment over his arm. As Johnny and Lucille tagged after the others, he checked them.

"Spare a minute, John?" He ignored Johnny's grimace. He did not even hesitate over Lucille's being within hearing; people were as used as that to seeing the two of them together. "Did you hear Quine's talk?"

"Part of it."

"About how smelting ore from Red Mountain will go through Baker because there's coal nearby, down the canyon at Montezuma?"

"Look, Roscoe. I'm—"

"I've sunk five hundred dollars in that road of yours."

"You'll get it back."

"I don't want dividends ten years from now. I want ore down here at my works—not over in Baker."

"Don't let Quine worry you. The haul down the gorge will be a sight easier and shorter than over the pass to Baker. The ore will come this way."

"But the coal, man! Jesus H. Christ—begging your pardon, miss." Roscoe bounded to a bin and picked up a black lump. "Do you know what I pay now to get a ton of this in here? Now, here's what I figure. There must be coal somewhere as close to us as Montezuma is to Baker. Down on the reservation maybe. Did you ever hear the Utes talking about black stuff that might be coal?"

"No."

"Well, probably they wouldn't notice it, not using it. But there must be some. There's a lot of country off there that not even the trappers know about. What I figure is this. While you're talking to Otto Winkler about your road, maybe you could suggest—"

"What makes you think I'll be talking to Winkler?"

"Down at Ben Emmett's last weekend Pat was kind of complaining about how you maybe planned to snuggle up to the old boy."

"Complaining?"

"No affair of mine, of course," Roscoe said hastily. "All I started to say is this. Why don't you and me and Otto Winkler, and Pat too if he likes—why don't we set up a prospecting syndicate? As soon as the Indians are gone we'll send some fellers down to look for coal."

"You know I'd like to help. But with the road taking all my time and cash—"

"Cheap coal for our smelters will bring more ore over the road. You ought to be interested in that. Otto, too, if he buys a piece of your company."

Johnny grew exasperated. "Building a grade smooth enough and easy enough so that our freighters can undercut the rates to Baker is what will bring traffic."

"Road! Road! You talk like it was a cure-all or something. But it ain't going to find coal for us. Jesus H.—pardon—be reasonable, John."

"What you mean is that you want Otto to find the coal for you, or at least pay for the search."

"He can afford it," Roscoe said. "I can't."

"The way to make Winkler listen is to talk direct, not go pussy-footing around him."

"I dropped some hints while I had him down here."

"And now you're trying to pry me into making a few more."

Roscoe hung his head. But he was not abashed. "We've got to have cheap coal," he insisted. "Not just me—the whole town."

"The price will go down when the railroad comes in next summer."

"Not as much as if we had our own source close by. We can't keep chopping down trees to make charcoal forever."

"Sure, sure," Johnny said. Everybody in Argent had talked about the problem off and on, since there had been a town. Everybody believed, too, that coal beds existed on the reservation, although Roscoe Blair was the first person to try scheming a way to locate it at outside expense. That was fair enough; foreign capital was going to have to underwrite lots of these expensive jobs, at least for a while. Johnny's objection was not to the theory but to Roscoe's crude implementation of it—and to the timing. At that moment, John did not want to listen to another word about coal. Neither did Lucille, standing abstractly a little distance, waiting for them to finish.

To escape from Roscoe, John said, "I'll talk to Otto, but—"

"That's great, John, great. I knew you would. Now, look. You tell him—"

"If I can catch him outside," John said desperately, "I'll offer him a ride into town in my buggy. That'll give us a chance for a nice private talk."

He felt Lucille's eyes turn on him: *You want Otto Winkler with us?* But Otto would not be as unendurable as the memory of the rejection, huge between them in the lonesome buggy seat.

Shaking loose from Roscoe, he hurried her up the stairs—too late. Winkler and Fred Fossett had already mounted their saddle horses and were jogging toward town. The empty buggy gaped at Johnny like a well. Morosely he helped her into it. Neither of them spoke a word until they came abreast of the blacksmith shop at the lower end of Main Street. There, in spite of himself, Johnny drew rein.

"See that plowshare leaning against the wall with the drill steel, both of them waiting to be sharpened? And the picks and the hoes together?" He gave a rueful smile. "Talk about hinting! I showed those things to Fred Fossett just this morning, hoping he'd point them out to Otto Winkler. There's not another place in Colorado like this, farms and mines lying side by side. And our road linking them. Baker, pah! You couldn't grow a potato in those rock piles for all the silver under Red Mountain." He looked at her miserably. "Argent is a good town, Lucille."

"Of course it is, Johnny."

But she was turning her back on it. He said stubbornly, "Roscoe is probably right. There probably is coal somewhere down on the reservation, closer to us than the Montezuma fields are to Baker."

Believe what you want to believe. The faith that already was moving these mountains. Could it also discover coal? Or repair a life? She kept her eyes on her hands. "Perhaps we had better go," she said.

He flapped the reins against the horse's back. "What I was thinking," he began, so tentatively that she sensed that the idea had just that instant touched his mind, "is that we can enlarge the float for tomorrow. We can rustle up a trailer and take off the sides and put the silver back there for you and Nora to stand beside. Up front we can put a farm scene—a blacksmith's forge and some bales of hay and a cow maybe and Mabel or some girl with a milk bucket. We'll run streamers from the front wagon to the trailer—you know, connecting them up, farms and mines, the way our road will. Our company sign can stretch clear across both wagons and—well what do you think?"

The Argent solution: Make it bigger and it will be better. Johnny had absorbed the spirit with his breathing, until his own answer to any hurt was this road, dreaming it bigger and wrapping it around him like a shield. Don't fight yourself so hard, she thought. She said, "I think the float is perfect now."

"I want to be sure you win. A good-bye present."

She attempted to tease him back to lightness. "Good Riddance Day?"

He was offended. "You know better." He stared at the reins. "If you'd rather, Pat or somebody can drive the float tomorrow and take you to the dance after the dinner. And then he can ride over to Baker with you and Tommy Brice on Sunday."

"Is that what you want?"

"No."

"There's a good-bye present I'd like even better than the prize."

"What?"

"To have the next two days go exactly as we planned."

"Honest?"

"Cross my heart."

He would not let go. "I can't promise not to . . . harass you."

"That isn't the way we planned." She moved across the seat and tucked her hand inside his arm again. She owed him this much, at least. "Please, Johnny. My good-bye present."

He drew a deep, unhappy breath. "I'll try," he agreed without much conviction.

"5"

That same evening Pat Edgell came down from his construction camp at the head of the gorge to talk over the lines he and Johnny should follow in the coming interview with Otto Winkler. Disheartened and unhappy, John would have preferred postponing matters until after the weekend, but Pat was honed as sharp as a razor over a new batch of plans. Nothing would do but that they go to the corner room of the Dixon House that he lavishly rented for himself each time he visited town, and launch into what became for John an interminable and disturbing talkfest.

They were agreed on one thing only: they had undertaken a far more ambitious construction project than they could complete without additional help. The gorge was scarcely scratched, and they were already out of money. They had exhausted Roscoe Blair's five hundred dollars; they owed Walt Kennerly for packing supplies; purchase offers for the unsold stock in their road company's treasury were too low to meet the problem; and Fred Fossett had hinted strongly the other day that they had borrowed as much on their personal signatures as they could expect. Johnny had sold his mules and was living in Walt's lean-to shack at the livery stable. Except for splurges in town, Pat was living in a tent. Each was working, according to his own fashion, nearly every daylight hour.

Some time ago Pat had suggested that they double the capitalization of the company, thereby doubling the amount of stock available for sale. Johnny concurred that far. Where they separated was in methods of selling the new stock while they were still unable to get rid of the old, inadequate issue. It was Johnny's hope that Red Mountain's headlong boom would persuade Otto Winkler that the deal at last "iss ripe" and that in spite of his earlier refusal to invest Otto would now subscribe to a large block of the new issue. His backing and the increased showing in the gorge which the new funds would make possible should then attract other subscribers at increased prices.

Pat opposed the plan vehemently. As he talked and talked, his shallow eyes glinted like glass in the lamplight. For emphasis he would sometimes slap the table edge with his fingers; at other times he moved his empty shot glass across its varnished top with quick little jerks. Like Parley Quine, he wore a broadcloth shirt and tight-fitting striped trousers tucked into black, laceless boots. He was not alone in his mimicry. Half of the people on Red Mountain dressed as Quine dressed, talked the way Quine talked, hoped to work for themselves a silver miracle like the one Quine had worked. Pat even cultivated his tone of voice:

"Sure I tried to sell the little Jew last winter. But now we've out-grown him and he's lost his chance. I wouldn't even give him a smile now." As he talked, Pat squirmed in his chair, thrust out his legs and fiddled with the coins in his trouser pockets, sat up again and poured himself another drink. "Hell, you know as well as I do how that kike son of a bitch operates. If he thinks he's got us over a barrel he'll try to take control. Damned if I'll let him, I don't care how soft you talk just because he was your great white father or something when you were a kid. This is big—and it's ours!"

He was as full of schemes for keeping it theirs as a sheep was of ticks. His first step would be to form a town at the foot of a certain hillock near the pass to Baker. A rich new mine, the Summit Queen, had just been struck half way up the hillside. Before the news of the strike had passed out of the conjecture stage, Pat had ridden and walked and waded to the scene. On the small flat below the mine, working in slush and snow, he had staked out lots for a new town. "But it's not a fit place for a town," Johnny demurred. "It's in the middle of a bog." Pat waved airily, "Drain it." As soon as the snow disappeared, speculators would come in a rush, eager to buy property they could sell on a rising market to later arrivals. That was the history of booms, wasn't it? His flat, intense face broke into a wide grin. Remember the Jim Crow!

The allusion was to a promoter who a few weeks earlier had journeyed to Boston to sell stock in two or three of Red Mountain's more prom-ising claims. He had succeeded so well that he had also incorporated for himself a company that possessed no holdings whatsoever and shortly thereafter had wired triumphantly to friends in Argent, "Have just sold two-thirds interest in Jim Crow Mine. Please send someone out to locate it." In common with the rest of Argent Johnny had laughed in delight. Eastern suckers were fair game. But his road was no Jim Crow.

He shook his head, completely unconvinced. "We're not in the town-company business. We ought to be spending our time on the road."

"Forget that road for five minutes, will you?" Pat said impatiently.

"That's what we're here to talk about, isn't it?"

Pat gave a monumental sigh. "God, you're green. It isn't the fellow who grubs in the dirt who makes the big money; it's the fellow who swings the propositions. And believe me, we've got one—if you'll just let me play it right."

The words stirred echoes: early morning in a tent on the road construction job out of San Cristobal to Baker. Pat sour-breathed and grinning over a handful of stock certificates picturing steamboats loaded with silver ore plying Los Padres River, where no steamboat could possibly navigate. *Sure, it's a fake. Brighter'n a button, too . . . What we need is a proposition of our own.* And now he had it.

Johnny wandered to the window fronting the main street and looked across toward the bank building. No sign of life showed around Lucille's shop. Probably she was in the Bon-Ton, eating her usual late supper with Nora and Mabel. While his mind pictured her there, his ears kept hearing Pat's voice hammering away at him.

Here was the way to make money out of the road. First they would set up a new construction company called the Ute Gorge Contracting Corporation. The Red Mountain Toll Road and Transportation Company would execute with this new corporation a construction contract for building the way through the gorge, paying for the job with a major portion of the new stock to be obtained through the new capitalization. "There'll be a commission on the transfer, too," he said with a broad grin. As a representative of the construction company, he would then travel East to turn the stock into cash for operating funds—still another commission for himself and Johnny.

Johnny turned around from the window. Why not sell the stock directly to Otto Winkler and settle down to work without so much fuss?

"He'll want discounts and favors," Pat said. "He'll cut us out of the commissions."

"What makes you so sure you can do any better back East?"

"Red Mountain is hot stuff on the mining exchanges. We'll make it look even hotter." Pat waved his hand in an arc like a rainbow. This was what he liked: selling a bill of goods. Here's how it would work. To prove to potential investors that the Red Mountain Toll Road and Transportation Company was already in business, the construction company would run a highway from the meadows at the head of the gorge to Red Mountain City and from there on up another three miles to Summit City. That section would be cheap and easy to build—not like cliff-hanging in the gorge—and would give their stock prospectus a real talking point: three miles of graded highway through the heart of the mineralized country, connecting the proven area of Red Mountain's first big strike with that of its most recent find.

"If you build that section first," Johnny said, "it'll be another year before we can put wheels through the gorge."

"What of it? Red Mountain has made out so far on trails."

"The Baker people are building toward the pass right now. You'll be playing into their hands. At Summit they'll hook onto a road we build for them and suck the Red Mountain ore out their way."

"We'll collect tolls on our stretch."

"Argent needs the ore."

"Oh, for Christ sake! Who are we building this road for, Argent or us?" Pat glowered at Johnny, who had turned morosely back to the window. "What the hell is the matter with you? Did that girl turn you down or something?"

John felt as if a wedge was splitting apart his chest. "Yes," he blurted and wheeled around, eager, now that the fact was out, for the salve of words.

"That's too bad," Pat said and wagged his head. "But you can't let it spoil your whole outlook. Hell, you know as well as I do that it would be damn bad salesmanship to offer road stock in a highway company that so far has built only a scratch a few hundred yards long, dead-ending in a gorge. We've got to make this thing shine. That's where Summit City comes in."

Johnny returned to the window. Pat's voice went on breaking across his back. Holders of road stock would have first option on a certain choice block of lots to be reserved for them in the new town. A double lure, one speculation furthering the other. You couldn't ask for anything brighter than that, could you? They did not need Otto Winkler's help to put it over, either. If the sheeney so-and-so wanted a piece of the company, he could take his turn in line just like everyone else.

It seemed strange that Lucille had not emerged from the Bon-Ton. Perhaps she was not there. Perhaps she had been as tired as she'd said when he had let her out of the buggy in front of Mother Marsh's. Perhaps she was sitting in her room, thinking . . . what? That he and his road were the deadends that Pat said? Was that her reason?

He turned around, wishing the argument were over and that he could see her for just one word. But Pat sat between him and the door, drumming the table edge with his fingers and waiting for his partner's agreement. Johnny scrubbed his face with his palm. Maybe in the morning he could think better.

"Well?" Pat insisted. "How does it sound?"

"I don't like it," Johnny said.

Pat's shallow eyes turned as still and as hard as porcelain. "Now what?" he exploded.

Johnny dropped into a chair and stared at the floor. He knew that he couldn't make Pat understand, but somehow he had to try. "Do you remember that article in the Baker paper about our road? I read it first on my way back from Denver, over at the stage stop on the San Cristobal fork. The article that said that people building the road out of Argent were irresponsible."

"Newspaper shit. It doesn't amount to—"

"Ewer picked it up and wrote an editorial, practically challenging us to come out and say what the road is—whether it's a responsible deal or nothing but a promotion."

"I see," Pat said between his teeth. "The editorial said a lot of other things, too. It said that maybe Hedstrom was fed to the Indians so they would stay quiet and a war scare wouldn't hurt the sale of stock. But there wasn't even a company when Hedstrom was—whatever you want to call it. Ewer is the one who's irresponsible. He'll say anything to sell a paper."

"That's not all he said," Johnny muttered, still staring at the floor. There had been another editorial saying that Uncle Stupid, meaning the federal court, had taken Hedstrom's slayers away from Argent's jurisdiction and then had turned them loose on the grounds that it couldn't think of anything else to do, though any schoolboy in Argent could have offered a few practical suggestions.

Pat's palm slapped the table like a pistol shot. "We've been friends for a long time, Johnny. But by God sometimes you make my ass ring. What's Al Ewer to you that you're still spookin' away from him like a lost colt every time he opens his yap. That Hedstrom business is over and forgotten and it's time you grew a little backbone and forgot it yourself."

There was no use arguing. "All right, forget it," Johnny said. He felt drained and indifferent. Standing, he tucked in his shirttail preparatory to walking out. "Even so, we still don't see things the same way. You want a proposition. All I want is to build a road."

Pat leaned across the table, his index finger pointing like a pistol.

"You talk about remembering. Well, I remember when I owned a third of Argent. I let it get away from me—my own fault, sure. Now I've got the makings of another proposition that may be even bigger and by the Lord Harry this one won't get away. Don't you make the mistake of forgetting it either, when Winkler has you cornered up there in the gorge tomorrow and starts soft-soaping you like he was the second coming of Christ, letting himself be crucified all over again just for you."

"It's my road," Johnny said. "The charter is in my name."

"It's fifty-fifty."

"If you want to have a vote by stock—"

"You try overloading it with Otto Winkler and you're damn right we'll have a vote. I'll put both plans in front of what stockholders we have and they'll see quick enough which way will increase the value of their holdings the fastest. Christ, Johnny, grow up!"

They glared at each other, red-faced and angry. Johnny was the first to drop his eyes. Pat leaned back and hooked one elbow around an upright of his chair.

"You let things upset you too much, Johnny. But there's more skirts than one in the world. And more bankers than Winkler and his errand boy Fossett. We'll make out if you'll just relax and use your head." He smiled but his procelain eyes stayed as hard as ever. Gently he warned, "I'll be there tomorrow to see that you do, too."

"6"

Sure enough, out he ambled from the Dixon House when John arrived to pick up Winkler in a spring wagon rattling with a score or so assorted lengths of freshly sharpened drill steel, some loose planks, a wheelbarrow, and two kegs of blasting powder. He climbed into the seat. To divert Johnny from resuming their argument about the road, he began chattering about the parade that afternoon, and the best way of securing the silver ingots, which could not be placed until the last minute. Johnny played along. They were deep in talk when Fossett and Otto Winkler joined them.

"Morning, poys." Otto's black eyes were amiably paternal as he greeted the two young men, former employees who were now striking out on their own and needed, as he supposed, a helping hand. Obviously he expected deference. "Vell now, hvat great t'ing do ve zee?"

Johnny jumped down to help him into the wagon. Pat, however, gave the transportation king of the St. Johns no more than a bare nod and stayed on the seat. Since Johnny needed the other half of the seat for driving, the calculated rudeness forced Winkler not to join them after all or else rattle along in the wagon bed with the supplies. He decided to go. Waving Fossett's little grunts of protest silent, he ascended awkwardly to a jouncing seat on the planks. Fossett followed less amiably, with open glares at Pat, who looked blandly back and grinned and chewed on a matchstick.

The two did not relish each other. Fred Fossett was a vain little man who found his chief satisfaction in making people think he controlled private channels of approach to important business figures. He had begun his mountain career as Otto Winkler's paymaster, journeying by buggy to the different construction camps with small kegs of gold and silver coins. He lived in terror of holdups. But he had never forsaken his duty, even taking the kegs and his pistol to bed with him when he felt that other security was inadequate. Rumor said that he had personally gone to Denver for the cash necessary to open the Argent bank, and put the currency into a half-ton iron safe and the safe into a baggage car, where he had insisted on riding with it. At South Arkansas he had wormed his iron monster into a crowded wagon train by promising to help chop wood, wash dishes, and curry horses—him a pink-handed bank president! But he had brought the safe to Argent without losing a dime—"Or spending one," Pat had sneered.

Their enmity dated from a practical joke during the construction of the road from San Cristobal to Baker. Exhausted by bucking his way through an early snowstorm, Fred had been dozing in his damp clothes beside the stove in the boardinghouse. Stooping as quietly as a mole, Pat had loosened the paymaster's bootlaces and then tied them to the chair legs. Stepping back, he bawled "Fire!" Fred jumped up, dazed, and started to run. He fell flat, the chair thumping him across the hips while twenty men guffawed. One cannot be ridiculous and stay important. Though Fred had pretended to laugh with the others at the joke, resentment had bred lasting distaste. He was prepared to swallow it if necessary, however. His bank would handle any transaction that emerged from this inspection trip—his first really big piece of business. It was potentially so big, indeed, that he could not make out Pat's attitude and kept staring at him like an affronted schoolmaster, trying to make him realize his place. All Pat did was laugh.

Angry and embarrassed, Johnny clucked the team up the street toward the gorge. The silence grew painful. To break it, he drew rein on reaching a fork in the road at the edge of town. Ahead of them, the Ute River slashed into the basin through a slit hundreds of feet deep but only a score or so wide. The road that forked to the right bridged this chasm and then laboriously climbed the slope between the river and a deep side canyon in a series of sharp zigzags.

The left-hand fork of the road swung far away from the slit in a long, slow curve. No side canyon hemmed it in and it gained altitude on an easy grade that lifted it only half as high, in a comparable distance, as the other fork. But a quick gaining of altitude was not the main consideration.

"That right-hand road," Johnny said over his shoulder to Winkler, "goes as far as the Mineral Patch Mine, yonder on a bench out of sight. The rest of the way to Red Mountain is by high trail above the cliffs. It's the shortest route, but not the best one." There was no need explaining road theory and economics to Otto Winkler, but Johnny was so nervous that he kept on chattering in spite of himself. "When a freight team goes around an elbow, like those zigs on the Mineral Patch road, the trace chains go slack and only the wheel horses are pulling. A big outfit can't make it except with a pusher." He meant a heavy pole extended behind the wagon, to either side of which horses were attached with a special harness so that motive power could be supplied from the rear. "That kind of freighting is awkward and slow, and what do you do with the pusher when you're coming back down? We decided that in the long run it would be best to start a brand-new grade where teams could have a straight-away pull the whole distance."

"That's why we went to the left," Pat said, to keep in the picture.

"We?" Fossett said with prim sarcasm. "As I recall it, Edgell's original plan, before Johnny returned, was to use the Mineral Point grade as far as possible."

"That," Pat said coolly, "was in the winter before things opened up, when we thought we might have trouble raising money."

"You're not having any trouble now?"

"Not so much that we have to beg for it, no."

Winkler's eyebrows went up. John said hastily, after a murderous glance at Pat, "What he means is that we don't want to compromise, just for money. We want to do the job right the first time. A smooth grade means that even in this gorge we can hold ton-mile costs below anything Baker can match, because they'll have to lift their freight over the pass. That means that practically all of the Red Mountain business will come to Argent."

He thought of the coal at Montezuma as he said it, but decided against mentioning Roscoe Blair's idea of a prospecting syndicate. Mere hopes of coal and smelters would not impress Otto Winkler. He never counted his chickens before he could at least hear them pecking inside the shell, and right now the chief problem was to prove to him that the road was feasible on the strength of what already existed.

"Vell," Otto said, "ve zee," and waved him on.

The two gray horses took the hill at a swinging walk that brought out scarcely enough perspiration to darken the hair on their necks. They reached a bench and followed it toward the crowding cliffs. The steepening slopes forced them closer and closer to the drop-off into the canyon bottom. Presently a rib of granite vaulting upward toward the peaktops blocked their way. On the last possible flat spot, trees had been cut away to make room for a few tents, a cookshack, a forge covered with a canvas fly, and a corral. Here Johnny stopped. The rest of the way around the rib they would have to cover on foot.

Masons were shaping stones to use in a retaining wall somewhere ahead. While Otto paused to watch them, Fossett whispered in Johnny's ear, "What's the matter with Pat? He acts almost as if he doesn't care whether Otto comes in or not."

"He's just feeling his oats. Don't worry. I'll handle him."

"I hope so. You know how Otto is. Sometimes he forms prejudices. I've seen it spoil deals before."

Without waiting to be guided, Winkler walked on, his bearded head riding forward on his neck, his hands clasped characteristically behind him. The way dwindled to uneven knobs, the spaces between filled with gray rock fragments that smelled still of powdersmoke. Planks had been laid on these rough foundations to make smooth pushing for men bringing up wheelbarrow loads of stone for more masonry. On the outside of the path a safety rope had been stretched between iron pegs set into the rock. Beyond the fragile barrier was a drop of three hundred feet or more. On the inside, the cliff rose enormously. As Winkler strode along, rock chips came rattling down ahead of him.

"Hold it a minute!" Johnny called up to three workers suspended in bosun's chairs fifty or sixty feet over the roadway, and preparing blasting holes by swinging short-handled sledge hammers against pieces of drill steel. Otto eyed the festoon of ropes draped down from the precarious ledge that gave them access to their work and then estimated the amount of rock they would have to cut away in order to achieve a roadbed wide enough for ore wagons.

"Ummm," he said and moved forward on the narrowing path. Curving like the center hoop of a gigantic hogshead, it brought them abruptly to a natural platform hardly large enough to hold the four of them as well as the great heap of building stones being carried up in the barrows. Otto stopped dead. "Himmel!" he grunted.

A tributary stream plunged down a side canyon behind the rib. The band of strata on which the men stood extended like a sill to meet its glassy slide. When the stream hit this flat lip, it shot forward into space as if intending to hurl itself hissing across the canyon. Air currents annihilated it. Shattered and diffused, the water dropped in wind-eddied gossamers to the Ute River far below.

Cautiously Winkler advanced to the edge and peered down. A jumble of house-sized boulders fretted the river in its narrow bed, rousing it to a thunder that swelled and faded in their ears according to the drift of the wind. Obviously there was no way to build a road down there. Slowly Winkler let his eyes rise up the opposite wall. Its steep sides, nearly a mile deep were an alternation of furrowed, exfoliating cliff and talus slopes where forests mauled by old avalanches clutched for a hold. Above the cliffs, almost at timberline, where the slope started to level back to the rounded ridgetop they saw a single file of moving dots. The Red Mountain trail ran there, above the cliffs, and evidently several riders were traveling down it to town for the parade and dance.

Johnny tried to gauge from Winkler's face what he was thinking. "If we built the road over there," he admitted, "we could avoid a lot of blasting. But freighters would have to fight the zigzags to get up there. In winter snow would pack in the cuts harder than iron. Worst of all, if we ever want to run a branch road up the left side of Ute Peak yonder—if mines get going in the basins on the back side or if we decide to hook onto the San Cristobal road—then we'll have to drop clear into the canyon, cross, and climb again. This way we're on the proper side to begin with."

Otto looked up the gorge. No road was possible in its bottom and one along the top would be uneconomical. So John Ogden had decided to hang one in the middle, along the cliffs.

"Himmel!" he grunted again.

"It'll go!" Johnny insisted. He squirmed on the balls of his feet in his excitement. For the moment at least this was his dream, his baby, and he wanted them to see it as he saw it. "We'll build up rock abutments from this platform here to the top of the falls and then go across on a log A-frame bridge." He eyed Otto anxiously as he elaborated on the engineering involved. Decisions about how far to cut back into cliffs and how far out to extend masonry involved nice problems in road alignment and economics. John had fretted a long time over this critical stretch and he hoped Otto approved. But the man just stood there watching, his moist thick lips working in and out behind his whiskers. The bridge over tributary Wolf Creek was just the start. Otto would want to see it all. Yard by yard Johnny moved their scrutiny ahead, showing exactly where the grade would go, admitting the full number of ribs that would have to be cut through and to what height, pointing out the ragged spot where the canyon to the left of the peak would have to be bridged, and then showing how the grade would tiptoe around the front of Ute Peak to the meadows at the head of Red Mountain Creek. "It looks hairy, but I know it'll go," he insisted again. "I've had a transit on the whole route and there's not a pull anywhere more than eleven per cent."

"Ummm," Winkler said.

"Anything up to twelve per cent is safe," Fred Fossett said, to prove he knew road problems, too. "Above twelve it's cheaper to use pack trains." He took off his spectacles and wiped away the mist that had blown onto them. The nose clips of the glasses had left small red indentations in his sallow skin. "Quite a sight, isn't it, Otto? I even memorized what Al Ewer wrote about it after he'd come up here. 'The entrance of Wolf Creek'—this side canyon is called Wolf Creek —'the entrance of Wolf Creek into Ute Canyon is the greatest combination of wild, yawning chasms, mighty towering cliffs, merciless, grinding waters, with gentle, misty sprays, great chaste, spreading bridal veils, variegated rainbows and ghostlike spray domes that has ever been discovered on this continent, if not in the world.'"

Johnny grumbled, "Ewer always talks too much."

Fossett kept wiping at his glasses. "I'm not sure he is this time. A sight like this could develop into quite a tourist attraction." He glowered at Pat, who was smiling. "You needn't laugh. As soon as the railroad reaches us next summer, tourists are going to start coming into these mountains. They could make an appreciable difference in the tolls the company collects."

"Stagecoaches, ore wagons, tours—we'll be able to handle them all," Johnny said.

And still Winkler gave no inkling of what was going through his mind. Wheeling abruptly, he walked back along the pathway to the gentler side of the rib. There he paused and looked up at the highscalers.

"Hvat wages you bay dem?"

"Three-fifty a day," Johnny said and rushed on before Otto could go ummm again. "I know, ordinary stiffs got only two dollars a day over on the San Cristobal job. But Red Mountain wasn't competing for labor then. And these aren't ordinary drillers. They're the fastest we can get. They could be pulling down three dollars for a ten-hour shift at the Ram. Good men just won't hang over these cliffs all day long for less than three-fifty."

"The masons?" Otto asked.

"Three."

"Muckers?"

"Two-fifty."

"Ummm." Otto's lower lip protruded redly as he added up what he had seen. "Forty t'ousand dollars you vill t'row in that gorge."

"About," Johnny admitted. "But there's no other way to do the job right."

"Plus," Pat said, "another five thousand for building, this summer, from Red Mountain City to Summit City."

Otto's eyebrows lifted again. "Summit City. Hvat iss?"

"A bog hole," Fossett interposed.

"It's the only flat ground next to what looks like a bigger strike than either the Ram or the Dixie Girl," Pat countered. He looked straight at Winkler, his shallow eyes glinting. "We're forming a town company up there. Holders of road stock will have the privilege of first pick of the building lots."

"Privilege?" Fossett sniffed.

"You don't have to buy the lots if you don't want. We figure most people will. There's going to be a humdinger of a rush up there this summer. Property is bound to jump in value for those that get in quick."

"Speculative," Fossett grunted.

"Anything wrong with that?"

"Ummm," Otto said and climbed ahead of Pat into the wagon seat. Pat grinned at him. "Want to ride horseback on up the gorge to my end of the job tomorrow? You can see Summit City, too, if you don't mind a little hike."

"Enough I zee," Otto said and it was the last word they got out of him as they returned him to the Dixon House.

After they had left him, John jerked the horses toward the livery. "You sure cooked that deal up brown," he said furiously to Pat.

Pat sitting now in the seat Otto had vacated, hugged one knee in satisfaction. "If you mean I let the great Winkler know he'll have to pay a fair price for a share of the best proposition on Red Mountain, I sure as hell did. Relax, Johnny! The day will come when you'll thank me for this favor."

"You may have scared Otto clear off."

"Oh, no. This is just his act to jew us down. Don't fall for it. That stock will sell like hot cakes back East, whether he comes in or stays out." Pat's face grew animated with still another idea. "I tell you what. We'll have the new photographer take some pictures of the girls in their princess duds standing on the float next to that pile of silver bars. We'll use copies of the best picture in our prospectus. I'll warrant that one photograph, plus figures about the mines printed up in a neat pamphlet, will sell more stock than Otto Winkler will ever buy, at twice the figure he offers."

"Maybe," Johnny said. Pat sounded plausible, as he always did, but behind the flow of words Johnny kept hearing the phrase "steamboats on Los Padres." Well, Pat had twisted the initiative out of Johnny's hands and now the next move in the dickering was up to Otto. Meanwhile, the idea of photographing the float intrigued him. Lucille's picture helping tell the whole country about Red Mountain! He wished he'd thought of it. You had to hand it to Pat for one thing; he was never at a loss for ideas.

"7"

They worked like beavers putting the finishing touches on the float and in the shared concentration they forgot some of their animosity. The afternoon before, Johnny had tilted a slab of granite against the back of the driver's seat and had mounted a Burleigh rock-boring machine on its metal column with the drill steel pointing against the slab. From the smelter he had borrowed the tree-trunk pedestal that had supported the pigs at Roscoe Blair's ceremony. He had painted it red as symbolic of the mountain and had inserted a crowbar painted silver. They fetched the silver bars from the bank vault and piled them around the bar, wiring each one for additional stability. They then lined the wagon with evergreens and covered the harness tugs with white bunting. They painted the horses' feet silver, put bells on their collars, red rosettes and pompons on the headstalls of their bridles. A banner stretched out the length of the wagon read "The Silver Queens. Red Mountain Toll Road and Transportation Company."

The lunch hour passed unnoticed as they worked. As parade time drew near, the two Cornishmen showed up in their outlandish clothes, both of them half drunk. After considerable difficulty, Johnny got them planted behind the silver tower, one holding a pick and the other a mucker's blunt shovel. Then they drove to Mother Marsh's boardinghouse to pick up the girls.

While Pat rode herd on the Cousin Jacks, Johnny pushed through the low picket gate, hurried past the scraggly lawn with its border of enormous, velvety pansies and, after the most peremptory of knocks, entered the parlor. Mother Marsh greeted him with a wan smile. She was a gray, flat-chested widow who coughed a great deal. After her husband's death in an avalanche she had sold his claims for enough to purchase this building. Johnny felt fortunate in having been able to secure a room here for Lucille. Mother Marsh was very strict. Women, mostly wives waiting for their husbands to come down from the high basins, stayed safely in her downstairs bedrooms. Bachelor clerks and junior engineers, if sufficiently recommended, could occupy the floor above, which they reached by an outside staircase. She did not serve meals. She had enough to do, she said, to tidy the place every day. "I keep a clean establishment," she stated on all occasions and generally added, "There's no excuse for bedbugs. Just mix blue ointment and kerosene in equal parts and wipe it on the bedsteads. That's all it takes—blue ointment and kerosene."

On Johnny's approach she said, "Oh, it's you. Oh, I hope it doesn't rain. You must take something warm for them to wrap in. Those costumes, I declare! Oh, girls!" She pattered down the hallways. "Oh, Mrs. Montgomery! He's here!"

The two of them came self-consciously into the parlor. "Wow!" he said. The severe, simple tunics they wore fell in soft straight folds almost to the floor; other folds belted them and crisscrossed on their fronts, lifting and subtly emphasizing their breasts. They had coiled their hair on top of their heads. The down at the nape of Lucille's neck, which he had never noticed before, gave her an unexpected look of intimacy, so that Johnny just swallowed and stared until she blushed and Nora snapped brusquely,

"Is there a parade or is the show in here?"

Flustered, Johnny gestured them ahead of him outside. The Cornishmen whooped and waved their tools. Pat beamed and even Nora exclaimed over the float. Then she glanced at the dark clouds leaning across the edge of the mountains. "Wouldn't you know?" she said in dismay.

The usual afternoon shower: you had to expect one this time of year. "It won't amount to much," Johnny said. "We ought to beat it back, anyway."

But of course there were delays. It took time for the photographer to set his camera on its tripod, stiffly pose his subjects, pop his head under the black cloth cover of his machine for a look through the cyclops lens, pop out to scold the Cornishmen for hamming, count one-two-three and squeeze his rubber ball, and then pop his black plates into the covered cart, labeled "Views," for the first of the mysteries that would reproduce the frozen look of this moment forever more.

Meanwhile the parade was slowly assembling. First rode Gaw and his deputies. After them marched the band in their new red coats, followed by two buggies pulled in single file by matched pairs, one for the mayor and Otto Winkler, the other for Fred Fossett and the chairman of the county board of supervisors. Behind the buggies marched the volunteer fire department in shiny black helmets, red shirts, white belts, and dark trousers, pulling their new engine by means of long ropes masked behind red and white bunting. Hotchkiss's Department Store had rounded up nearly every little girl in town, had dressed them as angels—no bellyaches—and had put them, their wings rapidly becoming bedraggled, on a flat-bed hayrick. Next in the line was Pat and Johnny's float, its eight big horses carrying themselves with the dignity that flows from strength and breeding. Behind them came the Argent Guards.

The Guards had expended considerable ingenuity on their offering. The saw blade was mounted in the middle of the wagon. The front end of the float was the facsimile of a log cabin. The rear end was a thicket of bushes. Two "Indians" thrust their heads up out of the cover, brandishing tomahawks. A watcher struck the blade in warning. Out of the cabin jumped a militiaman holding an enormous ten-gauge shotgun. In panic the Indians ducked back out of sight. Each few hundred yards the tableau was repeated.

"I hope they don't shoot that blunderbuss in the middle of things," Johnny muttered to Pat.

"They will," Pat said. "Didn't you hear them practicing this morning?"

In a series of jerks, stretching and compressing like an accordion, Argent's first parade crept up the street. Puffs of wind from the approaching storm blew dust around the legs of the tootling bandsmen and flattened the flimsy dresses of the Silver Queens to their legs, to the noisy delight of the onlookers. The saw blade clanged. Crowds of small boys ran beside and behind the different units. The streets were crowded. Many of the mines had closed so that the workers could come down for the celebration. Farmers and soldiers were up from the low country. Their applause and shouts and comments made Johnny envious. They liked his and Pat's float fine. But they liked the Guards' entry better.

The idea was for the parade to travel the full length of Main Street to the town's upper end, make a tight turn, and come back to the Dixon House, where the judges occupied a flag-draped section of the verandah. After the judging, the results of which would be announced at the dance, the honored guests would dismount and the parade would disband. The spectators naturally clotted most thickly on both sides of the street near the judges' section. As the Guards came abreast of the throng on their way up the street, the Indians made another attack. This time the militiaman, braced from behind by two companions, pulled the trigger of his oversized gun. It had been loaded with enough powder, Pat later declared, to blast out the entire rib of rock at Wolf Creek Falls, and had been wadded with at least seven issues of *The True Fissure*. It went off like the crack of doom. The shooter was knocked flat by the kick, the Indians jumped up in the air and fell down as if dead, spectators shouted, and every dog in town began to bay. A storm of newspaper shreds fluttered across the street, "The biggest circulation *The True Fissure* ever will have," Johnny said.

His horses, already excited by the crowds and the noise, began to plunge. Because they were going uphill he was able to control them, but he feared that if the gun roared again on the downgrade there might be trouble.

There was. As the parade completed its turn and began congesting in front of the Dixon House, he saw little possibility of maneuvering the float up beside the hotel. Furthermore, the thunderstorm was already bouncing premonitory rumbles back and forth between the upper cliffs. To save time he pulled up in front of the bank for the silver to be unloaded. Nora decided to leave for her restaurant. Pat lifted her down. "Come on up here," Johnny said and assisted Lucille into the seat beside him. And then, while the Cornishmen were struggling with the wires holding the silver pigs to the crowbar, the Guards again blasted the blunderbuss.

It went off almost in the ears of the lead team. They begun to run.

"Hang on!" Johnny whooped at the Cornishmen and sawed on the reins. He dared not let them pound down Main Street to almost inevitable collision with some of the vehicles beginning to move out into the thoroughfare. He swung for the corner. A gust of wind both aided and hindered him. By blowing dirt and straw and paper in front of the horses' faces it helped twist the runaways around the bend. But it also stretched them down Silver Avenue at a dead run.

The maw of the livery stable loomed across the end of the street. Afraid that the stampeders would bolt straight into it, John tried for another twist. He hit the brake as hard as he could, bawled "Gee! Gee!" although the horses probably did not hear or understand the command, and again hauled furiously on the reins. A Cornishman cried "Mother Mary!" and at the last possible second habit prevailed. The leaders swung around in a curve as tight as a pencil shaving. The wagon rocked after them with a groan of wood, hind wheels skidding sideways. It hit the elevated wooden sidewalk broadside on. Boards splintered. The rock drill and granite fell overboard. Just as the wagon itself was about to topple, the forward thrust of the horses restored its balance. It jerked toward the other side of the street, then was snapped straight again by the tugs.

This was Crib Street. A sporting house squatted on either corner. Stretching along the block were eight or ten log cubicles where the girls plied their trade, a single door and window opening into a tiny parlor and behind that a bedroom. Most of the occupants were out front in low-necked, knee-length, spangled black satin dresses, showing themselves to the men down from the mines. One had snatched the hat from a passer-by and was trying to stimulate trade by making him wrestle for it.

"I didn't have much choice," Johnny howled in apology to Lucille,

clinging ashen-faced to the seat beside him. He had no idea whether
she heard or, if she did, whether she knew what they were traversing.
Men whooped. Two dogs charged out barking at the wheels. The wagon
banged into a rut. The jolt was more than the shaken pile of silver
could adjust to. Pedestal and all toppled over the low sideboard. The
wires burst; silver pigs rolled heavily. One of the Cornishmen gave a
stricken cry. Jamming his plug hat down over his ears, he put both hands
on the tail gate and vaulted after his treasure. He tripped and tumbled
end over end. The hat stayed on and Johnny had a fleeting glimpse of
him wavering to his feet, apparently unhurt. The other, crouched on
his hams, clung in a paralysis of fear to the back of the seat.

A broad still pool of the river glimmered ahead. "We're hunky-
dory now!" Johnny cried. The approach to the ford was smooth. The
horses pounded down it full tilt. A sheet of spray flared over the footboard. In the deep water the horses had to slow. Clawing and splutter-
ing, he dragged them to a halt. Blinking his eyes clear, he looked at
Lucille, drenched and pale beside him. "Are you all right?"

She gave him a tremulous smile. At that moment a run of rain
hissed in a foam of white bubbles across the surface of the pool. Johnny
peeled off his coat and put it around Lucille's shoulders. Her dress was
soaked; wet hair lay plastered across one cheek. Her lips looked cool
and moist. Pulling her abruptly to him he kissed her so hard he could
feel the ridge of her teeth.

Behind them the remaining Cornishman said querulously, "Would
you mind too much getting out of here?"

"8"

After helping regather the silver and leaving Lucille at Mother Marsh's
to dress for the testimonial dinner, Johnny changed his own drenched
clothes and then walked disconsolately along the crowded sidewalks to
the Bon-Ton for a late supper. Nora had run out of food early, had
drawn her shades, and locked the door. When Johnny's knocking went
unheeded, he swung with the assurance of familiarity into the alley and
entered through the kitchen. Not many people remained in the dining
room, which suited his mood. Nora was relaxing briefly at the long
center table with her family, who had come up from the farm for the
dance: young Tommy and Mabel, Ira and his new wife, who wore a
shawl around her shoulders to hide how rusty her dress was. The Angel
Gabe was there, along with two or three regulars. Walt lounged in

his usual chair, and Harmon Gregg was on hand, too. Poor devil, Johnny thought. The lawyer was always hanging around, looking wistful; he had even turned down an invitation to the testimonial banquet on the excuse that the speeches would make him sleepy. Everyone knew his real reason, just as everyone understood that Nora was Walt's girl and would turn aside intrusions without rancor yet with complete efficiency. But maybe Harmon figured that there were no laws against looking and hoping.

Nora had expected Johnny and had saved him a plate. He sat down with it hungrily. In spite of his running feud with Nora he enjoyed the Bon-Ton. What made it different from the other eating places in town were the little home touches the proprietress offered her womenless clientele. Once when Johnny had commented admiringly on her extra pains she had retorted snippily, "I'd rather enjoy a few little things today than the big ones you talk about for tomorrow." Although laundry difficulties made her competitors content with oilcloth, she covered her long center table and the smaller side ones ranged along the walls with clean cotton cloths. Her tumblers and tableware had no water spots; her chairs did not wobble on their legs. The chimneys and the tin reflectors of the coal-oil lamps set in brackets on the walls were always polished. With Lucille's help she had put up net curtains at the windows. A parrot cage, covered with a cloth each evening, hung beside the glass; pots of geraniums and ivy plants stood along the sill.

She favored her regular clients, selling them meal tickets at a discount. Drunks she despised and would not serve. A chosen handful were allowed to sit around in the evenings after the dishes were cleared away to yarn or play cards or listen to the banjo one of them occasionally brought around. Sometimes Nora would play a hand of hearts or sew on a button for them. She learned their favorite dishes and tried, with considerable ingenuity, to produce them. Toward the tag end of winter when everyone was hungry for greens and none could be obtained, she had made herself the talk of the town by sprouting several pounds of beans in one of the hot springs. In gratitude for these touches, the men carried out the slops for her and Mabel, cut firewood, cleaned the soot out of the stove chimney, and even did dishes when the regular Mexican helper was recovering from one of his periodic hangovers.

As Johnny wolfed down his pot roast and boiled onions, the others joshed him about the runaway. While they talked they kept hearing the clang of the saw blade. The Guards had parked their float on the side street by the Dixon House; drunks and small boys were amusing themselves by pounding on the erstwhile alarm. Little Mabel Brice said indignantly, "I wish they'd stop that noise." She was almost four-

teen now and liked to be considered grown-up. She was wearing her
first party frock, one that Lucille and Nora had patterned, with restraint,
after a picture in one of Lucille's books. She had shaken out her pigtails and had done up her hair in a bun at the back of her head. She
kept patting at it until finally her brother Tommy scoffed, "How do
you think you're gonna dance, holdin' your head cocked like that?"
Tommy regarded the pretensions of the entire affair with masculine
scorn. Although he wore clean jersey trousers and had been forced by
his stepmother to polish his boots after a fashion, he stated emphatically that he intended only to watch. "You'll have to dance with me at
least once," Mabel insisted. "It'll be a cold day in hell," Tommy said.
Their stepmother reproved, "That's no language to use to your sister."
Johnny covered a faint smile behind a piece of bread; respectability
sure wasn't going to take hold of her by half-measures.

Mabel said, "Weren't Lou and Nora lovely?"

"The town was looking at them," Johnny agreed.

"Your float will win the prize."

"The Guards' float was funnier," Johnny said and listened to the
clanging. An uncharacteristic bitterness slipped from him. "Seems like
I'm always being beat by that saw blade."

Mabel did not notice the awkward silence. "Why don't you marry
her?" she demanded.

"I would if she'd have me," Johnny said.

"I'd have you," Mabel declared. Her round cheeks turned bright red
at the laugh that followed. Defiantly she repeated, "Well, I would."

"That's my sweetheart," Johnny said. "I'll remember this about four
years from now."

"Nora says no woman in her right mind would take a man if this
town has to go with him."

The old anger leaped between them. Before he could empty his
mouth for a retort however, Nora interposed, "Have you seen what Ewer
did with Lucille's style notes in today's paper?"

Deliberately Johnny finished eating, pushed his plate aside, and then
reached for the copy of *The True Fissure* lying farther down the table.
"Style Notes" was the heading of the article on fashions Lucille had
been writing for the paper, the first such feature any of the mountain
newspapers had yet printed. Johnny read it faithfully each week, amused
by the vital trivia of prettiness, yet proud of her in spite of his amusement: "Stuffed birds will ornament fall and winter bonnets," "Sarah
Bernhardt has decreed that the tiny bouquet de corsage must be worn
on the left side of the neck of the dress."

He found the familiar heading on the inside page and began to read
while others watched him in a kind of tongue-tied embarrassment. He

was well launched before he discovered that he had been tricked, as Ewer had intended that every female follower of the column should be tricked, into outrage, so that once again the masculine mountains would ha-ha in delight over the *Fissure's* latest.

The proper material for bustles has lately been the subject of discussion among the matrons of Vinegar Hill. Paper bags have received considerable support. They are economical; the material has a desirable stiffness; properly inflated and secured with string, the bag sticks out splendidly and makes the skirt hang well. While recognizing these virtues, this column nevertheless feels obliged, as a civic duty, to report an incident which occurred last Sunday morning and which illustrates the perils attending the unwary use of paper bags.

While dressing for church on the Sunday in question, one of our better known society figures asked her husband to tie on her inflated bustle. Entering church, the lady preceded her husband to their pew. She sat down grandly while the innocent man leaned over to place his hat on the floor. There was an explosion like distant thunder. Half crouched, the poor innocent, a perfect picture of amazement, looked at his wife as if to demand, "Are you trying to scare me into getting religion?" She meanwhile, blushing prettily, turned around to those behind as if to say, "I didn't know it was loaded." The minister announced in a loud voice that the next hymn would be "Sing the Loud Hosannah." After church the deflated matron led her unfortunate husband rapidly toward home before our fashion editor could pursue the subject further. Ah, well, style is style and girls will be girls.

Johnny growled, "Where's her regular column?"

"On the back page," Walt said.

He found it and somewhat mollified read about dresses of grenadine trimmed with bands of embroidered gauze in millefleur colors.

Nora said, "That was not a very handsome trick of Ewer to play after he'd persuaded her that publicity in the paper would make it worth her while to write a column every week for nothing. But I suppose he knew it was the sort of crudeness that would appeal to this wonderful town of yours, and of course a laugh makes anything all right."

Johnny flared back, "If you're going to go blaming the town for everything Ewer does—"

"Oh, quit the jawing," Walt said and broke up the quarrel by hauling on the age-darkened leather fob attached to his loudly ticking, thick silver watch. "The speeches must be about over by now."

Gabe Porcella picked up the diversion, saying he hoped that the din-

ner was good enough and the ceremonies impressive enough that Winkler would be inspired to invest in Pat's and Johnny's road. "What did
he say when you had him up there this morning?" he asked and the
others waited expectantly for the answer.

Johnny did not feel like pursuing that line of talk either. "Not
much," he said and sought a diversion of his own in Gabe's appearance.
He had evidently clad himself just before supper from the stacks of
black trousers and coats and celluloid collars piled in heaps, by size, on
the counters of Hotchkiss's store. He looked dreadfully uncomfortable.
His coat bunched between his shoulders and his heavy red hands hung
like misshapen knobs out of his short sleeves.

"What're you all decked out for?" Johnny said. "You can't dance."

"I got to find me a woman somewhere," Gabe said. "I'm four weeks
behind in my laundry already." The others laughed but he was completely in earnest. "It's been a bad spring up on the mountain, trying
to make do without any of the things we need. You think it's wrong of
Ewer to shuffle those style notes. It's a sight worse the way he boomed
the mountain before he should have."

"Worse?" Johnny challenged while Nora regarded him with a mocking smile.

"You bet it was worse. And the Baker paper was just as wrong. Both
of 'em kept writing these big reports about the Red Mountain strikes,
and both of 'em claimed their town was on the best route to the mines.
What they thought they were doing was talking people into coming
their way for the benefit of the merchants. But the people went on up
the hill before the snow was gone. Oh, it was awful. Some came on
snowshoes, but most just waded, and you know how plowing through
snow makes your legs swell up and ache. They couldn't go to work in
all that snow. They just sat and suffered. There wasn't food enough
or clothes or anything. Next year will be worse, unless there's a road.
There's got to be a road."

"There will be," Johnny said.

"There weren't even places enough for them to sleep. At nights
they were practically in layers on the floor of my store, using flour
sacks or horse pads or anything they could find for covers. Every other
public place up there was jammed the same way."

"I didn't notice anybody sleeping," one of the other customers said.
"They sat up all night, afraid of missing the next rumor about the
latest strike if they went to bed. I never saw such crazy running around."

"While the groceries lasted, I'd swap them for firewood or anything
else, and I got a great big stack of wood out back and then people
who were too lazy to cut it for themselves took to swiping it. So I bored
holes in a few logs and loaded 'em with black powder for a lesson and

forgot and put a stick in my own stove. Ruined it. One of the lids just missed me."

Again Gabe looked bewildered at the laughter. "It wasn't funny. You heard about Hank Ahern? I was feeling peevish the day he tried to bum me for a stake and his eyes made me feel mean and I told him to keep goin'. No one would take him in, and that night it was so cold the snow squeaked. I guess he was afraid to go back where he had been turned down before. He found the outhouse behind the cabin Parley Quine was renting. That's where Quine found him the next morning, froze so stiff we had trouble unbending him so we could put him on a sled to haul him out to bury him. First man to die on Red Mountain. That's how we started our cemetery."

"Progress," Nora said.

"We had to snowshoe, pulling the sled with ropes. Several fellows reached the grave ahead of us. While they were standing around waiting, that big dog of Quine's tangled with another dog and they fell into the grave fighting seventeen to one. The men crowded up, laying bets. The dirt was soft from fires we'd built to thaw it for digging and one side of the hole caved and three or four of them fell in with the dogs. Well, we got 'em out. We put Ahern in and his hat over his face and spruce branches over that and then . . . Well, he was the first."

"Gabe, Gabe," Nora said and laid her palm on the back of his knobby red hand. Then, lest anyone remark the softening, she added scratchily, "But when the road comes everything will be perfect."

Gabe nodded vigorously. "I'll never forget the thaw. I woke up in the middle of the night and heard this little ringing noise and couldn't figure what it was, and all the rest of the night I kept rarin' up on one elbow, listening. In the morning I found it—snow water dripping off the roof onto an old tin plate. It sounded just like the bells of a pack train of jacks. That was the day damn near the whole mountain went out with shovels to open the trail. And pretty soon we did hear bells, real ones, and here was old Walt, no one else would of made it, and if ever anybody wanted to kiss a mule, that was the time. Men lined up outside the store with their baskets and sacks and empty syrup cans, and while they waited for us to get things unpacked and sorted, they talked about the best way to cook bacon and how the prettiest sight in the world is a slapjack coated in butter and drowned in sweetenin'. And the prettiest sound was the rumble of whisky barrels rolling across the wood porch of the saloon."

Mabel was tired of storytelling. She opened the front door and put her ear to the crack. "Listen!" She whirled around, vibrant with excitement. "The music has started! Let's go! Nora, hurry!"

"9"

Miners and farmers and soldiers packed the verandah of the Dixon House, watching the dancers come and go. Johnny passed with the others through the lane they left to the door, through the lobby with its brass spittoons, and into the Grand Ballroom, glowing with chandeliers and festooned with evergreens. He had supposed he had grown used to not having been invited to the dinner, but when several heads turned to see who had arrived, he felt as conspicuous as a stuffed bear. He thrust his hands into his hip pockets and glared. Go on and gawk. It was a public dance. He had bought his ticket.

Lucille left the young Guard she was with and hurried to the newcomers. She exclaimed over Mabel's hairdo, teased Walt for not having provided the float Nora and she rode with gentler horses, and then said with a smile that was completely for John,

"You're late!"

Her black hair was done in a way he had never seen before, curled into ringlets and powdered with diamond dust. She was flushed from excitement and dancing, and he was racked by jealousy.

"Miss me?" he asked. The words, meant to be light, sounded sullen in his own ears.

Her eyes lowered. "I missed the Bon-Ton. The speeches were so dull. But Mr. Winkler was cute. He likes you . . . Schonny." Her eyes raised again, unexpectedly, so that he received their full impact. "He sat rolling bread into balls, as bored as I was, and whispered to me about your father and Saguache and what a good worker you were when you were a boy in his store. He said you were the youngest foreman he had ever put in charge of a road crew."

"Did he?" Johnny said, immensely pleased. Then he blurted, "What about the road? Did he talk about that?"

Her eyes dropped again. "Not really."

"Tell me."

"He just said that it was an ambitious job and . . . that it was too bad Pat isn't as stable as you are."

"So he's not going to invest!"

"He didn't say that."

"If he's not satisfied, he should talk to me directly, not through you."

"You asked," she said rather tartly. To distract him she tucked her fingers inside his elbow. "Let's walk around the room."

Only an occasional group chatted and laughed on the floor between dances. For the most part each man, at the conclusion of a number, took his partner to the row of chairs along one of the walls and deposited her there to await for whoever was next on her card—or, if there was no card, for whoever reached her first. It was a motley line of young wives, matrons growing thick through the middle, grandmothers, and tots who reached scarcely to the belts of the sunburned fathers or older brothers who gallantly pushed them around the floor. Women were outnumbered five to one and so no one was a wallflower. Between dances most of the males gathered in a tight knot at the side entry. A great deal of loud laughter echoed there, and there were surreptitious journeys to whisky bottles cached outside under wagon seats or behind loose boards in the alley fence. Before the evening was finished, so Johnny surmised from past experience, there would be several fist fights, the result of exuberance rather than of malice.

Touring the room as he did with Lucille was not customary. He heard the rustle of her dress. It clung to her, showing the movement of her legs. When she wheeled abruptly once to speak to a friend, he glimpsed her sheer silk stockings. She was the handsomest woman on the floor, the most beautifully gowned. He put a thumb in his waistcoat pocket and smiled benignly at the watchers.

Professor Delius's Silver City orchestra filed back into their stand and struck up a tune that sounded vaguely familiar to John.

"A round dance—a waltz!" Lucille exclaimed. She faced Johnny, put her left hand on his shoulder. "The Boston Dip! Remember?"

She and Nora had practiced the step with Walt and him in the Bon-Ton after hours, with a banjo to carry the melody and the humming of the girls for orchestration. Johnny had a natural grace and sense of time and had learned fast. Walt, though, had soon plunked himself down at the table and had sulked. "Public love-making," he grumbled. "Don't be stuffy," Lucille had chided him. "Everyone in the East is doing it." Even so, Johnny hesitated here in front of practically the entire town. Then, as her eyes dared him, he pulled her hand almost to his left hip and drew her close, as she had taught him. They stumbled at the start, then found the elongated step, the swaying, the quick reversals. Other dancers paused to watch. Over near the door someone yelled "Wa-hoo!" and as the piece ended there was a ripple of applause. Lucille stepped away from him almost reluctantly.

"Johnny, that was fun!" She was flushed and short of breath and very pretty. Then Harmon Gregg wandered up and said, "I believe the next dance is mine, isn't it, John?"

Johnny danced with Mabel, hurried back to Lucille, surrendered her

again, and stood miserably by himself at the end of the room. Tommy
Brice sidled up to him, self-importance big in his eyes.

"Hey, Johnny. You know what? Old Man Hedstrom is over there."

Johnny declined even to glance in that direction. "It's a public party.
He can come if he wants."

"He's packin' quite a load."

"That's Gaw's worry."

"He's got a bunch of punks with him and they're talkin' about givin'
you the bum's rush. Gabe and the feller who plays the banjo sometimes at the Bon-Ton, they're gettin' up a bunch to bounce 'em if anything starts."

"Thanks, Tommy." Johnny let his hand drop on the boy's shoulder.
Tommy tried to spraddle his legs at the same angle as Johnny's, cock
his head the same way. "That's interesting to know."

The music stopped. Johnny reclaimed Lucille. They were beginning
another circle of the room when a roll of drums drew attention to the
orchestra stand. Al Ewer, round and slow and strangely diffident for a
man who courted so much attention through his newspaper, announced
in a barely audible voice that the float of the Argent Guards had been
adjudged the winner of the contest. There was a din of cheers. The
saw blade reverberated outside and a moment later the shotgun
blasted its triumph. Lucille looked up at Johnny's long face.

"It was a good float, Johnny. It said what you wanted it to say."

"I should have tried harder. That idea of theirs really was better."

"I wouldn't want a thing different."

"Even the runaway?"

"Especially the runaway."

He looked at her, hungry and dissatisfied and utterly unable to find
words for what he felt. Then Sheriff Gaw appeared with the start of
the music, said "Dance, ma'am," and took her off without waiting for an
answer. The fiddles started earnestly sawing their way through another
log of music. Walt and Nora danced by, exchanged a few words
with Gaw and his partner. At last the piece ended and Lucille came
back to Johnny alone. She was subdued and silent as the music struck
up once more, and when their dancing brought them near the main
entry, she said apologetically,

"I'm afraid it has been too big a day."

"Why?"

"I've developed a headache. Do you mind taking me home?"

Instantly concerned, he led her into the lobby. There he saw Nora,
her coat on and her slipper bag in hand, waiting with Walt beside the
door to the room where the ladies had left their wraps. Belated suspicion rushed at him. He halted.

"Gaw put you and Kennerly up to this, to get me out of here, didn't he?"

"It's been a long day. Nora was tired too."

He gave a badgered gesture. It seemed to him that the eyes of every man in the lobby were weighing him, that any instant now he would hear a taunting cry, "Oh, Johnny, save me, save me!" She did not know what she was asking, the way women always ask, softly gelding one's manhood.

"Everybody will think I'm running from—"

"Does it matter?"

"Yes, it matters. I'm not—"

"I will not stand here arguing with you, John."

"But you are arguing, just saying that."

"Not any more. I'm going. You can come or not as you see fit."

"And have you mad at me either way."

"No."

"Disappointed then. That's worse."

She grew exasperated. "Why do you act as if I had to account to you? I'm not responsible for any of this."

Woman's alternatives: whatever he did, he lost. "Oh all right," he said as ungraciously as possible.

Stiffly she went into the coat room. A moment later she was back in her wrap and street shoes, carrying her dancing slippers in a blue satchel. In silence she handed the bag to Johnny and in silence they went outside, past the glowing cigars on the verandah and on to the corner. Walt sauntered discreetly behind with Nora. *Not to take Nora home,* Johnny thought resentfully, *but to see that nothing happens to me. What do they think I am?*

A hundred yards to the left was Mother Marsh's roominghouse. Up the steep street to the right was Vinegar Hill. A round moon floated detached and remote above the peaks of the amphitheater. A silver light as palpable as mist filled the basin. Sounds from the town fell thin and lonely. Johnny paused. His lungs felt too small. He swallowed.

"It's lovely," she whispered and he knew that she was apologizing.

"Our last night," he said.

"Please!"

"Shall we walk up Vinegar Hill?"

"I'd better go home."

"Is that what you really want?"

"It's what I have to want."

"But you will never tell me why."

Mutely she shook her head, turned and walked rapidly toward Mother Marsh's.

"10"

Walt and Nora watched from the corner. They saw the glimmer of light as the door to the roominghouse opened. A moment later Johnny's square figure returned through the picket gate and moved slowly toward the livery stable, where he shared a lean-to shack with Walt. As shadows engulfed him, Nora said, "That didn't take long."

They turned toward the Bon-Ton. Walt swore softy. "Gaw should have let them fight. Now Johnny is going to be tied up inside himself tighter than ever."

"The town is forgetting," she said indifferently. "Johnny is lucky there was no fight to make them remember."

"I don't think Johnny will forget, no matter what the town does." Walt hesitated a moment over a confidence, then let it escape. "Do you know what he asked me to do for him? He wanted me to go to the reservation before the Indians left and try to find out from Shavano whether or not they burned Hedstrom. He said he was afraid Shavano wouldn't tell him the truth if he went himself. And when Fossett came back from treaty-making, Johnny's first question was whether he'd learned anything about how Hedstrom died."

"You didn't go?"

"No."

"Why not?"

"Of course the Indians burned Hedstrom—or worse. Johnny knows that. But he keeps hoping. Why stop the hope by rubbing a charred bone in his face?"

"Perhaps he should look at the truth. The way things are, he keeps trying to make himself bigger and bigger for fear he looks small in the town's eyes. He can't get away from Young Hedstrom that way."

"Shame is a pretty powerful thing," Walt said and asked, "How much of this does Lucille know?"

"He told her some of it himself. Sometimes he acts proud of it, rather than ashamed. But do we have to keep talking about John Ogden?"

"Is Hedstrom the reason she won't marry him?"

"I don't think so," Nora said speculatively. They had reached the Bon-Ton. Walt opened the door with his own key. The tablecloths were ghostly. They walked quickly through to Nora's room and shut the door. The blinds were already down and Walt had to strike a match to find the lamp. There was no need this evening to worry about waking Mabel. Her family were camped at the fairgrounds and she was going there after the dance to spend the night with them. With a sigh of relief Nora took off her coat, loosened her hair, shook her head, and ran her hands up the back of her neck. Walt caught her wrists and kissed her. She responded absently.

"I've wondered about it," she said, "and I don't understand it."

Walt let his lips nibble along her jaw line to her ear.

"Stop that!" She turned her head but her lips stayed close. "Lucille came here to Argent ready to be sold a bill of goods and Johnny sold it to her and I don't know why she won't have him."

Walt addressed himself to the top button of her bodice. "Maybe he's the one holding back. Maybe he doesn't want his children ready-made."

"I don't think that's bothering him one bit."

"He's married to that road. Maybe she doesn't want to compete with it. I thought you didn't want to talk about John Ogden."

"A woman always wants to understand marrying." And then she said, "At least Johnny has the road. What are you married to?"

His hands grew still.

She went on digging at him. "You'd never give away enough of yourself to be married to anything."

He search her face. "Are you telling me you've had enough?"

"Harmon Gregg wants to marry me," she said, but stayed close to him.

It was he who pulled away. He sat on the brass bedstead and reached behind him for a pillow, upending it so that he could lean his head against it and watch her. He kept his face expressionless.

"I thought I ought to tell you," she said.

"Has Harmon proposed or are you working on intuition?"

"He proposed this afternoon, just after the parade, while I was worrying about the soup."

A shadow of pain crossed Walt's face. Then he shrugged. "You're free to walk away any time. We agreed on that in the beginning."

"You said you didn't want to be suffocated the way John Ogden's father was," she reminded him bitterly. "You learned from that, you said."

"And you didn't want anything that would tie you to this town."

"I still don't."

"Then why Gregg?"

"Because it's a man's world," she flared passionately, "and the only way out is some man's way."

She stepped out of her dress, shook it straight, and hung it carefully behind the curtained alcove that served as her wardrobe. He lay back, content for the moment just to watch. "Go on," he said.

"You've listened to John Ogden talk about these mountains. They're a brand-new world where you can capture rainbows and remake lives and be rich forever—if you're a man. But not if you're a woman. Who would take a woman seriously if she tried to go East to sell claims or if she promoted a toll road or set up a township company or ran a string of pack mules? Johnny Ogden certainly wouldn't—him and his fine new world."

Walt smiled. "I reckon that's about right."

"See! You're laughing already! The only thing a lone woman can do is run a restaurant to fill your belly. Or be your whore."

"Or wife."

"The rules are all yours. I can't play the game myself. But I can get someone to play it for me, my way. Unlace me."

He stood up. "And that's Harmon Gregg."

"More and more mining business is coming to him, especially from Red Mountain. If Otto Winkler moves in and builds that road and if the mines prove out at depth half as good as the promoters are saying, who is going to be any closer to the inside of things than a lawyer? He'll know what claims are going to be tied up in litigation. He can let information leak on the quiet. He can buy or sell before anyone else—a hundred things."

"You're shivering."

"Get in and pull up the covers."

"Is this Harmon's idea?"

"I'll let him think it is."

"Poor Harmon."

"I'm saving money here in the Bon-Ton faster than you think."

"But not fast enough evidently."

"I don't intend to stay by a stove the rest of my life. But where can I go by myself? What do I know—a sodbuster's colt? Somebody has to go with me." She rolled over and raised herself on her elbows and looked him full in the face. "You won't."

"With you writing the ticket?" He shook his head. "You wouldn't want me to."

"You wouldn't go in any event. And I won't stay." She waited, but he said nothing and the hardness returned to the corners of her mouth. "I'm going to help Harmon Gregg bleed as much money out of Red Mountain as we can, and then we're going as far away from here as the trains run—to our own new world."

"I hope they run that far," he said.

She kissed him with a swift wild passion. There was a glint of tears in her eyes.

"You're crying," he said in amazement.

"Not for you," she said.

He pulled her head onto his shoulder. "Relax. You fight things even harder than Johnny does."

"I get lonesome."

"I know."

"I hate myself sometimes."

"I know how that can be, too."

"Hold me, Walt."

A moment later she raised herself again and said vehemently, "If I do marry Harmon I won't cheat on him."

"You haven't married him yet."

"I don't think you care."

"Would you do things differently if I said I did?"

"That's not an answer."

"Should I let you cut my heart out, the way Harmon Gregg's is going to be?"

"I hate you."

"You're a cold-blooded little so-and-so."

"Am I?" Her arms went around his neck. "Am I, Walt?"

"11"

The morning dawned cold and still and as bright as a new knife. It was Sunday. The celebration the night before had lasted late, and as yet the chimneys hadn't started to smoke. In the deserted streets the steel shoes of the horses rang so loudly that Lucille was embarrassed, certain that aroused sleepers were peering outside and swearing at the lack of consideration. Then the houses dropped behind and the road to the Mineral Patch claims began climbing, in a ladder of steep zigzags, up the triangular snout of forest and rock that protruded between the main gorge and a precipitous side canyon on the right.

Not a word had been said since they had left the livery stable. Young Tommy Brice and Gabe Porcella were up ahead with the pack horses. Gabe had arrived with a sore nose and a puffy black mouse under one eye. He had fought the night before with one of Old Hedstrom's friends, but his eagerness to recount the experience had dulled against Johnny's grumpiness. Now he rode slumped in the saddle, his

big head rolling loosely to the horse's walk. He led two pack horses of
groceries and hardware by a rope looped over his right arm. Behind
came Tommy, leading two more horses. One was loaded for Gabe's
store with several dozen eggs and two kegs of butter from the Brice
ranch; the other horse carried Lucille's sample kits and personal gear.
Each time the little cavalcade bent back on itself at a zig, Tommy
would look down on Lucille and grin from ear to ear. He never before
had journeyed any appreciable distance away from his family, and he
felt grown-up and important to have two horses entrusted to his care.
The ostensible reason for his trip was to deliver the produce to Gabe
and then ride on over to Baker with Johnny and Lucille to see the
country. Actually, of course, he was serving as a chaperon of sorts.

Lucille came next, riding the sidesaddle on which she had taken
practice gallops each morning for the past week. She wore a green
velvet habit borrowed from Mrs. Fossett; Johnny would return it and
her horse the next day. Johnny himself brought up the rear. He was
being difficult. He was angry at Pat, for one thing. Pat was to have
ridden as far as the Red Mountain construction camp with them,
but had not pried himself loose from the gambling houses until just
as Johnny was saddling the horses. He had fallen into bed like a log.
"Now he won't go up until Monday," Johnny had complained to
Gabe, loudly enough for Lucille to hear. "I'm missing a day, too, and
that means a whole shift is shot to hell on both ends of the road."

The remark had made her feel just fine, of course. Crisply she had
told him, "Gabe will take us as far as Red Mountain. Tommy and I
can go on from there by ourselves."

"A boy and a woman alone on that pass? And Tommy by himself
coming back? Don't be ridiculous."

"Then perhaps Walt or someone—"

"I said I'd go."

"I don't want to be a burden or make you miss your work."

"The men can manage, I guess. And I'd like to see how the Baker
company is coming with its road on their side of the mountain."

"Is that your only reason for going?"

"That's the only reason you've left me," he had retorted and had
helped her mount with an icy politeness more stinging than rudeness
would have been. *Johnny, don't,* she had thought desperately, and
then had matched his edged courtesies with equal sharpness, crying all
the while, *Why, why?* It was last night's parting over again, an ache so
overwhelming that instinctively it sought relief by striking at whatever was linked most closely to the pain. *Johnny, Johnny.* This was
not the ending they would want to remember.

Please ask me again.

And tell him—what? The truth? Have that shadow lie beside them on their wedding night? Watch his eyes when she brought Lennie to Argent and the boy stepped forward in his grave, shy way, small hand uncertainly extended as she said, "This is your new daddy, Leonard," while the silence demanded, Where is the old one?

What would that do to Lennie? To her? To John?

Don't tell him anything. And then wake up each morning to the dread that this would be the day he learned?

Johnny, don't harry me so. No, no, no!

By the second zig they had climbed far enough to meet the sun. Approaching it, they had to use their hands as shields against its brilliance. Then silently they would wheel back into shadow. Pressed downward by the upper warmth, the chill air flooded in a silent tide through each gully, nipping at Lucille's nose and fingers and booted feet. Then they would veer again toward sunlight. While she waited for the thread of warmth, she wiggled her toes inside her stockings and listened to the sound of the horse behind her and watched the town below.

It was shrinking to a toy town, a crosshatching of a few streets lined by tiny cubes of houses. From here one could not see the littered alleyways and the manure heaps that so annoyed Nora. Rather, the town appeared trim and sure of itself, chopping its pattern cleanly out of the forest and striding undeterred to the foot of the hills. To her, it had been a good town. She had sold more dresses than even Johnny had predicted. Zest was part of the reason; defiance was another part. Argent might be new and isolated and crude; the mountains might be alive with many forms of death; nonetheless the threats could be met proudly with a gown that was a symbol of softer graces left behind only temporarily, graces that would yet prove stronger than granite. There had been more women in Argent to feel that way than a casual glance at the streets would suggest. Within her own time Lucille had seen the town almost double in size, and a surprising segment of the influx had been wives who knew good clothes—wives of army officers stationed at the cantonment at the agency; of geologists and engineers, of accountants and ambitious merchants. Even the madam of one of the sporting houses had come to the shop during the slack hours of one early morning and had authorized her girls' charging one dress each to her account. Lucille had been outraged initially by the woman's presumption, then touched by her generosity in lending brightness to bleak lives. But Nora had sniffed. "If she keeps them in debt, they're not so likely to get independent and strike out on their own."

A good town, but not inexhaustible. After the first excitement, sales had dropped quickly, and she should not have stayed as long as she had.

They passed the silent mines at the Mineral Patch. The road dwindled to a trail that zigzagged even more tightly until it had almost reached the tree line. Then it straightened out on a long slant toward the ridgetop marking the edge of the gorge. Just short of the top Johnny spoke for the first time, eagerly.

"Close your eyes until I tell you to open them."

She obeyed. She felt the sun strike her face, she felt a soft wind flowing from her right, she sensed the curve and leveling off of the trail.

Johnny said, "Look straight ahead over the horse's ears. Now!"

The view leaped at her. The gray, snow-spotted cap of Ute Peak towered close ahead. Beside it on the right was the deep, colored notch of Red Mountain Creek. Through that she could glimpse green meadows leading back to hillocks looking shaggy and black under their covering of spruce. Above the hillocks flamed the three peaks.

"Oh, Johnny!" She halted the horse and started to glance back. Her breath froze. Directly under her toes, so it seemed, the gorge dropped a thousand feet to a thread of water, dull silver in the shadows.

He grinned at her. "If you'll ride on up to that flat place, it won't seem so spooky."

He was twelve years old again, showing off his territory and strutting because he had startled her. She managed to make a face at him. Her muscles stiff with dread, she rode on to the outthrust he indicated, an acre or so of fairly level meadow grass and flowers. There she drew rein again.

"Can we rest a few minutes?"

"Sure." He helped her down and hooked the bridle reins of both horses to the branches of a low, wind-twisted tree. Gabe and Tommy disappeared around the next bend as he led her across the flat toward the canyon's brink. Fearful still of such heights, she drew back and found a seat on a fallen tree. Johnny stood at the very rim, staring moodily at the gray-brown cliffs on the other side. A vision of him falling, hands flung out and body tumbling over and over, made her shut her eyes.

"Johnny, don't go so near the edge!"

He retreated a step, humoring her. "You can see where the road will run." He pointed to the thin scar it made as it climbed out of town, to end abruptly at an enormous buttress of rock. His finger rounded that, crossed the top of a pluming waterfall, moved along the great slabs of creased rock.

She sat stunned. A wilderness of stone and roaring gulches. It had been appalling enough to hear him talk of miles and time. But now to see the effrontery of the scratch! She looked from the edges of the town to the tips of the red peaks.

"It's so far!" she protested.

He picked up a handful of pebbles and threw them absently, one by one, far out into the void. She watched each one course its tightening parabola, then plunge faster and faster until it disappeared. There was no sound of it striking below, just the rush of the cataract and the hum of wind in the evergreens. For the past month those two sounds, still indistinguishable to her, had pervaded sleep and wakefulness until they were as integral as breath. But in Chicago she would not hear them.

"Do you remember," Johnny asked, "what you said yesterday about me not letting a mistake spoil what I believe in?"

She nodded mutely. Her father's voice: After a mistake like that no decent man will ever look at you.

"It wasn't a mistake," he insisted.

Wasn't it? To do what the moment said to do?

"I thought the court would clear us. But it didn't say anything—wrong or right—not anything."

He waited for her answer but there was only the deep drone of the gorge.

"That's why I've got to build the road. Don't you see that?"

For four years she had lived with shame, pressing it into a knot inside her, encasing it with silence and aloofness lest the raw touch of hope unravel it again. That voice: If my friends knew that my daughter— Here no one knew. She had been happy. There had been moments when she had even forgotten.

"We haven't time enough," Johnny said, almost wildly. The thought that he too might occasionally be frightened had never before occurred to her. "We haven't money enough."

"Mr. Winkler—"

"I don't know what he's going to do. Something's bothering him. He told you that Pat isn't stable. And Pat thinks Otto wants to hog the show. Pat's full of schemes. I don't know if his notions will work or when. The road doesn't matter to Pat. Not as a road to help open up the mountains. If it makes him a dollar, that's all he cares."

She looked across the void at the great blank wall of rock. To hurl yourself at indifference, to bleed your heart away and have no one to care.

"We're partners, Lucy. He's been my friend ever since I came to Argent."

The things you count on dissolving around you. *I know, I know.* But what words were there to tell him?

"What am I going to do?"

The pain turned and twisted. She tried to press it back into its knot.

"I need you, Lucy."

For four years she had schooled her eyes to dryness. But now the knot unraveled.

He stared at her. "I didn't mean to . . ."

"Johnny, my Johnny."

"Don't cry."

"Not ever again. Not if you'll always love me."

And she believed it.

IV

"1"

Lucille stayed in Baker for two weeks. During that period she took orders for a third more dresses than she had sold during a similar period in Argent. From Baker she returned directly to Chicago, to supervise the handling of special patterns and to ready herself and Lennie for the move to the mountains. Nearly every day she wrote Johnny an enthusiastic letter about her plans and hopes. Occasionally there were intrusions of doubt. Was he sure? She must not be a burden. She knew how worried he was about money. Couldn't she help him by retaining her agency with the dress company? She could accept orders at their home without inconveniencing him while he was away at work; and after the new road was finished, it would not be hard to travel now and then by stage to Baker, where business had proved very good indeed. He wouldn't really mind, would he?

His pride minded bitterly. The suggestions came as the Red Mountain Toll Road and Transportation Company was slipping closer and closer to bankruptcy. On payday the third week following Lucille's departure he was not able to rustle up enough cash to pay his workers on time and had to stall them off for two days, until he could sell dabs of stock here and there at sacrificial prices. The week following that he could raise no cash whatsoever. Finally, after long arguments and using his residence lots on Vinegar Hill as collateral, he persuaded Linc Hotchkiss to let the workers charge groceries against Johnny's account for the remainder of the month. At least the men co-operated. He gathered them together at the new bridge over Wolf Creek Falls to explain the situation. There, where their own eyes saw the white rags on the new survey stakes marching upward along the gorge, they agreed to give the job a chance.

Their wives proved more difficult. Johnny shrank from the scorn in their eyes whenever he chanced to pass one of them on her way to market. The same self-contempt rankled in him when Lucille wrote about her dress agency. An employer ought to be able to pay his workers. A man ought to be able to support his wife. Out of submerged memories of Saguache his mother's voice railed again at his father: "Did you bring me out here to live like a Mexican? Are you willing for your son to work in Otto Winkler's stables to help support your family? If people in Altoona knew . . ."

Finally Winkler offered a solution of sorts. Shortly after Lucille had begun writing about the dress agency, Fred Fossett traveled to Saguache to see Otto about many things, including the road. Johnny learned of the banker's return one Saturday morning when a messenger rode on horseback to the road camp near the falls. Johnny, so the summons instructed, was to stop by the bank on his return from work.

The offhandedness of it was one more wound to his self-esteem. Wasn't the matter important enough for Fred to see him immediately?

Furious at Fred rather than at himself for being so vulnerable, Johnny hovered irritably around the workers who were blasting out foundations, just beyond the new bridge, for a combination toll station and store. The latter addition was his own idea. He felt sure that stagecoaches and private pleasure vehicles would linger at the brink of the cliffs so that tourists could admire Wolf Creek's spectacular drop into the gorge. Why not add to the station a counter over which the tollkeeper could sell liquor, cigars, post cards, rock specimens, and souvenir teaspoons? Pat had degraded the proposal: "Peanuts." But in Johnny's estimation nothing was peanuts to a company ear-deep in debt. Doggedly he went ahead cutting out the space he wanted. If Winkler invested in the road, he would approve of the store. Otto knew the value of pennies. That was how he'd climbed where he was.

When quitting time at last arrived, his humiliation made him perverse. Instead of going directly to the bank, he deliberately turned his back and walked across the street to join the queue lining up for the afternoon mail distribution. Let Fossett taste a little waiting and see how he liked it.

The post office occupied an inadequate cubicle of varnished tongue-and-groove boards in the rear of the drugstore. The line of men crawling slowly toward the single barred window wavered between glassed-in displays of guns, hunting knives, fancy liquors, books, and ranks of gaudily dressed dolls with china-blue eyes, presumably intended for children but generally purchased by drunk miners for the doll-faced chippies down on Crib Street. Mounted deer and elk heads stared superciliously down from the walls. On the flat top of the post-office cubicle, directly above the window, a stuffed bear reared on its hind legs, holding an enormous gilt key. No one understood the significance of the key or the bear, but at least it gave people something to talk about during the line's slow creep.

A single clerk handled the distribution. Half the men in the line never received mail from him. But they appeared each evening anyway, and when the clerk crossly told them, "Nothing," they invariably insisted, "Are you sure? I was expectin' . . ." and looked around with self-conscious grins while the harried man repeated the pretense of again riffling the stack of letters to check.

Johnny picked up one letter from Lucille and two bills. The clerk asked, "Red Mountain, too?"

"Might as well," Johnny said. Normal deliveries went up the mountain three times a week, by government contract, on Walt Kennerly's pack train. Johnny added one more trip each Sunday, purely as a favor, when he rode to Pat's end of the highway to see how work was progressing there. Each time that he picked up a sheaf of first-class letters he hefted it in his hand, gauging how much heavier it was than last week's. This bundle was especially big. Before long Red Mountain would need daily service, just as Argent already needed a separate post-office building with space for boxes so that a man could get his mail whenever he wished.

The letters weren't all. As Johnny tapped them into a neat pile, the clerk said, "There's a package here for Walt Kennerly. Do you want to take it?" He exhibited a flat, rectangular box of cardboard, its corners badly crushed. He leered wisely. "I'd let it wait for the regular pack train, except it looks kind of special."

The address on the mailing label was in Lucille's handwriting. The return read, *Paris Dress Salons, Chicago.*

Oh my God, Johnny thought. *That's the dress Walt ordered for Nora.*

But Nora was going to marry Harmon Gregg.

Her ending of their affair was the reason Walt had moved to Red Mountain. He'd said that he needed to put the transfer barns at that end of his freight run in order, but everyone in Argent knew better. He could not endure to walk by the Bon-Ton and see the lawyer with the soft brown whiskers sitting in the chair that once had been his.

Walt won't accept that, Johnny started to tell the clerk. Then he checked himself. Lucille was the one who had felt Nora needed the lift of a stylish gown and had persuaded Walt to buy it. Perhaps Lucille could figure out a way for her still to have it—a good-bye present or something. Anyway, it was not up to Johnny to do the refusing.

"I'll take it," he said. He could store it somewhere until he'd had a chance to talk to Walt or Lucille or both. Clamping the box under one arm, he moved across to the less crowded side of the drugstore and began fingering open the flap of Lucille's letter.

An exasperated voice plucked at him. "Jesus H. Christ, Johnny, are you coming or aren't you?"

It was Roscoe Blair, the gaunt, bald-headed owner of the smelter below town.

Mildly surprised by Roscoe's agitation Johnny asked, "Coming where?"

"To the bank. We've been waitin' the best part of an hour."

"We?"

"Fossett and the rest. A stockholders' meeting. Jesus H.—"

Summoned like an errand boy. Whose company was it? "Fred doesn't own any road stock. I don't know why he feels privileged to call a meeting."

"Come off it, John. Winkler . . . Jesus, we're busy men, too."

Johnny grew ashamed of his own toploftiness. Acting like Fossett because he was irritated by Fossett! He put Lucille's letter into his pocket unread. The box was less convenient. Then he saw Jules Halverson, Walt's regular hostler down at the livery stable, where Johnny was now living. He gave Jules the box.

"Take this down and put it on my desk, will you? I'll be along after a while." He grinned apologetically at Roscoe. "Let's go see what the boys in the back room will have."

"2"

The space where the tellers worked was separated from the public's part of the bank by brass bars and a wall of pine lumber painted mahogany. Behind this showy sanctum was Fossett's office, separated from the tellers' room by a door whose upper half boasted the only ground-glass panel in Argent. The teller who ushered Johnny and Roscoe through the inner space would not allow them to touch the door themselves, but himself tapped out a signal on the glass. A sound of permission reaching him, he thrust in his head and announced the visitors.

They shuffled in, feeling muddy and clumsy. The office strutted. It had its own nickel-embossed stove, cold now, in one corner. A rectangular rug brightened the center of the floor. Fred's rolltop desk occupied part of one windowless wall; beside it towered the ponderous black safe which he personally had escorted by wagon train across the divide and through the old reservation. Above the desk was a large framed etching of a thoroughbred racehorse. Several brass spittoons gleamed here and there, including one in the empty coal bucket, in case any visitor was tempted to use that receptacle. Tobacco smoke twined a diaphanous ceiling below the plaster one. Mayor Rubin, Linc Hotchkiss, Sheriff Gaw, George Yount, the town's elder lawyer, and two or three more sat in the uncomfortable straight-backed chairs. Still other men leaned beside either frame of the open window.

Pat was not on hand, even though this was supposedly a stockholders' meeting. Neither was Harmon Gregg. That absence, coupled with the presence of George Yount, who held no stock, was strange.

Johnny nodded to the crowd and then glanced at Fossett. The banker wore a stand-up collar, a high-buttoned coat with short, narrow lapels and rimless pince-nez spectacles which he habitually took off so that he could rub the red spots on either side of his nose. On his desk was a sheaf of impressive-looking letters opened out flat and held down by a long, slim, gold-handled envelope slitter. These letters were one of Fred's newer stage properties. He liked to have visitors think he was in constant communication with important people. And the way things were developing, I golly he was.

"You're late," he said crossly.

"I'm here now," Johnny said and remained standing, although Gaw offered his chair.

Fossett pursed his lips, picked up a crinkly-sounding letter, glanced at it without reading, dropped it onto the desk, leaned back in his swivel chair, and asked how the drillers were coming with the big rib beyond the falls.

Johnny told him, although he knew the question was an opening only and that Fossett would not listen to the answer. Sure enough, as soon as a little door of silence opened, the banker thrust his foot into it.

"Winkler is ready to make an offer."

Johnny grinned uncomfortably at his principal creditor, Linc Hotchkiss. "I'm ready to listen to one," he said.

The situation was simple enough, the banker told him at some length, though obviously the rest of the men in the room had heard the full statement earlier. Winkler had computed the amount of money necessary, first, to pay the debts of the Red Mountain Toll Road and Transportation Company and, second, to complete the highway. The total came out approximately double the amount which could be raised through sale, at par value, of the stock remaining in the treasury, assuming the stock could be sold for anywhere near par, which was unlikely. Fossett pursed his bloodless little lips. No doubt Johnny would recall one of Otto's favorite aphorisms: "Too soon you yump and hvere do you land?" Johnny had perhaps permitted enthusiasm to —uh—let's say, sway his judgment.

"We can increase the capitalization and raise more money by issuing more stock," Johnny said. Fossett didn't have to tell him what he already knew.

"Possibly," Fossett conceded. But Otto preferred a different approach. He wanted the same number of shares as were currently authorized to represent double the capitalization. In other words, he would ask each stockholder to turn back to the company his certificates and in their stead receive half as many shares of twice the face value of the old issue. Each man's investment would thus remain the same, and Otto could advance the capital needed (twice the original estimate, remember) without paying twice as much per share of stock as the original investors had. That was clear and reasonable, wasn't it?

"Go on," Johnny said. He did not like the way the other men in the room kept studiously watching the floor.

The road company's articles of incorporation, Fossett said as if he were talking to a client of less than normal intelligence, had authorized 10,000 shares of stock. Of this total, John held 2550 shares and Pat Edgell held 2550. Minor stockholders, most of whom were represented here in this room, owned a total of 920 shares. Some of their shares had been acquired through barter. Linc Hotchkiss, for example, was due 150 shares in exchange for supplies advanced, and Harmon Gregg had been given 100 shares in return for legal work. Winkler and Roscoe Blair had each paid cash for their holdings. The rest of the minority issues were sprinkled about in odd lots ranging from 15 to 75 shares each. In short, after several months of active promotion, 3980 shares of the company's stock still remained unsold in the treasury.

"I haven't heard anything yet," John said gloomily.

Fossett ignored the jibe. Winkler, he continued, was prepared to buy at the new par value of ten dollars the 3980 treasury shares, the money to be devoted entirely to construction expenses. He would also buy Pat's 2550 shares for $4500. Obviously the latter offer involved a high discount—something less than half the original par value. However, since Pat did not personally own any part of the charter from the state and had worked less than a year on the project, Fossett felt that the proposal was generous in the extreme.

Johnny exhaled slowly. "Pat won't think so."

Again Fossett went on as if he had not heard. Winkler was prepared to buy other holdings at the same rate, though he hoped the individuals concerned had faith enough in the project to keep their interests. (The eyes of the listeners met briefly, then dropped back to the floor. *They had to ride along,* Johnny thought, *if they hoped to get their investment back. Probably they would succeed; with Otto behind the road, it had a chance.*) Fossett's voice droned on. If Winkler gained both the treasury stock and Pat's quarter interest, then Otto would own, in round fractions, two thirds of the company. Johnny would retain his quarter interest and the minority would have one twelfth.

"What will Otto pay for my quarter interest?" Johnny asked. He met Fossett's eyes squarely. "The franchise is in my name."

A thin steel blade appeared ever so lightly in Fossett's voice. "He won't be held up because of that," he warned. "After all, he can easily secure another franchise."

"For the other side of the gorge?"

"Yes. He has—uh—friends in the legislature. And the Red Mountain mines are becoming important enough that the state probably would not consider it a matter of public good to maintain an exclusive franchise for a company that is unable to meet its commitments." He paused to let the thrust sink in and then continued unctuously, "But of course Otto would rather not be forced to that measure." (*My side is the best side for a road,* Johnny thought.) "Furthermore, Otto would rather not become involved in the company except financially. He has so many interests now that he can't possibly give to either the construction or maintenance of the road the regular supervision it needs. He respects your work and your integrity, Johnny. He hopes you will continue with the plans you have already laid out. You will of course retain your position as president of the company. Its importance is such that Otto feels the company will be justified in paying you a salary of a hundred and fifty dollars a month, in addition to the value which your stock eventually may have." The banker's lips lifted in what he probably throught was a smile. "Regular income is something for a potential bridegroom to think about."

"I see," Johnny said. *Guarantee that I'll be a good boy and then kick Pat out in the cold.*

"I don't think Pat will sell."

Fossett shrugged. "He may, after he has considered the alternatives."

"Why won't Otto buy just the treasury stock and let Pat alone?"

Fossett made a deprecating gesture. "It's nothing personal. Pat's a fine fellow. We all like him." (*You don't like him,* Johnny thought.) "But Otto feels that where long-range business considerations are involved Pat isn't—uh—stable. He feels that over the years it won't be to the best interest of either Red Mountain or Argent for Pat Edgell to have a substantial voice in the affairs of the company. You'll have to admit he'd likely be . . . dissident."

Peace, it's wonderful, Johnny thought. So were 2550 shares of stock at less than half price. Still, Pat had not put out one dime for his stock. Steamboats on the Los Padres: Winkler knew how Pat operated. And Winkler would be investing more than forty thousand dollars.

"There are other ways of raising money," Johnny said.

Fossett clucked. "I assume you are referring to Pat's involved scheme for setting up a separate construction company, granting stock purchase options to holders of town lots in Summit, and whatever other frills he can dream up overnight."

"It's not as bad as you make it out."

"It is completely unsound, and you know it."

"It lets us keep control of our own affairs."

"If it works. But will it? And when? How many people are living in this great new Summit City he is banking on?"

"The Summit Queen claims have been tied up in litigation," Johnny admitted. "That slowed things down. But Pat figures that as soon as the mine has a chance to show its potentials, then a real rush will start, like the one to Red Mountain."

"Pat figures!" Fossett certainly knew how to sneer, with his tongue, his eyebrows, his pince-nez, his whole face. "Even if a rush does develop, which is highly speculative, setting up this folderol and going East to float a stock issue will take time. Pat's ability to secure proper underwriting is even more problematical. Under the very best of those circumstances, you cannot complete the road before the end of next summer, can you?"

Johnny squirmed unhappily. "I guess not."

"But if Otto takes over he'll move in every bit of equipment he has. Experienced foremen—expense no object. He'll do everything within his power to assure a connection with Red Mountain by wintertime."

A spark jumped through Johnny. "This year!" Then he gave his head an incredulous shake. "I'm not sure even Winkler can do that."

"Winkler and you together," Fossett corrected and smiled his pursy smile. "It's a challenge, isn't it?"

"I . . . All I can do is talk to Pat. He's still my partner."

"No," Fossett said, his smile vanishing. "That's not all." His pince-nez circled the room. "That's why we're here."

The men stirred in embarrassment and kept on staring at the floor. Except for George Yount, the lawyer. He leaned back in his chair,

one elbow hooked around an upright and looked both bored and
impatient: Let's get down to cases.

Fossett said, "According to your articles of incorporation, unsold
stock in the treasury has no vote. Is that correct?"

"Yes," Yount replied, not waiting for Johnny. "I've been over the
whole thing. Ogden and Edgell each own the same number of shares.
In case of a dispute, decision will rest with the minority." And now
he too looked from man to man.

Fossett nodded and took up the account. Johnny had a weird sensation of weightlessness, as if his muscles had absconded.

"Before the Red Mountain Toll Road and Transportation Company can execute a contract with a construction company or offer
options or do any of the other things Pat is promoting, the move will
have to be approved by a majority vote. If Ogden and the minority
holders vote against him, Pat's proposals will be blocked."

"Which is what we'll damn well do!" Roscoe Blair cried and turned
beet-red when everyone frowned at him.

"Everyone of you?" Johnny asked.

They nodded, one by one.

"Where's Harmon Gregg?" Johnny asked.

"He left for Red Mountain about noon."

"Did he know about Winkler's offer?"

"Yes." Fossett said. "I explained it to each of the minority holders,
in order to learn how they felt."

"Harmon—"

"You might as well know it now, Johnny. Gregg is on Pat's side.
Even so, they're outvoted. You are the one in control."

Why didn't Harmon come talk to me? Johnny wondered. That
hurt. After the way they had grown to know each other while waiting
for the murder trial . . . "Suppose I vote with Pat?" he demanded.

Mayor Rubin jumped from his chair. "Then you'll be voting
against what's best for Argent, and you know it. Do you want Baker
taking away ore that is located in this county and rightly ought to
stay in this county for processing? That's what'll happen if we don't
put a road up that gorge and put it there fast."

"Otto will support this town against Baker," Fossett said smoothly.
"If he has to, he'll build a road up the other side of the canyon and
make sure Argent retains the business to which it is entitled."

"This town will back him, too," Roscoe Blair shouted. "Jesus H.
Christ, John think of the rest of us. I've got to keep ore moving into my
smelter—"

"Why worry?" Johnny said sourly. "Fred says Otto will keep ore

moving to you on the other side of the canyon. You don't need either
me or Pat."

"Your side is better and quicker," Roscoe stormed. "Why do you suppose I invested in your friggin' road in the first place? If I have to shut
down for half of next winter, I'm ruined. Damned if I'll lie still and
get screwed like that just so Pat Edgell can turn a boghole up at Summit into a private bank account. Jesus, John!"

"Pat won't lie down either," Johnny said. "He's got Harmon up
there right now, cooking plans. If I try to freeze them out, they'll
sue me until—"

"There's nothing they can do," Yount advised, "I've studied every
clause. You can block any move Pat tries, and pretty soon he'll realize
he has to sell."

"He'll be getting forty-five hundred dollars," Gaw pointed out reasonably. "Hell, I'd enjoy a screwin' like that myself."

Johnny cracked his knuckles. "He's my friend," he said, almost to
himself.

"We're all your friends," Fossett told him.

"We just want to do what's best for the town *and* for you," Linc
Hotchkiss pressed.

"We're sure of our investments this way," another voice insisted.
"But Pat's way—"

The words were pellets, spattering him. The faces were white staring
blobs in the gathering dusk of the smoky room. Everyone was talking
at once. The murmur rose and fell, and in it Johnny heard again the
growl of the crowd meeting at the saw blade when he had ridden into
Argent after Young Hedstrom's surrender. Almost wildly he straightened.

"I've got to think about it," he said to Fossett.

"Of course," the banker agreed. "But I should start word back to
Winkler by—say, Monday."

"The day after tomorrow!"

"Otto is a busy man. I happen to know he's involved in deals with
Evans and David Moffat—big figures in Denver." The banker picked
up a rattly sheet of stationery, implying that he too was big. "He won't
wait on—uh—peanuts."

"Like my road?" Johnny snarled.

"Like Pat Edgell," Fossett said and pretended to become engrossed
in his letter.

Chastened, the audience filed outside like sheep behind the teller
who, at some mysterious signal from Fossett, popped in to shepherd
them past the tills.

"3"

As soon as he could free himself from the invitation of the others for a drink and more talk, Johnny turned up Silver Avenue toward Vinegar Hill. He walked so rapidly through the late twilight that in spite of his barrel-sized lungs he was out of breath when he reached the flat space where his house was being framed by a single rheumatic carpenter, the best he could afford to hire. Panting a little, he stepped onto the flooring. His bootsteps echoed. He tested the solidity of the studs by striking them with the heel of his hand, and gummed his skin with pitch from the raw lumber. From the frame of the kitchen window he noted again the boulder that would have to be blasted from the ditch that was to bring his pipeline from the creek. Normally when he visited the house after work, he added touches here and there, accomplishing as much in half an hour as his carpenter did in two. Tonight, however, it was too dark. Besides, he felt too upset for pounding nails.

He went to the doorway. The rim of the sky was apple-green. The last slanting light molded into sharp relief each fold and ridge in the upper parts of the peaks. Here and there in the town, lamps were blossoming. He could smell wood smoke, hear vagrant noises—a cow bawling, children squabbling, the clatter of a horse's hoofs, a robin's late caroling. Pervading it all was the incessant thrum of running water. Yet when Lucille had been here on a similar evening, she had whispered beside him, "It's so still!" Alpenglow, the curve of cliff, lift of trees, the feathered plunge of waterfalls. "It's beautiful!" That had been before his proposal, before any sign of a house, before she had known that this was to be home. He had sent rough building plans to her in Chicago—"It's small but arranged so we can add an ell"—and she had suggested only minor changes. "Each time I look down this characterless city street," finished one letter, "I think of our view. My darling, how can I wait? I love you so."

He remembered her latest note, still unread in his pocket. Smoothing the wrinkles, he turned it to catch the fading twilight. He could barely make out the hurried, excited slant of the letters. She had despaired of being ready on time, she wrote, but at last she was beginning to work her way clear. The most marvelous idea: she had been able to obtain, largely on credit, a quantity of choice, lightweight merchandise that took little space for shipping and yet sold at high

mark-up: egrets, pompons, French gloves, corsages, costume jewelry—
"I hope you'll understand."

That's just dandy, John said to the letter.

"Lennie is growing excited, too. I think he is beginning to realize
at last that he is going far away, where there are tall mountains—even
with pictures it is hard to explain a mountain to a child who has never
seen one—where he will have a new home and a daddy who will
love him very much. You *will* love each other, I know you will, darling, he needs you so and he *is* sweet-natured, a little shy but he *wants*
the three of us to be happy. He asks me a dozen times a day what
you and the house and the town and the horses and the big rocks
look like. But to be honest, he thinks mostly about the train ride and
a hill he can coast on with a sled all by himself; last winter when he
was on a sled he had to be pulled by his mother. For once I'll be
glad to see winter come—with you, my dearest Johnny."

Leonard. The name had no shape to it. Sometimes John would
pause in a street and watch small boys playing in their yards, their
mothers hanging laundry nearby. A tenderness would touch him and
he would want to lean over and rumple their hair. Lennie. "Gettin'
yours ready-made," the jokers said. He didn't mind. But there was
still no reality to it. As yet the room the boy was to occupy consisted
of nothing more than boulders at its corners for the floor sills to rest
on. Where would Lennie sleep? At this rate where would any of them
sleep? At Mother Marsh's? For that matter, where would people come
to see the pompons and the French gloves? To the unfinished parlor?
Oh, elegant.

If Winkler bought into the road company, if Pat Edgell left, then
President John Ogden would be paid a salary. He could hire another
carpenter. He could complete the house.

Viciously he kicked at a loose board and walked through the darkness down the hill past Fred Fossett's new home. A lamp with a
crimson shade glowed warmly through a crack in the draperies covering
the fine bay window.

"4"

Most of his nights he spent in a tent at the road camp, but when he
came to town he reoccupied his bed in the lean-to shack at the livery
stable. Since he did his book work here, he rather grandly called the
place his office. It was hardly private. After Walt's shift to the mountain,

Jules Halverson, the chief hostler, had moved in with Johnny for the sake of company. They cooked their own meals. Neither could afford Nora's Bon-Ton more than occasionally. Besides, Johnny had felt ill at ease in the restaurant after Walt had been given the gate. His presence embarrassed Harmon, too. Of course the lawyer and John were still good friends; just the same, when evening caught him in town, he preferred to sit around the stable, adding up figures or yarning with Jules and Walt's bookkeeper and with the blacksmith.

This night, however, no one was around. Feeling lonesome, Johnny fired up the stove, added more grounds and water to the coffee pot, sliced a leftover baked potato for frying, and cut two thick slabs off the ham butt hanging in the screened cupboard. He was just dishing it up when he heard voices and a loud guffaw outside. A moment later Jules came in alone, grinning behind his scraggly mustache. He looked guilty when he saw John. He wiped his mustache on the back of his hand, asked foolishly, "When did you blow in?" just as if he hadn't seen John at the post office, turned red, sniffed, looked at the ham and said, just as inanely, "Supper cookin'?"

"What have you been up to?" Johnny asked. Not that he really cared.

"Nothin'," Jules lied and went outside for an armload of wood, which he dumped in a cloud of dust into the box beside the stove where the food was sitting on the warming shelf.

"For Christ sake, Jules," Johnny said and it was the last word spoken while they wolfed down the meal and washed the dishes. Afterwards Jules produced a stained deck of cards. "Casino?" He'd be happy to play the game every night of the year if he could find a partner.

Johnny excused himself. "I've got to write a letter." He retreated into the bedroom part of the shack. Two wooden bunks filled with Colorado feathers, pine shavings, were nailed into the corners at one end of the small rectangle. A rickety table and a curtain-covered wardrobe of unpainted pine boards occupied most of the other end. From the table drawer Johnny produced a pad of writing paper. Sitting down, he placed the stiff guide sheet under the topmost leaf of the pad, so that he could see the heavy black lines through the white paper. He carefully picked a speck of lint from the point of the pen nib, dipped it into the ink bottle, and then sat and stared. How did you write it? *My Dear Mrs. Montgomery: It is a man's responsibility to take care of his family. I do not need your pompons. Just Winkler's cash, that's all. I do not need Pat, either. Nearly every road job I've been on I've worked with Pat. When I was in jail and could not form my own road company, Pat did it for me. But I do not need him*

*any longer. I do not need French gloves and costume jewelry. Just
Otto Winkler's cash, that's all.*

He grunted an obscenity, stood restlessly up, sat back down. Tilting his chair, he regarded indifferently a bundle wrapped in newspaper that had been pushed partly out of sight on the wooden top of the wardrobe.

*But Pat will bog down in propositions. Winkler will guarantee the
road—by snowfall, if we're lucky. That'll mean a lot to the mountain
and to the town. My town.*

Lucille, what shall I do?

He wrote half a dozen words, wadded the paper savagely, and hurled it into a corner.

By and by he tried again. One way to start the words was to say that the dress had come for Nora. Work around the edges of heartsickness, surprise it sideways, and—

He stopped. Standing, he lifted the bundle from the top of the wardrobe, placed it on the table and pulled back the newspaper wrapping. A brown, rustly silken thing.

"Jules!" he bawled.

Jules shuffled in. He grinned hopefully. "I was wondering when you'd find that."

"Is this the dress Lucille sent for Nora?"

"Now look, Johnny. When I got down here with the package, Chris had just finished shoeing Gaw's black mare, the one with the cracked frog, and him, Chris that is, and Lew were sitting on the bench out back where I'd done my laundry and—"

"Why isn't it in its box?"

Jules was offended. "That's what I'm telling you."

Chris Christofersen was Walt's blacksmith. Lew Arnett was bookkeeper, mule packer, and freight expediter. Jules's laundry consisted of three blue cotton shirts, two pairs of denim overalls, miscellaneous socks, and one suit of woolen underwear, bright red with white buttons and copious drop seat.

"You know them long-handled union suits I wear?" Jules asked.

Johnny turned cold. "If you clowns—"

That was exactly what they had done. They felt justified. When Jules had brought in the box with a Chicago Dress Salon label on it, they had easily surmised what was inside and they had wondered at some length about what use Walt would have for a Paris gown now. Old Walt, turned down for a dude lawyer. Women surely did take peculiar turns. At that point Lew Arnett had noticed Jules's red drawers hanging on the line. The shift hadn't taken a minute. Then Lew had produced a new mailing label. With this they covered the address to Walt Kennerly (but had left the Chicago return) and had substituted Harmon Gregg's name, as though the package had been designated for Harmon—as if Harmon were the one who had ordered clothing from Chicago for Nora.

"We made up a note to go with it," Jules said proudly. "We spoiled the first copy and Lew wrote it over. He's got a good hand, fancy curls and things at the ends of the big words, you know. She'll think for sure a lawyer or somebody smart wrote it. Here, let me read it to you."

He produced the folded, ink-stained original from his shirt pocket. "The note'll be right on top of the drawers, see, when she opens the package." He doubled over, slapping his leg in delight. "Oh, I'd give anything to see her readin' it. Anything!"

"She's going to think Walt did this," Johnny said. "And that I helped him."

"Listen," Jules said. "We all thought up little bits of the saying. Lew put it together. Then we gave the Cunliffe kid fifteen cents to deliver the box to the Bon-Ton and tell Nora that old chinwhiskers was right sorry not to bring it himself and be with her when she opened it, but he was in a hurry to go to Red Mountain. Oh, it's rich! Listen:

"Darling Nora, I send this gift to you in ardent—[Lew said what it means but I forget]—in ardent hope that it will always shelter and beautify your fair form. Those who see it fitted to your stately figure will gaze after you impelled by a power they can't resist. They will admire its handsome color and style as it bends and waves with the motions of its lovely wearer. I have but one request [this is the part I thought up]—(and now Jules could hardly read for laughing)—that my hands be the ones to put it on you and button it tight. Your own Harmon."

"You bastards," Johnny said.

"Aw, Johnny, it's just a joke. She's got it comin'. Marryin'—"

Johnny pushed the newspapers back around the dress and bound the package with a piece of twine. "If she's had a busy night, I can maybe get this to her before she opens your box."

"Aw, don't go spoilin'—"

"It can't be spoiled any more than it is."

"What makes you so sure Walt still wants her to have a dress?"

"He's the one to decide that." Johnny jerked the string tight. "But you didn't leave him any chance. When Nora sees that label she'll know something came from Chicago, and she'll guess Walt's the one who ordered it, not Harmon, you fools. Now he's going to look like a sorehead, jobbing her because he got turned down."

"Aw—"

The dress threatened to break out of its clumsy wrappings. To safeguard it, John pushed the bundle into an empty wooden case labeled "Giant Powder." "Next time pull your jokes on somebody who's around to defend himself."

He vanished into the dark. Behind him Jules cried righteously, "I'll bet Walt would see the joke. You're just too darn touchy for your own good, that's what you are."

"5"

She had lifted the red union suit part way out of the cardboard container and then had let it fall back in a crumpled heap. The open note lay face down beside it. Johnny placed the powder box on the bed beside the pile.

"Those clowns—I don't know what to say," he said for the third time. "I suppose I shouldn't have given Jules the package in the first place. But they didn't really mean any harm."

To his surprise, Nora smiled, though the skin beneath her eyes looked drawn. "I appreciate you coming. I thought perhaps Walt was involved and was . . . trying to tell me something. I couldn't imagine what."

"Like you say, it is a crude town some ways, I guess."

She patted his hand. "Don't fret about it any more. And now please take the dress away with you."

"Walt's not going to want it."

She gave her head a mute shake.

He persisted. "Lucille will be disappointed. She went to a lot of trouble."

"Johnny, please."

Take it where? Throw it in the river or something? Give it to one of the girls down on the line? Lucille would be sore. "Why not stash it away until Mabel can wear it?" he suggested hopefully.

She grew angry. "Do I have to explain as if you were a child? I simply cannot accept that dress now."

"I don't see why. Harmon knows—" He stumbled. Harmon knows what? That she had been sleeping with Walt? Lamely he added, "I mean, you could explain to Harmon that it was ordered before you and him took up."

Hard spots of color burned on her cheekbones. "What Harmon knows is that after I've made a bargain, I keep it. Now take the dress and leave."

To his utter discomfiture he saw tears in her eyes. He picked up the powder box and edged toward the door. "I didn't go to make you feel bad," he apologized. "For that matter, neither did Jules and the boys. A joke . . . I mean—well—" He did not really know what he meant. "I don't know why it's always so hard to talk to you."

Perspiring and awkward, the box clutched to his front, he started through the restaurant toward the street. Her voice stopped him.

"Johnny."

He turned.

"Sit down a minute."

She seemed perfectly calm again. He slid into a chair at one of the small tables ranged along the wall, the box balanced uncomfortably on his lap. Nora sat opposite him. Two belated diners in the front part of the restaurant glanced incuriously at them and went on chewing their pot roast. He could hear Mabel rattling around in the kitchen.

The table was covered by a clean cloth only recently unfolded. Nora placed a thumb on either side of a crease and, as her thoughts coursed, pressed down and outward, smoothing out a tiny section of the white ridge.

"Perhaps the reason that you and I have always fought," she said, "is that we're so much alike."

"Us! Alike!"

"We both mean to have our own ways, regardless." She loosened her thumbs and the crease reappeared. "We won't accept what has been handed us. We keep trying to straighten things out our way, no matter what it costs." She placed both palms on the table and tried to flatten out a larger section of the ridge. It resisted. "I suppose you are wondering why I am marrying Harmon after . . . after . . ."

He shifted in embarrassment. "It's your business."

She lifted her hands and the crease sprang erect and she ran a finger along its top. "You've got your road to Red Mountain." Her eyes met his squarely, the way they often did just before she lashed him with her words. "I'm going to build my own road too, to my own Red Mountain. Walt wouldn't have gone all the way with me. Harmon will. That's all I'll ever say to anyone about it. Now please go."

He sat motionless. "A proposition," he said bitterly.

"What do you mean?"

"You're the reason why, when Harmon heard about Winkler's offer, he went to talk to Pat instead of coming to me."

"To find some way to keep you from knuckling under to Otto Winkler. Yes, that's why."

"Thanks a lot," Johnny said and stood up and went outside. At the intersection where the white flagpole reared dimly, he paused. He seemed surprised to find that he was still carrying the powder box.

"Now what am I supposed to do?" he muttered.

"6"

He left the livery stable early on Sunday morning. By a little after nine o'clock he had reached the slit at the head of the gorge where Red Mountain Creek burst through the rust-colored dikes guarding the way to the meadows above. After leaving the town of Red Mountain, Pat's Argent-bound section of the road skirted these meadows and followed the creek through its narrow chasm. Once past the gateway it was to swing around the side of Ute Peak, high above the foaming cascades of the stream, and join Johnny's section on the cliffs half-way down the main gorge.

To avoid having to ride the two miles from Red Mountain town to the job and back again each day, Pat had pitched, as a shelter for cooking and eating, a gray, patched tent at the last flat where the meadows ran up against the dike. Beside it was a prospector's shack of logs and shakes that he had repaired somewhat for use as an office. When Johnny reached the shelters, both were deserted. On a Sunday morning that was to be expected. But when he went inside the shack, a sense of abandonment oppressed him.

Overhead, a festoon of strings reached from the shake roof to the sides of the hutch. Their purpose was to guide away drops of rain water seeping through the cracks. One of the strings had slipped its moorings and dangled straight down above the table. Water dripping from it had stained a sheet of scratch figures being cast up as a preliminary cost table for the week. The last entry was Tuesday. Tuesday evening would have been about the time that Pat had learned there was not going to be cash for paying the workers this week. On receipt of the message he had evidently halted the job. Or perhaps the men had. That was understandable. But why hadn't he come to town to consult about possible remedies, such as the one Johnny had set up with Linc Hotchkiss? Pat hadn't even acknowledged Johnny's message. It was almost as if he were glad of the holiday, so that he could turn to other things. The Summit City bog, probably.

Stepping out of the shack, Johnny looked glumly along the raw gouge of new road that skirted the meadows on its way to Red Mountain City. He had not wanted the company's slim resources expended on this part of the construction. Earlier in the summer, when Pat and he had decided to split their forces and tackle the job from both ends, Johnny had suggested heading from the dikes straight down the gorge—finish the hard part first. Pat, however, had argued in favor of completing the easiest stretch so as to make a showing. He had done a respectable job, too; Johnny admitted that much. He had kept back at the base of the ridge, away from the soft meadowlands. Treacherous spots were thoroughly ballasted, drainage ditches were adequate, the culverts stout enough to handle the floods that would bawl down the hillsides after each hard rain. But the finishing touches weren't there. The surface was messy with stones, shattered tree limbs, dirty mudholes. "Easy cleared," Pat said, which was true. He always postponed cleaning up a job. By contrast, Johnny liked to complete each section of the construction as close behind the advance push as the exigencies of the work allowed. But in this case he had yielded to Pat's argument that they needed quick results to impress investors. Now they had it, two miles of first-class road, mister, right in the heart of the richest silver district in Colorado. Step up and buy a share of prosperity. A proposition: two miles of road that had no connection at either end and would not carry wheels until—when? Pat had waved the question aside. The stretch had to be built sooner or later, didn't it? So far as traffic was concerned, what difference did the order of the building really make? Nothing, Johnny thought—except that his instincts just didn't operate that way.

He walked between the jaws of the dike and around the corner onto the face of the peak. Within two hundred yards Pat's gouge petered out against a slanting slab of gray-brown cliff. Bleakly John peered on down the chasm to the end of his own section, miles away. Blasting and masonry would be needed every foot of the distance. Did Otto truly realize how tremendous these cliffs were? Yet he had promised a connection by snowfall. Was it merely big talk, like Pat's? That wasn't Winkler's way. Yet if the job weren't done by winter, then what was the advantage of selling to him?

Otto would at least try. Pat wouldn't.

As long as they tried, it was a road. When they spent precious time on other schemes, it was a proposition.

Pat wouldn't admit that. As long as there was a road on paper, he'd think he was keeping his part of the bargain. *Don't be such an*

old woman, John. We're partners. We'll build the road—we, not Wink-
ler. And it'll be ours.

Perhaps Walt would have suggestions. Distraught, Johnny returned
to his horse and started for Red Mountain City.

It should have been a pleasant stretch, especially after the tumult
of the gorge. The red peaks shone ahead. Snow streaks glinted on
their sides. Relieved for a time from its headlong rush, the iron-colored
stream coiled indolently through tall grass and scrub willows. Beaver
dams created several ponds, indigo-blue under the depthless sky. Instead of soothing Johnny's restlessness, however, the rich serenity swelled
it into an ache. So much to do, so much promise—and yet for some
reason he had been unable to convey to his own partner what he
dreamed and felt about this majestic sweep. What was the lack? Was it
in him?

The unusual despondency generated self-pity. Even this meadow
turned into mockery. Here too, in his earlier buoyancy, he had seen
promise. If the beaver were trapped out, their dams destroyed, the
willows grubbed clear, and the stream channel straightened, as pretty
a farm as a man could want could be created on the reclaimed land.
During the summer and autumn months, dairy and beef cattle could
be held for the Red Mountain market. Wild hay could be cut for the
freight teams. Afire over the possibilities, John had told Ira Brice of
the place and Ira had talked grandly about getting right at the job.
But so far Ira had done nothing more than ride up and look and
grumble about how bad the horseflies and mosquitoes were. He'd come
back when the swamps dried out a little, when . . . That was the
trouble—when-when-when: always the excuse for delay: we'll get at it
when something else happens: Pat, Harmon, Ira Brice: when . . . when
we've got a proposition, then-then-then . . . all of it talk while the
days slid like water through a man's hands. If he tried to reach out and
close his fist around what he saw, things went wrong: Hedstrom, the
growl of the town, headlines in the newspaper; ghouls; betrayal; and
Pat's eyes flat and hard and eager: it's a real proposition, John.
When . . .

Winkler would do it now.

"7"

Red Mountain City—City was an official part of the name and no
one sensed any incongruity—sat at the base of the hillocks that rolled
downward from the red peaks to the east and from the red pass

to the south. Johnny had visited the settlement nearly every week and still he marveled at its growth. Everywhere trails zigzagged upward, to timberline and even beyond. Some led to bright-hued freckles of dump rock beside the hopeful mouths of prospect tunnels. Others fed actual mines whose piles of waste were growing so large that they had to be held in place with massive log cribworks. Beside every dump stood a sprawl of tiny buildings with steep tin roofs and sheet-metal chimneys. Dominating them were the burgeoning Ram, standing just above the town, and, a little farther south, the equally rich Dixie Girl. Other rich mines inevitably would be developed, each crying to ship its ore out and bring its materials in—more food and hay, more powder and iron rail, more chemicals—more of everything they needed to realize their hopes. And they needed it now. This was no time to finagle and speculate.

The town was equally eager—and equally limited by lack of transport. When Gabe Porcella sold a needle for ten times what it cost in Denver, he blamed the increase on freight charges. As yet no one had ventured to pack machinery for a sawmill up the precipitous trails from either Baker or Argent, and every building had been erected out of the materials that lay at hand. Woodcutters had devastated the timbered hills that boxed the upper end of the city. Only trees too small or too crooked for use remained standing, like Nature's last sad question marks over what was happening. Slashed and discarded logs lay in tangled heaps. A chute led down the steepest hillside into town, and although it was Sunday several men were busy lowering logs down the slide by ropes. The houses that were being constructed from such materials were, for the most part, shabby and small and makeshift. Many boasted side frames only and were roofed with canvas. Others were covered with dirt. Many of the tiny windows were unglazed or covered by greased paper; doors often consisted only of hanging burlap or deer hides. It was the Angel Gabe's pride that his store and the office of the Ram were the only buildings on the mountain that possessed floors of honest plank, brought up from below by Walt's mule trains. But the thing Johnny noticed was that now there were two full blocks of buildings in various stages of construction, and that a side street was beginning to sprawl down toward the creek, where Walt had built his stables. Also, of course, there were other cabins scattered around in the distant trees where lone prospectors lived beside their tunnels. The district's population must number in the hundreds by now. And no road. Think what it would be when the highway came. *Pat, we can't fool around.*

The first house he reached, although built of logs, was fancier than most. A split-rail fence kept stray burros away from the doors. Inside the plot the tall bunch grass of the meadow had been trimmed by a scythe into a vague semblance of a lawn, and the gravelly red soil on either side of the porchless front entry had been spaded into a flower garden. White curtains showed through the small windows, and from previous visits Johnny knew that the walls of the two rooms had been covered with muslin to hide the crude chinking between the logs. The muslin itself was decorated by geologic maps splotched green and yellow and red.

The cabin belonged to Buck Shaffer, one of Pat's workers. Buck's wife Jenny was out back hanging wet clothes. She was bony and plain and had sorrel-colored hair to which she paid little attention. She was very intense. She traveled at a running walk, as if she had far more to do than she could possibly attend to, and her eyes held a look of profound absorption. She often passed friends on the street without a sign of recognition, and the next moment corraled a nonplused stranger and burst into talk. She nurtured tremendous convictions. Every so often she beset the men in the neighborhood to rise and act on some pet project. Most recently it had been to gather up the discarded tin cans that littered the town and bury them in pits abandoned by the earlier placer miners. Many people considered her teched. But Jenny Shaffer kept a neat, cheerful home.

She saw Johnny and came trotting toward the fence. There was nothing for it then but to stop and riffle through the bundle of mail for the letter he had seen addressed to her.

"It's from Mother!" She wiped her red, moist hands on her apron, preparatory to opening the envelope. "Bless you, John Ogden. It isn't many in this camp who takes thought for little things. Everyone acting like gophers, hoping to find a mine like the Ram and be as high and mighty as Parley Quine. But you and Pat, you heed what's best for the camp."

"Is Buck around?" Johnny asked, hoping to divert the flow and then perhaps learn from her husband what had been going on since work on the road had stopped.

"He's surveying toward the Summit Queen with Pat," she said and rushed on. "Mines, mines, and what'll help the mines—no thought for anything else. They want their clothes clean and then dirty the only water we have, working their mines. I was telling the street just yesterday that if we don't do something about our water—"

"Surveying what toward the Summit Queen?" John interrupted.

"The road, of course." She regarded him as if it were he who was a little mad. "It's a grand thing for Pat to do. He might have gone prospecting or taken a fine job in the Ram or—"

"What road?"

"It's a grand thing of Parley Quine, too, though I must say *Mister* Quine does give himself more airs than some people might like. But we have to have a road outside, and if Quine is willing to help, I say give the devil his due. Menfolk! They come rushing up here to get rich and give no thought to what might happen when winter comes. Oh, we don't blame you. We know you and Pat worked your hearts out in that gorge. It took big men to admit this early that it was a failure and to turn around while there is still time and build a road through the pass to Baker."

"Is Pat saying we can't put a road down the gorge by winter?" John demanded. Half an hour ago, looking at the cliffs in the chasm, he had wondered about the same thing. But now anger was rising. "Well, I'm saying we can."

"Oh, we're not blaming you. Like I was telling the men when I went up and down the street persuading them to turn out today and help, it's a blessing we have you and Pat in camp. There's not a doctor on Red Mountain, I said, and if you're sick—that's what I told them straight, even if they don't like to face the truth—if you're sick next winter how many doctors do you think will ride up that trail to see after you? If you break a leg, I said, how do you think you're going down the hill? On muleback? But if we volunteer extra work on Sundays, I said, and get behind John Ogden and Pat Edgell and build a road to Summit, then we can join onto the road that's coming up from Baker, and that way sleighs at least can get in and out all winter. Trails! The one to Argent was closed several weeks last spring, wasn't it? I asked them. How are you going to pack food and fuel over a trail that's closed? But they never think of things like that on time. Well, I can tell you we women think about them, even if there are only fifteen of us—seventeen, counting the two Mexican girls at the laundry. But not counting those two you-know-whats. Oh, I gave them a piece of my mind, the men I mean, and if I do say so as shouldn't, it was a big crew that went out this morning to help. Parley Quine brought down shovels and bars and the like from the Ram. Bless him, I say. And bless Pat for seeing what had to be done, and you for coming to help." She tore open the envelope with a triumphant flick. "That's where Buck is," she said.

"I—" But she was reading now. With a mute gesture of despair, he rode on up the street. Blessings. Savior . . . on a different road, away from Argent.

The arms of the street closed around him, as if to suffocate him. A headlong town, born overnight, careless and unoriented still. Tree stumps, chips, logs, barrels, and boxes were strewn everywhere. Rain had fallen the evening before. Paper, horse manure, and straw lay half drowned in puddles beside the muddy pathway. In spite of Jenny Shaffer's cleanup campaign, rusty tin cans, old bones, rags, more soggy manure and more limp paper fouled the spaces between the buildings.

Business houses could be distinguished from residences only by signs crudely lettered on the doors or on boards that protruded over the pathway to supporting poles at the edge of the street. One cabin, mocking its owner, labeled itself the DELAWARE AND LACKAMONEY. As if in sympathy the man in the adjoining shack had painted the top panel of his door white and advertised in black letters, CASH TO LOAN. Underneath the legend pranksters had drawn three circles to represent pawnbrokers' balls and had painted the names *B. Ware and I. Steele, Props.* A cardboard sign in the tiny four-paned window of a cabin across the street invited, PLAIN SEWING, RIPS AND BUTTONS. Then came the settlement's largest building, the log COSMOPOLITAN HOTEL: EATS. Across from that was Gabe's store, open for Sunday shopping, and next to it the peaked canvas roof of the Tiptop Saloon.

Not all the townsmen had volunteered for roadwork, Johnny noted with sour satisfaction. Many were using their Sunday leisure to work on or around their cabins. Hammers clanked, handsaws chewed. Far up the slopes he could see tiny dots pushing wheelbarrows; he could hear the distant, earnest *thunk* of axes. Still more men stood aimlessly gossiping in the middle of the street, careless of horsemen—a street that seemed curiously deserted because of the absence of wagons. The common costume consisted of slouch hat, red shirt, and canvas trousers tucked into high laced boots splotched with yellow clay.

Several of the idlers called greetings and began drifting toward the post office in Gabe's store in anticipation of the mail he brought. Dismounting, he pushed brusquely through them. Remarks about the new road assailed him: "You gonna shift headquarters up here, Johnny?" "I'd a gone with the tree choppers this morning but my old woman . . ." "Pat sure called the turn, didn't he?" Johnny kept shaking his head and pushing. He did not even stop to talk to Gabe, who looked up from selling a pair of rubber boots and signaled for him to wait.

Walt was not in the store. He was not in the Tiptop either. Only a few men were, sitting listlessly at the card tables or leaning against the bar. Sunlight heated the canvas roof intolerably. Last night's crowd had churned the earthen floor, still without sawdust, into a paste two inches deep. Johnny backed out after a glance, mounted, and started toward Walt's barn. Up ahead and to the left, dug solidly into the hillside above town, were the spreading buildings of the Ram. King Quine. Blessings on him too. He still owned a quarter interest in the mine, and had sold the rest for more than enough to build such roads as he wished. Otto Winkler was no longer necessary.

But Winkler would stay with Argent. Parley Quine's pull was toward Baker. Something more was due Argent, was it not? Or at least Argent had seemed to matter most back there at Tally's, with the Utes yammering outside for a white man's bones.

He turned the corner and no longer had to look at the Ram. Walt's corrals lay at the foot of the slope beside the creek, the fence cornering out in a pool so that the stock could reach water without the necessity of pipes or troughs. Although the steeply gabled rectangular barn had been completed only two weeks ago, Walt was already adding a wing. Even that extra space wasn't going to be enough, to judge from the amount of hay and equipment piled outside and protected only by sheets of pegged-down canvas. Johnny's expression turned wry. A hell of a Walt, men said. They were right, too. While everybody else scrabbled, Kennerly sat tight. No stock promotion schemes, no quarreling partners, no clashing loyalties. Just Walt, playing it alone. And growing.

He had always been a loner. Though he had packed material for the road in the gorge and was willing to wait for his pay, he had not been willing to invest. Though he had rented horses to people wanting a look at Pat's paper Summit City, he had not purchased a single lot. Why get involved? Whichever road was built, whoever built it, his wagons would roll over it. Sit tight and win.

Perhaps Nora should have thought about that a little sooner. Perhaps Johnny should have. What kind of advice was he likely to get from a man who was never willing to commit himself to anything? He started to turn around. Then he heard the tapping of a hammer inside the dusky maw of the barn and checked himself. He had to talk to someone, if for no other reason than to be rid of some of the pressures that were swelling and churning inside him.

"8"

On Friday Walt had gone to Baker and had purchased a light express wagon for making deliveries around Red Mountain. Yesterday, Saturday, he had taken it apart and had packed it from Baker across the pass on muleback. Now he and his hostler were putting it together again. Engrossed in the task, Walt did not hear anyone approaching until the hostler drawled, "Well, look who the cat dragged in! Hi there, Johnny!"

Deliberately Walt stayed bent over the wheel nut he was tightening.

Baker wagon, Johnny would accuse. Well, Walt had got a better buy in Baker. Reason enough, wasn't it? Except that Pat Edgell and Harmon Gregg and Parley Quine and everyone else, seemed like, were turning toward Baker. And the boy's eyes would cry, *Why?*

Ah well, it had to be faced. He straightened, his face impassive behind its golden mustache.

"You're looking fat and sassy," he said. Actually John looked like a kicked dog. *He's heard about the road*, Walt concluded. He was tempted to tap him on the shoulder with the carriage wrench and tell him, Don't take it so hard. But demonstrativeness was not easy for Walt. When possible he even avoided the ceremony of shaking hands with a person whom he really liked. So he simply came around the end of the wagon and grinned.

"What do you think of her?" Not that he cared, as Johnny did, about the first this or the first that. Still, the wagon would be the talk of the town when he drove it outside later that afternoon, to make sure it was functioning properly.

"I'll be—!" Johnny walked completely around the vehicle. "A wagon!" A corner of his mouth turned bleakly down. "And no roads."

Walt glanced at his helper. "I can finish tightening up, Ike, if you want to go out for lunch."

Ike rolled down his sleeves and disappeared. Johnny patted the rim of the wagon box. "Pretty as a schoolmarm," he said. The body was painted blue. The slim spokes were red, with a thin yellow line down each one. Walt had brought the whole thing up without a nick. "Funny nobody downtown told me a thing about it."

"I bought it in Baker," Walt said.

"Baker!"

"There was nothing suitable in Argent at the right price." Reason enough. But just the same an unnatural flow of talk wagged Walt's tongue. "I need a cart around town and I didn't have time to wait. Deliveries are a nuisance. You bring up sixteen mules, two of 'em loaded for Gabe, and if he isn't ready to receive right that minute, you come down here and store the stuff and then when he wants a sack of flour and six gross work gloves it's too much to walk with and not enough for a mule that ought to be out earning his keep on the trail. Or the Ram wants a barrel of nails and a dozen shovels. There's more and more little stuff like that moving around and no transfer company yet to handle it. So I got me a wagon."

Johnny wasn't listening any longer. "How's the road over there coming?" he asked.

"Fair enough."

"Do you think they'll reach the pass by snow?"

Walt hesitated. But there was no use hiding plain truth. "Probably," he said.

"Do you think Pat can push a road from here all the way up there in time to hook onto it before snow flies?"

"If Quine backs him strong enough he probably can."

"Quine!" Johnny flared. "You know damn good and well he's mixed up with the Baker syndicate that's building the road up from Baker. If he can talk Pat into building from this side, then the Baker crowd get a free connection. And Pat plays along because that way he'll have a road through Summit and can boom his townsite." His frustrations spilled out like gall. "Town heroes—saving the sick and comforting the women, like Jenny Shaffer was telling me a minute ago. Tell that one to Sweeney."

Walt sat on the edge of a feedbox. Poor kid. This was worse than he had anticipated. Absently he hooked his index finger through the closed end of the carriage wrench and let the other end swing *tink-tink-tink* between his legs against the wooden side of the box.

"What's the matter, Johnny? What's eating you?"

"Nobody from Red Mountain ever came down to give me a day's work in the gorge," Johnny cried. "Why should they be doing it for Pat on the way to Summit?"

"The circumstances were different."

"A road's a road."

"They thought from your own actions that you had the one in the gorge under control. Besides, how could a gang of unorganized volunteers blast down a cliff rib? They'd stand around in each other's hip pockets. But anyone can work a shovel or chop a tree. Then when we heard you'd run out of money and were quitting work, Jenny and some more took panic. Rushing out to do something made the boys feel useful. They'll relax. If half as many volunters show up next Sunday, I'll eat this wrench."

"It's the idea of the thing," Johnny said, refusing to let go. "I don't want free work. Just . . . oh, support, a little faith from the ones who'll benefit from what we're doing. But if this whole damn town is going to turn its back and follow a pure promotion like a bunch of sheep, to hell with them."

This was a case of the plain sulks. It was unlike Johnny, and unwholesome. "It sounds . . ." Walt began. He had to say it. ". . . it sounds like you've picked up a bad case of green-eye."

"What do you mean?"

"You're jealous."

"Oh for Christ sake."

"Maybe *you* want to be the town saver."

He hated to have to watch. Johnny humped up like a pet colt being spurred for the first time in its life. "What a hell of a thing to say!"

"That doesn't mean it isn't going to be said by more people than just me."

"By who?"

"You ought to know better than anyone how a town can pick up one side of a story and twist it around to suit themselves."

Johnny's voice sank almost to a whisper. "Hedstrom, you mean?" Then it rose again. "That hasn't a thing to do with this."

"Hasn't it?" Walt retorted.

Johnny glared at him, then heeled around as if to fling himself from the stable. But at the sill he halted, looking up at the red peaks. "I'm only trying to build a road the best way I know how. Why won't people let it go at that?"

Walt did not answer, just sat there letting the wrench tink against the wood. Johnny turned around. His resentment was melting now into bewilderment. Twice he tried to say something, lacked the words, and swore helplessly. "Everything is . . . I don't know, so damn mixed— nobody tells me anything. I come up here and find—" He swore again. "Did you ever feel that what you'd counted on had been . . . well, cut from underneath and you had to step . . . but if you did step you'd fall?"

The carriage wrench hitched in its rhythmic tapping. Arizona: carrying water to an abandoned crevice in a canyon wall. But that story, which he had never told to anyone, would mean nothing to Johnny. The boy was too wrapped in his private agonies for someone else's ancient aches to mean much. And it didn't seem that Pat's turning toward Summit was by itself enough to account for Johnny's dismay.

"Has something else gone wrong downtown?" Walt asked.

"You didn't talk to Harmon Gregg when he came through?"

Nora's new man? Why the hell should he talk to Harmon Gregg? The wrench struck out a stronger rap against the box. "No," he said.

"*We* might get a road through the gorge by wintertime, too," Johnny told him. He folded his arms on the wagon box's rim and stared into the empty bed. "Winkler might come in." There was a long pause. "But he wants Pat out." Somewhat incoherently, while the wrench *tap-tap-tapped*, he told Winkler's terms. When at last he fell silent and there was no other response than the tapping, he raised his head. "What am I going to do?" he demanded in anguish.

Why ask me, Walt thought resentfully and gave the wrench a savage little swing. Saguache: Deborah Ogden: take care of him, Walt: *Oh hell and damnation. I won't get mixed up in this.*

But he would.

One of the women who had taken care of him back in Ohio had developed a routine for teaching her foster children how to make decisions. She'd rule a sheet of paper in half, label the left-hand space "For" and the right-hand space "Against." The children were supposed to write down points in the appropriate column. The lists complete, they would check off the left-hand points against the right-hand ones. A real big point was sometimes allowed to even off two little ones. But, she would say as the children sat around the kitchen table with the oilcloth cold and slick beneath their fingers, feelings did not count. Only logic. The column that ended containing the greatest number of unchecked logical points was winner. Walt had never considered the system worth a damn. For one thing, the woman had known how to stack the columns her way.

"You've got to look at every side," he said. "Yours and Pat's, Winkler's, Quine's, Red Mountain's, everybody's. For instance, Quine has about as much money as Winkler has. So that checks off."

"Quine wants Baker to get the road."

"It doesn't matter much to Red Mountain which way the road goes."

"The hell it doesn't. You know as well as I do that as soon as the road is built, you'll be able to freight ore down the gorge a sight cheaper than you can lift it over the pass to Baker. Parley Quine nor Pat Edgell nor anybody else can change that fact, I don't care what kind of road they build."

"Freight's just one item," Walt said and made a check against Johnny's point with this: "Next summer the railroad will be finished through Los Padres Canyon to Baker. Then ore can be taken to Montezuma, only sixty miles and downhill all the way, and smelted there where the coal is handy a lot cheaper than it can be smelted anywhere near Argent."

"By next summer we'll have a railroad too," Johnny said stubbornly. "Maybe there's coal somewhere on the reservation; prospectors are out looking. Anyway, Winkler is nobody's fool. He wouldn't be putting that much money in the road if he didn't think he'd get the traffic. A solid road, built right. All Pat wants is a speculation."

What was it Harmon Gregg had said about Johnny once? Virgin eyes? Greenness, Pat would put it. Walt slapped the side of the box with the wrench. "Winkler doesn't need to hold two thirds of the stock to have control of the road."

"Fossett says he doesn't want Pat to have any voice whatsoever—"

"He'll sell Pat's stock and some of his own to friends whose votes he can count on. In fact, he can unload more than half of what he buys and still keep the management under his thumb."

Johnny sniffed dubiously. "If stock was as easy to sell as that, we wouldn't be in this bind."

"You're not Winkler. He has a reputation clear back to Denver and beyond. Just the fact that he's taking over the company will make the stock rise in value. He'll run it up still more by parading exactly the same statistics about Red Mountain that Pat is parading, but when the figures come from Otto Winkler, they'll sound better. That's just the start of the snowball. Right now the mines can afford to ship only high-grade ore. When the road is open to wagons, they'll be able to move lower grades, in effect doubling or tripling their production just by picking up stuff that today they're throwing on their dumps."

Johnny stirred impatiently, as much as to say he didn't need this kindergarten lecture. But Walt plodded right ahead:

"What I'm saying is, the opening of the road will raise the price of stock in every one of these mines up here. I'll bet a hat to a horse turd that Otto owns some mine stock right now, or is planning to pick up some in whichever of these prospect holes is showing good color. Then when the mine stocks rise in value, they'll pull the road stock up with them. All of this time Otto is unloading a little road stock here, a little mine stock there, making himself a killing—particularly on the twenty-five hundred shares he squeezes out of Pat at less than half price. Look at it straight, Johnny. Otto isn't going to depend on tolls alone to pay back his investment. He's speculating just as much as Pat is."

Johnny stood stock-still, absorbing it. Then he gave his head a shake. "No," he said. "It's not the same. Winkler will build a good road and then take the profits. Pat'll try to take the profits first, with just enough road to make a showing."

"Pat's still your partner," Walt said.

Johnny winced. "That's the thing that bothers me."

"He started the company moving while you were in jail and couldn't do it yourself."

"Don't you think I've been telling myself that all the way up here?"

"Pat's going to be ugly. He's going to rub it in." Pulling his lips flat back against his teeth, Walt mimicked Pat's harsh, finger-pointing anger. "The great white father, the great Otto Winkler, bleeding for poor dear Johnny and the poor dear people of Argent who want a road so bad. Big-hearted Otto, coming to their rescue with forty-thousand pieces of pure generosity. And you fall for it. You sell out to that sheeney cold-decker . . . Use your head, John. Pat's not going to lie down and take this, not when he's got a juicy deal of his own beginning to steam."

John's eyes were stark. But he would not yield. "There's nothing he can do. He's outvoted."

"He doesn't have to sell. He can sit there like a lump and make you swallow him. Maybe he can bluff Otto out."

"We won't bluff. We'll vote down whatever he's up to with Quine. He'll see quick enough what's what. He won't bite off his nose to spite his own face. Not Pat."

"Will you sell your interest in the company to Quine?" Walt asked. There was no answer. He looked up through the silence. Johnny's face was dumfounded. "Will you?" Walt insisted.

"Why should I?" Johnny burst out.

Walt shrugged. "Why should Pat sell to Winkler?" The wrench *tap-tap-tapped*. "You'd better be set for them to spring that on you."

"Quine's from Baker," Johnny said, as though that settled everything.

"Winkler's from Saguache."

"Quine'll keep pushing the road toward Baker, the way he is now, making use of Pat to further his own company. They won't pay any attention to the gorge until they feel like it. Argent'll be stuck with a trail while Baker gets the smelter traffic. You're damn right I won't stand for that."

So now it's Pat who's being used to further Quine's selfishness, Walt thought sardonically. He took the wrench by either end and thrust his thumbs against the middle as if to bend the forged steel. Who do you think was used when that white boy was handed over to the Utes? Who, when Winkler saw that the red heart of the peaks was good and decided to steal the road?

". . . everything I've worked for," Johnny was saying. "You must think I'm crazy!"

Ah, well. No use holding up mirrors in the dark. Johnny's complete focus on his own enthusiasms obscured everything else. It wasn't that he wouldn't see; he couldn't. And when there were brighter dreams to look at, in the dark, perhaps that was best. Walt tossed the wrench with a clang into the empty wagon box and stood up.

"I guess that's it then," he said. The woman in Ohio had lied and even as a child Walt had known she lied; feelings were the points which could not be checked off.

Johnny clutched at the reassurance. "You mean you think I should go along with Winkler?"

"That's what you want me to say, isn't it?"

Johnny went to the door and looked out at the peaks. After a moment he turned back. "If Winkler takes over, will you buy a little stock in the company?"

"Me?" Completely startled, Walt temporized. "If Winkler wants it all——"

"He'll let you have a few shares if you ask. Or I will."

"Why me?"

"Just to share," Johnny said. Just to show you mean what you say.

Again resentment rippled through Walt. *Haul me around where I don't want to go: no.* He retreated into aloofness.

"I've got mules to buy, a wing to add to this barn. I haven't any cash to spare."

Johnny nodded. His burden alone. His shoulders stirred a little as he accepted it. "If I aim to see Pat and get back, I'd better start," he said and stepped outside.

Memory tumbled through the dusk of the barn: the pitch-blackness inside a covered wagon at the agency, the rustle of a dress; and outside the roll of hoofs fading along the road to the besieged post at Curecanti. Her voice: Be good to me, Walt: and somehow he had not been and she too had slipped away from him like everything else. No enthusiasms, no blindness—and still the mistakes, the darkness.

"Johnny!" he called. "Wait up! I'll ride along with you!"

"9"

Constraint kept them silent as they turned the corner by Gabe's store. Then, seeing the men congregated there, some bemused with mail, Johnny said, "A package came to you from Lucille."

Pain squeezed Walt before he could brace himself. He didn't answer.

"I didn't know whether to bring it up or not," Johnny went on. "Don't."

"Lucille went to a lot of trouble with it."

"It's over," Walt said. A brief wound to his vanity, perhaps, that he had been supplanted by a milk-toast lawyer. But at the very beginning they had agreed that if an ending came they wanted it quick and clean. "Finished," he said. So that Johnny would understand without mistake, he added, "Like Alice." That was the way you did with squaws. You gathered up your war bag and walked out of the lodge. It was hard to believe that scarcely a year had passed since he had walked out on Alice.

"You say the damnedest things sometimes." Johnny chided. When Walt just shrugged, he demanded crossly, "What am I supposed to do with the dress now?"

"Let Lucille decide," Walt suggested and turned the talk into different channels. "When is she coming out?"

"The end of the month."

"How's the house?"

"Slow. I don't know where I'm going to put her. And the kid."

That was Johnny: Jump first and then wonder. "How about Mother Marsh's?"

"I hope not—that old lady sitting in on every breath, gathering gossip and giving advice."

"Fossett might rent you a couple of rooms in that big new house of his."

"It's a thought."

The trail pushed them into single file and their listless conversation faded entirely. They passed axmen and shovelers and then came up to a gang who had hooked a log chain around a heavy boulder and were pulling it from the right of way with a team of horses. "G'up! G'up!" The stone yielded stubbornly, the moist earth heaving up in raw chunks and the exposed roots of the soft mountain grass showing yellow in the breaking clods. "Whaw now! Whaw!" The waiting men thrust in log braces and levers and crowbars. The horses were unhitched and moved aside. "Ready? Now!" In intense concentration the workers threw their chests onto their pry bars, two of them even leaping off their feet so as to ride their full weight on the levers. "Again!" The stone toppled ponderously down the slope into the gully bottom. The workers raised a cheer.

Johnny pulled his shying horse back onto the trail and spurred on, wordless. Nobody, he had said hotly to Walt in the stable, nobody from Red Mountain City ever gave us a day's free work. Here they were giving eagerly to Edgell and Quine for something in which he, John Ogden, had no share.

They wound upward among the hillocks, the deep creek channel to their left and reaching far above that into the cloud-dappled sky the red of the peaks. Rounding a timbered elbow they saw ahead of them a small dump of colored waste rock, a hutch of brush and logs, and the mouth of a low tunnel closed by a padlocked door of heavy planks.

"Why, that's Aino Berg's claim!" Johnny exclaimed as if taken by surprise. "Locked up. I wonder where Aino is."

"At the Ram, working for a stake. He still thinks he's going to strike it here. I don't know. Everybody else has moved across the creek to the side of the peaks. That seems to be where the veins run."

Just as they reached the flat in front of the padlocked tunnel, the three men they were looking for jogged out of the spruce above them. Johnny pulled rein and waited. The trio approaching had time to adjust their faces to whatever plan was in their minds. Pat came wreathed in smiles. Behind him, bland and cool on a high-headed thoroughbred horse, was Parley Quine, indifferent to a new brush rip in the side of his expensive shirt. His dog Joseph trotted at his heels. Harmon Gregg brought up the rear, awkward still in a saddle and, in spite of the fore-warning, looking embarrassed behind his silky goatee. Well he might, Walt thought with quick dislike, well he might.

"It's old Johnny!" Pat cried. For just one instant his glance flicked at Walt: Why's he here? and then his eyes went back to his partner. "What do you know! Old Johnny!"

Underneath the simulated heartiness he was as wary and as tense as Johnny was. The tips of his teeth shone in the stubble of beard that had been growing since he had stopped the work in the gorge. He sat hard back against the cantle of the saddle, the toes of his mud-en-crusted boots pushed forward in his stirrups. Walt had watched him that way before when the boogers were riding him, and he knew that in that state Pat was almost impervious to reason.

His words all but crackled as he laid the welcome on. "Old Johnny! I'm glad to see you, boy. We were on our way down to Red Mountain City, hoping maybe you'd come up on your regular trip. And here you are. You're lookin' good, boy."

Johnny knew Pat, too. He did not answer a word. He was white and nervous, as though the speeches he had undoubtedly been rehearsing on the way had slipped his memory and he could not pull them back.

Pat noticed the silence. The wariness tightened in his eyes, but his voice kept up its warm rattle. "Did you see the road workers back yonder? How about that? We'll be hooked up at Summit and running wagons over the pass before the leaves fall. I told you this was the way for the road to go. Did you see? Twenty-two volunteers!"

"Twenty-four," Quine corrected.

"Yes, sir," Pat said and then let Johnny have it. "This is the road Red Mountain really wants."

Johnny glanced at Harmon and then at Quine. "This is between Pat and I." He remembered Walt. "Thanks, Walt, but . . ."

"Sure," Walt said and jerked his head for the other pair to follow him away. Sit out of hearing with Harmon Gregg and recall the feel of Nora's breasts and talk about what—the weather?

Pat's abrupt savagery stopped them. "Oh no you don't." Then he smiled again. "You're always in such a hell of a hurry, John. Let's all listen. Parley's in this too. He's going to take seventy-five hundred dollars' worth of treasury stock. That'll guarantee us a road both ways out of Summit City, to Red Mountain town one way and to Baker the other. Then we really will be set to push ahead with both our town company and our construction company. I told you this was big, John. Now maybe you'll believe me."

John moistened his lips. "I guess Harmon told you, too. Winkler will put in better than forty thousand dollars. That'll guarantee a road through the gorge for Argent City."

"And Winkler will own the road." So far Pat had kept his temper, perhaps because Quine was watching him. But it was beginning to jerk loose now. "You'll be Otto's errand boy, like Fred Fossett and every other toad in these mountains that can't stand on his own feet. You do what I say and we'll own it. It'll be our road."

"Winkler will give you forty-five hundred dollars for your stock," Johnny said. "Cash money."

Idly Walt wondered whether Pat had ever seen as much as five hundred dollars in cash. But his mouth wrinkled as if the offer were beneath disdain. "Does he want me to wrap it up like a present and tie a ribbon on it, too?" he sneered.

Parley Quine interrupted smoothly. "If you two can't get on together, which sometimes happens in business even between friends, and if for the good of the company one or the other of you ought to pull out, I'd just as soon take Ogden's stock for my seventy-five hundred."

Very neat, Walt thought. Outbid Winkler on the same number of shares and do it with flair enough to make Otto look cheap in Johnny's eyes.

"I'm not going to sell," Johnny said.

"Why should I?" Pat flared.

Johnny swallowed. "There's nothing else you can do."

"When Parley votes the shares he buys—"

"He can't buy any."

"What's to stop—"

"The majority will vote against selling him a single share."

"Don't be a goddam fool. We'll sue you ragged in every court in Colorado."

"George Yount says it's airtight."

"Gregg says different." Pat jerked toward the lawyer. "Don't you?"

Harmon looked miserable behind his whiskers. "We'll certainly look into the matter."

"Agh!" Pat chopped off the hedging with a downward stroke of his hand. He swung back on Johnny. His temper was completely loose now. He put both palms on the pommel of his saddle and leaned forward as if to launch himself. "If Otto Winkler thinks I'll jump through his hoops just because you do, by God he'd better start thinking again. I hold as much stock as you do. I have as many votes as you have. Stockholder meetings—rubber stamps, for Christ sake. I'll stamp 'em. I'll get injunctions. I'll push every breath you take back down your bellies. Every one. Tell Winkler so. Tell him there are some things he can't buy. I'm one, understand. This company is another, understand. We're not all gutless, understand. Tell him!"

He was raving. Harmon looked uncomfortable. Quine interrupted by jostling Pat's horse with his own and suggesting suavely, "Take it easy, Pat. I think Ogden is just trying to bargain."

"No," Johnny said, white still from the tongue-lashing. "I—"

Quine went right ahead. "Gregg tells us that Winkler is offering you a salary for your work, in addition to letting you hold onto your stock. For a man about to be married—a ready-made child to support—a salary is a temptation. We appreciate that."

Johnny flushed, shamed by the innuendo—unmanned by a woman.

Blandly Quine continued, "We want you with us enough that I'm ready, for one, to match Winkler's . . . generosity. I'll raise my ante for the treasury stock to—say, eighty-two fifty. We'll agree you can regard the excess as salary. Finish your house, take a little honeymoon trip——"

"I'm not bargaining," Johnny said.

Walt came unhappily to his aid, challenging Quine, "Why don't you buy all of the treasury stock, the way Winkler is? Is it because you don't want a road down the gorge to compete with your highway to Baker, and you know eighty-two won't even scratch—"

Pat snarled, "This is no business of yours, Kennerly. You had your chance to come in with us when we first started talking road. But you nursed your nickels, and now you can stay out, see."

Johnny seemed scarcely to have noticed the exchange. He was regarding Aino's tunnel as though the words he needed might be locked up somewhere behind the planks. Moodily he said,

"This is where I first got the idea for the road."

"Should we put up a plaque?" Pat sneered. "Don't bullshit me. What you got up here was a two-bit contract to build a two-bit burro trail and that's all it ever was, a pissy little burro trail, until Quine made his strike. That's when a road grew out of it. Right while you were in jail, that's where you were with all your goddam nobleness, in jail, and it's me that made what road there is out of your stinking trail and it's me that'll make something worthwhile out of the road, but not if you keep on thinking like a two-bit trail builder."

"I applied for the franchise as soon as I was off the hill," Johnny said. "It was a road then. Ask Gregg. A road for Argent. Not Baker or Summit or anything roundabout, but a road straight down the gorge to the town that I've had my stakes in ever since there was a town."

Don't talk to them, Walt thought. *Your check marks and theirs aren't even about the same things.* He looked at Aino's claim and on up among the tree-spiked hillocks toward the pass. Could anyone really know what it had been like for Johnny that September day, the aspens as clear as gold, when the boy had walked past here with a pair of blankets across his shoulders? What prophecies in this immensity of light, beside these peaks? And now the surge of the days was drowning it. *Don't try, Johnny.*

Urgently he interposed, before Pat could begin storming again, "It doesn't look to me like there's anything useful left to say. Maybe we'd better turn this over to the lawyers and——"

"I said keep out of this, Kennerly," Pat flared. "There's plenty needs saying. There's——"

And Johnny went on as if he had wound himself up too tight to run down. "I went outside for supplies to open a way up here. And then . . . then . . ."

"Hedstrom!" Pat sat back in the saddle and hammered at him with those hard, flat eyes. "By God! I think you're getting to where you're actually proud of that. By God!" He had to work for the breath his rage needed; he used his oaths like a pump. "Well, by God! My name's not Hedstrom, see. You're not going to throw me to that Jew Indian just so you can point up the gorge and say to your seamstress, 'That's what I did for this town.' You won't get away with it, by God you won't."

Seamstress. Johnny's face muscles tightened. Without speaking another word he reined his horse around and started down the trail.

Walt spurred ahead of the others to keep them off his back. The jostling of the horses threw him beside Harmon Gregg. They regarded each other with animosity, and Walt said, feeling he owed the lawyer this jibe at least,

"You're the fellow who said last fall that you'd bet on John Ogden. Something must have changed your mind."

Harmon flushed, knowing well enough the something to which Walt referred. "He's obsessed," he growled.

"That's because you didn't clear him in the courts. You sidestepped and now he's trying to clear himself."

"Some day he'll choke on that road."

Pat overheard the remark. Loudly he said, for Johnny to hear, "You're goddam right he'll choke. And I'll be the one who shoves it down his throat, by God, I will."

Quine said, just as loudly, "Imagine a skunk like that—selling out his own partner the way he sold out Hedstrom."

"Anyway," Walt told Harmon, "you can't call him innocent now."

"No, you certainly can't. This time he knew what he was doing."

"I mean that when the things you've worked for get twisted out of shape and the hopes you've had get shrunk in the laundry of other people's schemes and the men you thought you knew turn out to be less than you supposed they were—that's when the fuzz goes off the peach."

"So?"

So I hope he doesn't turn hard and mean or dry up inside like me, Walt thought. But there was no way of saying that either. They rode on, silent. The little donkey trail the prospectors had made for taking supplies to their claims wound out of the hills and zigzagged down the slope to where the volunteer workers had uprooted the boulder. The men had eaten their lunches after the triumph and were just now straggling back to work. Pat and the other two stopped to talk.

"Well," Walt said to Johnny's back, "I guess that's that."

Johnny twisted around in the saddle. "You saw how he was. What else could I have done?"

"Don't worry about it."

"I . . ." Johnny didn't finish. The trail turned so that the peaks were straight ahead, glowing crimson in the rush of the afternoon sunlight. The next bend brought into sight the log-and-canvas settlement of Red Mountain City, the meadow with its blue beaver ponds, and on beyond them the abrupt deepening of the gorge. He smiled suddenly. "Now we can work—real work for a change." They passed half a dozen axmen chopping a roadway through a tight barrier of blue spruce. "We'll build a better road," he said.

Walt gave his head a wry shake. It had been wasted breath to tell him not to worry. He would carry this day with him just as he carried Hedstrom's death with him. Perhaps Pat was right. Perhaps the time would come when John would even grow proud of these things, pointing up the gorge and saying, That's what I did. You've got to relax, Johnny. But the boy never had been truly at ease since his mother six years earlier had turned her back on what he had grown to believe. That thought brought still another with it: *I do fall in love with the damnedest women.* Which hurt bled deeper, the kind he brought to himself by holding back, or the kind Johnny invited by embracing too much too eagerly? The ageless cry of grief that the things we wish were so are not so. Did life always end in betrayals, no matter what a man did?

I

"1"

In his first zest over putting to work the new equipment Winkler was
sending in, Johnny thought he'd not waste valuable time going outside
to meet Lucille and his new stepson. She had written him not to. A
narrow-gauge railway now ran across the divide and as far as Gunnison.
The stage ride from there to Argent would be a lark, her letters assured
him. She knew now what to do; they'd make it all right, he must not
delay his work for Lennie and her.

Until the day of her arrival, the words sounded logical, but in the
end his eagerness to see her supplanted even the road. He rented a
buggy and drove as far as the agency to meet them. Or rather, as far
as the former agency.

Everything was transformed. Cushman, his staff, the cavalrymen, and
their camp followers had gone with the tribe on its long march to a
new reservation in Utah. The lounging of the Indians had given way to
a bustle of overalls and sunbonnets. To dust, wheels, oaths—teamsters
and farmers and men bound for the mines—to canvas tops, highsided
trailers, horses and mules and oxen. The agency and military buildings
had been pre-empted by a federal land office, by a hotel and eating
places, by sharpers advertising their readiness to locate farms and survey
homesites, to equip any sort of activity. I golly, Johnny thought. A
person forgot this bursting energy up in the gorge where the road butted
against brown granite cliffs and nothing appeared save what was needed
for immediate work. A year ago he'd foreseen this, had helped bring
it about. Now Winkler was promising that by winter they'd have these
hoofs, these wheels moving to Red Mountain. Yet Pat had turned his

back. Well this was the way, no mistake. They'd see. By winter . . . and
the restlessness gnawed him again.

In his heart he was sure now that he could not finish so soon. To that
extent he too was standing on falseness, not delivering what was
promised. True, the promise had been Winkler's, not his. But it was
John Ogden's performance which the towns and the men would be
watching: Red Mountain, Pat, Harmon, *The True Fissure*, Argent.
As he tied the buggy horse to the hitching rack, the gorge scarcely
visible in the blue distance, he soothed his uneasiness by making his
own promise to the air: Anyway, we'll give it a run for its money.
Why doesn't that stage hurry up? I've got to get back.

It bucketed in with its usual flourish. Lucille sat on the top again. A
small, dark-haired boy was crowded between her and the driver.
"Johnny!" She came over the wheel to him careless of whether her
stockings showed or not. He held her in a bear hug, feeling the round
sweet press of her body, and he wanted to say, *It's been too long,* and
he wanted to say, *You should have been here when I rode down from
Aino's that day.* But most of all he wanted to say, *You've come back,*
for now he knew that during every day of his waiting he had recalled one
woman who never would have returned; and in the deepest, most remote part of his hurts there had lurked an instinctive doubt of Lucille,
too. But he did not know how to bring any of this off his tongue. Too
many faces staring, the boy looking down on them, bewildered and
frightened and alone.

"Mommy!"

Reluctantly Johnny let her go. "Surprised?" he asked.

"I hoped you might . . . Oh Johnny." She reached up, tiptoe, and
kissed him again, so vehemently that he grew embarrassed.

"Mommy!"

They broke apart, shy now. John gripped his new son under the arms,
no more body than a lath, and swung him down. "Isn't it fun to
have Daddy surprise us?" she said brightly. They had agreed by mail
that Lennie was young enough to start calling him that—or rather
her intentness had been such that Johnny had assented. He offered his
hand. The boy looked uncertainly up at his mother. She nodded and he
held out limp fingers. Johnny waggled them and said "Hi," and felt
inane. How did one talk to children? He shrugged apologetically at
Lucille. She looked in dismay at her small son, and suddenly the three
of them were strangers.

"We'd better load your baggage," Johnny said.

Words to mask the bigger wordlessness. She chattered: "I brought so
much that I'm ashamed. I sorted and re-sorted—not just clothes but

linen and blankets and towels and things we'll need in the new house
—and still it filled two steamer trunks. And a barrel for the dishes."

"Besides these suitcases?" he said in mock amazement, swinging the
grips into the buggy.

"Three trunks really," she amended.

A pleading ran underneath the words: laces, pompons, kid gloves.
Stiffly he said, "I wrote you I'm drawing a regular salary now."

"The things were ordered, I couldn't turn them back, I—" She
stopped. None of the excuses really explained. That was why the flow
came out so easily; it had been diligently practiced in advance. Now
it sounded completely false. She placed a hand on Lennie's tousled
head, brushing back the long dark hair. Another man's son. With much
more difficulty she spoke the truth. "We don't ever want to be a burden
to you."

She had her pride too. Grudgingly he yielded an inch. "We won't
argue about it here," he said.

He let Lennie give the soft nose of the horse a tentative pat and
then started to boost him into the middle of the seat. Lucille demurred.

"He'd like to sit on the outside so that he can see the rocks with the
moss on them and the little animals and the water bugs on the pools
when we cross the brooks."

The outside of the seat sounded fine, put that way. A faint animation
lighted Lennie's tired face. He had his mother's fine-spun black hair and
blue eyes, but someone else's high cheekbones. The soft chin was
probably babyhood's lingering impreciseness. Johnny said, "I should
have thought of that," and swung him—"Upsadaisy!"—onto the outside. As he settled into his own seat and gathered the reins, Lucille
put her hand through the crook of his arm. Her fingers squeezed. Again
he understood. The boy was not to come between them ever. But she
still didn't have to peddle pompons.

He clucked the horse alert. The mountains ahead were green with a
yoke of oak brush and aspen. Above that light greenness were black
collars of spruce, and higher still, above the timberline, perched the
soft gray cap of distant rock streaked with white. "That's snow up
there in those gullies," Johnny said to the boy. "I'll bet you don't see
snow in Chicago in the middle of summer."

Lennie did not answer. He had already fallen asleep against his
mother's shoulder. "He's only four," she apologized.

"Was it a pretty bad trip?" Johnny asked.

"For him, yes. I knew what was at the end. But Lennie was trainsick
most of the way across the divide. When finally we did get a hotel
room in Gunnison, he was too frightened to sleep. Some drunks were
arguing in the hall. One of them fell against the door or was pushed.

Lennie thought they were trying to break in. He wouldn't go to sleep for hours. This morning we started inside the stage but the cigars upset him, and after we persuaded the driver to give us a place outside, the sun made his head ache."

He patted her knee. "I like kids," he said, trying to be reassuring.

"He'll love you, Johnny. I know he will. But he's exhausted now."

She was taking Lennie's remoteness too hard. He said cheerily, "He's only four—to quote a famous authority."

She couldn't manage a smile in return. "I don't want you to be . . . disappointed."

He hooked the reins around the whip socket. "Does this seem like disappointment?" He kissed her hard. "Whew!" he said and grinned. Then he turned contrite. "It was too much for you to tackle alone. I should have gone to Chicago. We could have been married there."

"I didn't want you to leave your work."

"Your family must think—"

"They're happy for me," she said quickly.

"I could have come as far as Denver."

"Sssh! I want to be married where my home will be, among our friends."

His gloominess returned. "I guess Nora is still figuring to be your maid of honor even if Harmon doesn't show up. It'll be kind of awkward if he does, after that scene with Pat. You got my letter about it?"

"Not in time to answer." Her hand tightened its pressure on his arm. "I ached for you."

"It was the only way to be sure of the road. Now Argent is sure." He tried to buoy himself. After all, this was a happy time. "You won't believe the stuff we're moving in. High-scalers climbing around those cliffs like ants—"

"You're not taking chances, are you?"

"Not me." He slapped the reins along the horse's back. He was not used to being fretted over. When he had thought about the matter at all, he had supposed such mother-henning would annoy him. Actually he found the concern warming. He'd better not talk too much about the work, however. She might rebel.

"It's getting to be a social occasion around town to ride up as far as the falls on the afternoons we blast," he said. "We break dozens of tons of rocks each round—the most of any powder job I know of. It's a sight, it really is. First a couple of boulders whip out as if they were going to sail clear over the mountains, then the smoke puff comes, white and black boiling together, and the roar, and the rock face crumples as if somebody had pulled it loose with a string, and—well, it's a sight."

She pressed closer, smiling. "Now you're talking like my Johnny again."

"We'll be ready for another shot on the day after tomorrow in the afternoon."

"Oh, I want to see it."

"Al Ewer prints my name in the paper once in a while now. I guess he figures it doesn't read like quite such a dirty word beside Winkler's name and Fred Fossett's."

"It never did, John Ogden. I'm proud of it."

"You're stuck with it, beginning next week. I reckon the details are getting squared away. At least Nora and Mrs. Fossett have been bustling around .enough."

"Poor Johnny. Doing your work and mine."

"Did I write you that they decided just the other day it would be better if we were married in the Fossett's front room instead of in the church? The church preacher, though," he added hastily. "Not the town justice. Old Spec Alden. He's a pretty good sort for a minister. I went bear hunting with him once. We didn't know there were two bears in the thicket. We found out in a hurry." He regarded her anxiously. "Do you mind?"

"Of course not. Just curious. Why did you decide against the church?"

"I thought it would be more—homey. We can stand there in the bay window with flowers in back and the guests—oh, the women have doped it out. They'll tell you. Anyway, it's better than rattling around in an empty church." That was what he feared, emptiness. Bitterly he said, "I don't know for sure that even Walt is going to show up to be best man. He says he and Nora split up without hard feelings, but just the same he moved to Red Mountain. Pat sure won't come down. Everything's a mess. I don't know why things go wrong this way, I swear I don't."

"I don't need people crowding into a church for me to have faith in what we're doing, Johnny."

"You're not even going to have a honeymoon."

"I told you I don't mind. I know your work has to come first, now. I'll collect later. That's a promise."

"Where'd you like to go?" he said, trying to recapture gaiety.

"Some place far back in the mountains."

"Not Denver?"

"No."

"San Francisco maybe? Some city?"

"Just you and I—not another person. We'll camp by a little blue lake perhaps, with trees around the shore. Nothing to do. No road—just us."

"You're wonderful."

"I love you."

"How much?"

She caught his chin, turning it clumsily because of Lennie's weight on her shoulder, and pulled down his head to kiss him. "Every bit of me, darling."

Lennie roused and stirred and fell asleep again. The warm dust clung to the revolving tires and then slipped back in feathery plumes. The horse's muscles rippled easily under its silken skin. Awareness of her shoulder against his expanded into desire.

"I knew you'd be like this," he said and sighed. "I wish we were getting married tomorrow instead of next week."

She snuggled even closer. "I know it's a long time. But . . ."

"I suppose." Fred and Margaret Fossett were timing their vacation trip to Denver so that the newlyweds could have an uninterrupted stay in the Fossett home, and every one of the banker's arrangements had been keyed to that. During the honeymoon, Nora would care for Lennie, taking him to the Brice ranch for part of the time. If they pushed the boy too hard, he might think he was being abandoned.

"It's best the way it is," he conceded. "We've got to give the tyke time to get used to these people and places. It's a big change."

She brushed back Lennie's hair. "Some day he'll know how lucky he is," she murmured and looked into Johnny's face. Impulsively she told him, "You're the kindest man I ever knew."

He felt the curve of her hip against him and sighed again and kept his hands on the reins. "Me?" he said and took refuge in stale banter. "I thought it was my beauty you loved me for."

"2"

The town was even busier than she remembered. Activity strained and hammered: cement foundations, brick and sandstone walls, high mansard roofs: schoolhouse, courthouse, a fraternal hall. Business establishments flared from Main Street up new transverse thoroughfares. New residences crowded around the foot of Vinegar Hill. But the animals were what appalled her most. "I never imagined anything like it!" she told Margaret Fossett, in whose guest room she and Lennie were staying. Each morning the two of them were awakened by the clatter of mules starting for the high country. Many of the animals noisily dragged along lengths of pipe and iron bars and lumber attached by ropes to either side of their wooden saddles. One train even carried a monstrous reach of cable coiled from animal to animal. In the evening the endless strings poured back into town with their loads of ore. For a wild hour before sunset the streets swarmed with galloping saddle horses, lurching freight wagons, and squeaking express carts that raced each other pell-mell for the hay and grain of the crowded corrals and stables. "No," Margaret Fossett said dryly, "and I don't suppose you ever imagined anything like these flies, either."

In this milieu Johnny grew more and more tense—or perhaps Lucille learned to recognize a tenseness that she had not fully appreciated during the days of their wooing. He was the one who had said not to push Lennie. Yet on the second afternoon following their arrival in Argent, he left his work early and showed up at the Fossetts' with a rented mare for her and a pony for the boy. He wanted them to ride up the canyon with him and see his blasting. But the moment he lifted Lennie onto the shaggy little beast—Lennie, who had never been on a horse before—the boy turned rigid. When the pony took a step, he screamed for his mother. For half an hour Johnny cajoled and then grew pinched about the nostrils. By this time it was too late to see the explosions.

Lucille tried to revive his earlier generosity. "To requote a famous authority, he's only four."

"It doesn't matter."

But it did matter. The next day he came in a sedate buggy and morosely drove them as far as the falls, to see what little was left to see. Again Lennie was frightened: the heights, the hissing plunge of the water. So the three of them stayed self-consciously on the horse-hide seat while his new father pointed out a rib of cliff half a mile away. Drillers dangled there like spiders; rubble pushed over the cliffs by the roustabouts plummeted downward with comet tails of dust; a line of two-wheeled carts plodded upward with supplies, turned, and came back. The work in the upper part of the gorge had been stopped, he said, in order to do away with packing supplies up the old zigzag trail. Now the full energy of the project was being concentrated on this difficult stretch beyond the falls.

"There won't be another blast until after we're married," he grumbled. "It takes that much time to clear away the muck from the old shot and drill the holes for a new one."

"I'll see it on my honeymoon," she promised. But he stayed disappointed. It worried her. When first she had looked across the canyon at the beginnings of this road and he had proposed, she had realized rather nebulously that in accepting him she must also accept his work. But she was just now beginning to understand how total the acceptance must be. She did not like it. Was he disappointed in her because she had not left Lennie behind yesterday, forsaking everything else in order to see him as he wished to be seen, full-rounded against the boom of the power he released, the cliffs he destroyed? *It's the road that gives him meaning, not I:* and for a moment she was afraid and unsure, and she thought in sudden inchoate misery: *Have I crossed that divide to make another mistake?* Severely she took herself in hand. Wedding nerves. Every woman moving into newness felt this sacrifice of identity. She did not really know the stranger who was to be her husband, the exile that was to become her home. But she would—she must. *Her father's unblinking stare: Have you told him the truth?*

She touched his wrist. "I'm sorry, John."

"It doesn't matter," he said again and gradually under her questions and her deliberate enthusiasm—"The canyon is so tremendous, Johnny; I don't see how you dare"—gradually he loosened a little and for a time was more like himself.

Lennie, however, stayed constrained and distant. Johnny fretted about that also. "I don't know what's wrong," he said after they had returned to the Fossetts'. "I generally get along fine with kids."

"Nothing's wrong. He hasn't had time to take in everything yet. Think how overpowering things must look when you are as small as he is. You said yourself he mustn't be pushed."

"I know, but . . ."

But-but . . . Too many contradictions rose to unsettle and disturb him. The day following the disappointing trip to the falls, the county commissioners rode to the same spot for an examination of the highway. Returning, they bluntly expressed doubts about the road's being finished by winter and intimated that in this eventuality the county might take over the project and complete it as a toll-free thoroughfare.

"That franchise came from the state," Johnny fumed. "The county can't revoke it. Pat's behind this—him and Quine—trying to scare us, that's all."

"Then don't give them the satisfaction of being scared," Lucille said.

"The trouble is we promised to finish. We—"

"Leave it to Winkler," Fossett advised and nodded mysteriously, as though over secret information. "Otto has channels."

"I don't know why he made that promise in the first place. I don't know why he doesn't come over here to see what's happening. He said he'd be here at least for the wedding."

Unexpected, urgent meetings in Denver had called for a change, Fossett explained. Otto had, however, sent this little token; and the banker gave to Lucille, as her first wedding present, a replica of a silver tray designed originally for some sort of fair in Denver. It was round with a filigreed rim. Embossed in the center was a mountain peak haloed by a legend in ornate script, "From the Silver St. Johns." Under the peak was an entwined monogram, JO and LM, and the date of their marriage-to-be.

"What do you know!" Johnny said, partly mollified. "Old Otto, sending us that! Real sterling!" But the nervousness soon pushed back through. "Just the same, he sure ought to come himself. He ought to see the road and talk to the commissioners. . . . You don't suppose he thinks we should have postponed the wedding until the road is finished, do you?"

"I suppose he just can't get here," Lucille said, a touch impatiently.

And then Johnny worried about Walt. Kennerly was supposed to attend a brief rehearsal at the Fossetts' house the evening before the ceremony. He did not appear. The other principals waited stiffly in the brand-new plush parlor, sipping coffee and making small talk punctuated by long silences. Nora, who felt the others were blaming Walt's absence on her presence, grew scratchy, as John termed her difficult moods, and took exception to every remark he essayed. Fossett's dignity was injured. "Doesn't Kennerly realize our time is worth something?" Each time he said it he hauled from his waistcoat pocket a thick gold watch whose ticking was audible throughout the room. "Now, Fred," his wife pecked at him. She managed to flutter although she was growing overweight. "Now, Fred, there's no use upsetting others because you're upset," and she pattered around refilling cups from a hand-painted pot until Lucille felt that one more swallow of coffee would turn the inside of her mouth to fur.

Only the minister remained calm. His name was Barnabas Alden. He was called Spec for no reason that Lucille could discern, except perhaps that Barnabas wasn't a usable name. He did not wear glasses. He was rather short and chunky. He had square white teeth tipped with gold. He smiled a great deal and spoke with extreme articulation, thumping precisely on accented syllables. He was dreadfully earnest. Even his heartiness was intense, and yet he did not mind telling stories on himself or hearing them told. Johnny liked him—but Johnny wanted to like everyone and so became vulnerable to each fresh discovery that not everyone else was equally determined to be friendly in return.

Some years earlier, Argent's Protestant townswomen had submerged denominational differences to institute the building of a small white boxlike community church. It was a simple cube in shape, with three narrow steps leading to its double doorway; and overhead rose a square, squat tower on which a pointed top sat like an afterthought. Structures of equally modest scope had been built in Argent in weeks. The erection of this one, entirely by volunteer labor, had required a year. Barnabas

Alden, a Baptist, had then been summoned from San Cristobal to take charge. An early snowstorm had turned his crossing of the mountains into an ordeal and he had arrived so used up that the dedicatory services had been postponed from Sunday morning to Monday evening.

In spite of the unusual hour, curiosity had filled the church for the dedication service. Thereafter congregations had dwindled, partly because of the airs of the Baptists who felt that since the minister was of their persuasion they could run things to suit themselves, and partly because of male indifference. Alden healed the denominational rift. "Then," he reminisced into the silence of the Fossetts' parlor, "I decided to go where the men were and give them the truth burning hot." He invaded the saloons. The throng in the Pastime welcomed him boisterously, thumping their shot glasses and beer mugs on the bar and shouting for a temperance lecture. "Oh, I blistered them. 'You are here to strike it rich,' I said. 'There are richer lodes in heaven.' They roared, 'Hear, hear!' 'Wouldn't you be ashamed to have your mothers and fathers and sisters see you now?' I asked. 'Yes,' they roared and waved their glasses. 'Should you be less ashamed with the eye of God upon you?' I asked. 'No!' they cried. 'Then what do you propose to do?' I demanded. Someone, I believe it was Pat Edgell, climbed onto the bar and offered two motions, first that everything I said was true, and second that the next round of drinks should be on the house. Both carried unanimously. They then took a handsome collection for the use of the church. The next Sunday I noticed several of them in the congregation."

"Then there was the funeral," Johnny said. He did not go on, but he had told Lucille the story earlier. A sporting-house girl had died and her colleagues had been determined that she have a Christian burial. Barnabas Alden was prevailed on to preach the sermon. The audience, almost entirely from the tenderloin side of town, had filed in defiantly, as if to say, "The trumps are in your hand; go on and play them; we'll endure it for the sake of the departed." But Alden had not taken advantage of the occasion and after his short talk the audience had filed out completely won. Some of the Baptist ladies had been less pleased, however. In our church!

Fossett looked at his watch. Nora said crossly, "I've had enough, thank you," to Mrs. Fossett's third proffer of coffee. John squirmed and said desperately to Barnabas Alden, "Then there was that first Chamber of Commerce dinner. I was fresh in from the agency. I didn't know there was a preacher around or your name or nothing about it. Linc Hotchkiss was master of ceremonies. He stands up and looks straight at me and says, 'Mr. Alden will ask the blessing.' I'd swear he said Ogden. I golly, I like to faint right there. Pat is sitting next to me. He nudges me and says, 'Come on, Reverend, shake a leg.' Linc says again, 'Mr. Alden!' I golly! I start to crawl up on my feet, trying to remember how the Lord's Prayer goes or 'A Mighty Fortress Is My God' or something I can get untangled with. Then I hear Spec boomin' 'er out. I'm telling you, that *was* a blessing. I came in strong on the ay-men, believe me."

Nora said, "Very amusing. But can't we talk about something else for a change—weddings, for example?"

Mr. Alden smiled his square white smile. "I once went through a ceremony without a ring that had been forgotten. I suppose we can rehearse without the best man. Fred, if you'll act as understudy—"

Afterwards, when the outsiders had gone home and the Fossetts had discreetly withdrawn from the parlor, Johnny fussed and fussed. "I can't figure what happened. Walt's generally dependable. If he doesn't come tomorrow—"

"Fred will fill in the way he did tonight. Don't worry so."

He scrubbed a rueful hand across his face. He looked very tired. "I'm rattled, I guess."

"Why? You used to be the one who was always convinced that every-thing would turn out all right."

"I was never married before, maybe that's it." He took a nervous turn around the room, paused at the bay window and stared through the net curtains at the blackness outside. "The day I went to the agency to meet you a letter came from Mother."

Why didn't you tell me before? Lucille wondered. "Is she opposed?"

"Not exactly. She wished happiness and the rest."

"She asked if you are really sure."

"How do you know that?"

"I'm bringing you another man's child. Any mother would ask."

She waited for his assurance, for by now she was feeling badly in need of buoying. He did not notice. He was staring out the window again. "She complained because I hadn't given her any inkling—just wrote and announced I was marrying. She said her own son had grown to be a stranger to her, like his father before him. Well, I guess I don't write as much as I should. Seems like I hardly think about her for days on end, and that's wrong." He turned abruptly, searching Lucille's face for something he had lost. "But she's been wrong too. She would never do any of the things my father had his heart on. You could even say she helped kill him, because . . . because . . . Maybe I told you. She wouldn't . . ."

"Yes, you've told me," Lucille said. Her heart continued its sinking. Was he marrying her so that she could fill his mother's lacks, deny his mother's rejections? "Is this what has been bothering you all week?"

"Not really. I just got to remembering. I—oh, I don't know what's the matter. Things start straight and clear, and end muddled. The road's behind schedule. Walt doesn't show up. Pat . . . I don't know. Sometimes I feel like I was just part of a man, shrunk down below size and trying to reach farther than my arms will stretch. I swear I don't know what's wrong."

His eyes pled: *Straighten me, Lucille. Make me whole.*

Not you, Johnny, she entreated silently. *Don't you let go.* She put her palm across his mouth. "Don't talk like that. You're the one who made me believe. Remember? It was when I realized that, that's when I knew I loved you. Hold me, Johnny."

They clung together. His strong fingers rubbed the back of her neck. Gradually some of the tension eased out of each of them and at last he stepped back from her.

"I got upset, I guess. It's going to be all right."

"Of course it is," she said. But after she had taken him to the door and while she was listening to his footsteps fade down the street, down Silver Avenue, the terror returned. How could she presume to make him whole when she herself was less than complete?

"3"

Walt finally appeared the next afternoon, about an hour before the ceremony. He led behind him, right to the Fossetts' picket gate, a pack mule loaded with wet, muddy containers full of flowers. There were masses of long-stemmed blue and white columbines, scallop-edged ferns gathered from the shadow of a great gray rock where the sun never shone, and handfuls of huge white and purple violets in nests of pale green mountain grass.

Nora met him on the porch. For a motionless time they looked at each other across the galvanized pail of columbine that he held lightly in front of him. She broke the wordlessness first. One of her dark, heavy eyebrows moved in the way it had and she said, "You're late again."

He smiled faintly. "They'd have wilted on me if I'd have been in too big a hurry." With a clatter he put the dripping cans and buckets on the clean front porch and departed silently to change clothes.

Nora was all bristles afterward. "Just like that man—bouncing in when everything is ready, making a mess and then acting as if he's doing us a favor!"

Lucille said, "He meant well. And they are lovely."

She was very pale as they started scurrying about, borrowing vases from the neighbors and banking the ferns among the evergreens and delphinium spikes and trailing vines that until now had constituted the decorations. Nora forgot the welter of her own thoughts long enough to look at her sharply.

"You go up to your room and lie down," she directed. "We'll tend to this."

"4"

The minister stood with his back to the bay window. She saw only a white glare and a black silhouette. She smelled the fresh greenery. She heard Mr. Alden's words falling around her like cold drops of rain. She did not listen to them. *Johnny—.* His shoulder was touching hers. She was as intensely conscious of him as if he were attached to her own nerve ends; yet at the same time each sensation she possessed seemed to be retreating from everything outside, from the glare the words the fragrance, turning inward to a vast unanswerable question. *Johnny—.*

Johnny said, "I do."

The silhouette shifted toward her. The drops fell and ceased. She stood numb. There was a soft demanding sound, the clearing of the minister's throat.

Behind her Lennie sneezed.

Lucille gripped the Testament her grandmother had given her to carry. *Forgive me, Johnny.*

"I do," she said to the expectant silence.

"5"

Nora closed the Bon-Ton to her regular trade and held the wedding supper there. They indulged expansively in the town's two great luxuries, tinned oysters and champagne, exclaimed over the wedding cake, laughed loudly at their own broad jokes, and in general tried to make the restaurant seem fuller than it was. Johnny and Lucille sat close together at one end of the long central table. He laughed when the others laughed, but in the pauses she saw his eyes go around the flushed faces like a schoolteacher taking attendance. Walt was sitting just beyond Lucille. Harmon Gregg was at the far end of the table with

Nora. In between were the Fossetts, Linc Hotchkiss and his wife, Barnabas Alden and his bony-faced Gwen, bald-headed Roscoe Blair and his daughter, who, with Mabel Brice, joined the merrymakers at the table and intermittently jumped up to serve. The wedding of Hardrock Johnny Ogden, founder of the town, practically. And this was the roll of the guests.

Lucille squeezed his arm. Fossett saw the byplay and said with a leer through his nose glasses, "Well, if anything is going to get done this evening, we'd better be moving along."

The table sniggered. Margaret Fossett reproved him, "Fred!"

"I mean, if you and I are going as far as the new hotel at the old agency, we'd better start." He winked at the others. "What did you think I meant?" The table guffawed.

Obediently the newlyweds ran through the gauntlet at the door. A shower of rice followed them into the beribboned buggy. Passers-by stared; two or three whooped coarsely. The horse took them at a run to the corner of Silver Avenue and then slowed to a walk on the steep slope toward Vinegar Hill.

"That's done," he said at last.

"It's just beginning," she countered and then blushed. But he detected no double meaning where none had been intended.

"Was it all right?" he asked anxiously.

"It was perfect."

He seemed unsatisfied still. When they reached the Fossetts' home, the horse wanted to turn into the carriage house behind the dwelling. Johnny twitched it on up the street through the fading summer evening to Vinegar Hill. Their house was completely framed now, and she knew its present condition intimately from daily visits. Nonetheless he wanted to take her in again, trailing the skirt of her new suit through the sawdust.

On the porch he said, all at once shy, "Wait!" Gently he picked her up and carried her across the threshold. There he kissed her and set her down. Perhaps he intended originally to walk again through each room, but the failing light frustrated him. They bumped into sawbucks and leaning planks. The echo of their footsteps sounded foreboding to her. She started to say, "Let's go back," and feared he would misinterpret and remained silent. "Ah well," he conceded at last and led her outside again.

Still he seemed in no hurry. She began to wonder why, especially when he simply sat down on the edge of the porch and motioned for her to join him. They watched the darkness flow up the sides of the basin to the peaktops. There was no moon. The sky blazed with stars. A meteor flashed. "Hey, did you see that?" he demanded. She did not answer. He sighed audibly. "Well," he said with what seemed downright reluctance, "I suppose we'd better go."

He lighted a lamp in a wall bracket in the Fossetts' hallway and left her there where the arched entry of golden oak opened into the parlor. "I'll be back as soon as I put up the horse," he said. She wasn't quite sure what to do. She went into the parlor, took off her plumed wedding hat, laid it on a marble-topped table, and sat on the plush sofa. Putting up a horse ought not take this long, ought it? Endlessly later she heard the back door bang and water splash as he washed his hands in the kitchen. By match light he groped his way into the dining room. He saw her just as the wavering flame went out. "Damn," he muttered.

What is he waiting for? she thought in dismay. *What is he missing?*

He found his way into the living room and lighted another lamp. For a time they sat on the sofa, talking desultorily. He seemed to be listening for something outside. Twice he consulted his watch. Presently he said, "Well," once more, picked up the lamp and gestured toward the stairway.

What *is* the matter? Her cheeks were burning.

The coverlets of the bed were turned back, the blinds drawn. He seemed not to notice. Methodically he lighted every lamp in the room.

She said with great difficulty, "I'll step across the hall. I'll be back in a minute."

At first he did not comprehend. Then he shook his head. "Wait."

"Johnny, what on earth——"

He looked at her as if he could not quite believe such naïveté. "Don't you know about shivarees?"

"Oh!" She began to laugh almost uncontrollably. A charivari. "To tell the truth it never crossed my mind. But of course! This town!"

"What's so funny?"

"Nothing. I was upset. I couldn't understand . . . It's all right."

She laughed until tears came. He gave her only a gloomy smile in return. "Didn't Nora drop any hints about them coming?"

"No."

"Maybe they won't," he said and cracked his knuckles and listened. "In some places in Pennsylvania they call it a belling," he said absently. He blew out a lamp. "Well, I guess it's time to go to bed. I mean to look like we were."

He finished extinguishing the lights he had so carefully struck.

For what seemed ages they sat in darkness on the edge of the bed. Her hand crept over and laid across his. "Darling . . ."

"They wait until they think we're—well, you know."

"You can at least kiss me, can't you?"

"I suppose," he muttered. But before he could forget to listen, before he could turn to her, an infernal din of horns and bells and clanging tin erupted beneath the window.

Johnny shot to his feet through the darkness and peeked from behind the blind. "Why!" he cried exultantly. "It's a whole mob!" There must have been lanterns in the crowd for he began listing names. "Gaw, Rubin, Sim Galloway, old Gabe, clear down from the mountain—Ewer even!" He turned back, patting the bureau top. "Where's that lamp? Ah!" The light flickered smokily up, as if he had just crawled out of bed to it. "Listen to that racket, will you! That's why they weren't around the Bon-Ton or anywhere. They were planning a real surprise." He jerked off his coat and tie. He let the blind go up with a tearing clatter and raised the window. Leaning out, he yelled into the uproar. "All right, all right, you coyotes! The carpet's up!" meaning, We're ready to dance. He swung back, his hair tousled, his face glowing. "Listen to that! We could have filled the church after all."

Johnny, Johnny, she thought sorrowfully. He had not been afraid of what might happen should the serenaders come at the moment of his love. He had been afraid they would not come at all.

He caught her and pulled her to him, his triumph too insistent for him to notice any aloofness. She had to share. *Johnny, Johnny.* Had his isolation from his town been so hard that a blowing of horns could mean so much now?

"Ah!" He laughed and kissed her and laughed again. "You're wonderful, darling. I knew they'd love you and give you a welcome." Did he mean, And give me, John Ogden, a welcome back among them, too?

The whooping and calling went on unabated. With a wry and sudden bitterness she thought, *It's all backwards. I'm the one who's making an honest man out of him.*

Fair enough. She rumpled her own hair for appearances, held him for a moment against the din, then broke away. "It's time to meet our guests," she said and took him by the hand and led him toward the stairs.

II

"1"

She soon saw him completely upset again. Before the wedding, though Johnny had not known this at the time, Harmon Gregg had gone to Denver on behalf of Pat Edgell's and Parley Quine's Summit Toll Road Corporation. In Denver, Harmon had petitioned the legislature for an exclusive franchise to operate a road from Red Mountain City to the pass, there to meet the highway building from Baker. If the franchise was granted, Johnny would lose his somewhat shadowy rights to the upper stretch of country between Red Mountain and Summit. That was exactly what happened. A week after the wedding, word came that the franchise had been awarded to the rival company; furthermore, the new charter specifically revoked any prior grants to the area between Red Mountain and the pass. Although Johnny was willing to admit that the wording of his own franchise was vague concerning that upper section, he was furious over Harmon's having gone behind his back—especially since Harmon had obtained Johnny's original charter and knew its weaknesses. He came home in a towering rage.

"That two-faced, self-generating bas—"

"I don't like that kind of language," Lucille said.

"—sat right there at my own wedding supper and never said one word about what he was up to."

"He didn't want to spoil the party."

"He needn't have come at all."

"You were worried that not enough people were coming."

"You're splitting hairs."

"I'm just pointing out how unreasonable—"

"Next I suppose you'll want me to kiss the son of a bitch and make up."

"I told you I don't like—"

"Well, I don't like hypocrites."

"Flying off the handle won't help——"

"This is business. You don't know anything about it. Don't meddle."

"John Ogden, if you ever again talk to me like—"

"I—"

"Oh, Johnny—"

"I'm sorry, sweetheart."

He put his arms around her and she let him kiss the soft hair behind her ears, and their first quarrel did not quite come to a head. But the fresh glimpse it gave her of the rawness festering inside him alarmed her anew. Under the exuberant pressure of his body when finally he had embraced her on their wedding night, or more accurately dawn, she had felt a surging confidence that she could soothe his dissatisfactions with love and patience and understanding. Fulfilling him would be her own justification as well. By sharing his life, by building with him, she could build also for herself. Now she was learning how much she had underestimated what she was up against. No soft snuggling of bodies as a gentle accompaniment to the joys of work accomplished were going to make John Ogden whole again—make an honest man of him, she thought wretchedly once more. He was too sorely roweled by his road—or rather by the ill-submerged guilts that drove him to this road for his own form of justification. Betrayals had fed on betrayals until now they were grown monstrous from their own cannibalism. How was she to find any share of him in the midst of that?

If he'd just relax a little while! she thought desperately. A trip, a fresh perspective . . . Instead he grew more tense. George Yount, the lawyer he consulted about the franchises, advised him against suing to recover the lost section of road. Johnny's claim was not clear-cut, and anyway he and Winkler might have trouble enough retaining the main section through the gorge.

That was exactly what developed. On learning how vigorously the rival road company was pushing across the pass from Baker, the merchants of Argent let out a wail of dismay. Red Mountain City lay in Argent County; Red Mountain business by rights was Argent's business. But the new road was going to pull traffic away from them. If the gorge project had been handled properly in the beginning . . . Pat's situation was discussed in the saloons with nods of sympathy. Thrown out by his own partner! After that what could Pat do but fall into Quine's arms and work against his own town? No sir, Pat Edgell wasn't to blame. That damned Indian-lovin' Ogden—

Helplessly Lucille watched him fight the twinings of frustration. He'd come home exhausted, sit on the edge of the bed, pull off one cracked, powder-stained boot, then hold it in his hand and stare at the speckled wallpaper. His eyes looked trapped. "Those stove contractors!" he'd growl finally and drop the boot with a thump.

"Those what?"

"Those backcappers that sit on their butts around a stove and tell how they'd run things. They couldn't run slops through a pig. They want a road and they sob for poor Pat. Well, poor Pat wouldn't have finished a road through the gorge until Christ"—he glared at her and went defiantly on—"until Christ grew horns. Yet to hear them talk Pat is the genius that should be building it now. What do you have to do to suit this town, anyhow?"

"Come to bed, Johnny."

The next morning the remoteness still would be in his eyes. When he pushed his chair away from the kitchen table, dabbed at his lips with a napkin, tousled Lennie's hair and kissed her good-bye, he was already thinking of the new day's worry.

Honeymoon, she thought.

What shall I do?

She wanted desperately to talk to Nora. But Nora was selling the Bon-Ton and preparing to move across the pass to Baker, there to marry Harmon in another ten days. Johnny blamed Nora entirely for Harmon's swing to Pat's side and vowed he would not attend their wedding, even though both of them had been a part of his own marriage.

"That's petty, John. Nora's and my friendship has nothing to do with your road problems."

"Nora has. She's right in the middle of this."

"You don't know that."

"I know quick-profit Nora. From the day she got here she's hated this town. All she wants out of it is money enough to get away. She told me so herself. Ask Walt. And she accuses me of betraying a friend!"

"Walt wouldn't give her . . . oh, what's the use?"

"That's what I'm beginning to wonder."

"What Nora does needn't spoil us, need it?"

"Not if you leave her out and stay out yourself."

Stay out! Why had she come? Vehemently she protested.

"I won't stay out of what concerns you so much. I'm your wife—or would be if you'd let me."

"You know I love you. But—"

"If we're going to quarrel every day I might better have stayed in Chicago."

Instantly he was contrite. "Don't, Lucy!" he begged. "Don't you go back on me too."

They clung together while doubt and fear evaporated in the quick urgent warmth. But now she knew the warmth could not last—not this way. She did not talk to Nora. And they did not go across the mountain to Nora's wedding.

"2"

Pressure by the merchants and the mounting gossip in the saloons and billiard parlors led the county commissioners to continue discussions about expropriating the gorge project. John hurried a letter off to Winkler, and then rushed outside to snatch that week's new copy of *The True Fissure* from the delivery boy so that he could read what Ewer said about the county's proposal. It was encouraging. In a short editorial, couched with unusual mildness, the paper advised the commissioners to make haste slowly; Otto Winkler was not a man to be scuttled lightly.

Johnny's state of mind was such that even that was too little. "I'm the one who's building the road," he said bitterly. "When something goes wrong, I get kicked. But when it's right, Otto gets the pats. There's no pleasing a town like this."

She started to say there was no pleasing him and then bit the words back. She was learning to buy peace with silence. But perhaps the price was too high. She had thought marriage and Argent would bring her renewed life, not suffocate her afresh. Indeed, on those empty days when she walked alone up Vinegar Hill to the unfinished house that soon would be hers to turn into a home, she sometimes did not feel married. She held no real part of her husband and she was beginning to wonder if she ever would. Bleakly she turned away from the bustle of saws and hammers and looked up the gorge. From here she could not see the scar of the road, only the vastness of the chasm, split at its upper end by the rearing triangle of Ute Peak. Somewhere beyond, out of sight—out of reach?—the three red mountains lured. His straining grasp for them was his life, not she.

"I hate you!" she flung at them aloud one day. But as she started back down Vinegar Hill to wake Lennie from his nap and begin supper, her violence echoed at her in her own ears and she grew discomfited. That had been Nora's cry at the mountains, so Johnny had told her, after the mule had been beaten and the soldiers had been taking the Brices back to the agency: It's cruel and it's brutal and I hate you. Now Nora was trying to flee them.

Meanwhile, Lucille had come here from emptiness, seeking fulfilment. Each of them twisted by unhappiness in different directions and finding what? Only more emptiness?

Johnny, what can we do?

Although the wedding had not brought Winkler to town, the letter about the commissioners' threat soon did. The Fossetts returned with him, earlier than anticipated. While the men met with the county officials in the courthouse, Lucille awkwardly entertained Margaret Fossett in Margaret's own house, using Margaret's own hand-painted china. Margaret tried to reassure her. They were not to worry about the early return. There was plenty of space for them all. Until the Ogdens' own house was finished, they were to keep right on living here as if—

She paused, a shrewd, gray, well-fed wren. "What's the matter, child?"

"Nothing," Lucille said and then began to talk. "I hate it!" Even her lips were wan. "I hope the county takes the road. Then perhaps we can begin again at something, together. This way—"

"This is Johnny's way," Mrs. Fossett said. "If you try to turn him from it, you'll turn his love away too."

Lucille's eyes dropped. "I know I shouldn't have said that. It's just that I feel so helpless sometimes, so defeated by things I can't even touch."

"I know. You don't have to tell me." Margaret's own gaze lowered. "I think that if the women in this town were to tell the truth, most would admit that very often they feel they can't endure living here, swallowed by these mountains, so far away from"—her hand fluttered over the teapot—"from woman things."

"I thought I would like it," Lucille said.

"I'm not sure the men truly want to stay either. There's excitement for them, of course, and adventure. Some of them believe they've found a kind of freedom they never had before. And always there is the hope of a rich strike. But a strike for what? It's a means for going somewhere else."

"Johnny would stay."

"Ah, Johnny." Mrs. Fossett gave her fluttery little laugh. "There are always the Johnnies, the ones who see a little more shine on things than the rest of us see. Yes, he'll stay."

"What shall I do?"

"Trust him, child."

Lucille looked at the circling pattern of the Brussels carpet. "He won't let me."

"I've known him since he was scarcely more than an overgrown boy. I've heard my husband and Otto Winkler talk about him many times. I've seen for myself how kind he is and generous and full of fun when people will let him be. He does go rushing off in tremendous hurries sometimes, but Mr. Fossett says that he is as honest as the day is long, and that's rare in a person as ambitious as John Ogden is. How many men his age do you think Otto Winkler would turn completely loose on a project as big as this one?"

Lucille did not answer.

Mrs. Fossett controlled a small sigh. "Besides, he loves you."

"I love him. That's what makes it so wretched. We quarrel every day unless I make myself be still. That's no kind of marriage, is it? Is it?"

"You should have had a honeymoon," Mrs. Fossett declared. Her plump fingers stopped their perpetual smoothing at the bombazine skirt that stretched tight across her lap. "Learning to know a woman is work enough for a man. While he's doing it he shouldn't be distracted by ordinary jobs. Especially John Ogden. It's not too late for a honeymoon, either."

"Oh, I wish . . ."

"I'll speak to Mr. Fossett about it. He'll speak to Mr. Winkler. And I'll speak to Johnny."

"Do you think . . ." Lucille checked herself. "He won't go. I know him that well by now."

And of course he didn't go. The commissioners had proved recalcitrant. A connection with Red Mountain had been promised by winter, and a connection there must be—or else. "Else what?" Johnny fumed, telling Lucille about it, not noticing her listlessness. "Does the county think they can build any faster than we are?"

Fossett, convinced the law was on their side, wanted to appeal against the commissioners to the courts. Legal action would stall all progress, however, and no one desired that. A day of acrimonious argument in the courthouse dragged by. Then Winkler engineered a compromise. He granted the impossibility of blasting out by winter a roadbed wide enough for wagons, but he would put up a bond guaranteeing a graded trail four feet wide that could be kept open throughout the worst of weather. He patted his dark little fingers on the edge of the desk, guttural, persuasive. Such a trail would afford easier travel and be freer of snow than the old one on the west side of the gorge. Packing on it would be duck soup for men like Walt Kennerly, men who had already established their main barns in Argent and would not willingly move to Baker. If a wagon road was completed across the pass that fall by the rival company, it would be hastily done, full of corner-cutting and consequently a breeder of trouble. The haulage distance from Baker to Red Mountain was greater than from Argent; the pass would be stormier than the gorge. Under such conditions mules operating out of Argent could hold their own with wagons coming from Baker; the merchants in Argent could retain the trade they were fretting about. Then the following spring, at no expense to the county, the gorge road would be completed so magnificently that Baker transporters simply would not be able to meet the challenge.

"Oh, he's a fox, Otto is," John said exultantly. "The commissioners were painting themselves into a corner with their talk about finishing the job and turning it into a free public highway. They'd have to order a vote on a bond issue and even if it passed they'd not be able to do the job as well or as fast as we can. The whole move was politics. They were glad to have an out, and the bonded trail gave them one. To save a little more face, they said no tolls were to be collected until a real road is built. Otto gave them their crumbs and now we're set. Now we can really go!"

But not on a honeymoon, Lucille thought.

Mrs. Fossett was outraged. "That trail isn't going to perish if John Ogden leaves for a few days. I'll talk to Otto Winkler myself!"

"Please." Lucille restrained her. This moment of victory was no time to pull him away. "Everything is clear at last for him to move ahead the way he wants to. It would be wrong to make something else look more important now." What she had to do, somehow, was find a way to join him in those hopes and drives to which he had not yet admitted her.

The next day Winkler and Fossett and Johnny visited both ends of the gorge project, examining each in detail. When Johnny returned he was afire with eagerness, yet he seemed uneasy too. Evidently something had been settled which pleased him; yet it was equally apparent that he did not think the decision would please her. He avoided her eyes. He played too enthusiastically with Lennie; he answered her questions vaguely and thought up excuses for escaping outside—he must curry the horse, chop a supply of stovewood. What was it he did not wish to tell her?

"Where are you going now?" she demanded as he edged once more toward the kitchen door.

"I'd better check on how much grain there is. I might need to order some before I . . ." He caught the slip and amended it to ". . . before the feed store closes."

She tried to keep him from seeing how the clumsy lack of frankness cut at her. Coolly she told him, "You're not a very good pretender. What's on your mind?"

He tried postponement. "When Winkler comes for supper we'll talk it over together."

She made him stay. "We won't be able to talk freely at supper—in someone else's house, at someone else's table. That's what you're stalling for, to keep from talking. But I want to hear now."

Pinned down, he began an elaborate exposition of road problems— transporting supplies, housing workers, supervising . . . She did not really listen. That glow in his eyes again: not since she had crossed the divide with him the previous spring had she seen him so expectant and assured and vibrant. A new attack. His arm swung broadly toward the gorge as he explained. Earlier, after Winkler had decided to finance the road, he had advised Johnny to abandon temporarily Pat's beginnings in the upper end of the gorge and concentrate his effort on the big ribs beyond the falls, so that he personally could supervise the heavy, tricky blasting involved. A trail, however, would move faster if separate crews worked simultaneously from both ends toward the center.

The excitement in his voice, the drive: my Johnny. But she was worried too. He was taking too long to come to the point that somehow concerned her. She pressed him, although just below the level of active awareness she was beginning to sense and struggle against what was coming.

"I'm telling you," he said and went on talking about road construction. The most difficult blasting at this end of the project was finished now, he said. During the work the foremen had grown familiar with the sort of problems that still lay ahead. At the upper end, however . . . He looked uneasily toward the door, as if instinctively seeking escape again. To gather a qualified crew and line them out properly would require close supervision. Under the circumstances—the recent political pressures—a race against time—

"I see," she said. A wedding trip for him. While she stayed here below.

"I know you don't like it. I don't either. But after what's happened . . . well, Pat and what came of it—it's my responsibility."

"How long will you be gone?"

"It's hard to say. We haven't—"

"A month?"

"Well . . . probably."

"Until winter?"

"I'll come down weekends, Lucy. There'll be other days when I can get away. After it's done we'll go for our honeymoon anywhere you wish. This time nothing will stop it. I promise."

A *lake*, she thought. *Covered with ice.* "Take me with you," she said.

He looked at her as if she were not quite sound. "To the head of the gorge?"

"Why not? Our house isn't finished. We have to live somewhere."

"The Fossetts don't mind."

"I do."

"You'll live in a tent up there."

"We'll be together."

"No other women around. No playmates for Lennie—"

"It's you we need to know," she said desperately. "How can we do that on weekends?"

"You've no idea what it's like."

"I've too good an idea what it's like without you. Since we've been married we've not been together. Not really. Now I want to be."

He stood oxlike, as if a wife at Red Mountain was a possibility he could not quite believe in. A tent. A galvanized tub for bathing. An outhouse behind the willows. What was he thinking: his mother: I'm going to live like a white woman?

"Is it so strange," she said, "for a wife to want to be part of her husband?"

"Up there where——"

"Where you're happy. You aren't happy here. Neither am I."

"You really mean you'll live like . . . like—"

"Do I have to give bond too?" She could have wept her exasperation. "But—"

She put her hand furiously across his mouth. "Don't say that again!"

He pulled her palm from his mouth and clamped his iron fingers hard around her ribs. "You're a funny one," he said. But he wasn't going to argue about it any more. A great ringing laugh broke from him and he swung her in a circle. "But you surely are nice to have around!"

"Just keep me around," she said against his neck.

Around and around. Her ankle struck the edge of the ironing board, toppled it with a clatter. Lennie ran in to see what was happening and stared at them sitting on the floor among the clutter, Johnny rubbing her bruise and both of them laughing their heads off.

"Mommy?" he said uncertainly and she held out her arms, pulling the three of them together.

"3"

Her decision sent a flurry of cluckings through the townswomen. A lady like Lucille Ogden, just married, fresh from the city—the child, too: really now—no notion of what roughing it involved; John Ogden ought to have his head examined, indeed he ought. Margaret Fossett declared that Lucille never again would be able to repair her skin or her fingernails or the damage to Lennie's manners. Vera Hotchkiss prophesied that neither the mother nor the boy could endure so much work from dawn to dark, while Abigail Rubin, the mayor's wife, predicted that within a week they both would be bored to distraction with so little to do.

Nora, back in town briefly to sign papers about the sale of the Bon-Ton, was even more direct in her disapproval.

"I hope you realize what you're doing," she told Lucille.

"I don't see why everyone acts as if the world is coming to an end," Lucille retorted. "A woman ought to be able to live wherever a man can."

"Oh, they can," Nora agreed edgily. "I've done it. But it's always on the man's terms. Don't give in to them, Lucy."

Lucille's head lifted. "Johnny didn't ask me. I asked him."

"Why?"

She almost said, So that I can be with him. But she sensed how the corners of Nora's eyebrows would lift: Johnny's terms. She sidestepped. "I thought a mountain honeymoon would be . . . different."

The eyebrows went up anyhow. "A very touching thought."

Although she was not working now, Nora's face looked thinner, its skin stretched tighter across the bones than when she had been driving herself at a day-long run in the Bon-Ton. She was having her honeymoon in Denver, in connection with Harmon's legal work filing the townsite plats for Summit City. Parley Quine, she admitted, had not liked the arrangement, saying that Nora's travel expenses were not a legitimate part of the fee, but she had made Harmon stand his ground. If Summit City was going to be as big as the men said it was going to be, they should be willing to act big.

"So should Johnny," she advised Lucille now. "Don't start out by giving him too much."

"He won't take what I do try to give him," Lucille said defensively and told her about the trunk of merchandise that had arrived and was at the livery barn, awaiting storage in the attic of their new home. "In the gorge we'll—"

"In the gorge you'll be another machine for building roads. I know John Ogden. He wants the world, but he wants it the way he dreamed it, not the way it is. That trunk of yours isn't part of what he figured and so he pushed it back on you. But what he does want he'll take, the way he did with Hedstrom and Pat."

Lucille turned cold. "He had to do those things."

"In his mind he had to," Nora said. "Naturally, he wants everyone else to think he had to. There's only one way about anything—his way. That'll hold double for you, now that you're his wife. He'll be so sure you want things the way he does that he'll be surprised and hurt if you even begin to object. Don't let him start. Don't let him drag you around."

"You've grown hard," Lucille said sadly.

"I've always been practical," Nora retorted. Briskly she pulled on her long gloves, smoothing the wrinkles out of the wrists. "I got away from home. Now I'm away from that cookstove." She picked up a cardboard box holding the dress Walt had ordered from Chicago. She had changed her mind about it, she had said earlier; it would be just the thing for Denver. "Pretty soon I'll shake away from these mountains."

"Isn't it strange?" Lucille murmured. "The last thing I'd want now is to leave the mountains."

They touched cheeks, a farewell kiss, and each in her heart pitied the other.

"4"

Johnny took them to Pat's old camp where Red Mountain Creek left the high meadows and plunged through the rust-colored dikes into the gorge. Lucille went in excitement, warning herself that whatever developed she must not even appear to complain. John was equally determined not to give her cause. He brought up a brand-new tent for the three of them to sleep in. It had a frame of waist-high yellow planks to keep out the wind, and a floor of boards covered with sheep fleeces so that they would not have to step from bed onto icy earth. He stretched cords overhead to hold clothing, and over a homemade dresser he hung a small rectangular mirror whose frame he had stained to look like oak. She had a kerosene lamp for reading at night and heat from a small collapsible stove. Lennie's bed was a canvas cot. Hers and Johnny's was a pole bedstead piled deep with wild grass he mowed in a twinkling with a scythe. When he held her they seemed to sink softly into a rustling, fragrant cavern; and when the mattress grew matted it was an easy matter for her to fluff it up again or for Johnny to cut more hay and then overlay it with spruce tips. "Now this is what I call bed making," he said with a mischievous leer at each new mowing, knowing that she would pretend a prim disapproval.

Her kitchen and the dining room were apart from the bedroom in Pat's old patched gray tent. In it Johnny built a rough pantry for foodstuffs, a box for wood, and a bench beside the entry for the washbasins. He repaired Pat's tilted sheepherder stove and the loose-jointed stovepipe. For additional cooking space and to provide a hearth for heating water, he prepared, from rocks and drill steel, an outside fireplace like the one she had seen at Brice's ranch. "You'll probably find this handier than you think," he suggested. And she did, not minding for more than the moment of actual discomfort the smoke in her eyes or the cricks in her back from bending. But she did sometimes wish that her husband, in his eagerness to help, did not always seize the broom and sweep the tent floor or the hard-packed earth around the fire pit just as she was preparing to dish up their supper.

She had neighbors. Aino Berg and another taciturn Finn, leaving the Ram's dark tunnels to work outside for Johnny, moved into the decrepit shack that earlier had served as Pat's construction office. Occasionally Lucille did bits of laundry for the pair or took them fresh bread; and although she saw them only in the mornings or after work, it was reassuring to have signs of their living nearby—their crosscut saw and canvases, their drying overalls, even their discarded cans. Four other workers rode down from Red Mountain City each day, tethering their horses at the log manger which Johnny had built and which he kept supplied with hay at the last wide point on the road, where the new trail began. The quartet always called jovially and waved their lunch pails as they trotted by. Walt's long mule trains passed regularly twice a day over the old trail beyond the creek, now and then crossing over to drop off mail or newspapers. Other travelers occasionally paused to gossip or ask directions.

Meanwhile she was mastering a new craft. She learned how to bake soda biscuits in a Dutch oven, piling hot embers on its iron-rimmed lid. She kept a bean pot continually simmering, and stewed what seemed great vats of the savory potato-onion-bacon-diced-meat concoctions that Johnny relished and called cowboy mulligan. She even learned to bake pies of dried apples or dried peaches. He'd linger over these and his strong black coffee and declare, "About one more week and I golly, you'll be able to hire out as cook to a construction camp." He meant it as a compliment.

Her days settled into a placid routine. Since she did not attempt to prepare any lunch of consequence for Lennie and herself, her afternoons were generally free. Occasionally she walked with the boy as far as another pair of tents in the meadow below town. Ira Brice had at last moved up and with his son Tommy was preparing a pasture in which he could hold dairy stock and beef cattle for supplying the mines. While the males built fence, the women gossiped. From Mrs. Brice, Lucille learned, among other things, that machine grease could be washed out of fabric with cool rain water and soda, and that rusty flatirons could be polished like glass by first rubbing the hot iron with beeswax on a rag and then scouring it with paper sprinkled with salt. Generally, though, she preferred to walk up the hillside back of the tents, harvesting along the way masses of late asters and deep blue gentian from places where trickles of water oozed out of the gravelly earth. When she passed through groves of evergreens, the smell of lichen and of rivulets flowing under gnarled roots filled her with a kind of subdued exaltation.

On one of the rare occasions when Johnny stayed in the tent to do the paper work he hated, she left Lennie in his care and ventured higher than usual. A swift lightning storm caught her at the fringe of timberline. Half frightened by the strange tigerishness that gripped her, she crouched under the arching boughs of the nearest tree, listening to the gigantic crash of the thunder and watching blades of fire slash the swollen bellies of the clouds. When the storm feathered apart, she was above the mist in the gorge. The ridges glistened with new hail, and a sense of the bigness of the world stifled her. So much, so much . . . She ran back toward the warmth of the tent, her skirt picking up the cold wetness of the grass.

Lennie throve. He had always been a lonesome child and he stayed so. But he was happy. He dug make-believe roads in the hillside with a spoon. He watched chipmunks by the hour, tossing them bits of bread and taming them enough that they would sit up like busy little men, turning his offerings around and around in their hands as they nibbled just beyond the touch of his reaching finger. He enjoyed seeing the Finns pitch horseshoes in the twilight, and sometimes he sat wordlessly beside them as they smoked their last pipes while the stars winked on in the deep, brooding sky. With Johnny he was more reserved, partly, Lucille thought, because of the tensions he had sensed in his stepfather at their first meeting and because of the quarrels he had overheard and had magnified in his imagination. Johnny worked diligently to dispel the restraint. He carried the boy pickaback to the aspen-pole corral where they confined their saddle animals and the cow he had rented in town. He put him on Lennie's own pony and patiently walked beside him, holding him in the saddle as the lethargic animal plodded around and around the enclosure. She knew he thought Lennie excessively timid—too much grandmother back there in Chicago—but he never pushed and gradually the boy took to watching for Johnny to come striding up from work, the swing of his step showing his eagerness to be with them.

Her husband's energy continually amazed her. Each morning he was out of bed before she was convinced that the canvas overhead really was echoing the first faint gray of dawn. He built the fires, set buckets of water on the firepit to heat, filled the woodbox, and milked the cow. While she cooked oatmeal and steak for his breakfast, he drove the hobbled horses from the dew-wet meadow into the corral, for he wanted her to have something on hand to ride in case of need. At night, after ten hours on the trail, he packed in more water, carried out the ashes, tended stock, and played with Lennie. For recreation after supper he whittled. Any reading other than local items in the newspaper seemed bloodless to him. Instead, he produced a piece of what he called "dish timber" in which he had seen a shape and carved it into woodenware— ladles with long, graceful handles, forks, boat-shaped biscuit dishes, pie- crust crimpers, and the like. Only rarely did he attempt some figure that had no practical use. "I sure did miss this in jail," he said once out of a long silence. It was the only reference she heard him make that late summer and early fall to the Hedstrom affair.

On Sundays he soaked a bandana in kerosene, tied it around his head to ward off mosquitoes, and helped Brice dynamite beaver dams. Or he went to Red Mountain City to assist the townspeople in building a cofferdam that would divert the creek that now cut awkwardly across Main Street. She learned little things about him that surprised her. For instance, he was very fleet of foot. An itinerant worker on the Baker road wandered into Red Mountain City one day and challenged the best local sprinters to a foot race, a hundred and fifty measured yards with a flying start. The visitor trounced them so thoroughly that he ran the last few yards backwards, thumbing his nose at his gasping opponents, and his backers returned to the Baker road camp with most of Red Mountain City's loose cash in their pockets. A delegation there- upon visited Johnny, asking that he meet the taunting victor in a return match the following Sunday. They waved their arms and argued: the Baker crowd, Pat Edgell and Parley Quine included, were bandying scurrilous remarks about Johnny throughout the mountains; victory in a foot race with their champion was his chance to retort. Johnny shook his head, and they went off muttering to themselves. No doubt he would be called a coward, and Lucille had supposed him sensitive to that sort of attack. The only explanation he vouchsafed her, however, was to grunt, "It doesn't mean a thing." She was pleased, but she was also surprised.

By walking down the old trail on the west side of the gorge she could reach a sunny spot from which to watch his work on the new trail. What she saw frightened her. The figures of the men were dwarfed by distance and by the enormous scale of the gray-brown cliffs. Cantankerous mules carrying supplies seemed always on the point of jerking their handlers off the threadlike footing. Boulders plunged awesomely. Drillers, Johnny among them, inched like bugs onto the sheer rock. The blasting terrified her most. She ever saw it, never wanted to. Generally it came so late that she was back at the tent preparing supper when the boom whipped back and forth between the great walls. Then she watched anxiously through the tent flap until she saw the crew returning around the corner of the dike and could tell from the way they moved that no one had been hurt.

At first she had supposed that the prodigious effort and the driving need for haste would increase Johnny's tensions. Instead he relaxed. Gradually she understood why. Though a dozen problems faced him each day, they were problems that could be solved without setting up conflicting loyalties. He was headed where he wanted to go and he had a fair chance of getting there, which he'd not had earlier when trying to complete a whole wagon road by fall. Now he could drop serenely into bed at night, confident that what he was doing was both good and possible. With the knots in his life thus untied he could arise each morning with an unflagging zest to get back onto a job that in her imagination quite possibly could kill him. Yet a surer disaster would be an inability to come to grips with the work at all. As she grew aware of this she no longer had to bite her tongue quite so hard each morning to keep from saying, "Be careful, darling."

In mid-September four inches of snow fell. The unexpected, glaring whiteness alarmed her. She had not bargained for this. How could they live in tents in winter weather?

Johnny laughed the fears aside. "These early storms generally don't amount to much. The weather's even better after they clear the air."

So it proved. Although nights were frosty and the stars shone like iced diamonds, by day a balmy Indian summer soothed the peaks. The soft sky was a profound blue; the whispering aspens turned to a flawless yellow. Contented again, she twice persuaded Johnny to saddle their horses for Sunday picnics in alpine meadows. Held back the first day by Lennie, they rode a short distance only. The next time they left the boy with the Brices and rode, just the two of them, along a scary trail high above the chimneyed mine buildings and boxlike houses of Red Mountain City. Swinging around a ridge point, Johnny led her deep into a cirque between the scarlet peaks.

"Our lake!" she gasped as they passed between two big boulders. He grinned, pleased that she should remember, and halted to let her look. The tiny tarn, rumpled by a breath of wind, flashed sunlight back at the sky. The stunted willows along the brook that drained the lake were no taller than the horses' knees. To the side and a little higher, a few warped evergreens grew where a bank of rock gave protection from the wind. Above the trees, mossy tundra swelled toward slopes of red scree—sliderock, as Johnny called it, that had tumbled from a rim of weather-shattered cliffs.

He tied the horses to one of the trees, unloosened the flour sack in which she had packed their lunches, and spread blankets. In the open the breeze had carried a nip, but the windless sunshine behind the rock was luxury. Lazily she reached across his lap to arrange the sandwiches. He kissed the nape of her neck. She pretended to duck. He pulled her around. She cracked a hard-boiled egg on the back of his head, and they wrestled until he chose to pin her beneath one muscular forearm.

"Beast," she said. Where the intense blue of the sky met the lifting red of the peaks, a thin line of pure light shimmered, as if the fusing of two such vehement colors melted all distinctions away.

His palm moved across her abdomen. "When are we going to have a young one of our own?"

Unhappiness touched her. Not yet, she thought. Through the needles of the trees she could see, far up the slope, small dumps of waste rock where restless prospectors had been probing for the hidden heart of the mountain. Nothing yet for them, either.

"When God wills," she said.

"God helps those that help themselves."

"John! You ought to be ashamed!" Then: "Somebody will see us."

"We'll watch the horses. They'll let us know in time."

Afterwards he ravenously ate his sandwiches and one of hers and obviously would have enjoyed more. His horse, bored, bit hers in the rump. The victim squealed and kicked. "Hah, you!" Johnny yelled and threw pebbles at them. Then he stretched out on his back, pulled his hat over his eyes, and went sound asleep. She leaned on her elbows, watching him. Nora had been mistaken. Coming here, high and remote from the pressing uncertainties of town, here where they could see their trail clear-cut ahead of them, had been completely right.

"5"

Thirty days hath September; October would have frozen a brass monkey. Pat Edgell and Parley Quine pushed their road upward from Red Mountain to Summit City and there hooked onto the highway coming across the pass from Baker. The first commercial traffic consisted of six wagons loaded with coal, half of them bound for the Summit Queen Mine, which was operating again, and half for the Ram. As many important persons as could be prevailed on to endure the weather added dignity to the occasion by riding along behind the coal wagons in buggies. There was to be a ceremony of welcome at Red Mountain City and afterwards a dance in the town's new schoolhouse.

Lucille caught the look of mingled yearning and envy that touched her husband's face as his men gossiped about the coming event. The first road—and he'd had no share in it. But he drove the moodiness away almost as soon as it came. For weeks he had known that his rivals would finish first—a road, not a trail, they kept crowing in the Tiptop —and he was braced. Credit where credit was due, he said to his men. Anyone who wished could leave the gorge early to take in the ceremony and the dance, and could return as late the following morning as their hangovers demanded. No, he didn't reckon he'd attend the doings himself. Time was growing to be a short bite. Unless Lucille would like . . .

Of course she would have liked. The increasing cold was pinching her tighter and tighter inside the gray tent roof. Mrs. Brice weeks ago had returned to the lower valleys and now Lucille almost never saw another woman. She was as starved for entertainment, for variety, as the workers were. Nora and Harmon Gregg, riding high at Summit, would be at the dance; Nora had written a note saying she hoped that she and Lucille could see each other there.

If Lucille likes . . . He glanced at her. Pat would be there, too, mocking him out of those flat hard eyes, grinning and making little spitting noises between his teeth. *A highway, not a burro path.* And Quine, as bland as butter, the big shaggy dog everlastingly grave at his side. *It's all ours, boy, not Winkler's, and we didn't trade a single thing to the Indians for it.*

"Ride out into this cold just to dance?" she said. (In her mind she saw the lift of Nora's eyebrow.) "I'd rather stay here and pop the rest of the corn Walt brought up last week."

Johnny accepted the offer with no comment, as if it were exactly what he had assumed. They popped the corn. He took two or three fistfuls, tossed the sweet white flakes one by one into his mouth, and chewed abstractly, almost without conversation. About eight-thirty he went outside, checked the horses, looked off toward town, came back in and said, "Brr!" Then he grunted, "I'm ready to turn in." By nine the lantern was out. But he did not sleep. He lay on his back staring up into the darkness, turned, and soon was on his back once again. The bed rustled dryly; the mattress of grass was brown now and the spruce tips were packing; but there was no longer any fresh grass in the meadow to cut and not enough daylight in this season of lengthening nights for him to spend it hunting fresh boughs. "Can't you sleep, Johnny?" she whispered finally. He did not answer. But she was sure he had heard.

When the celebrating workers reported back on the job the next day, they bore signs of battle—bruised cheekbones, swollen lips. The fight evidently had ranged up and down most of the street in front of the schoolhouse. "They called us the Jackass Express," one of the men explained to Johnny. It seemed that several sacks of the newly arrived coal had been carried into the schoolhouse—"The biggest thing next to the Ram that ever hit this camp," an alderman orated, meaning the coal—and after several toasts, cheers and more speeches, Pat Edgell had tossed out chunks of the fuel as souvenirs to a forest of reaching hands. Then someone had inevitably shied a piece at someone else, all in sport naturally, and the unscheduled part of the program began. The narrator smiled painfully. "It was quite a waltz," he finished and glanced askance at Johnny to fathom his reaction. Jackass Express. (You see, Lucille told Nora across the miles, we couldn't come. But the eyebrow stayed lifted.)

Johnny shrugged. "They shouldn't have thrown that shirttail full of coal around quite so careless. They may need it later."

Aino Berg gave an appreciative chuckle. "Ja, ja!" When Aino did grasp a cryptic remark, he wanted everyone to know that he did. "Maybe dey don' drive no wagons over the pass when the big snows come."

"Or through those boggy stretches on the other side in the spring thaws," the bruised narrator said and looked more directly at John. "There was some talk in town about 'em giving the hardest parts of their road just a lick and promise, so they could finish fast and bring those wagons in mainly to promote a stock deal at Summit City. Do you reckon there's anything to the story?"

"I do," Johnny said and then shrugged again. "The main thing is that nobody'll ever say that about our job." And off they went, in high camaraderie, to attack the last hundred or so yards of granite that still separated the converging ends of the trail.

Fearsome yards. Wind roared through the gorge, often carrying pellets of snow. The canvas roofs of the tents boomed and shook above their plank half-walls. Smoke from the outdoor fireplace was dashed into wild tendrils and pots would not heat. How much longer work could continue was problematical. Johnny drove himself and the men relentlessly. The icy dawns had scarcely turned the sky to steel when they hurried into the maw of the gorge; cold darkness had advanced again before they returned. He'd stand beside the stove for a moment, rubbing life back into his hands, then seize a lantern and plunge outside to his chores. Finally, in November, he sent the rented cow back to Argent with Walt, and even Lennie was wise enough not to fuss at the canned milk.

She was amazed that none of the men whimpered. Johnny could transfer conviction. He never said "Go on," but rather "Come on," and somehow they could see ahead of them the same shining that he saw. They stuck, and one quieter Wednesday morning he remarked casually to her as he was pulling on his gloves, "We'll be shooting about noon today."

Normally they blasted at quitting time. And he never before had told her on what days the blast would come. She glanced curiously up from the dishpan and saw the deep, waiting pleasure in his eyes.

"You're through!"

"Oh, some cleaning up," he said. "But this shot's the one we've been waiting for."

By now she knew the routine of the mountains. "Which one?" she asked obediently.

"The last one," and the triumph broke through to fire his whole face.

She remembered that immediately after her arrival in Argent, she and Lennie had failed him when he had wanted to show her one of his explosions. Since then, dreading their roaring destruction, she had stayed away from watching them. But now she promised, "Lennie and I'll walk down the old trail to see!" She tightened her damp hands against the rough canvas of his coat. "You've done it! At last!"

He misunderstood. He thought she was relieved that the waiting was over. "Now we can go home," he said and gripped her shoulders in return until they hurt. "No more tents, ever."

Home. After he had left, she tried to taste the word. She could not. She had never seen any more of that house on Vinegar Hill than its walls. There had been no easy way to leave Lennie so that she might ride down and check on what was happening there. While she stayed remote here in the gorge, Vera Hotchkiss and Margaret Fossett were furnishing the house for her, consulting with her by letter or word-of-mouth messages carried by Walt about the divan and carpets, the chairs, bureaus, beds. Expenses frightened her. "It's too much," she kept saying to Johnny, and he kept waving it aside with his usual impatience for the strictures of money. "Fossett told me to charge whatever I needed at Hotchkiss's. Those two women know that. Now just leave things to them." And that was home. She turned her glance around the tent—the streak of rain-caused rust wavering down the stove-pipe; the brown-edged elliptical holes in the plank walls from which drying knots had fallen; the grayed fleeces on the floor which she simply had not been able to keep beaten clean. *No more tents, ever.* Here she— here they—had learned to refashion their living; and yet she knew that as soon as she returned to Argent the mists of time would rise and she would begin to forget, without wanting to, just as surely as John would forget through no desire to remember. *Home,* she thought, and the pain of loss dropped her onto the edge of the bed.

Lennie climbed up beside her. "What's the matter, Mommy!"

She pulled him close. "You'll always remember living here, won't you?"

" 'Member chipmunks," he said. The nimble, striped little creatures had long since hibernated, and he missed them. Johnny had told him once that they would not return until warm weather came again. On windless afternoons when the sun swung around so that the impact of its pale beams rested against the wall of the tent and Lucille said, "It's warm enough now to take that jacket off," he'd run out to see if they were back, even though she had tried to explain about summer. He missed the cow, too. " 'Member Bess," he said.

"We'll see Bess by and by," she promised. "As soon as we go home."

"Home?" he asked.

He didn't know what it meant either, in spite of the chatting she had done with him during each long day while they kept house and waited for Johnny's evening return.

She jumped up. "This is silly," she said. "We've lots to do to get ready to leave."

She flew at her work, rebuilding eagerness out of her own zest. Shortly before noon she prepared a sandwich for each of them, bundled Lennie in wraps, tied a wool scarf around her own head, lifted Johnny's binoculars off their nail, and walked down the old trail. Soon they reached a niche into which they could crowd for warmth and from which they could look across the abyss.

Though she often came here, it always took her a moment to relocate the infinitesimal scratch which the men were dragging across the huge face of the cliff. In following the contours of Ute Peak, the trail swung away from her vantage point. To see the spot where it would join the lower section she had to strain her eyes across the widest part of the gorge. Without the glasses, the men who were attacking either side of the last stone buttress seemed no more than grains in the vastness. Even when the binoculars pulled them into bolder relief, she could not determine what they were doing. They'd move a step or two forward and then back. They'd point and make pounding motions. They'd wave what seemed to be exasperated directions across the rock at each other. All of them wore black caps with earflaps, canvas coats with sheepskin collars. She could not even be sure which of them was her husband.

They began a curious bowing as though doing obeisance to a great gray-brown god. At last she realized that the upper crew, Johnny's crew, were lighting the fuse ends that protruded from drill holes tamped full of dynamite. "Soon now!" she said breathlessly to Lennie, who could not bring the glasses to focus and was growing bored and whimpery.

Nothing happened. The men on the lower section disappeared behind a swelling of stone. Johnny's crew retreated a distance and just stood there. The binoculars' field of vision would not embrace both them and the site of the coming explosion. Not knowing which to watch, she abandoned the glasses entirely and tried to force her eyes, watering with the cold and the straining, to see everything at once.

After endless heartbeats, a small white puff appeared. A handful of what seemed pebbles flew into the air. A sharp crack, followed by a deep reverberation, disturbed the emptiness. The puff swelled in a kind of pouting minuet of rage and turned dark. A small segment of cliff crumbled and slipped indifferently into the chasm. Wisps of dust rose from its plunging to link with the smoke and then drift hazily off toward the ridge top. The rumble of the sliding rock faded into the everlasting thrum of the cascading stream. By squinting she could barely see that the threadlike ends of the trail were now tied together.

"Was that Daddy?" Lennie asked uncertainly.

Excited, she raised the binoculars and brought Johnny's group into view. They were executing a small caper. She could not tell whether any of them glanced in her direction. She took the scarf from her head and tossed it exuberantly. "Wave!" she urged. Lennie raised both mittened hands and stirred the air, laughing because she was laughing. Bending, she squeezed him, then straightened and found the men again in the glasses. They were moving forward to see what they had wrought. This time she was sure it was Johnny who was in the lead.

She took Lennie's hand. "Now let's go back and wait for them."

The crew returned earlier that afternoon than usual. Puzzled and actually a little fearful, she stepped outside. They whooped greetings, red-faced from cold yet smiling from ear to ear. Nothing was wrong.

They merely wanted approval and she and Lennie were the only immediate audience they had.

"It's done!" she said, smiling from proud face to proud face. "You've
been marvelous, every one of you!"

"The Yackass Express!" Aino Berg shouted. "Tonight we bray!"

They were turning a slur into pride. Lucille glanced warmly at her
husband. He dismounted and her smile faded. "Aren't you going with
them?"

"I'd better start packing," he said. "As soon as the rubble is cleared
out of the way, we'll want to start moving down."

After a moment more of bantering the others trotted on, reluctantly,
Lucille thought, and wishing that John were along. Did they suppose
that she was holding him?

"You can catch up," she urged. "Lennie and I'll be fine. Go with
them, at least for a little while."

"It doesn't mean anything," he said.

"Go for their sake. They've worked hard for you—with you. Now
you should celebrate together."

Tempted, he stood indecisive. Then he returned to his first determination. "And listen to the jokers in the Tiptop tell us that over Baker
way it's a road?" He shook his head. His tone wasn't bitter so much as
unsatisfied. "When we finish the road, then we'll celebrate." He patted
her rear gently, as if it were she who needed encouraging. "This . . ."
He gave a shrug of dismissal.

He went into the sleeping tent. Absently he thrust another stick of
wood into the sheet-iron stove, although a spot the size of a dollar
already glowed ruddily in its top, and stood holding out his palms.
Anticlimax was in the unguarded wryness of his lips. She did not really
understand his mood, and a sense of helplessness desolated her. Such
terrible effort, reduced by the size of what he had attempted to mere
second best—like the puff of powder smoke she had seen blossom in
the gorge, dwarfed against the cliffs to a smudge of what she had expected. Was that what was troubling him? If so, his ambition had made
him unfair to himself.

"Did you see Lennie and me watching?" she asked. Waving a scarf,
cheering the best they could. *Don't belittle, Johnny. We know how
much work it has been.*

He shook his head. "The shadows were wrong. It was just a blank
wall over there." He roused himself and looked around the tent. "If
the weather holds we ought to have the muck cleared out of the way
and be headed for home on Sunday. I don't reckon you'll be sorry."

No more tents, ever. She rebelled. This was not second best.

"Of course I want to go home," she said. "But this has been"—she groped for some shock to make him see—"a perfect honeymoon."

He simply grew wryer. "It's not the honeymoon I wanted for you, though."

She tapped a foot in exasperation. "Don't always fight yourself so."

He smiled. He wasn't angry or truly dejected. He—she didn't know what: withdrawn somehow, in abeyance, like a leafless winter tree with the sap running back down into the ground. "Some day," he said vaguely and then could not find words to convey this pause, this interim, this fruitless time of dying before he could reach out again. Gesturing for an understanding he could not create through words, he fled from his sentiment into the twilight to feed the horses and gather chips for starting the morning fires.

Lennie twitched his mother's skirts. Normally John took the boy with him for the evening routines.

"Is Daddy angry?" he asked.

"Of course not," Lucille said brightly and bundled him into jacket and mittens. "Run along and catch him."

"6"

He had gauged the timing well. By Saturday night the rubble was gone and the bumpiest of the knobs were smoothed away. Rather late on Sunday morning, a gray, raw day, Walt appeared with mules. Together Johnny and he carried outside the bags and boxes she had packed and then struck the tents, dropping months of living into a small disorder of containers and crumpled canvas. The lashing of these remnants onto muleback seemed to take forever. Numbly Lennie and she waited beside a flickering fire of yellow scrap lumber. The boy was wrapped until he appeared round. Mucus from his nose drained stickily across his mouth. She wiped at it; he ducked and whimpered; his face was chapped.

"Are we going home now?" he asked each time a loaded mule was moved out of the way. "In a little while," she'd say as still another empty-saddled animal was led up beside the boxes. The tumbling of the tents had frightened him, and it was clear that he was very dubious about a change that could so easily obliterate familiarity. Sitting down beside him on a log end, she told him another story.

At last the cavalcade was ready. John helped Lucille into her saddle and swung Lennie onto the shaggy pony. Perhaps the boy could safely have handled the phlegmatic creature alone; he had ridden nearly every day during their sojourn here and of late had manipulated the bridle reins by himself on brief adventures across the meadow above the tent. If the pony traveled single file between two other horses, there should be little danger. But Johnny did not ask her to face that decision. Nor did he ask if she wished to be the one who led the beast. As if the responsibility had always been his, he coiled the halter rope in one gloved hand, mounted, and tugged the pony into place behind him. Lucille fell in next, her feet so cold in her tight boots that she thought her toes must crack off. Walt brought up the rear with the mules.

The short stretch of wagon road which Pat had completed during the early summer led them around onto the front of Ute Peak and then funneled abruptly into the trail. Lucille had seen Johnny's work only from across the canyon. From there the way had appeared desperately narrow, a mere eyebrow on the beetling face of the cliff. During the night when apprehension leaped hand in hand with imagination, she had expected to be frightened by this icy ride to town. But as they moved ahead to where watery sunlight struck the tawny rock and the wind quit searching through her bones, she found the way far more secure than she would have believed. Much of the trail was wider than the four feet specified in Winkler's bond. Here and there turnouts appeared where pack trains bound in opposite directions could pass. These spots were already roomy enough for wagons.

The creek dropped much more rapidly than did the road. Soon it was foaming hundreds of feet below them. The aspens and alders along its banks were bare of leaves, stiff exclamation marks against the boulder-roughened, avalanche-scarred, brush-clotted slopes. And yet there was no sense of peril. Footing was solid and smooth. The thin legs of the laden mules twinkled delicately. Ahead of Lucille, Lennie rode easily in his small saddle, his short legs in their galoshes sticking out like pegs. His eyes regarded the chasm indifferently, although when first he had seen water plunging into it earlier in the summer, he had clung to his mother in terror. For months since then John had plodded patiently back and forth with him and the pony, until now Lennie placed unhesitating trust in the link with his stepfather. Seeing them thus, fully at ease, bound by the rope John had taken up on his own volition, Lucille felt a surge of tenderness compounded partly of thanksgiving and, she would admit later, partly of relief. The fear of discovery no longer lurked so cruelly. Lennie had passed from being an abstraction, an unknown x in the equation of Johnny's marriage, to being a person in his own small right, capable of commanding affection for himself and not just through her. This the propinquity in the gorge had wrought. For this, no matter what Nora said, she would have lived in any number of tents.

Out of the growing warmth, the growing security, temptation leaped. *I should tell him the truth,* she thought. *There's enough behind us now, in the living we've done here, there's enough so that he'll forgive.* Simplicity and directness. The high red peaks: hope unclouded, genesis afresh. *Some evening when we're sitting together, home, and the right minute comes, then*—an inexpressible relief filled her; this one deceit excised, this one concealment faced, finished, done—*I'll tell him!* The self-promise soared like an exaltation.

Johnny turned in his saddle to talk over her head to Walt. "What do you think of her so far? Think you can keep stuff moving all winter?"

Lucille caught his eye and smiled. Of course his prodigious effort meant something, no matter what he said. Only against the vast cliffs of other concerns did it seem shrunken. Now he was seeing it properly in front of him and like any worker who knows his work is good he wanted approval. Walt understood that and nodded.

"Like shooting fish in a barrel," he agreed.

"We can widen her in a hurry next spring," Johnny pressed on. "The grade's set—not a pitch steeper than ten per cent anywhere. We can move in supplies from either direction, and work right off the trail without having to hang our high-scaler from sky hooks."

They reached the spot where the final blast had ripped away the separating granite. The rock still smelled of powder smoke; the protrusions on the inner wall still showed the white scars of their travail. Some sort of ceremony could have been held here, Lucille thought—the cutting of a ribbon, the shaking of hands between aldermen. But Johnny himself had eschewed it by sending no notice to newspapers or city councils, and she felt she was beginning to understand his reticence without fully liking the reason. Once he had refused to meet the Baker foot racer because, so he had said, it meant nothing. For the same cause he had declined to celebrate with his men the opening of the trail. Casual challenges, incomplete efforts did not match the expectations he had set for himself. To his own hungry ambition the trail was a step, not an end. Only the final road, he felt, would bring him a clear, unambiguous justification of all he had done for the sake of this road; and he did not wish anyone to suppose, from his own premature hurrahing, that he was willing to settle for less than completeness. So much publicly. Yet in this privacy of friend and family he could still humanly want, still humanly need a word of assurance that what he had done thus far was good.

Obediently Walt was giving it to him. "It's sure an improvement over the old trail," he said. They both looked across the canyon. "That one's a bitch-kitty in the wind. Longer than this one, too."

"This one saves about forty minutes for saddle horses—more for a pack train."

"In a year," Walt said agreeably, "that's a lot of time."

Johnny grinned and wiped his nose on his coat sleeve. "So you like it?" And again: a boy coming into the kitchen to show off the first boards he has ever nailed together, the first uncertain cultivating of the still inexpressible but fate-fixed, thrusting future that lay in the loam of his shaping mind. "You think it'll do in a pinch, huh?"

A protest formed in her. In his insistence on completion he was unfair to himself. This embryo road from Argent to Red Mountain, this growing link from what was to what he had seen could be, was his assurance of tomorrow just as certainly as the guide rope to Lennie was her and the boy's assurance that pain did not have to last forever. The trail, like the tents, did matter. In his refusal publicly to admit it there was a kind of inverse arrogance that she would not have expected of him, a wrapping of himself in a horny carapace of false humility lest he be cut again by scorn and misunderstanding. He was too afraid of ceremonies turning hollow—afraid of an empty church at his own wedding, of an unattended ribbon-cutting to mark the opening of his trail. Full whoop or nothing. If we can be proud of you now, she thought, why won't you give others a chance to be? Sadness came, and she said again, silently this time, across her son's head, across the linking rope, *You fight yourself too hard, Johnny.*

"7"

The trip was too long and too cold for excitement to be sustained. As their discomfort grew, clouds drifted across the pale sunlight. When they reached Argent, snow was falling, enough of it blanketing the streets to deaden the sound of the horses' feet. The few people who were about, muffled to the ears, were too intent on their own affairs to do more than glance at the riders without recognition, without enthusiasm. Tired and cold and physically dejected, the travelers turned up Silver Avenue to Vinegar Hill. As yet there was no fence around the yard. The men rode directly beside the porch to unload. Although Lucille ached from cold and Lennie snuffed from tiredness, they stayed outside until the family could enter together. And still Johnny searched for assurance. "What do you think of that jigsaw work along the porch eaves?" he asked her as he stacked the sacks and boxes carefully away from the white paint of the wall, so fresh yet that it smelled. "Best carpenter in town done it. Same one Fred Fossett had for his porch."

"It's lovely," she said, trying not to shiver. "It's just what I'd have picked if I'd been here."

"I hope you'll like the furniture."

"Of course I will."

Walt departed with the mules. The front door was unlocked. Johnny pushed it open, then gestured to lift her. She hesitated.

"Is it bad luck to be carried across twice?"

"The first time was practice," he countered. "This is real." He swung her lightly up and over the threshold. Lennie thought it was a game. "Me, too, Daddy!" "Why sure, son," Johnny said, swooped him high and placed him beside his mother.

The parlor was blessedly warm. "I told the carpenter to have a fire going here and in the kitchen," he explained to her surprise. He grinned broadly, pleased with himself, and rubbed his hands briskly together. "You two look around while I bring in some more coal and wood."

With Lennie she wandered from room to room, exclaiming over the divan with the Paisley shawl across its back, the heavy oak table and sideboards in the dining room, the marble-topped commodes bearing gilt-edged basins and pitchers in the bedrooms. When she reached the kitchen, John was eating a piece of bread and drinking a glass of milk. Someone, Margaret Fossett probably, had set the new-made bread in the warming oven, a pitcher of milk in the cooler, staples in the pantry, and a covered pot of stew ready for heating on the zinc-topped table.

"It's wonderful!" she said and put her arms around his neck and kissed him between chews. "I can't wait to start the curtains and plants and pictures and the rest. Only . . ."

"Only what?"

"We didn't need so much so soon."

Impatience tightened his mouth. Money again. "Fossett okayed it." He smiled sardonically. "Big time now—got to live big, the banker says. President of a road company." The smile vanished. "And no road."

It was in the open at last: second-best. He had pounded at those stubborn cliffs as furiously as he had known how, but Pat, whom he had discarded for the sake of accomplishment, had reached Red Mountain ahead of him; and Johnny was afraid of what his town would say, even if the trail did prove better than Pat's road. How could she possibly fight such a mood? Bending over Lennie, she found time by taking off his wraps and galoshes, and was relieved when the boy whined, "I'm hungry."

"We'll all feel better for something hot." She bustled about heating a bit of the stew, warming milk, making coffee. They did feel better for it. More contentedly she went into the parlor and sat on the new divan, her fingers and toes still tingling with returning warmth. Lennie crawled up and put his head in her lap. An overlooked spot of mud on one stocking leg dragged a stain across the new fabric. Dismayed, she started to rise, intending to fetch a cloth.

Johnny restrained her. "It'll brush off easier when it's dry."

Drowsily the boy asked, as she settled back, "Are there chipmunks here?"

"Out back," Johnny assured him. "But they're in their holes now, warm like this, sleeping and eating the seeds they stored up for winter. Remember how you watched them filling their cheeks up on the mountain?"

"I'll like it when they wake up," he said and, curling like a chipmunk himself, he went to sleep.

Lucille's hand moved absently across his long hair. "It needs cutting."

Johnny smiled at them. "He's a good tyke. That's a hard ride for a youngster and he went the whole way without hardly a peep."

The familiar pain twisted her. She tried to deny it. *I've got to tell him.* Yet the resolution that had come to her during the first excitement of actually riding onto that longed-for trail was crumbling back into fear. Watch the regard in his eyes turn, each time he looked at the boy, into a question? Feel the same question in his hand when he reached out in bed to embrace her? *I can't.* Here, her new home on Vinegar Hill, the tents forgotten, the pressures which she thought she had fled tightening again—*second-best?* No. She deserved more, too. So did Lennie, from the life for which he had never asked.

"What's the matter?" Johnny said in consternation.

"Nothing." She squeezed back the tears. "Sitting here—all this—so much more than I dreamed——"

There was a knocking at the front door. Johnny opened it onto a thin, gauche young man with an enormous jib of a nose and straight black hair combed back along his narrow skull. Pimples blossomed on his long sloping chin. Simply being looked at made him ill at ease. He stamped the snow off his feet, wiggled, and introduced himself as Sam Varnum, reporter for *The True Fissure*. Al Ewer, the paper's editor, had encountered Mr. Kennerly on the street. Learning from Walt that the Red Mountain trail was open, Ewer had sent Varnum up the hill for a story.

"A reporter?" Johnny said. "Al must be getting pretty big." Bitterness edged his voice. "Too big to come after picayune stories like this one himself."

Varnum started to hee-hee obligingly, realized vaguely that tensions were at work here which he did not understand, and ended the laugh on a gurgle. It was an unsatisfactory interview. His pride hurt by what he considered Ewer's indifference toward the trail which he himself considered inadequate, Johnny gave the underling a few dead statistics about dates and mileage. Varnum writhed in embarrassment, not knowing how to warm him up. In desperation he turned to Lucille.

"If you don't mind—your angle—first woman—how does it feel to be —hee—a pioneer?"

"We took the first child through the gorge too," Lucille said, brushing back Lennie's long hair. He was still asleep on her lap.

Varnum brightened. "Human interest—oh, that's fine." He wrote vigorously in his notebook. "If you care to amplify?"

She remembered Walt's remark. "Smooth and easy."

"Ummm," Varnum mumbled and wriggled unhappily, not even bothering to write. Here in the warming room, it sounded too smooth, too easy. He had even run out of questions. Lucille grew annoyed, more at herself and at Johnny than at the reporter. Make him see, so that through him Argent can see. She cast back in her memory for pictures that would tell. She tried to describe how the drillers had looked hanging to the ends of their ropes, how boulder after boulder had been wrenched from the cliffs and swallowed in the abyss as completely as if there had been no disturbance. She told how small it had seemed from the old trail. Tiny men resolutely forcing themselves farther, one almost had to think, than men were supposed to go. But they had gone; they had created a way for other men. It was not tiny; it was tremendous.

"Perhaps I think so," she said, "because I came to the St. Johns recently from a flat, settled country. For that very reason I can perhaps appreciate more clearly than the people who live here just how tremendous the project really is. Some day other people from the East will discover it. It'll be a road then. They'll come clear across the country to see it—not because it carries ore or hay or food, but because they want to look into that huge canyon and at the cliffs and up at the spires rising against the sky. It'll be beautiful. But mostly they'll be proud because—oh, how can I make both of you understand this? —because they're men and this is something that other men were able to dream about and then go out and do. The hard part was in not being stopped at the very first. It was going all the way through. That's what the trail is: the proof. From now on it's just a matter of . . . growing."

She stopped, abashed suddenly by her own vehemence. Mr. Varnum was staring at her with his mouth open.

"My!" he breathed. He shut his lips and his notebook with a tiny pop. "You're very—hee—persuasive, Mrs. Ogden."

"A conscientious reporter would ride up the trail and look for himself, Mr. Varnum."

"I—" He stood up and squared his thin shoulders. She thought he was offended, but then he blurted. "By Jove, I shall."

Johnny ushered him out the door. When he returned he smiled gloomily. "That was quite a spiel."

Was that all she had given him, a spiel? "It was true, wasn't it?"

"Maybe you should be the stock salesman."

She flinched as if she'd been struck. "If that's what I've come home to, I'd rather be back in the tents. At least we knew how to value ourselves."

"I deserved that," he apologized. Wandering to the window, he stared up the gorge, his hands thrust deep into his pockets. "Just the same, it's still only a trail. And there's not a damn thing I can do about it now except stand around and wait for spring."

A winter of this discontent? "You expect too much of yourself, Johnny." There: that, too, was in the open now.

He swung around. "Why shouldn't I expect?" he cried. "There's everything a man could want here. I've always said so. But something always gets in my way and I can't seem to take a tight hold on any of it."

"Why not look at what you do have? Must you always be straining for something extra?"

He glared at her, uncomprehending and hurt. "When I quit wanting, I'll be as dead as . . ."

He didn't finish. *As Hedstrom?* she wondered and for a long time there was no sound in the room save the chuckling of the stove.

III

"1"

Al Ewer's newspaper called snow "the beautiful": "This sparkling new blanket of the beautiful will enable our young people to indulge in street sleighing and heart slaying side by side." And afterwards, when skies cleared and frost crystals seemed all but visible in the moonlight: "The beautiful in weather like this makes our summertime bachelors think of two in a bed, spoon-fashion." Until Christmas week, however, there were no real storms—only hints. And then, early on the Thursday afternoon before the holiday, the beautiful began again to sift over the basin, huge cottony persistent flakes. "This is it," Johnny announced. "This is the real McCoy."

Later that same day Gabe Porcella rode into Argent from Red Mountain. Johnny brought him to the house, to thaw and to repeat his errand to Lucille. Once inside the front door, trapped by the upholstered furniture and the colored carpet, Gabe grew as awkward as a bear. He brushed at his snow-crusted trousers and refused to sit down, but placed a folded copy of *The True Fissure* as a foot pad on the floor beside the parlor stove and stood on the paper with his back to the heat. The wet wool steamed and smelled. His great round face and heavy soiled hands were shiny from frostbite. Lucille never ceased marveling at his gentle ugliness—the orange sideburns that curled bushily almost as far as his eyes, the tufts of orange hair that grew down the backs of his paws to his knuckles. Probably, she had thought once, there were big tufts of orange hair even on his toes. The Angel Gabe—how incongruous a name, and yet how fitting.

Red Mountain City, he said, had decided on a community Christmas. The trouble was, they'd had the idea too late. Although Gabe had tried during the fall to lay in an ample stock of obvious necessities, he really hadn't thought about present-giving. Then some of the women had taken to fretting.

"Jenny Shaffer for one, I'll bet," Johnny said.

Yes, Jenny had barged in, true to form, and had called a meeting to decide what should be done. Those attending the discussion had determined to hold a service and a hymn-sing on Christmas Eve. Some had voted to gather in the Tiptop; the saloon offered ample room and was a place that lone prospectors from back in the rocks wouldn't shy away from visiting. But the ladies had insisted on the schoolhouse.

"I should think so!" Lucille said, and Johnny winked at Gabe.

"They voted to put up a spruce tree and decorate it with paper roses," Gabe went on. "We'll take the preacher, that feller Alden, up there Saturday afternoon, the day before Christmas. He wasn't excited about it exactly—me and John stopped by his house on the way here—but when Johnny said—"

"He just needed jollying," Johnny put in. "He'll go."

"He has a service here the next morning at eleven," Lucille reminded them.

"He can leave Red Mountain early enough to make it back down in time," John assured her. "That's not the problem." And he nodded for Gabe to go on.

"It's the presents," Gabe said. "We went by Hotchkiss's too, and by that new general store and the drugstore and everyplace else. Present-y doodads, stuff and junk at a reasonable price to put under a tree so everybody'll have something to open, that kind of item is powerful short around here. People have snapped it up for their own Christmases. We figure we'll need three hundred items. At least that's what I was told to order."

"Three hundred up there now! I thought lots of people left for winter."

"A few with kids did, but more come in. More kids, too."

"Things are humming," John said. He was excited: Hardrock Johnny: the push, the verve, the reaching: "Fellows that took summer jobs to make a stake—tree cutting, road grading, mill building or whatever—they've gone back to work on their claims. Winter's a good time, no interruptions or anything. Snow don't bother the inside of a mine. The main properties are opening new levels every week, but they can't hire from among the prospectors they were using during the summer, so they have to raise wages and bring men up from the towns. The men, some of them, bring families. That means more cabins, more supplies —oh, winter never slowed a real boom. No sir. And this one's real."

"How many women live there now?" Lucille asked.

"Thirty-six," Gabe told her.

"Children?"

"Eighty-nine, near as we could come, sitting around a table marking 'em off by fives, trying to recall who has what." The Angel gave his great round head a wag. "Of course, all of 'em ain't in school. Even so, they're about to bust the seams of the schoolhouse we built last fall. I wouldn't of thought it. I wouldn't of thought of such a passel of presents, either, even though there's some folks saying around that I should of seen what was coming and been ready, and what Red Mountain needs is another store that'll tend to its Ps and Qs."

He steamed gently. His red face mourned. Johnny said to Lucille, "What we're hoping is that you can make up a committee or something out of the ladies here in town and go call at different houses and see what you can rustle. Pocket knives, scissors, combs, clothesline, mirrors, alphabet blocks—then wrap 'em pretty—it's the idea mostly."

"Tin cups and tobacco plugs will do for the loners," Gabe suggested.

She felt herself growing excited in turn. Impulsively she patted the hairy back of his hand. "The Herald Angel. I'm sure we can do something." She turned to Johnny, speaking before she reflected. "My trunk!"

He looked blank. "What trunk?"

"In the attic!" The merchandise which she had brought to sell and which he had refused to touch. It still rankled his pride as a symbol of . . . she was not sure what . . . of, perhaps, his inability to assert full control over the destiny on which he was determined. His mouth tightened, as it had when she'd mentioned money.

"That's dude stuff. Red Mountain—"

"I realize part of it isn't suitable. But gloves, material for shawls, a bit of lace to brighten a Sunday dress . . ." *Take it, Johnny. Let me share in this too.*

He gave a churlish shrug. "If that's what you want—"

She laughed radiantly, out of pure pleasure. She had selected those things with anxious concern and they had been refused; now, to have them mean something again! She whirled toward the hatrack and umbrella stand in the hall. "While you two bring the trunk down from the attic, I'll talk to Margaret Fossett about a committee. Some to gather, some to wrap. Oh, this is fun!"

Later she was amazed at herself for not having read the portents sooner. But they were so busy: tramping through ankle-deep snow, knocking on doors, explaining, growing more and more thrilled with the way people participated as soon as they understood, pulling their collections up Silver Avenue on handsleds, setting up work tables in the Fossetts' living room, exclaiming over the donations, cutting paper, laughing, snipping ribbon, trying to picture the faces in the crowded schoolhouse, drawing, from the vision of this warmth they were providing, a dearer and private warmth to carry with them into their own family celebrations—how could she have suspected, really?

Throughout the period snow continued to fall, sometimes in wind-driven fury, sometimes in vagrant, almost absent-minded flakes, but with never a break or promise of a break in the low, peak-swaddling clouds. After they had finished wrapping late Saturday morning and Johnny came to estimate the transportation needs, one of the ladies expressed doubt about Gabe's being able to get both the presents and Barnabas Alden to Red Mountain on time.

"The trail's sheltered," Johnny said. "There won't be much trouble. Now, if they were trying to come over from Baker . . ."

He surveyed the mound of brightly wrapped gifts. "Bulky but not heavy—about three mule loads," he decided. He walked with Lucille from the Fossetts' to the path leading to their own home. Very casually he said, "I don't know how soon I'll be back."

At first she assumed that he referred to going into town to rent mules and to help Gabe pack. He'd be late for lunch. Then realization stunned her. Instinctively she sought his denial. "What do you mean?"

"There's a moon tonight. If the clouds break, we may be able to come down after the party in the schoolhouse. Anyway"—he gave her a placating smile—"I'm bound to have old Spec back in time for his eleven o'clock service tomorrow."

Her first real anguish. When he would have left her before to go to the gorge, she had been able to accompany him. That dislocation had been necessary. This time . . .

"This is the night we were going to put our own presents around our tree," she protested. "Lennie has the cranberries ready to string—he's even counted them, as high as he can count. He'll be up at daylight tomorrow. We've talked and planned—"

"Some of those kids up there won't have anything to plan on, except this load."

"It's Walt's job to take the mail."

"This isn't mail. Besides, there isn't another delivery until Monday."

"Gabe can get men without families to help."

"Alden wants me to bring him back. I know the trail."

To have to fight the mountain this day! "Our first Christmas."

"Christmas is tomorrow," he said, too reasonably. "I'll be back at least by eleven o'clock tomorrow morning."

"It's the way you've done it."

"I've tried to make things as easy on you as I could."

"You"—she almost said, betrayed me—"you lied."

"Lucy—"

"When you brought Gabe to the house yesterday, you knew then that you were going. You never said a word. You let me think—"

"It was storming. I didn't want you worrying and stewing."

"You were afraid I'd make a scene and things wouldn't get done the way you wanted them."

"Oh, for—" Much too righteously he said, "What's wrong between us that we can't postpone cranberry stringing for a few hours?"

She had not been allowed to share. She had been used. "You took my merchandise—"

"That was your idea. I never wanted that goddamn trunk around here in the first place."

"Johnny! It was for you—"

He'd had enough. "I've got to go."

"Why? Why?" The ruthlessness in him, the inflexibility: that was the terror which this calculated deception had opened under her, not mere disappointment; and it was something that could not be masked by calling it a postponement. "Red Mountain isn't your private responsibility, is it?"

"It's my trail."

"It's Winkler's trail. You're just hired help—for everybody, it looks like—except me."

His mouth pulled thin. "Gabe didn't go to Baker for what Red Mountain needs. He came to me. I'm not going to let them down."

"It's your pride." She tasted the cold wetness of snowflakes softly striking her lips. "If I swallow my own pride, if I beg you not to—"

"Don't!" he said and before she could make him choose so irrevocably that afterward there would never be retreat for either of them, he swung about and strode heavily through the deepening blanket, down Silver Avenue toward town.

"2"

The house breathed emptiness at her. She staggered in from the back shed with a bucket of their precious coal and fired the stove until the *huff-huffing* of the flames in the pipe frightened her. She sat on the cold floor and played tiddlywinks with Lennie. She brought their few gifts from the closet and laid them on the bed for wrapping and then fled from them. Desultorily she leafed through old copies of the newspaper—the beautiful, two in a bed spoon-fashion; not my bed on my first Christmas—and a dozen times, interrupting everything else, over and over she pulled the draperies aside and looked again into the wind. The storm had whooped itself into a gray whirl of confusion. Snow reached halfway up the new picket gate. The branches of the evergreen in the fence corner drooped heavily. Beyond that the twilight thickened impenetrably. Such weather, Ewer had not dared write, made one think of blocked trails and avalanches and slipping horses.

After supper she strung popcorn and the hoarded cranberries with Lennie. "Is Daddy sleeping in our tent?" he asked.

"The tent isn't there now."

"Where is he sleeping?"

"I don't know."

"Do you like Mr. Gabe?"

"Of course. He's Daddy's friend."

"He's ugly."

"Not inside. He's very kind."

"Was it kind to take Daddy riding in so much snow?"

"Daddy wanted to go, to help make the people happy."

"Couldn't they be happy without him?"

The popcorn crushed in her hand. "It's time for bed."

He protested. "The snow sounds like brooms on my window."

"I'll sit with you."

She stayed a long time. He would fade toward sleep, then rouse with a start. "Listen!"

"It's just the wind."

"When will it stop?"

"In the morning."

"When Daddy comes to open our presents?"

"Yes." If only all stormings could end so satisfactorily. "I'll tell you the story of St. Nicholas again. Then you must sleep."

Finally he drifted off. She watched him until the room grew too cold for sitting. Slipping away, she bundled into a scarf and coat, put on overshoes, and stepped outside. The wind made her gasp, but she bent against it with a vague intention of reaching the gate. Halfway there, pummeled and breathless, she halted. No man-made sound ruffled the deep roar of the storm. The wan luminescence from the obscured moon, teasing vision only to block it short of realization, was more oppressive than total dark would have been. A chaos of nothingness— the town at the foot of the hill might as well not have existed; by planting his house so far up this slope Johnny had isolated himself from the warm windowpanes of his neighbors. Loneliness and despair

filled her and she floundered back to the warmth of the nickel-plated
stove.

The storm died and the clouds broke apart without her knowing it.
Johnny stabled his exhausted horse and on the back porch removed
his snow-encrusted outer clothes. Coming into the kitchen, he washed
his face in warm water to dissolve the ice in his eyebrows and eye-
lashes. When he entered the parlor, he saw her asleep in a chair, the
scarf still looped about her neck. Her first inkling that he had returned
was the pressure of his cold fingers on her hands.

"Darling, why aren't you in bed?"

For an instant she stared at him without comprehension, then wordlessly pulled him close. A moment later she pushed him back to look
at him. "You're all right?"

"Of course."

"Didn't you reach Red Mountain?"

"A little after five, just as the party was about to start."

"You said if the storm kept up you wouldn't come down until
morning."

"I took to missing you."

She let him hold her against the wool of his shirt while she absorbed
the unexpectedness of his return. As she awoke more fully, questions
intruded.

"Mr. Alden——"

"Fine form." Johnny loosened her enough to swing his hand and
imitate the minister's thumping pulpit tones. " 'The true dangers of
these silver mountains and of these eager camps are not sin and temptation, not the thunder of the avalanche or the blast of giant powder,
but tragic delusion. A concentration on Mammon, a blind search for
false veins—' " He yawned. "You can hear it tomorrow if you want. It's
good for another run, I reckon."

"You both came down in this storm? Just the two of you?"

"Mike O'Driscoll came along to help shovel."

She shuddered. "How could you see? Those cliffs, the ice— You
should have waited for daylight."

"The storm broke up there before it did here. The moon was bright
on the fresh snow. We had pretty fair sailing most of the way."

"Were the people surprised when you showed up?"

"Yep," he said, pleased with the sensation the arrival had caused.
"Only about half as many as we'd brought presents for were there. The
rest either figured we wouldn't buck the storm or they didn't want
to buck it themselves. Gabe's going to put what was left over in a grab
barrel in his store. Good for trade. Like premiums."

"You say the worst things. This is Christmas."

"Our Christmas," he said and rumpled the back of her hair. Suddenly serious, he whispered, "Forgive me, Lucy."

With a last touch of vindictiveness she wanted to ask, Was it worth it? But not tonight. And then, without asking, she had her answer. He gave a chuckle of absolute satisfaction.

"There hasn't been so much as a bobsled over the pass from Baker since this storm began. We went up through the worst part of it with a preacher and three mules and came back the same evening in the dark. That ought to show even Parley Quine which way the best shipping route lies."

The wind *whoo-ed* in the stovepipe; the draft flat rattled. Never mind, never mind. He had come back. He had proved his point and had come back to tell her that he was sorry.

"What time is it?" she asked.

"Going on two. Why?"

"Then it's Merry Christmas."

"That's right." He pulled her to her feet and rubbed his chin with its sandpaper whiskers affectionately along her jaw. "Let's go to bed," he said.

"3"

The sun came out again; the snow packed by day and froze at night. Everyone went sledding. The drop from Vinegar Hill down Silver Avenue to the river was the most popular run. After each snowfall broom brigades rushed out and swept the way clear. John built the frame of a sled for Lennie, had a blacksmith weld on runners, and patiently dragged the boy about until finally he grew bold enough to join other small children on the gentler slopes. A man's game was to jam snow into seamless sacks, carry them farther up the hill to a precipitous slope, and try to ride them to the bottom sitting astride. Lucille never saw anyone succeed.

Mixed groups went out on toboggans in the evenings, packed tight, gripping the handrails, shrieking, and racing downhill so fast that to Lucille even breathing seemed impossible. Sometimes there were disasters. One toboggan hurtling down Silver Avenue ran into a donkey; the impact scattered its occupants far and wide and broke a young man's leg. Ewer of course used the occasion for one of the vulgar puns that offended Lucille but always made Johnny laugh, much as he disliked the newspaperman: "A load of coasters struck the gable section of a jack at Dixon's corner last night and got ass-ended from here to Tincup. Condolences may be sent to Tony Sloan at Mother Marsh's, where the pieces are being reassembled."

Lucille liked sleigh rides better. Johnny was fond of loading whomever he could persuade to come along into a multi-seated rig and driving up the Red Mountain road as far as Wolf Creek Falls, to see the tremendous sheath of ice which the cataract had built up out of its own spray and through which it now plunged. The uphill pull made the horses sweat; frost gathered on them in white bristles. Harness bells tinkled and everyone huddled close together under the bearskin robes for warmth. The heated stones put at the start in straw at their feet never stayed warm long enough. At the falls some man invariably produced a glazed jug, saying, "I guess we'll have to use this on the way back." The ladies shivered and held their hands in their muffs and looked studiously at the scenery until finally one would say, "Well, just a tiny bit . . ."

The town's inordinate love of surprise parties, practical jokes, celebrations over every sort of anniversary, and even of violence was caused, Lucille decided, by an almost total lack of outside entertainment. They fought monotony on their own. Bachelor clerks and storekeepers amused themselves by drinking too much. Laborers lounged disconsolately around billiard parlors, tobacco stores, saloons and houses of ill repute. Variety halls advertised flagrantly in *The True Fissure*: "Emmett's is the place for amusement. The girls are rounder, rosier, and more beautiful than anyplace else in the St. Johns, and will take you through the mazy waltz with refreshing movements that will make you feel you don't care whether school keeps or not just so the girls are there." Temperance drives—the one that winter was called the Murphy Movement—corralled several pledges, but Johnny was unimpressed. "It's a new kind of fun," he said. "They'll backslide next payday." He was everlastingly coming home with tales of brutality: a brawler biting off the tip of his antagonist's nose during a fight in the freight office; the drunken charcoal burner at Emmett's "who thinks this feller belches in his direction on purpose, makes a rush at him, hits the stove instead, upsets it, and smokes out the whole can-can finale."

Against this raw new setting the townswomen erected ancient defenses. They held genteel "afternoons," serving each other tea and biscuits beside their parlor stoves and on Sundays snaring such men as they could. They fostered home musicals, amateur acting, whist clubs, literary and debating societies. The husbands participated to a point, but sooner or later rebellion broke out in the form of what the men considered a hilarious joke. One cold evening when the whist club met at Mayor Rubin's new home, someone filled the twelve pairs of overshoes on the porch with water that froze solid. At the literary society, subjects such as "The Influence of Electricity on Religious Thought" were proposed for discussion so solemnly that Lucille was never quite sure whether the proponents were serious or not. One meeting was turned into a kangaroo court and Fred Fossett haled before the bench charged with attempting to kiss the chambermaid at the Dixon House to the great distress of the dignity of Argent. He was convicted when Johnny, acting as prosecutor, showed the audience Fred's incipient bald spot, obvious proof that the maid had plucked him in self-defense. As a fine he had to treat the society to a champagne supper already prepared and waiting at the new Bon-Ton. "A put-up job," he protested with a pale attempt at a good-sport smile. Lucille sympathized with him fully and ignored Johnny and sat beside Fred at the head of the table. Afterwards, though, she had to admit that it was the most enjoyable of the society's sometimes stuffy midwinter meetings.

One who chose to find the town crude and cruel, as Nora had before moving across the pass to Baker, could cite ample evidence. And yet, and yet . . . even the air tastes better on this side of the mountain, Johnny had said the morning that she had sat on the top of the stage with him during her first crossing of the divide. Now when she stepped from the house into these days of towering radiance, it was possible to believe that the air had in fact just been minted, that the world had been created afresh during the night. Expectancy became a state of the lungs and blood. Despite what Margaret Fossett had said earlier about most women wanting to leave Argent, more and more people were beginning to plan toward permanence. The city council discussed such improvements as a public park, street lighting, and a water system. A bond issue to create the water works during the spring was passed and called forth a rash of plans for new kitchen and bathroom facilities. Certain apparatuses normally not mentioned in mixed society became the subject of drawing-room discussions; and *The True Fissure* boldly used the word "sewer" in a headline.

Other discussions revolved about utilizing water from the town's hot springs in a municipal bathhouse. Miners in particular ascribed high therapeutic value to the faintly odorous liquid. At regular intervals they journeyed down from the hills, soaked in the dingy log-and-mortar dips operated by private enterprise, and returned rejoicing to their prospects. This exasperated the town's new doctor, Jess Carstairs. "Those hard-rock stiffs," he snorted, "spend most of their time in cold tunnels, living on canned vegetables and occasional weekends of sin. Eventually they get so full of aches that I'm at last able to persuade them to knock off for a while, rest and eat a few square meals of wholesome food. But do I get any credit? No. They go back up the hill prais-

ing the water. Everybody's looking for magic, when the most magical
thing on earth is a pinch or two of common sense." Such talk was
considered disloyal, however, and plans for a tony bathhouse financed
by the city went ahead in spite of Carstairs and a few similar backward
conservatives, not including John Ogden.

In mid-February, when temperatures were so low, Johnny said, that
even Ewer wouldn't associate with them, *The True Fissure* aired
another civic problem:

> The deep snowfall brings the burro question again before the
> public. During the summer months every one of the unfortunate
> animals is claimed by someone and put to hard work. In winter,
> when the cost of feed is high, they are turned out to rustle for them-
> selves. Compelled to subsist on scraps thrown out of kitchen doors,
> they become perfect pests. They bother the restaurant owners. They
> hang around the residential section, eating clothes off the line, brooms,
> or anything they can find to swallow. At night their prowling for
> food disturbs the sleep of our citizens. During the day they are driven
> from place to place by rocks and dogs. Something must be done.

The ladies of the debating society proposed arguing the question at
their next meeting. The men captured the floor and amended the
proposition to read, Resolved that a jackass has no rights a human is
bound to respect. Underneath the not very funny humor that resulted
there was nevertheless a real earnestness about the welfare of the city.
A delegation called on the council and eventually a pound for stray
animals was established. A pound law to finance the place was passed
and a contract entered into with Ira Brice for providing hay. In the
spring the impounded animals would be auctioned to help meet any
operating deficit. "A town that didn't give a damn," Johnny said in
deep satisfaction, "wouldn't have done that. I'll bet there's no pound
over in Baker." There wasn't, either, as *The True Fissure* proudly
pointed out.

Another proposal concerned a theater. Toward spring a group of
wandering actors appeared and rented the empty loft above the bank.
Lucille was convinced that they had chosen this apparently unpropi-
tious season with deep craft. Argent was starved for novelty. Every organization in town fell over itself to provide free labor. Volunteers built
a rough stage and set up a row of candle footlights. Rude benches were
packed in from wall to wall; sets were hammered together and enthusiastically daubed with paint. The plays—a different one was put on each
night for a week—were incredibly bad. The actors hammed, forgot their
lines, bandied drunkenly with the audience. Spectators who found
themselves close to the stove nearly melted; those farther away nearly

congealed. Crowds of miners returned each night, nevertheless, applauding the leading ladies by stamping so violently with their hobnailed boots that a large piece of plaster was dislodged from the ceiling of Fred Fossett's office directly below. Those who considered themselves competent dramatic critics (this included all the ladies and most of the men of the literary society) deplored the performances and said that their only good was to emphasize the need for a civic opera house that would attract worthwhile companies. By this time, however, the city council was sinking under projects. They passed what Linc Hotchkiss termed a whereass of approval and let the matter drop.

"It's too near spring," Johnny said. "You've got to start these things when people haven't private projects to be thinking about. But it'll come. As soon as the railroad's here, Argent is going to be the metropolis of western Colorado. Mines, farms, water works, opera houses, anything you can think of—and our road from Red Mountain feeding it all. You wait!"

"4"

The railroad! Sometimes Lucille wondered whether there was anything else in Argent to talk about. Theater parties, practical jokes, barroom donnybrooks, and the swamping incidents of daily life were but trivial interruptions in that one absorbing topic—when the railroad comes. The advent was no longer a faraway dream. During the previous fall, narrow-gauge tracks, bound from Denver to Salt Lake City, had been pushed vigorously across the erstwhile Ute reservation. They missed Argent by thirty miles. A mere skip. About the time of the first frost, grading began for a feeder line up the Ute River. Though heavy snowfalls soon halted the work, speculation was only intensified by the hiatus. In preparation for spring, company engineers and auditors rambled around seeking bids on moving earth and cutting ties, on providing draft horses and hay, on maintaining boardinghouses for the construction crews. Tax rates were discussed with the county commissioners, freight rates with the managers of the principal mines.

Talk, talk, talk . . . every life in town would be touched. Many would find jobs; all would share in the tumbled prices. Housewives dreamed of new draperies bought from their trimmed budgets, of fresh lemons from California. Prospectors dreamed of profiting at last on the low-grade ore bodies they had found. Lennie and every other small boy in town could be enthralled instantly into goodness by prospects of a roaring ride on the iron horse.

The excitement gripped Johnny especially. Inactivity was hard on him—and on Lucille, who had to have him underfoot. He fretted continually about not earning his salary. At the first sign of a snowflake he was off like a shot to line up shovel crews and make sure that travel along the trail remained uninterrupted. Each time Walt put a mule train through while the Baker road stayed closed, he exulted. But when Pat succeeded in transporting an entire sawmill across the pass on sleighs and Red Mountain City could at last provide its own sawn lumber with no assistance from Argent, he was utterly dejected.

The railroad from the outside gave him something concrete to think about. He needed the release. Between storms he had little to do other than wander from stoveside group to stoveside group and join their speculations about the future. To be in the middle of everything was as essential to him as breathing; and when he heard the railroad's rumored completion time of July first he immediately promised, to Lucille's alarm, that he would duplicate the feat: his road to Red Mountain would also be finished by the first of July. The seeds having thus been sown, the reaping began. Showmen and town promoters, Johnny included, launched ambitious schemes for a double-barreled ceremony of welcome—road and railroad—to coincide with the town's normal Fourth of July celebration, a show so stupendous, in the minds of its planners, that Argent and Red Mountain would be the talk of the entire St. John mining country, perhaps of the state.

Ewer of course picked up the proposals. News was scarce during winter and he filled space in *The True Fissure* with whatever flights of rhetoric he thought might please his readers. Alluding to the lead ore in which the most dependable local showings of silver generally occurred, he cried at the city council in an editorial advocating the festival, "Let Gaiety Be Unrestrained Amidst Our Glittering Glades of Galena —a Gala Day in the New Golconda of the Rockies." Fascinated by his own alliteration, he then proposed a name for the event, using dollar signs for s's: "$HOWER$ OF $ILVER—THE TWIN CITIE$ $ALUTE! Argent and Red Mountain, One and Indivi$ible! Parade$, dance$, contest$—A REAL $TEMWINDER! $ilver Prize$ for victorie$ in hose cart race$, tug$ of war, drilling contest$, horse race$! Let us invite mines and merchants from every camp in the $t. John Mountain$ and from every new farming community along the Utc River to send teams, and let us make it worth their while to win!" Baker, the editorial went on, was already planning a ceremony to commemorate the completion of her railroad up Los Padres Canyon. Let Argent put that show to shame; let the rival town learn once and for all, through this triumphant display, that

Red Mountain's inexhaustible eam of $ilver were inextricably linked to Argent, $ublime queen city of the Rockie$.

The account pleased John enormously, for in effect it amounted to public recognition of what he was doing by his old enemy. As he read the editorial, Lucille watched his face and smiled. It was, she decided, a propitious time to tell him that she was pretty sure she was pregnant.

She began cautiously, almost diffidently. "The parade I'll remember," she said, "is the one last year."

He hurt her by not immediately grasping the reference. "This one will be better," he grunted and went on reading.

"Better than our float?"

"Oh." He laid the paper aside and grinned at her. "The runaway!"

"The silver bars rolling in the dirt!"

"And those two Cousin Jacks, drunker'n hoot owls."

"The rain."

"I golly!" He reached out and pulled her onto his lap. "That was the first time I kissed you—in the rain."

"But not the last time?" she asked and felt herself blushing like fire.

"Ah!" he murmured. "I'll show you."

And that was when she told him.

"Great . . . showers of silver!" was all he could think of to say at first. After that he would not let her go. Unfortunately she had planned to do a big ironing the next day, and since the stove would be roaring to keep her sadirons hot, she had decided to bake bread at the same time. She wanted to prepare her dough after supper. Johnny wanted to be tender. Telling him please to go down to the Pastime and talk about Ewer's proposed Shower of Silver with the boys, she boiled a potato, drained a quart of cloudy water from it, and into this put a cake of dry yeast. Johnny stayed doggedly in the kitchen, pouting and offended. She poured her liquid into a dishpan and sifted in enough flour to make a runny batter. To keep this from freezing, she placed it beside the stove, which Johnny banked for the night as anxiously as if he were preparing an incubator. Is he going to fuss like this for seven months? she wondered.

The next morning he grew fidgety simply because she rose ten minutes early to add more flour to the batter, which had swelled during the night and was beautifully bubbly. Exasperated at him and wretched with morning sickness, she kneaded it down until it was firm, set it aside to rise again. Unnoticed during the flurry of getting breakfast, the cat went to sleep on the soft warm dough. "I'll *warp* you!" She flew at the animal with a broom. Johnny leaped up to stroke her. "Don't get yourself so excited!"

"Will you please go away?" she railed. He crept off and that made her more miserable. Fighting it, she called silently after him, *Just let me be pregnant in a perfectly ordinary way. Don't make issues.* Despair welled up through the pangs of nausea. *Don't make me remember.*

She put the bread into pans, let it double in size, and thrust it into the oven to bake. She placed several irons onto the stove to heat. She dragged the ironing board into the middle of the kitchen. When Johnny came creeping back, ostensibly to collect some papers, the room smelled of starch and fresh bread crusts and steam and the scorched flannel cover of the ironing board. He kissed the back of her neck. Her temples were moist with perspiration. A strand of hair had come loose and hung down in front of her ear.

"Don't work so hard, darling," he urged.

She contemplated dropping the iron on his foot. "Just what else would you suggest at the moment?"

"We can take the stuff to some laundress."

"They shred it. Besides, we can't afford it."

"What we can't afford is for you to take chances—now."

"For heavens sake, John, that baby won't be born until nearly November."

"I'm going to hire you a servant," he stated firmly.

She grimaced. The house mortgaged, the furniture unpaid for. "I don't want a servant."

"It's not fitting for you to work like this."

The only fitting thing is for me to earn my way back, she cried wordlessly. "Johnny, please—"

"You leave everything to me," he said and bustled away.

She dropped into a straight wooden chair and rested her arms on the zinc-topped kitchen table. Her back ached. "You've got Red Mountain," she said at the door. "You've got that railroad to escape to." She couldn't even have a backache. Showers of Silver indeed. "I won't cry," she said and started to weep, then saw the cat and flew at it again merely for looking in the direction of the empy dough pan.

He did engage a servant, a phlegmatic Norwegian whom she formally called Mrs. Nylander even after they became firm friends. Mrs. Nylander smoked a pipe. When she heard her mistress approaching, she hurriedly stashed it in the pocket of her apron. Both of them then would pretend not to smell or see the clouds of tobacco smoke in the kitchen. Lennie was one bond between them. Another was the small bulwarks they erected against their husbands. It became routine for them to cast looks at each other and agree that men were impossible. Mr. Nylander, it seemed, forgot to fill the coal buckets in the mornings and came to Sunday dinner without a shirt, in suspenders. The real impossibility, Lucille sensed, was something else. Exactly what it was she never learned. Mrs. Nylander loved her husband, however, and the coal buckets and suspenders served in place of that which could not be talked about in public.

But even though she grew attached to Mrs. Nylander, days passed before Lucille forgave Johnny for hiring her. "I didn't come here to be a burden," she said again and again, and that brought up the egrets and pompons remaining in the attic. Wasted. "Why won't you let me help you?" she demanded in exasperation.

He always looked blank at such remarks and retorted in injured tones, "I love you, Lucille."

"I know you do. But——"

"What *is* the matter then?" he demanded anxiously.

"Nothing . . . everything."

"It's the baby," he decided proudly.

Men, she told Mrs. Nylander later, were indeed impossible.

IV

"1"

At long last spring strode up the river. Ice left the pools; snowdrifts grudgingly shrank to gray resistant crusts on the northern slopes; sticky buds swelled on the cottonwoods. Overnight, water began dripping from the rocks, springing from mossy crevices, pouring down the gullies. The basin burst into a misty green of promise that caught Lucille's heart each time she stepped outside and looked down the budding slope toward the awakening town.

Inside the town, however, she found spring less romantic. The winter-long packing of snow in the streets had, in places, built up the center of the thoroughfare higher than the edges. Each spring night this mixture of slush and mud froze solid. In the mornings it softened again. The wheels of ore wagons churned up great gluey chunks. As the ooze melted, it flowed onto the sidewalks and was tramped in sticky ribbons through the stores. Although slag from Roscoe Blair's smelter was spread on the crosswalks, wagons soon ground the makeshift paving down into the muck, and by afternoon women shoppers were in despair. They would gaze helplessly at the morass for a time, shrinking from spatterings by careless horsemen, and in final resignation gather up their skirts in both hands and mince across, lifting their feet, encased in little rubber boots lined with lamb's wool, like unhappy cats with paper tied to their paws.

In the high country, winter clung stubbornly. Dawns came blue and still, but as soon as the sun struck the summits, winds awoke. Long snow plumes blew out from the ridges. As the morning light descended the sides of the red peaks, so did the gales and presently, so Lucille was told, Red Mountain City was swept by blizzards howling under a cloudless sky. As winter's powdery snow compacted on the sides of the high glacial cirques, avalanches began to run, sliding like sibilant express trains into the bottoms of the cups and then funneling in gigantic battering rams through the outlet gulches. Each issue of *The True Fissure* mentioned the more famous slides by name and spoke casually of shattered cabins or trails littered with debris. But this was a mild spring. Damage was light; no lives were lost.

If Johnny noticed the pale pasqueflowers that popped out at the edges of the melting snowbanks or the fuzzy willow stems and the new light-blue tips on the spruce boughs, it was only as an accompaniment to the sap stirring afresh in his own blood. He crowded the ice line up the gorge; as Fred Fossett put matters in an unexpected flight of fancy, he even stepped on its toes for not backing up fast enough. He carried a high-powered rifle to work with him and shot icicles out of the way of the scalers. Whenever he suspected unstable cornices of snow he climbed dizzily up across the granite and jarred them loose with dynamite lest in taking their own natural course they sweep areas where his crews were working. "Couldn't he wait until after the weather has cleared the way for him?" the wife of one laborer complained to Lucille, out of sorts because her husband had to sleep now in the revived construction camp beside Wolf Creek Falls.

You don't know Johnny, Lucille thought. He could no more have waited than these streams could. "Won't it be great if we roll wheels into Red Mountain from Argent before they come across from Baker!" he exclaimed to her one morning. The tantalization of triumph: snow on the summit pass was deep and as it softened under the strengthening sun, horses trying to cross from Baker would sink to their bellies; meanwhile farther down the grassy south-facing hillsides the footing would liquefy into morasses. Throughout this time Johnny would be at work in the gorge. Not that he really believed he could carve away the remaining cliffs before the rival road dried out. But it gave him a target. With an almost audible shout of release he took aim at it with a self-reviving zest which Lucille at last had learned to understand. In the gorge, the ambiguity of human affairs no longer muddied the things he so passionately believed. These obstacles could be removed simply, by the exertion of mechanical power, and in this sort of power he could place his confidence.

His impatient energy at times alarmed her. To speed the melting of snow which pack trains had tramped hard along the higher section of the trail, he covered it with coal dust. The black powder absorbed heat; the snow under it melted rapidly, and the trail became the channel of a torrent flowing between the high snowbanks on either side, the water itself helping to wash away the remaining drifts. Meanwhile his own face was eroded almost as painfully by the morning blasts of wind and by the reflected sunlight. During one nine-day absence from home he grew a beard as protection. Convinced that wetting his face simply opened his pores to deeper scorching, he washed away neither the coal dust nor the streaks of charcoal he put under his eyes and down the ridge of his nose as a guard against snow blindness. The continual wading in slush pulled his voice like a bullfrog's deep into his phlegmy throat. He even scalped his new soft wool pants: when he rested from shoveling he leaned back against the snow; this froze to the nap of the cloth and pulled out little tufts when he straightened again.

Lucille was horrified when he returned home. His begrimed, weather-scalded cheeks were peeling in scaly flakes—parboiled dirt was the phrase that flashed into her mind. She flew at him with blankets and hot water. He submitted grumpily to having his chest rubbed with hot sweet oil and turpentine. More willingly he absorbed her favorite bracer—a pinch of ginger added to steaming hot wine that had been poured over sugar burned in a pan. He ate heartily of a tough steak cut from an old draft ox which everyone in town knew had been taken near death from an immigrant's wagon the previous fall and kept alive until meat grew scarce. Then he was restless again and wanted to walk down town and look at the store windows.

They fell in with other couples as they sauntered along the street. There was lots to see. The first sign of spring had quickened the town's yeasty growth. The wooden sidewalks along Main Street were being replaced by cement. The once protruding signs had, by council edict, been removed from above the walks and placed flat against the store-fronts. There was a sprinkling of new striped awnings with serrated edges. The men studied the enlarged hardware displays, the women the dresses hung on frames and set against bolts of cloth unrolled to show their patterns. Johnny paused to admire some babies' knitted hoods and flannel sacques. Again, as he had done several times before, he mortified Lucille by announcing loudly to the newcomers in their group that his wife was expecting. "October-November, I golly!" There were the usual exclamations, though she privately thought that by now her pregnancy could hardly be news anywhere in the St. John Mountains, and they all went into the drugstore to toast her with glasses of lemon phosphate before going home to bed.

In spite of his exertions, small wagons pulled by multiple teams reached Red Mountain City from Baker before the road up the gorge was open. *The True Fissure* scoffed feebly at the triumph: "Nothing is impossible. Leander swam the Hellespont and Pat Edgell floated an amphibious wagon over the Summit Pass. But regular travelers had better be cautious. That 'road' would mire a saddle blanket." The Baker *Herald* cackled in retort. "Argent still hopes for travel through Ute Gorge. The latest rumor is that John Ogden is setting up a series of snubbing posts so they can lower their jackasses down by the tail. Meantime a carload of highest grade ore has already been stored at our freight depot awaiting completion of the tracks through Los Padres Canyon so that it can be shipped to the new smelter at Montezuma. Poor Argent!"

Johnny read the facetiousness with a pained glower. Beaten! Although he had never expected to get up the hill first, he did not like the failure turned into public humor. Now the first wagon from Argent to Red Mountain would lack freshness. Resistant as usual to anticlimax, he did not wish Ewer even to announce the final shot that opened the gorge to travel of sorts. There was polishing still to do, he said; save the ceremonies for the Shower of Silver. But Ewer sent Sam Varnum along with the first wagon anyway, and kept dropping into his columns weekly notices of progress: "The one sharp curve at the falls where it seemed that the lead horses of long teams might have to be unhitched to make the swing has now been gentled." Or, "At regular intervals turnout points are being built, platforms with outward curving walls of well-joined rocks, so that the biggest wagons bound in opposite directions can pass each other without danger or inconvenience." And finally, "Drainage ditches are now completed, and every low place and rut in the roadbed itself is being filled with compacted layers of broken stone and loam. Transporters seeking a sure outlet for Red Mountain ore take notice: the most severe rainstorms will not delay schedules or result in missed trains on this road."

By this time the city council was meeting almost nightly to push plans for the forthcoming celebrations. Souvenir teaspoons of pure silver were ordered cast; there was to be a likeness of a locomotive's front end on the tip of the spoon's handle, a view of Wolf Creek Falls on the shank, and a picture of Argent's Main Street in the bowl. Handbills describing the contests and prizes were sent throughout the state. A silver railroad spike was prepared, to be driven in front of the depot. The governor was invited to deliver the principal address. He declined but promised to send the lieutenant governor in his place.

The frenzy of preparation put Johnny on edge. He wanted to think of something special for the road company to do, yet for days nothing suitable occurred to him. When he was home, which was increasingly seldom, he prowled through the dark house and woke Lucille in the middle of the night to tell her of heated notions that cooled off in the dawn. "Isn't the road enough?" she asked. Yet she knew that it wasn't; everything the job had meant to him and to Argent somehow had to be epitomized in one concentrated moment, and he kept fretting and fretting until inspiration came. Then he grew mysterious and teasing, up on his toes with pleasure. "Wait'll you see! Oh man! It'll take the play clear away from Baker. Just wait!"

Finally she wormed it out of him, as she knew he wanted her to do.

"The biggest, richest load of ore ever hauled on any road! But don't you tell Sam Varnum or anyone else!"

"Why not?"

"It won't be as fine a surprise if people can think about it in advance. I want to pop their eyes. We can! I'll bet that fifty claims and mines will contribute ore for a real shower of silver—not just bars from one mine, like we had last year. Fifty in twelve months! Wait'll the town gets a load of that!"

She smiled at him, wondering fondly whether any surprise could be as splendid in actuality as it shone now in this imagination. A child, Nora would have said, with a child's faith in the magic of surprises and of mere bigness. Just the same, that irrepressible faith was moving mountains.

"2"

Spring eased into summer; huge primroses bloomed on the gravelly banks; streams retreated decorously into their channels. Lucille's clothes began to fit uncomfortably, and she hated the lonesomeness of the evenings. During the last days of June and the first of July she did not see her husband. He was continually between the falls and the mountain, putting finishing touches on the road (the lieutenant governor's entourage would be driven over it after the ceremonies in town) or at Red Mountain City preparing a spectacular entry into town for his secret load of ore.

His idea was for all persons coming to the Shower of Silver by way of Red Mountain to ride down the new road to Argent in a united, impressive line. "Like pilgrims in the old days," Lucille had said, nodding her own excitement when he had told her of the plan. He hadn't been taken by the analogy, however. "This is new," he had grumbled. "A new Canterbury," she insisted. He didn't know what that was and shook his head. "Just plain new, nothing like it ever before, for those who are willing to buck it."

Returning to the mountain, he persuaded with ceaseless argument the driver of every wagon that went up the hill during the days immediately preceding the ceremony to lay over and return with what he called the Red Mountain Special. People already there or bound across the pass from Baker were also cajoled into joining the parade.

Anticipation fed on itself. By four o'clock on the afternoon of July third, when the vanguard of the procession was expected, townspeople began drifting to vantage points on Vinegar Hill to watch the arrivals swing out of the gorge and down the last broad curve into Main Street. Soon quite a crowd had gathered outside the Ogdens' picket fence. Sam Varnum, the pimply, long-nosed reporter from *The True Fissure* floated awkwardly among them, asking their impressions and scribbling furiously in his notebook.

Lucille was fussed and pink with pleasure. She had not expected any such turnout and she didn't know what to do about it. She asked Varnum and some of the men who were standing around to drag such movable chairs as she possessed outside onto the unkempt lawn for the ladies to sit on. Over and over she apologized to Margaret Fossett,

"What am I going to do? There isn't a lemon in the house, or enough tea—only a drop of sherry in the decanter."

"Just let them look," Mrs. Fossett said. "That's what they came for."

Sam Varnum, who had been eavesdropping, interposed with a whinny, "An event like this needs no folderol to give it significance." He looked at her with hangdog yearning; during the winter he had developed a hopeless crush. "I'm sure you realize better than anyone what that road represents. I hope—I hope—hee!" He absolutely choked.

Lucille turned an amused, puzzled glance on him. "You hope what, Mr. Varnum?"

"I hope he appreciates you!" he blurted and was so acutely embarrassed by his own temerity that he tipped his hat in consternation and oozed out of sight behind a nearby group of men, as if he had just recalled something vital that needed to be jotted down.

Mrs. Fossett's plump underlip went out. "Fancy now!"

Lucille blushed. Perhaps she had encouraged Sam a bit too much with her friendliness. But he was so strange and lorn a young man, so unsuited to the hurly-burly of the town. What dismay was he fleeing? she wondered occasionally. What impossible hope had he followed here? He was the butt of endless practical jokes and cruel rebuffs. Yet, given identity as a reporter for *The True Fissure*, he seemed able to endure them. He attended church faithfully, appeared at every gathering of the literary society, covered each meeting of the city council. Wherever he went he held his notebook in one bony hand as if it were a passport to a fellowship he could not otherwise attain. When he was not at meetings, he read avidly, seeking substance from the shadows of his imagination. But it was impossible to imagine him striding forth on any project wholly his own.

"He's such a sad, lonesome young man," Lucille told Margaret, "so eager to be agreeable. He doesn't mean anything."

"Oh yes he does. And he's right. I hope John Ogden does appreciate you. Not many women would have put up with what you have."

Lucille's head lifted. "I've loved every bit of it. I—"

A great shout from the watchers interrupted. "Here they come!"

A bristle of excited fingers pointed toward the gorge. "There! See them! There!" Around the buttress guarding Wolf Creek Falls, reduced to specks by the distance, came eight black horses drawing a high-sided ore wagon and trailer. Buggies, horsemen, democrats, a pack train, and still more wagons followed. And "Hey, a fire pumper and hose cart! Must be the ones from Red Mountain for the races!" Men afoot, donkeys. "The Baker fire company, too!" Slowly the serpentine slanted down across the hillside beyond the creek. Someone among the spectators waved a handkerchief. Others took it up, arms swinging in unison, a flutter of white against the green of Vinegar Hill. The men on the lead wagon spotted the display and stood upright to wave back.

"Sssh!"

The crowd froze dead still, ears straining. Faint shouts of greeting reached them above the creek noises. Varnum saw Lucille standing alone and slipped up beside her.

"Is that Mr. Ogden on the front wagon?" he asked.

"Yes. With Walt Kennerly."

"What's in the wagon?"

"Sssh!"

The faint, thin shout had come again. Together the watchers drew deep breaths and howled back. Lucille felt as if more air had been crowded into her chest than she could hold.

Lennie reached his hand into hers. "Will the train come next, Mommy?" he asked.

She shook her head. "The train comes from the other direction. But some day," she added, "there will be a train from that direction."

Varnum overheard the remark. "So John has talked to you about it— a railroad up the gorge, I mean?"

She nodded. Her gesture took in the entire town's wild excitement over rails at last arriving from the outside. "He was bound to think of carrying the tracks from here on into the heart of the mining country."

"John Ogden being the carrier?"

"Johnny is . . . Johnny."

Varnum wagged his head almost sadly. "Pushing that road up the gorge has been a prodigious effort. I know. I've followed your husband over it until my—hee!—tongue was dragging. And now, before he can even celebrate what he's done, it's being belittled by calls for more. Where's the end?"

"Look at that parade!" Her eyes turned his back toward the long, slow file. "The road is not belittled. It had to come first. If there's a railroad, it'll be possible because Johnny showed the way."

Varnum wrinkled his long nose dubiously. "Rails can't use the wagon road for a grade. It's too steep. Johnny admitted as much to me himself. To obtain a grade easy enough for locomotives—and I'm just repeating what Johnny said—the builder, whoever it is, will have to twist hairpin curves back on themselves and run tunnels and blast cuts. He'll have to build snowsheds and put in masonry footing every rod of the way. I can see how that would be a challenge to him. Johnny, as you said, is, hee, Johnny. But the money! It'll cost well over a million dollars. A million, Luci—Mrs. Ogden. Before that much capital moves in, the mines up there will have to prove themselves at a far greater depth than they've reached so far."

"That's what the wagon road will help them do," she said proudly. She could repeat her husband too, and more in accord with the rainbows he had seen, not the doubts Sam Varnum felt. "The road will let the mines move material up and ore down at reasonable rates. It'll help us show the whole world what we have. That's why we're celebrating."

"Hardrock Johnny. I know. I've heard him." Varnum wriggled unhappily, swallowed for courage, and tried to mimic John. He did not do it very well, in Lucille's estimation. "That's deep-rock up there and we ought to believe in it. We ought to be thinking ahead, thinking big. Nobody has touched the bottom of one of those fissure veins yet. Meantime prospectors keep locating new veins as fast as they can work through that tangle of landslide hillocks. Do you know what I think— Johnny, I mean? I think that before long there'll be a solid line of mines beginning at the pass near the Summit Queen and running along the side of the mountain as far as Corkscrew Gulch, maybe clear on around the peaks. Oh, nothing limited at all—I mean, that's me. And Johnny: down at the foot of the red peaks, on the flats, there'll be stamp mills, homes, stores—everything that's in Argent today, all crying for the stuff our farmers and merchants can send them and pouring trainloads of silver back down to our smelters. Trainloads, I said—I mean Johnny said, hee—trainloads running through this gorge!"

It wasn't like the reporter to talk so much, almost as if arguing with himself. She eyed him quizzically—the yearning, the uncertainty. "Are these things so impossible to believe, Mr. Varnum?"

"I—I—" He whinnied his nervous, maddening laugh and all but

wiggled out of his shoes. "He said they'll need—oh, hee—a newspaper up there."

So that was it! He was searching for confirmation of what, in his heart, he really wanted to do. Lucille gave him a radiant smile. "How wonderful!"

"Oh, hee!" Varnum's Adam's apple galloped up and down his scrawny throat. "I told him it would take more silver than I have in my pockets."

"If I know Johnny, he had a suggestion about that too."

"He did say that if I wished he'd mention the matter to Otto Winkler."

"Do you wish?"

"I . . ." Varnum's blush ran even across his forehead. "If I could truly believe . . ."

"Why not?" she countered and they both stared at the advancing procession, beyond it, and up the gorge through which it had filed. The beginning only. She could almost hear Johnny's voice as it must have rung in Sam Varnum's ears: *Why not? Three red mountains full of silver up there, hardly scratched yet. Everybody sharing in what's to come—nothing like it anywhere else on earth.* "Why not, Mr. Varnum?"

"I—oh, so much silver. If the price keeps going down the way it has the last few years—I mean, the economic graphs do show—oh . . ." Even Lucille had been in the mountains long enough to know that this was total heresy. He writhed under her glance. "I mean—oh, hee!" Self-depreciation and doubt struggled with his terrible yearning. "A newspaper of my own! It's something—ha!—to think about. Isn't it?"

Overwhelmed, he fled.

Solemnly Lennie watched the lead wagon turn off the hill onto Main Street and disappear behind the city buildings. The crowd began slowly to disperse.

"Is Daddy up front because he wants to be the first to meet the train?"

"We all want to meet the train together."

A man standing beside her chuckled. "Without your husband's road, ma'am, very few of those people from Red Mountain would be meeting the train." He was a newcomer; at least she did not recall having seen him before. But he knew of Johnny. "What Ogden told that reporter about Red Mountain isn't half good enough—if you'll pardon my having eavesdropped on you. Too much silver, indeed! Why, you'd think Varnum is a black Republican—on Ewer's *True Fissure!* Why, any fool knows that a growing, debtor section like the West can't have too much money in circulation. What we really need is to end the

Crime of '73 and institute absolute free coinage of silver—no half-measures like the Bland Act. It'll come. It'll come because men like Jack Ogden, with faith in what they're doing, are bringing the truths of our new West to the attention of the country. Yes, indeedy, this must be a proud day for you, Mrs. Ogden!"

Lucille smiled tremulously, not really grasping everything he said and certainly not daring—so many people listening to the speaker and nodding agreement—not daring to speak.

Margaret Fossett eyed her shrewdly. "You go right ahead and blubber if you feel like it."

I certainly will not, Lucille thought. "We're celebrating, remember?" she said in an effort at lightness.

Margaret smiled. "I hope you'll always feel this way about what Johnny does." Her face turned wistful. "It's the best wish I know for any wife." She blinked rapidly. "Now I am the one who's about to blubber," she said and fled down the hill.

The crowd dwindled away. Lucille went inside the house. It seemed full of whispers, yet lonesome. She placed her hand against the teakettle simmering on the kitchen stove; very soon it could be heated enough for tea. But she was too excited for tea. She returned to the living room and dropped onto the sofa. There had been no reason to expect that he would come to her immediately on his arrival; yet as the minutes dragged, her disappointment grew. He needed only to park his canvas-shrouded, secret wagon and help Walt care for the horses. That should not take long. Had something gone wrong?

She turned to the window overlooking the gorge. The last vehicle had reached town and only two belated horsemen were visible on the road. She scolded herself. It was ridiculous to feel this way, keyed to the point of borrowing trouble. Probably he was wandering along Main Street right now, wondering why *she* hadn't come to meet him. They hadn't seen each other for days; there'd been no opportunity for arrangements; that was the trouble. She picked up two dried leaves that had fallen from her potted geraniums and stepped outside to throw them over the porch railing. Nothing interesting stirred on Silver Avenue. Of course he probably was being stopped every dozen feet by people wanting to talk over plans for the morrow.

"I think I will have a cup of tea," she said aloud and hurried back into the kitchen. She shook the grate vigorously. But she did not put coal into the stove. She stood absorbed, the lid hook idle in her hand: *This must be a proud day for you, Mrs. Ogden.* She heard Lennie pattering in, wanting bread and sugar probably. *Here they come!—* the long serpentine of his victory. A proud day: and thoughts that generally broke free from their repressions only at nighttime shouldered into her consciousness: restoration—the day when the town officially admitted that he had earned back his self-respect. But have I earned mine?

If he wasn't her assurance of worth, then what was?

She fed Lennie his bread and sugar and sent him back outside. She had carried this guilt alone too long. She had to face it, as John had faced his. I'll tell him today. It was a recurrent temptation at times of high excitement, but at the irretrievable moment she had always shrunk back. Today, though—and then, when there is nothing hidden between us, when we have looked at it together—Johnny, you will look; Johnny, today you can afford to be generous—then: *it must be a proud day*: proud for both of us, Johnny, please Johnny.

She heard a step on the front porch. Her breath startled. She stood shaken an instant, then ran to the front door. But it was not Johnny. It was Nora, breathing hard from her walk up the hill.

"3"

The two women embraced, stepped back an arm's length to look each other over, and embraced again. "Umm hmm," Nora decided, after still another look. "When?"

"The last of October, I think," Lucille told her. "Or early November."

"I would have expected you to have gotten around to it sooner."

"Tch! And you?"

"We move too much," Nora said airily. "Later perhaps." She let herself be led into the kitchen while Lucille fired up the stove. Then she went through the entire house, exclaiming over this and that, and finally they settled in the parlor with their teacups. "It's beautiful," Nora said and squeezed Lucille's hand. "You look happy."

"I am," Lucille said and returned her visitor's scrutiny. Nora was thin. Her skin was gray. At rare instants when she was off guard, discontent showed deeper than ever in her eyes. But the obvious response had to be made. "And you?" Lucille asked.

"On the go," Nora said, airily still. "Where's Johnny? He was riding in that big lead wagon on the way down."

She might as well have said in the bladed way she reserved for him, The first man in town and still not home; why? Lucille pretended unconcern. "I really don't know when to expect him. He has lots to do for tomorrow. Did Harmon come with you?"

"He's at the hotel looking up old friends. Do you realize we haven't been back to Argent since . . ." Nora didn't finish. Instead she asked abruptly, "Aren't you surprised that I'd come here after—everything?"

"Friends don't need a reason for coming."

"Johnny may think differently," Nora said. Her shoulders moved in a brittle shrug. "We bet wrong—I did, rather. I was the one who persuaded Harmon to go to Pat. I think Johnny realizes that."

"It's past."

"Now," Nora said bluntly, "we want to make peace."

"All of you?" Lucille asked in quick hope. She was thinking of Pat. A very proud day: every sore healed.

"Harmon is embarrassed," Nora said. "I've a thicker skin."

"There's no need—"

"Oh yes there is. I intend to admit to Johnny exactly why I appeared to double-cross him. It wasn't really that, though. I simply misjudged. He's always so wide-eyed about big plans that I thought of course Pat's Summit City scheme would appeal to him. Oh, I knew he had some doubts, but Pat was his friend. So was Harmon. I was sure that if Winkler forced a choice, Johnny would stay loyal to them."

"Johnny stayed loyal to the road and to Argent," Lucille retorted.

"Or loyal to himself," Nora said, then smiled an apology for the impulsive sarcasm. Peace was her errand, she had indicated. "I still think the Summit scheme was a good one. But it's dead now. Without the Red Mountain Toll Company stock to boost it and with Otto Winkler turning thumbs down in Denver, it didn't have a chance." She paused, then finished, starkly, "We lost our shirts. Even my Bon-Ton money."

"Johnny will be as sorry as anyone to hear that," Lucille said in real distress, yet defensively too. "He never means to hurt. Never. You can't imagine the agony these . . . misunderstandings cause him."

"I know Johnny," Nora said and again the claws of her temper slipped their sheaths. "I know how he bleeds over getting what he wants. But he gets it." Again she checked herself, completely miserable. It was hard for her ever to surrender. Now she had to abase herself on a supplication that probably should have been her husband's. She did it, though. She spread her hands and smiled wryly. "I didn't come here to quarrel. Johnny has won and that's that."

"Will Pat . . . ?"

"Eat this kind of humble pie?" Nora shook her head. "Not Pat. He'll never forgive Johnny. He thinks he was cruelly framed."

"I'm sorry. It would have made tomorrow perfect if—if—"

"I don't imagine John will miss Pat or any of us tomorrow," Nora said. Her thin face turned hard and desperate. "If it'll make him feel any better, Harmon and I have had to leave Pat too." She rushed ahead before Lucille could speak. "Everything went wrong after the town scheme failed. Parley Quine blamed Harmon partly. They quarreled, and that made it impossible for us to do much in Baker or even at Red Mountain. But now we've come across another opportunity."

"Oh, I hope so."

"We need Johnny's help."

"Of course we'll help."

Nora smiled wanly and went on, "Some—speculators, I guess is the word—have been looking around the mountain for a property that so far has escaped attention but that might be developed on a large scale, under proper financing. They—oh, the details don't matter. To make it short, Harmon knows the Summit area pretty well because of the work he did on the town scheme. He was able to show the men several small claims that could be put together and operated as a unit, with a fair chance of striking an extension of the Summit Queen vein. That's what we call the property—the Summit Queen Extension."

It was one way of riding on a proven name, Lucille thought. But she simply nodded without speaking.

"We hope to issue bonds and stock enough to pay for development work at depth. Harmon would like to talk with Winkler and Fossett about it."

Lucille's heart sank. "Everyone is trying to sell them interests in claims and things. I don't believe—"

"We don't want to sell them anything," Nora said desperately. "I mean, we're sure it's a good proposition. If Winkler is convinced of its merits after his own investigation, naturally we wouldn't turn down his money. But the important thing now is not to have either him or Fred unfriendly. After the road troubles they might be. They were, about the town company. But if Johnny will—oh, go up to them with Harmon and let them know that as far as he is concerned, bygones are bygones, it might create a whole new atmosphere. Then if Winkler or even Fossett will write a note to some of the financial people in Denver, not recommending or anything, just introducing—Harmon couldn't bring himself to ask Johnny, but I can. It could make such a difference to our plans now."

A suspicion crossed Lucille's mind that perhaps this throwing of herself and Harmon on their mercies was not so candid as Nora was trying to make it appear, that the approach had been calculated as the one most likely to gain what they wanted. Immediately she fled the thought as unworthy. Though Nora's words sounded contrived, her eyes were stark. Compassion for her filled Lucille. Life had always begrudged her. Now it was taking even her pride.

"I'm sure Johnny will help," she promised once more. She turned possibilities in her mind, rejected one after another. "Tomorrow is going to be confused. Johnny—and the others too—are going to be so involved that I think tonight would be better. Are you going to the banquet for the lieutenant governor at the Dixon House?"

"We weren't invited."

"Herb and Abigail Rubin are in charge," Lucille said. "I'm sure that if Johnny mentions it to them, they'll be agreeable." She tried to ease Nora's mortification with a laugh. "Though if Johnny doesn't get home pretty soon to change his clothes, we won't be going ourselves."

Nora did not speak a word. Clothes, Lucille thought. Probably that brown dress from Chicago was the only thing she had—and if Walt appeared at the banquet, as probably he would . . . Brightly she said,

"For all of that, I don't know what I'm going to wear myself. I'm outgrowing everything." She paused and eyed Nora as if the notion had just struck. "There's a little summer thing that I brought in with me last year and then never had a chance to wear because we were up in the gorge . . ." In other words, the women of Argent would not recognize it.

"I couldn't," Nora said, barely audibly.

"Of course you can," Lucille said. "Here, let me show you. The petticoat I made too. I did the fagoting the way you showed me."

"W-well . . ."

They hurried upstairs, carrying on a mimicry of the springtime gestures and tones of a year before when they had bustled in and out of each other's establishments on Main Street. Lucille took the clothing from the wardrobe and laid it rustling across the bed. She didn't force the dress, however, but picked up the petticoat first—humble enough surely. "I made this while Johnny was away on the road. He's always away. I split some old silk stockings, turned the ankle ends up, fagoted them, and trimmed it with these little handmade French flowers. I didn't plan very well, though. I can't begin to get into it now. It should be just right for you."

"It's divine," Nora said. She laid the petticoat aside and held the dress up to herself, studying the shirrings and puffings, and then turned it inside out to see how it was lined and interlined, how it was bound, and how the steels were put in. "What perfect stitches!" The torment of lost chances drew her face. "Last fall I supposed that by now I would have a closet full of dresses like this." She shook the mood away, made herself say graciously, "In this I'll enjoy waltzing even with Otto Winkler. If he waltzes."

"Who knows?" Lucille said. "Last year he sat through the banquet covered with napkins from his whiskers to below the tablecloth. As soon as the speeches were over he left for bed. We'll have to catch him quick.

Just to be on the safe side I'd better send you a note about the invitation. Where are you staying? At your father's ranch?"

That was a mistake. Nora looked at the floor and shook her head. Probably she hadn't written the old man, or even her brother and sister that she was coming. "At . . . Badgley's," she said. It was the cheapest, dirtiest boardinghouse in town. She looked up, pleading for understanding. If it had been possible to back out now, she would have. But the only thing left was to say, "The Summit Queen Extension is a good proposition, Lucy; truly it is. If it wasn't, I wouldn't ask."

"The men can make up their own minds about the business part of it," Lucille said and hurried to change the subject. "Let me get you a box for the dress." They rustled with paper and string and went downstairs, talking about clothes and weather and new dance steps. She had to bite her tongue to keep from alluding to the ball last year, on Good Riddance Day, when it had been Johnny's turn to be humiliated. Now the talk had to stay impersonal, in order not to remind Nora even indirectly that while she and Harmon had been sliding downward, Johnny had been climbing.

As they were saying good-bye at the door, they heard horses' feet and the shrill laugh of women. "What on earth!" Lucille said. She stepped onto the porch and flinched. A pair of two-seated carriages had halted at the gate. They overflowed with men dressed in what appeared to be faded red union suits and with girls in low-bodiced gowns and hats over whose curling brims dangled feathery purple or crimson plumes. Johnny had evidently just jumped from one of the vehicles and was opening the gate. His work trousers, jacket, and shirt were draped over one shoulder; he carried his boots in one hand. The low shoes he wore clattered on the brown flagstones.

Nora glanced sideways at her. "That looks like the Red Mountain fire department under the feathers," she said dryly.

There were redoubled calls of parting. A woman in one of the buggies stood and waved drunkenly over Johnny's head at the watchers on the porch. A man beside her pulled her back. She struggled and swore.

Resolutely Lucille said, "They must have been practicing for the hose-cart races tomorrow. That's why he's late."

"Is Johnny running on the Red Mountain team? Against Argent?"

"Evidently." Lucille declined to be baited. She knew her Johnny. "Look at those clothes."

He had turned and was waving back at the shrilling crew as they dipped down the hill onto Silver Avenue. He was not wearing a union suit, she saw now, but pink tights stretched almost to splitting over his muscular thighs and leaving no doubt about his masculinity. The trunks were spangled by gold stars; the jersey, which his chest filled almost to bursting, was striped in black and had quarter length sleeves. The clattering of his feet came from short spikes in the soles of his shoes.

Approaching, he recognized Nora. His eyes turned wary and he instinctively shifted his clothing to shield himself. He was vulnerable now and he knew how she could scratch.

"Well, look who's here!" he said. "Hi there, Nora."

"Johnny!" She shifted her box and held out her hand. No trace of mockery edged her voice, though certainly it might have; she really did mean peace. "When did the Red Mountain boys put you on their team?"

"This morning." He fumbled his clothing out of the way and accepted the proffered hand. He smelled of sweat and beer. "You're looking good."

"You too. Whose place are you taking?"

"Mike Woodall's." He glanced at Lucille, using the opening Nora had given him to explain to her. "Mike's the fellow in these hose-cart races who runs ahead with a spanner wrench to the hydrant and cracks off the cap and helps couple the hose and then turns on the water."

"What happened to him?" Nora asked. "He's supposed to be the fastest runner on the mountain."

"He bunged up his leg. He was hurrying out of the Dixie Girl at quitting time yesterday to a practice race and he slipped on a tramming rail and fell and cut his calf on the sharp end of a sprag someone had left sticking out of the wheel of an ore car. The boys needed someone to run in his place."

Lucille felt isolated, unsharing in a process that these two who had not seen each other for months understood perfectly well. She tried to bring herself back to them—to him. "Last fall," she said, "when some of the men up there asked you to run against a foot racer from Baker, you refused. You said it didn't mean anything."

"It didn't. That fellow was just a wandering pro—something to bet on, like a roulette ball, or which stinkbug will reach a crack first. But this Shower of Silver is a big thing. It wouldn't be right for the whole Red Mountain team to drop out just because of one man, would it?"

"You don't live in Red Mountain."

"Close enough so that I figured I was eligible for helping them out."

"I suppose your public spirit is why they brought you up the street in such high style?"

He sighed with elaborate patience. "We wanted to have a practice run to get used to the hydrants here, so did all the outside teams, but we didn't want to do it on Main Street and take the edge off the races tomorrow. We went down back of Crib Street to be private. Some of the girls heard us and some of the gamblers came to look us over, and afterward we went in one of the houses for a beer. The boys wanted to whoop it up, but I said I was coming home. It seemed to them like a good idea to bring me. Shucks, there wasn't any harm in it."

Nora said, drawing his attention back to her, "The Baker company is pretty cocky. They won everything in sight at their celebration. They think they'll win this one, too."

"Yeah? What's their best time?"

She laughed. "Heavens, I don't know. Harmon might."

Johnny's eyes lighted. "The old billy goat!" he said. "How is he?"

"Fine, he's in town, tending to some business. He wants to see you."

"Why sure," Johnny said. Her interest in the races had softened his guard. "The old billy goat! I want to see him too."

Now was the time. Nora's eyes appealed to Lucille who picked up the cue. "Do you suppose," she asked Johnny, "that we can get banquet tickets for them? Then we can go together."

Did he hesitate a split second, remembering how she and Harmon had left him for Pat? If so, he recovered quickly. This was his day. He had won. And Nora had been adroit in feeding his self-esteem as against his wife's disapproval. "I reckon we can arrange it," he said, just a little grandly. "Everybody and his uncle is going to be there anyway. Two more pieces of fried chicken won't matter. We'll meet you in the lobby at seven-thirty. Old Harmon! Has he learned any new jokes?"

"I'll leave that for you to find out," Nora said.

They chatted a moment or two longer. Then Johnny went inside and Lucille walked with Nora to the gate. "Thanks, Lucy, for everything." She smiled indulgently. "I'd forgotten how priceless he is."

No doubt condescension now helped soothe the wounds her pride had endured earlier. But this was a bit too much to swallow. "You always used to fight with him for his airs," Lucille reminded her.

"I probably will again—that cockiness of his that if you follow his way to Red Mountain your troubles will be over. Well, today he's right. Today I'm not going to fight." She shrugged ruefully. "He's due a little cockiness. Pat Edgell would never have built the road so well. Don't be too mad at him, Lucy."

"Only enough to let him know he can't come home to me that way again," Lucille promised. They touched cheeks. "It's wonderful to have you back, Nora."

"It's wonderful to be back." Each smiled into the other's eyes. They understood each other and liked each other in spite of it.

"4"

When Lucille returned to the house, Johnny was posing in front of a mirror. He held one foot thrust forward, head back and scowling, arms folded across his chest and his hands under the muscles of his upper arms to make them look larger. But at least he had taken off his spiked shoes to save the carpet.

"Pretty elegant outfit, huh?" he said, experimenting with his other foot forward. She knew he was clowning in an effort to make her smile. "The team had its picture taken in these uniforms, some sitting on a bench and some standing behind them. There's a photographer's tent set up next door to Wayne Snively's saddle and harness shop. If we've time tomorrow, let's you and I and Lennie go in for a family picture. We can send copies to our parents. My mother has never seen a picture of you. Or of me neither, for that matter. And your father—"

"Johnny, you cannot go through the streets in that costume."

"What's wrong with it?"

"Look at yourself."

"It does bind in the crotch and armpits." He grinned hopefully. "I was wondering if maybe you could let it out a little so I can sprint around the corner down there without the whole thing splitting."

"It would serve you right if it did."

In injured dignity she carried the teacups into the kitchen. He followed, contrite and yet impatient also.

"I'm sorry about those girls. But what could I do? It was the only chance the boys had to practice and afterwards I couldn't just pick up my marbles and come home. If I'm going to run with them—"

"It isn't only the girls."

"Then for gosh sakes, what—?"

"Red Mountain isn't your private responsibility, is it? There were other people who could have gone up with Gabe Porcella last Christmas. There are others who could run now. Why does it always have to be you?"

"They asked me."

He said it as though the answer was self-evident. Lucille rattled the stove. This tail-wagging eagerness of his to have everyone, Crib Street and everyone, accept him! That was the true difference between his earlier refusal to meet the professional foot racer and his present readiness to become a part of the group that tomorrow would be representing the district with which he had identified his amazing energies. But there should be more toughness in him than this mere uncritical amity.

"You have some responsibility to Lennie and me also, you know."

"What's that got to do with—?"

"Parading up the street with those girls!"

He was bewildered. "You just said it wasn't the girls."

"You don't have to go along with everything everyone suggests, do you? You can say no once in a while."

"Look, Lucy. I didn't touch one of them or anything like that. There wasn't time, for one thing. Anyhow, I wouldn't. You know that."

"Do the neighbors know it?"

"It's too late to go around worrying about the neighbors if they don't know it."

"Daddy!" Lennie came racing in from feeding chipmunks in the back yard. "Daddy!"

Johnny swooped him toward the ceiling, glad of the distraction. "Hey, you're getting heavier than a yearling bull!"

Lennie laughed in delight, then put his legs around Johnny's middle, learned back, and studied him. "What's that funny suit?"

"It's a fireman's racing suit—red for Red Mountain." He swung the boy around onto his shoulders pickaback and went bucking around the kitchen in his stocking feet. "Away we go!" Winded, he said, "Oof! You're too many for me." He lifted the boy down. "Run and bring me my slippers, will you?" Lennie bounded away. Johnny gave Lucille a conciliatory smile, using her son as a bridge back to her good graces. "He's really growing husky."

You win, Lucille thought. *Just as Nora said, you always win.* That impervious innocence: who else would drive home in broad daylight with a clutch of befeathered whores and assume that no one would look askance. And of course it had been all right. Naïveté that complete truly was its own guardian.

"Hug me!"

He grinned uncertainly. "Anything to oblige."

"Tighter!"

"I'll squeeze the young 'un."

"Don't ever forget us—any of us."

"I wouldn't do anything to hurt you. You know that."

Lennie skipped back with the slippers and they broke apart, oddly embarrassed. Johnny rumpled the boy's hair by way of thanks and shifted the talk to neutral channels. "Sure was a surprise to see Nora. Wonder what got into her to come?"

"She wants your help," Lucille said and told him something of what Nora had admitted.

Johnny nodded. During the spring on the mountain he had learned of her and Harmon's struggles, though he had said nothing of it to his wife. "They made their own bed," he said.

Don't we all, Lucille thought. Her earlier resolve about Lennie, forgotten during the afternoon's surprises, flickered back across her mind. But this was not the proper time. Later tonight, after the party, perhaps.

One of the words that had occurred to her with the resolution returned and she used it now. "Be generous, John. They've had a hard time."

"Oh, I'll take them around to Winkler. There might be something in the Extension deal at that. There's a hell of a lot of silver up there." Red Mountain, where everything was possible—almost. Too casually he asked, "Did she happen to say anything about Pat?"

Almost everything. But not that. "No," Lucille lied.

He sighed a little and turned away from it. "I suppose we'd better start getting ready," he said.

"5"

The evening turned out wonderfully. Johnny glowed with well-being. Two speeches mentioned him by name, and there was a great deal of banter and curiosity about his secret entry in the grand parade. Lucille reveled in compliments. Even Nora seemed content. The borrowed dress suited her, and the excitement brought color back into her cheeks. She didn't seem to mind that she and Harmon were placed at an overflow table hastily contrived from three planks placed on sawbucks. Their seat neighbors flattered them satisfactorily. Two couples newly arrived in Argent hung wide-eyed on Harmon's grand descriptions of the Summit area of Red Mountain; and one of the lieutenant governor's undersecretaries played up to Nora most reassuringly.

The meal completed there was even a reconciliation of sorts with her family. After leaving the dining room, the guests stood gossiping in the lobby or stepped outside for a breath while the tables were being cleared away for dancing. Too full of exuberance to stay in one place, Johnny circled the hotel to see what was what. A crowd of miners in ill-fitting coats bought out of piles on the department-store counters that very night, and farmers with new hats set squarely on their heads, craned their necks on the narrow verandah to glimpse the swells inside. The Brice family were among the watchers. They didn't even know that Nora was in town. Why, Johnny exclaimed, she was right inside the door. And this was everybody's day to celebrate, including theirs. Trampling down hesitations, he herded them into the lobby and confronted her.

Oh dear, Lucille thought, *Nora won't like this.* She had never seen Nora look directly into her stepmother's eyes, let alone smile at her. The only reluctance Nora had expressed about leaving Argent with Harmon was over the thought that Mabel would have to go back to the ranch. "Keep an eye on her for me, will you, Lucille?" she had asked. Lucille had tried until she realized that Mabel and the new Mrs. Brice got along fine. But Nora had never quite believed it.

She wasn't likely to believe it now. Mrs. Brice kept her red hands out of sight in the pockets of a sleazy new overcoat of which she was obviously proud. Mabel was in gingham; Tommy's shaggy hair curled over his collar. A gold button gleamed in Ira Brice's collar. He wore no tie. His fleshy chin and heavy jowls waggled as slackly as ever to the gusts of his talk.

"You're by God lookin' pert, daughter, that you are. Allus did say high altitudes and high livin' would agree with you." He laughed loudly at his own humor and stared around at the banqueters, many of them in dress suits and white bow ties. "Just as spruce by God as any of these society folks. New dress, ain't it?"

He shook Harmon's hand and called him son. Mrs. Brice stood at his side, silent and overpowered. Trying to put her at her ease, Lucille asked her when the family was planning to move to their new ranch on the meadows at the head of the gorge.

"Tomorrow." The single word cost the woman all the aplomb she could muster.

"Aren't you staying for the parade and the races?" Lucille said.

"We can't."

"We're taking fourteen milk cows up," Tommy explained, "and twenty-one yearling steers for beef. I'm driving the cattle. Pa, he's driving a wagonload of hens." He glared at the smiling watchers. "We got a contract with Gabe for all our milk and butter and eggs. Better by God than a silver mine, Pa says."

"You don't have to get them there tomorrow, do you?"

Tommy was loyal. "Pa says there won't be no goddamn ore wagons in our way if we push the cattle up that new road while everybody's prancin' around down here."

Johnny interposed. "Let the kids stay, Ira. We can find 'em a ride as far as the ranch without any trouble."

"Oh yes," Nora said, putting an arm around Mabel's shoulder. "They can ride with Harmon and me when we go back to Summit."

Brice wanted the watchers to know who ran the family. Importantly he demurred, "There'll be lots of settlin' to do. No time for gallivantin'."

Mrs. Brice said unexpectedly, with more defiance than she generally mustered against her husband, "Let them, Ira. They don't often see their sister. I can drive the wagon tomorrow. And I can do the chores alone until they get up. Let them see the parade."

That was when Nora for the first time smiled at her stepmother.

"W-well . . ." Brice began.

While he hesitated, Professor Delius and his Silver Serenaders struck up the first tune. Johnny winked at Lucille and asked Mabel if he might have the dance. With his head he motioned for Tommy to take Nora onto the floor. Lucille understood: Get them out of the way so that they couldn't increase Brice's resistance by pleading with him. She slipped her hand inside Mrs. Brice's arm and steered her toward the doorway into the ballroom. "Don't you want to watch?"

Mabel almost spoiled the plot by turning shy. "My dress . . ."

"It looks mighty pretty to me with you in it," Johnny said.

That was enough. She was nearly fifteen. She loved to dance. She loved Johnny. The combination was irresistible. She lifted her arms to him and he swung her onto the floor. Lucille tipped off Walt and he asked Mabel for the following dance. With that as an example other young men, who badly outnumbered the available girls, fell in line. "Good as anybody," Brice said proudly. "Suppose she might as well stay around iffen she wants." Meanwhile Walt danced correctly and silently with Nora. Winkler stopped for an affable exchange with Harmon, and this in turn thawed Fossett. Even Parley Quine, who had maneuvered a seat at the speakers' table, granted Johnny and Lucille a nod. But Lucille did notice that although Pat Edgell was said to be in town, he did not appear at the dance.

At one o'clock in the morning they dragged Tommy and his reluctant sister home with them. *Now*, she thought when she and Johnny were alone at last in their bedroom. He was prowling restlessly, chattering of this small incident and that, still high on the crest of his excitement. *Now is the time to tell him.*

It was hard to start. She watched herself in the mirror as she groped. "You were wonderful about Tommy and Mabel, John. But mostly about bringing Mrs. Brice to see Nora. Not many are that generous with her."

"She's making old Brice a good enough wife, I guess. Besides, he's not in much position to complain. He's lucky to find any kind of woman."

"You could have been mean about Harmon and Nora, too, and no one would have blamed you. Instead, you welcomed them back." She drew a deep breath: *welcome me, Johnny.* "I—"

He was not listening. He had picked up the red racing tights and jersey from the chair onto which he had dropped them earlier and was examining them dubiously. "Can you loosen these?"

She held herself until her face was under control, then turned. "Let me see." Somehow she made herself concentrate on the seams. "I'm afraid that if I try this late to piece in a gore or gusset, I'll only weaken them."

"Unhh! If they bust loose in the middle of the race!"

"They held while you practiced."

"Yes."

"You'll have to take the chance. Or not run." But of course he would run. She handed the garments back. "Johnny, I've something—"

He wasn't listening. He dropped the tights and turned to her, joyless now. "Lucille, I'm—afraid."

She did not understand at once. "If you really want me to try to loosen—"

"I mean, suppose the whole day splits apart?"

"It won't." Dismay overwhelmed her. *Not you, Johnny.* She ran to him, not for his support so much as for hers. That tremendous confidence! "What can go wrong?"

"I don't know. Pat. Old Hedstrom. They're both around."

"They weren't at the banquet. You were. Everything went perfectly. You saw how much people admire what you've accomplished."

"That was a hand-picked bunch with a stake in the road. The ordinary fellows in town . . ."

"Everything you've done is for the town. They know that." She shook his shoulders. She could not let him see how this unexpected, this incredible self-doubt was tormenting her too. "Of course you're nervous. You've aimed at this day so hard for so long that it would be strange if you weren't nervous. But you don't need to be—especially not with the whole wagon load of ore under you. Don't you see?"

He managed a smile. "I hope everyone believes the way you do."

She buried her face against his shoulder. "Hug me."

He picked it up. "Anything to oblige."

"Tighter."

"I'll squeeze the young 'un."

"You'll see. That's what you're always saying to me—to the town—to everyone. Now it's your turn to listen. You'll see."

"Lucy—"

"Oh Johnny."

They clung together, still afraid but able this way to endure it. She could not tell him now, however. Would she ever be able to? *We die alone,* she remembered someone's having said in a book. *We ache alone,* she added. And with strange desolation she thought for the first time in weeks of Leonard's true father and wondered what road he might be traveling this night, carrying what burdens, what joys.

"Johnny, Johnny—tighter, darling. Squeeze him!"

"6"

His hand shook her awake again before she had closed her eyes, it seemed. Sunlight was pouring through the curtains. The doubts of last night did not show now, except in tenseness behind his eyes. "Big day! Big train! Rise and choo!" He was dressed in a new frock coat and string tie and had already started breakfast cooking. The children were bickering in the kitchen, shrill with excitement. She dressed like a sleepwalker and did not rouse fully until they had driven in the buggy to Badgley's boardinghouse for Harmon and Nora. There Johnny left them to go to the livery stable for his float, and Harmon took over the reins.

He turned back to Main Street, where other buggies were filing back and forth, showing off while waiting for the festivities to begin. Torpedoes banged. A blast of giant powder high on Vinegar Hill sent echoes rolling among the cliffs. The horses stepped out arch-necked and nervous. Lucille drew a deep breath. It was a glorious day, windwashed blue save for cloud puffs above Ute Peak. *Even the air tastes better:* how many times had she thought those words since first she had heard Johnny say them?

Flags fluttered overhead on ropes stretched across the street from roof to roof. Fans and streamers of red, white, and blue bunting crowded the fronts of the buildings. More bunting festooned the two platforms which had been erected at the lower side of the intersection of Main and Silver, where the old flagpole of whitewashed pine still stood. One of the platforms held a block of granite as enormous as a wagon for the rock drilling contests. The other platform would serve as a grandstand for committeemen, speakers, and their wives. Right now smart-aleck boys strutted on it, mimicking the coming orations. When they saw Tommy riding with women in a buggy, each thrust out a little finger, put the other hand to the rear of his head and minced along calling, "Ohh, yoo-hoo!" Lennie giggled, Mabel pretended not to see, and Tommy leaned out to make an inelegant noise with his tongue. Nora dragged him back by his suspenders. "You'll be a gentleman for the rest of today if it kills you." "I'll kill them," he grumbled back.

The parade was scheduled to form at the depot. Actually, the train bearing the lieutenant governor's party and mayors and aldermen from towns along the way had arrived the evening before. In order not to turn next morning's symbolic ceremony into anticlimax, the cars had halted at the Narrows. The visiting dignitaries had been taken by carriage to the hotel for the party. They had slept at the hotel also, for the narrow-gauge line as yet boasted no sleepers. The next morning, the visitors, fortified by Mayor Rubin's party of Argent bigwigs, had been taken by buggy back to the train for its grand entry into the town proper. Of course work trains had been puffing in and out for days, but everyone understood that these did not count. This was the first regularly scheduled run, passenger and freight combined, to cross the divide to their urgent young city.

All steps now turned down Silver Avenue toward the new depot on the meadows near the river bank. Bandsmen in scarlet coats straggled out of the courthouse basement, clutching their shiny instruments. The twenty-three members of the Argent fire department pulled their pumper from its house, eleven men in black helmets, black trousers, and red silk shirts on each of two long ropes, their leader stalking in front with his leather speaking trumpet. Here and there were Knights of Pythias, resplendent in plumed helmets, orange sashes, silver swords. In front of the beer-garden tents hastily erected on vacant lots, heavy-eyed musicians were already thumping out their alluring dissonances. A long line of breakfast seekers waited outside the Bon-Ton. A tall man with a gold-handled cane, a pearl-gray high hat, and fierce black mustaches waxed to a point walked among them, introducing himself as the confidential physician to the late Rajah of Kashistan and selling tigermar, made by mixing, in secret formula, the marrow of tiger bones with the healing herbs of the mysterious East, a sovereign remedy, friends, for every ill.

"That bunco artist," Nora said, "drifted into Baker last week from Passaic, New Jersey. I still claim that stuff he peddles is nothing but hog lard and perfume. But he certainly has found himself a market here."

She openly estimated the number of customers outside the Bon-Ton and for an instant regret touched her face. Harmon saw it. Some of the carefree forgetfulness of the morning faded from his own expression. "Probably it would have been a better silver mine than the one we're chasing after," he said unhappily.

"Well," Mabel said, "I'm glad I'm not looking at all those jaws chewing ham and eggs." They laughed, a bit too quickly.

Pedestrians slopped over from the sidewalks into the street, darting among the horsemen. Runabouts, democrats, and rattling farm wagons pulled by big brown mules jockeyed for position; movement toward the depot slowed to a good-natured, bantering creep.

The station had been buried under evergreen boughs and bunting. "A good thing, too," Lucille said privately to Nora. It was a shiny, brown-trimmed yellow building with scrollwork along its eaves. Johnny, who had checked its progress every time he was in town, considered it as bright as a button. Lucille thought it an eyesore. Today, though, no one noticed the building. Attention focused on the parade entries.

Lennie jumped upright. "There's Daddy!" he called and pointed at Johnny, lounging beside Walt on the high seat of the huge green, double-tongued wagon-and-trailer outfit which yesterday had led the procession down the hill. Although the vehicle had traveled to Red Mountain and back over the new road, it gleamed spotlessly and must have been washed that morning. Eight enormous Norman horses, groomed until they shone, tossed their heads under plumes and rosettes. Otherwise there was nothing to see. A drab gray canvas stretched across the top of the wagon and along its sides.

"What's in there that made him so excited?" Nora wondered aloud.

Harmon smiled mysteriously. "You'll see."

His wife looked at him in surprise. "Did Johnny tell you?"

"No, but I heard up on the mountain."

"Tell us."

"I promised not to."

She looked at Lucille. "Do you know?"

"I promised not to say, too."

Nora pouted. "I'm certainly not going to get out of this buggy now and walk around with a megaphone spoiling his big surprise. He's always so grand about everything."

Teasing would not budge them, however. Johnny waved. They all waved back and then, giving way to the press behind them, moved with the other spectators into the open fields beyond the depot. For the sake of the celebration the final five hundred yards of newly laid rail had been torn up from its ties. The iron would be replaced by crews racing toward each other from opposite ends of the gap. At the central point a red pennant fluttered from a short staff. Beside the staff and matching its height stood a stack of champagne cases, guarded by three marshals and destined for the winning crew. Small boys and quarrelsome dogs bobbed and eddied.

The crack of a starting pistol sent workers surging onto either end of the grade. Spectators whooped. Diminutive switch engines pushed up flatcars loaded with shiny rails and fish plates and spikes. Workers seized the steel and lined it up on the ties. Wrenches spun, sledges arched. A great black-haired Irishman who had been exhorting the crew that started from the depot watched his gang fix the last rail in its place and with a hoarse shout of triumph wrenched the pennant from its standard. A ragged cheer rose from the crowd. Shamefaced, the defeated crew bolted its last rails onto those of the victors. Ballast would have to come later; never mind, the first official train could roll.

Brakemen waved blue flags. Down by the Narrows the locomotive gave a mighty cough of self-importance. Steam whooshed; balloons of black smoke surged heavenward. Slowly, with a noise that made every horse throw up its head and every woman surreptitiously clutch the edge of her carriage seat, the monster advanced on the depot. More evergreen boughs swathed it. Proud elk horns decorated the great square box of its acetylene headlight.

Seven boxcars preceded the lieutenant governor's special coach. Town merchants had been persuaded to order goods in carload lots for this first rail shipment and were taking advantage of the opportunity to advertise themselves with legends of red letters painted on streamers of white oilcloth. The locomotive bore the city's official slogan: ARGENT, THE TOWN WITHOUT A BELLYACHE. Then, THIS CARLOAD OF COOKSTOVES FOR HOTCHKISS, ARGENT'S LEADING GENERAL STORE. PLOWS FOR VAN DUESEN, THE FARMER'S FRIEND. COOL KEGS TO BEN EMMETT FROM PINK-STAFF'S GOLDEN BREWERY. Next came one that made Nora draw in her breath. STUDEBAKER WAGONS FOR THE RED MOUNTAIN TRANSPORTA-TION CO., W. KENNERLY, PROP. "A whole carload!" she said before she could check herself, and Lucille saw Harmon's eyes go completely miserable.

A shout of "Look!" went up from the crowd. Several urchins, evidently hired for the purpose, had leaped the drainage ditch and were racing toward the passenger coach. A strip of dirty canvas stretched beneath its windows. Apparently everyone had supposed it connected in some way with the celebration and no one had disturbed it. The boys jerked it loose and fled for the willows along the river bank. Laughs, whoops, finger pointing: the dignitaries next to the windows inside practically stood on their heads, leaning out and trying to decipher the words painted there in drippy white letters: DEAD FREIGHT. From mouth to mouth rumor flashed that Pat Edgell and his roughs from Red Mountain were responsible. Oh dear, Lucille thought and looked toward the canvas covering the side of the big freight wagon. If the jokers had got at that . . . but surely Johnny and Walt had checked. Dismay touched her afresh. Why couldn't she smother last night's unreasoning fears?

Explosions erupted. According to plan they should not have been touched off before the train glided into the depot. One handler of anvils beside the track, however, could not contain his enthusiasm. He had long since tamped coarse-grained black powder into the square depression in the tail of one of his anvils, had inserted a fuse, and had turned another anvil upside down onto the first so that their flat faces exactly coincided. Beside himself with excitement, he set fire to the fuse. The powder exploded with an infernal bang. The top anvil lofted ponderously through the air and nearly crushed a small black-and-tan dog. Half the horses in the field threatened to stampede. Friends of the shooter yelled in joy and reset the anvils for another blast.

From every direction more anvils boomed, firecrackers snapped. The bell in the tower of the firehouse tolled its iron-lunged *bong-bong-bong*. At sawmills and smelter, at the mine workings high in the canyons steam whistles blared. Bandsmen raised their horns. Harmon sawed on the reins of the rearing horses, and Nora said petulantly, "Couldn't they be just as happy without so much noise?" Lucille watched Johnny. At the train's approach he had stood on the wagon seat. In utter raptness he was watching the round face of the locomotive, gold medallion bearing the figure "1", elk horns jaunty, the balloon stack's upper rim painted red, smoke, pistons steaming, *huff-huff-huff*, smooth glide of strength: cookstoves for Hotchkiss, plows for Van Duesen; when first he had arrived in Argent the entire town had been supplied from two wagons. She saw his head turn toward the deep V of the gorge. Only ambition? Only self-justification in this day, in that look? Or did there ferment in him the inbred restlessness of a race that had found it could lift itself from stagnation and, having made the first lurching step, could not now check its own straining acceleration toward more and more? Otto had tried to hold him back the other day when they had lightly discussed the possiblities. Not yet: you yump too soon und hvere do you land? *But you'll do this too,* she thought with quick fierce pride and looked, as he looked, toward the stolid bulk of Ute Peak athwart the way to Red Mountain. *Just don't be afraid.*

Perhaps the engineer decided to play a small joke of his own; or perhaps the noise fooled him into stopping too soon. Anyway, he halted while the end of the train still hung out into the fields. Before the conductor could wave him on, the visiting dignitaries started hopping awkwardly to the ground. Forming an uneven line beside the car, they removed their plug hats. The noise dwindled, the horses subsided. Formal speeches would come later in town, but the first order of business was a sanctification of the parade. A Catholic priest appeared from the depot, sprinkled holy water, and intoned a blessing. Barnabas Alden, his hair so newly cut that the scalp showed white behind his ears, followed for the Protestants. He began on the President of the United States and slowly worked down to the lieutenant governor and the mayor, swaying side by side under the R in DEAD FREIGHT and looking badly in need of intercession. From there Alden went on to the treasures of the mountains and the bursting granaries of the fields. "The way he's using that scattergun," Harmon grumbled, "he sure ought to bring something down."

Alden, his eyes shut and face lifted, entreated earnestly, "Amidst these manifestations of Thy endless bounty, O God, teach us to be humble. Make us mindful that it is not given to sinful man to be truly the master of his own destiny. As we reap this silver harvest which Thou hast provided, let us always be aware that our own unaided strength and feeble vision are not enough to build heaven on earth, but that Thy hand is the only sure guide, Thy commandments the only unfailing rule."

Lucille continued to watch Johnny. He was not listening. Neither was anyone else. Just before the prayers he had scuttled froglike across the load to the back of the wagon. Although he now sat with his head bowed, his fingers were working at the knots that held the rear end of the canvas shield to the side of the wagon. Walt meanwhile had edged sideways in his seat and was jerking at the ties holding the front end. These furtive manipulations had attracted almost everyone's sidelong attention, and Alden's peroration went almost unheeded.

"A-men!" said he and a ripple of automatic amens returned to him. Simultaneously Walt and Johnny pulled the tie ropes free and lifted the canvas to reveal a load of ore that looked like other ore which Lucille had seen on dozens of sleds and wagons—rough gray chunks that here and there showed the gleam of galena. But it was not the same as ordinary ore. A gasp ran through the crowd, followed by a burst of hand clapping.

RED MOUNTAIN TO ARGENT

The Richest Single Load of Silver Ore Ever Hauled!

Net Weight, 15,032 pounds. Value, $12,278.62

Underneath this was a long list of contributing mines and claims, ranging from the giant Ram and Dixie Girl, which had added half a ton each, down to single-man operations that had been able to afford only a small sackful of hand-sorted ore apiece.

"Just a year ago," Lucille boasted, "it was silver bars from one mine. Now it's ore from fifty!"

"Progress," Harmon murmured.

"You contributed," she retorted, seeing the name Summit Queen Extension down near the end of the list.

"How much ore did we give?" Nora demanded.

"Two hundred and fifty pounds."

Nora calculated rapidly. "That's close to two hundred dollars. We can't afford it."

Harmon's bitterness grew. "To participate in the richest load ever? It was a bargain. Johnny knew how to shine it up, too, playing one outfit off against the other. The Dixie Girl was joining in, so the Ram had to. The Summit Queen was contributing five hundred pounds; obviously the Extension had to be at least half that good."

"I wish I'd talked to him," Nora said testily.

Harmon glanced at Lucille. "When he turns on that old missionary fire—home-grown, eagle-soaring, Argent style, upward and onward to Red Mountain, the best of everything and there's something wrong between your ears if you don't believe it—well, he's hard to resist."

Lucille eyed him suspiciously. "You're being cynical."

"Not really." He looked at Walt's carload of wagons and then back at Nora. "I've got to believe him."

"Do we get our ore back?" Nora demanded.

"It'll be smelted and each mine will receive its production costs. The profit—well, you'll see."

Mabel sensed the tensions. Trying to help her sister, even at the cost of doubting Johnny, she asked, "How do they know what that load is worth, right to the penny?"

"The lot from each mine," Harmon explained, "was carefully sampled and assayed by the same procedure the mines go through when they ship individually to some smelter or refinery. The figure is pretty close."

"They can't be certain it's the richest load ever."

"It would be hard to prove it isn't. This is hand-sorted to be rich."

Nora said, "Just like John Ogden—the biggest of everything on the strength of an assumption."

The old envies, Lucille thought, the old lashing back at a grudging world. "Yesterday," she said, "you told me not to be mad at him."

"And today I'm not following my own advice," Nora admitted. She smiled and patted Lucille's hand. "Don't heed me. If things turn out even a quarter as well as Johnny is trying to make us believe with that wagon, I'll never be mad at him again. That's a promise."

The blare of bands ended further talk. Harmon broke loose from the crowd and dropped his passengers at the hotel. By the time he had stabled the horses and had returned through an upstairs window to a place on the dirty, crowded roof of the verandah, the parade was laboring up from the depot. In fits and starts it turned the corner for the march along Main Street. During the jam-ups the horses had to stop, heads tossing. Just as the band in the lead ceased playing, the richest load ever hauled was forced to pause beside the flagpole where once the alarm gong had hung. Conspicuous on their high seats, elbows on knees and long wrists dangling, Johnny and Walt grinned amiably down on the crowd.

Out of the press a harsh voice bawled, "Hey, Johnny!" Lucille saw him stiffen. *Save us.* She pressed the back of her hand against her mouth. Oh, who would . . . ?

"Hey, Johnny! How about showering us with some of that silver!"

She saw Walt glance at him. Still he did not move. Walt hooked the jerkline over the brake handle, reached back, and picked up a fragment of ore. A forest of hands raised toward him. He tossed it out and the shouts redoubled. Rousing, Johnny picked up a chunk of his own. "Hey, Walt! Hey, Johnny! This way! This way!" Suddenly the great wide smile she knew so well broke across his face. He threw out the chunk, reached for more, and waved it in both fists above his head. "Come on up to Red Mountain and dig your own!" he called back. "There's plenty there for everyone!"

Beside him Lucille heard Harmon exclaim softly, "By heavens, he's done it! He's made the town forget!"

Nora retorted—out of awakened envies, out of the sight of Walt high on the wagon seat?—"Has Johnny forgotten too?"

"He can now," Lucille said hotly and then the band blared again. The big horses strained into their collars, the wagon lurched triumphantly past the flagpole, cries, and hands reaching: It's done.

Gaw and the town marshal cleared the street. An imported orator from the lieutenant governor's party climbed onto the speakers' platform and recited the Declaration of Independence. Firecrackers banged. A team of packers from Walt's stable led out a string of half a dozen mules and gave a startling demonstration of how fast a ton of sacked ore could be loaded by hand.

"Archaic skills," Harmon said, struggling to restore neutrality. "Men bring them to perfection about the time they are no longer needed. Then they become folklore. Some day grown men will probably be playing cowboy."

Next, paired rock drillers stripped to the waist bounded lightly onto the huge block of granite resting on the platform opposite the speakers' stand. They raced against time: how deep could they drive steel in fifteen minutes? One of each pair knelt, holding and turning the steel while his mate swung the double-headed sledge in crushing arcs. When the bit grew dull, the handler reached for a sharper, longer piece from the pile beside him and inserted it into the hole. When the striker was winded, the two changed places. Neither interruption caused the least break in their rhythm. The miners jammed around the base of the platform, most of them dressed in bowler hats and with heavy sums wagered on the outcome, were fascinated. When results were announced they flung up their arms and howled. Thirty-six and five-sixteenths inches in fifteen minutes! Zowie! But Lucille was bored. So was Lennie.

"Where's Daddy?" he kept asking.

"Pretty soon," she told him. The parade marshals pushed the crowd back onto the sidewalk and strung smooth fence wire to hold them there. Brass horns gasped through an ill-pitched flourish, and the Baker fire laddies plummeted down Silver Avenue, dragging their cart. It was laden with two hundred feet of hose and its wheels were higher than the runners' shoulders. Their eyes stared, their mouths gaped. The course was seven hundred feet long from a standing start. They sprinted three hundred feet downhill, rounded the corner at the flagpole, and then were to run four hundred feet up Main Street to compensate for the easy beginning. As the Baker crew hit the corner, a dog rushed out, barking excitedly. A fireman kicked injudiciously at it, sprawled head-long, and threw his teammates off balance as he scrambled out of the way of the wheel. Demoralized, the racers creaked to a halt before reaching the hydrant at the finish. The Argent crowd hooted in derision and delight.

The Argent team followed, running beautifully. The lead man had the cap off the hydrant by the time the cart raced by. Two teammates loping behind it caught the end of the hose and sat back on their heels, letting the moving cart unreel the line. While men up ahead screwed on a nozzle, the ones behind coupled the hose to the hydrant. An arm flew up. Give us water! The lead runner, waiting tensely at the hydrant with his spanner ready, gave the wrench a twist. The hose swelled and writhed; the men on the far end pointed the nozzle into the air. A white spout gushed high and descended in a rain that made the spectators whoop and duck. The timer shouted and the man at the hydrant shut off the flow. The watchers in the crowd who were experts about such things looked at each other and wagged their heads. That was going to be hard to beat.

A team from one of the new farming communities down the river followed. Inept—strictly no contest. Tremendously exhilarated, Lucille gave Harmon one hand to hold and leaned as far as she dared over the edge of the roof. She could not quite see the start. Then suddenly her husband shot into sight, running like an antelope, the big spanner held easily in his right hand. *His pants*, she entreated as he leaned into the corner, *please!* They held and he dug in, head bent and arms pumping as he breasted the slope. He was at the hydrant, wrench ready, seconds before the cart rattled by. When the water spouted, no gesture from the timer was needed to inform the crowd who had won. Bowler hats sailed skyward and excited miners from the hilltop, rich with bets won, hoisted their team onto their shoulders and carried them to the judges' stand to receive the silver speaking trumpet that was their prize.

"And him about to be a father," Nora said, good-naturedly this time. "He ought to be back in short pants."

The firemen vanished to change their clothes. The chairman of the board of county supervisors took over, reading in a low monotone a speech his wife was said to have written for him. The shower of silver from Red Mountain, he droned, was a true shower, dropping like a gentle rain upon the hearts beneath, hearts thirsting for knowledge, thirsting for the refinements of the cultured life that now was within the reach of all. The ore in the wagon from Red Mountain was to be smelted and the bullion sold. After costs had been deducted, the balance, by directive of the generous mines who were the donors, was to be used to equip one reading room in the Argent courthouse and another in Red Mountain town hall. The listeners cheered the announcement vociferously. Those who whooped the loudest, Lucille thought, were probably the ones who read the least. For that matter, Johnny himself seldom read anything but the local newspapers if he could possibly find anything else to do. But the reading rooms sounded impressive. Furthermore, they were the only philanthropy upon which the contentious and reluctant donors had been able to agree.

As the speech drew to a close, Johnny appeared on the rooftop, dressed once more in his frock coat. Lennie ran to him. Johnny swung the boy onto his shoulder and worked a way to the edge to look out across the town. The crowd was scattering, intent on lunch before assembling again at the fairground for horse races and a baseball game. As they wandered happily away, many glanced up and waved and called. Hey Johnny!

Finally he turned around, Lennie still perched on his shoulder. His burned, dark face, flushed still from his exertions and his triumph, beamed upon them.

"Isn't this," he demanded, "the best doggone Fourth of July you ever did hear of?"

"It is, it is!" she said joyously and looked up at Lennie's contented smile. Spoil this—hey Johnny? No, she need not ever tell him. They'd gone the full way with him and now his victory was big enough to embrace them too.

V

" 1 "

The summer days that followed the Shower of Silver rushed breathlessly. It seemed to Lucille that she had scarcely adjusted to one of Johnny's new ideas when he came striding home with another. The entire town was that way, afloat on optimism. Nothing was impossible; mere flicks of the wrist! The runaway spirits soared so high that on September 1, 1882, Al Ewer took chill notice of them in an editorial boxed on *The True Fissure's* front page.

Lennie as usual was waiting for the paper boy and ran into the house with their copy. Busy setting the table, Lucille glanced only long enough to catch the editorial's headline. ARE WE GROWING TOO SPLENDID? She could imagine Johnny's outrage: That backcapper, running down his own town again! Largely by means of insults that offended a few people but amused more, Ewer had turned his thin little weekly into a daily read throughout the county. Like everyone else in Argent, Johnny recognized the tactics, yet each day he scoured the pages from end to end and regularly found in them something to laugh at or be exercised over. Tonight, she judged, he would not laugh.

About six he bounded up the steps, glad as always to be home. He shied his hat at the tree in the hall, missed, and let it lie where it fell as he strode into the parlor. From that she knew that he had stopped again at the Silver City Club, a new male social organization with ornate club rooms in the loft above the bank, where once traveling actors had presented their plays. Now, so he had told her, the plank floors were soft with deep-napped, dusky carpets and the windows were mysterious behind scalloped draperies from whose lower edges gilt tassels hung. There was a dining room where sandwiches and coffee could be ordered, and a fine mahogany bar backed by the largest mirror in the St. John Mountains. On the wall opposite the mirror, duplicating itself in the glass, hung an oil painting, life-size, of a rosy and buxom female lightly draped under a strip of gauze that floated sourcelessly down from the upper left-hand corner. Johnny considered the picture a classic. "Real as anything," he declared to Lucille. "You feel like you could reach out and tweak her nipple just like this." She pushed his hand away, pretending primness. "Then it must be art."

At first she had been upset by the frequency with which he came home smelling of whisky. She had kept the worry to herself, however. She knew how much the feeling of acceptance, of belonging, had meant to him when the leading businessmen of Argent had invited him to be a charter member of the group. Hey, Johnny! He'd pulled it off. The stain removed, the cry no longer a derision. Hey, Johnny—or rather Jack. More and more men were calling him Jack now, as though he had grown too important for a diminutive nickname. He seemed to like the change, just as he liked to sit around the club and talk about the town's potentials. Twice he had asked her if she didn't think he ought to grow a mustache—"If you do I won't sleep with you"— and in the two months since the celebration he had gained nine pounds in weight. He was learning to smoke cigars. She disliked the smell of them on his breath and in his clothes even more than she disliked the smell of whisky. But at least, she consoled herself, he never let his pauses at Silver City Club slip so far out of hand that he had to be led home, as she'd heard many members did. The worst that happened was that sometimes he fell asleep in his chair after supper.

This night he kissed her enthusiastically and she smelled the liquor again. Then he saw the paper over her shoulder and pulled away to reach for it.

Mrs. Nylander was in the kitchen preparing to dish up pork chops and tiny new potatoes and green peas brand-fresh from one of the new farms below the Narrows. If the food was held back it would toughen and Nylander would be irritated.

"You'd better wash, John. Everything's ready."

"Listen to this," he growled and began reading the editorial aloud. "'Each day in Argent a sonorous new association takes form, relying for support mainly on the sesquepedalian verbiage of its stock prospectus. Every person in town has a scheme for making a million, but too few have the willingness to make an effort' . . . What's the fat son trying to do besides show off his big words?"

"Can't it wait until after supper?"

He went right on reading. "'We have grown spectacularly, from a

few hundred discouraged residents during the Indian-troubled days of
1880 to an estimated population of thirty-five hundred, not including
the residents of the mines within riding distance of town or of the
farms below the Narrows. Our fine new transportation system has put
us ahead of every other city in the St. John Mountains. Other solid
new developments are taking place—the new illuminating gas company, the Opera House Association, and the toll road being built to
the recently discovered mines in Killpacker Basin. . . .'" Johnny
glanced up, somewhat mollified. "At least he gives credit to two of the
things I'm in."

Nylander came from the kitchen and loudly banged the serving
dishes onto the table. Lucille steered Johnny to his chair and put a
serving spoon into his hand. Then, while his food grew cold on his
plate, he continued reading the editorial.

"'It's not this handful of well-planned, well-financed enterprises that
we are talking about. It's the host of others that surround us, most of
them still in the prospectus stage. Paper roads and paper tramways have
been projected into every gulch in the mountains. The town has been
snowed under by a flurry of paper breweries, paper lixiviation works,
paper foundries, and even a paper factory for casting bricks out of
smelter slag. Paper lumber companies propose to saw millions of board
feet from our forests, and paper irrigation canals are grandly platted for
watering every dry mesa in the lower part of the county. Most grandiose
of all is a paper railroad tunnel eleven and three-tenths miles long
under the range to San Cristobal. Supposedly it will finance itself from
the metal veins it intersects and eventually it will save us a total of forty
miles on the run to Denver. That's what we call being splendid—an
eleven-mile, twenty-five-million-dollar tunnel to spare our traveling business men seventy minutes on the train.'"

Johnny paused and looked up. "The San Cristobal tunnel might not
be such a crazy idea at that. We were talking about it down at the
club and—"

"If you don't eat those chops they'll be like rubber."

He took a few obedient bites and began reading again, mumbling
because his mouth was full. "'Even where a few schemes have gone
beyond the paper stage, the results do not always reflect credit on our
fair city. Stamp mills have already been built in the vicinity that are
monuments to extravagance and ineptness if not worse—our readers
can name them without our help. Excitement replaces prudence and
cautious management is sneered at as parsimony. So many patent proc-
esses are appearing for leaching silver from ore in one easy movement
that we confidently expect to be invited one of these days to write a

so-called news story of a special sassafras tea that will physic out dollars already minted.' "

Johnny swallowed and grinned. "He knows how to put a thing neat, you'll have to hand the fat son that."

Lucille glanced at Lennie. "For family reading, really!"

" 'Some of these projects,' " he went on after sampling the peas, " 'are mere shell games designed to mine silver out of suckers, not out of true fissure veins. We have as little love for such bunco artistry as the next man, but right now we're not talking about the unadulterated fraud. We're talking about the ham-fatter who has seen the tremendous strides we've taken in two short years and thinks nothing more remains to be done but incorporate a new company and cash in. We're talking about these splendid fellows who expect to create more miracles simply by sitting in a leather chair above a bank—' That's a dig at the Silver City Club!" Johnny growled.

"There's pie for dessert and Mrs. Nylander wants to clean up so that she can get home."

" '—above a bank and talking big while they wait for the Lord to drop plums into their laps. At the risk of crowding in on Mr. Reverend Spec Alden's territory, we'd like to suggest to the county of Argent that the Lord doesn't operate that way. He put the plums here, all right, but we've got to roll up our sleeves and spit on our hands and pick them ourselves in the sweat of our brows. If we're too cocky and too proud for that, we don't deserve any plums.

" 'Let us remember in our hurry to grow rich what Alden said in his prayer at the Fourth of July celebration—a celebration to inaugurate what can be our finest decade: "Teach us to be humble." There's nothing quite as humble as honest toil. It is what made us great in two years, and it is what can make us greater still. How about it, Argent? Less foam and more beer! Let's go!' "

"Now will you please eat your supper?"

He laid the paper aside. For the next several minutes he wolfed his food in silence, a hangover from construction-camp days when it had been ritual neither to speak nor to loiter at the table. As she watched him, loving him and exasperated by him simultaneously, phrases from Ewer's editorial turned in her memory. *In two short years.* They had been married little more than one of those years and the first part of the period they had spent in a tent. So much, so fast. *Teach us to be humble.* And immediately following that thought came a memory of Margaret Fossett's voice saying, after Johnny had become one of the incorporators, along with Fred Fossett and Otto Winkler, of the St. John Illuminating Gas Company, *Aren't you proud of him?*

Of course she was proud of him. This was one of the developments that Ewer had called solid. The new company had at once hurried an engineer to Denver to buy huge retorts into which coal could be shoveled and gas produced by a process she did not try to understand. Down by the river, men were laying foundations for a brick building that would boast the first iron roof in Argent; and Johnny's erstwhile road workers were digging trenches along the streets for pipe lines, so that subscribers could tap the gas as soon as it began to flow. It would be far different from candles or kerosene; from carrying round gallon cans downtown for fuel or standing in line behind the coal-oil wagon as it made its weekly deliveries through the residential sections.

In addition, there was the quarry. When the Opera House Association had been formed to erect out of native red sandstone a building for every form of cultural activity, Johnny and Walt Kennerly had immediately filed a stone and timber claim to a quarry site they knew of. Now their teams and men were preparing the quarry for operation. An even greater feat, in the minds of many townswomen, had been his idea of using the railroad to haul out of the basin, for dumping below the Narrows, the vast manure heaps in which tumultuous, teeming, spirit-corroding blue-bottle flies had hitherto multiplied undisturbed. Waldo Trumbull, the former waterman, had contracted to do the work; Johnny had been his surety and had helped him round up the necessary carts and mules for taking the refuse to the cars. So much to make lives easier, and so soon. Of course she was proud. It's done, she had thought at the parade. But the push went on, the everlasting drive.

His free-swinging expansion embraced his own home. On August 4, one month after the Shower of Silver, he had brought carpenters up the hill and set them to work adding onto the house a new room for Lennie and an office for himself. Now she lived with the bang of hammers and the rasp of saws, and there were moments, particularly when an unexpected silence came, that her breath caught. Instinctively then she stepped onto the porch, drying her hands on her apron, and looked down on the town, so small and patterned with its rectangular streets, beneath the huge, chaotic shaggy aloofness of the peaks. The tumult of things, the rush. The sensation, when activity ceased to produce its own anesthesia, not of guiding the events they had started so much as of being carried headlong by them. Could they stop even if they wished? No. Every bit of it—gas company, quarry, house alterations—was being waved alive on borrowed money. Each thing had to be swept through to completion in order to justify itself. Behind the glow in his eyes when he came home to tell her what he had done that day were the names of strangers who meant nothing to her, yet were making all this possible—Denver and eastern capital produced magician-like for him by either Fred Fossett or Otto Winkler. And Johnny saying, the yeast forever bubbling in him, You can't make money without spending money. So much. Of course she was proud of him. But she did not like the silences that sometimes fell when she was unprepared for them.

He had surprised her lost in reflection one afternoon and had offered a penny for her thoughts. It wasn't a thing that could be captured in words, really. But she had tried. "Before I'm used to one thing, something else happens. Each is marvelous, but . . . it's like a superstition, as if we should knock on wood each morning when we wake up. If something goes wrong, if one thing starts tumbling—"

Fretting about debt always irritated him. Impatiently he had interrupted, "Building two more rooms on a house isn't going to cause a collapse." He eyed her affectionately, seeking as always a clear and easy explanation for whatever he did not understand. "It's Henry," he decided.

Henry was the unborn baby. A week or so earlier she had let him feel it stirring inside her and instantly his assumption that it was a boy was totally fortified. "Girls kick too," she had warned. He had remained unconvinced, however. "Like that? I'll betcha!" and he had named it after his father. So sure, so eager. And so anxious that every difficulty resolve itself without friction. He squeezed her hand. "We're not sending Lennie away just because he's moving into a room of his own. Henry is not going to displace him."

"That's not what I mean. And don't always excuse everything because of"—perversely she would not use the name—"of the baby."

"If it isn't Henry, what is the matter?"

"I don't want anything to go wrong."

"What can?"

"I—I don't know."

Why couldn't he be content? Was it because it wasn't really done after all?

She fled from the fear to a more rational explanation. Ever since the Shower of Silver, she told herself, he had been suffering from anticlimax. For more than a year he had concentrated his enormous energies like a burning glass onto finishing the road; he had reveled in the celebration that signalized his accomplishment; and now that it was over he felt restless and dissatisfied without knowing why. The routines of maintenance did not fill the emptiness. Besides, he had built the road too well. Carved for most of its length from solid rock, it now demanded little from him. He needed challenge, the music of inception. He actually had said that to her once: when first he started a big job, it was as if he could hear band music in a distance so filtered by tree leaves and the drift of the wind that he couldn't quite catch the tune and felt he must hurry around the corner into the park before the notes faded and he missed it. What park? she had wondered at the time and then had realized that probably the image went back to Altoona and a park arched with elm leaves where a band could sound like that to a small boy. Always the boy, always the music around the corner. That was what he had been straining for with summer's rush of projects, and her mistake was to let him think that she might want to hold back and catch her breath for even a moment. Of course she was proud of him. And so far he had not grown splendid; he had stayed himself. Wouldn't he always, being Johnny?

He pushed back his plate with a sigh of contentment and carried the newspaper to his favorite chair in the parlor. By the time she had seen to things in the kitchen and had rejoined him, he had read the editorial through again.

"The trouble with Ewer's spreading this kind of thing," he said, "is that it scares off capital. We've got to bring in outside money so that we can do these jobs."

To be uncritical was also like him, she thought. Although his need to be at work kept him from speculation for speculation's own sake, still he was willing to let the wildest sort of schemes run on unrestrained about him, lest brakes applied to one venture slow down all of them. On this score he found Ewer's editorial downright disloyal; and having been mellowed by alcohol and a good dinner, he proceeded to pontificate. What he was doing, she imagined, was repeating sentiments he had heard in the Silver City Club.

"Not every seed you plant in a garden grows," he said. "You don't know which will make it and which won't; but Ewer, he figures each idea has to sprout or it ought not be planted. Well, that's not the way to get the most growth possible out of these mountains."

She picked up her crocheting. "Weeds grow in gardens too."

He stared at her suspiciously. "Such as?" he demanded.

"The new smelter competing with Roscoe, for one. You heard Walt say, right in this room, that it's run by crooks and he hates to deliver ore to it. I hate for your road to be used for dishonest things."

"That's as crazy as blaming a gunsmith because somebody gets shot with one of his pistols. Walt—" Johnny stopped abruptly, banged his hand on the arm of the chair and brayed a laugh that was not quite mirthful. "I golly! I got so het up by that editorial, I forgot. Walt's getting married! Walt! Walt Kennerly!"

She could not have been more startled if he had said that Red Mountain was turning black. Her hands dropped into her lap. "That school-teacher!"

"The redhead. Yup, that's right."

"She hasn't been in town a week."

"That's what I said when Walt told me. He claims it's been eleven days."

"Poor Walter!"

"Oh, Molly looks like a pretty tasty dish."

"Is that her name?"

"Molly Gilroy. From Denver."

She pictured him, a gorgeous figure still, tall and golden-haired and lonesome. "It won't last," she declared.

"What makes you so all-fired sure?"

"Miss Molly began setting her cap for him the minute she laid eyes on him. Everyone noticed. It was disgusting."

"You women! You've been pairing Walt off with every unmarried female for forty miles around. Then when a good-looking outsider comes in and does in eleven days what you couldn't do in a year, you start seeing rabbit snares under every bush. Well, Walt's no rabbit. He's been around. He knows what he's doing."

"Will she keep her teaching contract?"

"They're talking about being married in Denver in October."

"Has she thought about how hard it will be for the school board to find a replacement this time of year?"

Johnny yawned. "I don't guess it's our problem."

"You'd think so if Hen—if the baby was in school."

He grinned. "Now who's rushing things?"

"It shows what kind of person she is."

"Walt's talking about building a house here on Vinegar Hill. You might as well start getting used to her."

"It won't last that long," Lucille said again. She still could not quite absorb it. She remembered Johnny's telling her that back in Saguache men had called Walt "Cautious Cat" Kennerly because he drew back from their reckless enterprises: too chancy for me. "If this isn't taking a chance, what is?" She glanced at Johnny and was deeply troubled in a way she could hardly have explained to herself. "What has changed him?"

"He's not so different," Johnny grumbled. "I was after him again today to go in with me on incorporating a railroad company to build from here up the gorge to Red Mountain. Not Walt. He gives me the old Winkler treatment: 'You yump too soon und hvere do you land?' I said to him, 'Goddamn it, Walt——'"

"Don't swear." She glanced toward Lennie.

"I—oh, all right. Anyway, I told him that we ought to draw up our articles and plat a track profile and enter it in Denver before somebody else beats us to it. Not Walt. He says it isn't as simple as locating a wagon road. We'd have to hire surveyors and engineers and make more than just rough estimates, and where is the money coming from? I said Fossett maybe could help us. All we needed at the start was a franchise. You know what Walt said? He said, 'And then hope lightning hits you the way it did your wagon road,' as if it had been luck or something. Then he said, 'Why should I promote a railroad that'll put me out of business?' I told him, 'It's going to come eventually. You can't lick it, so you might as well join it.' Not Walt. He just looked out the window at the gorge and grunted. 'That's a lot of rock.' Too chancy for him. He hasn't changed."

But to her Walt had changed. She turned it in her mind, trying to understand what the difference was and why it gave her this strange sadness. "Is Walt rich, Johnny?"

He roused himself. "Huh? Oh, I guess so. He owns a lot of wagons and draft stock and I suppose he's got more hauling contracts than any other freighter in the mountains."

"Is he in debt?"

"Kennerly? Not him. Too chancy. When he yumps he wants a landing place for both feet. Most of this stuff he didn't even jump for. He was just sitting there on the mountain and it fell in his lap."

"Did he leave Nora because he thought her ways were too chancy?"

"Maybe she's the one who left him." Johnny yawned prodigiously. "It's their business, I reckon."

"But now he's sure he can manage Molly Gilroy. Is it because he's rich?"

"Perhaps he just wants to get married."

She resumed her crocheting. After a time she asked without looking up, "Isn't it when we grow too sure of ourselves that we make the most mistakes?"

Johnny did not answer. The paper had slipped from his lap, the editorial about splendor face down on the floor, and he was asleep in his chair.

"2"

Early the next month he went to Denver to be best man at Walt's wedding, and for five days the empty house talked back at her. If she turned up the lamp wicks high enough to drive the shadows into their corners, the chimneys smoked. Looking out the windows was no help.

Johnny had isolated the house on the hilltop. Frost-nipped, golden tree leaves hid the homes at the foot of the slope, and the lights in the center of town gleamed as remotely to her loneliness as the stars themselves.

He had been gone before, of course, and for longer stretches; but those absences had been connected with his work, with the intertwining of their lives. But this departure had no association with her; it was to attend a marriage she wished was not happening; and when she awoke with a start in the middle of the night and felt the emptiness in the bed beside her, it was as if somehow he had slid wraithlike beyond her touch, no matter how far she extended her hand.

There had been no way to help it. Walt and Johnny both had urged her to come, saying that the train ride would be nothing compared to the colossal discomforts of her earlier trips. She had refused. "Misshapen like this? I'd be embarrassed to walk down the street, let alone into the church." The real deterrent reached beyond vanity, however. "It's too close to my time," she finally admitted. "A month?" Johnny objected. She nodded. "I don't want to risk spending a day and a night on a train each way without a doctor near. Oh Johnny, we can't take chances. Everything has to be right this time." She hadn't realized what had slipped out until he picked up the words. "This time?" Her breath caught and she made a vague gesture, letting her silence lie for her.

The thought that some mysterious danger might threaten her or the baby alarmed him. Excitedly he vowed to stay home and not let her face such chances alone. But she herself had insisted that he go. Except for the Fossetts, no one else from Argent would be witnesses for Walt when he stood up with Molly Gilroy. "There's Nylander," Lucille had said, reassuring him. "I won't be alone."

So he had relaxed, promising to be back on the fifth night unless something unforeseen occurred. From sunup to sundown the five days were endurable. But after Mrs. Nylander had gone home, after the friends who dropped by each evening to make sure she was all right had departed, after Lennie was asleep, then the house began its talk. *Liar*, it said. She stirred and tried not to listen. *Pretender*, it said. The lamp flame wavered: *Remember*, it said. Shadows flowed out of the corners. The other emptiness. The other waiting. *Why haven't you told him? I can't. You've got to. I do not. It's over, it's done. It's not; you can't forget, ever.*

She jumped up and made bread. Each one of those late, lonesome nights she made bread, kneading her fears through her thrusting hands out into the softly resistant, absorptive dough. Her kitchen filled with bread. Some she gave to Nylander. The rest she took to Barnabas

Alden, thinking he would know families who could use it. The minister was grateful, but behind his smile she could see him wondering what on earth was prompting her to such relentless baking.

Each evening just before sunset she went onto the front porch and listened to the high thin wail of the locomotive's whistle as the narrow-gauge train bustled through the Narrows. The fourth night she told Lennie, No, Daddy isn't coming yet, and then she stayed outside, looking down Silver Avenue until dark. The fifth night she wrapped a shawl around her shoulders against the October chill and carefully descended the slope. As she was passing the Fossetts' gate she saw him striding toward her, his long mountaineer's step heedless of the uphill pitch. She was astonished at how she was trembling.

"Johnny!"

"Why, sweetheart!" He was surprised and pleased, and dropped his grip so that he could hold her with both hands as he kissed her. Then he began to tease. "Miss me?" He stepped back to look. "Hey now! I've got to hug you sideways. How's Henry? Still kicking?"

"Johnny! Not in the middle of the sidewalk!"

After supper she tried to lead him into descriptions of the church, the bridal party, the bride's family, Molly herself. He answered in mono-syllables. One would almost suppose he had not seen the ceremony. He was far more interested in talking about Denver, its population, the size of the buildings, the streetcars pulled along rails by horses, the amazing Brush electric lights, the evening swish and gurgle as men smoking cigars or small boys squidging mud between their bare toes stood outside their homes squirting hoses to lay the dust or wash the cottonwood leaves off the flagstone sidewalks. "Two hundred and fifty thousand shade trees in the town," he declared, impressed as always by statistics of size. "Irrigating ditches running along beside 'em—two hundred and sixty miles of ditch, they claim. Business is booming too, thanks to good crops and the silver mines. Everybody I talked to wanted to hear about Argent and Red Mountain. Yes sir, capital is out looking for a place to lay its head and I let a couple of the big boys hear of a nice soft pillow or two I knew about. You'll see!"

"Is Molly still dragging Walt to San Francisco for a wedding trip?"

"I wouldn't say dragging is quite the way to put it."

"You know he'll be a fish out of water in a city like that. When will they be home?"

"When they feel like it," Johnny said. He was bursting with another kind of news. "You know what one of those pillows was? The railroad! Yes sir, we incorporated the Argent, Red Mountain and St. John Railway Company! Tomorrow we'll start surveying for the plat so we can apply for the franchise."

Of course she was proud of him. But why couldn't he rest? The wagon road had been in operation less than half a year and already he was turning his back on it, as though somehow all that it once had meant to him was still not enough. "When will you start building?" she asked.

"Not for a while. It'll take planning. And lots of money. But it won't hurt us to be ready."

"Did Walt—?"

"No."

"Or Otto?"

"He's got too many other irons in the fire, he said."

"Who?"

"Fred Fossett and three fellows Fred knew in Denver." Johnny paused, his eyes turning reflective. "You know something: I think Fred would like to move to Denver if he can find himself a good tie-in with some bank there."

"Margaret always said she never wanted to stay in Argent any longer than she had to." Elaborately Lucille folded the baby dress whose collar she had been crocheting. It was hard for her to breathe. Those statistics he had been rattling off about Denver. "Are you thinking of . . ." Her voice faltered.

"Of leaving Argent? Good grief, no." He eyed her sharply. "Why do you ask? Do you want—?"

"Johnny, no." She could tell him this much: here was where each of them had gathered up the rubble and had rebuilt their lives. Where else could she have done it—or he either? "This is the only place where I mean anything to anyone. This is home. Don't. . . ."

In alarm and some bafflement he watched her turn her head so that he could not see her cheeks, her eyes. "It's Henry," he said and came to her chair and awkwardly patted her shoulder. "Don't worry. We aren't going anywhere away from here, not permanent anyhow."

"3"

The rest of autumn's crisp blue days hurried by on each other's heels. Toward the end of the month the first snowstorm whined around the corners of the house and when the weather cleared, frost-ferns crusted the windowpanes. Lucille asked that her bed be brought downstairs and set up near the parlor stove; the upstairs rooms were too hard to keep warm. The baby stirred vigorously. Johnny cut his inspection trips along the road as short as possible. On the gray afternoon of

November fourth he returned early only to be called away by a construction problem connected with the new quarry. Hastily he filled the nickel-scrolled parlor stove with coal, forgot to check the dampers, and departed with a promise to return as quickly as he could.

Coal gas accumulated inside the iron maw. A spark flared and it exploded. The door flew open, the stove pipe toppled. Lucille, Lennie, and Mrs. Nylander ran in from the kitchen and halted in dismay. A mist of soot filled the air, settled gently on the carpet and the furniture. After the first numbness disappeared they laid their plans of attack. In spite of Mrs. Nylander's protests, Lucille crouched awkwardly down with a mop bucket, swishing angrily and weeping in frustration. Suddenly she paused.

"It's coming! Get Dr. Carstairs! Send for Mr. Ogden! Oh hurry!"

Nylander threw a shawl over her head and rushed down the street, pausing en route to leave Lennie with Margaret Fossett. Lucille meanwhile pulled back the sooty bedspread and huddled miserably on top of the blankets. The first spasms passed. She arose and grimly cleaned the bedside table. Johnny arrived first, horrified and frantic with self-castigation. The pains came again. He scrambled upstairs, found a clean bedspread, flew back, and fanned it out to lay across her. Soot eddied afresh. Lucille glared at him. Her temples were moist.

"John Ogden, if you've tracked up the rest of the house." She clutched his hand. "Oh Johnny."

Dr. Carstairs arrived and sent him outside. Presently he was told he could return. Lucille looked ghastly. "Everything's fine," the doctor said with moronic cheerfulness. "It'll be a while yet. Might as well get this mess looking less like a mess."

Nylander set methodically to work. Carstairs meticulously polished the smallest, most useless ornaments in the room. Johnny sloshed water, stood in the way, fussed, and flew into incoherent alarms each time Lucille tried to sit on the edge of the bed and help. Finally Carstairs took him into the kitchen, found whisky for John and coffee for himself, and inveigled the distraught father into telling stories about the early days.

Five hours later the baby was born. It was a girl.

He saw her first, and then they let him come into the parlor to see Lucille. She could tell from his eyes that she must have looked dreadfully spent. "Why," he said, laughing uncertainly, "you've got a smudge of soot under your ear they missed. Here, let me wipe it away." She felt the brush of his finger, but what they said after that she never remembered. She started sliding into a deep eiderdown of sleep. Rousing herself with a start, she asked him to fetch Lennie.

"This time of night?" he protested in surprise.

"Please," she begged, and added as he hesitated, "This is my Fourth." He did not recognize the allusion and she had to rally again to explain. "My Shower of Silver—my job done."

"I golly, that's right. Counting the time I laid off the road for winter, it took you just about as long to get her built, too."

She hadn't said it for the sake of joking. "You will bring Lennie?"

He glanced at Carstairs, who studied her face a moment and then nodded.

He vanished and she drifted back into the eiderdown. A voice sighed through the cavern. *Humble.* At each spasm she had heard it. *Teach us.* Toward the end she had reached for the sound like reaching for a hand to grip. *Thy endless bounty.* Amen. Amen.

An instant, and there they were. "I thought you were asleep," Johnny said. "Look, hon. We can wait until——"

She motioned for Lennie, sleepy-eyed and awed, to come to the bed and for Mrs. Nylander to put the baby into her arms. To Johnny she said,

"Can we name her Katherine?"

"Sure, if you want. Why?"

"It just came to me." That was true. *Thy bounty.* And then the name had been there, sounding itself in her ears. Katherine. Brand-new. No ties, no associations—a life begun completely afresh. Katherine. "I like it."

"Why sure," he said again, mystified still but in no wise intending to raise any issues.

She turned her head to her son. "This is your new sister, Lennie. This is Katherine."

He stared solemnly. "She hasn't any hair," he said.

"Take good care of her always. Then she'll take care of you." Joined so they were safe. At last. She looked up at Johnny and smiled. "I can sleep now," she said. She heard him start to tiptoe away with Lennie. Her eyes opened wide. "We won't ever be arrogant, will we?"

"Why no," he said without the faintest idea what she was talking about.

He hovered around the kitchen for a time, but when Mrs. Nylander assured him that Lucille was not likely to arouse again that night, he put on his hat and hurried proudly downtown. The Silver City Club had long since closed, but there was still a group in the Pastime. When one of Walt's teamsters twitted him about this-yere Henry we heard tell of, he was outraged and offered to fight the house.

"The finest girl you'll ever see," he declared belligerently. "Why, her feet aren't as big as my thumb. Now what do you say to that?"

I

"1"

As much snow as Johnny recalled seeing fell during the early months of the next year. The icy drifts delayed work on the opera house, but by hiring extra crews he managed to lay pipelines for the illuminating-gas company before the ground froze. Under the shelter of the iron roof the retorts were installed in jig time, and on February 21, 1883, Johnny tossed in the first shovelful of coal. Five days later the first jets of light were turned on in the main business block—the residential section would have to wait until spring.

The event occasioned another banquet at the Dixon House. Here, appallingly nervous, Johnny made his first speech. He used the opportunity to announce another triumph for the town. During the ensuing summer, a telephone line was to be built by the Ogden Construction Company (that slipped in incidental-like—new company and all) from Argent to Baker through Red Mountain. The new line would connect with other wires already being pushed into the St. Johns from the outside. "Argent, the bride of the true fissures," he proclaimed while Lucille listened proudly, "the home of opportunity." And so on. Reporting the event in the next issue of his paper, Al Ewer wrote,

"As the party was breaking up, we took a poll of twenty guests, asking who had done the most for this country, the Almighty or Jack Ogden. The vote came out even-Stephen. You can count on both of them to deliver the goods. If as much could be said of every bunco artist, slick spieler, and ham-fatter who infests our hotel lobbies, we'd feel better. Then we would agree completely with Jack Ogden's optimism and say with him that there is no limit which Argent cannot reach."

Lucille was shocked at the remarks as being irreverent. Johnny shrugged it off. "Al always does walk way out on the edge."

"He doesn't have to call you Jack, does he?"

"It doesn't matter, I guess," Johnny said and smiled at the baby on his lap, "as long as the young 'un grows up to be proud of her old daddy."

As he well knew, a major part of Ewer's approval stemmed from his success in keeping the gorge road open during storms that closed the rival highway to Baker. Pat Edgell and his partners had lost interest in bucking him. They did not hold their crews out in the teeth of the blizzards, and once the men had been turned loose they were hard to regather. The drifts got ahead of them. Mines that had been shipping to Baker found themselves faced with closure as ore they could not move piled up in their storage bins. In desperation even the Summit Queen and the Ram turned to Argent during one two-week period of stagnation.

The most critical challenge came in March. A dry, powdery snow fell for two weeks without cease, piling deeper and deeper on old frozen crusts. Finally, the mass in Corkscrew Gulch slipped. In a wave that hissed like rolling sugar it foamed down the gulch and buried the road eighteen feet deep about a half a mile below the town of Red Mountain.

Johnny was ready, even at home. During a crisp cold spell during an earlier storm he had ordered new stores of groceries, coal, and firewood. Lennie had gone with him, sniffing the delicious smells of the store and riding up Vinegar Hill on a sled driven by a Mexican timber cutter from a camp near the river. He remarked later that the poor man had been sick and had "throwed up," a process that fascinated him. The next day Johnny heard gossip in town to the effect that the wood-cutters had vanished from Argent during the night, no one knew why. "Lucky we got our supply of wood when we did," he remarked to Lucille and forgot the matter. More than a week passed before anyone realized that smallpox had broken out in the woodcutters' camp and that the well had fled with the sick groaning under straw in their sleds, for fear they would be arrested and confined to the terrifying mysteries of the pest house.

Word of the Corkscrew avalanche reached Johnny while he was at supper, trying to cajole Lennie, whose appetite was listless, into cleaning his plate. He left immediately for the high country, so that he could begin clearing the road at daylight. It was a laborious job, and he was afraid that for the first time that winter traffic might have to turn to Baker. The blockade, two hundred yards wide, was too soft for a trail to be packed hard across its top and far too deep for shovelers to throw snow out over the rim of the trench they dug. Johnny decided to start burrowing at it from the Red Mountain side. He hired every available cart in town. One by one he had them backed into the cart, filled, driven out, and dumped into a nearby gully.

He was on snowshoes, planning a way to bring carts to the lower side of the blockade and so be able to attack both ends simultaneously when he saw Sheriff Gaw and a deputy riding up from below. They led an empty-saddled horse with them. Their faces were as shiny as polished apples from the cold; their eyes were grave as they motioned for Johnny to approach.

After he had slogged over, Gaw said with a glance at the slide, "Big one, ain't it?" and then immediately added, "I reckon I got bad news for you, John."

If the house had burned or if Winkler had sent word that the road company was bankrupt and shoveling must stop, Gaw would have used a different tone. This was the way it came out when someone was dying. Or dead.

"Who is it?" Johnny said.

Gaw had spent most of his ride up the canyon figuring how to break this and he clung to the pattern. "Do you remember those woodcutters who were camped in that shack by the river?"

"*Who is it?*"

"Seems like one or more of 'em had smallpox. That's why they run off. One of 'em was at your house with a load of wood. That must be where the kid picked it up."

Johnny made himself ask it. "Kathy?"

Gaw looked surprised. "The kid. Lennie."

"Oh," Johnny said and then asked swiftly, lest Gaw had heard the relief in the word, "How is he?"

Gaw gave his head a shake. For a moment they stared in silence at the slide's tumbled surface.

"He was a good tyke," Johnny said. Then he asked, "How's Lucille?"

"Taking it hard, I guess," Gaw said. "She's at Fossetts' with the baby. Doc Carstairs is with them, or was when we left."

Fear rushed to Johnny. "Doc won't put them in the pest house, will he?"

The isolation building was the most dreaded structure in Argent. A steep-roofed, rectangular plank box, it stood alone at the Narrows behind the sandstone boulders that had been heaped up as a barricade during the Indian scares a few years earlier. Argent had no hospital. Bachelors with broken bones or wounds stayed in their boardinghouses, most of whose proprietors would bring up trays and see about laundry. Those with miseries or severe sickness could find perfunctory nursing at various establishments, Mother Marsh's among them. Married people and children stayed home. None of these expedients was suited to a potential plague, however. Its victims were isolated in the pest house, to be fed and cared for by some man or woman who had survived the disease previously and was immune. The doctor called once a day. No one else, not even members of the afflicted's family, was allowed near the building. Very few wanted to go. The boldest of Argent's adolescent explorers gave it wide berth even when dared. The terror in Johnny's question was the irrational superstition of the mountains. Despite ample evidence to the contrary, a trip to the pest house was firmly believed to be a one-way journey.

Gaw gave his palm a commiserating spread. "They haven't said yet."

The deputy put in, "We brung a horse. When Jules Halverson at the livery said you'd sent yours back, we figured there wasn't no way in or out of Red Mountain and you'd be afoot. So we brung this bay of Walt's. It's a good walker."

"I'll be damned if they do," Johnny cried. "I'll see Carstairs. "I'll—" He started to kick off his snowshoes, then took hold of himself. "I'd better go tell Buck Shaffer what to do." He rebuckled the webs and clambered back onto the slide. Abruptly he paused and glanced back down at Gaw. Somehow he felt he must say something. But what? He grinned a vague apology. "I'm beholden to you," he said politely and stumbled on.

During the ride back through the gorge he learned as much of the grim night as Gaw knew. Lucille had been alone with the children, Mrs. Nylander having stayed home because of a cold. Lennie had awakened feverish, complaining of a headache and backache. She kept him in bed, but by afternoon he was so bad she began wondering if she shouldn't call the doctor. The snow and wind were beating around the house, however—

"We got it up here too," Johnny said. "Had to knock off work about three-thirty. I wondered how they were getting on down there." He beat a gloved hand softly on the saddle pommel. "I should have gone down."

"You couldn't of known," Gaw assured him sympathetically and went on. Hot fires were burning in the stoves and Lucille hadn't wanted to leave them unwatched in the house. By twilight, though, she had been desperate. Lennie's fever had reached 105; he was delirious and vomiting. Somehow she had to fetch Carstairs.

"That goddamn telephone company that come in here from outside," Johnny said. "They were willing to string their wires downtown where they could go from roof to roof, but would they do anything in the residential section? Ground was froze too hard for poles, they said.

Some of us who knew we'd often be away asked 'em. But no, God damn them."

The path was drifted bad, Gaw said. When Lucille reached the gate, carrying the baby wrapped in a blue blanket, the snow was piled around it too tight for her to open it. She laid the baby down on the snow and wrenched and tugged until her hands bled, and she kicked and wallowed, but she couldn't pull the gate wide enough to go through. She couldn't climb the fence, either. She sank so deep in the soft snow she couldn't step across and she was afraid of spearing herself on the pickets if she slipped.

"I'll never let her go through another winter on that hill," Johnny said. "Never."

Seemed like she must have lost her head then, Gaw went on. Instead of going back for a shovel, she waded to the corner of the fence on the southwest side. The snow had drifted across the pickets there. She took off her overcoat and spread it above where the pickets were and lay down on it and rolled across the fence, by God. How she managed with the baby beat anything. But she did. Never stopped to pick up the coat. Just held the baby against her and slipped and slid down the hill. Fell twice, maybe more. No, nothing had happened to Kathy.

Luckily both Mrs. Fossett and the maid were at home when she reached there. Fred was still down at the Silver City Club, gassin'. Lucille left the baby, they got her into a coat, and on she went. Carstairs had his suspicions right off the bat. He got hold of Fred and told him not to go home—the family maybe exposed thataway. Then he put Lucille in his cutter and headed up the hill.

Gaw wagged his head with the sorrowful relish that afflicts some purveyors of disaster. It had been pretty bad, he reckoned. Lennie evidently had missed his mother and had gotten out of bed to look for her. They found him lying in the hall. They put him back to bed of course and Carstairs had stayed throughout the night, as much for the mother as for the boy, Gaw reckoned. He'd done everything that could be done but it wasn't no use.

By the time Johnny and his companions arrived in Argent, the undertaker had been notified. As Johnny rode on up Silver Avenue, Carstairs popped out of the Fossetts' house to meet him. Over the doctor's shoulder he could see a square yellow sign nailed to a porch pillar. Lucille was inside, Carstairs said, asleep at last under sedative. At the moment nothing more could be done.

"Are you going to put her in the pest house?"

"Not unless she actually comes down with the disease," Jess Carstairs assured him. He was a homely man with a lipless mouth and a short square chin. He looked dead tired. "The maid has already had smallpox, and Margaret was exposed when Lucille left the baby there. So she said that Lucille might as well stay on—they can shut her off in the guest room. Of course Margaret is increasing her own chances of infection, but the alternative for Lucille was so dismal that I took her up."

The guest room was where Johnny and she had spent their wedding night. He stepped off his horse and hooked its reins to the square stone hitching post.

"Where are you going?" Carstairs said.

"To see her."

"There's some risk. To you, I mean."

"I was as exposed to that woodcutter as she was."

"But you weren't as exposed to Lennie," Carstairs said. He scrubbed his face with his palm, then shrugged. "The health department, which is me, has definite requirements about quarantine, but as Lucille's doctor I don't like some of them. She's going to need you when she wakes up. I'll allow it under two conditions. One is that you don't go any nearer to her than the head of the stairs. The other is that you promise not to leave the premises again until after the quarantine is lifted."

Johnny glanced up the gorge and hesitated for perhaps eight seconds. "I guess they can clear the road without me. But I won't promise about the head of the stairs."

"Be patient with her, John. She's had a rough go. To tell the truth, she came closer to hysteria than I would have expected of her. Carrying on, blaming herself—it's her fault, she sinned, both of you were too sure of yourselves, Lennie was damned from the beginning—they get like that sometimes." He watched Johnny closely, as if to catch his reactions. Seeing nothing but worry and grief, he finished, "Don't let it upset you. Perhaps I've said more than I needed to, but I want you to be braced in case she seems . . . irrational. It's not going to be easy."

"Anything that helps her," Johnny said distractedly and tried to order his thoughts. "Can I go home for some clothes and papers I'll be needing?"

"No. We're chinking your place tight right now. No one goes in until it has been thoroughly fumigated. You'll have to ask one of the stores to send you whatever you think you'll need to wear. Perhaps Fred can help you with your business affairs."

Johnny snapped his fingers in apology. "That's right, I forgot Fred. Where is he?"

"He's moving into the Dixon House. It'll be all right for him to toss things onto the porch for you, but neither you nor anyone else inside is to send out a note or letter of any kind."

Johnny swallowed. "Everything's done. Everybody . . ." He gestured helplessly.

"Where the common enemy is concerned, people generally do band together," Carstairs said and then grew brisk. "I don't believe Lucille will wake before morning, but if I'm needed for any reason, Margaret understands and so do the people across the street. She's to signal them with a candle in that front window upstairs and I'll come right away."

He waded off through the snow. Johnny walked onto the porch. Automatically he removed his snowy galoshes, glanced up Vinegar Hill toward his own home, then knocked on the door and pushed inside without waiting for an answer.

"2"

The next morning he aroused in the blankness of disorientation to find Margaret Fossett shaking his shoulder. He was asleep on the divan in the parlor. During the next two weeks it would be his bed, but for this one fuzzy moment he thought he was still on Red Mountain and he wondered what on earth she was doing there. Then awareness overwhelmed him.

"Is she . . . ?"

"Yes."

He wheeled toward the stairway. Margaret pattered after him, fat and fluttery. Lucille was waiting in the doorway to the guest room.

"You're not supposed—"

They clung together wordlessly. He stroked Lucille's hair and finally tried to pull her head back to kiss her eyes. She resisted, keeping her face buried against his shoulder so that he could not look at her. Finally Margaret was able to cluck them apart. Lucille retreated into the doorway, Johnny to the head of the stairs. Her eyes were desperate. Savagely he turned on his hostess.

"Get out, will you?"

"Johnny!"

"I'm sorry." He flailed his arms.

"It's all right," Margaret decided, recovering herself. "I knew Jess Carstairs was a fool, but I said I'd try."

She disappeared. It was possible then for him to stand with one hand on the newel post and watch Lucille in the doorway and just by being there to encourage her words to come. It was painful, a disjointed phrase at a time, but none of the hysteria or self-blaming Carstairs had mentioned. Most of the time she kept her puffed, dry, reddened eyes away from his. The funeral arrangements seemed to be what was primarily on her mind right then. He could not tell her anything, and so had to go outside and ask the neighbors to send for Alden. With Margaret Fossett shuttling back and forth like an overstuffed walking megaphone, they decided to dispense with church services until a memorial could be held later. The rest had to be done according to the health regulations. What these were Alden explained as well as he could and then departed, leaving behind a large brown envelope full of comforting pamphlets. Lucille turned them listlessly and dropped them onto her dresser.

Silently, hour after hour, he sat on the top step while she sat as silently in a wicker-bottomed chair just inside the doorway. About eleven o'clock she heard what he'd been afraid of, the distant crump of powder explosions. Without anyone telling her she knew what it was, the frozen earth being blasted loose. She drew a shuddering breath, jumped up, and shut her door. Johnny rose to follow her, then halted. "Damn!" he said and went outside. From the porch he asked a boy playing with a sled to fetch Walt Kennerly—"Quick!" When Walt appeared, he asked him to bring up a cutter with a buffalo robe. At two o'clock that afternoon he defiantly put Lucille into the sleigh and drove with jingling harness bells along back streets, through weather almost warm enough for thawing, to the cemetery. Only a few people were gathered around the brown scar in the white field—Alden and those professionally concerned, Walt but not his bride, Fossett, and, to Johnny's surprise, Sam Varnum. Health rules, he thought. Or maybe the townspeople thought that since the Ogdens couldn't come, they wouldn't have to appear. He hoped the slight would not add to her hurt. But she did not seem to notice.

He halted the sleigh apart from the others. They did not descend from it into the snow. Everyone pretended they weren't there. Alden recited the prayer and added a few remarks, probably for their sake's. Johnny did not heed. He was sure, from the violence with which Lucille was trembling, that she did not either.

Afterwards he worried a little over Varnum and *The True Fissure*, but not one line ever appeared in the paper about the violated quarantine. No one ever mentioned it to him, either.

"3"

Ten days after the posting of the yellow card, when Johnny's restlessness was ready to explode, Harmon Gregg sent to him by messenger from the Dixon House a long letter marked on the outside "Private and Confidential." Its purport was that the merchants and county supervisors in Baker were disgusted by the mismanagement of the toll road between their city and Red Mountain. Very quiet discussions had been started about inviting Johnny and Winkler to take over its operation. Harmon had been appointed emissary. Was there any way they could talk about the proposal?

The message was like a roll of spring wind through the stagnation of Johnny's confinement. He rushed upstairs and told Lucille through the doorway. Perhaps this would strike a spark. So far nothing had. Friends came by every day to leave baskets or covered dishes of food on the cement bird bath on the lawn. Fossett appeared punctually each morning and afternoon to shout across the fence to his wife on the porch for as long as she chose to shiver there and shout back. Johnny gossiped with everyone. Each visitor asked about Lucille and looked up to see if she was at her window. Only rarely did she appear and wave back. But surely the numbness could not last forever.

Harmon's newest proposal did not seem to penetrate it however. Discouraged but still excited, Johnny went back downstairs and called to a passer-by to tell Mr. Gregg at the Dixon House to come right up. When the lawyer arrived, he motioned him into the alley. There they could talk without danger of eavesdroppers. Johnny stood downwind from him and when Harmon eased closer and closer in his earnestness, Johnny warned him away. "Back up or Gaw'll have you in the hatch." Every so often he glanced hopefully toward Lucille's window, but he did not see her.

Harmon tried to be adroit, but he was too eager. Johnny kept his nose wrinkled and his head shaking negatively. No, no, neither he nor Winkler would be interested in working on a road owned by anyone else. No, Winkler would not be interested in purchasing the two pieces of road, from Red Mountain to the pass and from the pass down to Baker, at the prices their owners would undoubtedly ask. It would be more to Otto's and Johnny's advantage to spend the same amount of money improving the Argent road, reducing tolls, and diverting still more traffic to Argent, away from Baker.

Harmon squirmed. Well, yes, that was what the Baker supervisors had feared. For that reason Baker County was prepared to buy that part of the road within their limits, up to the summit pass in short, from its owners. Feelers had been put out; the road company was willing. Now if Argent County would purchase Pat's section from Red Mountain to the pass—yes, Pat had indicated a willingness to discuss terms—then would Johnny and Winkler talk over a maintenance contract with the two counties, a percentage of the tolls, say?

"No," Johnny replied.

Harmon blinked.

"A lot of that road will have to be rebuilt to meet our standards," Johnny explained. "We won't sink that much money into something the county owns just for a percentage of the tolls. We wouldn't want a bunch of county supervisors in our hair all the time, either. But if both counties—Argent and Baker both—are willing to assign the franchises to us outright and give us the full tolls, then I'll go to Otto about it. Not otherwise."

"Why not ask for the whole moon?" Harmon grumbled.

"It was your idea, not mine," Johnny said and actually made himself appear to be stifling a yawn.

Harmon argued, "There are others in town who'll jump at a maintenance contract on county property in return for a percentage of the income."

"But they won't rebuild," Johnny retorted. "They'll sit there on their thumbs, fobbing off, on a traveling public which deserves better, the same wore-out, poorly located, slap-dab-built old road. They'll shave every corner they can, just like Pat and the Baker outfit have been doing. But we'll rebuild. We'll give you something we'll guarantee to keep open—something to be proud of. You tell 'em that."

"I don't think Argent will want to buy for your sake a road that'll help move ore into Baker."

"It'll also help move Argent hay and grain and beef and lumber over the hump to Baker. Besides, this is the short way down for ore. If that advantage doesn't help our smelters here buck the smelters on the other side of the pass, then we don't deserve the ore. But we'll get it."

Now that everything was in the open, he was almost abashed at himself. His demands were bolder than they probably would have been if he had thought more about the proposal. He had been caged and confined too long. His bursting desire to be back at work had boiled out in this one sudden, irresistible reach upward to control every wheel route into Red Mountain. The elemental unhappiness of his wife he could not control, but this he could, and he turned to it with a fierce reassertion of himself.

In the face of the unexpected thrust Harmon did little more than go through the motions of trying to resist him. Harmon was simply an errand boy. He let Johnny bowl over a few straw men and then said well, he'd go back to the various people concerned and do what he could. And then, coloring above his chin whiskers, he asked that if anything did develop, Johnny and Otto remember that it was he who had started the ball rolling. The usual commissions and so on. . . .

"I thought the Summit Queen Extension was shaping up pretty well for you," Johnny said.

"It was too slow," Harmon scuffed a galosh toe in the slush. His color deepened. "Nora—we thought we'd be better off letting the claim go for one of these other opportunities that might shape up faster. The mountain is loaded with them, thanks partly to what you've done. I marveled at that road through the gorge all the way down here. I know now that you were right, Jack. Pat Edgell would never have built it that well." The flattery was too crude. Harmon knew it and quailed under Johnny's candid stare and the words dwindled off into a grimace of embarrassment. "Well, that's the size of it. I'll let you know what the supervisors say so that you can get in touch with Winkler."

He trudged away through the slushy alley, an old-moving man barely into his thirties. Sadness for him filled Johnny. Surely this was not what Harmon Gregg had come to Argent for—or what had led Nora to marry him. Johnny had seen many men in the mountains twisted by greed from what they might have been. But Harmon had been twisted by longing. He hadn't heard with his own ears the sirens singing up there; all he'd heard was a woman telling him what he should listen to. But if a man was bound for hell he at least ought to arrive under his own steam and not be rolled there like a ball.

Never mind; the prospect he had opened was worth considering. Johnny hurried back upstairs to tell Lucille how he had manipulated the offer—his own road stretched out to arch the entire range. There was satisfaction in Harmon's being the agent, too. For it was Harmon who had applied for the original franchise with its vague pretensions of reaching to the Summit Pass; it was Harmon who had helped Pat nibble away the upper end; and now it was Harmon who was bringing it back, along with the Baker stretch to boot. Under the circumstance it was hard not to feel cocky. Yet as he swung around the newel post and saw her through the doorway, he grew hesitant. *Don't belittle it, Lucy*, he thought. *Don't sit there grieving as if it isn't worth listening to.* That sightlessness was what bothered him most, that acting as if everything had come to a dead end.

She was nursing the baby. "Is she all right?" Johnny asked, as he did twenty times a day.

"There's nothing wrong with her appetite at least," Lucille told him.
She ran a palm over the soft fuzz of hair. "She's as cool as a cucumber."

"Four more days and we'll be sure. God, they drag."

"No one else is going to catch it."

"I know you're right. Just the same—"

"There doesn't have to be any more paying. Lennie was enough."

She talked that way sometimes, as if the disease had been a deliberate,
malignant balancing. Well, Carstairs had warned him. A shock like that
coming so shortly after Kathy's birth, the panic in the snow, returning
to find the boy sprawled on the floor—any mother would have lain
awake on her wet pillow. Johnny had talked endlessly to her about
everything he could think of: the gas company; the opera house; Spec
Alden's campaign for a bigger church; the snowslide below Red Mountain; even Jenny Shaffer's cockeyed plan to build a row of triangular
log breastworks along the hillside above Red Mountain City so that if
avalanches ran there, they would split themselves into ravels against the
points of the triangles and not pour onto the town in a solid wave of
destruction. But Lucille did not listen attentively. He would notice
that her mind was elsewhere and then his own voice would trail off
and he would sit in uneasy silence on the top of the stairs wondering
what to do next. This waiting! This confinement! If he could get her
outside where she could breathe air, see sky! As he shifted from one
uncomfortable position to another, he would feel her eyes and think
that she was on the point of telling him something. "A penny for your
thoughts," he had urged her a time or two. Always she'd shrink.
"Nothing . . . nothing."

Remembering those hours of her indifference, he was diffident about
telling her of this newest plan, lest she think that pointing ahead was
somehow disloyal to Lennie's memory. More than once she had asked
him, "You did love him, didn't you?" And he'd said, "He was a good
tyke. You know I did." But damn it, nobody could brood forever. It
wasn't like her. That was the true curse of the quarantine, turning her
inside on herself. As soon as they were out with life's chores to do,
death could be held to size.

And so, stumbling at first but soon with a soaring of enthusiasm as
his imagination took command, he told her what he had proposed to
Harmon. "I'm pretty sure Winkler will go for it," he said, "because
anybody can see hvere we'll land this time—one company working one
road clear across the mountain the way it ought to be worked." He
smiled reminiscently. "It's like picking up something you thought you'd
lost. I can still remember finishing the San Cristobal job and leaving
Baker with a man-sized hangover and walking back over the pass and
thinking, the minute I saw the opening, Here's the way a road across

these mountains ought to go. A linking, you might say. These town jealousies over Red Mountain cut things in half." He wagged his head critically, forgetting how intensely he had been a part of those jealousies. "Oh, I'll admit the competition to get the ore is what made it possible for us to build the roads as fast as we did. But just the same, a road ought to be a linking. And that's what we've a chance of making it now, a highway for everybody in any direction."

He was chattering. Realizing it and seeing her stir, he paused self-consciously. She curved little Kathy over her shoulder and patted the gas out of her, then let her loll her eyes, unfocusing, toward her father. Johnny made small noises. Lucille placed the girl in the wicker laundry basket that had been pressed into service as a bassinet and for a moment stood looking abstractedly down on her. Johnny sighed. Once again she had not heard a word he had said.

She turned to him, a cryptic half-smile on her lips. "Red Mountain— the solution to everything."

His defenses sprang alert. "What do you mean?"

"Take me with you."

"I don't . . ."

"This summer. If you're going to be building roads and a telephone line, you'll be up there more than you'll be at home."

The house on Vinegar Hill, Lennie's brand-new, empty room . . . But to move a baby onto the mountain! "Do you think it's wise for Kathy—"

"You told me once of a woman who took up six-month-old twins in boxes on either side of a donkey."

"That's right. Sophie Di Carlo. On the old trail."

"Surely I can take one baby almost four months old on my lap in a stagecoach over the road her own father built."

He turned the idea rapidly in his mind. Not yet, he thought. Winter was too rough still. "It'll be easier a little later—in May, say. She'll be six months then." He saw her face stiffen: that house: the ghosts of its fumigation coiling along the base of the walls. Quickly he said, "If she can ride on your lap on a stage, she ought to be able to ride the same way on a train."

This time it was she who said, "What do you mean?"

"The two of us will go to Saguache to see Winkler about Harmon's proposition. Take Nylander along to help. I'll show you my old home, if there's anything left of it. Then we'll go on to Denver. I want you to see that town. You won't believe—"

For the first time in ten days animation touched her eyes. But she still could not quite let go. "It's extravagant."

"It's good business. I never had a chance to do anything when I was back for Walt's wedding. I ought to meet some of the people Winkler has sold road stock to and explain this new expansion, and I ought to see the bankers Fossett got in on the gas company deal and the telephone line." He drew a deep breath. "You and I never had a wedding trip, except up there to the head of the gorge. This'll be the one I promised you."

She wasn't listening again. Her lips trembled. "Oh Johnny, we were happy there."

"We will be again." The sky and the mountain: motion, completion. "But no tents this time. We'll build us a cabin near town and—" He could not finish. She came through the door to him, and they forgot that for another four days they were not supposed to act that way.

II

" 1 "

The telephone line which Johnny built from Argent to Baker via Red Mountain was completed in September 1883. The major camps of the St. Johns—Argent, Baker, and Red Mountain, plus San Cristobal and Sylvanite to the east and west—were now linked by wire. To signalize the event the telephone company decided on a five-way musical concert, to take place at three o'clock on Saturday afternoon. Each town was to provide its own music. The company would make available at each of its offices instruments by which the general public could listen to the various performances free of charge.

Imbued with the notion that all civic projects of such magnitude should be commemorated by speeches and parades, Johnny wanted Red Mountain City to usher in the musical with flags and floats and appropriate orations delivered from a bunting-draped platform in front of the town hall. Sam Varnum, who earlier in the summer had followed Johnny's advice and had borrowed money for starting a newspaper on the mountain, endeavored to assist him.

Sam was, in his loneliness, a perpetual assister. His restless mind, unsettled, in Johnny's opinion, by too much reading, was always raising the sort of questions that seldom occurred to the very people with whom he was most eager to mingle. His agonizing self-consciousness led him ruthlessly from one gaucherie to another. Undeterred, he kept on struggling to find protective coloration by identifying himself with this febrile district into which he had been spun by the outrageous carelessness of the western ferment. In Argent he had used his position as Ewer's reporter to sit in on every sort of organized activity—town council meetings, church socials, the Opera House Association, politics of every hue, or whatever else might draw groups together for, in his words, "serious considerations." Transplanted ten thousand feet high to the torn and frantic sides of Red Mountain, he discovered that similar groups had not yet taken form and he set about endeavoring to create them. The area did not respond. By September he knew sadly that it would probably not respond to Johnny's plans for an organized town holiday and parade. But Sam tried anyway, printing excited feelers in his paper and consoling Johnny when the reaction proved as phlegmatic as anticipated.

"There's no civic cohesiveness," he told Johnny one morning as they stood in the street talking about it. He pointed with his long jib of a nose. "Look at it—not the town alone, hee, but the whole mountain. Did you ever see anything so lacking in pattern?"

Johnny looked. And of course he did not see at all what Sam was trying to indicate. What John Ogden saw was the activity, the energy, the rush. Certainly there was plenty of that. The tall-chimneyed, metal-roofed buildings of mines in various stages of development sprawled from the sides of the meadows by the Brice ranch to the top of the pass. The forests had been devastated. Slashed and broken tree trunks sprawled like jackstraws. Fire had added to the desolation. Charred stumps rose forlornly in bramble thickets and swampy patches of broad-leafed skunk cabbage. Spindly evergreens that here and there had escaped both axmen and blazes held out bent arms like mourners.

At the lower side of each mine a huge log cribwork held dumps of waste rock from sliding onto the roads and the buildings beneath them. Spidery trestles ran like thin tongues from black tunnel mouths to the ends of these dumps. A continual procession of antlike men with candles on their caps in place of antennae pushed loaded cars out of the tunnels to the ends of the dumps and returned to be swallowed again. Near each of the dumps stood drab plank boardinghouses for bachelor workers. Married men lived in small log cabins constructed wherever there existed a bit of ground that could be flattened. Passage between each home and its outdoor privy was assured during the deep snows of winter by patched, sway-backed wooden tunnels. A few of the houses boasted ramshackle fences and bits of flower gardens. All were surrounded by heaps of rubbish for which no community means of disposal existed. Beyond the area served by Red Mountain City's municipal reservoir, drinking water was a continual problem; each little stream ran thick with rust-colored mud from the dumps.

Roads wound crazily in every direction, churned by ore wagons and bouncing express carts. Although all of the major surface lodes had been discovered, the tents of hopeful prospectors still gleamed under the scattered trees. Every so often in swampy hollows not pre-empted by mine buildings, one encountered a saloon or livery stable. A few whiskered, muddy-booted men were always slouching around these places, whittling and watching like half-wild animals whatever movement occurred in the vicinity. Fat brown groundhogs whistled among the boulders; flocks of black and white jays shrilled erratically along the ravines. Periodically the air shook to the din of steam whistles announcing shift changes, or to the muffled crump of underground explosions. On each vagrant breeze floated smells of crushed rock and willow bark and spruce needles and horse manure.

In the three undulant, climbing miles between Red Mountain City and the top of the range, four small post offices had been established as matters of convenience—Tin Cup, Castle, Beartown, and Summit. Each consisted of an unplanned ganglion of cabins, a dark grocery store, a saloon, and more livery stables. Red Mountain City remained the heart. Here were the huge transfer barns of the freight lines that toiled up from Argent and Baker. Here were the apothecary and clothing stores, laundries, two hotels, several restaurants, hardware, assay and blacksmith shops. The main street was named Mountain Avenue. On it Sam Varnum had built a newspaper office scarcely large enough to turn around in. Two lawyers, an insurance agent, and a dry little title and abstract recorder moved into neighboring offices during the same summer. Pat Edgell, after selling his road interests, set up quarters for what he called the Red Mountain Investment Company, a brokerage concern for locating claims, leasing mine dumps, and swapping titles. There were a fire department, a sheriff's substation, a jail and a town hall. The last-named building housed the ill-equipped, ill-lighted, dusty "reading room" called forth by last year's Shower of Silver in Argent.

The streets wandered. When one cabin owner refused to move out of the way of an extending thoroughfare, the highway simply bent around him; now and then he gave up a panel of fence to multi-teamed freight wagons whose jerkline riders tried to shave the corner too closely. The edges of the town fused without distinct boundaries into the mine compounds and the dumps of colored waste rock. As space grew limited, some of the shacks anchored themselves to the hillside with lengths of iron cable.

Within the town itself, nationalities congregated into districts. As in all of Colorado's mining camps, Scandinavians and Cornishmen sprouted like grass wherever mineral was found. Other sections filled with Italians and Irishmen who had been imported as laborers on the railroads and who had drifted up to the mines on the completion of the tracks. In between these crowded sections there oddly remained a few neutral vacant lots filled with debris; here children and donkeys congregated. Married white-collared workers, accountants, engineers, and mill managers who did not live huddled next to their places of business, moved away from the town proper around the toe of a hillock on which a few evergreens remained standing and on the edge of the meadows built cabins somewhat more substantial than those occupied by the laborers.

Here Johnny erected for Lucille a three-room summer home of peeled, varnished aspen logs. The structure was well under way when they returned from Denver; until it was habitable they lived uncomfortably in one of the hotels. From the cabin's shady porch they could look across the meadows and out through the notch of the gorge to the distant farmlands on the old Indian reservation. Sometimes after rainstorms the sun would lay an almost unbearable dazzle across clouds caught in the canyon lower than the house was, while above them the scarred red flanks of the three peaks glimmered with wetness as if crystals had been set into the rock. In the fall the aspen leaves lining the slopes above the meadows burned gold and orange. Lucille said she loved the view and the house, and Johnny believed her. Only rarely did he surprise her sitting idle, hands in her lap, her mouth sad as she looked toward the drop-off point into the gorge, where Lennie had lived with them in the tents only two years before.

No one knew how many people dwelt between Red Mountain City and the Summit Pass. The city fathers talking to traveling journalists, said it was somewhere between three and four thousand, of whom less than twelve hundred were women and children. Sam Varnum, who boasted a subscription list of three hundred and twenty-two, put the population at half that. Voting registration gave no clue. The population was largely illiterate and had scant interest in politics. This caused great wastage to office seekers who looked on the map for centers of population, bought beer for Red Mountain clambakes, orated to large and docile audiences, and were mystified by the scant garnering returned to them at the polls. The wisest counter at all was the deputy in charge of the sheriff's substation. It depended, he said. If you counted as residents those who held jobs for as long as six months straight, together with their wives and children if any, you'd get one figure. If you threw in wandering bunco artists, traveling seamstresses, fiddle-footed prospectors, hustlers floating around one day ahead of last week's board bill, adventurous youths from the East out to see the elephant, and rambling hardrock stiffs who worked until they got mad at the foreman and then went down the hill talking to themselves, the total would come out considerable different. Like week days. When only a sprinkling of folks were moving up and down Mountain Avenue

on their routine business you'd think there was hardly enough popula
tion to pay for heating the jail. But on Saturday nights when they
swarmed in from every hillock you had to push hard to travel from one
end of the street to the other; you got pushed back while doing it, too.

As Sam Varnum pointed out to Johnny, this floating, phlegmatic,
clannish population lacked the particular brand of American missionary
zeal that he was used to, the eager civic-mindedness that found its own
justification in swelling with pride over its accomplishments. Few of
them expected ever to own a telephone, so why get excited? Tugs-of-
war, hose-cart races, or water fights between rival mines; rock-drilling
contests, boxing matches, or foot races on which they could bet—
these might attract crowds of spectators. But parades and such-like in
which they participated as a town—no, it just wouldn't come off.

"They don't care," he told Johnny. "After all, how many of them
are here because they want to be?"

"I am," Johnny said. "Lucille is."

"You're in a minority. The workingmen are here because the jobs
average fifty cents a day more than they do in Argent. The engineers
come because as long as the mines are roaring they can command
higher salaries than anywhere else. The wives come to be with their
men. But there's not one of them who isn't thinking about leaving as
soon as he feels he can afford to. Now, there's no pride in a town
everyone wants to leave. Without pride, there's no interest in town
things, like a good theater and clubs and parades."

"Some people—the Fossetts for one—used to talk that way about
Argent," Johnny retorted. "But look how solid Argent is turning out."

"Argent has more than mines to fall back on. Red Mountain hasn't.
The minute the mines peter out, this entire district will die."

Johnny glowered. "Maybe you'd like to pull out too."

"I'm the one who's trying to promote the things a lasting town
should have." Sam's bony face grew sad, and this time he did not
whinny. "But lately I swear I've been wondering why."

Johnny tilted his head toward the red peaks. "Don't sell out too
soon, Sam. We haven't scratched what's in those babies yet. The mines
won't peter out soon enough to bother you or me. Pretty soon the grab-
and-run boys will realize it." He clapped Varnum on the shoulder.
"You'll see a town here that'll match any of its altitude in the United
States. And you're the boy who brought in the first newspaper, to
grow with it. That's reason enough for not getting discouraged, isn't
it?"

Sam stammered and shuffled. "I never knew anyone like you. The
whole world's perfect. But—hee!—it isn't."

"Sure there's things need improving," Johnny conceded. "That's what's good about living in a new country—seeing those things and being able to do something about them. You just wait."

He walked off so jauntily that as Sam stared after him he actually smiled and later went doggedly inside his narrow office to write an editorial on the long-range view.

The town, however, persisted in its short-range view. The parade died stillborn; the city's share in the musical almost collapsed as well. Although Sam and Johnny did their best to persuade the city council to hire a band for the performance, the officials authorized only a single cornet player. But if Red Mountain's populace were not proud, they were at least curious.

Private subscribers held telephone parties in their homes; Lucille invited a full dozen women, including Nora, to drop by for tea and listening. Businessmen—Gabe Porcella, Walt Kennerly, Sam Varnum, Pat Edgell, and other office owners along Mountain Avenue—agreed to open their doors to the general public. The telephone company bolted onto its outside front wall the two wooden instrument boxes which it had not yet sold. No one knew quite what to expect; but by early afternoon of the day scheduled for the musical such throngs had assembled that it was evident not everyone would be able to hear.

Johnny was among the first to reach the heart of town. Officially he had no connection with the event, but everyone knew who had set the poles and had strung the wire. Everyone knew, too, who had urged a real civic turnout. Whatever happened, he would be tied to it.

"I told you we should have held a parade," he chided one of the councilmen he encountered outside the town hall. "Look at this mob!"

"Regular Saturday crowd," the man rejoined.

"But are they going into the Tiptop or down on the line? No! Look at 'em, ganging up wherever there's a phone to listen to."

It was true. A frustrated barker and a banjo player and drummer were performing listlessly in front of the Tiptop, trying to lure trade. Down Red Street the girls waited in low, short, spangled dresses. But they were receiving little attention. The crowd was packing into Mountain Avenue and queueing in front of the available instruments. Johnny was particularly surprised to note how many women were on hand and how much more excited than the men they seemed to be.

At the invitation of the perspiring manager of the local office, he was invited to be one of the first to listen on the company phones. He had used the new-fangled invention before, especially during the construction of the line, but it continued to excite him. At the appointed moment he heard the mayors of the five connected cities address each other by name and give hollow laughs to fill the tremendous silence of the space between them. Then the music took up, horns in San Cristo-

bal, a piano and violin in Baker. As soon as he had been assured by the
first note that everything was functioning well, he passed the receiver
to the next man in line.

"What do you know!" he exulted. "San Cristobal sounds like it was
right in the next room, don't it?"

It didn't. The thin, reedy notes sounded infinitely remote. Electrical
disturbances popped and hissed. As Johnny wandered from queue to
queue, he noticed that many a listener on first catching the alien
sounds jerked the receiver from his ear and stared at its black orifice
in profound suspicion. Invariably the gesture led the person behind to
cry impatiently, "Come on, huh, give someone else a chance, huh!"
A few stood rapt and had to be tapped on the shoulder. One or two
knowing ones declared that these back-country lines couldn't hold a
candle to the ones in Denver. Only an occasional bold and original
soul ventured to speak back to the thing. This they did by pulling their
heads away from the mouthpieces and emitting stentorian bellows.
Their explosions raised ghostly retorts from listeners at the far ends of
the wires. Then other listeners would crowd in to hear and with no one
thinking to speak, silence would fall again, save for the disembodied
notes of the wired musicians.

At last the town's moment arrived. "Red Mountain, come in!" cried
the voice of the far-off master of ceremonies.

Every listener in town wheeled toward the telephone office. A great
shout ran through the streets. "Eric! Eric!" The cornet player, who had
dressed himself in a red bandsman's coat embroidered by black frog-
gings and who for half an hour had been sweating and swallowing and
moistening his lips over this instant, aimed his trumpet at the indicated
mouthpiece and cut loose on "The Battle Hymn of the Republic."
The stampeding blast splintered into an unbelievable sharp. Recovering, he soared on at race-horse speed. His performance created a far
deeper impression on the townspeople than had music transported
many miles over snowy peaks and through sounding canyons. They
craned their necks to see the musician, caught the undoubted tune with
their own naked ears, and compared it with what was coming through
the telephone. "That's Eric! Begorra and I'll be go to hell, that's Eric!"
The men behind them thereupon seized the black earpieces for a turn,
and at Gabe Porcella's store two Swedes fell into a terrible fist fight.

The performance passed across the range to Sylvanite, where a con-
tralto sang "Listen to the Mockingbird." In Sam's newspaper office
Jenny Shaffer stepped up for her turn and listened with a look of exaltation until the pointed coughing of those behind her made her yield.
"A miracle!" she exhaled to the crowd packed around her. "The whole
wide world brought right to our doorsteps." Her brown, protuberant,

slightly mad eyes ranged from face to face. The room was so full that breathing was uncomfortable. "I declare I'll never feel lonesome up here again," she said and turned to Johnny. "Bless you, John Ogden! The whole wide world!"

"2"

The exuberance which the afternoon brought him was soon shattered. As he walked back into the house, he found Nora bustling around the parlor, helping Lucille clean up the remnants of her party. Nora should have been in good spirits, he thought. Harmon and she had earned a reasonable commission off the road deal to Baker when Winkler had taken it up; they had spent most of the money on a lavish trip to New York, and now they were back concocting more schemes and talking of wintering in California. But she never admitted to any satisfactions when Johnny was around. Lucille once had suggested that perhaps her truculence was a defensive reaction to the way in which she and Harmon had had to abase themselves before Johnny for that modest garnering from the road. This afternoon, when Johnny repeated Jenny Shaffer's remark about the wide world, omitting the blessing part lest Nora pounce on it as pride, she gave him another of her sniffs.

"Never mind bringing any wide, wide world to me. I'll go to it. I imagine that's what Jenny meant, too. Thanks to the telephone, at least her voice has a chance of getting away from Red Mountain once in a while. It's the only way she can leave, poor thing."

Jenny's husband, Buck Shaffer, now held a good job as foreman of the Toll and Transportation Company's Red Mountain shops and corrals, and Johnny did not consider the Shaffers poor things at all. "So what's the matter with Red Mountain now?" he demanded testily.

"If you'd look around at your feet once in a while instead of always up at those peaks, you might see."

"Stop it, you two," Lucille chided.

Johnny was too outraged to heed. "I'll tell you what you'll see if *you'll* look. You'll see a city that didn't even exist when you came into this country not so long ago, hating it and bound not to like it, no matter what happened. You'll see your old man and your brother and sister living good on ranches they couldn't have had without these mountains. You'll see hundreds of jobs that wouldn't be here without them."

"Bigger this and more of that," Nora retorted, relishing the ease with which he let himself be baited. "That's the answer to everything, isn't it—except how to live in this forsaken hole like a human being. What's here except cruel, grubbing ways of getting money to take somewhere else?"

"There's more here than silver."

"Name it."

"I wouldn't bother. You wouldn't see if I did."

"Stop it!" Lucille snapped again. "You two may enjoy picking at each other, but the rest of us find it tiresome after while."

They subsided then, but Johnny remained indignant most of the evening. "That female backcapper," he growled after Nora had swished out. "Milking the cow and then cussing it."

"Try to be more patient with her. She's frustrated and unhappy. The things she reached for aren't turning out the way she hoped."

"That road commission—"

"I'm afraid even money isn't going to be her answer."

"Quick-profit Nora? Don't make me laugh!" Johnny shifted his chair so that he could catch the light from the Aladdin lamp and picked up Varnum's newspaper. Obscurely he growled as he settled down, "She'll come around. You wait!"

"3"

He had occasion on the following Monday to remember that irritable sparring with Nora. He'd ridden up town early on errands. First he checked with Walt about a shipment of insulators. Then he hitched his horse outside the blacksmith shop and went inside to see about repairs to some fresno scrapers he used in his road grading. While he was there, the steam whistle at the Ram cut loose with a scream of alarm. He peered through the blacksmith's grimy window. Black smoke was leaning like a pillar over the cluster of buildings surrounding the mine's main adit.

Instantly he jumped for his horse. Before he was in the saddle the roof of the compressor house collapsed and orange flame sprouted around the roots of the smoke. The bell on the fire house tolled; other volunteers sprinted hatless and coatless to their stations. Within five minutes the winding, crib-supported road to the Ram was a bubbling clot of riders, wagons, and staring, breathless runners. Among them were a handful of women. They ran holding up their skirts in both hands, their long hair tumbling. Soon the steepness of the slope caught them and they had to pause, leaning on posts or boulders and sucking in long, shuddering gasps of air.

"Mr. Ogden!" one panted as Johnny rode near. "Please!"

Her face was so beet-red and wet that a moment passed before he recognized her as the wife of Rudy Pruitt. Rudy had worked briefly rebuilding the road from Red Mountain to the summit; but when the project had moved too far away from him to reach it easily from town, he had left John and had found employment tramming ore at the Ram instead so as to stay near his wife and twin boys.

"Why, Mrs. Pruitt!" Johnny exclaimed stupidly, startled at the way she was breathing.

"Please!"

He removed one foot from its stirrup. She thrust one of hers in, seized his extended hand, and swung herself behind him, astraddle like a man, careless of the long expanse of undergarments exposed. None of the people past whom they galloped seemed to notice. He dropped her at the switching sheds where the tracks emerged from the mine. The sheds were aflame. The buildings nearby were beginning to smolder, as was the log crib holding back the hill above the tunnel entrance. The tunnel itself was a giant flue, sucking in smoke and heat. Soon the timbers within the mine entrance would be burning.

A still-harnessed, terror-wild mule burst through the smoke. A man clung to the singletree. He had unhitched the animal from the cars he had been tramming along the tracks inside the mine and had let the animal pull him into breathable air. As he emerged he fell. The mule dragged him a few yards. Then his grip broke loose. He rolled, got to his hands and knees, and started to crawl. Smoke curled from his denim overalls. Johnny spurred close, jumped down, and with two others dragged him clear. They beat out the sparks. He was still conscious.

Above the tunnel entrance workers with wet cloths about their faces were setting dynamite. One of them waved. Parley Quine and the mill foreman began pushing back the spectators. "We're going to shoot! Get clear!"

Ellen Pruitt screamed, "No! No! No! They can't get out!" Her husband, Johnny remembered, was another trammer and perhaps he too could follow his mule to safety.

Quine said, "Ma'am, no one in there will be able even to try to get out if we don't stop that smoke."

The powder *whoomed.* The air filled with dust. Windows shattered in the mill building. A ponderous mass of earth slid across the tunnel mouth. More dynamiting and frenzied ax work by a score of volunteers isolated the blaze from the stamp mill itself. Firemen poured on water and within two hours the conflagration had collapsed into a tangle of black rubble emitting feeble curlicues of smoke. Meanwhile the size of the crowd waiting for the tunnel to be reopened had steadily increased. Johnny was disturbed to see Lucille arrive in a buggy with the wife of the mill manager, who lived two doors away from them. Lucille was pregnant again, and he did not think it fitting for her to witness such scenes. His protests increased when the tunnel was cleared and a rescue squad started inside.

"For heaven's sake, John," she said. "The baby isn't going to have red birthmarks or withered fingers. That's a superstition."

"There's no use taking chances. Besides . . ." He faltered, not knowing how to clothe in words the dismay that had been growing inside him. The tiers of stern and agonized faces waiting around the tunnel mouth shocked him profoundly. There had been other accidents, of course, the crushing and maimings that mine work always brought. But none had blazoned itself so. Black smudge against the red hills: *You*, the steam whistle had screamed across their sky. This was not part of his bargain, life for silver, and he felt as if somehow the mountain had betrayed him as well as the men swallowed inside its maw and he did not want her to look at it. He did not, he knew suddenly, he did not want her ever to say to him what Nora had said just the other day. A forsaken hole to live in.

"We didn't move here for you to go through things like this. You're not ready."

"It won't leave just because I leave."

A handful of miners, blinking, their faces begrimed, stumbled outside. The candle lanterns on their caps and in their hands burned palely in the sudden sunshine. The spectators cheered.

They went to friends and shook hands. Then words jumped through the crowd and smiles faded. "A dead end . . . three of them." Johnny watched Ellen Pruitt. Some fool had let her twins come up, straw-headed boys about the age Lennie would have been. She was standing like stone behind them, her hands on their shoulders. The stretcher bearers appeared, sober and important under their burdens, blanketed lumps one after another. Two had been found asphyxiated belly down against the rock floor. One had been curled up inside his tramming car behind a suffocated mule. Noses in the crooks of their arms, faces puffed and discolored by this ending of air at a tunnel mouth which they had supposed, if they paused to suppose anything whatsoever, was bathed in the morning's renewed miracle of tranquil light. One's arm dangled over the edge of the stretcher. Apparently either the shirt sleeve or the finger ring was familiar. One of the twins ran forward. Parley Quine caught him and sent him back. He looked up at his mother.

"Why can't I see Papa?" he asked.

Her eyeballs rolled up inside her head and she sank like a dropped handkerchief. Instantly the crowd pressed around. The mill manager took charge. "Stand away! Do you want to smother her too?" At that the shrieks of the twins redoubled. Some women gathered them in and led them away.

Johnny's face turned gray. "He worked for us a while this summer," he said to Lucille. "Scraper crew. I got the very fresno he used down at the blacksmith shop right now, being fixed."

She pressed his hand. "I'll go see her this afternoon," she promised.

A forsaken hole. He scowled. "Lucy, this isn't the kind of thing I want you to—hurt yourself with."

"It's the kind of thing a woman who's been hurt can do best for another. Please let me."

That night she told him about her mission. She had gone by buggy to the Pruitts' cabin, bearing a basket of food and a sack for any laundry that needed doing. She'd found that one neighbor was already taking care of the twins. Another was inside with Mrs. Pruitt. But it was Aino Berg who had met her at the door.

"Aino?" Johnny said incredulously. "He isn't related to the Pruitts, is he?"

"He said he was representing the Miners' Benevolent Association."

"The what?"

Lucille wasn't sure herself. But she was sure that she had been greeted rudely. "He looked at my basket and at me," she said indignantly, "just as if we hadn't lived side by side all fall down at the head of the gorge, and he said as cool as you please, 'We don't need your charity, Mrs. Ogden; we'll take care of our own.' It was his tone that made me want to shake him. 'I came to see Mrs. Pruitt,' I told him, just as cool as he was, 'and I'm going to see her.' 'Are you a friend?' says he. 'That makes no difference,' I told him. 'I lost a boy not many months ago and I know how she feels. I intend to talk to her.' And then I said, 'I always thought you were a gentleman, Aino Berg.' He let me in."

She told him how meagerly the house was furnished and how grateful Mrs. Pruitt had been for the visit. Twice she'd said that her husband had often spoken of what a fine man John Ogden was to work for and she was touched that they had remembered her now in her time of trouble. She too was uneasy about Aino Berg. She had never laid eyes on him before that afternoon. He was there to persuade her to let the Miners' Benevolent Association assume charge of her husband's funeral at no expense to her and to let the association represent her in negotiations with the Ram Mining Company. The permission was important, Aino said. Of the three men killed in the accident, her husband was the only one with known survivors. Although the association was appointing itself to represent the other two casualties also, its achievements would be more impressive if they flowed visibly to a widow with two children. Whatever minister she chose, from either Argent or Baker, would be brought up to conduct services in the school- house. A fine carriage with plumes would be provided to carry her and the twins and her close friends in the funeral procession. Furthermore, the association would exert every effort to secure from the company an adequate settlement for one who had given his life to the cause of labor.

"It sounds like a union," Johnny said. He had never heard of such a thing in the St. John Mountains. The fact that one could have been formed without his knowledge right while he was living there made him feel as displaced as if he'd paid a routine call for a routine object at a familiar place of business and a total stranger had thrust out his head to demand what he'd come for.

Mrs. Pruitt, Lucille went on, didn't know any more than Lucille did about the Benevolent Association, and to that extent Aino's proposals made her suspicious. On the other hand, the pomp was tempting. Lucille predicted that the woman would accept. Then she asked,

"Why should Aino be mixed up in a thing like this?"

"He's sour," Johnny said and explained something of the man's misfortunes.

A company from somewhere in the East, Johnny could not recall where, had obtained title to the ground surrounding Aino's claim and had made him repeated offers for the holding. Aino had always refused, fully confident that some day his prospect would make him rich. But he had neglected to file on water rights. The company obtained control of the stream he used when he wasn't off working for a stake, shut him away from it, and so brought him to terms—a small down payment and a note for the balance. Shortly thereafter the company had filed bank- ruptcy. Many months later Aino had collected two cents on each dollar owed him. A new company secured the bankrupt firm's assets for a song and was now setting up an obviously speculative venture. Harmon Gregg was doing their legal work. Out of the bitterness of his disap- pointment Aino had bred a conviction that the entire sequence had been a plot designed solely for cheating him. "The little man don' stand a show," he told Johnny. "The law is money law. I develop dat claim and dey give two cents, ya, and I am supposed my head to bow in tanks. Ya. Well, the president of the old company and the vice- president of the new company the same man is. He yost better not walk on my claim. I see him put one foot dere and I kill him, I swear to God I kill him."

"Poor Aino," Lucille grieved. "Of course he's hurt and angry. But why is he angry at us?"

"I don't know," Johnny said, "unless he thinks we're part of the money class, as he calls it."

"You started with no more than Aino had."

"I was luckier."

"Or smarter," she amended proudly.

The next morning Johnny set about familiarizing himself with the miners' association. Very few business people had heard about it. Walt hadn't, Harmon hadn't, Parley hadn't; even Sam Varnum at the newspaper hadn't. Gabe Porcella had picked up odds and ends of talk around his store but had paid no attention. Now, however, the group had moved into the open and its antecedents could be fitted together. One of its officers was a veteran of the railroad strikes in the East in '77; another had been active in fomenting the Chrysolite troubles at Leadville. Aino was a third. He had fallen by chance into a discussion group led by the former Leadville miner and at once had become one of the association's most ardent supporters. As yet it was small. Though not clandestine, it had been biding its time, waiting an opportune moment before advertising itself.

The funeral for the victims of the Ram disaster provided the occasion. They did things up brown, Johnny had to admit. Completely shaken by the fatalities, every employee at the Ram walked off the job to march to doleful band music behind the widow's carriage. This kind of parade evidently the town would support.

Immediately after the ceremony the president of the association approached Parley Quine to discuss death benefits. Parley told him to go to hell. The company would pay Mrs. Pruitt the standard allowance for such unhappy events. (This was an ill-judged statement; there was no standard and the association knew it.) But Parley would not deal with a representative of an organization which the company did not and would not recognize. Elated by the violent rejection, the association thereupon presented to the weeping and grateful widow a sum that depleted their treasury but won loud approval from workers throughout the district.

By evening, thanks to the telephone, the entire St. Johns area knew that the Miners' Benevolent Association had stepped forward as a protector of the defenseless. The matter occasioned far more talk than the fire had. Newspapers took sides. Ewer admonished the association: if it confined itself to benevolences, as its name suggested, all right-thinking, humanitarian men would approve; but if it ventured to dictate policy to the employers, if it was in short a labor union, it would soon find public opinion solidly arrayed against it. At Red Mountain, Sam

Varnum was more restrained. He admitted gently in print that certain practices maintained by the companies might be legitimately the subject of review with representatives of the workers, but he questioned whether the association had been well advised to capitalize so blatantly on sorrow.

As for Johnny, he was bewildered. "I don't see why there has to be so much shouting," he said plaintively to Lucille. "If there's a problem, the people concerned ought to sit down and talk it out. This public agitation gets everybody excited and interferes with work. That isn't good for the men or for the companies." And he added, after a few minutes' abstract staring up at the red flanks of the peak, "That damn telephone! If the news hadn't swept all over the mountains the same day, there wouldn't have been half so much stir. Folks would have had time to cool off before they took to shouting. Without so big a stage to strut on, the association wouldn't have been so hot to put on a show. It makes you wonder if these inventions don't do almost as much harm as they do good. For a fact."

"But the news did sweep," Lucille said, "and the association did put on its show. Now they're feeling sure of themselves. What do you suppose they'll do next?"

Johnny thought it over. "There's not much for them to do," he said and grinned at her with that serene confidence of his. "Once we've had time to catch up with ourselves and straighten out a few kinks that need straightening, there won't be anything left for them to get sore about." And he added, "It's just like with Nora. They've got to realize where their bread's buttered."

"4"

Eventually he came around to saying privately to friends like Walt and Sam Varnum that as far as his family was concerned, at least one good came out of the Ram disaster: it opened an outlet for Lucille's reawakening energies. In Argent before Lennie's death she had joined vivaciously in the town's parties and discussion groups. On the mountain she had been more withdrawn, not willing to mingle in festive affairs and not finding among most Red Mountain wives any enthusiasm for more serious pursuits. Then, almost overnight, the Pruitt tragedy—and Jenny Shaffer—offered a new field.

Like Lucille, Jenny had gone to the stricken household to offer help. Later they had chanced to meet on the porch of Gabe Porcella's store when Ellen's funeral carriage had gone by followed by its procession of marching miners. "It's showing off they are," Jenny said crisply, "making use of poor Ellen's sorrow for their own ends." The excited talk occasioned a few days later by the death benefits paid the widow had increased her impatience. "Fiddlesticks," she had said, encountering Lucille outside the apothecary's. "So the company did pay more for a man's life than it ever paid before. The only reason the Ram sent its stuffed shirts to her was to take the starch out of the association's boasting. So the association boasts anyway, claiming in every saloon that if they hadn't jarred the Ram, Ellen would have nothing from the company. Fiddlesticks twice! If either one of them really wants to help folks in trouble, they can find plenty. But they won't. Plain Christian help isn't a good way to make a show against each other, and a show is all either of them wants. Bad cess to them both, if you'd like my opinion."

She went on to tell of Jake Lesch, his leg crushed by some logs he had been hauling to his cabin and his wife taking in laundry and watching three young hellions too old to keep close to the house and yet too young to go out and work for the family's bread. Of Job Dilthy's girl, three weeks in a fever, no one knew why and no money for sending her to Argent to stay where Dr. Carstairs could keep an eye on her as he recommended. Of the unheated, vermin-infested "rest homes" where bachelor men coughing their lungs out with miners' consumption holed up for a day or two of relief before dragging back to their wet, dark jobs. A schoolhouse not half big enough, one stove for three rooms, and in one of those rooms a blackboard made of rubber boots split open and nailed flat to the plank wall. Befouled streams. Rubbish everywhere. No churches. Just Barnabas Alden, bless him, and that Catholic priest, yes bless him too, coming up by stagecoach on alternate Sunday afternoons to hold service in the reading room in the town hall.

"I keep telling the street about these things," Jenny rattled on. "I keep saying they can't expect anything better than they're willing to pitch in and work for themselves. But do you think they'll stir? Humph! I asked them, up and down our block I asked them, do you think anything extra is going to come to you now that Aino Berg and those other radicals have strutted in to take care of your problems? Do you think the companies are going to come down here and clean up these sinkholes we live in? Fiddlesticks! If we don't pull on our own bootstraps, nobody will."

"I'll help," Lucille said and hurried home to tell Johnny about it.

He started to say that Jenny Shaffer had been trotting intently around town on one good work or another for so long that no one regarded her seriously any more. But something about Lucille's face checked him.

"Why sure, sweetheart," he said. "If you and her can help some poor soul rest a little easier, that'll be fine. Just let me know if I can do anything."

At first Lucille hardly knew what to undertake other than prepare baskets for families Jenny told her about or read to ailing children so that their mothers could escape to do necessary errands or step next door for a cup of tea. Even this soon ended. Winter was edging near and they had to move back to Argent. She took her new bent with her, however. Always a churchgoer, she now became an active worker. Her goal was the erection of a church at Red Mountain, especially after she learned that the Catholic diocese in Baker was planning a building of their own—"You don't want *them* to be ahead of us, do you?"

When Alden said that finding a permanent minister would be difficult unless decent living quarters were provided, she raised her sights to include a parish house. She persuaded the Altar Society to embrace both buildings as official projects. She initiated socials and rummages to raise funds; she browbeat publicity out of Al Ewer; she corresponded voluminously with the church's Home Missionary Society, hoping to locate groups in the East who would help sponsor the new church.

Red Mountain's own reputation proved to be her greatest handicap. The place was said to be rolling in silver. Why didn't it provide for its own needs? So she tackled the mines. The managers referred her to the home offices and she was surprised to learn what Johnny of course knew, that the majority of the working properties were controlled in Denver or the East or even in England. Answers to her solicitations came slowly, circumlocutory letters accompanied by small checks: "Appreciate your good work . . . primary responsibility to our stockholders . . . In the face of dropping silver prices, we are obliged to remember we are operating a mine, not an eleemosynary institution . . . Much though we sympathize with your goals . . ." These discouraging results she relayed in a weekly letter to Jenny Shaffer, who was trotting about Red Mountain City on the same errand as earnestly as the deep snow and the interruption of other inspirations allowed.

At least, Johnny told Walt, Lucille wasn't oppressive about her efforts. She romped with Kathy; she was nearly always home when Johnny returned; she made sure that Nylander cooked the things he liked the way he liked them. What pleased him most was the way the abstraction had left her eyes; she sang around the house again. As far as Johnny was concerned, that was reason enough for a dozen churches. He would not have interfered for anything in the world except her pregnancy. That worried him.

"You've got to slow down," he said again and again. But she kept right on going until almost to the very day late in April when a second girl, whom they named Flora, was born.

For a time the prospect of moving an infant and a toddler to Red Mountain City almost kept her at home. As she grew stronger, however, her enthusiasms rekindled. Late in June they returned to the aspen-log house, and in July she was making arrangements to take the Argent Striders on a trip through the mountain town and the Ram so that they could see at first hand how the workers lived on whom so much of Argent depended. The Striders, she hoped, would then join her drive for church funds.

The Striders were a social club of ladies who took energetic picnics once a week to study botany and invigorate their figures. Mostly they hiked through the glens near town, but on special occasions they chartered stagecoaches for excursions to more distant beauty spots. To give this trip an extra fillip, Lucille arranged with Walt to provide saddle horses for a gallop about Red Mountain's more interesting environs. She also urged Walt to accompany the group as escort. His tall frame, his sad eyes, and his golden hair had always titillated the townswomen. The Striders would be pleased to have him join their excursion, and a day's wholesome vacation from the work he buried himself in, Lucille thought, would be good for Walt in his present unhappy state.

His marriage had been the misfortune that she had predicted from the beginning. Within a year the cold and, so gossip insisted, the deliberate shrewishness of Molly Gilroy had driven him to the purchasable solace of one of the girls on Crib Street. Injured but brave, Molly had gone home to Denver. Lawyer Yount collected "evidence," and she easily won an uncontested divorce and heavy settlement. After that Walt had grown more aloof and more taciturn than ever. At a loss to himself he sold the incompleted house on Vinegar Hill to a hay and lumber dealer and moved back to an austere room beside his stables in Red Mountain. A black moodiness ruled him. On rare occasions loneliness led him to an evening gathering at one of the homes beyond the toe of the hill. For a time he would seem to loosen up. Then what Johnny called his surlies would possess him again; he would rise in the middle of someone's sentence and stalk outside without a farewell to his hostess. Sometimes he would vanish for days at a time and on his return would never say where he had been.

With Johnny and Lucille only he was at ease. He knew he could come to breakfast on Sunday mornings and lounge around the table without having to make conversation. Lucille said she thought he wanted to help Johnny do something. "Help me do what?" Johnny asked. That was the trouble, she said; there was nothing special. "But he needs to be needed." She also thought he was still in love with Nora. "Nonsense," Johnny retorted. "He talks to her like he talks to anyone else—when he talks." "That's what I mean," Lucille countered. "He's too careful." To Johnny this was illogical. "Why can't you women stick to your own romances and let poor Walt alone?" he grumbled.

The eleven Striders who were coming up for the excursion, Lucille told Walt, were all married; he needn't be suspicious; they simply wanted a dependable man along to see after the horses. He promised her to join them and she was delighted with her triumph. On the strength of it she prevailed on Johnny to make ice cream for refreshments. "If he can provide horses for us, you certainly can turn a crank for a little while." Having promised, he could not locate a hand-cranked freezer anywhere in Red Mountain, perhaps because no householder there had supposed that ice and cream would be simultaneously available in that remote spot during the middle of summer. But Lucille went herself to the Brice ranch on the meadows for enough ingredients to make several quarts of custard, which she poured into lard pails and set in the creek to cool. Complaining prodigiously, Johnny gathered ice out of an old prospect tunnel. He chipped the rock and talc out of it, crushed it, packed it in a galvanized washtub, and added salt. He nested a lard pail of custard in the ice and by hand rotated it back and forth, back and forth, back and forth until the contents froze. These he stored in more salted ice and tackled another lard pail. By the time the Striders appeared he could scarcely lift his arms. And then Walt did not show up. Instead he sent the horses over with his two homeliest hostlers, aged seventeen and sixty-four. "You're sore!" Johnny said to Lucille. "Wait'll I get hold of him! I'll murder him! He did this just so I'd have to wrestle those pails!"

The party was a success nevertheless. With everyone save the hostlers ignoring the stares of the townspeople, with rising rears and flapping elbows, the cavalcade jounced along Mountain Avenue and up the curving road to the Ram. Although the superstition of the miners quailed at having women underground, Quine let them go far enough inside to feel the darkness, to hear the drip of water and the clang of drill steel, to see on the wet rock walls the eerie flicker of their own shadows in their own candlelight. Emerging, they saw the charred logs of the cribwork, mementos of the fire. How good it was to get off the hill! Lucille told Johnny later. Thankful for the sunshine, they galloped to the site which she and Jenny Shaffer and Spec Alden had selected for the church, a slight knoll, still crowned with firs, rising conveniently between the town and the extension where she lived. Afterwards they dismounted stiffly at her home and ate ice cream. As they boarded the last stage for Argent, the peaks above them blood red in the evening alpenglow, each of them vowed to help the church become a fact.

Nothing much happened that summer. Carpenters were undependable. Most of Red Mountain's above-ground construction work had to be pushed through during snowless months; those carpenters who did hire out to erect the church and the parish house often vanished the next day for higher-paying, hurry-up jobs at the mines and mills. Sometimes Johnny would send over men from his projects and then have to pull them right back to cope with emergencies. What with one interruption and another, the roofing, painting, and furnishing of the buildings had to be postponed until the spring of 1885.

By then enthusiasm among Lucille's volunteers was waning and not enough money came in for her to do the things she wanted. The church had to be content with a single coat of paint—"That's one more than half the buildings in Red Mountain have," Nora told her in cold comfort—but what truly distressed her was the fact that there could be no bell for the white belfry she had added to the plans despite opposition from her frugal board of trustees.

Johnny saw the disappointment coming and set about remedying it. Wiser than she in the ways of the mountains, he did not walk down the street with his hand out, baldly soliciting money for a church bell. Rather, he plotted a giant surprise. The suspense plus the glow brought to their vanities by being in on the know wrung cash from a few select individuals who otherwise had no interest in the spiritual condition of the mountaintop. A fine, clear-toned bell of nearly half a ton weight was ordered cast in Philadelphia. Johnny sent back two pounds of Red Mountain silver bullion with directions that this be melted and added to the metal, to insure still more mellowness. The bell was then shipped to Baker, lest its arrival in Argent be detected and the surprise spoiled; the cost of the freight turned out to be almost as high as the price of manufacture. Walt then carted the bell up the mountain without charge, concealing it in the middle of a load of mill castings.

At two o'clock in the morning before the dedicatory services, he and Johnny and Sam Varnum hauled it around to the church. They awoke the new minister, swore him to secrecy—he was too young, bewildered, and excitable to have been trusted for any longer than this—and with labored grunts and strangled oaths managed under no more light than the full moon and, later, the beginnings of dawn, to hoist it into the belfry.

Johnny slipped undetected back into bed, pretended to awake when Lucille stirred, and then sneaked from the house once again while she was primping for the ceremony that would crown nearly a year and a half of her efforts. The Striders had promised to come up for the service and of course Alden and his deacons from the mother church in Argent would be there. Contributors to Johnny's fund were also very much on hand. Fearful of some premature spilling of the beans, Johnny and the minister lurked nervously inside the building, peeking out through a crack in the doorway. When the first worshipers started drifting toward the new edifice, they nodded at each other in perspiring excitement and sprang for the bell rope.

The sensation was tremendous. It was the first true bell tone—the bell in the firehouse was an inconsequential thing of blacksmithing iron—to float across the mountain valley. People poured from houses and boardinghouses to stare at the knoll. The mercurial Italian section decided the clang announced an emergency and began running up in their shirt sleeves. Dogs barked. The visiting Striders, just then disembarking from a chartered stage, wept openly. Lucille came flying down the gravelly path. "Johnny! You—you—oh Johnny!" The morning's congregation was at least triple what it otherwise would have been. People in all stages of dress jammed into the rear of the building behind the pews; others pressed their faces against the small-paned windows. The new minister was in transports until Alden dryly warned him that he wasn't quite as close to heaven yet as the unaccustomed altitude might lead him to believe. And indeed attendance dwindled during following Sundays to an average of forty or so. Johnny said that for a mountain mining camp that by now numbered four or five thousand persons, mostly Catholic, the turnout wasn't bad at all. But ever afterwards the new minister advanced to his pulpit looking just a little bit wistful, a little bit discouraged.

"5"

About this time, the early summer of '85, Johnny became involved in the box house.

The encroachments of the town and the need for more space had led Walt to move his freight operations farther out onto the meadows. The district's most famous madam, Slanting Annie, so named because of her club-footed limp, thereupon proposed to take over Walt's old stables. She planned to remodel the main barn as a variety theater. There would be a stage on which waitresses could double as a chorus line in support of whatever traveling burlesque comedians came through. In front of the stage would be space for public dancing and around this space tables for refreshments. Upstairs in the former loft, surrounding three sides of the interior, were the boxes that gave such establishments their name, curtained alcoves from which customers would look out on the scene below without being detected themselves. Here waitresses could hustle drinks and entertain. The erstwhile tack room adjoining the barn was to become a bar, the blacksmith shop a gambling hall. The outbuildings by the creek were to be fitted up for the girls.

Slanting Annie was a fixture in the St. John Mountains. Coarse, bony, forthright, hot-tempered, dishonest, and courageous, she had been among the first of her profession to arrive in Argent. Soon retiring from active participation, she had become an entrepreneur, setting up facilities and ground rules for later arrivals. Everyone knew her. The Argent city council sought her advice on municipal rulings for the tenderloin part of town and generally found her suggestions workable: "What's good for all is good for one—this one, me," was her favorite introduction to civic discussions. She had formed a branch establishment at Red Mountain early in its career. Now she envisioned something truly elegant.

Walt agreed to let Annie have his old stable for a modest down payment, balance in five years. She next came to Johnny for a loan to help with the remodeling and the purchase of equipment. "I could go to those tinhorns in Baker or Argent either, for all of that, and raise the money so." She snapped her fingers and rolled the ball of snuff under her upper lip. "But then they'd start edging in on me, expecting this and that in return. I want my house to be mine. I figure you won't be coming around all the time, screwing me here and screwing me there for your own benefit. Besides," she finished shrewdly, "a classy house that the men will appreciate and patronize instead of going off maybe to Baker and forgetting to show up for their shift the next day will be a good thing for the camp. I mean real classy, like Leadville."

This annoyed Johnny. Whenever Red Mountain felt expansive it compared itself to the pulsing, high-altitude camp of Leadville, in the central part of the state. "What have they got that we haven't?" he'd protest on such occasions. "Their mines and smelters and stores and whatnot are all jammed up in one place because that's all they've got —one place. We spread—Argent, Red Mountain, Beartown, Summit, Baker, a dozen basins and gulches on each side—add those together and it's a sight more than Leadville can hold a candle to. They ought to be comparing themselves to us."

Now Annie wanted a Leadville-style house, or better. Johnny talked the problem over with Walt, scratched around to raise the money she asked for, and had Harmon execute the papers tight enough so that he wouldn't have to worry about her trying to squirm loose. He made no effort to keep the transaction secret; he just did not get around to mentioning it at home. The news reached Lucille through the new Altar Society and when he came home late that evening she lit into him in outrage, unrestrained by the familiar presences of Harmon and Nora, who happened to be there for supper.

"Honestly, John, I have never been so mortified. Right after you and Walt brought up the bell for the church. Now you're fostering immorality."

"Me?" he said. "Why, it's just a plain business loan."

"You know the uses to which that . . . place will be put."

"Every camp in the mountains has them."

"But you went right ahead—"

He glanced uneasily at Nora, whose eyes were mocking him. "Now look," he said with elaborate patience, "you might as well say that Walt shouldn't let his wagons haul lumber up here because he knows Annie will use the boards in her cat house, or that Otto and I should close our road to her whores when they drive up—"

"That's not the same, and you don't have to parade that kind of language." She appealed to Harmon. "Isn't there a law?"

He squirmed unhappily, avoiding Johnny's eyes. After all, he was involved too. "The police powers legitimately exercised in regulating commerce," he began evasively and then threw up his hands. "I don't think any statute covers the specific situation. It's a social problem rather than a legal one, at least in this area."

"You're damn right," Johnny said and glowered at his wife. "What's so bad about it anyway? I mean for these poor honyaks that work all day in a wet mine and have nothing to come out to but an eight-by-ten plank room in a drafty boardinghouse or some stinking billiard parlor—"

"That's what I thought you'd say."

"Facts are facts."

"There's a rumor in the Altar Society that the moneyed interests in Argent are behind this and persuaded you and Walt to front for them, to give the men something that may help keep them quiet if wages have to be reduced. My own husband!"

He stared at her. "Oh for Christ sake!"

"You'll admit that there is talk of cutting wages."

He waved in dismissal. "This slump in the price of silver is temporary."

"Temporary for the last ten years. Now they say it's getting really bad."

The temptation for a jibe was too much for Nora. Mockingly she said, "Do you mean there are actually clouds coming up somewhere in this wonderful heaven?"

"No, there's no clouds," Johnny growled. "All anybody is trying to do is make things a little better for everyone—"

"Everyone!" Lucille flared. "Really, John!"

He grew completely exasperated. "You've got your church and the micks have their church for those a church means something to, and I helped put up both of them, especially yours. There's a reading room for whoever wants to use it, and I helped get that going, too. But not everybody on Red Mountain is hankering to spend their one free day singing hallelujah or reading books, and just because you don't like to think about what they'd rather do instead don't mean they aren't going to do it. Nobody told Walt or me to put up a box house so wages can be cut, for God's sake. We lent Annie that money just like we'd lend it to anybody who wanted to start a hardware store or an iron foundry or some other business that's needed."

"Needed!"

"That's what I said. Needed. I don't mean by me. I'm not going to patronize the house, if that's what you're thinking, any more than I'm going to buy mill castings every week because I've got money in the foundry. But some poor Cousin Jack wanting his ashes hauled—"

"Castings aren't immoral."

"Is rape?"

"Johnny!"

"All right, I apologize—no, I don't! A fact's a fact. For every decent woman up here on the mountain, there's four or five unmarried men, most of them uneducated and dumb, used to rough work and rough living. But you can walk down Mountain Avenue any hour of day or night and not have anyone look crosswise at you—"

"That's man-logic, I must say—excusing disease and misery and evil on those grounds."

"Even woman-logic ought to see that a lot of this high and mighty virtue that parades down the aisle on Sundays is able to get there partly because of the girls they scorn as not having any virtue."

She was growing very pale. "Of course you men defend it," she said. "You're the ones who create it. Without you it wouldn't last a week."

"If Slanting Annie knocks on the door of that Baptist Church next Sunday, will you women let her in?"

Lucille's eyes dropped to the table edge. "If she's truly repentant . . . Johnny, we've talked enough about it."

"Repentant? Ha! By whose standards? Who decides—"

He checked himself. She was more unsettled than seemed reasonable. Let it go, let it go. But he was too exercised himself to count on being able to hold back the things crowding to his tongue. To give both their tempers a chance to slack off, he seized the empty coal bucket and stalked outside. The embarrassment that always attends a family rift crippled the tongues of those left behind. Lucille spread her hands in apology.

"I'm sorry. I don't know what possessed him: the church and that . . . place in the same breath. I—I just don't know."

"No doubt it's his innocence," Nora said, aiming the taunt at her husband.

"That's right." Their eyes locked and Lucille realized afresh how much they hated each other. "Innocence never does discriminate. How can it?" Harmon turned to Lucille. "In his way, Johnny truly is trying to help. The one and only John Ogden—*rara avis*. He'd stand on his head in the middle of the street if he thought it would promote his town or his mountain. He isn't very critical about some of the things he picks, I'll admit; but that's the Johnny of it. And now, Nora, I think it's time we left."

"Please don't!" Lucille begged. She and Johnny had spatted before over routine annoyances, but this was the first contention to slice so deeply. She needed distractions while she steadied herself against his return. Accordingly she held them there, only to wish that she hadn't.

Nora was on edge. As Lucille had learned, Harmon's trick of dropping Latin phrases into his conversation was a deliberate reminder to Nora of her lack of education, as though this small assertion of superiority somehow compensated for the way she dominated him in other respects. She resented the pinprick out of all proportion. Perhaps too she resented his daring to step in ahead of her to mollify Lucille. It was she, Nora, who was Lucille's friend. To push her husband back into his place she ranged herself, to Lucille's dismay, against his defense of Johnny.

"I'll say he isn't critical," she snapped at Harmon. "And no one dares be critical of him or of what he does. As far as John Ogden is concerned, his way of doing things is the only right way."

"He's right often enough for me," Harmon said and struck back. "I bet against him once, in favor of Pat Edgell. It was a bad mistake."

Nora flushed. "It's not the only mistake that's been made."

"I'll still bet on him," Harmon persisted. "If you want to know the truth, I did the legal work for him in his arrangements with Slant— Miss Anne Siala, as her name turns out to be."

"My!" Nora sneered. "Don't we boys kick up our heels when we get away from home."

"Please!" Lucille cried again, hearing Johnny's footsteps. "Let's not talk about it any more. We've said too much, all of us."

He strode into the uneasy silence without noticing it, rattled a shovelful of coal into the stove and turned gustily about, brushing his hands together. While fetching the coal he had thought of a face-saving way for everyone to back off from the quarrel and he plunged headlong into it.

"I suppose things are different in Chicago." He meant the concession as a generous acceptance of Lucille's inability to understand the mountains, even after four years of living in them. "But up here we have a peculiar setup. Things happen fast, the way they did in Argent after the Utes left. All kinds of people come boiling in, floaters and shysters and ham-fatters along with good managers and honest workingmen. We can't keep up with ourselves. Almost before we've brought in a steam hoist big enough to serve the levels we're reaching, the mine is deeper than the hoist can go. Last year a mountain sheep couldn't climb into some of the basins behind the peaks; now there's trails into every one. The trails down here sprouted into roads, and now the roads aren't hardly able to move the ore. What we'll have to have pretty quick now is a railroad."

"I can practically hear the whistle blowing in the gorge," Nora said.

Braced for exactly that retort, Johnny took no offense. "Maybe not in the gorge first; maybe Baker, where construction will be easier and cheaper. But," he added as her eyebrows went up in the manner they had, "it'll soon go down the gorge to Argent, too. That's not what I started to say, though. What I mean is that when we get a railway, we'll bring in really big machinery and set it down solid and lasting and dig back through these mountains to kingdom come. We'll be able to move all the low-grade ore we can produce. Living will be easier. It won't be no trick for a family man to load his wife and kids on the train and ride down to Argent—"

"Baker, I thought," Nora interrupted.

"Let him have his say," Harmon told her.

"Or Baker," Johnny admitted. "They can see their friends and do their shopping and take in a show at the Opera House. For that matter, the friends and shows can chug up here in an hour or so. There'll be more and more jobs—a solid town, like Argent, that folks will take pride in. Socials, plays, gardens, churches, anything you can think of. This other stuff we were talking about," he glanced apologetically at Lucille, "is just a sort of phase. Growing pains." He grinned hopefully at them. Everything was fine, wasn't it? "See what I mean?"

"Steam cars to heaven," Nora said. "That's quite a pull for a locomotive."

"Do you always have to belittle?" Harmon chided.

Looking at the lawyer's expression, half envious of Johnny and half amused by him, Lucille remembered what he had said about her husband months ago, following his and Johnny's reconciliation: *He's as morning-fresh as young Adam still. He's had his snakes too, yet nothing, not even jail, has changed him. I hope nothing ever does. He makes you believe in yourself again, makes you believe that being a man has some glory to it after all. I'd almost forgotten.* Evidently he was remembering now. He proffered a cigar, lit his and Johnny's, stroked his chin whiskers into place, and began discussing, as they had before, the ways and means of railroad potentials and financing.

Nora grew bored and dragged him away early. As they walked by the light of a candle lantern along the rocky path toward the cramped cabin they were renting, at a bargain price in order to save money for another winter in California, Harmon said defiantly to her silence, "I'll bet he gets the railroad, too."

She shrugged. While listening to Johnny's grandiose plans and knowing now that even if they materialized she and Harmon would do no more than touch the fringes, she had felt quarrelsomeness ooze out of her into discouragement. "Feed on his crumbs again," she murmured. "Well, it's a meal, I suppose." She pulled her coat collar tightly around her neck and crossed her arms tightly over her breast so that his groping hand could not find the crook of her elbow. Oh, he hated her; but when lonesomeness grinned at him he clung tighter than ever, his impoverished spirit drawing nourishment from the very thrusting, angry vitality that was destroying it. Yet even this knowledge could no longer comfort her. Shivering, she looked toward the silhouette the peaks cut out of the night sky. In the crisp air, the star clusters looked almost close enough to touch. Almost, but never quite.

III

"1"

When definite proposals for a railroad did come late in the spring of 1886, they caught Johnny flatfooted. He had ridden to the Argent home late one April afternoon, dead tired and soaking wet from a week-long battle with melting snow. As he sagged in a kitchen chair with a hot toddy, the telephone rang. Lucille called to him.

"It's Fred Fossett."

"This time of afternoon! Can't he wait until morning?"

"He says it's urgent."

"I probably misfigured by five cents on that last draft," Johnny grumbled and went to the telephone. When he came back he told Lucille she'd have to reconcile herself to a late supper again. Fossett wanted him to attend a meeting at the bank "instanter," as Johnny put it. "No, Fred didn't say what it's about. Otto is there, though. Came in on yesterday's train. So something's up."

In addition to Winkler he found four other men in Fossett's office—it had a new carpet now and a large flat-topped desk. Two of the men he knew well, Parley Quine and another of the principal owners of the Ram. With them was heron-nosed, round-orbed Daniel Ide, manager of the big smelter at Montezuma, who occasionally visited Red Mountain in search of trade. The fourth man, introduced as Alastair Monroe, was straight and ruddy, with long, bushy hair behind his ears and a strange, clipped way of pronouncing his words. He was, Johnny learned, fresh from England.

A long discussion had evidently been going on in the office and Johnny had been summoned to provide a modicum of extra information. Fossett was spokesman. He removed his pince-nez, rubbed his nose, replaced the glasses, rattled some papers on his desk, looked impressive, and at a nod from Winkler gave Johnny a summary of as much of the meeting as it was presumed he needed to know. An English syndicate had taken an option on the Ram. Engineers had been examining it for the past two weeks, trying to determine its worth. A tentative figure of two million, one hundred thousand dollars had been arrived at. Fossett had difficulty keeping his face impassive as he let the figure slide off his tongue. Johnny didn't even try to be indifferent. Ragged Ass! Wow! He whistled aloud and glanced at Quine, leaning negligently in his chair, his hands folded across his checkered vest.

The figure, Fossett continued, was predicated in part on being able to double the Ram's output by installing new machinery and building a huge new concentrating mill to handle low-grade ores. It was further predicated on being able to move the concentrate from the mill economically, in volume, to the smelter at Montezuma. That implied a railroad from Baker over the pass to Red Mountain.

"And on down the gorge to Argent!" Johnny blurted.

They regarded him like a ring of disapproving owls. Daniel Ide, the smelter manager, looked as if he'd enjoy reaching out and pecking at him with that heron's beak.

"Iss not ripe to Argent," Otto said.

Johnny flushed. Maybe he had yumped too fast. Coal at Montezuma, easier construction from Baker—no doubt the pass was the logical route for a start. He nodded apology for his haste.

Fossett let the stern silence sink in—after this keep your place, Jack— and went on. The problem now being considered was the cost involved in building the railway. Since it would serve every mine on the mountain, it would be built not by the Ram but by an independent company, formed perhaps by Otto Winkler. The group in the office realized that accurate surveys would have to wait until spring. Meanwhile, however, Johnny was familiar with the area. "Possibly," Fossett said with his pale, important smile, "in traveling back and forth over the pass, especially while you were rebuilding the wagon road to Baker, you considered that some day a train might follow that approximate route."

Johnny smiled. Possibly! "I know almost to the foot where the track will have to go."

"Then perhaps you can suggest a rough estimate of grading and installation costs."

"Not forgetting," the manager of the smelter interposed, "the cost of spurs to each of the large mines."

"Off the top of my head? Now?" Johnny asked in agitation.

"Oh, spend three or four days if you like. Remember this is preliminary. We want only enough to start the ball rolling." Fossett removed the pince-nez and rubbed his nose again, benignly this time. "Bear in mind the interlocking considerations. The sale of the Ram may depend on the construction of the railroad, and the financing of the railroad may depend, in part, though of course the other mines are involved, on an assured tonnage from the Ram. The balances are delicate."

In other words, Johnny thought, don't scare off the underwriters by making the figures too high. On the other hand, don't frighten possible contractors by suggesting that the railroad will pinch them at every curve.

Otto might have been reading his mind. He smiled behind his grizzled beard and said, "The Ogden Construction Company on the part from Red Mountain to Summit might like to bid, eh?"

Johnny swallowed. "Might."

"Figure it dot vay, eh?"

Fossett said hastily, "No promises, of course."

Quine put in, "And no gossip. Premature rumor would upset the stock prices of every mine on the hill. Let's save the announcements until things are definite."

"There's just one thing more," Fossett said and paused. Whatever the thing was, he did not like dragging it out into the open. He cleared his throat, pretended to study a paper, glanced at Otto, who nodded, and then said, "In making your cost estimates, take as a rule of thumb a wage scale for unskilled labor of three-fifty per ten-hour day. Adjust other labor categories in proportion."

Johnny scowled at him. "I've always paid at least four. So has everyone on the mountain."

"Have you," Alastair Monroe interrupted in his clipped accents, "noticed the recent silver quotations? They have dropped below a dollar an ounce for the first time since '76."

"They're not going to stay that low," Johnny protested.

"We trust not, or we wouldn't be studying this investment," Monroe retorted. "I appreciate that your western legislators and businessmen are working on the problem." He granted Otto a mechanical smile in recognition of Winkler's recent trip to Washington as a delegate of the new Silver League to lay a memorial before Congress. "Everyone decries drastic wage readjustments. It is nevertheless well to be forearmed. To keep your western mines open at all, it may be necessary for your workers to share the sacrifices of the owners."

When Aino Berg talked on the mountain about sharing, Johnny thought, he did not mean quite the same thing. Aloud he asked, "Will the Ram cut wages if your syndicate buys the mine?"

"I can hardly say before we buy," Monroe reproved him stiffly.

Fossett interposed soothingly, "Figure both ways, John—three-fifty *and* four. The difference may not be as critical as we fear. Besides, by summer, the whole picture may change."

Figure low anyway, Johnny thought as the meeting broke up. When he started toward the door, Fossett caught his arm.

"There's another change in the making that you and Lucille may be interested in. If these deals go through, I'll be one of the bankers handling the transactions. It will probably mean moving to Denver, to take a vice-president's position in one of the banks there."

"Leave Argent!"

Fossett waved a deprecatory hand. "It'll be a wrench, I'll confess. But Margaret always has hankered for city living. And I'll be in a better position to serve you, in case your company does decide to bid on part of the railroad construction. Or on any other jobs."

Belatedly Johnny remembered his manners. "Denver is a great opportunity for you, I guess. But we'll miss you. I don't know what Lucy would have done at times without Margaret. As for bidding—I golly—sure I'd like to. But those wages—"

"These are preliminary figures, nothing final," Fossett repeated and gave his conspiratorial nod. "The main thing is to consider what a railroad will mean to the camp. Remember the changes you yourself have helped create in less than six years. They'll be as nothing compared to what will be possible when we begin using modern methods to handle really big tonnages. I mean big! That kind of prosperity rubs off on everyone. Another thing—once a railroad has crossed the pass to Red Mountain and has stimulated business and has increased the demand for the products and services Argent can supply, then an extension of the tracks through the gorge will almost certainly be ripe. Think of that!"

Oh sure, Johnny said to himself when he stood outside, looking through the twilight toward the gorge. *Think about it, beat the drums: heaven by the silver stairs—at thirty-five cents an hour.* Wages on Red Mountain had never been that low. To Fossett, rattling paper in an office chair, the figures were no more than marks on a cost sheet, just as in the old days when he had been Otto's paymaster, coins had been no more than discs of metal to take from a barrel lashed to his buggy seat and drop grudgingly one by one into the waiting hands. But Otto should have known better. Otto should have been able to measure three-fifty against a sack of groceries, against a pair of rubber boots in the Angel Gabe Porcella's hairy orange fist.

Oh damn! Why, whenever you thrust your head into sunlight, did there always have to be a shadow behind you to boot?

Slowly he started up Silver Avenue toward Vinegar Hill. As his blood began to course after the stuffiness of the office, his stride lengthened. After all, three-fifty was better than no job whatsoever. Besides, the drop would be temporary. As Fred said, the prosperity which the railroad brought would rub off onto everybody. Silver could not stay below a dollar forever, that stood to reason. Only at sunrise did the shadows seem longer than natural. As things developed, as the light climbed, the doubts shrank. The main thing was to get out and work, to take advantage of everything the red peaks held. Things would turn out; they always did if a man had faith enough. He began to smile as he thought of Lucille's face when he told her. A *railroad, just like we always said*. Baker first, then Argent. She could keep a secret. Surely the warning to keep quiet had not been meant to include her. Oh, wait until she heard!

"2"

He presented his figures at another meeting in the bank, was summoned twice more on successive days to answer questions, and at last was free to return to his road. He reached Red Mountain City on a sunny afternoon, the streets quagmires, log foundations oozing moisture, vacant lots of pale young grass and disintegrating containers afloat on lique-faction, snowbanks on the peak sides dripping crystal down the rusty gullies, creeks brawling, the rocks and even the sky looking washed by this insistent sudsing of the year's first deep thaw. He contemplated riding around the toe of the hill to learn how the aspen-log cabin had withstood the winter; soon now Lucille could plan on moving up. A railroad!

First, though, he had errands to do. He stepped off his horse into ankle-deep goo, hitched the animal and sloshed to the sidewalk—cement now rather than splintering plank. There he came face to face with Aino Berg, who had halted his own progress and was waiting for him. They exchanged pleasantries and Aino asked after the children.

"Fine. Another one next September or October."

"Big family: dot's goot."

"Lucille will be up again for the first part of the summer. She'll admire it if you drop around to see her and the girls."

"Ya," Aino said and puffed in silence on his short-stemmed black pipe. Possibly his being on the street at this time of day meant that he was working night shift now. More probably it meant that he had no job. Though he was a good driller and expert timberman, mine managers suspected him of being an agitator and were reluctant to hire him save when extra demands required extra hands. Johnny used him when possible, but sooner or later Aino drew his time, saying he had work to do for the Benevolent Association in its tiny upstairs office over the watchmaker's shop or that he must attend a meeting in another town. Regularly Johnny expostulated with him—not about unionism, concerning which Johnny pondered very little one way or another, but about wasting himself. The talks had no effect. In spite of that, the two men liked each other. Memories of trail-building days in the gorge were still close enough that they could stand together as they were doing now, sheepskin jackets open to the sun, wet gloves dangling from their pockets, the earflaps of their caps turned up, and feel no constraint over inventing conversation. Aino puffed a full two minutes before removing his pipe and asking in his singsong voice, the inflections rising at the ends of the sentences so that every statement sounded like a question.

"I tank the Ram is sold?"

"Yeah?" Johnny said noncommittally.

"Two–tree weeks dose foreign engineers sample every breast and stope, measure every gallery and winze. They write on pads and ask the foremens questions. They tank maybe some pollack knocking hung ore out of a chute or tramming the cars are deaf and dumb. They talk to each odder. Ya!"

"Yeah?" Johnny said again and eyed the sun for time. "I've got a million things to do. Tell you what, Aino. If you're looking for a job when we start repairing culverts—"

"Tree-fifty a day?"

Deaf and dumb, hah! You sure walked into that one, Johnny boy, he told himself. Too blankly for conviction he asked, "What do you mean?"

"Everywhere rumors," Aino said. "For months we hear wages are to be cut. Now we hear as soon as the Ram is sold, the new owners will start. Then, no stopping anywhere."

"Wages are the owners' business," Johnny said mildly.

"Englishmen," Aino said. "What do they care? The Dixie Girl—Boston. What do they care? The Summit Queen—St. Louis. My place—what was my place—Denver. Ya! You tell me one claim on this mountain hiring more dan ten mens that is owned by people living here." He tapped at Johnny's shirtfront with his pipestem. "Yoost one."

"In the beginning we didn't have capital to develop our mines. We had to import it. We've been over this before, Aino. It's money that makes jobs."

"Forty-two per cent dividends the Rose Marie pay last year. How much per cent stay for the mens that dig the ore?"

"That's rumor too. Did you see the Rose Marie's books?"

"We know—"

"Who's we? The association?"

"The Mine and Mill Workers' Union now. Ya, union!" Aino puffed defiantly. "We know ore when we see it. We know mining costs. We know what pay we get. The rest—foreigners." Anything beyond the St. Johns was foreign to Aino. "The Ram was the last mine owned at home. Now it goes. You and Kennerly, ya big Walt, you two, now you are only companies who live here who hire many mens. What you going to do?"

"About what?"

"About wages. Whose side you on?"

Pressure. More pressure at Argent in the bank. Johnny felt himself bracing. "Red Mountain's side," he said.

"Hah!" Aino grunted. He stood puffing silently. This time the minutes dragged. Johnny stirred and squinted again at the sun.

"Look, Aino. I—"

"You know the foreman at the Smuggler. Kip Nellis?"

"Nellis manages to run the Smuggler without my advice," Johnny said. He did not want to hear what he sensed was coming. The Smuggler was a marginal producer, plaything of speculators, open for a few months and then shut for a few more while its promoters sent out another prospectus fishing for sucker dollars. The Smuggler was one of Harmon's law-edge clients. It was also a mine where a test case on wages might be tried first; it employed leftover workers who might not generate an organized protest against a reduction in pay. Thus a precedent could be established. Naturally the union was on guard— though, Johnny thought with quick impatience, just how the Benevolent Association had come by its assumption that the workers of Red Mountain possessed some God-given right to four dollars a day, no less and to hell with the owners and their problems, was more than he could figure.

"Nellis," Aino said imperturbably, "posted a notice yesterday at the Smuggler portal to drop wages. 'You drop us,' the mens say, 'we drop you.' They poot him in a dump car and poosh him to the end of the trestle. Oh my, he cry and beg. They let him out and he run down the side of the dump, slip and fall and not come back for his lunch box. Ya."

The main thing Johnny felt was sadness. A threat. The Smuggler workers should not have thumbed their noses like that. Nor should Aino have recounted the tale in just that fashion.

"That's the way trouble starts," he said.

"Ya," Aino agreed and they stood for another moment within arm's distance but no longer looking at each other. Johnny moved first.

"Well, Aino, come around and see us some day."

"Umm." The Finn waited until Johnny had started back through the goo toward Sam Varnum's newspaper office. Then he called, "Don' forget, Yohnny!"

"Forget what?"

"Kennerly and you—dot's the only ones left."

"3"

Johnny waded on across the street, intending to ask Sam Varnum for such additional information as the newspaperman possessed. But when he was inside the shop—Sam had added a small private office to the minuscule reception room—he found that he had been anticipated. Kip Nellis was there, Parley Quine, Joe Dyer of the Dixie Girl. And Pat Edgell.

Johnny's "Morning, gentlemen" should have been enough to include Pat, but Pat would not let it be. He stared so unblinkingly at John that the others noticed, his intent being, as John knew from other encounters, to belittle his old partner into nodding first. Johnny always did, for a small hope buried deep inside still believed that some day Pat would come around again. So this morning he once more gave Pat the satisfaction of a particular greeting. Pat's lips curled then and he inclined his head the barest fraction and glanced at the others to see whether they had noticed that he'd won.

They weren't interested in private feuds. Joe Dyer, who sat next to the window, barked in his bulldog voice, "We saw you talking to Berg, Jack. Telling you how to manage your own business, wasn't he?"

"We talked about wages," Johnny admitted.

"Huh!" Dyer grunted. He was round-faced, hard-headed, heavy-handed. When his temper was wound up, there was scarcely any possibility of interrupting him. "Like I was telling Varnum, that four-dollar base rate is obsolete. It went into effect at the opening of the boom when everyone was in a sweat to reach the veins and build their surface installations while the weather was good. But those exceptional amounts of construction are over. Every day now hustlers are pounding on my office door looking for any kind of work I have. Who the hell does that benevolent union think it is that the law of supply and demand don't work for them the same as it does for everybody else, for Christ sake? Why don't you print those figures, Varnum?"

Parley Quine stirred restively. "The paper comes out on Friday. That's not going to help much with the marchers tomorrow."

"Marchers?" Johnny asked.

Pat taunted him. "You mean, Jackie boy, that something can happen here in your private town and you not know?"

"Never mind," Dyer growled and swung to Johnny. "Yes, marchers. The union is drafting a resolution to present to a mass meeting tomorrow afternoon out in front of their hall. The resolution is supposed to say that if wages drop anywhere, there'll be a general strike. The idea is to catch us flat-footed right at the beginning of spring when we're as busy as cats on a tin roof, and put the fear of the Lord in us. But hell, they couldn't keep it secret. Not every worker at the Dixie Girl is sold on these radicals. The thing was reported to me as soon as Aino Berg and those other agitators started floating the scheme around. Well, I say we make our own agreement to call their bluff and not give them a dime."

Pat sucked on his teeth and spit. "Absolutely! I've got clean-up leases on five dumps hanging fire that I can sign tomorrow if the people concerned know that wages will drop into line."

"Dumps!" Quine scoffed. He paused, obviously wondering how much to reveal, and then shrugged. "Everyone on the street seems to know that an English syndicate has taken an option on the Ram, and so I guess I'm not spilling any beans to say the syndicate may let the option lapse if they think there's a union here strong enough to hold costs higher than they are anywhere else in the Rockies." He glanced at Johnny. "If the Ram deal goes under, there's not likely to be a railroad."

"Railroad?" Their heads swiveled in surprise. "From Argent?"

"That wasn't supposed to be made public," Johnny objected. He shifted to Dyer, who evidently had arrogated to himself the position of spokesman for the employers. "Have you tried talking to the union about a compromise?"

Dyer slapped a big palm on his own knee. "Not a dime!"

Quine said to Johnny, "Whether you like it or not, the railroad is a public matter now. At Fossett's bank you did your figuring two ways —four dollars and three-fifty. Which are you going to tell Aino Berg it'll be? It's a stand you'll have to take."

"A railroad?" Pat insisted, jealousy leaping through him.

"From Argent?" Nellis demanded again.

"From Baker, if anywhere," Johnny admitted and heard Pat's whuff of mockery.

Impatiently Quine explained the proposal. It took them off Johnny's back long enough for him to face his own thoughts. *The only ones left.* He glanced out the window. Aino was still out there, pacing back and forth.

As soon as the talk fell away from the railroad, he tried to compromise.

"We talk about sharing a drop in profits. Why not promise to share a rise, too? I mean, give the men a written promise that when the price of silver climbs back to a dollar, the wage cut will be restored."

"A dollar!" Nellis yelped. "Give 'em our shirts, too! No, sir!"

"A dollar ten," Sam suggested.

"The exact scale is something that can be worked out with the union," Johnny said.

"I won't recognize the bastards for a minute!" Dyer shouted.

"Shut up," Quine told him, "and let Jack talk."

"I know you," Dyer snarled back. "You're interested in buying peace until the Ram is sold and you've got your quarter interest safe in your pocket."

"You're damn right I'm interested," Quine agreed blandly, without offense. "So is Ogden interested in his railroad. If you don't want to ride along with us, then maybe we'll have to talk to Aino on our own." He swung to Sam Varnum. "What stand will your paper take? Or will we have to go to Ewer for our support?"

Sam blushed to his ears but held his ground. "You don't have to steam roller me. I think Johnny has a point. I've seen labor trouble in the East." His eyes grew abstract, remembering. "Nothing poisons a town faster. We don't want it here. Johnny's way might be the solution. Except for one thing: What makes you so sure that—oh, hee—the price of silver will go back up?"

Johnny scowled. "Why, it stands to reason."

"Or to faith," Sam murmured. "I receive exchange papers from the East and—well, not every economist thinks the government's support of silver is a good thing."

"Are you crazy?"

"I'm just trying to look ahead. In the last thirty years the gold supply from California and Australia and right here in Colorado has increased I forget how many fold. I can look it up if you want."

"No," said Dyer.

Sam whinnied but went stubbornly on. "As gold grows more plentiful, more and more countries are leaving the silver standard—France, Switzerland, Belgium, Italy, Austria, Germany. And you know Gresham's law."

"Never heard of it," Dyer declared. "State or national?"

Sam squirmed as if he were the one who had blazoned his ignorance. "It's, hee, an economic postulate. The inferior metal drives out the more precious—"

"Inferior!" Johnny bleated. "If you think it's so inferior, why did you come up here to live off it?"

"Damnedest crap I ever heard!" Dyer snapped. "Put a silver dollar and a gold dollar in the same pocket and they'll get along. If anything, the silver will be spent first. The laboring people trust it. They'll hoard a twenty-dollar gold piece, but they'll spend and enjoy two hundred silver dimes. That's what makes prosperity—money in circulation."

"Bimetallism, that's the answer," Nellis said.

Quine waved them silent. "It's nothing we can settle before the marchers come down the street tomorrow afternoon. But this proposition of Ogden's about a sliding scale is one which we can settle. Personally, I'd vote to go along with it."

"It means the men will have to start right off with a reduction." Sam glanced at Johnny. "Do you think Aino and the other union officials will accept that?"

The only ones. But facts had to be faced. "I don't know about the union, but I think the workers themselves will agree if we can make them realize how much depends on a temporary cut."

"In other words," Quine said, "our first problem is to spread our side of the story among them in time to undercut the union spielers."

"We can call workers' meetings at each mine in the morning," Dyer suggested.

"They'd think it was just management talk," Nellis demurred.

"What about you, Sam?" Quine demanded. "What stand will you take?"

"I—hee—I'll support what's best for the majority."

"A strike that stops production and causes layoffs and lost wages isn't good for anyone."

"No," Sam admitted. "But—"

"Suppose," Quine pressed, "that you bring out a newspaper extra first thing tomorrow morning announcing the possibility of a railroad."

Dyer slapped his knee. "Great idea! Let the honyaks read that while they're standing around waiting to march. That'll give 'em something to think about!"

"If Winkler and the others agree to the announcement," Johnny temporized.

"Get on the telephone and explain," Quine urged. "Tell 'em I'm okaying it as far as the Ram is concerned."

"The extra will be only about the railroad," Varnum said. "Nothing about wages."

"Gutless!" Dyer growled.

"It'll be more persuasive if it's subtle," Quine soothed and hooked his thumbs blandly in the pockets of his checkered vest. "Then after they've got Sam's story under their belts, I'll stand up there at their street meeting and give 'em a little talk. They know me. They'll listen. Let Jack talk to them, too. He's another old-timer."

"Me?" Johnny said. Speechify workers he might be hiring one of these days? "I'm no talker."

"Tch!" It was Pat. With soft venom he said, "Why, Jackie, you can talk a man right out of his own road and make it sound noble. The good of the country and our Jackie boy sitting up there shining his halo over it all."

The small hope that had lived so long inside Johnny died then. He looked straight back at Pat. "Why sure," he said, and felt hate's iron bands clamp around his chest. "Why sure I'll talk to them about what's best for the country. Not everything that's been tried around here has been."

"4"

Winkler agreed to publishing a story about the possibility of a railroad provided that the problem of costs was emphasized. A meeting of mine managers called to discuss the sliding scale was less productive. After two hours of wrangling over the points where adjustments should begin and how much they should be, Quine waved a hand in dismissal.

"As I see it, we want the union to come to us first. Let's hear what they have to say and start from there. Maybe we won't have to slide anything."

That was agreed. But after the meeting broke up, someone, Nellis perhaps, grew alarmed at the prospect of a march of dissatisfied men through the middle of town and appealed to the sheriff's substation for more protection than the local constabulary could promise. The substation called Argent. The next morning Charles Gaw, recently elected to his fourth term as county sheriff, responded in person with six deputies. Characteristically he met the unprecedented situation by marking time. He posted his deputies as inconspicuously as possible and told Johnny over a cup of coffee that his only plan was to improvise as need arose.

Johnny told him not to worry. "There's not going to be any violence. Have you seen Varnum's extra? His newsboys are hawking it right now up at the Ram's loading docks, where the parade is assembling."

He pulled the single sheet from his coat pocket and smoothed it on the counter of the restaurant where they were waiting. The single word RAILROAD! spread blackly across the entire page top. The story itself leaped nimbly over the contingencies on which the project depended and concentrated on interviews hastily concocted the evening before with John Ogden about expenses; with Quine and Dyer about the stimulation to production; with Harmon Gregg and Bert Sesnon of the Rose Marie about the new enterprises and new jobs that would be called into being.

"Dyer," Johnny added to Gaw, "wanted Sam to come right out and say a strike now over a four-dollar minimum wage would scare the railroad off, which it probably would. But Sam hung back—wouldn't say anything at all about wages. That's what Quine and I'll have to do in our talks." He grimaced, thinking of Aino. "I admit I don't like it. Still, it's got to be done for the good of the camp. The men will understand that. They may growl for appearances, but there isn't going to be any real trouble."

"Sounds like you've outfoxed them all down the line," Gaw conceded with some relief. He consulted his watch for the seventh time. "Anyway, they're late starting, and I guess that's a good sign. I mean, if they were organized to come out swinging, they'd be here by now." He scratched his lantern chin and regarded the syrupy street outside. "I suppose they calculated that spring, when work picks up, would be a good time to show their muscle. But you'd think they would of remembered what this place is like in a thaw."

"Listen!" Johnny interrupted. They cocked their ears toward the doorway. Distant cheers and catcalls: Gaw dropped a quarter on the counter to pay for the coffee and reached for a toothpick. "Sounds like school's about to start," he said and led the way outside.

By mutual agreement the mines had offered no opposition to the men's knocking off half a day to attend the mass meeting. A press of workers ranged along both sidewalks in front of the union headquarters, located in the echoing top floor of a two-story, false-fronted dun building, its paint scaling and dirty crusted snowbanks heaped against its shady side. A lumber wagon had been parked at the curb as the speakers' stand. Hastily lettered banners on its side insisted, "A fair wage for a fair day's work," and "Strength in union." Gaw, who was taller than Johnny, elevated himself on a sidewalk steppingstone, craned his neck to spot his deputies, and glanced along the street toward the marchers.

"Not even a band," he remarked as he stepped back down. "Kind of amateurish, ain't it?"

"It's a march of strength," Johnny told him, "not a parade."

"Next time they ought to have at least a bass drum to thump 'em along."

And indeed the ranks did straggle. The mud was part of the reason. Every few yards one or two marchers wearied of the sloshing and veered aside to the concrete walks. Varnum's extra had been another drain. Many marchers walked with a copy of the paper rolled in their hands and waved it sheepishly to acquaintances among the spectators. But the most telling weakness, Johnny decided, was the lack of tradition which Gaw called amateurishness. Save for funerals and socials the union had had little opportunity to act in concert. It was by no means accepted by the bulk of the mountain's conservative, clannish, and suspicious workers. Under the stares and occasional good-natured jeers of the spectators packed along the sidewalk, the paraders grew miserably self-conscious. *Almost as if they're ready to apologize for showing up in the first place*, Johnny thought. And he wondered unhappily, *Maybe the whole thing would have caved in without us going to this trouble to kick it apart.*

By Gaw's estimate, five or six hundred men at last gathered raggedly around the lumber wagon. To judge from the expressions of the union officials as they conferred in the doorway to their headquarters, they had hoped for more. Nevertheless two of them climbed resolutely onto the wagon and with upraised fists shook out florid rhetoric whose purport was summarized in the banners at their feet. When the last one had finished, Quine imperturbably climbed over a wheel hub onto the wagon bed and asked if he might say a word or two. The two officials, nonplused by the unexpected boldness, stuttered a denial. A few marchers hooted but were cried down by the majority. Quine stood slackly, thumbs in the armholes of his vest, until his very blandness brought quiet.

Then humorously, without rancor, he began to talk. The town hero, discoverer of the Ram, already a legend. He didn't say anything in particular: the old days, Angel Gabe keeping store in a tent, and Quine arriving to share a fungus-grown cabin with, at conservative estimate, four thousand three hundred and twenty-one rats. From that to a city: industry, jobs. Quine did not actually say that the Ram had wrought it all, but the impression was there, mellowed by the common touch: Ragged Ass Mine. He did not quite say that anyone in the crowd might have done what he had done and be standing where he was standing, feeling the same responsibilities about the future. The idea was clear, however; and although he never used the word "wages" that shadow too was plain.

Finally he asked permission to introduce his good friend Jack Ogden, who had been around even longer and had done more than any other man to boom the town—"has done," Quine said as they leaned forward to listen, mouths hanging—"and will do, if you'll give him a chance!"

They whooped and hollered as he pulled Johnny to the edge of the wagon and left him there, feeling as self-conscious as any marcher slopping through the mud, but grinning in an eager amiability that brought answering smiles from an audience turned sympathetic by Quine's unction. He wasn't much at speaking, he told them, but here, in front of his fellow townsmen, he didn't need to be. Quine had explained to them how their city had grown in the past, higher in its altitude and its prospects than any other city in the land. The red mountains would tell them the rest—those three red mountains right back of them, the mountains they looked at every morning and evening. This was no time for backcapping. "Not even scratched yet!" he cried. "Nobody knows how far those veins reach!" But a railroad would help the mines to grow and the workers to prosper. Patience, faith, and a short sacrifice, geared to the price of silver, for the sake of the long-range good—those were the keys. Those would bring the iron tracks. And then—but how could he say it? "Just wait!" he told them, his eyes glowing. "You'll see!"

A few of them applauded vociferously as he jumped down from the wagon. Others glanced at each other and spread their hands uncertainly. Quine, his shoulders leaning negligently against the wall of the building, gave him a wink of unabashed cynicism. Simultaneously Aino Berg stepped out of the doorway to confront him.

"So," he said bitterly, "I was wrong about you. Ya, wery wrong."

His voice got under Johnny's skin. "What do you mean?"

"I did not tank you sell us out so cheap."

"Aino, I——"

"Fifty cents a day out of our pockets so you can look up dere—ya, dose fine red peaks, all heaven—and say, 'My railroad.'"

"That's not the way of it and you know—"

"Lackey!" Aino said. He swallowed as if spitting out the strange word came hard, but he managed. "Quine's lackey. Dyer's lackey. You like the taste of boots, ya?"

"Why, Aino! Tch, tch!" It was Pat Edgell's voice coming from the crowd pressing behind their shoulders. "You ought not bite the Great White Father's hand that way."

Johnny warned, "Let it alone, Pat," and turned back on Aino. The eyes of the bystanders rubbed like sandpaper. "Where you were wrong about me," he said, "was thinking I'd sit still and let you close every mine on the hill to suit a minority's end. That's what your union is up here, a minority. Count 'em!"

"I count one at a time. Right now I count you for what you are. Lackey! Vinkler's lackey!" Turning, he went heavily up the stairs.

Pat laughed softly. "Sucker!" he mocked.

"Let it alone, I said."

"Aino's more than half right at that. Quine and the boys sure did use you to pull their wage chestnuts out of the fire for them."

"Let it alone! You were sitting in the same room when I agreed to do what I could to help."

"Oh, you're always helping," Pat said. His flat eyes laughed; he made little sucking noises with his tongue against his teeth. "Some people just don't like the way you go about it." His face grew still. "Young Hedstrom, for instance. Me, for instance."

The hatred leaped naked. The cordon of faces pulled tighter and tighter. Somewhere in the back, bright-cruel with anticipation, a voice yelled, "Sic 'im, Johnny!"

Quine pushed between them. "Easy does it," he urged. He took each by an elbow, motioned with his head for Dyer to help, and shouldered them clear of the tightest part of the crowd. "Easy!" He aimed them toward the town hall, where, so the union officials had been given to understand, a committee of managers would await, unofficially, to hear the union's resolution about wages. "Let the union fight among themselves. That's what we want. But you're both on the management committee and this is no time for personal grudges to mix us up."

The insistent voice drowned the incoherent protests they tried to make. Dyer rolled over like a landslide and swept Pat off. Quine let go Johnny's elbow and said more affably, "I know how you feel. Edgell always was a sorehead. I had to dump him, too, you know. But up there in the hall, while we're waiting, you sit in your corner and let him sit in his. After we've settled what we're there for, then you can claw all you want. Fair enough?"

Johnny was still too unsettled to manage his words very well. As if searching for help his gaze lifted to the peaks, dropped to the hillocks through which the road wound past Aino's lost claim on its way to the summit, and settled bleakly up ahead on Pat's back. "I never went to fight him," he said thickly. "But when the things you do get taken and twisted and—"

"Sure, sure," Quine soothed. "The good of the country. We understand. Just take it easy, that's all. Very easy."

"5"

Time dragged. When the waiters in the town hall grew restive, Dyer rumbled, "Don't worry. The delay is a good sign. They're probably out beating up the boondocks trying to find signatures for their resolution. It isn't worth a damn without signatures. You've seen the fool thing, haven't you?"

They had. Dyer had bribed a union member for a copy of the document earlier in the day. It was a curious mixture of awkward formality and truculence: "Whereas $4.00 a day has been the established base wage in the Red Mountain mining district since the district's inception; and whereas the cost of living here is higher than elsewhere in the St. John Mountains due to transportation difficulties; and whereas, in comparison to the profits taken from the mines, $4.00 is no more than a fair return for a fair day's wage, be it resolved that the undersigned members and friends of the Mine and Mill Workers' Union hereby go on record as demanding. . . ." The threat "general strike" thereafter appeared three times.

The union's strategy, as Joe Dyer divined it, was to collect enough signatures to make the demand really sound like a demand. It was his and his committee's hope that enough defection had been sowed in the street to thwart the scheme. Reports from watchers stationed at strategic spots indicated that the end had been achieved. What next? All the managers could learn was that a hundred or so men were locked in the union hall, arguing and shouting at each other. To what end, the committee could not learn. An immediate strike while some cohesion still existed among the workers? A total capitulation? The managers argued among themselves and in their nervousness began tossing recriminations until Quine again moved blandly forward as peacemaker.

The hours limped. Quine thumbed a book brought from the reading room. Pat argued in one corner with a tax assessor who had dropped by to see what was afoot. Dyer started a pinochle game. Johnny played seven rounds of checkers with the manager of the Rose Marie and was so unsettled that he lost all but one.

Finally a little man with a gold collar button gleaming in his collarless shirt popped in the door. "They're comin'!" The waiters started to align themselves. Dyer rumbled, "You're not a damn bit excited. Sit still." They went back to what they had been doing and managed to appear almost indifferent when three members of the union appeared, bowler hats in hand and mud crusts to the tops of their knee boots. Dyer gave them the barest of glances.

The spokesman of the three twisted his hat in his hand and said that the union had unanimously passed a resolution which they would like to present.

Dyer shook his big round head. "We cannot surrender any of our responsibilities for the successful operation of the mines which the stockholders have entrusted to us. Wages are part of those responsibilities. We cannot accept any dictation about them."

They weren't dictating, the man said; they were presenting a few suggestions. If the managers would read—

"Let's see," Dyer said and held out his hand.

The others tried to read over his shoulder as he skipped through the revised document. The same whereas clauses. But the resolution part had been amended to "be it resolved that the undersigned representatives of the Mill and Mine Workers' Union hereby go on record as suggesting to the management . . ."

"Well, now," Dyer rumbled, "that's more reasonable. Now maybe we can talk."

Johnny read the list of official signatures on the resolution. Aino's name was not there. An ineffable sense of loss filled him. "Why didn't Aino Berg sign?" he asked the union spokesman.

The man shifted uncomfortably. "Aino resigned."

"Tch!" said Pat.

Some fulsome talk rolled around and the delegation departed. Behind them Dyer let out a roar of triumph. "Ha! Let's adjourn to the Tiptop! Drinks on the Dixie Girl! Ha! They're done!" He shredded the resolution and dropped the fragments into a cuspidor. "If the union ever had any prestige in this camp, they've lost it now. Representatives—that's the best they could do for signatures! 'We suggest!' The gutless wonders! Ogden, Quine!—great work, boys, great work! We won't even have to pretend to set up a sliding scale. They're through, the punks! Drinks on the Dixie Girl! Ha!"

They trooped to the Tiptop, but Johnny stayed only long enough to make sure that Aino was not at the dark corner of the bar, where he sometimes stood for an hour or more, nursing a single drink. Nor was he at any of the other saloons in town or at Slanting Annie's. The sense of loss growing in him, Johnny sought out Jan Pekkarine, a bearded patriarch who whittled on a bench outside the steam baths and watched the comings and goings in the Finnish section. No, Jan said, he had not seen Aino since morning.

Telling Lucille about it the next evening in Argent, Johnny said,

"Absolutely not to be found, as if he'd up and melted. Then I had a hunch. I went to where the road takes off toward the pass. It was almost dark by then. But a fellow was out sawing wood in front of his cabin. He said Aino had gone by on foot an hour or so earlier."

"Afoot over the pass at that time of day?" Lucille protested. "Why didn't he come to Argent? It would take him most of the night to walk to Baker."

Johnny was silent, staring at the same memory that had come to him the evening before at the foot of the tangled hillocks when his informant had looked up from sawing to say, "Why, yeah, I saw him a while back." And then Johnny had seen him too, six years ago, squatted outside his tunnel mouth, the black assay stain of insufficient silver on the copper sheet between them and he heard himself talking of bringing in a single mule train of supplies so that the boys could hang on a little longer against the teeth of winter and Aino's voice: *This place might amount to someting* and Aino's eyes: *A man might be someting too*; and from that Johnny's seeing had fled to the red slopes, tall chimneys smoking, corrugated roofs, dump cars grinding across the trestles. Well, he had said back at himself, Aino picked wrong, that's all. The side of the creek where Aino had filed on his claim never had produced anything.

Lucille's voice roused him. "I asked you why he went to Baker."

He shook himself. "I don't think he did."

"You said he started that way."

"His old claim is up that road."

"What's at the claim?"

"Nothing. The speculators that got hold of it never ran a foot of gallery. His same old plank door is closing the tunnel mouth, only Aino doesn't have a key that fits. I'm sorry now that I didn't follow him. But when I first decided where he was headed, I thought he'd rather be alone."

"The middle of the night—what on earth could he do there?"

"There was a moon. Maybe he figured to sit on a stump and look."

"And then?"

"He'll come back," Johnny said. "He hasn't hardly been off this mountain for the past six or seven years. He doesn't know anything but mining. No family—where else can he go?"

Lucille pictured the silvered loneliness at the claim. "Poor Aino," she grieved. Then she read her husband's face. Reaching out, she took his hand. "But what else could you have done?"

"I don't know," Johnny said. "I asked myself that all last night, and I just don't know. You can't block progress, like Aino tried to do."

IV

"1"

When, late in August 1887, the tracks of the Baker Northern Railway Company were open for travel across the pass, Red Mountain City did not parade or even dance in the streets. But there was dancing on flatcars and even on the station platform. No one planned it. It just happened, spontaneously, some eighteen hours ahead of what should have been the more exciting, formal arrival of the first scheduled passenger and freight combination.

The summit lay three miles in airline distance from Red Mountain City and twelve hundred feet higher. To gain this elevation in so short a distance, the Ogden Construction Company graded and laid six miles of curving, looping, narrow-gauge track. Completing the job in the short months of open weather available used up most of two summers, and even then Johnny had had to hire an extra hundred Mexican shovelers for grading out the last spurs leading to the principal mines. Barroom Cassandras laid bets among themselves that because of heavy snow in the late spring and heavy rains during the early summer he wouldn't make it on time. But he did, and he was feeling right pleased with himself when the work train glided down the hill from its final inspection run. Everything was clear for the morrow.

A fair-sized crowd was on hand when the engine eased with its three flatcars to a halt beside the brand-new depot, painted, naturally, a deep red. The smoke from the locomotive's flaring stack could be seen for miles streaming downward along the crimson slopes. Loiterers gathered. Lucille saw the smudge, kissed the three children—the new baby Henry was not quite a year old—told Nylander to put supper in the warming oven, and drove over in a buggy to pick up her husband. She found Winkler there, and Fred Fossett, whom Winkler had brought with him from Denver to go over certain accounts. Harmon Gregg and other hangers-on hovered near him. Sam Varnum was also on hand, escorting four visiting journalists—Al Ewer of *The True Fissure*; a man from Hillsdale, a farming community several miles below Argent; a bearded reporter from a Denver newspaper; and most awesome (Lucille could tell from Sam's voice as he made introductions) a slouched and cynical dude who was preparing a story for *Century* magazine on all the Colorado mining camps.

Clinging like mustard plaster to the dude's elbow was Rudolf Gassner.

Lucille made a face to herself. Rudolf Gassner was the newest and most aggressive member of the Argent city council. He had said thinly at the council's last meeting, remarks duly printed in *The True Fissure*, that letting Baker voices sound alone in the ears of the outside reporters during their Red Mountain visit would be a disaster to Argent, a town already suffering enough from the faithlessness of her one-time booster, Jack Ogden. To prevent further damage, Gassner had appointed himself official guide for the journalists. About two minutes after her introduction to the group, Lucille divined that his charges were thoroughly sick of him. With real pleasure she turned her back as if Gassner didn't exist and talked eagerly to Winkler. On this trip Otto simply must take time to stop by the house and see Henry. After all, he was the baby's godfather. Otto beamed and nodded.

Johnny exchanged some final words with the engineer and jumped from the cab. He waved at the idlers, unabashedly kissed his wife, shook hands with Winkler and Fossett—"If I'd known you were coming up this early I'd have fixed it for you to take a ride"—and then was surrounded by the word-pumpers. They worked on statistics for a while—elevations, depth of snow to be fought, yards of cut and fill, tonnages of freight that could be anticipated. With their cool eyes they measured the tiny flatcars and the dude from the East annoyed Johnny by saying, "I rode a narrow-gauge clear from Salida and they still seem like playthings. Aren't you being overoptimistic in thinking that by themselves they can revive the silver mining industry?"

"Improve it," Johnny said stiffly, "not revive it. It doesn't need reviving."

The dude lifted his eyebrows. He obviously enjoyed tormenting the natives. "As I walked through town earlier this afternoon, I noticed several empty houses and half a dozen places of business boarded up, including a restaurant and an assay shop. How do you explain that?"

Johnny glowered. "That's typical of you backcappers—counting the empty houses instead of the full ones. Look at those chimneys smoking up yonder, why don't you? That's what you came to write about, isn't it?"

Before the dude could retort, Sam Varnum jumped to the rescue. "The explanation needs no laboring. Small properties have been consolidating lately for the sake of efficiency or have been absorbed by larger neighbors. They do their own assaying, to answer your question, and a public shop is no longer necessary. As we introduce better machinery, ton output per man increases. The Ram's new management, for example, is producing more ore from greater depth than the old company did, yet at no increase in labor force."

"In spite of this increased productivity," the dude persisted, "I understand that wages are still depressed."

The reporter from Hillsdale picked it up. "What about a rumor I heard in town, Mr. Ogden, that as soon as the railroad is operating, you will raise your own wage scale and that the mines may then follow?" He smiled apologetically. "Not to be snooping into your business, but our farmers are interested. They naturally feel that if wages are better here, they can sell you more apricots and beans, beef and mutton— you understand."

Johnny glanced uncomfortably toward Lucille. He was in a trap of his own making. She was frequently coming home with wrenching tales learned through the Altar Society or Jenny Shaffer or through her own visiting, of families who could not buck emergencies of accident or illness on the pay they were bringing home. He had quietly discussed with a few of the mine managers the advisability of passing on to the men some of the savings wrought by increased efficiency. Opposed to the suggestion was the compromise which he himself had helped push through in the spring of '86, a compromise which had nearly destroyed the union and which explicitly tied wages to the price of silver.

"It's silver that's depressed, not wages," he told the reporters glumly. "If we could pry some action out of Washington, you'd see a different story overnight." He concentrated on the dude. "Put that in your magazine for the gold bugs back East to read."

The Hillsdale man kept pushing. "I hear that Joe Dyer at the Dixie Girl is the main obstacle to a reconsideration of the scale."

A miner's voice growled from the background, "Dyer! You could colonize ten thousand souls the size of his on the point of a pin and each one would still have as much room as a bullfrog in the Atlantic Ocean."

Al Ewer, rounder of face and shaggier of mustache than ever, grunted "Haw!" in appreciation and recorded the saying in his notebook. Al knew the mountains and what the mountains liked. Long since, Johnny and he had gotten over their differences, and Johnny appealed to him for help now.

"Several of the mines have been stockpiling their ore for weeks, waiting to ship it on the railroad. A lot of that ore is of lower grade than was ever shipped before. If the railroad proves able to handle it, more and more marginal areas will come into production." He nodded vehemently at the dude. "That'll open up more jobs. That'll bring in more people." He looked at the Hillsdale reporter. "That's what'll push up wages, too." He saw Sam Varnum smile wryly and knew why. The old theme: *Make everything bigger and watch your troubles fade away.* Belligerently he demanded, "That's right, ain't it, Sam? Ain't it, Al?"

Sam shrugged. "If it's not, we've surely been fooling ourselves."

Nor was Ewer quite ready to join the defense. "Speaking of bigger and better transportation," he said, "what about the railroad between here and Argent? Have any dates been set yet?"

"A very good question," Rudolf Gassner snapped, "and one that lots of people in Argent want answered."

Mainly bald-headed Roscoe Blair would like it answered, Johnny thought. The completion of the railroad through Baker was going to siphon away to Montezuma most of the Red Mountain ore that Blair had been treating. He was convinced that the whole thing was the plot of a smelter monopoly. First the monopoly would crush him personally; then it would fasten its tentacles on the entire St. John Mountains, in order to replace Democratic office holders (Roscoe was on the county Democratic central committee) with Republicans devoted to plunder, pelf, and by some unexplained connection, to the English monarchy. Blair wrote frequent letters of alarm about the scheme to *The True Fissure*, demanding exposure of all wickedness in high places, and when Ewer needed filler material he sometimes printed a letter for comic relief. Johnny, though, didn't find the matter very funny. Blair's chief political ally in his cries for action was Rudolf Gassner; and since John Ogden had allowed himself, in their view, to become a tool of the Montezuma cabal, Johnny was the one who received some of their most energetic thumps.

No one took the pair very seriously, but in time their stridence did grow tiresome. After all, Blair could have made better use of his energy in trying to find new business among the mines near Argent. Walt Kennerly was adapting without fuss, wasn't he? Walt stood to lose a lot of ore haulage to the railroad; but instead of bellyaching he was replacing some of his wagons with stagecoaches, convinced that during summers a considerable number of sightseers would ride the Baker Northern to Red Mountain and that he could make a good thing out of whirling them on down the gorge to Argent. But that sort of adjustment was too imaginative for people like Roscoe Blair and Gassner. They just sat and howled, like the dog on the burr—too dead to move.

"I've run one grade survey down the gorge at my own expense," Johnny told Gassner mildly. It had been a hair-raising feat, dangling surveyors on ropes over the cliffs so that they could direct other danglers where to put daubs of paint on the rock in lieu of grade stakes. A forbidding six-and-a-half-per-cent climb had been the gentlest he could work out; and attaining even that meant tunnels and tight curves that would reduce locomotive efficiency. Still, it could be done. "I know how to build the road," he said. "All you have to do to get it started tomorrow is find me the money. Do you think maybe the Argent city council, instead of complaining would guarantee, say the interest on a bond issue, just to help get what it claims to want?"

Gassner went up on his toes in outrage. "Why on earth should the town hand feed you?" He swung his sarcastic regard toward Otto Winkler, standing quietly with Lucille to one side of the bickering. "It might be edifying, at that, to know just how much support Baker and Montezuma gave you, at the taxpayers' expense, to bring the railroad *their* way."

No muscle of Otto's face moved, yet the jet eyes and the pendulous lips managed to express profound contempt. He had turned completely gray during the past few years, his skin as sallow as stale dough. He had always possessed patience; to it he had gradually added an abhorrence of the sort of altercation into which Gassner was trying to drag him now. (He didn't even like ceremony. If the mountain towns wished to celebrate the completion of the Baker Northern, that was their affair; but Otto refused to appear publicly. And indeed Baker would launch tomorrow's train with speechmaking, but Red Mountain, to Johnny's resigned disappointment, had taken its cue from Otto and was not planning anything.)

To Gassner's slur he replied quietly, "Jealousy is not goot mit any-ones, towns or peoples."

Gassner flushed. "You're begging the issue. It isn't a matter of jealousy. It's a question of morals."

That was a fool thing to say, Johnny thought and looked anxiously at Otto. The least shadow of unhappiness touched Winkler's face, as if what he had to do truly hurt him.

"So?" he said. "Der support Montezuma gifs iss beds of coal. Hvat you gif is der biggest canyon der mountain in. If you und Roscoe Blair don't like der goot Lord's arrangements, maybe letters you should write to Him in His heffen, und not to der *True Fissure*. Eh, Ewer?"

"It would save type," Ewer agreed and everyone snickered. Gassner's cheekbones turned as deep a red as the mountain. To mollify him,

perhaps, Ewer returned to the question of the railroad through the
gorge. Had Johnny's survey resulted in any definite plans?

Again Johnny looked at Otto. He did not say a word and it was
Johnny who had to answer.

"No," he admitted and glared at Gassner's snort of I-told-you-so.
"There will be one, though. As soon as we have more population and
more tourist travel and more produce moving up from Argent, there'll
have to be a railroad. It just isn't reasonable to leave that eight-mile
gap unconnected."

The Hillsdale man asked, "Do you agree with that prophecy, Mr.
Winkler?"

Otto stood motionless, hands clasped behind him, bearded head
lolled slightly forward, his underlip showing moistly. Then he said, his
big smile breaking suddenly,

"Schonny, dese gentlemen might like to see dot turntable you built.
Noddings like it anywhere else in der world, I dink. Dot's a story, eh?"

"Why, sure," Johnny said. For a flickering second, disappointment
at Otto's evasion touched him. But almost at once pleasure took over.
That turntable was unique, and he had planned it where the professional engineers had failed. Furthermore, it was solid and direct and
tangible, its tensions reducible to clear formula. This he could move
about with at ease. This he could explain to reporters with their remote
eyes and their notebooks as bottomless as wells. Sly old Otto! He
knew how to avoid those pits. And he'd gotten Johnny out too.

"Why, sure, we can ride up on the train now and see it if you want."

His smile broadened—absolutely new. Not even Lucille had seen it
yet, though he had drawn a dozen plans of it for her on scratch pads
and tablecloths. He gave her a questioning glance. She nodded, caught
by the quick excitement, and with an answering impulsiveness he
swung his arm in a gesture like a great hooked scythe, tumbling everyone on the platform toward the three empty flatcars standing behind
the sighing locomotive.

"Let's everybody go!"

That was how the dance started, though even then no one had any
real idea of making a mountain-wide party out of the ride.

"2"

The engineer tooted his whistle to draw still more people and then
took the train down to the wye to turn it about for its climb back up
the hill. At that point Lucille had a second thought—"My clothes!"—

but a brakeman produced coveralls into which she wriggled in the ladies' waiting room in the depot. Baggy though they were, the striped garment caught the line of her hips in such a way that Johnny whistled "Hey now!" and gripped her tight as he boosted her up the gritty iron steps into the cab of the busy little goat, as the crew called the diminutive work engine. The two "foreign" reporters and Harmon Gregg followed, finding room in the half-empty tender.

People racing down the street scrambled onto the flatcars. When they were aboard, the engineer motioned with his head toward the Johnson bar: did John want to drive? Oh, absolutely! Proud as a boy, he slid onto the padded leather cushion and leaned out the window to see the track ahead, every sleeper laid, every spike fixed by his decision and by the labor of his men. Otto's company, but not Otto's rails. Tonight at least the road was Red Mountain's.

He twisted a valve, eased the bar. The locomotive moved "as gentle," the engineer said, "as a duchess passing cups." Johnny grinned. "First time I did it," he admitted, "I jerked out the hind shack's false teeth and had to buy him a new set. We entered it in the books under fish-plates. Get it—plates?" They all held their noses and he laughed in delight.

The engine buckled down to work, cylinder cocks spitting. Pulling his bandana over the lower part of his face as protection, the fireman threw open the firebox door on a seething red mass that made Lucille shrink. He stirred it grandly with his rake, seized his shovel, and threw in coal. In spite of the reinforcement, speed slowed. The grade was steep, the curves compressed. Johnny opened the throttle still more. The engine shook and roared; cinders stormed and even the smoke seemed to strain. The cry of the wheels changed subtly with each change in the radius of the curve or the type of support underneath. To Johnny every tone was a problem mastered: when to cut through the point of a hill instead of bending around it; how high to lift the outside rail on the curves; how much expansion gap to leave between the joints; when to change from culverts to pile bridges, when to resort to trestles. Trained engineers had platted each foot of the way, but he had not let a single solution slide by without worrying out its reasons for himself. Often he annoyed the men with his picking at details, but sometimes, because he knew the country better than they did, he was able to offer refinements or check losses.

"We used red spruce for ties," he told the group in the cab. "Most of it for this end of the road came from that hill over there at the head of the gorge—above where we lived in tents, Lucy. Well, after while the spruce got hard to snake out. So this feller Wolfinger cuts some ordinary fir that was easy to reach and drags it through the red mud below an old prospect dump and lets the mud soak in and cake on good, and delivers the fir as red spruce. I was off in Baker seeing about a new commissary crew to take over the cook shack. A couple of junior engineers hardly out from behind their books at the state university accepted those fir pieces and when I got back there was three hundred and seventy ties had to be tore out and replaced. Well, I guess they know what red spruce looks like now."

"Did you fire them?"

"No need. They were mortified enough. Turned into right smart hands."

The rails rounded a low bluff, ceased their climb, and tilted slightly downward. Another track came down to join them at an acute angle from the right, from the direction of the summit. The stem of the wye beyond the junction was sheltered by a round log building whose roof looked like an inverted funnel. The track on either side of the structure was protected by snowsheds that extended outward from it like stubby arms.

"There's a turntable in there," Johnny explained. "We had to roof the table so's blizzards couldn't pack into the works and stop operations in winter."

"A turntable big enough to swing this whole train?" the Hillsdale reporter asked skeptically.

"Just the engine," Johnny answered. He all but effervesced with pride; this was his creation. "Watch!"

He halted the goat just short of the switch where the tracks joined. The crew set the brakes on the flatcars and uncoupled the engine. Johnny clattered it on into the shed, under the round roof. There the turntable spun it completely about. He ran back out again; the switch was thrown and the goat headed up the track toward the summit. Immediately above the flatcars he halted the engine and grinned amiably down out of the cab window on the mystified excursionists below. The switch was thrown again, the brakes on the flatcars released. They coasted by gravity through the sheds and halted. The engine backed up, hooked onto the opposite end of the cars from where it had been a moment before and went huffing on up the hill.

"Typical of Colorado," the dude reporter said, the purse of his lips showing that actually he was impressed. "Ever since I got in these mountains I haven't known whether I was coming or going. I suppose you flipped us like this to save building a long curve."

Johnny nodded. "The only other way to make the grade would have been to run clear across Corkscrew Gulch yonder and bend back in a muleshoe—that's what we call a narrow-gauge horseshoe curve. It would have meant another half-mile of rails and two high trestles, one with a bend in it. The trestles probably wouldn't have lasted anyhow. About every fourth year a hell of a snowslide peels the gulch; you notice there isn't anything bigger than a willow bush in it. We had to shy clear and this is what we came up with." Or rather he'd come up with it. He had just been wrestling on paper with the problem of turntables and wyes for the end of the line at Red Mountain City, and it occurred to him that the two devices might be combined high on the side of the peak as a way to avoid the gulch. "They tell me there's not another one like it in the world," he said. "I was too dumb to know that. So I happened to think of it when trained engineers didn't. It saved money too."

"Why have the turntable? Why not just run out onto the stem of an ordinary wye, throw the switch and back on up the hill?"

"You can't back up in snow. Anyway, backing isn't safe in this country, where there are so many blind curves and places for rocks to roll onto the tracks."

The demonstration was completed, and sunset was pinking the high, thin cirrus clouds. He might as well have returned. But a deep sense of well-being kept him pushing the goat upward in a triumph of smoke and flying sparks. They rattled past the spurs dropping toward the larger mines and hooted the whistle at the wagon roads leading to the hill-enfolded post-office hamlets. Shifts had changed. Day workers were outside enjoying the twilight. Hearing the busy noise of the train, they drifted curiously toward the track, wondering what errand was bringing it along so stridently at this time of day. Their wives looked out of cabin doors or hurried with them toward the grade crossings, drying their hands on their aprons as they went.

The regular engineer pointed toward a pair of knee-length feminine drawers fluttering from one trackside clothesline. "The widow Cafky. She hangs 'em out for Sugarfoot as a sign she's ready for a date."

"That's a damn lie!" the fireman cried. "She don't hang out nothin' but a blue towel."

"Whatever it is," said Johnny, "why don't you go get her? We'll pick you up on our way back and you can take her along for a night on the town."

"You mean that!"

"Sure. Get going before we hit the trestle!"

"Who'll fire?"

"Harmon will."

"We all will," Harmon amended.

"Gee-rusalem!" Sugarfoot breathed. He swung down the steps, jumped from the slow-moving goat, sprawled flat, picked himself up, and galloped off through the skunk cabbage.

The townspeople on the flatcars were waving to the watchers along

the line and shouting, "Come on! Come on! Let's have us a party!"
The watchers stared. "You mean? . . . Look at old Sugarfoot go! A
party! Why not?" Men on the flatcars leaped impulsively off and, like
Sugarfoot, ran down the roads hollering and waving their hats: "Party
in town! The train'll pick us up on the way back! Everybody out! Party
in town!" No time to hesitate over dishes or babies or how one would
feel on the job in the morning. A patting of hair, a bundling of
children, a gathering of coats. Some reached for mouth organs, some
for fiddles. Some ran for the neighbors. "Oh hurry!" A scrambling up
the hillside to wait for the return: the thin, high song of approaching
wheels to eager ears laid against the rails; a flicker of yellow light through
the gathering darkness. "Here she comes!"

Harmon and the reporters had fired manfully. Often, as they braced
their feet against the floor and swung the scoop, they hit the edge of
the firebox door with a corner of the shovel and sprayed the cab with
coal—to the scorn of the engineer, who, however, contributed nothing
but advice. But they maintained steam. At Summit they picked up
another flatcar from a siding and loaded it with people. Then Johnny
turned the train on the wye and relinquished the throttle to the
engineer, for whom he found a volunteer fireman. With Lucille he
walked back along the flatcar until he spotted Winkler. They joined
him, sitting in a row and dangling their legs over the edge.

At the Beartown siding they picked up one more flatcar loaded with
merrymakers, and still another at the Dixie Girl spur. Above them star
clusters shone; below, cabin lights followed the curves of the hillocks to
the prickly brightness of the town. Now and then the engine whistled
softly as the engineer signaled for the shacks to club down on the hand
brakes as he slowed to pick up partygoers waving frantically on the ties
ahead. Then on again. Wheels clacked. The headlight's beam slanted
against fir branches and red granite walls. When the stoker opened the
firebox door, red light threw a weird, shifting glow against the drift of
smoke and steam. At the rear of the car where Johnny sat, an Italian
played softly on an accordion.

For a long time he did not speak. Then memory touched him and
he said to Winkler, "Come to think of it, this is what brought my
father West—building railroads, I mean."

Lucille said, "I wish I'd known him. I wish he could have known his
grandson."

Little Henry, Winkler's godson. Otto had given him a cup made of
silver mined from the Ram, the same ore that was building this railroad.
"He's not a year old and he's already pounded a dent in it," Johnny said,
in no wise apologetic. "He's a right husky boy."

Ewer wormed up beside them. "I swiped a saying from that dude reporter and wrote a poem about this ride for the *Fissure*," he said. "Want to hear it?"

"Sure."

"'A jackass would have to have hinges to negotiate those curves,'" Al declaimed. "That's not the poem, just the introduction. This is the poem:

> It doubles in, it doubles out,
> Leaving the traveler still in doubt,
> Whether the engine on the track
> Is going on or coming back."

"That's rich, Al."

"It's a great road, Johnny."

"We'll get a greater one down the gorge."

"Now that I've seen the turntable and the rest, damned if I don't believe you can do it. When?"

Johnny glanced sideways at Otto. "When things are ripe enough."

Winkler did not answer. Perhaps he had not heard. He sat humped under his cloak, gray and shrunken and remote, staring into the night, his lower lip pendulous and his bearded head shaking slightly from side to side.

Much later Johnny grumbled to Lucille about the unresponsiveness. The train had pulled into the depot; the musicians had formed themselves into a band; dancers were frolicking in the waiting room, on the platform, even on the flatcars. Johnny and Lucille were among the latter, above the shifting figures and clapping hands on the platform, not dancing so much as moving somnolently back and forth at the end of the car, bumping occasionally into the round brake wheel. Otto long since had slipped away to the hotel.

"Poor old Otto," he said. "His wife sits home in that farmhouse at Saguache, taking care of her cats and chickens and her parrot, and lets him go off alone to build his roads. I like my wife handier, for nights like this."

Her palm tightened against his back. He could see the shine of her eyes in the dim glow from the waiting room lights. "I'm proud of you, Johnny."

The restiveness took hold of him again. "It's only half done, though, and everybody in Argent knows it is, I don't care what kind of poems Ewer writes."

"Don't worry about it now."

"A road through the gorge is the most logical thing in the world. But every time it comes up, Otto sidesteps. Haven't you noticed?"

"You're always telling me how cautious he is: look before you yump."

"Just the same, it's hard to see every bit of it there in front of you and still have to wait."

"You'll do it, Johnny. I know you will."

He pulled her closer. The engine made little clicking noises; the peaks were a darkness against the dark of the sky. A bright star whose name he did not know hung moist-looking above the V of the gorge. Wait. Wait. But not now. Like she'd said, that was tomorrow's worry.

"Let's go home," he said.

V

"1"

He prospered while he waited. The toll station beside the gorge road reaped an increasing harvest of silver coins. He improved the stone quarry and extended the gas-company lines. He became fascinated by and built two aerial tramways that carried iron ore buckets on cables stretched between wooden towers striding down hillsides and across gulches. He added to the log house in the mountains and to the white and green clapboard one in Argent, until the latter became the show mansion of the town, many-gabled, with bays and turrets and shady porches inside the ells.

His returns from the hills to these houses were great events for the family. The children clamored to romp with him. Dutifully he picked crumbs off the wads of spruce gum they brought him and popped the amber mass into his mouth as if he truly enjoyed it. During the winter he coasted endlessly with them on Vinegar Hill, and in summer led them on their ponies endlessly around the hillocks of Red Mountain. He showered the girls with more toys and picture books and flaxen-haired dolls than Lucille thought they should have, and made more plans for Henry than the boy could possibly grow up to fulfill.

Seldom could she make him relax for long. Sometimes, on impulse, he would pile the entire family into a wagon and drag them off to camp beside coiling trout streams in the unspoiled forests along the lower slopes of the mountains. In the fall he liked to hunt with Walt or Spec Alden and other cronies. He learned to breathe deep on these outings, he said. But in two or three days he chafed to return, convinced that during his absence something at home or on the mountain had crumbled into fragments without his overseeing eye. Occasionally he took Lucille to Denver on his business trips, and once they went with Nora and Harmon as far as California; but the same itching restlessness always brought him home sooner than he had planned when leaving.

In town he drank a good deal and played poker for sizable stakes at the Silver City Club. Generally he lost; no one seemed to have trouble divining when he was running a bluff. Attracted by his phenomenal zest and physical strength, the discontented wives of recently arrived engineers or merchants sometimes endeavored to start flirtations. Often he wasn't aware of what they were up to, and always he returned to the mountains unperturbed, leaving them puzzled and sometimes angry. He was completely in love with his wife. In 1889, during the eighth year of their marriage, she bore him his fourth and last child, a boy whom they named Walter. Only occasionally did John think to mention Lennie and then generally when Lucille's abstraction made him aware that once again she had been to the cemetery with flowers.

Neither of them forgot the dread of the pest house, however. When Jess Carstairs inaugurated a drive to add refinements to the new county hospital, both participated eagerly. Lucille and the Altar Society worked diligently throughout February and March of 1890 to prepare an evening's entertainment in the Opera House. They acted *The Wild Irishman,* and Lucille herself recited dramatically Shamus O'Brien's "St. Peter at the Gate." Afterwards there was a dance. The net for the hospital turned out to be $113. She was disconsolate.

"Such an unresponsive town! Everyone agrees we need that equipment. But who does anything?"

"You went at it the wrong way," he said.

She bridled. "You could do better, no doubt."

"Sure."

"I dare you."

"All right." His increasingly florid face grew excited. He knew his town. "A real stemwinder of a party! I'll show you!"

He spoke to the manager of the new Belmont Hotel, an imposing three-story building of red brick, standing on the site of the old Dixon House. The entire county was proud of the white marble arches above the windows on the front façade, of the golden-oak woodwork inside, of the lofty ceilings in the rooms, of the steam heat and the bathrooms and water closets on every floor. But they were proudest of the soaring rotunda encasing the lobby and of the grand staircase that rose majestically to a landing decorated with imitation marble statues of seminude Greeks. At the landing, the staircase split in twain and soared on to a promenade that circled the space below. People came from miles to look over the railing and to see the ballroom, which was also two stories high. Halfway up one wall was an alcove where musicians in stiff white shirts and long-tailed black coats played for formal affairs.

At first the manager of so much magnificence was dubious about turning the hotel over to the kind of party Johnny proposed, but the purpose behind it finally won him. Next Johnny visited the tenderloin side of town and talked to Argent's six leading gamblers. They needed no persuasion. Briskly they set up dice and twenty-one tables in the rotunda; roulette, faro, and poker in the ballroom. *The True Fissure* then stridently invited the town to buck the tiger for the sake of the hospital. The games were guaranteed honest. The gamblers would retain a small percentage only of their winnings and turn the rest over to Carstairs. Players who chanced to win could donate as their consciences dictated. To keep the games going as long as possible, the hotel bar agreed to serve a high-priced buffet supper (profits to the hospital) at one o'clock, and the musicians agreed to play at least until three.

The affair glittered. Lavish gowns were hurriedly ordered or made; hairdressers and barbers were frantic; and at Ewer's earnest entreaty Lucille consented to serve again as his fashion reporter, describing in advance, as a form of publicity, the silk embroideries, appliques, lace-trimmed basques, hairdos, and whatnot that would appear on the memorable evening.

Anyone who was anyone bought tickets. Those who weren't came to mingle with them. A string of stagecoaches rattled down from Red Mountain; a special train came up from Hillsdale. Toward dawn, after the empty champagne bottles had been toted away, the various committees in charge of the event gathered with the hotel manager and the gamblers to make a rough estimate of the take.

Lucille sat up with the rest of them. Wearing a new diamond brooch Johnny had given her and dressed in a cream-colored silk, cut décolleté, that had stunned every woman there, she had had a wonderful time. She had cautiously played roulette with chips whose value she did not know and had lost. For the first time in her life she had grown giddy on wine. She had danced waltzes, schottisches, fox trots, polkas, and two-steps. Now she was flushed and tired and headachy. She wanted to go to bed, but she was still keyed up by the excitement; and the suspense of the growing figures kept her sitting up over one of the green baize tables, her chin in the palm of a shoulder-length white glove, while the gamblers clicked through their figures with impassive efficiency.

The hospital was richer by nearly four thousand dollars.

"Why," Lucille protested, "that's more than thirty times what we made with our Altar Society benefits, and not half the work!"

"You wanted money, didn't you?" Johnny said.

"It's too bad it had to be this way."

He held himself, knowing what she would say if he pressed her. They had been through much the same contention over Slanting Annie's box house. Argument led nowhere. That was the way she was, and had been ever since Lennie's death. But considering the purposes of this party and the way she obviously had enjoyed the evening, he had not supposed she would raise the objections. Most of all he was embarrassed to have her do it in front of the people who had done so much to ensure success. He gave them an apologetic shrug and Carstairs came to his rescue, saying dryly,

"I don't imagine that the babies who will be helped by this money will grow up worrying about how it got here. Right, Spec?"

Put on the spot, Barnabas Alden smiled his square white smile and tried to straddle. "I suppose the real charm of such a party is that it lets people feel virtuous while doing an act which might otherwise be regarded as a bit—er—wicked, if you'll excuse the term for the sake of the argument," he added, nodding formally to the head gambler, who returned the nod just as gravely and said, "Every man to his trade, Reverend." Alden eyed him suspiciously, regathered himself and continued, "People will pay well for that kind of feeling—sin condoned. I confess that I wish it weren't so, but there it is. As for tonight, I can't believe that anyone will be hurt by their fling, while many others will be helped later. Let us hope therefore that the Lord will forgive whatever needs forgiving."

Again he bowed to the gambler, who bowed back, saying, "Thank you. We'll remember you in our prayers, too."

"Anyway," Johnny said cheerfully, "I'll bet there isn't another town in the St. Johns that could raise practically four thousand dollars for charity at one party. Good old Argent and Red Mountain—you'll need to get up early to beat them, you'll have to admit."

Thus assaulted, Lucille fell silent. But when they were finally home and undressing for bed, she picked up her objections again.

"I'll admit the party was fun. Just the same, it's too easy to get cocky this way. Unhook my top button, please."

Johnny unhooked them all and kissed her between the shoulder blades, above the corset stays. "What way?"

"Buying whatever we want. It's too easy. We have too much."

"Want me to unlace this sheet-metal corset? Too much what?"

"Too much everything. Stop that, it's late. Everyone of these towns thinks it can have anything it wants just by paying the price."

Rebuffed, he said sulkily, "You heard Carstairs and Alden. What you're doing counts some, doesn't it?"

"It's the way we do it, wantonly, throwing down silver dollars on the

roulette table with the big grand gestures because we think we're—
you're not listening. You don't care."

"Frankly, I don't know what you're talking about."

She sat down at her dresser and rubbed cream into her tired face.
"Don't you grow grand just because you can throw down a dollar—I
suppose that's what I really mean. Oh, Johnny, sometimes I'm afraid."

"Of what?"

"Of having more than we deserve."

Which the Altar Society hadn't had out of its work: maybe that was
what was still bothering her. "There's not much use doing these things
if you can't make them work out as big as possible," he said idly and
wandered to the window, bored with the talk. The first pallor of dawn
was lighting the teeth of the peaks lining the amphitheater above Vinegar Hill. "If we were in a road camp now, it'd be coming breakfast
time. Hungry?"

She shook her head. "Just tired."

"Well, I could use some eggs," he said and padded downstairs in his
bare feet to shake up the kitchen range.

"2"

At Red Mountain a few weeks later—a Tuesday morning, July 15, 1890,
while he was finishing a second cup of coffee, he glanced through the
window and saw a messenger boy peddling a bicycle furiously out from
town. "That's it!" he yelled at Lucille. He rushed outside. The red-
faced boy, breathless from strain manufactured in hope of a tip, held
out a yellow envelope.

"From Washington?" Johnny asked. Days ago he had made arrangements with the secretary of western Colorado's representative in Congress to have the results of the vote on the Sherman Silver Purchase
Act wired to him as soon as they were known.

"How should I know where it come from?" the boy said righteously.

Johnny ripped open the envelope, closed his eyes superstitiously
for a moment, and then read. "Wow!" He wheeled toward Lucille,
checked himself, and turned back to the boy. He pulled a silver dollar
from his pocket.

"When you tell your own kids about the biggest thing that ever happened to Red Mountain, remember today!"

He tossed the dollar into the air, letting it sparkle in the sun. The
boy jumped high to meet it. A nickel tip was average; dimes came from

drunks or at the announcement of births; quarters were simply dreamed about. A dollar! The lad didn't mount his bicycle but pushed it along beside him while he walked and stared at the pale glory cupped in his hand.

Johnny bounded up the porch steps, lifted each child high for a kiss, and put his arm around Lucille's waist. "Look at it, honey! Night letter straight from Washington—the biggest news in the St. Johns since—oh, since the Utes left without a fight. Four and a half million ounces of silver purchased by the Treasury each and every month! That's double what they've been buying under the old Bland Act. Watch silver prices now—and wages. I told Aino just last Thursday, over at Walt's stable. Of course, it isn't free coinage yet. Bimetallism, sixteen to one, that's what we want. But it's a start. The rest will come . . . Listen!"

The steam whistle at the Ram had begun to blow. The Dixie Girl picked it up. Soon the wail, punctuated by the crump of giant powder, was pouring onto the town from every side. He nodded benignly. "The telegraph office must be phoning the news to all the mines."

She smiled at him, fondly and a bit impatiently. "You didn't have to have that telegram. You could have waited a few minutes and found out like everyone else."

"I wanted to know first."

"And now?"

"Now," he said, "I want to talk to Winkler about him extending the railway down the gorge. If he moves fast enough, we could even get started this fall!"

"3"

He missed Otto in Saguache. Mrs. Winkler, rocking on the front porch between two canary cages, told him that immediately on receipt of the news of the Sherman Act, her husband had gone to Denver to talk to his bankers about various projects. "About extending the Baker Northern?" Johnny asked. She looked vague; Otto didn't bring his business home with him; she didn't know what he had in mind.

"I'll catch him in Denver," Johnny said. No hurry; Otto probably had a dozen projects on tap, including the gorge road. His memory aroused by the unusual visit to the sleepy town, he lay over another day and used the time to visit his father's grave. It was unkempt; the wooden marker was awry, rain-blackened, almost illegible. He hunted up the local coroner, who also doubled as undertaker and tombstone salesman, and made arrangements to have the plot cleaned and fenced, and a marble stone erected. That evening as he jogged out of town in a rented livery buggy to the railroad junction, he resolved that as soon as he reached Denver he would write his mother and sisters, both of the latter now married and starting families of their own in the East. Must be months since I've written them direct, he thought. Actually it had been more than two years and correspondence had been limited to Lucille's Christmas notes. A man ought not lose track that way. But that night in the smoking car he met a promoter with a scheme for building a railroad from Crested Butte into the Elk Mountains. They talked until nearly two in the morning and he forgot about the letters.

In Denver he sought out Fossett, ensconced now in a high-ceilinged bank office, and learned that Winkler had left, in the company of various financiers and engineers, for Montezuma. Fred put his fingertips together and blinked importantly through his pince-nez.

"You know, of course, that for a couple of years Otto has been projecting a railroad from Montezuma around the southern and western flanks of the St. Johns, to tap the new lumber and cattle and mining country over there. The line will be a hundred and fifty or more miles long—an ambitious undertaking."

Johnny's heart sank. "I heard. But I guess I didn't pay much attention —too far out of my field." He grimaced wryly, remembering the promoter he had talked to. "Seems like everybody's got a railroad on the make."

"A new proposal comes in here every week," Fossett said. "It takes considerable discernment to distinguish the few that are practical from the many that are pipe dreams."

"Has Otto talked any about extending the Baker Northern on down the gorge to Argent?"

Fossett skirted the question. "To tell the truth, he's been occupied with the Montezuma project to the exclusion of everything else." The banker dropped his voice and leaned across his desk. "This is unofficial and in confidence, but Otto is planning on pushing that Montezuma line completely around the mountains and hooking onto the Argent branch below the Narrows. If all goes as scheduled, I'm sure he'll give the Ogden Construction Company an opportunity to bid on the grading over Horsefly Mesa and on down Bobcat Creek at least as far as the San Miguel River."

He leaned back in his swivel chair and waited for Johnny's smile. It didn't come. Johnny glanced at the brief case on the floor beside his chair. It was stuffed with engineering studies of the gorge.

"I was wanting to talk to him about the Baker Northern," he said.

Fred picked up a piece of paper, rattled it, and laid it down. "Johnny," he advised like a father-confessor, "I realize that this gorge project has been on your mind since—for a long time. I hate to give you bitter pills to swallow. But if you'll accept my advice, and I know Otto Winkler as well as anyone does if I do say so myself, this isn't the time to go to him about a railroad in the gorge."

"I see." The taste was bitter all right. "The gorge is peanuts to him now. Well, it's not peanuts to Argent. Or to Red Mountain."

Fred sighed and took off his pince-nez and rubbed his nose. "Face the facts, John. As long as there are no coal beds or smelting facilities near Argent, the bulk of Red Mountain's revenue-producing freight— ore and concentrate—will go out through Baker and on down Los Padres Canyon to Montezuma. Sentiment can't change economics." Fossett held up a small white hand, checking Johnny's retort. "That's right—sentiment. Otto sat in the very chair you're in now, talking about you and the gorge. 'For Schonny, iss a thing of pride, not sense,' he said. I'm afraid he's right. Now hear me out! We're inclined to see things the way we want to see them, not the way they are. Otto's advice is more unbiased. Not being bound up with Argent the way you are, he perhaps views the gorge project more clearly."

A thing of pride! Was that the size to which Otto would reduce this? Bleakly Johnny said, "He didn't worry about my pride when he came in on the wagon road and the things that grew out of it, including the Baker Northern."

"He saw balancing circumstances."

"Circumstances are better now than they ever were. The Sherman Act has started silver prices rising again. Red Mountain is bound to grow. They'll want more products from the farms. There'll be more tourist traffic. These things feed on each other. I've seen it happen again and again, ever since I and Pat Edgell helped put that first road over from San Cristobal."

"Otto thinks that the development has reached its limits, at least as far as steam locomotives in the gorge are concerned."

"Do you?"

"I haven't studied the situation in detail. Anyway, it's Otto's business."

"Well, I've studied it and I know it's good. A thing of pride? All right, I am proud of Argent and of Red Mountain—yes, and proud of what I've done there. I aim to stay that way. From where I sit, it's when you quit being proud, that's when they might as well cart you off, because then you are through."

"No one said anything about being through. You can have the Horsefly contract if you want it."

"I'm not sure I do," Johnny said. An idea was beginning to bloom, springing almost full-flower from the talk he had had with the railroad promoter he had met en route from Saguache. He told Fossett about the encounter and about the fellow's cockiness concerning money. "He said Colorado is railroad-crazy right now. He rattled off a whole list of major projects that have been completed during the past four years. The Missouri Pacific, the Rock Island, and the Denver, Texas and Fort Worth have come into the state from the outside. The Denver and Rio Grande, the Colorado Southern, the Midland, and I forget what others he named are either building new lines over the mountains or are expanding services already established. Those are facts too, aren't they?"

"Yes," Fossett admitted.

"On the basis of facts like those, this fellow was ready to promote a line of his own into country not as good as ours. He says there's worlds of capital ready to listen to sound plans for opening areas that haven't been tapped."

"That is exactly what Otto is doing beyond Montezuma, tapping new country. After all, Red Mountain has one line."

"I'm not talking about Otto. I'm talking about me. Maybe about you too, if you've nerve enough." Fossett looked alarmed and rustled through his papers, but Johnny allowed him no chance to interrupt. "Suppose I build my own road—the Argent Southern, say—up the gorge and join the Baker Northern at Red Mountain."

Fossett rattled his papers in agitation. "A bank works with other people's money. It has to be more conservative than its officers sometimes wish."

"I'm not after the bank's money—yet. First, though, what's your opinion about this? Will Otto cut my throat if I pass up the Horsefly contract and strike out on my own?"

"What do you mean?"

"Will he enter into arrangements with my company to exchange rolling stock and sell passenger tickets straight through between Argent and Baker and in general let the two roads operate as a unit, the way they ought to be? Or will he break it in half at Red Mountain for fear we might suck too much ore traffic through the gorge?"

Fossett temporized. "No one can speak for Otto Winkler except Otto. Now let me ask you something. Do you really appreciate the magnitude of what you are proposing?"

"Oh, I know I'll need help. I'm just a roughneck builder. I don't understand corporation law or the ins and outs of underwriting and stock issues and the rest. But Harmon Gregg does. I can get him over right away, as soon as there's someone to talk to."

Fossett drummed his fingers on the desk. "Gregg's reputation isn't . . . uh, triple-A."

"I'll take care of the reputation." Johnny patted the brief case. "The story is here, black and white. I can outline it in detail so that investors can understand exactly what we're proposing. But there's got to be someone to propose it to. Will you help me?"

"I told you that the bank can't—"

"I'm talking about you, personally."

"I have no such amounts of money to risk."

"You have connections that are worth something." Cynically John measured the banker. Since moving to Denver, Fred had grown afraid even to breathe on his own. To hide his lack of independence he had developed his mannerisms to absurdity. He blinked more secretively than ever; he continually rattled letters he never let anyone read; he dropped names that by association might somehow make his own name roll more resoundingly. His life had shrunk to a big desk over which he could give small tugs of influence at important people. Even John Ogden's name had become one for him to use in talks with Denver mining men and construction experts! Young fellow I know in Argent, partner of Otto Winkler's in a road company: he'll get your job done. Johnny knew. One of the aerial tramways he had built had come to him through Fossett personally, not through the bank. Fossett had profited well from implementing the transaction, too. He'd not be averse to repeating, if Johnny knew him.

"The usual commissions," he prompted, "and a chance to get in on the ground floor when the company is set up."

"W-well," Fossett said and blinked and rubbed his nose. "Purely in a private capacity, of course, with no suggestion that the bank itself is recommending—well, perhaps there are a few names I might suggest. Auld lang syne, you and I, and all that. Yes, yes, I might."

"That's more like it!" Johnny cried, exultant again. What was it his father had used to say when things were going well?—the world by the tail on a downhill pull. More ways of killing a cat than choking it to death on hot butter. Yes siree. "I'll write Harmon to jump on the next train. Lucille, too. She and Nora might as well take in the town while we're working. I'll write Otto too. I don't want him to think I'm crossing him."

"No need mentioning my name to him in this small connection," Fossett said. He squirmed under Johnny's sardonic glance and sought to change the subject. "And John, if I were you, I wouldn't completely close the door on that Horsefly grading possibility."

"Oh that! Don't worry about Horsefly. If I'm going to be sewed up in the gorge, I'll let Otto know in time for him to find someone else."

Away he rushed to write his letters. He ate a lonesome dinner in the elegant new Brown Palace Hotel and toasted himself in French champagne, which he did not really enjoy. Afterwards, restless and yearning for someone to talk to about this stampede of new plans, he wandered about the lobby, neck craned. The entire Belmont Hotel, practically, could have been encased in the Brown's soaring rotunda. Wait until Lucille got a load of that and of the overstuffed furniture in the parlor suite he was moving to from his more modest single room, and the clothes the women wore in the restaurant and . . . oh damn this waiting. He should have brought her along in the first place, so that she could have shared the excitement from its beginning. Let's see now: when could he expect her? A night and a day and a night for the letter to reach the mountains. Three days—two if she hurried—to pack and make arrangements for the children. Then . . . Meanwhile there was nothing to do but josh with the redheaded girl at the cigar stand. A very lush little number. She had the drummers stacked up in lines, buying more perfectos than they could possibly smoke.

"4"

While he waited, he wandered about the city, feeling the warmth of his own energy reflected to him in its stores and factories. The electric street cars intrigued him. He rode them back and forth, wondering how they would perform in the mountains. Through Fossett he obtained an introduction to a vice-president of the tramway company and took him to lunch. The man asked half a dozen questions about terrains and distances and drawbar loads and shook his head.

"I'm estimating without proper figures," he said, "but I question whether a storage battery setup would pull the weight you want over the grades you suggest. The free water power you mention is no answer. You have to get the current out of the canyon. The size of wire needed to transmit direct current—that's what our trolleys use, direct current—the size increases with distance and power. You'd have to have a conductor as big around as your wrist. Carrying it up the sides of the canyon would require special towers. Paying for them and for the wire at the present price of copper would be prohibitive."

"You must be using fifteen or more miles of wire here in the city. That's as far as I'll need to carry my current."

"We also have five coal-burning power stations right beside the tracks rather than in the bottom of a gorge. No, I think you'd better stick to conventional steam locomotives."

So although Johnny considered that he knew steam fairly well through the Baker Northern, he went next to the railroad yards and talked endlessly to supervisors, roundhouse foremen, bookkeepers, and even dining-car specialists. He took what he learned to his hotel room and stayed up until midnight adapting as much of the information as seemed relevant to the figures in his brief case. In between bursts of pencil pushing he drank too much with chance acquaintances, tumbled into bed tipsy, awoke late, and began his rounds again.

Eight days after he had mailed his letters, Harmon and Nora arrived. Lucille was not with them—and was not coming, Nora said.

She handed him a letter from his wife. Little Walter was fretful and not holding his food well; she thought she'd move from Red Mountain down to Argent early this year and besides, being at loose ends in Denver while he was off at all hours meeting people did not appeal to her. They'd celebrate when he returned triumphant, ready to begin work on the project.

Johnny could not believe it. "Did you talk to her?" he demanded of Nora.

"I told her what it is like to be a stage property for a promoter." As she so often did, she was really talking at Harmon rather than to the person whom she was ostensibly addressing. "Pretending to play up to slobs you'd turn out of the house if you had your own way, flattering their wives, laughing at their crummy jokes—"

Johnny was offended. "If that's the way you feel, why did you bother to come?"

"I haven't a houseful of children to keep me away," she said while Harmon's eyes stayed on his shoes. "And even if the jokes are crummy, at least they're jokes."

"This is the biggest thing I've ever tackled—more than a million dollars, if we get the company going."

Her eyebrows mocked him in the way he had learned so well. "Would it be any bigger if she was here to clap her hands over it and make you feel strong and wonderful?"

He flushed. "There you go, twisting what a person says out of shape. I just meant she might show a little interest in what I'm doing."

Nora gave him an angry whistling swish of her breath. "Lucille lived in a tent to be with you and now she's living at Red Mountain to be near you. She has wrapped herself completely in everything you've done. The only success she's ever wanted has been your success. She came to a man's world where the only way a woman can live is on the terms laid down for her, and she's swallowed it all, the poor dear wonderful fool. Yet you have the nerve to stand there and talk about interest."

Harmon interrupted. "Forget it, forget it. If we're going to try to raise a million dollars together, we'd better act like friends while we're doing it. After we have the money, go ahead and scratch each other's hides off and luck to you both. But until then, lay off!"

"5"

They tried. They held in sequence long discussions with three well-known financiers to whom Fossett introduced them. More detailed talks with the men's lawyers and construction engineers followed. In each case a telephone call from a secretary dashed their hopes: "Unforeseen complications . . . Very sorry, but . . ."

According to Fossett, word somehow had buzzed around Seventeenth Street that Winkler had rejected the proposed railroad. That alone had been enough to frighten off conservative capital. "Otto didn't turn it down," Johnny fumed at Fred in the banker's office. "He's doing something else is all." Fossett picked up a letter and pretended to read. The rebuffs had chilled him thoroughly. "True or not," he said stiffly, "there the rumor is. In the face of it, though you realize I'd like to help you personally, I'm afraid I'm going to have to withdraw."

Harmon then endeavored to make contacts. The men he produced were far more enthusiastic than Fossett's acquaintances had been and entertained Johnny and the Greggs lavishly. In each case, however, Johnny drew back. Somehow the affairs smacked too much of promotion for the benefit of the promoters. In one instance, the costs of the underwriting seemed to him exorbitant; in the other, obtaining the capital would cost him the control he wanted over the road.

Aware of Harmon's disappointment, he apologized for throwing cold water on the two propositions. Nora shrugged it off.

"You're paying the bills; it's your privilege." Then her full lips twisted. "But it gives you an idea of how it is to always be hunting someone else's money to live on."

August passed and the first part of September. Silver quotations hit $1.20 an ounce. The city grew frantic with schemes, propositions, deals, plans, programs. In one morning three different speculators telephoned Harmon begging for appointments. Johnny and he discussed the reputation of each man and finally agreed to attend a party the following evening with the least objectionable of the trio. The affair was to start at River Front Park, where there was to be a spectacle of fireworks against twelve thousand square yards of canvas painted to show an "amazing, lifelike and authentic reconstruction of Rome during the days of Nero." Afterwards the group would move on to a private supper. The guests could bring female companions, or, if they preferred, the hosts would provide.

"I've been through this routine, too," Nora sniffed. "No thanks. But Harmon can coach you on how to eat your cake and explain to Lucille too."

Mechanically Harmon retorted, "Don't shove me into these things and take the money and then complain."

"Oh, I know it's terrible—the things one has to do in the line of duty," she scoffed.

"I've told you I've never been to bed with one of them—if that matters. Are you sure you can say the same—that baron, he called himself, in California?"

And now it was Johnny who interrupted, "Nix on it, both of you. If these fellows have the right kind of terms to offer, I'll talk to them about it in Slanting Annie's or anywhere else."

The day of the party did not begin auspiciously. First a telegram arrived from Winkler. He would be in Argent during the next ten days and would like to talk to Johnny about the Horsefly grade. Though Otto must have known why John was in Denver, he did not refer to the errand or ask about success. Indeed, he made no reference whatsoever to the gorge. *Awful sure of me,* Johnny thought resentfully. *Probably Fossett has told him I'm licked. Or Lucille told him. They think I'll go running back at the crook of his finger. Well, they'll see.*

A little later that same day he learned that the price of silver had broken drastically. Harmon was long-faced when they met at lunch. According to rumors the lawyer had picked up on the mining exchange, Wall Street speculators had been driving prices artificially high with the thought that the Sherman Act would panic India into heavy purchases of silver lest the policy of the United States Government result in still further rises. The Indians had not bought as anticipated, however, and now prices were cracking.

Johnny digested the information and shrugged. "It's good to get the water squeezed out of the market," he said. "Now it can readjust for a steady, long-range climb."

Harmon smiled without mirth. "I might have known you'd take it that way. But over on Seventeenth Street they're not so calm."

"What about the party tonight? Should we wait a while and see what happens?"

"Another meeting might be hard to arrange. Folks are jittery."

"That's why I like the mountains. People over there don't act as if it was an earthquake every time somebody on Wall Street squeaks."

"This may be more than a squeak."

"Then we'd better go listen to your friends, I suppose."

He went angrily, feeling abandoned by the market, by Otto Winkler, even by the wife he thought he could have counted on. He got very drunk. The fireworks stimulated him. When the rest of the group continued on to the plush Windsor Hotel for their supper, he slipped away with the redheaded cigar-stand attendant, who he had suggested be invited as his companion. It was his first act of unfaithfulness. He performed it harshly, perfunctorily, revengefully. The girl grew enraged with him. She threw things and used bad language in a loud voice and just before dawn they were requested to leave the room where he had registered them as man and wife.

When he awoke the next afternoon he learned from Harmon that because of his disappearance the promoters considered the party a success. With broad winks and assumptions of fellowship, they had asked when they could meet again—for business this time. Buddies, John thought with savage self-scorn. He got rid of Harmon and fumbled into his clothes. He was queasy-stomached, leather-mouthed, wracked by guilt. He hoped he could avoid Nora at least until he felt better. But as he was wobbling along the hallway, wondering whether he was hungry or not, he ran straight into her as she stepped out of an elevator. She looked him over sardonically.

"You need the hair of the dog," she said and took him to her room. Harmon was not there.

He gulped the first drink neat and burning. The next he sipped, alternating with deeper draughts of water. His hands shook but he felt happier—or would have except for the way Nora sat watching him, her lips curved in what wasn't exactly a smile.

"Don't keep looking at me like that," he said finally.

The curve deepened. She had him pinioned now. "You're getting rattled," she said.

"Not by you."

"By everything. You'd best go home."

He flushed miserably and dropped his eyes and took the refuge of adolescent boys. "I don't know what you're talking about."

"None of this is your style, Johnny. None of it will get you what you really want." Her smile, if it was a smile, turned bleak. "I know."

"I can manage my own affairs, thanks."

"I'm not going to tell Lucille," she said. "For her sake, not for yours."

He glowered at her. She was very like his mother, he thought for the first time in years. From the beginning she had been a denial of every-

thing he had seen in the mountains, everything he had believed in
and had reached for. She needed showing. He traced the soft curve of
her underlip, the brown ringlet that curled in front of one small ear.
His eyes dropped to the fullness of her breast. He put one hand on the
table. The feel of her flesh under it, the thrust, the dominance. He
swallowed.

The upsurge must have been plain on his face. Her eyes turned icy.
"Now you really are getting rattled," she said.
"Nora—"
"Please leave."
"Nora—"
"Not on your terms, John Ogden. Not ever."
"I could take—"
"Just try it."

He stood there trembling. "God damn you!" he cried. "You geld a
man just the way you turn down your mouth at him. Your kind always
do."

He stumbled from the room, threw into his suitcase those of his
things he saw during one wild, dazed sweep of his quarters, and caught
the night train for Argent.

"6"

He took Otto's grading contract. Grimly, aided by a mild winter and
early spring, he showed how rapidly and how well a rail line could be
pushed across Horsefly and down Bobcat Creek to its junction with the
next contractor's stretch. Within a year work trains were running halfway around the mountain.

One October day in 1891, motivated as much by curiosity as by
anything else, Johnny decided to ride a construction train as far as the
rails went. In the rattling caboose he encountered an electrical engineer
who was hitching passage to a new power plant at a lonesome siding
called Troy. During their gossip Johnny learned that the plant was
delivering electricity to a gold mine perched four thousand feet higher
in the mountains than the generators were. The wires gained this
altitude in a three-mile heave up one of the roughest slopes in the St.
Johns.

He whistled his amazement and asked what kind of towers were used
to carry so heavy a wire.

"It's ordinary wire," the man said, "not any bigger around than a pencil. We don't need towers. Poles are enough."

Johnny frowned. "In Denver a trolley-car official told me that you can't carry as much power as you're talking about over such a distance with plain wire."

"You can't carry direct current that way. This is alternating current—a new wrinkle. Our plant is the first in the country to transmit an alternating current commercially for more than a few hundred yards."

"What's the difference?"

He received thereupon a lesson in electricity that he did not fully understand. The figures were clear, however. The Golden Fleece Mine, recipient of the power, had been crippled by high overhead, principally coal—$2500 a month delivered. "Now we're doing the same work in the mill and compressor house, plus lighting the mine and running the trams, for five hundred a month."

"The trams!"

"Why not? All you need is a motor and a trolley."

"The locomotive would run outside the tunnel as well as inside?"

"Of course."

"Is it possible," Johnny asked, "to build an electric engine as powerful as one of these little narrow-gauge steam locomotives and run it off a wire no bigger than a pencil?"

"I suppose. Offhand I don't know of any engine motors that large, but by now the principles are familiar enough. Why?"

"Oh," Johnny said vaguely, though the pulse in his neck was beginning to pound, "it just seems that in this country, where coal is so hard to haul and water power foams around everywhere, we ought to be able to use some of it for moving our trains."

"I've always said so," the engineer agreed. "Steam men claim that the original investment in penstocks, pelton wheels, wire, and whatnot is too high. But probably you could save part of those charges through cheaper construction costs. An electric locomotive should weigh considerably less than a steam engine, to say nothing of a tender full of coal. I'd imagine you could get away with lighter rails, fewer ties, smaller trestles and so on. I'd think, too, that electric trains might be able to handle tighter curves on a grade. Even if you didn't save on construction, you'd certainly save on operation. For one thing, you wouldn't have to take a tender of profitless coal over every pass with you just so you could get back home again. You wouldn't even have to pay for the power. The water is free, once your turbines are in. To say nothing of electricity being cleaner and more efficient."

"I golly!" Johnny breathed, and he knew that for the rest of his life he would be able to repeat the engineer's remarks practically verbatim. "Do you mind if I look your plant over?"

"Glad to have you," the engineer said and regarded him quizzically. "If you're that interested, why don't you go back to Buffalo, New York? The city is about to bring alternating current from Niagara. And Pittsburgh. That's where our generators and transformers were manufactured. If you like, I'll give you a note to the fellow who came out and helped us with our installations."

"I golly!" Johnny said again. A thing of pride! "I'm practically on my way!"

"7"

He telephoned Lucille and told her that he would not be home for a few more days. Renting a horse, he rode through muddy forests, under sodden, fall-browned aspen leaves to the head of the track pushing out from Montezuma. There he found Winkler. They sat on an inspection handcar on a temporary siding and there Johnny told him of his newest plan.

"I know what you called my first idea—a thing of pride. Maybe it was. But this new alternating-current development changes everything."

"Iss no pride at all?" Winkler asked dryly.

Johnny grinned. "Sure. But now it'll work. We'll forget hauling ore from Red Mountain to Argent, though Roscoe Blair won't like that. Instead, we'll plan a light train for light freight—farm products and household merchandise—stuff like that. And passengers, especially in summer. Remember how passenger service out of Baker jumped when you advertised the Rainbow Tours to Red Mountain? Scads of people bought tickets just for the sightseeing. Lots of them continued on down the gorge to Argent on Walt's stagecoaches and caught a train to Denver from there. Scads more tourists will come up if they know they can finish out the trip in a comfortable, clean, cinder-free electric trolley —interurbans, I think they're called in the East."

Winkler eyed him wistfully, as if in the midst of this far bigger project Otto had lost the tingle of anticipation. "Der old Schonny—all excitements," he murmured. He pushed his moist underlip in and out through his gray whiskers. "But even light trains iss a big bite."

"This light train I'm talking about ought to save us at least a quarter of a million in construction costs."

"Dot's facts or hope?"

"I . . ." Johnny checked himself. Winkler never bought a thing on sentiment alone. "It's hope," he granted, "until we can bring in engineers who understand power design and can give us firm figures. That work will have to wait until next summer. Meantime I want to go East and study every electrical installation I can find, so"—Johnny made himself smile—"so ve zee hvere ve land hven ve yump."

Winkler's lip moved back and forth. "No," he said finally.

Johnny's heart sank. "At least give me a chance!"

"Der is noddings I can do. Silfer is down again und we must fight in Congress ofer und ofer. Der new mines I hope might open for my railway dis side of der mountains on, dey don' do it. If dis track already had not swallowed so much, I'd not keep on."

Otto Winkler talking defeat! Johnny jumped from the handcar and paced back and forth on the tie ends in agitation. "The things that built this country are as valuable now as they ever were, aren't they?"

"I tell you dis road takes eferyting I haf. I can noddings more do."

Johnny drew a deep breath. "Then I'll try to find financing somewhere else."

"Mit Harmon Gregg und his ham-fatters?"

"I deserved that, I guess," Johnny admitted wryly. "But don't blame Harmon too much for what happened last fall in Denver. I was the one that was in the sweat to get moving. I won't hit the fast-buck boys again. But I'll probably keep Harmon with me. I owe him that much and besides he has been familiar with this gorge road from the beginning." And then Johnny said the thing he knew had to come out sooner or later. "Just give me a chance. Don't murder me again in Denver."

Winkler bristled. "Hvat you say!"

"Last year you waved off what I was doing as a thing of pride. You killed it in the banks with a shake of your head. Looking back, I can appreciate why you thought I was jumping too soon. This time I'm going at it differently. I believe in it. I believe that in time electricity may bring us a lot more good than just trains. Maybe it's pride, but as long as there's something better I can put up the gorge for Argent and Red Mountain both, I've got to try. Otherwise I might as well have quit working when I'd finished building the first trail." He flung out his hand in despair at the emptiness of words. "Don't you see what I mean?"

Winkler's thoughts turned backward. The boy, not seventeen, cramped into the corrals at Saguache, hearing the song of just-beyond, crying out his heart in words too lead-footed to carry what he meant: *Please, Mr. Winkler, please let me go!* With a resigned lift of one palm Otto accepted his share of the responsibility, using the same words of consent that he had used before.

"Iss no picnic, Schonny."

"You'll help!"

"You get complete costs. Eferyting—facts, not hopes. Den I'll tell Fossett to go ahead mitt appointments."

"I golly!" This time Johnny did lift on his toes. "Wait till I tell Lucille! This is great! She hasn't been East to see her family since she came out for our wedding. Neither have I. Oh, this'll be great!"

"Schonny."

"Yeah?"

"Iss goot seeing excitements again."

Strange, Johnny thought as he rode toward Argent and had time to reflect on what had been said, strange that Otto's voice should have sounded so very sad. Ah well, he was old and trying to do a young job—tired, that was all.

VI

"1"

Excitements! Impervious behind his own verve, John ascribed Lucille's hesitation about the trip to a natural reluctance over packing up the older children, the girls, to accompany them on an extended trip in the middle of winter. He scarcely noticed the stiffness of Lucille's meeting with her father: tentative words, the sudden welling of tears, an impulsive embrace, and shyness again as the granddaughters were introduced. The visit with his own mother was no more satisfactory. Ill-advisedly, as he realized later, he told her what he had done about his father's grave. Deborah Ogden dabbed at her eyes. "Such a tragic waste! He could have given the world so much if he hadn't sunk himself in that wilderness. Now . . ." She let one hand lift three or four inches from her lap and fall back—the martyred relict. Lucille caught Johnny's eye and kept him silent. Later, though, he wondered aloud how often during the past fifteen years Deborah Ogden had given so much as a passing thought to her husband's resting place.

"Anyhow," he said as their train pulled out of the Altoona station, "they've seen the kids. Maybe now they'll believe us a little more when we write that we're getting along. Just the same, I wish Ma could see those red peaks. It seems—oh, I don't know—such a dead end she's always existed in."

"You were wonderful to her, Johnny. To Daddy too. I was proud of you and the girls." She watched the telephone wires go by, dip and rise and dip against the snowy fields. She seemed to shake away a burden. "Now we can enjoy things."

They came home just before Christmas, tired, sated with sights,

laden with gifts and new clothes. In addition Johnny was stuffed
with information which made him more certain than ever that the
electric line would work. In a long interview with Al Ewer he raised
every question and objection he could think of and proceeded to
analyze them judiciously and impartially—until the end. Unable then
to restrain himself, he gave his convictions their head. This bold new
concept would provide one more milestone on the road to achieving the
glorious heritage of the peaks. And so on. And on.

In print the interview was a sensation. On the afternoon it appeared
Johnny could scarcely make his way from the Silver City Club up
snowy Vinegar Hill to his home. Every few yards people stopped him to
congratulate him and ask more questions. Most of them boiled down to
a single point: When would work begin?

When indeed? He had learned at last not to jump too fast. If he
were to raise the money he needed on terms that would let the company
flourish, he must present figures as exact as persistence and integrity
could make them. The rough surveys of possible routes would have to
be polished until a sound choice could be reached among them, the
savings in construction balanced against long-range economies in operations. Where should the generating station be located? What of penstocks, flumes, lightning arresters, and motors? What size train would
best meet anticipated conditions? Could surplus power be sold to the
city of Argent, which was already planning to illuminate its principal
intersections and string an attention-catching series of arc lights up the
outside of the fire department's hose tower?

Little could be accomplished before spring. Snows were heavy that
March, the cold intense. The demands of keeping the road open to
Red Mountain became as taxing as any Johnny could remember. When,
on the twelfth, a new blizzard struck, he was tempted to roll over in
bed and let it howl itself out unchallenged. But he couldn't. The
Summit Pass was snowed in; no train had reached Red Mountain from
Baker in more than a week. If the gorge road was lost, supplies of coal
and hay and foodstuffs might become critically short. Groaning in self-
commiseration, Johnny pulled on his galoshes, tied a bandana around
his ears, jammed a black hat onto the cloth, and went outside to gather
his shovelers.

In the tollhouse by Wolf Creek Falls, where the crew paused to
warm themselves, they encountered Buck Shaffer and Gabe Porcella
bound down the hill to buy two sledloads of hay, beef, chickens, and
butter from Ira Brice.

"I lined out the boys at the upper end and come along to prove we
could make it through," Buck said, watching his mittens steam. "I knew
you'd be out down here."

"Don't bet too much on getting back," Johnny grumbled. "If avalanches start running, we're in trouble."

"There ain't nothin' to eat in town but tripe and stew meat," Gabe said. With his hairy fingers he worried little crystals of ice out of his orange sideburns. "I thought one reason you built the road up this side of the canyon is because it's sheltered."

"From the normal avalanche runs it is. But in weather like this, slides are liable to bust loose anywhere."

"You'll get us through."

"We'll try."

To make sure all was well, he took three of his men with him clear to Red Mountain. When the quartet started back the next afternoon, the air was warmer and Johnny remarked that sometime during the night the clouds should start breaking. If a chinook was developing, temperatures would stay high even during clearing weather. "Spring!" he said and grinned through his cracked, chapped lips. It couldn't come too soon to suit him.

A little below the head of the gorge they met Buck Shaffer and Gabe with their laden sleds, hay on the first, beef quarters and frozen chicken carcasses on the second. Ira and Tommy Brice, a husky twenty-two now and freshly married, had come along to help shovel through if necessary. Tommy was riding on the front sled with Gabe, Ira on the second with Buck. The two parties exchanged badinage while the sled horses caught their breath, then went their separate ways.

A few minutes later Johnny and his men heard a muffled *whoomp*. In the canyon below them powdery snow suddenly boiled off the evergreen boughs and the patches of untimbered hillsides. Instantly they knew that a wall of rushing snow was compressing the air ahead of it and whipping it into the gorge. The sound, Johnny told Lucille later "was like when our train going East passed another coming the opposite direction at sixty miles an hour. Only louder."

"There goes the Riverside," one of the workers remarked, referring to a familiar avalanche that plunged nearly each winter down the slope across the way.

Johnny looked back at the white mist eddying at the head of the gorge. "The hell it is!" he exclaimed. That wasn't the way the Riverside would throw out its cloud. "It's on this side!"

"Do you think . . ."

"We'd better see!"

They galloped back up the grade. At the head of the gorge a chaotic white mass covered perhaps five hundred feet of the road. The rest of the slide, yellowed here and there by earth and boulders, spotted by branches and broken tree trunks, lay in a sullen heap that filled the canyon almost to the highway level. "Jesus!" Johnny breathed. That mass was seventy or eighty feet deep.

They struggled to the top of the blanket covering the road. Nothing moved beyond. Johnny directed two of the workers to rush to town for help.

"Bring as many shovelers as will volunteer. Have Kennerly or Halverson start up two or three sledloads of firewood. We're liable to be here all night. Coffee—call my wife. Tell her to get her church people making sandwiches. And for God's sake watch out. They're likely to be cracking loose everywhere now."

"Sure." Risk a hundred to dig out four. No one said it, however. The pair ordered to town turned around with the horses. Johnny and the other worker wallowed on foot across the slide. At its upper fringes they found the wreckage of the first sled. It had been wrenched apart. Later they learned that its four panicked horses had bolted for town dragging the tongue and running gears and that a rescue party was already forming to learn what had happened.

Hay littered the slope. Gabe was sitting on a board at the edge of the road, rocking back and forth. He had taken off his gloves and was holding his huge round, snow-caked head between his bare hands. Blood oozed between his fingers. When Johnny knelt beside him he looked around, dazed and bewildered. Snow ringed his eyes, plastered his cheeks. The cut in his forehead was long but did not appear deep. The most alarming symptom was the strangled gasping with which he struggled for air. Twice Johnny spoke to him. Gabe just stared and shuddered. At last Johnny realized that he could not hear. The powder-fine, whirling, avalanche-driven snow had packed into every orifice in his head. Instinctively he had hacked away barely enough to keep from smothering, and that was as far as he'd gotten.

"How are we going to unplug him?" the worker said.

"Melt it," Johnny decided. He whittled slivers from a broken board and built a fire. He found a scoop shovel in the wreckage, melted snow in that, and collected the water in his hat. Gabe snorted in it like a horse, clearing his mouth and nostrils. The water did not help his ears, however. In between trying to read Johnny's questions from his lips, he leaned his sore head to one side or the other and pounded mournfully on it with the butt of his palm. No, he hadn't seen a thing—just an explosion of snow. He moaned and rocked, too dazed to be of help.

Johnny spread hay on some boards, made him lie down, and covered him with his mackinaw. "You stay tight; help's coming!" he bawled and started down the slope with the shovel, stepping in the tracks of the worker who had plowed along ahead of him. Just then the fellow let out a shout. "Here he is!" And sure enough Tommy was. A wad of hay had caught in the upper branches of a willow bush, forming a kind of roof. Tommy had been pushed headfirst into this small chamber where there was air enough to breathe. But he had landed with his belly across a log and his hands behind him. Snow sat on his back like a wrestler clamping him in an armlock. All he could do was holler. He was doing it with vigor, although the sound that reached the searchers and set them digging was like a weak fluting blown through cotton.

He insisted he wasn't hurt, only bruised and winded. "Thanks, boys, I was beginning to get restless." He gaped around. "Where's Pa?"

Johnny shook his head. The other worker said, "You can't never tell what might happen. Look at you. These slides are full of freaks."

Tommy leaned over and spit and wrinkled his mouth as though he did not like the taste. "That's right," he agreed. "What had we better do first?"

Johnny and the worker looked up the opposite slope. A streak two hundred or more feet wide showed where the Riverside avalanche annually stripped vegetation from the hill. It had already run once this year. It might be ready to break again.

"There's not much three of us can do with just one shovel," the worker said nervously.

"We can use boards," Tommy said.

Johnny looked at the worker. "Gene, how about going to Red Mountain for help? They can get here quicker than the Argent people. Bring some of those long steel bars they use in construction. We'll need 'em for probes. I'll stay and help Tommy."

Tommy took the one shovel. John made a clumsy scoop from a splintered board. Rather hopelessly they tried to estimate where the second sled had been when the avalanche had picked it up and dumped it over the edge of the road. Even accurate knowledge would not have helped a great deal, however, for after the vanguard of snow had foamed into the canyon it had been squeezed like toothpaste by the following mass and had turned and flowed heavily some distance along the trench, its whiteness stained by tangled mats of debris.

How long could a man keep breathing under snow? Quite a while if he had air holes. Twenty-six hours for old Dan Eisley at the Virginius two years ago. When rescuers had dug him free he had shaken himself like a dog and asked querulously what they'd been waiting for. But they'd had a fair notion of where Dan might be.

Tommy was not as sound as John had supposed when first they had found him—jerky, increasingly incoherent, riding the wires of his nerves. Alone, he'd have shoveled at headlong speed without pattern, as though he supposed that in an hour or two he could clear out the entire snow heap by himself. Not that the faint scratches of order meant much against this chaos. But perhaps pattern was any rational mind's instinctive defense against Nature's meaningless catastrophes. Johnny picked out a direction and aimed Tommy along it.

"Let's trench here," he directed. Tommy nodded and began, an ant who had never been informed how large the world is. Johnny glanced again at the swath of the Riverside above them and at the bit of board in his hand and at the steady rhythm of Tommy's shoulders. Then he too began to dig.

"2"

By midnight more than a hundred people had gathered on the flat where once Johnny and Lucille had lived in tents. They used the remnants of Aino's shack for shelter. Fires burned beside it and along the edges of the slide debris. When diggers grew exhausted they waded back for coffee the women served and sat down, heads hanging while they caught their wind. Gabe had been taken to the hospital. Tommy should have gone, but he had insisted furiously that he was all right— call him when they spotted the old man, would they? He was asleep in the shack on blankets brought by the rescue party. His gray, stolid stepmother sat beside him on the shack's one surviving chair, smiling wan appreciation at the men who stopped by, blowing at their coffee and telling of different rescues they knew about which had succeeded. Lucille was outside by a fire, trying to keep Jenny Shaffer busy serving coffee and sandwiches and turning the gloves that were drying on a bit of clothesline stretched near the blaze.

Johnny had left the gorge for food only once, a little after darkness had fallen. At midnight he might have gone again, had not the probes just then found a dead horse. It lay alone, torn completely from its harness. Yet its position perhaps furnished a clue. The swarm of shovelers concentrated on sinking a circular terraced pit around the animal, until other probers found two sides of beef a hundred yards away. The unexpected diffusion threatened to paralyze the attack. But Johnny lined the men out between the two points and they settled back to their urgent, almost conversationless digging. Lantern holders moved back and forth. The full moon behind the clouds spread a shadowless phosphorescence. The trench grew so deep that three lines of shovelers, standing on ledges one above the other, were needed to relay the compacting snow aside.

To Johnny it was a strange and warm and wonderful fellowship.

Death generally had its own way undefied. But here they were meeting it on its own ground, united in the last thin hope of tweaking victory from under its careless thumb. Many of the shovelers would not have toiled so for wages, but they did it now to assure each other of the worth of the common life they were defending. Aino was there and Pat and Parley Quine, Walt and Alden and Sam Varnum, even Al Ewer, slack-fat and hollow-eyed from fatigue. As long as they could convince themselves that any chance remained they nodded cheerfully and went wherever Johnny suggested. But after midnight the minutes dragged longer, the scoops weighed more heavily. The clouds broke; the temperature rose. "Chinook," the men told each other. They shed their jackets and glanced uneasily toward the Riverside. This quick warmth would make the new snow settle fast. If icy crusts lay underneath, the heavy top layers might slip at any time.

One by one the diggers straggled out of the trench, sheepish and wagging their heads. Johnny paused to watch each one go, then bent again to his shoveling. At length only Aino and he and four or five others remained, probing short laterals off to the sides of the main cut. Blocked by a huge spruce, Johnny dropped to his knees to gouge out an exploratory cave beneath its rough, pungent bark. He wobbled in a mist of weariness. Sometimes he started to topple and had to catch himself with the shovel and lean on it while the dizziness passed.

During one of these moments he felt a touch on his back. Jenny Shaffer had found her way into the trench with Spec Alden.

"Everyone else is out, Johnny."

He straightened. "Have they found him?"

She shook her head, her coat collar caught by one hand under her pointed chin. She looked far less substantial than the moon-silvered walls that would soon be melting away under the spring sun.

"It's no use."

He was surprised at how his chest hurt. He must have been bent over too long. "You can't tell," he insisted. Buck might be alive behind the tree right now, hearing the scratch of the shovels and trying to call.

"If more are hurt because of him, then I will weep," she said.

Alden said, "Lucille is waiting for you, John."

"Buck would want you to," Jenny told him.

They put him in a sleigh and wrapped a buffalo robe around his sopping trousers. Lucille held one wet wrinkled hand that had no feeling left. As Walt picked up the reins to drive them to the log house at Red Mountain, Johnny tipped back his head to look up the long sides of Ute Peak. "If we hadn't cut so much red spruce out of there for railroad ties," he muttered, "maybe the trees would have held the snow from running. It never ran here before."

Lucille pressed his hand between both of hers. "Rest, Johnny."

His eyes stayed lifted. "God, that slide came a long ways." He could see its course in the moonlight, a mere wrinkle in the huge expanse. The slope was tall and serene. The cloud streamers were edged in silver. "One more minute either way would have been enough," he said.

"You did everything anyone could."

That was the trouble—the insignificance. A hundred men: nothing. Bone and tissue and strength; a dozen straining, believing years. And the mountain did not care.

"Like spitting on us," Johnny said. His head rolled forward onto his chest; the whites of his eyes showed under the iris. "Funny it took me such a hell of a time to see it," he said and tried to laugh but was shaken by coughs until he fell asleep.

He slept until eight o'clock that night and awoke with a headache and knifing pains in his side. He tried to eat a bowl of soup Lucille brought him. His throat was so sore he could scarcely swallow.

"I suppose this will be in all the papers," he complained.

"Both editors were there," Lucille said.

"It won't read so good in Denver—two wagons lost and two men killed right where the trolley may run."

She reproved him. "To Jenny and Mrs. Brice it's more than statistics."

"Suppose it had hit a train. That'd be more than statistics, too."

"The men around the fire said the chances were a million to one. They said a slide had never run there before. Besides, they said, you can build breakers that will split it if it ever does come again."

Johnny swung his feet over the edge of the bed and reached for his socks. "You're not getting up now!" Lucille protested.

"I want to go to the maintenance station."

"At this time of night?"

"Night?" He looked out the window and scrubbed his face with his palms, reorienting himself. "I don't remember ever before waking up in the evening." He lay back, staring at the ceiling. "We've got to open the road as soon as we can."

"They've already started."

"Not a cut, though. I want to tell Buck . . ." The slip turned in on him like a snake. He lay still while the self-horror eased away. "I want them to dig a tunnel."

"Morning is time enough to send word."

"The snow is plenty deep. When air starts through the tunnel, it'll freeze on the inside. It's a shady place. I'll bet a tunnel will last until August. A real tourist attraction. People will flock from all around to see it." He swallowed at his sore throat. "Dead men at the bottom. Not every highway tunnel can make that statement."

Sadly she said, "Don't fight it so, darling."

He closed his eyes but did not sleep. He sensed her sitting beside the bed, watching his face. Presently he looked up.

"I'm tired, Lucy."

"Of course you are."

"Never like this before. Used up. Done."

"I've seen you drop into bed like a log lots of times."

"I always woke up ready to go." He thought about it and was frightened. "Now all I want is to lie here."

"You'll be yourself in the morning."

"It'll happen again. And then one day I'll stay tired." He turned his head toward the wall. "I'm getting old, Lucy."

He was not quite thirty-four. But he had always been prodigal of himself.

"3"

The depression of his spirits lasted through a siege of pleurisy. It was his first serious illness. The pains first astounded and then outraged him. He chafed, fell into moods of black despair, and made life miserable for Lucille. But when spring came he bounced joyously back. As the land turned green again, he stalked intently up and down the canyon with his surveyors and engineers, spending his energies as recklessly as he ever had, despite Lucille's remonstrances.

The number of tourists leaving the train at Red Mountain and descending to Argent in one of Kennerly's open buckboard stages rose seventeen per cent that summer. State-wide promotion of the scenery by the Baker Northern and by the stage company accounted for some of the increase. The tunnel through the snow had its effect as well, and the drivers made the most of it. On the way down they halted their matched four-horse teams at its upper mouth and used their whip handles to point out the gouge which the avalanche had slashed through the trees and brush on the peak's flank. They then urged the horses into the tunnel's chilly entry. The iridescent, marbled surface of the walls and ceiling, pocked by the marks of picks and shovels, cast blue and green gleams of light. Soon the light faded and the passengers saw only each other's pale faces and the dazzling glare that marked the outlet ahead. Water dripped. The cold sank deeper. Here and there lay shattered gobs of snow that had fallen from the ceiling. Travelers given to claustrophobia turned rigid. Two women and a fiercely mustached man fainted dead away, each on a different occasion, and had to be revived on the outside.

After emerging into sunlight, the drivers halted again and pointed downward at the huge compacted mass of snow and boulders and shattered trees in the canyon bottom. The surface was dirty from its own debris and from dust and pine needles blown by the spring winds. The under part was hollowed into a huge cavern through which resoundingly rushed the iron-colored stream. The thaws had exposed the horses, the drivers said, but most of the beef, and two men yet remained hidden in the icy tomb. The passengers shuddered. To imaginative ones the shadows thrown by tree branches looked like protruding legs or arms. The oppressive weight of the tunnel still fresh in their minds, they rode on to the toll station at Wolf Creek Falls. There they bought numbers of picture post cards showing a stage similar to theirs emerging from the tunnel. To the stage's right a black X marked the fatal slide.

Some of the fortunate ones rode with Jenny Shaffer herself. Jenny had a horror that Buck would melt free, drop into the stream, and be lost. Every few days she rode a stage from Red Mountain as far as the lower end of the slide. Dismounting, she stared for an hour or so at her husband's vast shroud, then returned on an upbound stage. "She rides free," the drivers explained afterwards to the passengers. "The president of the road company—feller named Ogden, Jack Ogden—dang near killed hisself trying to dig 'em out after the slide run—he left standing orders for us to take her any time she wants to go. Later on toward fall, when the pile has shrunk down as much as it's likely to, Ogden's gonna take a party in and dig some more. It won't be easy. Or safe, if that arch collapses while they're on it. But he'll do 'er. The dangdest feller, Ogden is. He takes these things to heart. Smart, too. Ain't everyone would of thought of this tunnel. Biggest thrill in the mountains, folks claim. Why if a lot of hard rains don't go washing off the top of it, I'll bet it'll last till fall."

So much for Jenny. Ira's wife saw the mass just once, when she moved for the summer with Tommy and his wife from the river ranch to the one on the meadows below Red Mountain. Nora still remained to worry Johnny.

She and Harmon had wintered as usual in California. On their return they had stopped in Denver while Harmon went about setting up the New Hopes Tunnel Company. Using inside information about the route which the electric train would likely follow, he had purchased several hitherto unproductive claims along the right-of-way near the head of the gorge. As Harmon knew, a grade straight down the gorge would be prohibitively steep. Johnny planned to approximate the route of the old zigzag trail, finally swinging completely out of the canyon into the tributary creek beyond and continuing down it to Argent. Harmon's grandiose scheme envisioned a tunnel through the ridge into the tributary canyon. According to his prospectus, such a bore would certainly intersect rich veins. After it had been holed through and while the veins were being exploited, the tunnel could be leased for extra profits to the electric railway, which would thus save more than a mile of very snowy going. Privately John doubted whether Harmon could raise the six hundred thousand dollars deemed necessary, but since the trolley would benefit from the plan's success he played along, not investing because of his own commitments but giving Harmon information and employing him for legal work.

The slow progress of work in Denver bored Nora. Leaving Harmon there, she came on to Argent alone. She declined Lucille's invitation to stay on Vinegar Hill and took an expensive suite at the Belmont. As soon as Harmon had finished in Denver, she said, they would go to Red Mountain and build a summer home on the claims. It would be the first house they had ever owned. Always before, they had rented whatever cabin they could afford after their winter splurge. But at last they'd found something worth settling down and building for.

Lucille suggested to Johnny that he ought to take Nora to see the slide where her father had died. He refused.

"She don't need a guide. Everyone in the St. John Mountains knows where it is."

"But no one else knows as well as you what happened. Hearing it straight from you, the first time she sees the place, will be comforting to her."

"She was never so all-fired fond of the old man."

"Her conscience bothers her about that, too."

"Not as much as she'd bother me. I can see her now, looking at me the way she does and saying I've sure made a good thing of her father dying right at that particular spot, as if it was my fault the avalanche caught him."

"She and Harmon have changed, Johnny. That's why they've named the company the New Hopes."

He made an inelegant noise. "They named it New Hopes because it's a good moniker for a speculation."

"Truly it's more," Lucille insisted. "Nora told me something of it this afternoon. She said—don't let her know I told you this—she said Harmon left her for a while last winter."

"And then went back, I suppose. Poor old Harmon—can't live with her or without her. I don't know how he stood it this long."

"She's the one who went back to him."

Johnny stayed cynical. "Because the New Hopes sounded like a money-maker, I'll bet."

"Perhaps that had its part. But before Harmon took her back, they had everything out. They're going to make a real effort to start fresh again."

"They're starting. Not me."

"It involves you," Lucille retorted. "Without the electric railway, the New Hopes will collapse. They both realize that. Furthermore, Harmon hopes to be full-time attorney for the tram company, not just part-time lawyer for you individually. Nora as much as admitted to me that Harmon put her on the carpet and told her that among other things she could start betting on you for a change and not fighting with you every time you're together."

Johnny grinned. "What do you know! Old Harmon, growing a backbone!"

"New hope."

"If it doesn't let him down again," Johnny said. He shook his head. He could not face the slide with Nora. He had known her too long. That cold, implacable debris would represent to her everything that she had found wrong with the mountains since the day she had cried her hate at them while the soldiers were forcing her and her family back across the river to the agency. She had never ceased despising the circumstances that kept dragging her back to them. Whatever Harmon might think the New Hopes Company was, to her it was one more twist to the persistent old hope that this time, at last, she could escape. For the sake of that she would pretend to make peace even with Johnny's love of the mountains.

"I'll sign a truce with her if you want," he told Lucille. "But not at the slide. That's too much for either one of us to start over on."

"4"

A more ambitious tunnel than the New Hopes caught Red Mountain's interest during the summer of '92. Its name, derived from the claim on which drilling started, was the Joker. Parley Quine was the promoter. The purpose was drainage. As Red Mountain's principal mines had reached deeper and deeper, pumping water from their lower levels had grown increasingly expensive and inefficient. Quine proposed driving a tunnel from near the outskirts of Red Mountain City beneath the mines and draining off the water—"He's aiming to get his Joker in the Dixie Girl," Ewer wrote in *The True Fissure*. But after the bore had pierced eight or nine hundred feet, Parley found money harder to raise than he had anticipated. He stopped the work. Before this, however, at about the six-hundred-foot mark, drillers had intersected a small vein carrying a dusting of gold. Its values were only fair and the mineralized area did not appear extensive, but thanks to the tunnel already being there, exploitation was feasible. Uninterested in the small job himself, Quine leased the rights to Pat Edgell.

Pat took over the tunnel's steam compressors, notorious gulpers of fuel, borrowed money to build a small mill, put about fifteen miners to work, and found himself the center of an interest quite out of proportion to the size of his operation. Gold ores had never been a primary value on Red Mountain. Pat's lease was the first true gold mine in the region. Inevitably it suggested others.

No one was more vocal than John Ogden in proclaiming the significance of his enemy's work. "I always said we hadn't scratched the possibilities of those peaks," he exulted in Argent's Silver City Club. "I hope Pat makes a million and shows some of the backcappers around here what can still be done. Why, there's no telling what Harmon Gregg might find when he gets going on the New Hopes. With Gregg's tunnel opened, we might even buck Montezuma and in the next few years start Red Mountain ore down the trolley to Roscoe Blair's smelter. Then when Parley picks up the Joker again and pushes on to the Ram and the Dixie Girl and the Rose Marie—well, the millions that have come off that red hill won't even look like a good start to what's coming. You'll see!"

In spite of such grandiloquent optimism, speculators were nevertheless finding money surprisingly difficult to obtain. Inspired by Johnny's proposed trolley, a group of Argent businessmen decided to imitate it with a line that would tap nearby points of interest from a base at the town's principal hot springs, where a huge summer resort and health center was to be erected. The idea never got off the ground. "It's because of the way those Wall Street gold bugs depress the price of silver," one of the promoters raged in the Silver City Club. "It's back down to eighty-six cents, for Christ sake! I don't know why our western congressmen don't get off the dime!"

For the first time in his life Johnny found himself engrossed by politics. When Davis H. Waite, a newspaper editor from the mining town of Aspen, declared for governor on a Populist platform advocating free coinage of silver at a sixteen-to-one ratio with gold, Johnny became an active backer. He headed Waite's reception committee in Argent, escorted him to Red Mountain, and took charge of the rally there. It was held in the switchyard behind the depot. Johnny's committee built a table of planks laid on sawhorses and loaded it with bread, bologna sausage, and cheese. Barrels of beer beckoned at strategic intervals. A drummer and two horn blowers played vigorously; committeemen waved flies away from the food with their bowler hats.

The audience, mostly miners let off work for the afternoon, docilely followed the tacit rules for such occasions: the speeches first and then the rush to the tables. Accepting free cigars, they found seats on flatcars facing the one from which Waite would speak, on wheels that had been rolled aside for lathing, on broken pistons and freshly creosoted ties awaiting placement. Waite, a gaunt man with a prophet's long white beard and fiery eye, sawed the air with his oratory: "Gold is the money of monarchs; kings covet it; it accumulates in commercial centers like Wall Street and is used to unsettle values and oppress the debtor. Silver flows freely. It is not the treasure of the avaricious but the tool of trade. It is to the arteries of commerce what mountain springs are to rivers. It is the stimulant to industry and production in the thousands of small but honest businesses which in their aggregate make up the true wealth of our glorious nation!" Everyone cheered. Six barrels of beer were consumed, and although Johnny knew the indifference with which Red Mountain generally regarded elections, he assured his perspiring candidate that the rally would carry the day.

Politics slowed his work in other ways. Shortly before the election he went with Harmon to Denver on another of their increasingly frequent trips. Both the electric railway and the New Hopes Tunnel Company were chartered and incorporated now and could begin operations as soon as capital was available. Harmon contemplated a public stock issue. To lend radiance to his offering he had obtained testimonials from the mayor of Red Mountain, from the postmaster of Argent, from the engineering firm which had prepared his estimates, and from John Ogden, "that well-known, aggressive, and far-sighted construction expert of the St. John Mountains."

Since Johnny felt that his venture was less speculative than Harmon's, he hoped to finance it more cheaply by placing his entire issue of stock and convertible bonds with a dozen or so potent Colorado financiers. He had worked out three different grades for the road and exact figures for each route. He himself preferred the most expensive job, for he believed that the costs entailed in achieving a gentle grade would be returned through savings in operation and maintenance. The total for building this line came to $1,205,000. The figure frightened him a little. It had been one thing to talk of such sums when his proposals had been mere imaginings, but he had failed miserably on his first excursion into high finance and to see this solid total glaring up at him in irreducible black and white was awesome. "I came here with mules," he told Lucille one evening. "Now look at what I'm up against. Not with Winkler or anybody else's help. Just me. Sometimes I think I'm dreaming."

When Fossett saw the figures he waved airily and recommended capitalizing for a million and a half. A considerable part of the excess would go to him both in cash and stock for implementing the deal. That was fair enough, Johnny assured Lucille. Fred had worked hard throughout the summer and fall arranging interviews, entertaining prospects, presenting the facts. He had lined up more than a score of likely investors. But, he told Johnny, the usual election-year hesitations, would delay the actual putting up of the money until spring.

"Things are slow everywhere," he said. They were sitting in his office. In the distance they could hear the noise of a Democratic parade starting along Seventeenth Street. "The Denver Steel Company is holding back construction until we see more clearly what is developing. So are the proposed new cotton mill and the paper company. I don't mean to suggest a serious recession. True, silver remains depressed and agricultural prices are down. On the other hand, farm output is up. New irrigation projects are hard at work. The state's gold and silver production last year amounted to more than thirty-two million and this year will be higher still, thanks to the silver boom at Creede and those new little gold fields at Cripple Creek, behind Pikes Peak. Have you been to Cripple Creek? It's interesting. Several of our mining men are looking over possible investments there. You ought to take it in on your way home."

Johnny stirred impatiently. "Red Mountain is enough for me."

Fossett gave his pale, important smile. "Single-mindedness—that's how I described you to Evans and Moffatt the other day. You of course know who they are." He rattled a letter as if to suggest that it had just arrived from one of those bankers. "As I told them, that sort of tenacity can be a greater assurance of success than any other personal qualification. But they insist on waiting for the election . . . Here come those Democrats. I suppose we might as well watch until we can hear ourselves think."

He threw open the window. Firecrackers popped. The blare of a thirty-piece band rose stridently. Immediately behind the band came a square banner made of panels joined together like the four sides of a box. This was carried on poles and steadied somewhat by portable guy ropes tied to the corners. On the front was a portrait of Grover Cleveland; on the back, his vice-presidential candidate, Adlai Stevenson. On either side were cartoons of contented workingmen smoking cigars and carrying lunch pails from which fat chickens dangled. Behind the banner marched costumed Jacksonian clubs from throughout the central part of the state.

When the marchers came abreast of the bank, they halted—deliberately, Fossett sniffed. At a signal from the drum major they roared in unison,

Rah! Rah! Rah!

There are no flies on Grover!
There are no flies on Grover!
There may be some on Ben,
But there are no flies on Grover

Rah! Rah! Rah!

CLEVELAND—STEVENSON

The names were hard to yell and the sound that beat around the window was an inarticulated bawl ending in a triumphant "son!"

Fossett closed the window. "He's a 'son' all right. I suppose you're voting for General Ben Harrison and the Republican ticket."

"No," Johnny said, "I'm voting Populist," and told about the rally on Red Mountain.

Fossett looked as if someone had aimed a loaded pistol at his heart. "You must be mad! Don't you know what the Populists advocate?—graduated income tax, an enforced eight-hour day, and"—Fossett shuddered—"government ownership of *railroads!*"

Johnny shrugged. "Waite comes square out for silver, which neither of the old parties do. Bimetallism is our first need. The rest of Waite's campaign guff we can worry about later."

"You always were your worst enemy with these impulsive, ill-considered actions." Fossett took off his pince-nez and rubbed his nose in agitation. "If word of this leaks out in Seventeenth Street, it could spoil every bit of groundwork I've prepared."

"You've been sitting behind a desk too long," Johnny said mildly. "You'd better come back for another look at the St. Johns—the silver St. Johns. Anybody who's going to live off silver sure as hell ought to be interested in silver. If those gold bugs of yours aren't, then we'll find investors who are."

Fossett retreated—the commissions involved were too big to toss away over politics, Johnny surmised later to Lucille. "Well, perhaps they won't hear about it," he said. "In any event there's little we can do until the smoke clears after the election."

"Which is next spring as far as construction is concerned," Johnny grumbled. Now that every detail was ready, delay chafed him. If financing had been available, he could at least have ordered and assembled supplies, and have prepared construction camps at Red Mountain and Argent, for he planned to attack the grade from either end of the line the moment weather allowed. But without funds he was handcuffed.

He went grumpily home to Argent to vote. The first returns on election night suggested that the Democratic ticket had swept both the state and national offices. About midnight victory-flushed Democrats paraded through the town, waving kerosene torches. Johnny went home to bed. About two o'clock he was aroused by a whooping messenger on horseback. Democrats might carry the nation, but in Colorado Waite and the Populists had crept ahead and were going to carry the state by an estimated three or four thousand votes. "Hell's a-poppin' in town!" the messenger howled. "Come on!"

Tremendously excited, John and Lucille dressed and drove down Silver Avenue in the buggy. The press of people was too great for them to reach the center of Argent. Evidently the Democrats had started a bonfire near the old pine flagpole at the intersection of Main Street and Silver Avenue. While they had been feeding it with privies pilfered from Republican and Populist back yards, the telegraph office had picked up the latest returns. In wild triumph the Populists then took over.

Halting the carriage, Johnny helped Lucille stand on the seat. Over the heads of the crowd they saw the silhouettes of the celebrants leaping and gesticulating like imps against the deep red of the fire. Now and then one would dart into the crowd, seize a hat from the head of a chagrined Democrat, and sail it into the blaze. Presently resistance developed. When a wagonload of screeching Populists appeared with a Democrat's privy, the losers tried to block the way. A furious melée followed. The shrill of police whistles halted nothing. A wedge of Populists formed around their trophy. Using it as a battering ram they bowled their way to the edge of the bonfire and with a ringing cheer hurled it high onto the flames. The insecure heap of half consumed tinder collapsed against the flagpole. Heat had already charred its whitewashed surface. Now it too broke into flame.

The flagpole was the oldest landmark in town. The fire bell tolled at last. Volunteers, regardless of party, ran to their places. Johnny did not join them, although he had been a member of the department, either active or honorary, since its sole apparatus had consisted of leather water buckets. Buckets would have been as useful tonight as the hose cart. The crowd was so dense and in so obstreperous a mood that before the lines could be coupled a great shout arose, "She's falling!" As neatly as if dropped by axes, the ancient pole toppled in a magnificent spray of sparks up Main Street, straight toward the gorge.

Johnny held the horses steady. "It's time that old relic quit blocking traffic," he approved. "The council has been voting on it for years, but somebody always blocks it. Sentiment. Well, she's done for now."

He reined the horses about. In the darkness following the collapse she could not read his face. What was he remembering? she wondered and then decided, Nothing. Defensiveness always made him tense. But the easy way he was handling the horses and humming to himself showed that at the moment he was completely relaxed and cheerful.

On the porch he paused to look down on his town. The embers had been doused; the streets were dark. Only an occasional yell still disturbed the sibilance of wind and water.

"It's been a long haul," he said with deep satisfaction, "but silver has won, at least in Colorado. Now we can get to work."

VII

"1"

The investors Johnny had counted on were less contented. Fossett kept writing of delay after delay until in the spring of '93 Johnny went impatiently to Denver himself with a plan for action.

"We'll let them size up the worth of the country with their own eyes," he said. "Here's how I figure it. As soon as summer has come and the mountains are pretty, we'll take them to Argent by special train. I'll rent a broad-gauge car here in Denver for the run to Salida. For the rest of the trip to Argent we'll transfer them to a narrow-gauge varnish outfit all their own—parlor car, observation car, buffet, the works."

Fossett looked alarmed. "How many people can you afford to entertain that way?"

"Everybody you've talked to. Their wives and children. A real outing. We'll time it to hit the Shower of Silver in Argent—that's an annual Fourth of July celebration now, you know. I can have the lower construction camp laid out for them to see and perhaps a few hundred yards of grading toward the gorge. After they've had a look at that, we'll load them back on their special and take them clear around the St. Johns to Montezuma over Otto's new line. From Montezuma we'll go up Los Padres Canyon to Baker—that canyon'll pop their eyes. Next we'll come up the Baker Northern tracks to Red Mountain—an open observation car under those red peaks, over the turntable, past mine after mine working full blast—that'll show 'em a thing or two!"

"It should be impressive," Fossett conceded.

"I'll have the construction camp at Red Mountain ready, too. I'll buy some rails and lay a mile of line along the edge of the meadows to where we begin the rock work. If the special is too heavy to run along those light rails, we'll transfer the party onto a couple of flatcars and let the goat haul them to where they can see the beginning of the grade and the power-station site with their own eyes. Harmon Gregg will have a show on tap, too. He has ordered a lot of brick and will have started putting up his compressor house and other buildings at the mouth of the tunnel."

"Bricks have to be imported."

"Yes."

"Isn't that extravagant? Won't planks and sheet metal do?"

"Floppy old sheet metal don't look like much," Johnny said. "Harmon figures to hit the money hard while it's coming by."

"The investors are coming to see your railroad."

"Harmon realizes that, but it won't hurt to give the men in that group something to talk about on their way back to Denver. That's the whole point of the excursion. After we've shown them the proposed line, Walt will take them down the gorge to Argent in stagecoaches. Walt has finally decided to come in with me on the railroad, as I guess I wrote." Johnny smiled in pure pleasure. "Cautious Cat Kennerly! It's taken me fifteen years to bring him in on a deal but finally I've made it."

"Naturally. Your trolley will put his stage and freight lines out of business."

"He'll wind up the tour in fine style," Johnny promised. "A hair-raising thrill at the end of the most scenic ride in America—Argent to Montezuma to Baker, then Red Mountain and down that gorge to Argent. The Rainbow Circle I figure to call it. It'll bring a tourist boom to the whole region. I've talked to Winkler about it. He's all for it."

"Of course. A large part of the run will be over his lines." Fossett removed his pince-nez and rubbed his nose. "How do you plan to finance this? Hiring trains for such a junket isn't exactly cheap. In addition, you're talking of launching construction before you've sold a dime's worth of stock."

"That's not quite accurate," Johnny said. "Walt is advancing ten thousand dollars against stock. That'll more than take care of the train. I've sold my interest in the quarry and gas company. Most of the money went to pay for the engineering studies, I'll admit. But the Argent bank will loan my construction company enough on its due bills for me to set up the layout in Argent. I'm hoping your bank here will accept my share of the toll-road company and my franchise from the state for the trolley line as collateral for a loan to start the Red Mountain end of things."

Fossett temporized. "You're getting in pretty deep."

"I haven't missed on Red Mountain yet," Johnny said. "Not since the day I told Gabe Porcella I'd bring in a mule train of supplies for him to sell out of a tent. Now Gabe is grossing a hundred thousand a year in his store—mostly food and staple dry goods that'll soon be coming up to him on the electric railway."

"I know; I've read your statistics," Fossett grumbled. He rattled a letter and rubbed his nose. "I must confess our financiers here have been worrying about the sluggishness of the national economy. Still, I'm sure they'll be interested in the junket you propose. I don't mind telling you, John, that you're getting a name throughout the state for imagination and aggressive work. Such a reputation is probably the best collateral you could have. I think perhaps, after I've presented the case, the directors here will help somewhat. I'll let you know."

The directors did help—after the fashion of bankers. They scaled down John's request by twenty per cent and asked for more collateral. In the end he had to mortgage even the Vinegar Hill home. Nonetheless he was satisfied.

"It's enough to let me make the showing I want up on the mountain," he told Fossett as he prepared to return to Argent. "Do me one favor, though. Don't say anything to your wife about the house. The word might slip back to Lucille, and you know how these women are about their homes."

"2"

Six loaded freight cars was the maximum which the small narrow-gauge locomotives of the Baker Northern could haul at one time over the tight curves and steep grades of Summit Pass. During June, five of these trains arrived at Red Mountain City in addition to the regular runs. About two thirds of the cars were loaded with rail for John, one third with brick for Harmon's buildings at the New Hopes Tunnel.

By the time the iron began arriving, Johnny had already graded his right-of-way from the town toward the head of the gorge, grubbing out the stumps and burning the trash so that corner-cutting foremen could not use the junk as fill in the roadbed. Drainage ditches were installed; the fills were banked evenly to prevent settling and sliding; every culvert was equipped with a precise mud sill.

Soon everything was prepared so that the little goat which John leased from Winkler could shove carloads of ties, rails, bolts, and spikes out to the track's end. Waiting men passed out the ties, laying them evenly. Next came the rails, three men at the forward end of each piece, two at the rear. These were dropped onto the ties and bolted together by fishplates, enough room being left between the joints for expansion. Spikers next fixed the rails to the ties along a line carefully chalked by the gaugers. Ashes and cinders were used in damp spots for ballast.

It went swimmingly: 2640 ties, 532 pair of fishplates, 1408 bolts, 27 kegs of spikes, and 47 tons of thirty-pound rail to reach the New Hopes spur. Originally Harmon had planned to transport his brick to the tunnel mouth by wagon in order to have the buildings under way before the excursionists arrived. When he saw how fast the rails progressed, however, he decided to let the brick stack up in the freight yard until Johnny's work train could move it.

That was how matters stood on June 27, 1893—a mountain of red brick stacked near the depot and, running from the brick toward the gorge, the shine of the new steel rails, bright against the gouged red earth. On June 27, Red Mountain learned that the mints of India had stopped the coinage of silver. Overnight quotations dropped five cents and afterwards kept sagging. The Smuggler and two smaller mines received telegrams ordering them to suspend work. Men stood on every street corner shaking their heads. Some didn't know for sure where India was. Many didn't understand why a happening on the other side of the world should have created such instantaneous havoc in the Colorado Rockies. They looked up at the red peaks and scowled as if somehow the very stones had betrayed them.

Harmon Gregg, his face drawn and pale above his silky chin whiskers, explained to the workers he laid off at the tunnel that the knock was bad because India had been the one remaining major country in the world with a silver monetary standard; now there were none and the repercussions were shaking every financial center from Bombay to Boston. Sam Varnum, pessimistic as always, said coinage wasn't the true cause of the trouble; the nation was suffering from overspeculation, and India's action had simply knocked the last of the props out from under the house of cards. Now everything would tumble.

Only John and Parley Quine and two or three others scoffed at the gloom: it stood to reason, didn't it, that the intrinsic worth of the mountains had not changed overnight? Perhaps it was a good thing that the Indians had abandoned silver; the action might jar Congress into doing something positive for the West. Varnum quoted their arguments at length in the paper, although he wasn't convinced that he personally believed a word they said.

As for Pat Edgell, he did not care at all. He was mining gold as hard as the space restrictions of his small vein allowed, two shifts a day, and the price of gold was by law as steady as a rock. In fact, his profits would increase if the sudden depression dragged down the costs of supplies. Already the frightened coal dealers in Montezuma were offering their product for thirty cents a ton less than it had brought in May.

On June 30 a telegram reached Johnny from Fossett: SITUATION SO UNSTABLE EXCURSION POSTPONED SO PROSPECTS CAN KEEP IN TOUCH DEVELOPMENTS HERE. TRIP TENTATIVELY RESCHEDULED JULY 15.

That was when Johnny felt his first pangs of doubt. On the first of July he suspended work on the railroad. Varnum appeared instantly with questions. Was the layoff permanent?

"Certainly not," Johnny snapped testily. "Everybody is rattled. What we need is a vacation—a good time. Things would be closing in a couple of days anyway for the Shower of Silver. I'm just going down early and enjoy myself. I recommend that everybody else do the same. As soon as the holiday is over we'll come back with a fresh perspective."

The celebration merely increased the area's dejection. Workers who in previous years had spent freely grew fearful for their jobs and decided to save their money. Those who did play got drunker and more shrill than usual, as though the sound of any sort of laughter was the last barrier against emptiness. Three floats scheduled for the parade were never completed; another broke down in front of the new bank building. The Argent baseball team lost its game to the Hillsdale farmers by a score of 13 to 3. Old friends meeting on the street after long separation thumped each other boisterously, talked rapidly for few moments and then grew embarrassed, reluctant to say what occupied their thoughts.

"Tough times, Johnny."

"We've seen 'em before, Luke."

"Yeah, I guess. Well, I'd better be jumping—a million errands."

Away they went, as if motion might help. Two doors down, the pattern repeated. "Hi there, Jack! Long time no see!" "Linc, you old horse thief, what da ya know?" . . . "See you around, boy." "Sure thing. Don't take any wooden nickels." Run again. And then: "Morning, John." "Mud in your eye, Al." And on.

But no one was really busy.

The event that irritated Johnny most was an act interpolated at the last minute in a variety show put on at the Opera House by various civic organizations. The auditorium was crowded. The local jokes, the stumbling dance routines, and the personal allusions by local performers were applauded vigorously by a home audience. But to Johnny's mind a routine built out of the town's despair was inexcusable.

Al Ewer produced the verses. A barber-shop quartet hastily learned them and donned tattered clothes to represent various classes of desti-

tute workers—miner, cowboy, locomotive engineer, grocery clerk. They
held their heads close together, rolled their eyes mournfully toward the
chandeliers, and wailed to the accompaniment of a bent saw blade
gripped between a fifth performer's knees and struck into doleful vibrations by a muffled stick.

> Prospectors tramping the St. Johns through
>   Listen to my tale of woe!
> Sat down one day their grub to chew
> And on the ground midst grass and dew
> Saw outcrops of silver which they knew.
>
>   Hard trials! Times are blue!
>   A silver dollar's not worth a sou,
>   All on account of the Gold Bug crew.
>   Oh! Listen to my tale of woe!
>
> Then thousands of miners to Red Mountain flew.
>   Listen to my tale of woe!
> They founded railroads and cities too
> And built an empire vast and new,
> Which Gold Bugs are vowing now to subdue.
>
>   Hard trials! Times are blue!
>   Silver is down to sixty-two,
>   The act of the villainous Wall Street crew.
>   Oh! Listen to my tale of woe!
>
> But the bugs shall learn their ills to rue.
>   Listen to my tale of woe!
> They shall hear free silver's hullabaloo,
> For we'll join and fight like a starved Zulu
> To skin Grover Cleveland, the big Yahoo!
>
>   He'll listen to our tale of woe!
>   Hard trials! But listen true!
>   Better times will soon ensue.
>   We drink to the death of the Gold Bug crew
>   As we make them answer our tale of woe!

The audience yelled and stamped. Johnny sat glowering, arms folded
across his chest. Afterward, as he and Lucille were undressing for bed
in the Vinegar Hill house, he growled,

"That was damn poor judgment of Al and of the boys to come on the
stage dressed in rags and remind us of our troubles. What we need is
entertainment that'll take our minds off our worries. You'd think this
town was getting set to bury itself."

"The troubles are there," Lucille said. "Laughing at them is one way to make them seem smaller."

"Like kids whistling in the dark," Johnny scoffed. "It doesn't take away the night."

"It helps take away the fear. What else would you have?"

"Work! Mining, cutting lumber, building railroads—the enterprise that made this country in the first place." He flung himself into bed and jerked up the covers. "If everyone in these mountains went back to his regular job in the morning, the panic would be over by evening."

"Who would pay for it?"

"There's as much money in the world today as there was yesterday, isn't there?"

She turned out the gas light and slipped in beside him. His chest and legs were tense. "Don't stew so, Johnny."

"It's those damn fraid-cats in Denver. They could have come as easy as not, but because a mint closes way off in India, they all of a sudden think they see holes in their pockets. They freeze, figuring that's the way to save what they've got, when anyone knows the only value money has is when it moves. They could stop this foolishness tomorrow if they would. Fossett's a banker. You'd think he'd show them a few straight facts."

"Let me get you a glass of milk. Then try to sleep. Things always look simpler in the morning."

"I don't want any milk. And it's simple enough right now. Everything I've said makes sense, don't it?"

"I can't understand any of it, darling. But I do know you'll worry yourself sick if you keep on this way."

"Forget it," he said and turned away.

He did not sleep. Toward dawn while he was in the kitchen getting himself milk, the telephone rang. It was Nora, asking whether Harmon was there.

"No," Johnny said. "What made you think he would be?"

"After the show several of us were sitting in the Belmont lobby talking. Finally I said I was going to bed. Harmon said he'd be along later; he wasn't sleepy, he was going for a walk. I woke up a few minutes ago and he isn't here. He—" Nora paused. Her voice was high and tight. "I thought he might have gone to your place to talk."

"Have you called anywhere else?"

"The hospital and the jail. And the Pastime. It's closed." (The Pastime never used to close during the Shower of Silver, Johnny thought absently.) "It's four o'clock, John. I don't know what to think. He hasn't been himself all evening."

"Sit tight. Lucille and I'll be right down."

He hung up and saw his wife, standing barefooted and cold and perturbed in the doorway. He summarized the call. "What she really wanted was for me to go look for him," he muttered as they hurried back upstairs to dress.

"Do you think . . ."

"Of course not. Anyway, she never used to be so all-fired worked up when Harmon stayed away overnight."

"That's the first cruel thing I ever heard you say. They're trying again. Where would she turn if anything happened to him?"

"Nothing has," he said and harnessed the buggy and drove Lucille to the hotel. As dawn started seeping into the sky he drove about the streets until he located the three night policemen. Each gave him a negative answer. Not knowing where else to turn, he pointed the horse along the road toward the Narrows. He had driven a mile or more and light was brightening enough for colors to show when he saw a lone figure walking toward him.

It was Harmon. Johnny halted the buggy and after a moment's hesitation Harmon climbed in. He did not speak. He sat humped and shrunken inside his thin overcoat. His shoes and trouser cuffs were crusted with gray mud. The only clay Johnny knew of like that was three miles farther on.

He turned the buggy and waited for Harmon to be the one to decide when to talk. "Did Nora send you?" he asked presently.

"She woke alone in a strange room and took to fretting. She'll be all right. Things always look simpler in the morning."

Harmon did not answer. The sun rose above the rim of the amphitheater and struck a dazzling radiance from the snowy peaks. Johnny tilted his head to watch.

"It's going to be another fine day."

Harmon shrank deeper into his coat. Suddenly he blurted, "John, I can't even pay my hotel bill."

Johnny smiled. "If that's the worst of things, I reckon we can manage."

"I don't see any way out. That new president of the bank, Bill Escher, was after me just before the show—"

"He's bothering everyone: has to call in some of their paper, he says. I told him my loan still has six months to run and I'll talk to him when the time comes. You're not due yet, are you?"

"Two more months. But then? If those Denver investors had come in and Escher and the others could see that outsiders have confidence in me—but to stake everything on their visit and then have them not show—"

"Hang on. They'll come." Johnny felt the muscles of his own

stomach grow tight again. Explosively he said, "What we need is to get out of this goddamn gloom and go back up Red Mountain and breathe some clean air. It'll give us a fresh perspective."

"That's what you said when you talked us into coming down here."

"Did I? Well, now I'm saying to go back."

"Jesus, Johnny!" Harmon cried, looking at him almost frantically. "Don't *you* go getting rattled!"

"3"

Less than a week after they had returned to the mountain, Johnny and Lucille to their aspen-log summer home and Harmon and Nora to the new white frame house they were building at the tunnel site, President Cleveland called the Congress of the United States to convene in special session on August 7 to consider the repeal of the Sherman Silver Purchase Act. That night three more Red Mountain mines shut down. In Denver, Governor Davis Waite cried somewhat incoherently to a mass meeting in Coliseum Hall, "If the money power shall attempt to sustain its usurpations by 'the strong hand,' we will meet the issue when it is forced upon us, for it is better, infinitely better, that blood should flow to the horses' bridles rather than our national liberties should be destroyed." The rafters rang. Ever after the governor would be called "Bloody-bridles Waite." But neither his tirade nor the resounding endorsement given it by the State Silver League helped Denver's banks. Between the twelfth and fourteenth of July, twelve of them closed their doors. Fred Fossett was a vice-president of one of the first to crash.

As soon as the news reached Red Mountain, Johnny wired Fossett, "What about the excursion?" No answer came. The fifteenth arrived and he frantically contacted the station master at Argent and the one at Salida. Neither had heard a word about the special train Fred supposedly had authorized for that day.

The bank in Argent failed. The Rose Marie shut down. The Ram laid off thirty-three per cent of its crew; the Dixie Girl eliminated its night shift. Each morning the Baker Northern puffed mournfully over the pass with a single car, baggage in the front half, two or three passengers in the rear. Each afternoon it puffed back with the entire car and sometimes the coal tender jammed by people fleeing the town. The prostitutes were among the first to leave. "That's the infallible sign," Varnum remarked as he and Johnny and Harmon Gregg were standing idly outside the shack by the depot which Johnny used for an office, near Harmon's bricks. Three befeathered girls from Slanting Annie's climbed into the coach, found seats, then leaned from the windows and thumbed their noses at the town. Sam thumbed back. "The rats and the sinking ship—" he said and blushed as red as the bricks at his own unwonted temerity.

"They'll be the first back when things improve," Johnny said. "They always are."

Each day, however, he saw two or three more empty houses in town. Often the occupants did not bother to take the cooking pots off the stoves, but simply threw a change of clothes into a grip and lit out for the low country. If they had the fare, they rode the stage or the train. Otherwise they walked down the gorge, suitcase in hand and blanket roll over one shoulder. Walt told his drivers that whenever the stages had room they should pick up women, children, and men who looked either old or sick. In Argent barrels appeared on the street corners marked FOR OUR MINERS. Gifts of clothing were put into these, taken to the churches, cleaned, repaired, and distributed. Twice a day restaurants passed out from their back doors whatever leftover food and stale bread they had. Farms down the river were besieged by men offering to do any sort of work in return for a meal and a chance to sleep in the barn out of the weather.

At Red Mountain abandoned dogs shivered forlornly on empty steps. Abandoned donkeys prowled the alleys. Abandoned cats slunk between the houses. Johnny took to stopping by Gabe's store every other day or so, it was generally empty of customers, to pick up bones and scraps for the dogs. The other creatures stood a fairer show of making out on their own until snow flew. Then—but by then things would have taken a turn for the better.

He wrote Fossett three urgent letters. Finally a hasty scrawl came back, misjudged words blotted out and forgotten ones inserted above carets. Sorry not to have written sooner but he'd been in Cripple Creek with certain individuals he was not free to name. (Johnny smiled; he could hear Fossett rattling a paper and looking important.) He was still working on the excursion, in a private capacity, being of the unemployed himself. Naturally he wanted the plan to go through —the commission and so on. If John would be patient . . .

"You see!" Johnny exulted, showing the letter up and down the street. "Patience, that's all. Fossett's in the know and he figures things will look up." To Harmon he added. "Fred's not just sitting dead like you were afraid maybe he was. He'll have those investors here in time for us to start work before winter, even yet. You wait!"

"Not much else to do," Harmon said wryly and wandered off to sit in the sun on one of his mounds of brick. He had been trying unsuccessfully to sell bits of the material here and there, without Johnny's knowledge in order to save argument. Johnny knew anyway and said nothing in order to spare Harmon's feelings.

On August 7, the day Congress convened, the railroad brought in the final three carloads of rail Johnny had purchased. He had written asking that the order be canceled, but evidently the rolling mill intended to make him stand by his contract. The sight of the cars and the clang of the unloading bred a rumor that John Ogden was about to resume work. Before he could stop the talk, sixty-three men had come to his office shack in the railyard, begging for jobs. It harrowed him.

"I've done a thing or two around these mountains," he said miserably to Lucille at supper, "and now people expect me to keep on doing. That's what's so hard—seeing their eyes expect and having to shake your head and watch the look go dead. I can't take it much longer. Why doesn't Fred do something?"

She managed a smile. "You read what he wrote: be patient."

"Sure." Like Harmon had said, what else was there to do?

Save for the rails, very little freight moved that August. Normally the mines would have been shipping as much ore as possible during favorable weather and bringing in coal to stockpile against winter. This summer, however, the few concerns still producing were holding their ore and concentrate in the hope that a decision by Congress to maintain the Silver Purchase Act would result in a rise in price. On the other hand, repeal might shut them down overnight and they did not wish to be caught with supplies on hand. Accordingly they bought only for immediate needs.

Pat Edgell alone prospered. He selected for his gold mine the best men from the hordes of workers who haunted his employment office and increased his ton output per laborer to fantastic levels. As soon as a silver mine closed, he visited its manager and bought whatever was salable at bargain prices. By the time Joe Dyer and other supervisors woke up to what he was doing and tried to emulate him it was too late; Pat had cornered, at a third its former price, every spare ton of coal on the mountain and had hired Walt to cart it to his fenced storage yard at the Golden Joker, as he called his property.

He dressed as Parley Quine had used to dress and strutted through the streets. Each time he saw John Ogden he called joyfully, "Heard from your banker yet, Jackie boy? When do you start work on your railroad?"

Endless days. Each afternoon a crowd gathered outside the telegraph office, waiting for word from Washington. Each afternoon it was a smaller crowd. By Sam Varnum's estimate, eighty per cent of Red

Mountain's population had evaporated during the summer. Now
scarcely a thousand persons remained.

On August 21 black figures went up in the window. The act had
been repealed in the House by a vote of 239–108.

The next morning Sam brought out an extra whose margins were
lined by black. He summarized the debates and the statement by the
president and the roaring protests from western politicians. Sadly he
concluded his editorial, "Write our senators. The Senate is our last,
forlorn hope."

Johnny read the piece on the porch of the cabin—a beautiful,
sunny morning. "Western senators don't need letters," he growled. He
heard the telephone ring and Lucille go answer it. He went on grumbling. "Eastern senators are the ones we need to get next to. I don't
suppose they'd read a letter from Red Mountain City, Colorado, but
just the same I've a mind to—"

"Johnny!"

Her scream lifted him from his chair into the doorway. She met him
there and clung to him, trembling so that she could not speak.

"What's the matter?" She grimaced mutely. "Who called? Lucy!"

"It was Tommy Brice. He wants us right away. Nora—oh, Johnny!"

"What's happened to her?"

"Nothing. I mean, she just came running to the ranch from their
house at the tunnel. She—poor, poor, Nora. Oh hurry!"

"What is the matter?"

"Harmon. He—" She burst into tears.

"Lucy!" He shook her shoulders, violently because he had already
guessed. "Get hold of yourself!"

"He put a shotgun in his mouth and—and—hurry, John! We've got
to go to her."

He stood there stunned. "Why didn't he wait?" he cried in protest.

"4"

He dropped Lucille from the buggy at the Brice's gate. Nora did not
appear, for which he was thankful. He waved for Tommy to join him
and in silence they drove to the home at the New Hopes, its upper
floor unfinished. *All that for two people,* he thought once again before
recalling that there were no longer two.

The deputy sheriff and a deputy coroner arrived a little later—
Tommy had done a good job of keeping his head. They went

through their routines, wrapped the body in a blanket, loaded it into the coroner's spring wagon, and rattled briskly away. John and Tommy returned to the ranch. Johnny's throat was dry. He kept swallowing at it and wondering why he had supposed it necessary for him to go to the New Hopes. The county people would have been enough.

At the Brice ranch they jumped stiffly to the ground and pushed through the picket gate. It creaked shut behind them, pulled by a clothesline to which was affixed, as counterweight, a heavy piece of broken casting salvaged from one of the mines. Nora slipped away from Lucille and ran toward them. She was puffy-faced but obviously had been persuaded to bathe her cheeks and tidy her hair. As she neared him, Johnny put his hands behind his back.

"What have you done with him?" she demanded.

Tommy told her. "We'll make the arrangements later. Don't worry about it now."

"Worry?" She grimaced over the word and swiveled on Johnny. "You're the one!" she said.

The concentrated venom of the thrust startled him. Her eyes looked wild, and his mind scrambled to excuse her. It must have been a horrible shock to hear the twelve-gauge roar as Harmon triggered it with his toe—Johnny remembered afresh how dreadfully white that one bare foot had looked—and to have run in and found him so. He gave her a vague shake of his head in lieu of the sympathy he could not articulate.

"You! You! You!"

"Nora!" Tommy laid a hand on her arm.

She shook it away. "He'd bet on you, he said. All summer I tried to tell him. I said it wouldn't work. I tried to make him leave. But no. You!"

"Nora!"

"It's time someone told him. Hardrock Johnny—that's what he called you. 'These veins go deep. I'll bet on Johnny,' he said. 'I started betting on him when I took his first case and he's been right every time.' Over and over he said it. 'They won't come,' I told him, 'those men from Denver won't come. We've got to leave while we can.' But no. 'I'll bet on Johnny.' You!"

Where did she think they could have gone? Johnny wondered absently. He started an automatic gesture of protest and in the nick of time checked the motion, letting her horror work itself out unrestrained.

" 'Johnny'll bring them,' he said. 'I'm betting on Johnny.' He bet wrong, didn't he? From the very beginning we've bet wrong, all of us. Silver! Red Mountain!" Her hands clasped her head, the fingers in the tumbling, thick brown hair. A detached, remote part of his mind observed, She's a good-looking woman still: that panther vitality: a wonder it hadn't devoured Harmon long ago. Her distraught gaze swung along the horizon, stopped on the three scarlet peaks, serene against a flawless sky. "I hate you!" she screamed. And then at last she began to weep.

Her brother and her stepmother led her to the house. Lucille stayed with her husband.

"Forgive her, Johnny. She . . ."

"Sure." But words were no good. Forgetful at last, he waved a palm outward in a gesture of helplessness.

She gasped. "Your hands!"

He looked at them, the palms and the backs. "I was kind of shook myself, I guess," he apologized. "I didn't think about cleaning up until after we'd loaded what was left of him in the wagon and Tommy was ready to leave and anyway I didn't want to go back in that house." He rotated his hands, still staring at them. "He should have waited," he cried. "The men'll come!"

He took a step as if to circle the farmhouse and seek a washbasin in the kitchen. Immediately he stopped. Not there. Turning, he went blindly through the picket gate, passed his buggy without pause, and strode along the lane. Lucille hesitated a moment, glancing toward the house where Nora was, and then ran after him.

An earth-covered log bridge spanned the creek where it crossed the lane. Johnny veered away from its approach and walked down to the edge of the water. Kneeling, he washed. The blood was caked and did not yield easily. Scooping up the fine, rust-colored sand from the creek bottom, he used it as a scouring powder. At length he straightened, half leaning and half sitting on the edge of the bridge as he pulled a blue bandana handkerchief from his pocket for a towel. The sun was warm. He felt the soft breeze, willow-scented, stir his hair. The meadow grass beyond the pole fence was ready for mowing, lush and fresh, shimmering like silver when the fitful breeze rustled across it. Tommy would make a good crop this year, he thought, the best yet. A good worker, Tommy. The place had looked half shabby as long as the old man had run it, but the boy was putting it into first-class shape.

He glanced up at Lucille's worried, questioning face. "We didn't bet wrong," he said. A little blood remained on the cuticles of two of his fingernails. He worried at it with the ball of his thumb. "They'll come," he said.

He climbed onto the bridge, crossed it and walked so rapidly toward town that every now and then she had to trot to keep up. He talked jerkily to her, not glancing around.

"You know what I think I'll do? I'll get Walt to go to Denver and help Fred boost the excursion along. Fred hasn't been back here for three years or more. He hasn't the feel for it. Walt knows. He can tell them. Probably they're scared of the price, too. Well, we can cut it by going to the steeper grades and still have a railroad that'll work. Labor will be cheaper, too. A round million—that doesn't sound so bad. While Walt's in Denver, I'll put the finishing touches on the survey— it's rough; we didn't figure to use it—and work out the rest of the details so that when they come they can see with their own eyes exactly what's what."

She caught his arm. She was panting. "Johnny, wait!" When she had halted him she said, "I have to go back to Nora."

His glance returned along the lane. He gave his head a shake of bewilderment. He had completely forgotten the buggy. Well, he was not going back now.

"You can drive the buggy home when you're ready, can't you?"

"Please come back with me."

"I've too much to do." He kept rubbing his thumb across his finger-nails. "We didn't bet wrong. Next thing, she'll be telling me Harmon never should have helped me out of that Hedstrom mess thirteen years ago."

"She didn't mean that."

"Yes she did. She all but said it. And if she's right, then I was wrong about Hedstrom. And Pat. And Aino. And everything else I've done here. Everything! Well, she's the one who's wrong. I'm going to show her so."

Despair darkened her eyes. "It's you saying those things, not Nora. Johnny, listen to me. You're upset. You're unreasonable. That's natural. But you've got to face—"

"She'll see," he muttered and stalked off toward town, leaving Lucille alone in the empty road.

"5"

The next day he bounded up the porch steps and into the house almost as cheerily as he had used to return home before the panic. He shied his hat at the hatrack, missed, let it lie, and smiled at her through the dusk of the room. She was sitting very quietly in one of the easy chairs he had extravagantly purchased in Denver and had shipped to the mountain over the Baker Northern. She was dressed with the painful neatness she might have used before visiting the dentist. The unnatural reserve scarcely touched his mind, however. He was too full of his own doings.

"Old Walt didn't like it much, but he finally agreed to go to Denver." Briskly Johnny rubbed his hands together. "Now I can start polishing up that other survey. You don't know how good that feels—having something solid to do again."

"Don't send him."

Surely he hadn't heard correctly. "Don't what?"

She stayed rigid in her chair. "Sit down, Johnny."

He stared at her. "Where are you going?"

"Nowhere."

"What're you dressed up for?"

"It helped me keep my courage."

"Where are the kids?"

"I sent them over to Jenny Shaffer's. Please sit down."

Mystified, he obeyed. "You're being mighty funny."

"It's about Lennie," she said.

"Oh?" he asked carefully. Lucille rarely spoke of the boy these days; Johnny rarely thought of him. He sorted dates rapidly. No, it wasn't the anniversary either of Lennie's birth or dying. She had not been to the cemetery since they had visited Argent for the Shower of Silver. So she couldn't be brooding too much. He risked an indulgent smile. "What about Lennie?"

"I hardly know how to begin." Her eyes were lowered to a thread she was picking at on the arm of the chair. Her fingers trembled. Abruptly she looked him full in the face. "Promise not to interrupt."

"Lucy, what on—?"

"Promise!"

"Sure, but—"

"Sssh!"

The words rushed: the entire shame. "I was wrong," she finished. She began again to pick at the thread, stopped, and folded her hands in her lap. "I should have told you long ago."

He went to the entry, put his hat on the hatrack, and for a moment looked at the red peaks through the glassed upper half of the door. Presently he turned back to her.

"Would you be telling me this if Lennie was alive?"

"Why do you ask?"

"Just wondering."

"I had to consider what was best for him too," she said in so small a voice he could scarcely hear.

"Why are you telling me now?" he persisted. It had been calculated.

She had decided; and then, while she dressed and while she waited for him to return from talking to Walt, she must have weighed the advisability of every word. And when he had come back, almost the first thing she'd said, he remembered, had been, *Don't send Walt.*

He dropped into a straight chair facing her and leaned forward, elbows on knees. "What does Walt's going to Denver have to do with it?"

"Can't you see?" she cried desperately.

"No, I'm damned if I can."

She groped for words. "Johnny, the wrong I did was not altogether . . . Lennie. What was worse was hiding it. Every morning when I woke up I felt the ache here, under my heart. Nearly every day I wondered, What if this is the day my husband finds out? I knew I was wrong. I tried I don't know how many times to make myself tell you, and at the last minute I always lost my nerve and hid it again. It's the one thing that has been false about our marriage. It needn't have been. I should have faced it."

He patted her hand. "Poor Lucy! You needn't have worried so."

"That's what I'm trying to tell you: *you* needn't worry so."

"Me!"

"About Hedstrom. Face it, Johnny!"

He pulled back. "What makes you think I do worry? Anyhow, they're nothing alike."

"Yes! You've been trying to hide it ever since—"

"Hide! The whole state knew. I couldn't have hid it if I'd wanted to."

"Not secretly, as I did. But you tried to deny the wrong by making it seem right for the good of the country."

"It wasn't wrong. The court freed me."

"No it didn't. And ever since then you've been trying to do what the court didn't. You thought that if Red Mountain turned out right, you'd be right. It's behind everything you've done. It's behind sending Walt to Denver. And it's going to break your heart unless you bring it into the open and look at it for what it is."

"That's why you brought yours out?"

"I couldn't ask you any other way to be honest."

He jumped to his feet and paced the room. "Nora! That's what's the matter—her hollering that I'd bet wrong. You practically agreed with her the other day in the lane. But you've got it wrong, both of you. The values I bet on were in those mountains before I started to Gunnison for grub. They were there before Young Hedstrom ever shot that Indian. They've always been there. They still are. It was Hedstrom, not me, who would have spoiled our chance to open this country for the prospectors who were lined up, aching to come in. It was Pat, not me, who wanted to turn the road into a private speculation. No, I wasn't trying to make Red Mountain right. It has always been right. What I did was what I had to do to keep it right—not the other way around, like you've got it."

His intensity rather than his words was what she followed. She could have wept for him.

"I know what you say is true, too," she granted. "But the two are so mixed together——"

He swung his hand downward, chopping her off. "Why you're bringing this up now—why you drag Lennie into it—why Walt should stay—how you think any of this will help put a trolley down the canyon—"

"It isn't that at all." She did weep now, silent tears salty on her lips. She wiped at them with the back of her hand. "It's to help you when you find you *can't* build the trolley."

He stopped dead still. "You!" he said at last, much as Nora had spoken the word the other day. "I never thought you would quit me!" He lifted his chin. "I will build it. You'll see! You'll both see!"

He swung toward the door. There he paused. He had been desperately hurt. The impulse to retaliate was more than he could down. Over his shoulder he said, "The next time you feel like making a confession, go see Spec Alden or someone in the business. Personally, I'm not interested."

Out he went.

VIII

"1"

After the funeral, Nora stayed in Argent with her sister Mabel, married for the past five years to the best blacksmith in town, the one to whom Walt gave most of his work. Lucille stayed also, opening the Vinegar Hill house and moving in with the children. She could help Nora, she said, and besides it was too near the opening of school to go dragging back up the hill now.

Johnny accepted the fiction. The aftermath of the quarrel had been grim. They had ridden properly side by side to the funeral and in front of the children had dabbed properly at the household routines, acutely conscious of each other, yet scarcely speaking when alone, each waiting for the other to yield. He saw the reluctant Walt off on the train, returned home long enough to kiss her cool mouth and leave her more cash than he could conveniently afford, and then rode back up the gorge. At Wolf Creek Falls he remembered her bundled against the cold on their winter sleigh rides. Lifting his head, he saw the old horse trail and the small flat where he had proposed. He spurred the horse on. At the spot where long ago he had linked the two sections of the new trail on this side of the canyon, he recalled how she and her son had walked along the opposite slope to watch the blast she dreaded—and how he had failed to see them waving to him from their cranny. At the head of the gorge he remembered Lennie feeding the chipmunks, learning to master the pony. He was in a savage mood when he reached Red Mountain City.

A week crawled by. Walt's departure on an errand everyone knew and Johnny's resumption of surveying brought a constant stream of unemployed workers. "I'm a miner by trade, Mr. Ogden, but now I'm willing to do anything." "Logging is my line, but to tell the truth I'd be happy to shake hands even with a wheelbarrow." "Four kids at home, Mr. Ogden, like you've got." "It sounds funny for a trained book-keeper, I suppose, but hoeing, cleaning up . . ." "Johnny, if I don't get work soon . . ."

Anything, Mr. Ogden. Anything. He could not face the desperate eyes. "If you'll leave your name and where I can reach you. Then as soon as Mr. Kennerly is back . . ."

Four more days went by. He slept fitfully. He was awake before dawn each morning. He dressed at the first light and walked through the shadowless dusk, the September frost pinking his ears, to the only café still operating. Generally he was waiting when the owner opened the door.

Invariably the fellow asked, "Any word from Walt yet?"

And Johnny would have to shake his head. "Today, I hope."

Finally he wired Walt in care of Fossett's home address. He was too nervous to return to his surveying. While he waited for a reply, he rode to the Dixie Girl to gossip with Joe Dyer. Joe looked about as tired as Johnny felt. He had lost eighteen pounds since the first of July, he said.

Johnny asked whether the Dixie Girl would stay open throughout the winter even if the Senate joined the House of Representatives in voting to repeal the Sherman Act. Joe scrubbed his round, weary face with the palm of a horny, big-knuckled hand. He couldn't say definitely; the decision would be up to the directors.

"But we can scratch along for a while, even at these prices. Hell, we've better'n two hundred thousand tons of ore in sight and half of it developed, ready to stope. With that expense behind us and by work-ing the higher grade areas, we can keep seventy or seventy-five men busy for at least another year." Dyer grimaced; six months ago six hun-dred men had been working in the Dixie Girl. "But it sure isn't the kind of mining we came here for."

"What about the Ram and the Summit Queen?"

"More or less the same story, I imagine."

"The mines that are closed must have comparable amounts blocked out."

"It's hard to say unless you see their annual reports. And some of those are private."

Johnny persisted. "Would you guess that the total of known ore re-serves on Red Mountain comes to a million tons?"

"A guess is all it would be."

"Just an estimate—round figures."

Dyer eyed him. "All right, if that's what you want. A million tons."

Johnny pounced on it. "And that's counting only ore already in sight!" He looked out the window at the soaring red slope. "Think how much must be under there that hasn't been touched yet. I golly!" Bet wrong? In the face of a million tons of known reserves? His gesture swept the smokeless chimneys along the flank of the mountain. "You can't tell me values like those will stay shrunk in half just because a bunch of fatheaded congressmen in Washington don't know their asses from third base! Of course silver will come back! It's bound to!"

"Don't yell at me," Dyer said. "I'd dearly love to believe you. But I don't know as my directors will let me."

That was the way all the managers on Red Mountain were, afraid even to spit on their own initiative. Disgusted, Johnny returned to the telegraph office. An answer was there from Margaret Fossett. Fred and Walt, her wire said, had gone to Cripple Creek and were expected back in Denver in another day or two.

Johnny scowled. Cripple Creek? Were they running out on him? He was tired of hearing about Cripple Creek. A gold camp, it presumably had not been hurt by the collapse of silver prices. Many of the miners fleeing Red Mountain declared loudly that they were going over there to try their luck. If the other silver camps in the state fed in equal numbers of men, the lines at the Cripple Creek employment offices must stretch dang near out to the plains. The camp couldn't possibly boast of that much gold. It was nothing but a flurry, breeding its own excitement out of the fears of the silver panic. He'd bet dollars to doughnuts that Cripple Creek didn't have any million tons of ore blocked out ready to be mined. What was the matter with Walt anyway?

"2"

The next day rain fell, a soaker that raised streams bank-full. In the evening, skies cleared, showing gleams of fresh snow on the peak tops. The regular equinoctial storm, folks said. For the next six weeks Indian summer should prevail—perfect deer-hunting weather, or working weather too, if there was anything to work at.

The predictions were premature. The next morning fresh black clouds boiled out of the northwest. Blasts of wind preceded a fierce deluge. "Somebody sure pulled that plug," Sam Varnum muttered, staring through his dripping window. The rain came in such sheets that the air shivered to its roar. The already soaked ground could contain no more.

Walls of water hurtled through every gully onto the meadows. One of them tore out the restraining cribwork at the Ram, swooped up the tailing dump and spread it in a knee-deep ooze over the lower two thirds of the town.

Eighty minutes later the gray storm veil moved on toward Baker. The sun shone on the wet rocks; eaves dripped a cheery tinkle. Camp-robber jays, swarmed out of their havens in the thick evergreen copses, ruffled their feathers and rejoiced. Less exuberantly, the remaining inhabitants of Red Mountain City crept from their homes to learn what had happened.

The train that was due at noon did not appear. "A good thing, too," the stationmaster grumbled, contemplating the mud that swaddled his yard. "This town has been crapped on, absolutely. You might as well try pushing an engine through two feet of wet blotting paper."

Sam Varnum mourned, standing in goop above his boot tops, "Here's the frosting we needed for our cake. No place to shovel it if we try to clear it away. Not enough wagons or teams left to haul it off. I'm trading in my newspaper for a pair of walking shoes. We're through."

"Why," Johnny said, "it's easy. Get me twenty men together and I'll show you."

They knocked some abandoned sheds apart and used the planks for building a low flume along one side of Mountain Avenue to the creek. Workers on either side of the trough shoveled mud into it. A fire hose played into the upper end sluiced the syrupy debris into the stream, still boiling along bank-full. The current swept the mud on in rusty eddies through the meadow, into the gorge and away. "They'll be growing onions in it next spring down at Hillsdale," Johnny said. As soon as a strip was cleared, the flume was moved sideways on its short underpinnings and the work resumed.

Inspirited by the speed with which the device worked, the town council inspected its dwindling treasury and authorized the hiring of up to a hundred men at thirty cents an hour until the streets and railroad yards were cleared. Even at those starvation rates men flocked to sign up. Sluice boxes were hammered together on every principal thoroughfare. When shifts changed, workers coming from the mines took over the shovels of those who had to report. Many shoveled without pay. Children joined in. With renewed vigor women scraped mud out of their homes with hoes and rakes and little fire shovels designed for feeding stoves.

Toward noon on the day following the flood, Johnny sloshed up Mountain Avenue to cleared land in front of Sam Varnum's newspaper office. Sam popped out to obtain the latest reports. Johnny did not hear the questions. He was standing as motionless as a pointing bird dog. "I golly!" Lucille was riding toward them on her chestnut saddle mare.

He was mud from head to foot, even his cheeks and his hat; but when he held up his arms to help her down, she slid into them without hesitation. "You're back!" Never mind why right now. Then a miner yelled, "Hey, Jack, does that go with the job?" and they stepped apart, embarrassed.

"I think the telephone line between here and Argent is the only one still open," she told him. "We heard about the flood immediately. I knew there'd be plenty to do. So I left the children with Nylander and came to help. At least I can cook for some of you."

"How's the road?" Johnny asked. "I've been too busy to send anyone to see."

"Not bad." Being carved from solid rock most of the distance, it had not washed. In places slides of mud and gravel and tree branches had rolled across it. These would block wagons, but her mare had picked a way through without difficulty.

"I'll get some men at it as soon as we're clear here," Johnny promised.

As far as she knew, Lucille continued, she was the first person to come through. She had expected to meet files of discouraged residents trudging away from this latest blow, but had not encountered a single one. It was amazing.

"Listen to them," Sam Varnum explained. The shovelers were knocking off work to open their lunch boxes. The brief relaxation brought forth banter and joking. "It's almost the first laugh I've heard on the street this summer. Johnny has showed us how to pick ourselves back up off the floor."

"They have something useful to do," Johnny said. "That's what makes you feel good—a job you can see leading somewhere."

Lucille beamed at him. "Having something to eat helps. Is there any food at home?"

"A little."

"Let's get more at Gabe's and I'll fix you something hot before you go back to work."

He stirred wretchedly. "You know there's nothing I'd like more, especially after you came alone all the way up the gorge just for that. Only, well . . ." He drew a deep breath and plunged. "The train didn't come in yesterday or today, so we figure the tracks are out. The telegraph and telephone lines are down between here and Baker, so we don't know how extensive the damage is or what's being done at the other end to repair it. Dyer and some more of us are going to meet here in ten minutes and have a look. I was going to pick up some sandwiches in the café to eat as we ride along. If we hustle, we ought to be able to

reach the Summit Queen tonight and Baker tomorrow night. With luck
we'll be back the day after tomorrow with a full report."

"That long!" She couldn't keep her disappointment quiet. "I might
as well have stayed in Argent."

"We have messages out trying to locate Winkler. We have to be able
to give him a full report as soon as we reach him, so that he can make
up his mind what to do about the railroad."

"Are you the only one who can go? Isn't there enough here for you
to do?"

"Everybody is edgy. Winter is close. No one has any supplies. Without a railroad, the mines will close. Then we will be through."

Without the Baker Northern to feed it, his electric railroad would be
through, too. That was what he really wanted to find out, she thought,
and he didn't want to learn the news from someone else. Did that mean
he had heard from Walt and that there was still hope in Denver—and
he hadn't told her? Her bruised pride stirred.

"Johnny—"

"I know you're disappointed," he said. He was restive. And then she
saw Joe Dyer splashing toward them, riding one horse and leading another for John. "But I've got to get those sandwiches or hold everybody
up. We'll have a good talk as soon as I'm back."

The mountain and the city named for the mountain—those, not she,
were the roots of his life; those were what had made him what he was.
She had known it since the Christmas Eve when he had left her to
bring presents to Gabe's store. Yet he had come back to her then and
would again. There was no use trying to fight for more now, here in
the middle of this street he had just salvaged.

She touched his wrist with her fingers, letting him go. "I understand." But she did wish he'd at least think, without prompting, to
share with her what he had learned from Walt.

He gestured unhappily, sensing her distress but not fully understanding its source. "Aino or somebody will ride back with you—"

"I'll stay, now that I'm here."

Her generosity increased his guiltiness. "I'm sorry." He wriggled almost like Sam Varnum. Dyer reined in beside of them, touched his hat
in perfunctory greeting to Lucille, said, "Everybody's waiting," and
shifted his big rump impatiently in the saddle. Johnny's glance appealed miserably for an understanding which she had already given
him. "I wish I didn't have to go . . ." he started. But he didn't really
want to stay, and under Dyer's irritable glance he let the sentence trail
into vagueness and a conciliatory smile.

"You'd better hurry for your sandwiches," she said to reassure him
and looked brightly at Sam, who was politely pretending to read last

week's copy of his own newspaper, affixed to the inside of the office window. "I'm starved from my ride. If Sam will take me to lunch—"

For a moment she thought the editor would refuse through some mistaken delicacy. But he measured the tableau and realized that right now the briefly reunited, parting husband and wife needed the distraction of an outsider.

"Hee!" he cried, unutterably self-conscious under Joe Dyer's hard-eyed, uncomprehending scrutiny of something that Joe would have trampled underfoot. "I guess it is lunch time, at that!"

With a great show of bustling they went into the café. Johnny purchased a paper sack of sandwiches, pecked her cheek good-bye and fled in relief from the awkwardness. After he had gone, Sam and Lucille silently stirred their coffee, their eyes unseeing on the stained table top. Trying to cheer her, as if she didn't know Johnny as thoroughly as he did, Varnum said,

"He's—hee, hee—amazing. Truly he is. That's not mud out there in the street as far as John Ogden is concerned; it's a mere temporary inconvenience. He never sees things as the rest of us think they are, but as they're going to be. We've too many realists, Lucille—too many mud-watchers. We need more dreamers like him."

Realists? She smiled wryly. "Dreaming is a part of his reality. It has taken me twelve years to learn that—and sometimes I still forget." Her mouth turned sad. "He expects so much. And then he gets hurt by the very things he tries to accomplish."

"All dreamers are hurt that way. Just the same, we need the dream—or at least someone like Johnny who can stand in the mud and assure us that a promise still does live somewhere under the red peaks. We've been stripped pretty bare this summer, Lucille, but as long as we keep the rags of the hopes we wore when we first stampeded up that road of his, we've a chance. That's what he's doing for the town—sluicing the mud clean, showing us that trouble can be washed away."

She winced. "That's why I'm afraid."

"I don't understand."

"If the time comes when he can no longer clear out the mud, then what?"

His eyes dropped from hers. Absently he traced with the end of his spoon on the tablecloth the crosshatching of rails and ties. "You mean—hee—Walt?"

She made herself ask it: "Has anyone heard from him?"

Sam looked up in surprise. "Johnny would have let you know, wouldn't he?"

"I was off in Argent getting the children ready for school and. . . ." She swallowed her pride. "Has John heard?"

"No." He looked levelly at her. "Don't be—oh, hee!—so foolish, Lucille. You've never been that far from him. You'd have been the first to know."

She smiled her relief and her penitence for the doubts that had invaded her during the solitary ride up the road she once had tried to share so fully with him. "Thanks, Sam." She patted his hand and stood up. "I must go straighten the house. After two weeks' of his batching, it'll be a boar's nest."

He blushed crimson under her touch and scrambled to his feet. "If the telegraph lines are opened soon and a message comes for Johnny while he's gone, I'll bring it right over to you."

"I'll appreciate it, Sam." The fear came again and she bit her lip. "I can't understand why Walt hasn't sent a word, either yes or no. It isn't like him to shirk what he knows is so important."

"3"

Walt had tried both to wire and to telephone on the day the floods struck. When it was evident that several days must pass before he could communicate that way and that mail service was also disrupted, he and Fred Fossett decided that he would have to return unannounced to Argent with his message.

Fossett accompanied him to the Denver railroad station. The one-time banker was in a more dreadful state than Walt would have believed without seeing him. A persistent cold kept him hacking into his hand-kerchief. Always thin, Fred was downright scrawny now. His eyes were bloodshot. In his agitation that afternoon he had broken his pince-nez. Without them he looked strangely naked and vulnerable. He long since had said everything that needed saying, but as he trotted along at Walt's elbow through the vast, odorous lobby of the depot, he repeated his argument over and over like a pendulum wound too tight and swinging wildly against time.

"I know it will be hard for John to understand, but I've done every-thing a human could—after all, I had a stake in it too. You couldn't budge the investors either, you know. You talked to them. You heard their opinions about what the Senate will do. They're some of the best informed men in the state. You've got to respect their judgment. You've got to make Johnny realize it isn't my fault that they simply will not finance anything connected with Red Mountain or any other silver camp now or later."

"Nothing to it," Walt said sourly. "Just sit down over a beer and tell him he's thrown away half his life."

"It isn't as if there aren't alternatives," Fred retorted and hacked and rubbed his eyes. "You saw Cripple Creek. It's the one sound mining camp left in the state. Gold! Fresh and vigorous—even Argent in its best days was never like that."

"No," Walt agreed, "it wasn't. Argent never had ten unemployed miners from everywhere fighting for each available job. We had more jobs than there were men who were able to do them. That's when you live high on the hog. That's what Johnny will remember—the days when anything you did was just a start toward something bigger."

Fred was offended. "That grading contract I've lined up for him on the Cripple Creek line—and for you and your wagons and livestock—isn't exactly small change. Not in these times. A lot of men would give an arm for it. Certainly John will be disappointed at having to leave Red Mountain. But what is there to stay for? Make him realize! He doesn't know how desperate the situation is. You saw that refugee camp in River Front Park where the city has been feeding unemployed miners since the end of June. You've seen the trains for the East pulling out with men packed aboard them like sardines, running from the blight that silver has spread across this state. They've even tried to float away on rafts down the Platte River. Silver is dead! Why should Johnny die with it?"

"Just saying these things isn't going to make Johnny Ogden believe them."

"That's why you're going back—to make him realize! Johnny's too young and has too many potentials to go on beating his head against a stone wall up on that mountain. This is a chance for him to start over again with a better than average contract. It could very well lead to jobs that'll be even bigger than his electric railroad."

And a better than average commission for you, Walt thought. He kept it to himself, however. Fred was in no shape for jibes. Besides, he really had worked hard to arrange this contract for both Johnny and Walt, and although the two of them would have to shave corners close to come out ahead on it, still it was something to do.

"We must have your answer immediately," the banker rushed on. "The company has agreed to delay because of the disrupted communications, but patience stretches only so far. Too many other bidders want the work."

"I was there when they said all that," Walt reminded him crossly. Fossett had been a severe strain on his nerves the past days, especially at Cripple Creek when they had toured the proposed project and

Fossett had kept up a steady drone in his ear, as if Walt were incapable
of sizing up an ordinary piece of work for himself.

The banker cringed at the rebuke. "I know I'm repeating, but the
point is vital." He snuffed and blinked his reddened eyes. "You know
that if you decide to come to Cripple Creek, Johnny will."

"No," Walt said, refusing the responsibility, "I don't know. Don't
count on it either; I'm not promising a thing."

"You've always been like the father he lost," Fossett urged. His lips
trembled; they were wet and swollen. Walt could scarcely bear to watch
him. "He respects you more than any other man in the world. Don't
let him down."

Disgusted and yet profoundly moved, Walt broke away from the beseeching eyes and climbed the steps to the car platform. Turning, he
promised, "I'll get the data to him as fast as I can, Fred. We'll talk it
over without anything left out, and I'll let you know his decision—
and mine too—the minute the wires are open." Harried still by the lips
mumbling their silent arguments, he wheeled down the drab aisle of
the coach, tossed his suitcase onto the overhead rack, and sank onto a
dirty red plush seat on the opposite side of the car from where Fossett
was standing on tiptoe, trying to catch his eye with one last entreaty:
Save me, Walter. Make Johnny come.

Dear Jesus, he murmured as he wiped his face on a handkerchief.
Perhaps Harmon was better off, after all. Then he thought angrily,
addressing Johnny, *Why did you make me come and go through this?*
And finally, squirming into a comfortable position and lighting a cigar
as the train jerked forward and Fossett's dejected figure dimmed into
the twilight, he repeated savagely, *Make him realize.* How? By telling
him what Fred had descended to, craven and abject and ruined and
holding himself naked out to their mercies so that if they denied him
they would have to carry this too on their backs for the rest of their
days?

"4"

Luck hadn't finished with him yet. In Gunnison he learned that sixteen
miles of track in one of the canyons which the train followed had been
rendered impassable by washouts. At the beginning of this gap the
train halted and passengers were loaded into an open buckboard stage
for transportation around the break. They were to spend the night as
the railroad's guests at a hotel favored by section hands and located

where the tracks crawled back out of the canyon. The next morning another train would pick them up and take them on to Argent.

Walt pictured the road the buckboard would almost certainly have to travel to make the circuit—the road he himself had supervised the building of into the Ute agency back in '75. The road the first stampeders had appropriated—the one along which Young Hedstrom had been taken to meet the Indians while Walt had stayed with Nora at Los Alamos. The hotel would almost certainly be Mort Tally's yellow bedbug corral.

Now isn't this just dandy, he thought.

Only two other passengers got into the buckboard. They had traveled with him from Denver and during the slow ride they had learned quite a bit about each other. One was a sullen drummer in striped silk shirt who handled a line of gents' ready-to-wear and who complained that he spent most of his time in these hick silver towns trying to collect overdue bills. The other was a pink-cheeked young man with pale red hair as fine as silk. He was from Indiana. He was perhaps twenty or twenty-one years old, and to his own awe he was traveling to Hillsdale to rescue a sick uncle. The uncle had written that he was completely on his uppers and wanted to come home to die. The boy's father, who had been bitten that way once before, had sent the youth West with the cash and strict instructions about how to bring the invalid back without letting him put his hands on so much as a dime.

The lad was full of enthusiasms. The romantic nature of the errand excited him. His reading had excited him. Riding now in the buckboard with a pioneer over a road obviously little used since the railroad had captured the traffic excited him still more. He confidently expected to see grizzly bears and Indians in every gulch. He plied Walt with questions and listened wide-eyed to the monosyllabic answers, not in the least bothered by the drummer's sarcastic interpolations.

"'Seventy-five!" the pink-haired youth exclaimed enviously, looking across the sagebrush at the crenelated rimrock of the mesas. "Gee! And all this was Indian reservation! What was it like, going across to Argent then?"

Walt hunted for a word. "Why," he decided finally, "we thought it was work, but compared to this I guess it was exciting."

"I'll bet!"

"Huh," the drummer said.

They topped a hill and Walt's mouth tightened. This was the place. It had been about this time of year, too, maybe a week or so later, and the fall coloring must have looked the same, russet oak brush and golden aspens. Thirteen years ago. Had Johnny been back since? Yes, of course, after the trial when he had returned with Harmon and

Lucille. An old ache that Walt had never lost grew suddenly large. Suppose he had returned with the soldiers: Would it have made any real difference?

The youth said insistently, "Did you ever see any Indian fights when you were going back and forth on this road and the Utes were still here?"

"No," Walt snarled, "You read too goddamn many books. We spent our time getting out of fights, not looking for them. You'd be interested in staying alive too, wouldn't you, for Christ sake?"

"Hah!" the drummer said and the boy gaped. "All I did was ask," he said plaintively.

Walt humped up on the seat. No, it wouldn't have mattered. Even that long ago Johnny had married himself too irrevocably to what he thought the red peaks meant for him to have turned back. So what reason was there to expect he would forsake them now merely because the allure had turned out less than he had expected when first he had stood up and said I do.

"How would you like to go to Cripple Creek," he asked the youth abruptly.

The fair cheeks grew red with protest. "I swear, mister, I plain don't know what you're talking about lately."

Walt grimaced. "I'm not sure I do either," he apologized and turned his gaze away from the russet brush and tried to think of something else.

Nora. The touch of her hand. For years he had not let himself dwell on it. But Harmon was gone now.

Would she like Cripple Creek? Quick-profit Nora, Johnny called her. Gold: the excitement born again. Would she go only for that? Should it matter why she went with him so long as she did?

Would taking her be running out on Johnny again? Would Johnny come too, if Walt shined the figures as Fossett said to do, and made the Creek sound quick-profit for all of them? Was that the way after the limping years, after the light had gone out on the red mountains, was that the way to make amends for the original desertion? Deborah Ogden's voice: *Take care of him, Walter.*

He groaned. *Why did you make me come?*

"What's that?" he said to the youth from Indiana. "What's that you asked about?"

Red Mountain City? Your uncle wrote once that it was quite a place? Well, yes. The town stood on a fiery hillside more than ten thousand feet above sea level. It was difficult to reach; its ores were stubborn to handle. In the whiskery joke of its inhabitants its year possessed two seasons, winter and the Fourth of July. But it was city or had been in the days of the stampede. High, wide, and handsome—nothing like it anywhere else. Why ask now?

"Gee," the boy breathed and it was plain that he was looking out of his cornfield eyes at all the things he'd read in his schoolbooks: courage, self-reliance, ingenuity, hard work, perseverance. "Along with greed," Walt said, "and hate and yellowness and betrayal. You don't think those things got left back home in Indiana, do you?"

The boy objected. "There must have been something extra to make that many people go to such a place and build a new city."

"Yes," Walt conceded, "but it wasn't the great wonderful mysterious secret thing you'd like to think it was. What made them go was a sort of urge, a frame of mind. One man that had it would take it up the hill with him and work his guts out, while the fellow next door with the same feeling would use it sitting on his ass scheming out ways to cheat the first one. A third fellow would save a life and the next one would kill just as fast and easy. Sometimes the same man would do both—not at the same time of course. The urge came out different in different people. But the frame of mind was the same." He sat staring between his knees, vaguely aware that he hadn't talked this much in an unbroken sequence in years. But the thought was one which, in his present state, he needed to work out—not for this corn-fed farm boy but for himself. It was to himself that he nodded confirmation and repeated, "Yes, that's right. That's what built Red Mountain—the frame of mind of the people."

The youth wrestled with it and found it vague. "What frame, exactly?"

Walt thought of Johnny during that first Christmas Eve in the cabin at the foot of Vinegar Hill, looking down at the map of the new townsite and pointing out what was really the stirring in his own viscera (otherwise only paper lots in a paper town) and saying—that voice!—: *I'll take those two.*

What frame? *Oh Christ,* Walt cried silently in his agony. "They believed," he said.

The drummer was tired of the conversation. He leaned over the edge of the wagon and deposited his quid. "In what?" he sneered as he straightened.

They fell silent. The horses were tired and plodding. They went slowly into Curecanti Valley and Walt saw the barren earth from which Tally's yellow shoe-box hotel once had reared. The structure had vanished. *That's progress at least,* he thought in relief. Then, after they had driven on to the point where the railroad tracks emerged from the canyon, he blinked. The structure had been reincarnated next to a grimy siding, as gaunt and yellow and strident as ever.

Mort Tally bounded out to meet the stage, a little grayer and a little more wizened than before, but his eyes as muddy-looking as ever and the creases in the back of his neck as black as if still full of the very same dirt.

"Hi ho, folks, hi-ho! Tally's for the best. Gents to the—" He stopped and stared. "Well, I'll be go to—! William—no, Walt Kennerly! Well, what do you know!"

The same washbasins out back—the same towels? The same catsup bottles, red-crusted about their necks. A red-faced, angry-looking woman emerged from the kitchen with thick white platters balanced along the length of one arm and slammed them onto the oilcloth. "Evening, Mrs. Tally," Walt said politely. "I guess you don't remember me, do you?" She glared blankly, snapped something about not having time to remember every section hand who fed their faces at her table, and vanished into the kitchen.

"Hi-ho!" Tally roared. "That's one on you, Kennerly! You're thinkin' of Freda. That was two ago. Me and Carrie—that's this one—got hitched last spring."

Each of her predecessors worn out by the same untiring stove, no doubt, Walt thought. Incredible how they resembled each other—perhaps because it took the same sort of person to endure Mort Tally's kind of life. "Pioneering," he murmured to the young traveler, sitting beside him and gingerly contemplating a serving dish mounded with gray string beans.

Afterwards they sat in a row on benches on the porch, sucking toothpicks and watching twilight darken while their suppers digested. Presently Walt asked their host, "That flat up yonder always struck me as a prettier place than this. Why did you move?"

"The railroad killed the wagon traffic, so I came down to make a killing off the railroad. Get it?" Tally laughed uproariously at himself.

"Must have been quite a job to move this building."

"Oh, this ain't the same one. I sold that to some sheepherders who wanted the boards for lambing corrals."

"You mean you could have started fresh and did the same thing over?"

"I liked the design."

"I see."

They fell silent again until Tally asked, "When's Jack Ogden going to start work on his e-lectric railroad?"

So the assault was beginning already, Walt thought resentfully. "Have you heard about that plan clear over here?"

"Most certainly. It's the only construction project left in this part of the country. Every day or so there's fellows go through, headed for Red Mountain to rustle jobs. I allus did say that when something needed doing Jack Ogden was the one who'd step up and do it. Like that time with the Utes. Yes sir!" He nodded sagely to himself until Walt's silence seized his attention. Suspiciously he demanded, "He is going to build it?"

"No," Walt said.

"Why, he's got to."

"No money."

"Those goddamn Denver loan sharks turned him down!"

"You might put it that way, yes."

"Are they crazy?" Tally jumped to his feet and blew agitated gusts of air across the end of his nose. "Why, that railroad could of been the saving of these mountains! What're they thinking of?"

He paced the verandah, declaiming about gold bugs and the oppression of the working classes. First the drummer and next the youth drifted off to bed. Before following, Walt stepped out from under the roof to glance at the night sky. He heard Tally wheezing beside him. Out of pure contrariness he asked,

"Tell me, Mort. Do you ever have any regrets about Young Hedstrom?"

The breathing paused, then quickened suspiciously. "What are you driving at?"

"Nothing. Just wondered."

"Well, wonder somewhere else." The wizened frame grew compacted with outrage. "Why should I have regrets? It was either that or get burned out. If we wouldn't of done what we did, there wouldn't be none of this here now." Tally's hand swept upward toward the face of the hotel, dark save for lamplight glowing behind the ragged lace curtain in one upstairs bedroom. "None of it!"

"That's one way of looking at it, I suppose," Walt said dryly and started toward the steps. Abruptly he paused. "How'd you like to go to Cripple Creek, Mort?"

"Cripple Creek?" Once more the gusty breathing hung suspiciously. "Why Cripple Creek?"

"Just wondered."

"Everything I've got is here in Curecanti. What the hell would I do in Cripple Creek?" Tally started to blow air angrily across his nose, then checked himself. More reflectively he added. "They tell me it's quite a place, though."

"Yes," Walt said, "it is."

"5"

One might think people had been watching each arriving train just to see Walt. The moment he stepped onto the depot platform, men converged on him, the question big in their eyes. He shook his head and watched the grayness settle back on their faces. As he strode on up the street, the suitcase swishing back and forth against his trouser legs, he went through the same misery again and again, until his only defense was to grow furious at everyone, at himself and Johnny and Fossett and especially at the dogged, insistent questioners.

As he passed the office of *The True Fissure*, Al Ewer hailed him. "No," Walt snarled before Ewer could speak, "they're not going to finance it. Period."

Ewer's thick shoulders sagged, but he made an effort to take the disappointment without blinking. "You don't have to bite my head off about it, do you?"

"Sorry," Walt muttered and nodded at the street in general. Every few yards one or more idlers watched them covertly, trying to divine what they were discussing. "It's just . . ."

"I know," Ewer said heavily. He motioned with a piece of galley proof he held in one pudgy hand. Obviously he had brought it out to show Walt. "I set this up, hoping it might help if those financiers had it to read when they came in on the excursion train to look it over. Want to see it?"

"No."

"Read it anyhow," Al urged unhappily. "Nobody else ever will. As a matter of fact, things have reached such a pass that I don't know whether what I wrote ever was true or not. Go on, read about how wonderful we are and tell me whether I'm dreaming or whether once upon a time . . ." His sourness turned completely bleak. "That's a good line—once upon a time. All fairy stories begin that way. Here, go on, read it."

Take your map of Colorado and place the point of your pencil on the spot in the southwestern part of the state which is marked Red Mountain. With a string draw a circle with a radius of fifteen miles. That is the magic circle. Within those thirty miles of diameter lie the most richly mineralized and scenically magnificent areas on the face of our great round globe. A dozen peaks tower as high or higher than Pike's famous discovery. Canyons seam the granite universe so deeply and precipices tower so loftily that if they were located in remote Tibet, scientific and geologic expeditions would be organized and thousands of travelers would annually circle the globe to see them. Here they can be reached with almost no effort. Here . . . but there is no use attempting to describe them. Printer's ink and tourist's camera fail before the majestic operations of God.

To the pioneers who first gazed upon these awesome grandeurs. . . .

That was enough for the general idea. No verses or off-color puns, either. Al was taking this hard. Walt returned the paper. "If I could find me a place like you describe, I'd move to it." He gave back bleakness for bleakness. "How'd you like to go to Cripple Creek?"

"Are you kidding?"

"Not entirely," Walt said. "The money boys will let us build a railroad over there but not here." He told Ewer something of the grading contract they could have. "Plus commissions for Fossett," he finished. "Which the poor devil needs. He's in bad shape."

"Have you accepted?"

"Not yet."

"Have you seen Cripple Creek?"

"I spent two days there with Fred, and three more riding along rights of way on a mighty pert blood-red bay filly that I can buy at a bargain if I go back."

"Is the camp as good as I read?"

"It's not bad."

"Newspapers?"

"There's one working and another talked about."

"Do you reckon I can find room for a third?"

"Did you ask about room in '79, when you first headed for Argent?"

"No," Ewer admitted. "I packed up and came."

"Sure," Walt said. "A frame of mind."

A moment of silent remembering went by. Then Al asked, "Does Johnny know about this?"

"Not yet. The wires were down. I couldn't reach him."

"There's something you should know then. You'd better come in where we can talk about it."

When they were seated inside the office, Al summarized what had been happening. "The flood raised more Ned on the mountain and on toward Baker and in Los Padres Canyon than it did here. About fifteen miles of railroad between Baker and Montezuma plain vanished. There's big chunks gone between Baker and Red Mountain. A train was on the way over the summit during the cloudburst. It ran into a washout and killed the engineer. The locomotive is still standing on its ear in the bottom of a gulch. Another locomotive is stranded in the yards at Baker. The river cut across lots and left it standing on an island. So the only rolling stock the Baker Northern has that can be used is a little work goat at Red Mountain. Winter is not far off, either."

"What is Winkler doing about it?"

"That's just it—nothing. His line around the St. Johns was hit hardest of any of the roads. When the people at Red Mountain finally located him at Sylvanite, he said he was too snowed under with his big line to make a move on Red Mountain before next spring. He also said that if the Ogden Construction Company wanted to tackle the rebuilding now and wait a year for reasonable recompense, he'd trust Johnny to go ahead."

"That's sure loading it onto John."

"He may never get his pay."

"From Otto? Why, Winkler is as solvent as—" Walt almost said, as the bank, then swallowed the words and asked instead, "Is Johnny going ahead?"

"He's trying. The trouble is, Baker is isolated, too. They've got crews working toward each other from both ends of Los Padres Canyon, but it'll be nip and tuck to finish before winter."

"How does Johnny expect to bring in rails and so on?"

"From what I hear, he plans to rip up his own rails and ties that he laid for the excursion, and use them to patch the line over the pass. It's lightweight stuff, but apparently it'll do for stopgap. The main problem is coal for operating the goat."

"That ought not take so much."

"A month's worth, with the engine steaming back and forth over the pass every day."

"We can haul it up from here in wagons," Walt said.

Ewer's face puckered. "You said something a minute ago about frame of mind. If I hadn't been sitting here the past summer, watching the guts dry up inside our people, I wouldn't believe what has happened to the frame of mind we once had. Everybody is scared to death for himself. Argent is cut off too, you know. There isn't much coal in town. Folks were waiting to see what happened before they laid in winter supplies. They won't sell the little coal they have unless they get bonus prices in cash. Johnny is broke. He can't pay until Winkler pays him. Nobody will give him a pound. I know. He telephoned every dealer in Argent this morning. There's to be a town meeting in the Red Mountain city hall at seven o'clock this evening and he wants to go there with a plan, he says."

"How does he figure to pay his workers?"

"Script, to be redeemed when Otto comes through. Gabe has agreed to take the script in his store for groceries and clothes."

"Christ A'mighty! Did those honyaks agree to that—Aino Berg and the union boys?"

Ewer spread his fat hands. "I don't believe it either. But you know Johnny Ogden—Hardrock—the one and only. He has pulled that lost, dead camp together somehow—frame of mind—and made them think they aren't lost. He stood them up together, sluicing mud out of their streets, and to see it melt away so smooth and easy lifted them like nothing else since the mints in India closed. Mud was something they could meet and fight together and they did it. Now they think they can do it with the railroad."

Walt smiled faintly, almost enviously. "That's John, all right." He stared thoughtfully through the window. "I didn't pay close attention, but from the railroad it looked like there's still a pile of coal at Roscoe Blair's smelter."

"That bastard! Roscoe was the first person Johnny called. Roscoe yelled him right off the wire—a fellow that heard Roscoe's end was in here an hour ago. 'Send you coal,' he squealed at Johnny, 'so you can fix the railroad to take ore to Montezuma? You know where you can put that railroad, Ogden, and if you want to come down here to my coal pile, I'll shove some of it up there for you, too.' Oh, he's a real samaritan in troubled times, Roscoe is."

"There must be coal in Baker."

"No, they're worse off than we are. There was one trainload on a siding, but the flood undercut the bank and dumped the cars in the river. Whatever else there is to spare is being used for the work trains in Los Padres Canyon. They aren't about to help Red Mountain."

Walt exhaled unhappily. "I guess that leaves just Pat for Johnny to try next."

Ewer scowled. "Pat?"

"When the silver mines began closing, he picked up their coal at bargain prices for his Golden Joker."

Slowly Ewer shook his sad, round head from side to side. "Can you see Pat Edgell getting Johnny in a bind and then letting him have coal at any price?"

"No," Walt admitted, "I can't."

"If the pinch is tight enough, can you see Johnny trying to take that coal?"

Walt thought about it and stood up. "I'd better go."

"If he knows the trolley has folded, will he change his mind?"

"I don't know." Walt worried his yellow mustache with the fingers of his left hand. "The Cripple Creek deal might help. But if those people up there—Varnum, Jenny Shaffer, Gabe, people like that—if they pull at him hard enough . . . I swear I don't know."

Ewer motioned with his thumb toward the telephone box on the wall. "You can ring him up if you want."

Walt hesitated. "Those machines spit and pop until you can't make sense out of anything. This needs serious talk, a lot of it in a hurry. That's why I came here instead of writing or waiting for the telegraph lines to be opened. I tell you what: Will you call the stable for me and asked Jules to hitch my fastest buggy horses, the blacks? I'll be right along."

"6"

He did not go immediately to the stable, however, but walked up Silver Avenue toward Vinegar Hill and then turned along a side street to a small frame house behind a bushy fir tree. He twisted the bell ringer and heard feet running. A young woman, very pretty, with unblemished skin and animated eyes, threw open the door. It was Mabel Brice, now Mrs. Robert Jebb.

"Walter! Come in!"

He set the suitcase on the porch and stepped inside the tight little parlor. He could smell apple pie in the oven and hear someone moving about upstairs. Twin toddlers appeared and watched him solemnly, sucking their thumbs.

"Hi, Mabel. You grow prettier every day."

She crinkled her nose. "You spread more blarney every day."

"Is Bob around?"

"He went to Hillsdale." Her eyes clouded. "He thought the farmers might have something for a blacksmith. The mines haven't."

"How is he?"

"Discouraged." She studied him and he braced himself for what he knew was coming. "Any news?" she asked.

He started to say, How would you like to go to Cripple Creek? but there was an end even to bitterness. He merely shook his head.

Her eyebrows moved slightly with the shadow that crossed her face and for a moment she regarded her lap in silence.

"So many people," she murmured. "Each day after the train pulled in they'd go to the post office and wait for Johnny's foreman here to walk up and then they'd follow him back to the shack, in case a letter had come. Now . . ." She looked up, her eyes grieving. "Poor Johnny."

Oh indeed, very poor Johnny, Walt thought and his accumulated resentment spilled over. Poor Johnny had feared this refusal. He had sent Walt after the tidings while he stayed on the mountain and played savior. It wasn't Johnny who must walk through town past their eyes and drive up the hill to the waiting faces. Oh no, not Savior Johnny, the Latter-day Messiah: *these veins go deep.* Oh no. It was Walt whom he had manipulated into announcing they were through. Dumb cat's-paw Walt. Poor Johnny.

"Next time he can pull his own chestnuts out of the fire," he blurted and instantly felt unworthy. "I'm sorry. But no one likes to bring bad news, and that seems to be the only kind these days."

"If there's anything I can do—"

"Yes, there is. I just can't face Lucille. If you—"

"She isn't here. She joined Johnny in Red Mountain after the flood."

"Oh. Well then." He grinned his relief. The knowledge made it unnecessary for him to stay any longer. Nevertheless he made no move to leave. Now and again he could hear footsteps upstairs. "How's Nora?" he managed to ask at last.

"All right, considering. The shock was the thing she really had to get over." Mabel hesitated, then admitted, "She does grow irritable at times. We're crowded. Bob isn't always the best of company nowadays."

"He has worries of his own."

"The twins aren't always this quiet. They're in awe of you."

"I don't suppose she'd go to the ranch at Red Mountain," Walt suggested, "or even to the one below the Narrows."

"Not while our stepmother is there." Mabel pursed her lips in distress. "I don't know why Nora can't be more tolerant. Dele has made a good mother to Tommy and me. We're very fond of her."

"You weren't old enough to feel the shame. Nora was. To her it was one more black mark against these mountains. I don't reckon either you or Tommy ever quite realized how much Nora hated to come in here and surrender to them. And she's never been able to escape."

"Do you want to talk to her?"

"I . . ."

"You've always loved her, haven't you?"

He sat stone silent.

"At the restaurant when you thought I was asleep in the pantry—I wasn't always."

"Never mind," he said hoarsely and jumped to his feet. "I've got to go."

"Why did you come?"

"So you'd see Lucille for me."

"Nora never really loved Harmon, you know."

"Why should I know? I never thought about it."

"There's so very little left, Walter. Don't turn yourself, don't turn her away from what the two of you can still find together."

He sat down as if his legs had dissolved. When he looked up it was to ask with a mirthless chuckle,

"How do you think she'd like to go to Cripple Creek?"

"Do you mean you might move there?"

"It's a possibility."

Mabel jumped up. "Why not ask her yourself? I'll call her."

She started for the stairs. Walt stopped her. "Wait a minute. I have to leave right away to see Johnny. Nora and I would need to talk pretty carefully—to make sure. We could do it on the way. So don't say anything about Cripple Creek yet. Leave it for me. Just ask her if she'd like to go for a buggy ride up to Red Mountain this afternoon."

"7"

When Johnny hung up after talking to Roscoe Blair at the Argent smelter, he was more furious than Lucille had ever before seen him. He went outside so white-lipped that her breath caught. For more minutes than she could gauge afterwards, he paced back and forth in front of the cabin. He'd start up the path toward the church where he had helped hang the bell, its windows boarded now, its pulpit deserted, and stop by the first red-barked spruce tree. He'd stand a moment looking toward the smokeless prickle of chimneys on the side of the peak, his head would toss like a tormented bear's, he'd swing his fists against the tree, and come back the path as far as the gate, pause, turn and repeat.

She resisted the temptation to run to him and perhaps it was wise. Slowly he gained control of himself. Returning to the house, he resumed his calls in a normal, quiet voice. He argued when he was refused, but he did not shout. "Yes, yes, I respect your position. What's that?—this thing crackles so. Oh. Well. Sorry I bothered you." It was almost as though he made the calls with no expectation of success. By lunch time that was the phase of the barren morning which worried her most: the heart was going out of him.

"That's it," he said finally. He dropped into an easy chair, one leg hooked over its arm. He riffled through a magazine, tossed it aside and went back to the telephone. "Myrt, this is Johnny. Try Denver again, will you? You're sure? Yeah, yeah. Sorry to pester you, but you know . . . well, let me know the minute you hear."

Lucille said, wishing desperately that she could distract him, "Come to lunch, darling."

He moved obediently, unfolded his napkin carefully, and sat without touching his fork. Finally he gave the table edge a slap with his fingertips.

"I just don't understand what has happened to Walt."

How many times had they been through this? "Please eat something, Johnny."

"Travelers and mail are getting through from Denver now. The paper says there's a wagon shuttling back and forth by Tally's."

"If you'd like to ride to town tomorrow, we could pick up the children and bring them back for the weekend."

"You don't suppose he's run off to Cripple Creek without letting us know, do you?"

"Johnny, no. Walt will come as soon as he has something to come for."

"That's what I'm afraid of—there's nothing."

"He and Fred both have a stake in this. They're working. Don't jump to conclusions."

"Fred is probably waiting for spring now. He knows what winters here are like. He knows we can't do much before snow flies."

"Then wait until spring to worry."

"You saw the state bank examiner up here yesterday, trying to pull in the assets of the Argent bank." He folded his napkin and stood up, his plate untouched. His eyes were wild. "Lucy, unless I can show them something solid to make them think I have a chance, they'll take everything we have—even the home in Argent."

"Doesn't the law say they have to leave a roof over our heads? This cabin?"

He waved it away distractedly. "I don't know bankruptcy law."

"If they don't leave the cabin, we'll move into one of the abandoned houses up here. There's one next to Jenny."

"With the kids?"

"We were happy in a tent once. Smile again, Johnny. You used to smile about that."

"We had a road to work for then."

"Don't you want a glass of milk and a piece of this cake?"

"I'm not hungry." He took a turn around the room, caught her eye and stopped. Contrite suddenly, he dragged a chair around the corner of the table, sat beside her and took her hand. "I know I'm being rotten to live with. Some day I'll make it up to you."

"You haven't a thing to make up. I know what you're going through."

"Believe me, it isn't the electric trolley any more—except that if we were sure about the trolley we'd have a better chance of borrowing coal for repairing the railroad. Every day these men beg for work to save what little is left. Then to call Roscoe Blair and have him downright glad of what has happened——"

"Roscoe hasn't spoken to us since you graded the road across the pass and he lost the Red Mountain ore to Montezuma. You shouldn't let an old story like that upset you so."

"His time will come. You can't turn your back on your own people and not have it remembered."

"I don't seem able to say anything that will make you feel easier and that's where I've failed," she said sadly. "But truly, John, we're better off than many people here."

"No. Because they're looking to us for help. And I'm licked. I don't know where to turn." He went into the kitchen for his hat. "I think I'll take a walk."

She jumped up and untied her apron. "I'll go with you."

"I'd rather be alone." He eyed her gray face and smiled sardonically. "Don't worry. I'm not going to . . . do anything. I just want to try to figure out some plan."

Before he could leave there was a knocking at the front door. It was Joe Dyer of the Dixie Girl. "Any luck with Roscoe?" he asked.

"No."

"That son of—excuse me, ma'am, but that's what he is, a plain, unvarnished, home-grown, buy-'em-by-the-gross son of a bitch. We used to bait hogs with the likes of him back home. Well, that leaves us pretty near the bottom of the barrel, don't it?"

"Yes."

"It's a bind. I keep telling the directors I can piddle along through the winter—so can the Ram and two or three others—but not without a railroad."

"You did once," Lucille reminded them.

"In those days we cut our timber right here," Dyer said. "Now we have to import it. We're set up for machinery now. That means coal for the boilers and air compressors. Other things in proportion. To pay for it we have to be able to ship ore."

"Lots of ore used to go down the gorge road," she persisted.

"Us send to Blair? At his prices? Ha!" Dyer shook his hard head emphatically. "Not by God until we've tried one or two more things." He turned to Johnny. "Let me talk to Pat for you."

Johnny didn't even try not to grimace. "Gabe already has."

"Gabe's too soft. He probably went in with his hat in those roast-beef hands of his and ducked his head and said pretty please. Hell, Pat would talk Gabe inside out in three minutes. I'll put the screws on him."

"Even if you try to buy for the Dixie Girl, he'll know the coal will end up with me," Johnny said. He saw Pat's round eyes laughing, heard the noise his tongue made against his teeth. *The Great White Father; isn't it just too bad.* "It's no use, Joe."

"Let me try anyhow."

Johnny hung fire, then gave in. "I've nothing else to suggest, I guess."

"Where'll you be when I finish?"

"At the office." Johnny meant his construction office near the depot. "About five-thirty."

"It won't take me that long."

"I want to walk along the trolley line and figure out the quickest way to lift the rails and ties." He made himself smile. The stiffness of it felt fatuous even to him. "In case we do get coal," he said.

Dyer let it go and departed. Lucille's eyes clung to Johnny. She knew he didn't intend to plan on anything about the rails.

"All right!" he cried in anguish. "I'm just going out to look at my railroad line one last time. Is that so strange?"

To look back. To remember how he had felt on looking forward. And then to come back and learn the results of Dyer's interview with Pat. The Great White Father. *What now, Jackie boy?*

He was terrified. And there was nothing she could do.

"8"

He was fifteen minutes late when he reached the construction office, for no particular reason except that he had not wanted to be on time. To his dismay he saw that thirty or forty men had gathered there, waiting for him. Dyer sat on some of Harmon's old bricks, his big hands holding one knee as he rocked slightly back and forth. There was no need asking about the interview. The look of his slabby cheeks, the silent grimness of the men about him, hands thrust deep in their pockets and their tieless shirt collars buttoned against the evening chill—those were words enough.

Dyer talked anyway. "He was polite, at first. Said the chances were too long. Suppose the line from Baker to Montezuma wasn't opened before winter, he asked me. Then what good was opening the pass? Or what if we didn't open the Baker Northern? He'd have donated his coal for nothing."

"He'd be paid in script like everyone else," Johnny said.

"I told him that and he laughed. Suppose Winkler can't redeem it, he said. There we'd be with our hands hanging down. Why should he risk a winter's production and his men their winter's wages for that? I tried to show him that the risk is minimum. I told him that if Jack Ogden can't do the job with the entire town behind him, then it can't be done."

"I imagine that impressed him," Johnny remarked.

"Oh my yes," Dyer agreed and deliberately tried to kindle Johnny's anger. "He sneered at me, 'Who do you people think Jack Ogden is— God maybe? I know Ogden thinks so, but how he feeds the rest of you that diet of crap I'll never understand.' Those are practically his very words."

The ring of faces glowered. Johnny did not let himself move a muscle. "We're talking about coal."

"I'm getting there," Dyer said, pleased with his strategy. "I told Pat that someone had to take the initiative. I told him you know more about construction than any other three men on the mountain and that the town is prepared to line up back of you. I said we'd rather he'd be reasonable, but that if we had to, we'd take the coal. Like eminent domain, I said."

"And then?"

"And then," Dyer said with a humorless smile, "is when he pointed at the door. 'Think about it,' I warned him. 'So you'll know straight that I'm speaking for the town and not just for Ogden or the Dixie Girl, I'll come back with a committee at half-past six tonight for your answer. We'll want to know it at our town meeting tonight when we make our plans and draw up our crews."

Johnny glanced around at the ring that had drawn closer as they talked. "It looks like we've practically got a meeting here."

Dyer nodded. "Why not? Now is when we have to make up our minds. I might add," he continued relentlessly, "that Pat is expecting you. When I was leaving he asked, 'Is Ogden on your committee?' 'What's that to you?' I asked. 'Because,' he said, 'when I tell you all to go to hell, I want Jackie boy there to hear me.'"

The listeners shifted and muttered.

"Why can't I settle for the railway?" Johnny said. He smiled to make the words appear facetious. "Why do I have to help round up the coal to boot?"

Dyer knew it wasn't facetious. His gray eyes narrowed. "Nobody else I've asked to be on the committee has backed out. There's Varnum, representing the civic organizations."

Sam writhed and blushed.

"Porcella for the merchants."

The Angel Gabe, massive and mournful in a sheepskin coat, grinned about like a shaggy hound hungry for notice.

"Berg for the workers."

Aino bobbed his head. His short-stemmed pipe raised a mist of smoke in front of his face. "Ja," he said.

"Me for the Mine Owners' Association. You for the job itself." Dyer's blunt voice defied criticism. "That ought to be representation enough. The son of a bitch will have to listen."

Jenny Shaffer came trotting into the circle. So many men gathered on obviously man-business would have deterred any other female on the mountain. But not Jenny. "Let me through, please," she snipped right and left and came through. "Can I see you for a minute, John Ogden?"

Dyer hauled a watch from his pocket by its leather fob. "It's quarter-past six," he demurred. The pinch of his nostrils added scornfully, Petticoats.

Johnny's bristles began to rise. "Don't shove me, Joe."

Their glances locked. Then Dyer shrugged. "You talk to him, Sam, before I get mad." As Johnny started after Jenny, Dyer ordered peremptorily, "We'll see you at the road to the Golden Joker at six-thirty sharp."

As soon as they were clear of the crowd, Johnny asked, "What's the matter, Jenny?"

"Lucille wants to talk to you."

His heart leaped. Perhaps Walt had called. "About what?"

"About this," Jenny said with a sniff, pointing her nose back at the crowd.

"What does she know about this?"

"Everyone in town knows by now."

"She wants me to let it alone?"

"She's afraid of Dyer. Go to her, John."

Behind them Sam Varnum called desperately for attention. "Johnny —oh hee! Wait up!"

Johnny turned around. "There's nothing to talk about, Sam."

"Don't let Joe make you sore."

"He doesn't need me on his committee," Johnny said. "He's running the show his way."

"We all need you."

"I can't say anything to Pat that hasn't already been said. If I try he'll be more contrary than ever."

"You can hold the town together."

"So can Dyer. Or you."

"No." Sam squirmed and laughed and hung on. "Do you remember the first time I interviewed you in Argent after you had opened the trail through the gorge—not even a road, only a trail? Lucille made me see it—what we were capable of. We. Not you or Dyer or Pat or me as individuals. We—as mankind. I know I'm being clumsy, but—hee! —listen to me. You helped us have confidence in ourselves as men. What the country up here demanded of us was beyond our strength. I used to question and doubt more than anyone. But we did it. You were always in the front, believing so hard that it helped the rest of us believe. That's why Joe can't let you turn back now. If you falter, everyone will and our last chance will collapse."

"You're asking more than I can give," Johnny cried in despair.

"Why? After what you have already given? They're expecting it of you now." Sam's hand made nervous little circles as he searched for words. "They're betting on you!" he cried.

Johnny winced. His glance fled toward the hillock that thrust into the edge of the town, went past the boarded church to the brown thread of path that led to his home. He saw a woman's figure walking toward them. Shadows from the trees lay too thickly on it for it to be recognizable. He turned away. His eyes lifted to the peaks, the last slant of the setting sun striking a passion of light from their crimson sides. Without glancing at Jennie, he said to her,

"Tell Lucille I'll be back as soon as I can."

"9"

Pat saw them coming. He settled a deer-hunting rifle into the crook of his arm and nodded to his foreman and to the nervous bookkeeper. They armed themselves with pick handles and followed him through the door. Outside the office, they lined up abreast to await the delegation. Other workers equipped with clubs and with fist-sized chunks of coal to throw hung over the board fence of the coal yard, watching.

It was a tacky kind of area. A string of small, rusty mine cars stood half in and half out of the black tunnel mouth. The compressor in its sheet-iron shed grunted a sullen *huff-huff-huff-huff;* when its air receivers in the mine reached the required pressure to feed the pneumatic drills, the compressor kicked off with a sigh. The little mill ground its ore with a monotonous thrum. Off to one side sprawled a junk pile: iron wheels, lengths of leaky pipe, splintered planks, and a huge circular saw blade with a zigzag crack across its rusted face.

The foreman and the bookkeeper were scared white. At least seventy or eighty men were marching up the road toward them. Those who had been at the construction camp earlier in the evening had followed the committee when it started out; others had fallen in as the group strode through town. As the crowd neared the Golden Joker, the men instinctively fanned as far apart as the terrain allowed. Several of them had picked up stones and sticks.

When they were within fifteen or twenty paces, Pat gestured with the rifle. "That's far enough!" he called.

His boogers were riding him, Johnny could tell. Johnny knew. He knew very well. Without really being able to see it, he could tell exactly how the skin stretched across the cheekbones of Pat's flat countenance; how his round, almost lashless eyes glinted like marbles; how his tongue was working against his teeth.

Pat's glance shuttled back and forth across the line. He had nerve enough, all right.

"Quite a committee you brought along, Joe," he said.

Dyer nodded. "Committee of the whole, Pat."

They stood silent, waiting for Johnny to speak. He felt weightless and dizzy. He raised his eyes toward the flush of the alpenglow fading from the mountaintop. The high slopes looked exactly as they always had, the heart of them not even touched yet. Perhaps no heart was there to touch. My peaks, he thought. My beautiful, beautiful peaks. What had failed? Were they going to betray him at last?

His glance dropped to Pat. We were friends once, he thought. What had gone wrong?

"You're just hurting yourself, Pat," he said, "being a dog in the manger this way."

"The Great White Father speaks," Pat mocked. "But if you don't open the Baker line, you can't build your trolley, can you?"

"I'm talking about the good of the town."

"Sure, sure. It's just a coincidence, isn't it, how the good of these towns and the good of Jackie Ogden always happens to be the same?"

"We're not going to argue. You can't shoot us all. We can take that coal."

"I can shoot two or three of you first." The gun muzzle moved along the line, pausing for a fraction on each man who held a stone. "I'm warning you."

"It's our last chance, Pat."

"Your way is always the right way, isn't it, Jackie boy. Now let me tell you something. You're not the only savior in this camp. I've got every man at work on that vein that I can economically crowd in there. I haven't cut wages five cents. The work is steady. We've enough coal to keep working at least until spring. Why should I ask my men to give that up on the outside chance that maybe you'll open the Baker Northern and maybe Winkler will redeem your script and maybe the price of silver will come back? You always were a conceited bastard, Ogden, seeing nothing but what you wanted to see, but by God this takes the cake."

"You're still talking about only one mine. I'm talking about all of our mines. We can get through the winter if you'll help us. Next spring, when things open up again—"

Pat's sudden shout of triumph cut him off. He had glanced over the heads of the crowd, had started and peered more closely through the twilight.

"Next spring! Ha! Not for you! You'll never build that trolley! I just got the straight word from Walt himself!"

"You're a liar! He isn't——"

"Look!"

Every head turned down the Joker road. Turning onto it was a buggy pulled by two black horses. There seemed to be three figures in it, though in the uncertain light it was hard to be sure. In any event, the vehicle seemed like a dozen others in the region.

"What's he talking about?" Dyer growled.

"Nothing," Johnny said. But it was Walt. No one else ever drove those prized black horses. And if Walt had good news he would have telephoned from Argent, knowing how much depended on it. His coming in person to talk meant that he was bringing only explanations.

Still, hope would not quite abdicate. Perhaps the excursionists would come next year. If they could hang on . . . He turned back.

"For the last time, Pat. This is bigger than you or me or—"

"Anything is bigger than you!" Pat crowed. "You've reached the end of the road, Jackie boy. You're done!"

Johnny took a despairing half step forward. A shiver ran through the watchers. Off at the right Aino Berg, the ancient sourness in him triggered loose like a cork in a popgun, suddenly yelled, "You devil!" and hurled the stone he held. It came within an inch or two of Pat's head. He ducked and fired spasmodically from the hip.

He did it very neatly. The bullet struck Johnny half an inch above the bridge of his nose. As he fell, another stone, erratically hurled, struck the empty ground between him and Pat, bounced at a sharp angle, and hit the discarded saw blade with a resounding clang. Before the reverberations had faded, Pat cried out, still bent forward, his arm extended, fingers splayed,

"You all saw! Self-defense! You saw him signal to Aino. I warned him, but you saw him start for me. I had to do it. You saw him!"

The men beside him gripped their pick handles. The men on the fence cocked their arms to throw. The tableau of confrontation held frozen for a moment until Gabe found his voice. "You'll pay for this, Pat!" A growl ran through the watchers.

Pat waved the rifle muzzle. "You saw him! Now clear out before someone else gets hurt. Hear me! Out! Everyone!"

"I'm going to him," Gabe said and moved forward with the gun fixed straight on his ruddy head. But the others backed off. Catching dread from each other, they whirled and streamed down the hill past the buggy.

It had stopped. On reaching Red Mountain, Walt had driven straight to Johnny's house. Lucille had come running out to Nora and him, urging them to hurry with her to the Joker. But because of his late start from Argent, Walt had pressed the blacks hard up the gorge and they were tired. If he had whipped them too strenuously at the end of the run, they might have balked entirely. Or have been spoiled. And they were good horses. He kept them at an easy trot, and when he heard the shot and the clang, he halted, not wishing to expose the women to anything dangerous. That was the way they were when the stunned, silent citizens poured by: the horses droop-headed with weariness, Walt holding the reins, and Lucille and Nora standing on tiptoe, straining to peer into the darkness and make out what had happened.